RICHARD I

He was England's most romantic and heroic king, a passionate and sensitive man, great warrior, poet and musician, and a charismatic leader, blindly adored by the knights he commanded, deeply loved by more than one woman.

In this masterly novel set in the time of the bloody Crusades and the intricate Courts of Love, the fiery Plantagenet rulers come to life: Richard's father, the boorish womanizer, King Henry II; his mother, a legendary beauty and a unique woman of the medieval world, Eleanor of Aquitaine; his brothers the princes, vying for land and loyalty and power. And at the very center is Richard himself and the woman he loved above all others, the talented and free-spirited Blondelza, mother of his illegitimate son, who mocked the laws of God and man.

LIONHEART!

Great Fiction From SIGNET

- ☐ **THE RUNNING MAN** by Richard Bachman. (#AE1508—$2.50)*
- ☐ **SLEEPING BEAUTY** by L.L. Greene. (#AE1548—$2.50)*
- ☐ **WIFE FOUND SLAIN** by Caroline Crane. (#AE1614—$2.50)*
- ☐ **DEVIL'S EMBRACE** by Catherine Coulter. (#AE1853—$2.95)*
- ☐ **MINOTAUR** by Benjamin Tammuz. (#AW1582—$1.50)*
- ☐ **THE CURE** by Len Goldberg. (#AE1509—$2.50)*
- ☐ **KINGDOM OF SUMMER** by Gillian Bradshaw. (#AE1550—$2.75)*
- ☐ **NEW BLOOD** by Richard Salem. (#AE1615—$2.50)†
- ☐ **ROOFTOPS** by Tom Lewis. (#AE1735—$2.95)*
- ☐ **GAMES OF CHANCE** by Peter Delacourte. (#AE1510—$2.95)*
- ☐ **POSITION OF ULTIMATE TRUST** by William Beechcroft. (#AE1551—$2.50)*
- ☐ **LIONHEART!** by Martha Rofheart. (#AE1617—$3.50)*
- ☐ **EYE OF THE MIND** by Lynn Biederstadt. (#AE1736—$2.95)*
- ☐ **MY LADY HOYDEN** by Jane Sheridan. (#AE1511—$2.95)*
- ☐ **TAURUS** by George Wells. (#AE1553—$2.50)*
- ☐ **MIDAS** by Piers Kelaart. (#AE1618—$2.50)†

*Prices slightly higher in Canada
†Not available in Canada

Buy them at your local bookstore or use this convenient coupon for ordering.

THE NEW AMERICAN LIBRARY, INC.,
P.O. Box 999, Bergenfield, New Jersey 07621

Please send me the books I have checked above. I am enclosing $_____
(please add $1.00 to this order to cover postage and handling). Send check or money order—no cash or C.O.D.'s. Prices and numbers are subject to change without notice.

Name_____

Address_____

City _____ State _____ Zip Code _____
Allow 4-6 weeks for delivery.
This offer is subject to withdrawal without notice.

Lionheart!

A NOVEL OF
**RICHARD I,
KING OF ENGLAND**

by
Martha Rofheart

**A SIGNET BOOK
NEW AMERICAN LIBRARY**
TIMES MIRROR

PUBLISHER'S NOTE

This novel is a work of historical fiction. Names, characters, places and incidents relating to non-historical figures are either the product of the author's imagination or are used fictitiously. Any resemblance of such non-historical incidents, places or figures to actual events or locales or persons, living or dead, is entirely coincidental.

NAL BOOKS ARE AVAILABLE AT QUANTITY DISCOUNTS WHEN USED TO PROMOTE PRODUCTS OR SERVICES. FOR INFORMATION PLEASE WRITE TO PREMIUM MARKETING DIVISION, THE NEW AMERICAN LIBRARY, INC., 1633 BROADWAY, NEW YORK, NEW YORK 10019.

Copyright © 1981 by Martha Rofheart

All rights reserved including the right of reproduction in whole or in part in any form. For information address Simon & Schuster, A Division of Gulf and Western Corporation, Simon & Schuster Building, Rockefeller Center, 1230 Avenue of the Americas, New York, New York 10020.

This is an authorized reprint of a hardcover edition published by Simon and Schuster.

SIGNET TRADEMARK REG. U.S. PAT. OFF. AND FOREIGN COUNTRIES
REGISTERED TRADEMARK—MARCA REGISTRADA
HECHO EN CHICAGO, U.S.A.

SIGNET, SIGNET CLASSICS, MENTOR, PLUME, MERIDIAN AND NAL BOOKS are published by The New American Library, Inc., 1633 Broadway, New York, New York 10019

First Signet Printing, July, 1982

1 2 3 4 5 6 7 8 9

PRINTED IN THE UNITED STATES OF AMERICA

To Victor Chapin

CONTENTS

	Author's Note	ix
BOOK I	THE BOY *Told by Richard of Aquitaine, later Richard I of England*	1
BOOK II	THE GIRL *Told by Blondelza, the Glee-Maiden*	99
BOOK III	THE ROUTIER CAPTAIN *Told by Mercadier of Fouquebrun, Knight*	163
BOOK IV	THE MOTHER *Told by Eleanor, Duchess of Aquitaine and Queen of England*	203
BOOK V	THE BRIDE *Told by Berengaria, Princess of Navarre, later wife to Richard*	237
BOOK VI	THE SCRIBE *Told by Alexander the Monk, Chronicler of the Third Crusade*	281
BOOK VII	THE MAN *Told by Richard, King of England, called the Lionheart*	403
EPILOGUE	ANNO DOMINE 1204 *Told by Queen Eleanor, at Fontevrault Abbey*	455
	Notes and Acknowledgments	468

AUTHOR'S NOTE

Of the narrators of this novel, only one is invented: Blondelza. Alexander, Richard's foster brother, became one of the first medieval scholar-scientists, known as Alexander Neckham. Mercadier was the most famous of the mercenary captains of his age; nothing is known of his origins. The other characters in my story are, for the most part, historical, except for a few minor ones.

Richard's illegitimate son, Philippe of Cognac, became a renowned warrior, fighting on with King John after Richard's death; he is the hero (Philip the Bastard) of Shakespeare's *King John*.

The physical characteristics, at least of the men, are described in painstaking detail by the contemporary chroniclers, though our ideas of the women can be gleaned only from the songs of the troubadours.

I have kept the familiar English forms of the famous names, such as Richard, John, Eleanor, William—and the French Alys—though in the twelfth century there was no English language as we know it now, and nothing resembling modern French. Most of the other proper names I have used are those in the langue d'oc, the language of southern France and of the troubadours.

As to the interpretation of Richard's character, his most recent biographer, John Gillingham, observes:

> He was the first king to become a folk hero . . . none of his predecessors possessed the magnetic quality which attracted legend and story. But Richard certainly possessed it. No sooner was he dead than the process of legend-making got under way. Most remarkable of all is that the legend-making still goes on today. It is only in the last thirty years that the story has gone around that Richard was homosexual. Although this is now generally accepted as the "plain, unvarnished truth" repeated in works as staid as the Encyclopaedia Britannica, it is in fact no more than a highly colored assertion which

cannot be substantiated—in other words, a new legend which tells us more about our own time than it does about the character of the man whom it ostensibly concerns.

It is difficult to separate legend from fact, and indeed, Richard's contemporary chroniclers portrayed him as a man without flaws; even the hostile scribes (mainly French and Arab) were glowing in their accounts. Their descriptions of his looks, his strength, his kingliness, are here, in my portrait, considerably toned down, in the interest of a fuller, more human portrait of the man.

The high Middle Ages offer tremendous scope to the historian, and particularly to the novelist. There were the Crusades and, in counterpoint, the first seeds of religious dissent, the Cathar movement, so widespread that it threatened Rome itself. There was, above all, the troubadour culture, which mirrored that code of knightly honor which we now call chivalry, and was the highest expression of what is known as Courtly Love. I have attempted to incorporate all of these elements into my novel.

BOOK I

THE BOY

*Told by Richard of Aquitaine,
later Richard I of England*

CHAPTER 1

I CANNOT REMEMBER a time when there was peace in our family. It began with my mother and father, who could not agree on the smallest things, or so it seemed to me as a child. Not a day went by without harsh words or flashing eyes. Except, of course, on occasions of state, when they sat side by side upon their thrones, or presided over a feast table lined with dignitaries and ambassadors. They were both masters of irony and innuendo, and the tension between them crackled like lightning, even in their silences.

And so we children were not close either; not even allies, as might be expected. We were enemies, growing up together.

My oldest brother, William, died early, long before I was born, and the second son, named Henry after Father, became the heir to England and all the Angevin possessions on the Continent. After him came my sister, Mathilda, and then me. Geoffrey, Eleanor, who was Mother's namesake, Joanna, and John completed our family, a large one; it seems Mother and Father were able to agree on one thing, at least!

Henry was clearly Father's favorite, always getting the best gifts, the most indulgence, and the rare caress. He was the image of Father as well, even to the carroty hair and bowlegs, even to the rages. I used to think, when I was quite small, that my big brother had suddenly gone mad; he would, without warning, turn bright red, his eyes starting from his head, and throw himself upon the floor, shrieking and beating with his fists upon the stones. Often he would beat his head too; there was a permanent bruise upon his forehead, an angry purple lump. In later years, from vanity, he wore his hair in a long fringe to hide it.

No one could stop these fits; the nurses wrung their hands and clucked helplessly, while the serving-folk stood about in a circle, trembling and anxious, and we children retreated to the farthest wall. Once Mother slapped him hard, across the face, a time-honored remedy for hysterics, but it did not work. He turned and bit her in the leg, right through her gown and shift. "Like father, like son," she said bitterly.

We knew, finally, that Henry was *not* mad, when we saw our father in a rage. *He* was not locked up, he was even King of England—so we knew. And he was worse, being bigger and taking up more room on the floor. No, this was the famous "Angevin rage," as it came to be known later and written about by the soberest scholars; there was even a note of admiration in their writings! We are all tainted by this terrible temper, though I control mine, making myself sick at the stomach instead. I have seen little Joanna stamp her foot and pull her sister's hair or claw her cheek, and John, the baby, turned quite blue in his tantrums, even in his cradle; he would hold his breath until they feared for his life, and had to be turned upside down and thumped on the back to start him breathing again. Perhaps it is true, as the legends say, that we are descended from the Devil; I have heard Mother say so often enough, since it is on Father's side, the Angevin side.

The Angevin country begins between Normandy and Brittany and continues down through Maine and Anjou. It is low country, much of it lying in the valley of the Loire, with a huge peasantry and many petty knights, all owing allegiance to the great counts of my father's family. Dark tales have been told of this family through the years, tales of witchcraft and sorcery. "From the Devil they came; to the Devil they will go" was one churchman's stern warning. Mother, for one, often found it a handy saying.

"Blood is thicker than water" was another saying; my nurse, Hodierna, was fond of this one. I seem to remember her saying it every day, smiling gently and pushing me toward my brothers. Hodierna was my wet nurse, and her milk must have been more potent than either blood or water, for it was her son, Alexander, suckled along with me, who was my dearest friend. We were born on the same day, September 8, and as close as twins. He was a thoughtful, grave boy with straight dark brows and fine, shining brown hair; brown all over he was, like a drawing, hair, eyes, and skin, without a hint of color, even in his lips. I used to envy him, for I blushed like a girl, often for no reason. Alexander had a trick of tossing his head, very like a restive horse, to shake back a lock of hair which was forever falling over his forehead and into his eyes. I called him "Saracen" once, for my father's Arabian stallion, and told him why; he nodded and looked thoughtful. Afterward, whenever his head flicked up in the familiar gesture and I caught his eye, his still, serious face would break into a wide white smile. He had a slow, quiet way about him, a kind of authority; my brothers could not goad him into a cross word, though they set me off like tinder.

Most of the anger between us Angevin offspring was among the boys; Henry was two years older than I and Geoffrey a year younger, all close enough to be uncomfortable. John, of course, was nine years younger than I was, and did not come into it in those days, though he made up for it later. Even my sisters squabbled among themselves. The one closest to me in age, Mathilda, was sent away early to be reared in the household of her betrothed, Henry of Saxony, as is the custom with noble girls. She wept bitterly to leave home, and I along with her, for I was very fond of her; I was still young enough to weep without embarrassment.

"I feel for Mathilda too," said Eleanor, touching my hand. "A woman's lot is not an enviable one."

I stared at her. She, Eleanor the Queen, was the most envied woman in Christendom. She had been born to wealth and power, the heiress of the largest and richest domain of France, Aquitaine. She had ruled France too, earlier, as wife to Louis Capet, and now she was England's queen, and, with my father, suzerain of most of the lands of western Europe. She was very beautiful, even allowing for the exaggeration of the troubadours, tall and graceful, black of hair and eyes, with skin like cream and a dazzling smile. When she walked among them, the people, high and low alike, cheered her, looking as though they might fall upon their faces for love.

Then I remembered Father, with his string of mistresses and his many bastards, and remembered too Louis of France, whom men called "the Monk," who went to bed with a hair shirt and a prayer.

I had a little picture that I had found at the bottom of an old traveling chest, a likeness of Mother from long ago, in the days of her first marriage. The paint had faded and flaked, and the parchment was curled at the edges and dry; no one had thought to cherish it, for the artist was unknown and sadly lacking in skill. Still, one could see the likeness, though the chin was too long and the fingers like sausages. Mother was on horseback and dressed in armor with a

Crusader's cross upon the hauberk; the face was very young. They had called her, on that Crusade, "the Amazon Queen." The Crusade had failed, and the marriage too, and shortly afterward they were divorced.

I cannot think why she married Father; he was not yet King of England, only the third in a shaky, war-torn succession. Perhaps she fell in love with him; the poets write of such things. He was a lusty youth, with at least one bastard son in tow, and a fine knight proven in battle and tournament. He might even have been attractive, though it is difficult to see now; certainly he was a far cry from Louis the Monk! That ruddy coloring and stocky, powerful build are much admired, and his restless energy and commanding presence still draw all eyes. He is shorter than she, and she goes in heel-less slippers so as not to tower above him; they sometimes look, walking together, like a lady with her pet bear!

She is older than he by a good bit, though of course it is never said. But he was nineteen at his coronation in London, and she already had two half-grown daughters at the French court. It makes no matter, for one could never tell; Eleanor's face is as smooth as ivory, and her slim carriage might belong to a young girl, while Henry, our father, has had white hairs in his beard since I can remember, and a face beaten by all kinds of weather and seamed with the ravages of his choleric temperament.

He must have loved her too, once; how could he not? But I never saw any signs of it, unless jealousy is a sign. I have seen Father rage like a wounded boar over a verse that praised her red lips or her black eyebrows, and I have seen him gnash his teeth when she smiled upon a fawning courtier. But then it is true that he falls into rages at the slightest thing, if he has a mind to it. The very mention of her first husband will send him into a fit, for instance. Though that is partly envy of Louis's possessions, all the lands of the Vexin, and the beautiful city of Paris, which he deems too fair for "that pious ass," as he calls him.

I never saw Mother show resentment or rancor over Father's doxies, until the time of our youngest brother's birth. In my innocence I used to think that she did not know about them. There was a new one every day, and he flaunted them before the whole world, uncaring. Henry and I used to place bets on every new face at court; the pages did too, and the men-at-arms. There was one old Crusader, missing an arm, who used to hold the bets for us and pay up at the end of the week, taking his cut; it augmented his pension. Until Rosamund Clifford, "Rose of the World," as the English called her later.

I remember well the day of little John's birth; I was just old enough by then to take everything in, just turned nine years. He was born in our manor at Oxford, my birthplace too. Mother liked that little manor; it was new-built, and small enough to be comfortable. She had furnished it with precious things from the East, thick rugs with glowing patterns, low, cushioned chairs, and silk hangings at the walls. Her chamber on the second floor was the loveliest room I had ever seen, all delicate pinks and violets, with a low ceiling, two large windows, and a fireplace in the wall.

I was the only one of us children with her at that time, for a wonder, and I was happy, having her all to myself. We had been there nearly a week; John was taking his time, already showing the contrary nature he was to become famous for later. "Hurry up, you little knave," Mother would cry, rapping at her huge belly. "I am getting sick of dragging you about." She said such things in front of me now, for I was a big boy and growing up; it made me proud.

"How do you know it will be a knave, and not a damsel?" I asked.

"Because he kicks so hard," she answered, smiling.

Every afternoon she came out into the tilting-yard to watch me at practice, for the December weather was unusually mild. I had had real lessons this last year, from one of our finest knights, William the Marshal; before, I had just picked it up in scraps and pieces, watching the squires that were up for the next dubbing. Father had neglected us shamefully; we should have been started much earlier on our training, at six or thereabouts, like other noble boys. Still, I was coming along well, and could hit the quintain squarely nine times out of ten. There was not a real one here; I had rigged up a bale of straw with a Saracen's head painted on top and hung it with iron weights I had found in the stables. It was not a real tilting-yard either, just a little courtyard where the dogs were let loose to run. I did not have a horse even, and had to make do with my Welsh pony, getting old now, and too small for me; my legs nearly touched the ground, for I was growing fast. She was clever, though, the pony, and knew all the intricate paces; I called her Guinevere, after Arthur's queen. The watching must have tired Mother, so near her time, but she gave no sign, and sat through it all, clapping her hands at the end of each session and saying, "You will be the finest knight in the world, my Dickon." The praise warmed me like wine. I saw myself in full shining armor, astride a purebred Arabian stallion, setting out to find the Grail, or to slay dragons (I was sure there were such beasts, in other parts); most often I dreamed of freeing the Holy Sepulchre, of taking Jerusalem, picturing myself riding in glory through her golden gates, with Alexander at my heels.

"You will be my squire," I would say to him. "And someday, in some great battle in the desert there, you will do some great deed, like killing ten infidels, or saving my life maybe, and I will knight you on the field." He only smiled, and tossed back his errant lock of hair.

Alexander was with us there, for his mother, Hodierna, was midwife as well as nurse, and Mother valued her ministrations, and was fond of her besides. We had not many in train, outside of our soldier guards, just some half-dozen ladies, a Jew physician, Abram, and Mother's troubadour, Bernard. Not counting the manor servants, who came and went like shadows, or the musicians, brighter shadows. I knew all these folk by name, of course, as I knew the soldiers; what else had I to do to fill my days? My tutor had been left behind at Windsor, with a quartain fever; I had not looked inside a book the whole time!

At the week's end, the weather changed; a strong wind blew from the north all one night, rattling the shutters, and the next day the courtyard was rimed with a pale frost and slippery. It was still not really cold, but the sky was heavy with scudding clouds, through which a sulphurous yellow sun shone, evil-looking. Inside it was drafty and dark, and the fireplaces smoked; we coughed and shivered.

There was nothing to do. Alexander and I played a game of chess, but I won, as usual, boring us both. He wandered off somewhere to read, and I tried a new song on my lute. The melody would not come right, though in my head I almost had it, and finally a string snapped, making an end to it. I flung the lute down, sighing, and went along the hall to climb the stairs and scratch at Mother's chamber door. There was no need; in the daylight hours her rooms were open to all. Sometimes, in her chambers in our larger castles, there was scarcely an inch to stand up in, so filled were they with all manner of folk, ladies and knights, minstrels, singers, peddlers with their wares, account keepers, cooks, scurrying maids, and most or all of us children. It was true of Father too, and I suppose of most great nobles. They lived, as it were, on show; there was never any privacy, even in the bath or close-stool. They were alone only when they lay in love, and Father was not so nice about that either; I had come upon him once, lolling half naked in the steamy laundry room with a wench still red to the arms with the hot water.

Here, the chamber was small, and no one about but two of her ladies, a long length of silk stretched between them on an embroidery frame, and Bernard de Ventadour, her troubadour.

The ladies looked up and smiled, one of them, Louise de Brécy, putting her hand to her mouth to cover the gap in her front teeth. Her husband, now dead, had knocked them out long ago in a drunken fit. I had never looked at her closely before, being ashamed; I saw now that her eyes were lovely still, darkly glowing in the light of the candles. All Mother's waiting-women had been with her for years and I thought of them as old; they were not, of course, they were just her age, except that they looked it.

Bernard was her age too, give or take a year; there was gray in his black hair and a purple pouch under each eye. Otherwise, he was a fine-looking man, with a trim figure and well-turned leg; his calling kept him young. He sat beside Mother, talking softly into her ear; there was a little smile on her lips as she sat before her mirror. It was the hour when she painted her face, before the evening meal.

Her dark hair lay on her shoulders, caught loosely in a net of golden threads; she sometimes wore it that way when she was at home, without fine company. It was thick and lustrous, with a wave, like mine, except that mine is Father's color, a kind of red. She saw me in the mirror, her smile widening; she held out her hand. "Careful, Dickon, it's sticky!" She wiggled her fingers, tipped in blue and red paint. I kissed the back of her hand, carefully, not touching the paint. I was used to it; from childhood I had watched this ritual, loving it. I loved to see her features, blocked out by the ivory-colored wash she sponged on first, emerge slowly into ruby lips and long, black-rimmed eyes, like a picture painted on an empty page. She was a master at it. She designed all the patterns for her tapestries and her embroidered stoles and cushions, tracing the lines out lightly on the cloth for her ladies to follow with their silks.

As I watched, she took up a little pan, filled with some dark, gummy stuff, and held it over a candle's flame; then, dipping a straw into it, she carefully beaded each lash. The effect was startling, widening her eyes to huge starry lamps. This was something new. Curious, I sniffed at the little pan; there was only a smell of burning. "Wax," she said, "and charcoal . . . the glee-maidens' trick. Bernard got it from one of his jongleurs." She patted his hand lightly and flashed him a dazzling smile. "There, it is finished," she said, wiping her fingers upon a linen cloth. "Give me your arm, Sir Poet. I am heavy as lead."

But as she rose, I saw, in the mirror, her eyes change; she clapped a hand to her side. "I think . . . Fetch Hodierna— the doctor." Her face was very still, as if she were listening; then she moaned, just once, a low, animal sound.

The Jew came forward then, moving quickly, though he was a gray-beard. He bent his head to her great belly, with that same listening look, then kneaded it twice, gently, his fingers long and expert; she groaned again.

"It is coming," he said, in his soft, sibilant voice. "Quick!" he hissed. "The midwife!"

I darted to the door, seeing as I passed them her women's startled faces, hearing the embroidery frame clattering to the floor.

I found Hodierna belowstairs, in the kitchens, and followed on her heels as she sped up the stairs to the chamber door. "No, Dickon. You cannot come in," she said firmly. "This is women's work. Go now, the both of you!" For Bernard stood there too, uncertain, wringing his hands. "Go now," she said, more kindly. "It will be over soon. This is her tenth . . ." She shut the door.

But it was not over soon. All through the rest of the day and into the night feet clattered on the stairs; maids carried buckets of water up, splashing on the flagstones, and piles of linen cloths, and ran down, aprons flung up over their faces, sobbing. Once I saw the cook, fat, white-faced under his tall hat, scurry up, clutching a long kitchen knife. What was it for . . . to cut the cord?

I looked at Bernard, who sat huddled on a bench near the fire, all his worldly poise flown. He spread his hands, shrugging. "I think it is a charm," he said. "To cut the pain." He tried to smile, his lips stretching in a sorry grin. I eyed him furtively; I had never seen a grown man in such a state before, trembling like a woman. Of course, his blood was not noble; he was only a farrier's son, or a tanner's, I forget which, come to high place by his art. He should not be here at all, I thought resentfully; it was as though he took our father's place.

And where was Father? It was his child, after all. Then, suddenly, something struck me, cold. There were looks I remembered, eye to eye, and secret smiles, the lingering touch of hand on hand. Could it be? Gossip had linked these two for years, since Bernard's first aching love verses. But I had never believed it, for she was my mother, and a queen. Now I remembered too how Father, some years ago, had banished this man from our court. Why? Dark thoughts rose up in me, like bile; my fingers closed on the wine goblet I held, thin, cloudy glass from Venice. The fragile stem snapped, and the glass fell to the floor, splintering, the red wine spreading like blood, staining the gray stone. Dark blood dripped from my hand too, and I sat staring at it, frozen. Bernard leaped up from the bench, his face all concern. He took my hand in his, turning it over, clucking like a nurse.

"It is nothing," I said. "A scratch only."

"It is your lute hand," he said, frowning. "And your sword hand too." And he tore a strip of silk from the white sleeve of his shirt and wound it tightly about my arm, above the wrist. Slowly the welling blood stopped.

"How did you know to do that?" I asked, surprised.

"From my campaigning days," he said, smiling at my surprised look. "I am a belted knight, you know," he added, with a sort of wry pride. "Count Raymond of Antioch knighted me at Beyrout."

"On Crusade?" I looked at him with a new respect. "On that same Crusade with my mother?"

"The same," he said. "But I did not know the lady then . . . I saw her once . . ." His voice faltered. He had been wrapping that same piece of silk about the wound, but his hands halted in their task. His dark eyes were looking far away, into a distance I could not see. "I saw her when she took the cross . . . from the Abbot of Troyes it was. All in white she stood before him, and her long hands like white flowers . . ." He did not speak then for a moment, and the far distances still glowed in his eyes. "There was a look on her face you cannot imagine, like . . . like a lamp lit from within." He shook his head as if to clear it, and bent to the bandage on my hand, tying it in a firm, neat knot. "I took the cross myself that day."

"Because of her?" I said, a little shy.

He laughed shortly. "Because of her." He shook his head again, and his eyes met mine, then veered away. "So many . . ." he began. "You cannot know . . . thousands took the cross that day . . . after the fair young Queen of France."

In an instant I saw them, poor petty castellans of the viscounty, with the mud and mire of their wretched small holdings still staining their rough tunics; coarse gawping mercenaries in pillaged rusty mail; foot soldiers in leather jerkins, carrying their crossbows in chapped red hands; and at their head a shining girl, all light and spirit. It was not the Mother I knew, but I believed him, and ached for those long-ago days, now lost.

Through the silence that was between us I heard the din from the dining hall; the manor folk still sat at supper.

"Will you not eat, sir?" I said, with a new shyness; I was ashamed at my thoughts of him. "They will be letting the cookfires die down soon."

"I cannot," he said.

"Nor I."

I do not know how long we sat, boy and man together, both loving her, both miserable with fear. Once I said, my words stumbling, "Is it always like this?"

He shook his head. "No . . . I know not."

"She told me always," I said, near tears, "that it was nothing, a confinement. Not half so bad, she said, as a toothache." I tried to smile.

Bernard wet his lips. "They say that women do not remember from one time to the next . . ." . His voice trailed off, his eyes straying.

I turned. A priest had come in the side door, with a boy, younger than I, carrying the pyx. Someone had sent to fetch them, for I heard the varlets' boots stamping in the passage. The priest and his boy went through the little doorway, covered by a painted leather flap, that led to the chapel. As they passed, I saw that their heads and shoulders were all powdered with snow. Seeing me stare, the priest signed me, his hand sketching a cross in the air.

"It's begun to snow, then," I said, thinking, Father will never get through now. We had expected him for three days; he had been patrolling the Welsh border, for he never liked to leave such tasks to others, and the Welsh were always troublesome. Wales was devout, though, and would call a truce in good time for Christmas; so we expected him.

And then cold fearful thoughts began to work in me, born of the silence and the waiting. What if, as Father rode by some walled town—half-armed and bareheaded, like as not (for he was always careless of his person, and arrogant in his strength)—what if a stray arrow, loosed from an unseen enemy atop the wall, took him in the throat? And Mother too, vanquished by that other enemy within her body . . . Where would I be then?

Suddenly there began, worse than all my imaginings, a dreadful shrieking, inhuman, over and over, and a sobbing, long-drawn-out wail. Numb with terror, I thought the whole castle would have come rushing in, but only one kitchen slut paused in the passage, carrying a great tray of dirty dishes. She cocked her head, listening, as the wailing grew soft and died away. Then she nodded sagely and said, "There. It is over."

I jumped up and ran to her. "Haumette," I cried, "is she— My mother . . . is she dead, then?"

"Dead? She? Bless you, lad . . . not her! Strong as a mare she is, our beautiful lady . . . she'll have a dozen more!" And she passed through to the kitchens, shaking her head and muttering, "Dead, is it? Boys!"

I stood then, irresolute, at the foot of the stairs, Bernard at my shoulder, not certain whether to brave the closed chamber door. Suddenly, tiny and thin in the cloaking silence, came a sound like the mewing of a kitten, complaining. I started up the stairs; the door opened and Hodierna stood there, her finger to her lips. The front of her kirtle was filthy, stained with wet and with blood; exhaustion pinched her face. She had to clear her throat twice before she could speak. "She is delivered," she said, hoarsely. "A fine boy."

I whispered anxiously, "Mother . . . ?"

"She is resting."

I let my breath out in a long, sobbing sigh; I realized for the first time that my face was wet with tears.

Hodierna's tired face moved pityingly. "Oh, Dickon, were you so frightened?"

She put out her hand to touch my face; I threw my arms around her and sobbed in earnest, my head buried in the soft stuff of her dress.

"Dickon, Dickon, you will wet all the top part of me too! Hush, lad, hush! All is well."

"The priest," I sobbed. "When I saw the priest—"

"There must always be the sacrament at a birthing," she said. "God must be there, to give . . . or to take. Hush, my sweeting. Hush! It takes more than another contrary son to get the best of Dame Eleanor."

I laughed shakily and drew my sleeve across my wet face. "May I not see her?" I asked.

Her face softened again. "A moment only . . . and be very quiet, she may be asleep." She looked past me. "Not you, Sir Poet! There is no place there for you!"

"Oh, no," said Bernard humbly. "I will wait outside . . . and pray." He smiled, his face twisting. "Now I will pray, now that all is over and there is no need."

"You can give thanks to the Holy Mother," said Hodierna, a little sternly. "Come, sweeting," she said, drawing me after her. "Softly now."

The air in the birth chamber was foul, choking me. Steam, smoke from the fire, bitter herbs, acrid medicines, and over all, the close rank-sweet smell of blood. The room was littered with flung napkins, crumpled; piles of dirty cloths stood in the corners, along with pots and buckets; one large tub had tipped over and made a puddle on the floor. The great bed was an island, though, fresh and white, smoothed over with sheets of some fine, thin stuff, linen or silk, with an ermine coverlet at the foot. Mother lay in the middle of it, her eyes closed; her long body barely raised the covering sheets, so thin was she now. I tiptoed to her side.

She was dressed in a new red shift, sheer as a veil; her fllesh beneath it gleamed like marble in the firelight. Great wax candles at the bed's head lit her face; it was small and still and empty, looking as if it had been wiped of life. There was not a trace of color, or of the paints she had so carefully applied as I stood watching. Her hair was wet and plastered to her forehead in little ragged tails, and her lashes lay like black feathers against her white cheeks. I could not see her breathe.

I held my own breath, not to disturb her, and made the sign of the Cross. The faint movement must have roused her, for she opened her eyes. In the black depths of them, red gleams showed, in the fire's glow. Her mouth curved ever so slightly. "Oh . . . I am so tired," she whispered. "So tired."

I heard that mewing sound again, this time at my elbow. Hodierna stood, her face bent over a tiny bundle, smiling. "Will you not look at your new little son, Lady?"

Mother reached out her arms slowly and took the bundle, bending weakly to its face for a long moment. Then she handed it back, her arms dropping beside her, as though they were too heavy. I could not read her wan face, but the little smile had deepened. "An Angevin, for sure," she murmured.

I bent over the bundle in my turn; a little, little thing like a doll, the smallest being in the world, all wrapped about in bands of white linen, with a tiny white cap upon its head. Between the two whites a wrinkled face no bigger than a child's fist, the color of a boiled shrimp. From beneath the cap showed a thin black fuzz of hair; cloudy dark eyes opened, staring balefully straight at me. Then the face crumpled, into a rage so like Father's that I laughed. It was Father's face, suddenly, shrunken and turned that new, new pink. And a wail came forth then, no kitten's now, but a brassy roar, angry.

Hodierna rocked him in her arms. "Now, now, there's a lusty little man . . . there's a fine rooster, hush, hush!" It wailed on, its face purpling.

"He wants his dinner, poor little John," said Mother. "Put him here, beside me." The baby stopped crying and nuzzled up against her, trying to find the breast, its small mouth open like a nestling's. Mother laughed again. "He knows what he wants, the little knave . . . though he did try to come out backward." Weakly she pulled a corner of the sheet up, to shield the tiny head; loud sucking noises came from under it.

I moved my eyes away, feeling an obscure pain I could not voice. Mother watched me, her eyes soft. She reached up and took my hand; her fingers were thin and cool, and held mine hard.

"What need have I of more sons?" she said, smiling small. "I have all I want."

CHAPTER 2

"IF HE WILL not come to me, I will go to him!" cried Mother. "Woodstock is but half a day's journey, at most." Her face was vivid with the prospect of action; she had been pent up since her churching, two days before. Now she was feverishly turning out her coffers, and bright heaps of color lay flung about the room as she pondered which gowns and kirtles to take with her. "This vair trim is all mangy here at the neck," she said, frowning. "And moths have gotten into the ermine cloak." She looked at Bernard, who hung about her as before, like a pet dog. "Will they do for your jongleur folk, do you think? The cloth is good."

"Too good for players," said Hodierna firmly. "It can be cut down for capes for the little princesses. The jongleurs can have the fur. The moth will not show from a distance."

"You are right, of course. Take what you will, then, of this coffer. Everything is out of style, or worn." She sank back on her heels, looking happy. "The rest I will take with me . . . they are like new, since I have grown slim again."

I looked at Mother, glowing among the tumbled silks. Impossible to believe that ten days ago she had been so close to death. For so she had, swore the Jew physician, calling her a Christian witch. And they had laughed together, Abram and the Queen, as thick as two thieves. "And can I sit a horse, then?" she asked him. "If the saddle be well padded," he replied. "It is your rear, not mine." And they laughed again. Mother would not have countenanced such words from an equal, and Father, saying them, would have drawn blows. But the Jew could get away with anything. "You have saved my life—for the tenth time," she said, grave now. "You deserve a knighthood."

"Bah," said the Jew. "Knight me no knights! I would rather have the price in medicines."

"And so you shall," she said softly. "A knight's ransom. I thank you, fair friend." And she pressed his hand.

Dark color crept into his thin cheeks, and his sad old eyes

burned like coals. Even a Jew, ancient of days, was not proof against Mother's charm. Only Father, I thought resentfully—only Father did not love her.

For word had come, finally, from Woodstock, barely eight miles away. He had subdued the Welsh rebels, and would rest there, in Woodstock Manor, hunting and keeping Christmas quietly. "I pray you keep well, and that the babe thrives," the letter ended. There was no mention of me, his son, and no word of cheer. Just his signature, big and bold, sprawling over half the page, "Henri, Roi."

Geoffrey, his bastard, who had brought the letter, would not meet our eyes. He was a youth of eighteen, and kind; I sensed he felt shame for our father. "No, madame," he said, in answer to Mother's questions. "He is not wounded or sick—only tired. The campaign was long and grueling."

"Still, one feels he might have pushed on, being so close."

"Woodstock was a haven . . . our first," said Geoffrey. "And then, the hunting is good in those parts. Father would rather hunt stag than Welsh," he said with a smile. "And, too, there has been much poaching thereabouts . . . he thought to see justice done."

Mother's lips were pressed together, her eyes bleak. "His justice! It is Christ's birthday . . . can he not show mercy instead?"

"Madame, I am sorry," said Geoffrey unhappily.

Her face softened. "Poor Geoffrey . . . it is not your fault. And you look weary, also. You must have food and wine. Come."

And so she had suddenly decided to set out, against custom, so soon after her confinement. The new baby, John, of course, could not be subjected to the bitter weather; he would be left with his wet nurse, a slatternly creature with a fierce squint in both eyes. "A foul wench," said Mother, with a rueful smile, "but the only one to be found in all the countryside. And her milk agrees with him."

We were up at first light, eager to be on our way, but by the time the sumpter mules were loaded, a round dozen of them, the winter sun was halfway up the sky. It was a fine, crisp morning, for England, the air clear and very cold. We were swaddled to the eyebrows in cloaks and furs, but still the breath in our nostrils froze in a thin crust and our gloved hands were stiff on the reins. The snow, sparkling like diamonds, was crusty and hard, and at every step the horses' hooves made a sharp crackling sound, loud in the empty countryside.

We rode in a great company, like a procession, for, besides our household folk, there went along with us some fourteen men-at-arms. Though there was little need, here in England, for armed escort; the land, once so lawless, was now at peace. Before my time, for long years it had been torn by the wars between my grandmother Mathilda and her cousin Stephen, the usurper. And for nineteen feckless years of Stephen's rule, the great nobles, greedy and harsh, had scarred the land with huge fortresses, from which they spread brutal oppression throughout town, field, and village. Armed bands of their mercenaries prowled the forests, raping and killing; no road was safe. Bandits slit throats for a farthing, holy shrines were thrown down; England was a wasteland.

Father had put a stop to all that. When he came to the throne, he hunted out these robbers' nests, hanged the lawless nobles, and set sheriffs in every shire, imposing a peace as harsh and brutal as war. Dukes were stripped of their lands and titles, their goods confiscate to the Crown. The land now prospered, the coffers of the kingdom swelled to bursting. In all the length and breadth of the shires, there was no justice but the King's justice; so much had he done for England.

And Father was not content to leave the administration to others; he was constantly in the saddle, riding to the lonely, stark moor country, or to the windy fastnesses of the north, or on down through the gently rolling meadows to the south. He would be up before dawn, and everyone else with him; a wonderful bustle and confusion, with men running about as though they were mad, bumping into each other in the half-light. Horses whinnied and snorted, armor clanked, spurs rang; Father would pace the hall, impatient, not stopping to eat breakfast but cramming a stale bun into his mouth with unwashed fingers and swallowing it down whole, while we children hung over the upstairs balcony and watched, envious.

And, where he passed the King left potent signs; the King's justice was never pretty. I was reminded of it again and again on this little journey, for at every crossroad at least one gallows bore its horrible fruit; not far from the castle three skeletons hung, rattling, picked clean long ago, the eyeholes showing blue sky beyond, and the white bones covered with thin silver rime. A fresh body hung beside them, stinking even in the freezing cold. Where the right hand had been was a blackened stump, so I guessed he had been an archer. Mother covered her nose with her furred cloak; above it her eyes looked sick. "A poacher," Geoffrey whispered, as though the poor dead man could hear. "Father caught him two days ago."

Something moved in the bushes, and a scatter of snow powdered the air. Two of our men-at-arms, lightning-quick, were off their horses and pouncing like hawks at the place. They came up with a small squirming bundle of rags; above it burned a pair of huge frightened eyes and a shock head, all bloody. Mother made a sign to bring the creature forward.

It was a boy, skinny and blue with cold, the thin rags barely covering his body. Under his matted hair was a great raw wound, still oozing blood, a brand mark that covered his forehead; in the swollen flesh one could trace a shape, the letter "p." He struggled weakly and pointed to the ground behind the bush; hoarse cries came from his throat. He looked to be about my age, but undersized.

"A thief, Your Majesty," said the man who held him, looking important.

"Nonsense," said Mother. "What is there to steal? He pointed at something . . . see what it is."

They dragged out another bundle, long and thin, stiff as a log; a woman, clearly dead, the face dark yellow against the white snow, and strangely beautiful in death, like a carving dug up from ancient earth. We could see she had been young.

"Your mother, boy?" asked my mother, her voice soft.

The boy nodded dumbly, his eyes black with hate and fear.

"And your father . . . ?"

He squirmed again, violently. The hands tightened on him, twisting the thin arms behind his back.

"Loose him," said Mother quietly. "He cannot go far. Can you speak, boy? Don't be afraid . . . no one will hurt you."

Set free, the boy stumbled and nearly fell; his feet, wrapped in old rags, were frostbitten and could not support him. But he straightened himself, finally, and stared defiantly at us.

Mother spoke again, gently. "What is your name, boy?"

"Will," he said hoarsely. "Will, after—" He jerked his head toward the gallows. "After him . . . my father."

"You are young for a poacher, Will," said Mother, still gentle.

"Father took me along to help. It was the first time . . ."

"Did you get a deer, Will?"

"Na," he said bitterly. "He got two rabbits . . . before they caught him. I skinned 'em," he added, a note of pride in his voice. "We was taking 'em home to Mum—" His words splintered into sobs, and he raised his arm to his eyes, crying.

"Two lives and a boy maimed for a brace of rabbits." Mother spoke low, but I heard her. She had let the fur cloak down, unmindful of the stinking air, and I saw her face, white and cold. "The king's justice is hard . . . but God's is harder. God and His gentle mother judge him—I cannot!" She crossed herself on head and breast, closing her eyes for a moment. Mother was usually private at her devotions; she must have been greatly moved.

"Come closer, Will . . . Have you brothers and sisters?"

"No, Mum." He had seen her face, and his eyes were changed, the fear nearly gone from them. "There was two little ones, but they died a while back. Alfred Priest-son said they starved."

Mother felt in the purse that hung from her belt. "Here take this, Will. It will not pay you for what you have lost but . . ."

She had given him a gold bezant. He had probably never seen one, and he looked as if he had been struck by lightning. "I thank 'ee, Mum."

"Will you come with us, little Will, and serve me all your days?" Will nodded, with a dazed look. "Take him up on a horse, somebody, and bring him to the kitchen. That forehead needs seeing to . . . and he must have broth too."

A guardsman swung Will up on the saddle before him. I heard the boy say, "Who be the lady, sir?"

"The Queen, lunkhead."

"*Oh-ee-ee-ee.*"

We rode on to Woodstock Palace.

CHAPTER 3

WOODSTOCK WAS A fair manor, small and strong, set within a high thick wall, and moated. In the midst of old, wild forestland, surrounded by tall trees, it lay like a jewel upon the bosom of a little hill, its stones white with snow and sparkling in the sun. Little icicles hung like fingers along all its turrets and towers, and ice cracked like glass on the drawbridge as we rode in.

Father had made a favorite of this place, for its hunting. Deer abounded in the forest; we could see the soft brown shapes moving swiftly behind the trees. Wild boar nested there too, in the deeper dark, dangerous prey with little furious red eyes. The gates were half-manned, so I knew there must be a hunting party out. Even as I thought it, there came the long low notes of a hunting horn, muffled by the trees, and the deeper baying of hounds.

"The master is gone after stag, Your Majesty," said the old steward when we had come into the hall. "They spotted a twelve-pointer yesterday."

"Yes, well, we cannot expect him before nightfall, then," said Mother. "Geoffrey, see that the little poacher is cared for—some warm food and clothes, and his wound tended. No, Hodierna. Stay by me," she said as the nurse started after Geoffrey. "I will need you, and there are goodwives in the kitchen to see to it . . . Show me to my rooms," she said to the steward.

The man's old face trembled as if he had the palsy. "They—they are not ready, Your Majesty . . . the beds are unmade."

She stared at him. "Well, send women to me, then, and be quick, my man. I must rest. Come, Dickon." And she swept past him and up the stairs. He looked, poor old thing, as if he might swoon where he stood; I wondered what ailed him.

The door to Mother's privy wing stood open, but within all was dark and smelled close; some perfume cloyed the air, and through it the scorched smell of guttering candles.

21

"The shutters, Hodierna," said Mother. "And light some braziers. The fire is out."

I ran to help Hodierna. "Give us a hand, Alex," I said, snapping my fingers to bring him to life. The sights of our journey had quite undone Alexander; he was ever squeamish. "You look green," I said. "You will have to get used to such things . . . war is worse."

"I will never go to war," he muttered, under his breath. I laughed a little, because everyone goes to war sometime, except varlets.

The catch on the last shutter, near the bed, was broken, and we had to wrestle with it to get it open. It fell back, finally, banging against the wall and sending a flood of light across the great scarlet-hung bed. The coverlets were tumbled, and a girl, young and blond, sat up in the middle, between the flung cushions, clutching a white bearskin to her naked shoulders.

Behind me I heard Mother laugh, a low harsh sound. "A white rabbit . . . I have never seen one skinned before!"

The girl on the bed quivered like a rabbit, indeed; the red hangings shook with it, and we could hear her teeth chatter.

"Well, doxy?" Mother's voice was like droplets of ice, hard and cutting.

"I . . . We—we never thought . . . He said—the King said you lay ill . . . too ill to keep Christmas." She drew herself up a little now. She had a kind of pathetic dignity; one could see she was a wellborn damsel, and not really a doxy. "I crave Your Majesty's grace . . . I am Rosamund Clifford, of Clifford House."

"Lord Clifford's daughter! And your father—where is he?"

"He is with . . . him, Your Majesty. With the hunt."

"And how came you here, Rosamund?"

The girl swallowed, the words dry in her mouth. "The King offered us Yuletide hospitality."

"In my bed?" Mother laughed again, but her eyes were not smiling. She gazed long on Rosamund, her face very still. "How old are you, Rosamund?"

"Seventeen, Your Majesty."

The voice was soft and small, but the words were like a slap. Mother was long past twice her age; I knew it, counting up.

Mother sighed, a long, sad sound. "It is pity of you," she said, "poor young child that you are."

For a long moment there was silence; no one dared speak. Then Mother said, without expression, "Go. Pick up your clothes from the floor where they lie, and go."

"Wh-where, madame?"

"I care not."

For shame I did not watch the girl as she slid slowly off the great bed, gathered her scattered clothes, and fled, but from the tail of my eye I saw her, thin white back and slender legs, bearskin and clothes clutched close, go through the door into the passage.

"Burn them," said Mother.

"What, Lady?" Hodierna was startled.

"Burn the bedclothes. And have my new linens spread . . . and coverlets from my coffers. Fetch them. Make haste! I am weary."

She sank down upon a bench that stood before her toilet table, staring into the mirrored surface of a polished shield that hung there upon the wall. "Hodierna, friend," she said, "my paints . . . fetch the box with my paints."

"Yes, madame." Hodierna turned back and spoke, hesitantly. "Madame, what of the Clifford . . . ?"

Mother's face went hard. "What of her?"

"She cannot run naked through the halls—it is not seemly. She must be . . . put somewhere."

Mother's mouth twitched as if she would laugh, but she composed it and said, "How can I tell how the King has disposed his guests? It is a small manor. Find her a chamber somewhere—a cubby-corner . . . No, I know! Put her in the King's chamber!"

"Madame!" Hodierna was scandalized. "All his squires' pallets are there."

Mother smiled then. "Yes. It is fitting. She will have no want of beds to choose from when he is tired of her in his."

"Come, help me, Alex." Hodierna took her son by the hand. "Bring those too." She pointed where smallclothes and hose lay, flung upon the chamber floor. There was a mended place, star-shaped, near the top of the saffron-colored hose. I remembered when Hodierna had sat mending them last summer; Father had caught the hose upon a nail the first time he had worn them. I felt the blood rise in my face, and turned away so that Mother should not see.

"Go now, Dickon, and find your own chamber," said Mother. Her voice was mild again; she was busying herself with some little bottles and jars that stood before her. "I will rest a little now, before evening. And find Bernard . . . I would have some music."

I had a room at the top of one of the turrets, a room that beforetimes all we boys had shared; it was small, so I was glad this day to have it to myself. I was already half sick from the tension that I could feel, stretching from Mother to wherever in the forest Father disported. My head ached and I trembled inside, as though my blood boiled, a strange sensation. It would not leave me, I knew, until the storm broke. All the afternoon I hovered by my little high window, staring along the forest road to catch first sight of the returning hunt.

They did not come back until twilight; torches were lit already in the hall when the drawbridge clattered with many hooves and Father burst in, laughing and bloodstained, carrying a huge trussed deer, still dripping blood. "Got him," he said, "after a fair chase." And he dumped the carcass onto the floor, where it bled into the Eastern carpet.

I had run in when I heard the horn; he started when he saw me. "Where have you come from?" was his greeting.

"From Oxford, sir. This morning. Mother is upstairs in her chambers."

"God's nails!" he swore, laughing a little. "And where is—" He broke off. "Never mind." He turned to a man behind him, richly dressed. "Lord Clifford, do you know my second son? Richard, he is."

"Your Grace." Clifford bowed; he was a little stout, but comely of face, his hair still as yellow as his daughter's. He had a frank and open countenance and did not look the panderer he was.

Father stood staring at me and biting at his fingernails. His eyes were bloodshot and bulged a little, as they always did after violent exercise. He had a measuring, moody look; I knew it well and braced myself. But he only said, quite mildly, "You have grown."

"Yes, sir," I said, just as mildly.

"How old are you now?"

"Nine years this past September, sir."

"You are too tall." There was no answer to that, so I held my tongue. "Do you feel the cold?" he asked suddenly.

I was startled. "No, sir. Not more than others."

"Thomas always said he was much troubled with the cold." He meant Thomas Becket, the Archbishop, and the tallest man in the kingdom. He was in disgrace now and exiled these last years; I thought it best to make no comment.

"And then," said Father, laughing a little, "your furred gown—"

"Sir," I said, "it is the fashion."

"Looks womanish," he said curtly, picking his nose.

I went red as fire and angry with it. "Sir, everyone dresses like this—all the best knights." Lord Clifford, beside him, had a great capelet of miniver, and ermine tails bordered the hem of his robe. I thought it most unfair. "This lord, sir, has two furs on him."

Father turned to stare coldly at Clifford. "Everyone but the King, eh? *I* cannot afford it." So saying, he swept out, snapping his fingers to his companions. As they followed, great pools of muddy melted snow stood in their footmarks. The old steward scurried out to fetch varlets to clean up. It was always like this with Father.

At dinner, Mother sat in the high seat, next to Father; her face was cool as marble and dazzling fair above a black velvet gown. I had never seen this dress before, and indeed never seen a woman in black, except a holy nun; it did not look the same on Mother.

I thought I saw her face quiver when Father rose to lead Rosamund to her place on his other side, but she said nothing, and nodded to the girl when she was presented. Rosamund was dressed in a blue surcoat with a red silk shift and green sleeves; the colors were too strong for her, and for each other, but I could see that she was fair. Her hair was fluffy and soft, like a child's, and the slightest breeze stirred it; it was loosened into curls about the face and braided in thin plaits behind, a new fashion. Her cheeks were rounded, her lips soft and full, though pale, and her eyes were blue and bright, a little small and close-set under straight blond brows. I have heard her called the most beautiful girl in England, but I could not see it, then or after. Most glee-maidens are prettier, with a livelier air, and she could not hold a candle to Mother.

Father, as usual, could not sit still; after the first course was brought in, turbot in an anise sauce with eggs, he took one hard-cooked egg, licked the sauce off it, and carried it about with him as he paced the room, pausing here for a word with the musicians, there for a jest with one of the soldiers who guarded the door. He did not sit at all during the entire meal, but wandered about as if he were plagued with an itch; once, absently, he plucked a whole chicken off a tray that was being borne in, spoiling the cook's design, and stood cramming it into his mouth while he went over the account rolls with the steward. Mother and the girl Rosamund, with Father's place empty between them, never once looked sideways at each other; I think that neither of them ate at all but merely pushed the food around on their plates.

I ate little myself, for I was still waiting for the tempest that I felt was bound to break about my ears; I think Lord Clifford felt the same, for his face was glum and he drank goblet after goblet of wine. I blamed the whole thing on him, and did not look kindly upon him. My half-brother Geoffrey had told me that Father had met Rosamund at her father's manor on the Welsh border, "and Clifford offered the customary hospitality," he added.

"And a little more, it seems," I said, with my most worldly air.

Geoffrey laughed wryly, and looked hard at me. "You are old for your years, Dickon."

I answered, rather smugly, that Mother had always said I was born old. But then, childishly, I burst out, "Why could he not have hid the wench away? He must have known what Father is!"

"For sure he knew!" cried Geoffrey. "And saw his profit thereby."

"She is so young," I said. "Only a maid."

"No longer," said Geoffrey, with a bitter smile. I remembered he was a child of such a union himself; it cannot be easy, bastardy. Geoffrey's mother had been a girl of the streets, a common whore, or so it was said, but Father had loved her well. She was before my time and long dead—at Geoffrey's birth Father had been only seventeen—but folk remembered her still, for the scandal, and for her outlandish name, Hikenai.

I looked for Geoffrey now, at dinner, for I counted him a friend, and near my age, and the folk at table were lords of those parts and their ladies, all old, to my mind, past thirty. Geoffrey sat above the salt—just—for, though he was Father's acknowledged son, he had no status; he smiled at me across the distance.

My near neighbor was a lady named Elgitha, a rich Saxon, monstrously fat, who had no French. My English was rough, learned from servants, and I understood only one word in three, though she babbled incessantly. After a while she gave it up, and talked across me to her husband, Father's sheriff of these parts. I was uncomfortable and would have preferred to be pouring the wine, like Alexander. In any other household I would be, along with other noble boys, but Father scorned courtly manners; his pages, except for Alexander, were all soldiers' sons.

The long dinner was finally over, and the tables and benches pushed aside for dancing; it took a while, for Father's hounds had been let in, and the rushes were fouled with half-chewed bones, and worse. I remembered that, long ago, Thomas Becket had called Father's court "the pigsty of Europe," but Father had only laughed. In those days Thomas could get away with anything, for Father had loved him beyond all other men.

The musicians had filed into the gallery and were tuning up. I hoped it would hold them all, and not give way; it was only a ramshackle wooden platform at the end of the hall, meant to hold a quartet at most. Mother had brought her own as well, and the place was so crowded they had barely room to hold their instruments without colliding.

They struck up a lively dance, a Moorish air from southern parts, one of Mother's favorites; she was already tapping her toes in time and wearing an expectant little smile. But Father flung his half-eaten apple to a varlet and gave his hand to Rosamund Clifford. She hung back, looking scared, but he pulled her onto the floor to lead the dance. Shocked faces lined the walls; none dared look at Mother, and no one followed the couple onto the floor. They circled once, twice, in lonely animation. It is a lively dance, and meant to be performed by several partners, meeting in concert. Still no gentleman led out his lady, though the tune was getting to those measures where all must take hands and weave in and out.

I knew the dance well, I had practiced with the jongleurs. I was about to take the hand of the Saxon lady, though she topped me by a head, just to save the day and start things going. But just then, at a flourish in the music, Mother danced out upon the floor, whirling in the arms of her troubadour, Bernard de Ventadour. The gasp was audible; such a choice of partner was against all custom, for a queen. But she had turned the tables deftly, and even Father knew.

He missed a step, and Rosamund stumbled and nearly fell;

27

it was a moment for cheering, but of course no one did. Mother, all pride and lightness, dipped and swirled, curtseyed and smiled, while Bernard, graceful as a cat, clapped his hands and tapped his heels in the partner's steps. They might have been professionals; indeed, in a way, Bernard was.

The dance was long and intricate; when it came to the part where all the company must take hands, there being no other dancers, Father stopped short, turned out his hands helplessly, grinning, and led the little Clifford, blushing, to a seat. But Mother danced on, improvising with her brilliant partner, their steps ever more complicated and fanciful, to the end of the saraband. Flushed and triumphant, she sank to the floor while Bernard bowed over her hand. The musicians, in their rickety gallery, threw down their instruments and applauded wildly, stamping their feet and cheering, though the poor mazed court stood wooden and stiff with terror.

Afterward Mother, smiling, drew me into her arms, crying gaily, "So, Dickon, would your mother not make a gallant jongleuresse?"

"I think," I said gravely, "that you would make a gallant knight."

CHAPTER 4

I NEVER SAW Rosamund Clifford again, or Woodstock Palace either; Father kept her there, for years, like another wife, and visited her in between his other mistresses. After our stop there, Mother, with blithe and courteous words and a bland face, gave over the keys of the castle to her and pushed on to Windsor Castle, with all her train, to keep Christ's Mass with her children.

Father did not even show up to make his farewells; he had gone off again at break of day to hunt, and left no message. It was another affront, but Mother showed no sign; she hummed a sirvente as she rode, and, at every little hamlet, threw gold coins to the crowds that lined the road. Her face glowed with happiness and health as the people cheered us and the new heir for England. I had almost forgotten little

John, still at Oxford with his nurse! Father, of course, had not thought to mention the babe; sons were little to him, he had too many. I felt pity for my little brother, and something of guilt too, and resolved to make it up to him someday. I did, and more ... But I am ahead of my story.

I had thought the rift between my parents too wide to mend now, but perversely, Father followed us to London, leaving his Rosamund to keep lonely Christmas. Father ever would have his cake and eat it too—and being King, he often did.

Henry and I were in the tiltyard, trying out our new mounts; it was Christmas Eve, and the weather, as perverse as Father, had grown mild again. The horses we rode were beautiful spirited Arabians from Spain, too small and light for a man in full armor, but perfect for us, and tournament-trained; they were Christ-gifts from the Archbishop, Thomas Becket, who knew good horse-flesh, having beforetimes served as squire-at-arms in a noble house. They were goodly gifts, and expensive, besides being just what we needed, now that we were learning arms in earnest. Henry was Becket's godson, and had lived in his house before Father fell out with him, so it was a fitting present. But I hardly knew the man, and counted him uncommonly courteous; he had sent gifts, too, to the other children, even the little ones he had never seen.

I had been six when Becket was exiled, but I remembered him well; he was not a man to forget. He was so very tall, with a stretched-out look, a dark Norman face, and deepset eyes of a surprising blue. His smile was rare, and wintry, but I think there was humor there. Once Mother stood beside him, herself a tall woman, and, looking up, said, "Master Becket, I am undone! You make me feel small and helpless."

"Madame," he replied, "you could never be helpless."

Long ago, when Becket was Father's Chancellor, he was a very worldly man, fond of rich clothes and show. He and Father hunted together, played chess together, drank together—and in great part shaped the policy that had made England prosperous and peaceful. Though there were some eighteen years between them and great differences of temperament, they were loving friends, never apart.

When the old Archbishop Theobald died, Father named Thomas as Archbishop of Canterbury, the highest office in the land, though he had only clerk's orders. And that marked the end of their friendship, for Thomas changed. From a worldly courtier, he became a holy man, taking his new position as a dedication to God and His Church. There was no more hunting, no more chess, and no more wine. Thomas put off his scarlet robes and wore the prelate's black, with a hair shirt underneath. He drank barley water and ate curds, when he did not fast. He spent long hours in his cell-like chamber praying, his arms stretched out in the shape of a cross, the whole long length of him lying prone upon the cold stones of the floor. What was more shocking, he opposed Father in all matters relating to the Church.

Father was wild. Except for his wife, no one had ever raised voice against him; he was the King! He must have been doubly enraged because he had thought, by raising his friend Thomas to this eminence, he had secured an Archbishop who would do his will against the clergy. Not so, as it turned out; within a few months after Thomas's anointing, the two men were at odds. Thomas refused to cut back the jurisdiction of the ecclesiastical courts, and would not put his seal to the constitution for the English Church drawn up by Father's lawyers.

Father haled him before the royal court at Northampton; he was charged with contempt, fined three hundred pounds, and threatened with exorbitant exactions. Thomas answered that he would appeal to the Pope at Rome, which would have meant excommunication for Father. Soldiers were sent to arrest him, but he got wind of it and fled the country in disguise. Father announced that he was henceforth in exile, arrested every member of his family, and seized all his assets. For three years now Thomas had roamed Europe, entry to his own land barred to him, the See of Canterbury vacant, and the parishioners of England without their highest shepherd.

My brother Henry was desolate; he had spent two years in Becket's care, and loved him greatly; he wept bitterly at his exile. He wept again at the gift of the horse; Thomas had written that the horse's name was Augustine, after the saint, "so that you will not forget the holy words that we have read together, my dear son." He added that "little Richard's mount will be too big, but he will grow into it—and he may name it himself." My horse needed no growing into, for I was as big as Henry already, and I named him Galahad; he was a snow-white stallion with dark blue eyes.

Henry had changed greatly; he no longer fell into his black rages, though he still teased Geoffrey and the little girls, and was quick to quarrel with me. He was past eleven now; his face had thinned and lengthened, and lost most of its look of Father. If it had not been for his white eyelashes and brows, he would have been a handsome boy. He was good at games and practice tilting, but he could not lift my lance or draw my bow; I had been given the squire's size at my last birthday, and had almost mastered them, for I was tall and strong for my age, with long arms. I saw it angered him, but he gave no sign, and handed back bow and lance with a shrug, saying he needed to practice. On horseback, though, we were evenly matched, for neither of us had had proper mounts until now.

We put them through their paces all afternoon, or rather, the horses did it themselves; they were trained to the tiltyard, and soon got the feel of this one. The men-at-arms and pages who had come out to watch us cheered at every sally; we were both of us flushed to the roots of our hair with triumph and pride.

At last, tired and happy, we began our last turn about the yard, having agreed already that it would truly be the last. "One more time," each of us would say when bested, "one last chance." It was settled that each should have three turns, and no more, at the quintain. It was a true one, which all the knights used, and unbelievably heavy; even when we were lucky enough to make a hit, the thing barely moved, as if swayed by a gentle wind. And, too, the light was failing; it was hard to see the target.

I had won the last contest, so this time it was Henry's turn first. He hit it two times out of three, glancing blows but true. "Fair hits!" he cried. "Two fair hits!" It was the best either of us had done so far; I could not help thinking it was an accident, in the poor light. But I said a little prayer to Christ's mother; I was born on her birthday.

Twice I hit, squarely on target, spinning the quintain strongly; it was better than Henry's score already, but they counted as the same. As I rode back to the starting line, all a-sweat and my heart pumping hard, I heard the gate creak open and the sound of hooves, but I did not check Galahad; I felt that fortune was with me, and it was now or never. Riding forward, spurring fast, I saw, out of the tail of my eye, our colors stream out against the sky; in that last split

31

second I knew it was Father, and my lance dipped. I righted it too far, and the lance crashed into the scaffolding that held the quintain, splintering the wood and bringing the whole structure down, while I, from the impact, lost my seat and tumbled backward to the ground.

The breath was knocked out of me; I lay still for a moment, while several soldiers rushed to take me about the arms and raise me to my feet. "Let be!" I cried, shrugging them off. "I am not hurt!" I had wrenched my ankle in the stirrup, and was bruised all over, but I managed to walk without limping to where Father waited, still in the saddle. I heard Henry shouting, "A draw! It is a draw, then!"

I bent my knee to Father, setting my teeth that I would not wince, for the pain shot right up my leg. "Welcome, sir!"

His brows were drawn down, and a strange look was on his face; it was not till later that I recognized it for concern. For he said, after his eyes had swept me quickly, narrowing, "Ho, sirrah! 'Tis the first time I have seen a quintain fight back! He got the better of you, for sure!" He laughed, and rode up to the fallen scaffolding, looking down at it. "Demolished," he said. "We will have to build a new one. I see I have a dangerous second son!" He dismounted, and for the first time in my life, I believe, I felt the weight of his mailed arm across my shoulders; his hand fisted my cheek playfully. "So, Richard, you would use the Saracens so?"

"Oh, yes, sir!" I cried softly. "But by then the enemy will not unhorse me!"

"Well spoken, boy!" His fierce little eyes looked hard into mine, and he said, "Not hurt, are you, boy?"

"Oh, no, sir!" I said, and truly I felt nothing then, so happy was I in his notice. "But, sir, you did not see the first two hits! They were square on target, and set it spinning roundly!"

"Mine too!" cried Henry. "You should have seen me too! It was a draw—the third time did not count. Did it, Father?"

"It would take a greater judge than me to count it," Father said, laughing again. "A strong hit! Oh, yes! A fair hit!"

I was smiling broadly myself by now, though I knew I would never hear the last of this accident; it would be all over the castle in an hour. "But, Father, what of my horse? Is he not handsome? And he never wavered, but sat back strong on his heels, digging in. Most beasts would have fallen. I have named him Galahad."

"And mine!" cried Henry. "My gray is bigger! Which do you fancy most, Father?"

His eyes measured. "They are both uncommon steeds . . . I cannot choose between them." He fingered his chin, scratching at the day-old stubble, little gold wires against the fading sun. "Did I order them?" he said suddenly.

"No, Father," said Henry, smiling. "They were sent from Spain. Gifts from Thomas." His smile faded as he looked into Father's eyes. "Father," he began, faltering. "Father, we *may* keep them?"

"What?" Father was staring into space, frowning. "What?" he said again, turning to look at us. "Yes, of course, keep them. Yes, indeed!" His face cleared, and he smiled. "It is a bribe," he said confidently. "A suit for peace." Both of us knew it was best to keep silence, and ran to keep up with him as he started for the castle. Absently, he put an arm on each of our shoulders, and we went so, on into the hall. "You are of a height," he said, surprised. "Richard, will you hope to fill Thomas's shoes, then?"

"Oh, no, Father," I said earnestly. "I would never be a churchman."

He laughed again. "You please me today, Richard. And what will you be, then?"

"The finest knight in the world, Father . . . like you."

"I too, Father," said Henry. "Knight me first . . . I am older."

"Well, we will see . . . there is time still. But you shape well. Both of you." I thought my heart would burst; it was the first praise I had ever had from him.

Father stopped short inside the hall, pushing us from him with a mock roughness. He snapped his fingers; his squire came running. "A bath," he said. "In my chambers. Hot. And draw a footbath for Richard here . . . mustn't let that ankle stiffen."

I reddened; I had not known I was limping.

Father laughed hugely. "It is an honorable wound, boy!" His laughter stopped, and he frowned again. "I wonder where Thomas got the monies?"

CHAPTER 5

"MADAME." FATHER'S VOICE was cold. "It is out of my hands. You see fit to pick up scum from the roadside—a felon and son of a felon—you must pay his bond fee. Did you not see the brass serf collar on him?"

"I saw first the ugly wound his King made . . . for nothing!" Mother was glad of a chance to show anger, it was plain to see; she had been mild as milk throughout this Yuletide holyday.

"Madame," Father went on, "he was caught in the act. But for his youth he would have been hanged. It is the law."

"For rabbit poaching!"

"Poaching nonetheless. Laws are meant to be obeyed."

"But they were starving!"

"Madame, take it up with this fellow—his master. I will bandy no more words with you." And, so saying, Father turned on his heel and left the room.

Even a queen, it seemed, could not lightly dispose a felon's fate. The branded boy she had befriended on the road was unfree, a serf, and his master showed up at Westminster, demanding redress. He stood before the Small Court now, a thickset Saxon farmer with a red face and a scowl. "I paid twelve pounds for them, man and wife, Your Majesty," he said stoutly. "Only some fifteen years ago . . . there was still a good bit of work in them. And now the King hanged the man on me, and the woman died . . . all that's left is the boy. He's worth a good bit to me, though he's puny . . . got a head for figures."

"You do not take much care of your property, Goodman, it seems," said Mother.

"I never set them on to poach."

"The woman starved, and two other sons as well. And this poor boy was well on the way—if he did not freeze first."

"They would not come away from the hanging-place," said the farmer, whining. "It's no fault of mine. Twelve good pounds . . ."

"I'll give you four," said Mother. "That's fair enough—he's only a lad."

"But worth more than his mam and da, Your Majesty. Kept my tallies. The whore-son Normans were only laborers."

"They were French?"

"Don't know about French, Your Majesty. Normans, they were—they *said*. From a place called Longchamps . . . couldn't hardly talk English."

"You cannot buy French subjects," said Mother sternly. "It is against the law." Actually it was not, but she had taken a dislike to the fellow. She went on, a chilly sound in her voice. "This is a matter for the sheriff's justice."

"Oh, ma'am," he cried, falling to his knees. "I didn't know. Bought the pair of them, man and wife, from another Norman . . . twelve good pounds I paid. Not knowing it was against the law, ma'am. Never knowing. Have mercy, Your Majesty!"

"Well . . ." she said, seeming to relent. "Christ's twelve days are not yet over. For Christ and His mother's sake, you shall have mercy. But get back to your land before Twelfth Night—or the sheriff will hear of it."

"Oh, thank you, Your Majesty, thank you." The farmer, pulling at his forelock, backed out. At the door, he turned and ran. Mother smiled.

I said, smiling, "Mother, you cheated!"

"Do you think that fellow did not cheat? They *were* starving, you know, all three . . . the poor little wretch is skin and bones. That such a fellow should have the mastery of French souls . . ."

Mother gave the boy to me for squire. I had no such thing, and it was not customary to have a squire till one was a full knight, so I was pleased. I went down to the kitchens to see how he fared.

Fat Haumette, the serving wench who had comforted me at Mother's confinement, had taken him under her wing. With food and cosseting, he had somewhat improved. He was still weak, and could not walk yet on his frostbitten feet, but there was a little color in his dark cheeks and his eyes had lost their dull look. The brass serf collar had been filed off, but the green mark beneath it would not scrub away, though Haumette had rubbed it with lye. " 'Twill take months," said Haumette, shaking her head. "Poor little varlet."

"Not varlet now," I said. "He is to be my squire. Will you like that, Will?"

"What is 'squire'?" he asked.

"Well, for now, it is to take care of my clothes, and help me dress, that sort of thing, waiting on me. And later, when I am a knight, you will arm me, and tend my weapons. You will accompany me to tournaments—and battles too. And see to my horse and my armor. You'll have a horse yourself then."

"Oh." A wide grin split his face; I saw, with the ugly scar on his forehead covered, that he was not ill-favored, though he was as dark as a Turk. "I would like that well," he said, in passable French.

"You speak our tongue?"

"My father—" He choked on the words, his eyes filling with tears.

"I forgot," I said. "You are Norman. From Longchamps."

"Father, yes, and Mother. I was born here, in Saxon country." He wiped the tears away. "I hate the Saxons!"

There was much hatred in this misused boy, and much fear as well; he never really got over it, and shied from strangers, like a dog that holds to one master. With me and with my mother he was a faithful, loving servant, and valuable in time, for he was no lackwit. We called him Will of Longchamps, or simply Will Longchamps. He never grew properly; whether it was a birth defect, or from the early beatings he endured, he was somewhat malformed. He was low of stature, with one shoulder higher than the other, and his legs too small and thin. He was awkward, and never a good squire, though he was willing. He rose much higher than that, in the end. Father, all unknowing, had done us a good deed, for he set in our path a creature shaped by cruelty, as the iron is shaped by the fire. Will Longchamps served me well, throughout my life.

It was a pleasant Yuletide, I suppose—at least till the end. Then Father fell into the worst fit I had ever seen, surpassing even himself. We were at supper in the great hall at Windsor; Henry and I had been allowed to stay up, though it was the kind of feast that goes on all night, for some of our kin were there, I forget who. Halfway through, the baked meats not yet handed round, a messenger was led in, nearly dead from weariness. He had ridden half across France, taken a fast

Channel ship, and ridden again, hard, to bring his news. It was not good.

When he had got his breath, the fellow told that Louis of France had received Thomas Becket in great honor at his court, hailing him as the greatest prelate of Christendom after the Pope at Rome, and proclaiming a holy-day so that all might flock to the great Cathedral of Notre Dame to hear Thomas's Yuletide Mass. Thousands had lined the streets where Thomas passed, stretching out their hands for a blessing, and Louis himself had knelt to him there and taken the wafer and wine from Thomas's hands. He had set aside the Palace of the Louvre for the Archbishop's dwelling, and there Thomas bode in high pomp and great honor, eating his curds and whey off the gold plates of royal France.

At the words of the quaking messenger, Father rose from his high seat, his face flaming into scarlet, the veins standing out. He had been holding a venison knuckle in his left hand; in his right was the knife from his belt, the meat knife that he used at table. For an instant he stood stock-still, both hands raised; then he moved the left one, flinging the venison joint into the poor messenger's face. The bone was jagged and bruised the man's cheekbone, and the grease spattered all over his fine jerkin, but he was lucky. It might so easily have been the right hand, which held the knife! "Get out! Get out before I kill you!" roared Father. "Out of my sight, varlet!" The man was a high noble, but he scuttled like a kitchen maid, while all the company sat startled into silence.

Father threw his trencher of bread, dripping with gravy, onto the floor, and his goblet of wine as well. Then he reached for Mother's, but she snatched it up, a cold anger in her eyes. He turned on her as if to strike her, but her eye held him. He threw himself, instead, upon the floor, knocking over his great chair so that it fell into the hearth and was charred, the loose cushion going up in flames. Father too was dangerously near the fire, but none dared to pull him away as he raged. All, risen from their places, were frozen in fright, nobles and servants alike, hearing his shrieks. I was sure that he would crack his skull against the stones, or that the flames would catch his hair.

His screams were incoherent; the only words we could understand were "That hound of hell! That hell-hound!" over and over. Finally Mother moved out of the trance that held us all; she pulled down a hanging from the wall, Susanna and the Elders, I remember, and threw it onto the fire to blanket it. And the troubadour, Bernard de Ventadour, base-born but braver than a peer of the realm, took hold of Father's feet and dragged him away from the hearth.

That is all I remember, for fear paralyzed everything. But I think I knew, even then, that I would never see Thomas Becket again.

CHAPTER 6

WHEN I WAS twelve years old I was betrothed to the Princess Alys of France, who was ten.

Except for little John, I was the last of all my brothers and sisters to be so disposed. Henry was already married, years before, at the age of six, to Alys's sister, Marguerite, though he barely remembered the ceremony and could not recall his bride's face. Geoffrey had been pledged to Constance of Brittany only this last year, and all my sisters were promised too. At least we boys had been given brides close to us in age; we were fortunate. Mathilda's husband-to-be, Henry "the Lion," Duke of Saxony, was older than Father, and Alfonso of Castile and William of Sicily were grown men before their brides, my sisters Eleanor and Joanna, were out of swaddling clothes!

For years Father had been dickering with various dukes and powerful landholders about my disposal in marriage; he hoped to add more lands to his already vast domain. There was talk of a betrothal in Spain at one time, but it came to nothing. This one now, the alliance with France, was a peace-keeping compact, much like Henry's marriage had been. Father had never had much luck with Mother's huge duchy of Aquitaine, my heritage. Various barons there were always in revolt against his authority; time and time again they had gone as far as skirmishes and sieges, sometimes taking castles or even whole villages and putting all the folk to the sword. One such episode had caused a breach of truce between Father and Louis of France; the Count of Auvergne had seized lands and hostages and refused to turn them over to anyone but Louis, saying all the Aquitaine lands were truly under the rule of France. Things had been touchy, at any rate, between Father and Louis, because of Louis's championing of Thomas Becket. Becket was still under French protection, and the Auvergne hostages had been sent to Louis.

Father felt it was time to make a gesture toward peace. This, my betrothal, was part of it; also, I was to perform homage to Louis for my Aquitaine lands, along with my two elder brothers' acts of homage for their possessions in France. And so we were all present, Henry, Geoffrey, and I, with Father, at the ceremony in Paris, though Mother was not. I never knew why; perhaps the long-divorced couple could not bear to look upon each other's face!

We were all very uncomfortable, I remember, because the court at Paris was so poor; it could not compare with one of our oldest, smallest castles, either in England or on the Continent. The walls sweated darkly with damp, though it was summer, and there were no hangings upon them, except a small coat of arms behind Louis's throne, which was only a large, carved wood chair, set on a small dais. There was a long narrow carpet leading up to it, by which we approached the throne and knelt in turn to place our hands between Louis's and receive the kiss of peace. The carpet was red, or had been once, and very worn; my toe caught in a hole and I pitched forward, only catching myself in time, and blushing redder than the old royal rug beneath my feet. Henry, behind me, smothered a laugh, and there was another one, tinkling, from somewhere near the throne; I felt hotter still. Somehow I got to the dais, my eyes cast down, and knelt before King Louis.

"You can look up now, my son . . . it is the only hole, I promise."

The voice was soft and gentle, pitched low so that the court did not hear, though I heard the same tinkling laugh again, beside him.

King Louis had the face of a saint, as they are pictured by our best artists, thin, pale, and lined, with large brown eyes that looked upon me with a great kindness. Curiously, the lines that marked his cheeks and forehead did not make him look old; he still had a boy's look, with a small head and fair curls clustering close beneath his crown, a narrow band of dark gold. He wore a dark brown robe, cowled like a monk's, but made of velvet, rubbed bare in places. His only jewel was a large cross of Eastern workmanship, studded with rubies, which hung at his belt.

"You are a handsome lad, Richard," he said, still almost in a whisper. "You resemble your mother."

I wondered if his eyesight was all it should be; Mother is so dark, and I am fair, with blue eyes. King Louis smiled, reading my thoughts, and went on. "Of course you have your father's hair—the Norman red-gold."

I should have bitten my tongue, but, matching his whisper, I said, "Perhaps, Sire, it will darken in time."

"Perhaps," he answered, his thin lips curving slightly. I saw he had humor, and was not dull, as men spoke him. I knew, as well, that I liked him; he was a good man.

"Place your hands in mine, Richard of Aquitaine," he said, raising his voice for the court, "and repeat the oath of fealty."

It was a long oath, the vassal's pledge, and had to be said first in Latin, and then in Norman. I had learned it by rote for the occasion, but with his hands warm upon mine and his eyes deep upon my own, I heard the words in all their true meaning, and spoke as earnestly as if I were pledging my faith to Arthur of old. I felt his lips, dry and cool, upon my own in the kiss of peace, and it was over; the King of France was my liege lord.

I stood to one side, while first Henry and then Geoffrey did homage for their lands; they spoke clearly, but I did not hear. I had seen the two princesses who sat below King Louis on the dais, like royal dolls, one dark, one fair. They were children still, but dressed in stiff, gem-encrusted gowns that spread about them like billowing seas; they must have been sitting on small backless stools or plump cushions, for their heavy skirts rose, ballooning, all around. They looked like jeweled pawns upon a chessboard—as indeed they were.

I wondered which was mine. I guessed it to be the dark one, for she looked smaller and younger, shy, with a small, triangular face. She did not look at me, or indeed, at anyone, but kept her eyes cast down, the dark lashes making half-moons above her cheeks; her mouth was prim. The other one was bolder, tossing her yellow hair and smiling; it had been she who laughed that tinkling laugh before, for when Henry knelt she did it again. I saw his head turn, and he must have frowned, for she made a little face at him and laughed again. I was sure she was his bride, and wondered if he would be happy; she seemed frivolous, or even foolish, though I had heard no word of any lackwits at that court. I stared at her when she was not looking, and did not like what I saw, though she was pretty enough, with small neat features and a long graceful neck. Her skin was very pale, like milk after the cream has been skimmed off, almost bluish, and blue veins showed at her temples.

All through Geoffrey's words I stared at the little dark one, willing her to look up, but she would not. After stooping to kiss his new vassal, Geoffrey of Brittany, the King motioned for him to stand aside with Henry, and then, stepping down from the dais, stretched out his hand to me. "Come, my son. Come, Richard." The brown eyes looked into mine again, and I smiled. "And now I must pledge away another of my jewels—my little Alys." The brown eyes were bright with tears, for today both daughters were to leave, going with us to be reared at our court, as is the custom.

Father had joined us too, and a churchman, magnificent in scarlet robes.

The churchman held out his hand, raising up the blond child, and brought her forward to stand beside me. So this was Alys, my betrothed! Hard to believe she was only ten, for she was tall already, for a girl, and preened herself, too, in many little womanly ways. She giggled during the whole of the churchman's words; he had to frown at her twice. The huge sapphire that Father had given me would not fit anywhere, even on her thumb; she giggled again, and let it slip to the floor, where I scrambled onto my knees to find it. I was scarlet with anger at her; it was not a good beginning.

Afterward, Father took a thin gold chain from around his neck and threaded the great ring on it, slipping it over Alys's head and down the front of her frock, inside. "Keep it warm, girl . . . until you grow bigger." And he laughed a rude laugh, the sort you always hear at betrothals and weddings, the rest of the company laughing with him. He turned to me. "Come, sluggard," he said, for all to hear. "Come kiss your bride."

"She is only my betrothed," I muttered.

He heard, and jabbed me in the ribs, laughing again. "It is the same," he roared. "Kiss hearty!" And he pushed me toward the girl, making me awkward. I bent to kiss her cheek; she turned suddenly and my mouth hit her nose, a tooth biting into the inside of my lip, bringing stinging tears.

It must have hurt her too, a little, for she put her hand to her face and looked at me with bright angry eyes.

"I am sorry," I said helplessly. She stared at me; there was none of her father's kindness in her face, but after a moment she shrugged, like a court lady, stood on tiptoe, placed her hands on my shoulders, and raised her mouth to mine. Her lips were thin and a little moist, and her breath smelled of some sweetmeat she had eaten earlier. Suddenly I felt more comfortable, with this homely reminder of our common child-state, and I bent again and kissed her firmly, like a lover. There were shouts then, and cheers, and Father pounded me on the back, laughing loud.

"My turn now," he cried. "My turn to kiss the bride!" And he put his two hands on her waist and lifted her high to meet his mouth, holding her there for a long moment. When he put her down I saw a little color had come into her pale cheeks, and her mouth looked bruised, but she smoothed her long yellow hair with her hand, and as she turned away, she smiled.

Father winked at me. "A fine lass, that, Richard . . . only needs a year or two. Fire under the snow, as the poet says."

Afterward, there was a long formal meal, a feast really, lasting till after dark; course after course was brought in, each more elaborate than the last, and a wine to match each one. We ate and drank far too much, all three of us new boy lieges. Henry was sick and threw up, and little Geoffrey fell asleep; my humiliation was of a more private sort.

My stomach churned from the rich food, and I was dizzy with the wine, but after a while it passed, leaving me merely lightheaded. When the musicians began to tune up for dancing, I rose boldly and walked over to my betrothed, Alys, offering her my hand. She stared at me, surprised. "I have never danced with a *boy* before!" she cried.

"Who, then?" I asked, putting on a high nose.

"Well . . . my dancing master, of course. And my sister, and our ladies." She looked a little shy for once, and more like the child she was. I almost began to like her.

"Well, then," said I, "I have the advantage, for I learned along with my older sister. And Mother too likes dancing well, and will sometimes partner me. I know all the steps," I finished, and bowed to her, as I had seen the courtiers do.

Alys too knew all the steps, and was a natural dancer besides. After a time, all the other folk stopped and stood back, watching us. Except that I sometimes had to bend to her, she being so much smaller than I, we must have looked well together. And she would grow; she was already tall for her age. Perhaps she would not make such a bad wife, after all.

She laughed suddenly, that odd little glassy sound again, and said, "You dance better than you walk . . . you are not even clumsy!" She had not the kindest heart in the world, that was certain. But the wine was still working in me, and I laughed along with her, hoping no one had heard.

We were panting when the dance came to an end, and I was glad of a chance to sit down for a moment and take another glass of wine. I should not have done it, for my head was spinning already; when I drained the glass I looked at her and saw two thin blondes, both gobbling down marchpane sweets from a silver tray. I shook my head to clear it and the two merged into one, little Alys, who was to be my fate. Her mouth was all sticky, with crumbs around it; I thought it revolting, for Mother had always taught us to eat daintily, and wipe our hands and faces afterward. I snapped my fingers at a page who was carrying a ewer and cloth, gesturing him to offer it. Alys stared at me. "I am not finished!" she said haughtily.

"So many sweets will turn your teeth black," I said. "And your skin will break out too, when you are older."

"That's a long way off," she said, shrugging, and took another marchpane.

A hand came out of the air and took the sweet in strong, thick fingers. A hand with curling red hairs bristling along the back, glittering rings, and black-rimmed fingernails, a hand I knew well; Father's. He laughed, a low, rich chuckle deep in his throat. "Give us a taste, little beauty," he said, and kissed the sticky lips. He sat on the bench beside her, edging me away. "Sit upon my lap, Alys, and you can have the lot."

She jumped up quickly, the little witch, smiles all over her vixen face, and plumped down upon his knees, twining her thin arms around his neck.

I stood up, for there was no room now for me on the bench. As I moved away, uneasy, I saw him pop the sweetmeat into her mouth, laughing. "But I get a taste of each one after . . . promise!" I felt an obscure, nagging distaste; she was such a child, still, and my intended bride. I had seen him behave so with his doxies!

My eye fell upon the other French princess, Henry's bride, the little dark Marguerite. She was all alone, sitting upon a small gilt chair, watching the dancers. When she saw me coming toward her, she cast down her eyes again; I had still not seen their color. I bowed over her hand, as Mother had taught me. "Will you dance with me, my sister?" She looked up at me then, startled; I saw her eyes were not dark, but a greenish-gray, with little flecks of brown in them, and very bright. "You *are* my sister now, you know." I held out my hand. She took it and rose. It was my turn to be startled, for I saw a tear spill over the brightness and snake down her soft round cheek.

We danced a few steps; the measure was slow. She was tiny, much smaller even than the ten-year-old Alys—though, counting in my head, I knew she must be at least thirteen; a woman already. I could not match my steps to hers, and stumbled twice. "I am sorry," she said, in a wretched little whisper. "I am too little for you. You are such a very tall knight."

"I am not a knight yet," I said, smiling, "though I am working at it—hard."

"Oh, yes, you are," she said. "When Father gave you the kiss of peace, it meant you were his knight—his liegeman."

"Oh, that. Well, yes. But I have still to earn my spurs, you know. There is a great deal to learn."

"I know," she said gravely. "I know all the stories—the romances. The Knights of the Round Table, that is my favorite of all," she finished shyly.

We were in step now and the tear on her cheek had vanished; her face had a little sheen to it, a smile nearly.

"And which of all the Round Table knights is your favorite?" I asked.

"Lancelot, I think," she answered, casting down her eyes again. "Although he sinned."

"But he sinned for love, you know. So God forgave him. Don't you think God forgave him . . . through His holy mother?" It was a constant theme among the troubadours and the court ladies, the sin of love. "Some say that it is not a sin even . . . love."

"Oh, I think it must be," she said quickly, breathily. Her cheeks had flushed darkly, like a rose, and I thought her charming. "It must be a sin . . . it is venal."

"It must be that you take after your father . . . is it so?"

She had hung her head; I put my hand under her chin to raise it and look into her eyes.

She stopped in the dance and said earnestly, "Oh, no. Papa is truly good."

"I think so too," I said, meaning it. "But, then, surely you are not truly *bad*, either . . . you have the face of a nun."

She smiled then, like a light breaking through clouds, and said, "It was what I wanted . . . long ago."

"But they would not let you?"

"Oh, no," she sighed. "I am a princess." The smile was gone suddenly. "Could we sit down, do you think? Everyone is staring."

And so they were, for we had stopped dancing. I began to lead her back to her seat, but a court lady lolled there.

"I know a little chamber. Come." And she took my hand and led me through a maze of halls and up some stone stairs. Her little feet made no sound on the stone; my steps sounded loud behind her, but no one followed us.

The room she took me to was very small and bare, with one window, high in the wall, and a crucifix, carved in an antique style. There was one low, narrow bench in the chamber; Marguerite sank down upon it. Her face was very white.

I stared at her. "Are you ill?" I asked.

"Oh, no . . . no!" She looked up at me; I saw that tears had come to her eyes once more and were spilling over. I had never seen anyone cry that way before, with a still face, and silently; girls usually get red and sniffle.

"Why are you so sad, Marguerite?" I asked softly.

"Not sad. Just nervous . . . frightened. Oh, so frightened!" She began to wring her little hands; her face was all wet with the tears now. "Oh, don't you see? I have always slept with my sister and our maids, in our own big bed. And now, tonight . . . I shall have to sleep with a boy! I am married now . . . and Alys said I shall have to go into another bedchamber and sleep with a boy . . . with Henry. And I am so frightened!"

I saw she was, truly. I wondered if she had seen him once in a fit. "Henry is not very frightening," I said. "He almost never has a tantrum anymore . . . and he is not as big as I am."

"It is not him, not Henry, but . . . the strange bedchamber," she wailed softly. "The strange bed . . ."

I saw suddenly that she was afraid of the act of love. I

wondered if all girls were; perhaps it hurt. I was very ignorant. But I said, trying to comfort her, "The bedchamber and bed will be strange to him too, remember. He is used to sleeping with boys, his brothers, and our pages . . . there are so many of us there is hardly room to turn, even in our biggest bed." I spoke lightly, hoping to make her smile. "And anyway," I said suddenly, remembering, "he was sick tonight and they have put him into a bed over the bath house, with Geoffrey. They have both had too much wine. Tonight you will sleep with your sister, Marguerite."

Her smile was dazzling; it enchanted me. She took my hand in both her own and pressed it to her cheek in joy. "Oh, thank you, Richard. Thank you!"

Her face was transfigured, beautiful, though the wet tears still gleamed upon it. I could not help myself; I bent and kissed it, over and over, and, at last, I kissed her lips, tasting salt. I did not stop, but kissed her again and again, and I fancied that her lips clung to mine. My hands, too, strayed over her body, as if with a will of their own. I felt the little fullness of her breasts, small and hard like unripe fruit, and all my lower parts turned to water, and I trembled.

She pushed me away, finally. "Is it not a sin—for us?" she whispered.

"Forgive me, Marguerite," I said hoarsely. "Forgive me . . . You looked. . . so sweet."

She looked up at me. "I wish it *were* you," she said. "I wish it were you instead of Henry."

"I too," I said miserably. "I wish it too." I did not touch her then at all, except to press my lips lightly, one more time, to hers. "Good-bye," I whispered.

"Good-bye, my Lancelot."

It was my very first encounter with a girl. The older pages had once had a byre-maid in one of the outhouses at Windsor, smuggled in, and were taking turns, she giggling, her rough skirts flung up over her head. But I was shy. Perhaps I would have done it, if I had been a little older and if so many had not been looking on. I still remembered her face, red-cheeked and dimpling, and her yellow hair.

I was in love with Marguerite, my brother's bride, for over a year, while she lived at our court. I trembled when I spoke to her, and turned red, but we were never again alone. Some of my best verses were written to her, though she did not know it.

When the young couple were given their own court to keep and their own castle, I wept bitter tears. And for a long time my blood raced when I spied a small, dark maiden, remembering Marguerite. I was sure that it was only such a one that I could love.

CHAPTER 7

THE TOP OF the hill commanded a view of the whole valley. I caught my breath, reining in my horse; I thought that I had never seen so fair a sight. Green, green, green it was, with great swaths of dark blue lupin crossing it like giant brush strokes. Narrower brush strokes, silver in the sun, were the little sparkling brooks and rivers that gave the land its name: Aquitaine.

"It is yours," said my mother, Eleanor, pulling up her palfrey beside mine. "Your domain. It begins here, in this valley. Or—" She glanced at me, her long eyes narrow and laughing above the high soft rounds of her cheeks. "Or it will be soon—as soon as I have got your father to the mark. He resists, as always. But it is mine to give—not his!" She shook her head a little, as if to free it from a troubling thought. "Let's not think of your father now . . . we are free of him for a little. He has his Woodstock and—" She broke off.

I knew Father was there, in Woodstock, with his Rosamund, and kept my face still and grave; I never liked taking sides—though I was on hers, of course, always.

"We'll take a holiday from England—and Henry. You'll see how merry we'll be! We'll have sweet music, and perhaps a little tournament or two . . . and we'll have a Court of Love!" She clapped her hands, like a girl; she could still get away with it—though, incredibly, she was fifty, by my count. I studied her as she rode beside me; she was slim and erect, with long legs and a lovely long neck. She had tied her veil behind her head, under her hair, for the day was warm, and the line of her jaw and chin was clean and sharp as a girl's; I wondered again how she did it, and thought of witchcraft. But just then she ducked her head, twisting to free a fold of her skirt from the stirrup; I saw a little crease below her chin, a blurring of contour that was not of youth, and I was almost relieved. She straightened again, head high, and the girl-look came back, proud and free. She was beautiful, Mother, her cheeks and lips warmed pinkly from riding and the sun; though it may have been partly paint, I could never tell with her.

In the level of the field, she reined up close to me again; I guess she felt like talking, her tongue loosened, like a child let out from lessons. She was still in that gay and teasing mood. "Who is your lady, Richard?" she asked, in a sort of wheedling way that I had heard her use with the gentles at court. "She is dark, like me, but with gray eyes. I cannot recognize her."

She was speaking of the love songs I had written, all to Marguerite. My face flamed suddenly. "It is no one," I said hastily. "No one at all. I made it up."

She wagged her finger at me; I would not get out of it so easily, I could see, my heart sinking. "But that is against the rules," she began playfully, but stopped at the sound of lutesong behind us. I thanked God for Bernard de Ventadour, her faithful swain. He bowed low in the saddle, still strumming his lute, and she slowed, turning to him and smiling. I bowed and made my excuses, then spurred my horse ahead to where some of our guard rode before us. Leave them to it, I thought. I never liked to watch Mother with Bernard, though God knows, it was little enough, when you thought of Father's misdeeds with women.

Behind me, Bernard's voice rose, rich and warm, growing faint as I galloped ahead. I envied him that beautiful voice, finer than the sweetest viol; my own was cracking now like a crow's, and would change from high to low without warning, making me burn with shame. I had been giving my songs to jongleurs to sing of late, though just months ago I had thought I sang pleasantly enough. Eleanor had remarked kindly that all boys went through it, it was part of growing up. Dear Mother—it was the least of my agonies!

The little Marguerite no longer tormented my dreams; she was far off now, keeping her own court with my brother Henry, and though she was still the secret lady of my songs, I could not really remember the shape of the gray eyes I praised.

There was no one to replace her, only a nightmare twisting

of white limbs, red lips, pink nipples; I was captured by lust, and there were no girls to satisfy it. Occasionally, I made do with one of the pages who shared our sleeping quarters; everyone did it, we were all in like case. Though to hear some of them talk, you would think they had tumbled every wench belowstairs.

No one took these games seriously, not even the priests who confessed us. My confessor let me off with a dozen paternosters and a good wax candle, saying that young blood must needs be hot. But Alexander called it a sin.

Though I turned aside his lectures, they troubled me, for I valued his high opinion. Alexander was worth twenty pages, and all my brothers together. Such carnal thoughts as mine did not trouble him, or if they did, he conquered them. He said once, quoting Saint Paul, for he read all the holy writings, " 'It is better to marry than to burn,' " and enjoined me sternly to think only of my betrothed. Alys! I could not even like her. At any rate, she was still a child, and even farther away than Marguerite. Father had kept her in England; he said she was too frail for journeying! The last we heard, he had taken her to Woodstock, to his Rosamund. I thought them a perfect match, two insipid blondes.

I had been thinking hard, and at the last rather moodily, so that I had not noticed the path narrowing. It seemed to curve downward too, into a little wood. I had lost sight of the guard ahead. Bemused, I looked behind me; nothing in that direction either. There must have been a fork in the road, and I had taken the wrong one, for here one must ride single file; it was not much more than a deer track. Tall trees stretched overhead, darkening the sky, and there was tangled undergrowth on all sides. Galahad snorted and shied as a bramble caught his foreleg. I bent and whispered to him, sounds of comfort and soothing, wordless. He was a good horse, and took heed, pacing himself.

Around a bend I caught sight of Alexander, ambling slowly on his mount, his head, as usual, bent over a book; he was alone. He heard Galahad's hooves, and turned to greet me. He smiled, his own sweet smile, but I saw that the frown of concentration did not leave his face; it was permanent already, the mark of the scholar, from constant reading in a poor light, and it spoiled his looks. I thought it a shame, for there was no comelier boy in all our courts.

"Have you lost the guard?" I asked, pushing past him.

"Oh, they're somewhere up ahead," he said, waving a hand vaguely.

"I hope so," I said, a little crossly. "It's not safe to ride alone in these parts . . . we are not in England now, you know! And you are not even armed." For myself, I had only my table dagger and an old sword which I wore for the feel of it, though it was practice-blunted. "Spur your horse, Alex," I said sharply. "We must come out of this tangle."

I began to gallop; the low branches swept across my face, stinging, and making my eyes tear. I saw some open space ahead; at the same time I heard a low strangled cry behind me. I whirled, reining in Galahad.

I saw Alexander halted, two rough fellows holding the bridle of his horse; one held an axe uplifted. Alexander, having nothing else, threw the heavy book he was holding into the face of the one nearest; the fellow let go of the bridle, and the horse reared, pawing so that other fell back too.

I drew my sword; it would not cut butter, so I shifted it in my gauntleted hand so that the heavy hilt lay forward. "Go, Galahad!" I said softly. In a moment we were upon them; the axe-bearing fellow did not have time to raise it. I brought the heavy hilt down upon his head, as hard as I could; he fell like a stone. The other, I saw in a flash, was armed with a curved Saracen blade, a wicked thing; he struck upward, at Galahad's throat. The stroke missed, but caught the horse in the breast, a long graze. When I saw the red blood well out upon the white smooth coat and heard the pain-filled whinny, black fury burst in my head. I pulled my dagger from my belt and stabbed the man in the throat. It was easy as sticking a trussed pig. I saw his eyes, upturned, before he fell; he looked surprised.

Both ruffians lay silent on the ground, sprawled like jointed dolls; it was clear they would not move again. I made to dismount, but then I heard a crashing in the forest and horses' hooves stamping. "There are more of them!" cried Alexander. "Quick! Cover me with your sword!" And he slipped off his mount, as quick as any knight, and snatched up the axe where it lay beside the fallen routier, handing me the scimitar as he remounted.

"Listen!" I said, holding up my hand. "They are retreating. Shall we go after them?" The crashing noises were growing fainter as we hesitated, but still we could hear that there were many of them.

"Sounds like a small army," said Alexander, smiling a little.

I lifted up my voice and shouted, "To me, England! To me, Anjou!" If the guards were anywhere near, they would hear. We waited a moment, then, "After them!" I cried. It was foolhardy, but I was young, and had been blooded, as you might say, like a battle steed; I was heady from the ease of my first killing.

We crashed through the thick underbrush, making as much noise as the enemies we had heard, or so it seemed, and came out, suddenly, upon a narrow road, bordering on burnt-out fields. Far ahead of us, and fast disappearing from sight, was a body of horsemen in a cloud of dust. "It is no use," I said. "We can never catch up. Let us go back and see what manner of men we have vanquished."

Alexander said, as I turned over the ruffians one by one, "They deserved it, by the look of them—villains for sure." Still, he made the sign of the Cross where they lay.

They were ugly customers, no mistake. One had the slit nose of a felon, and the other was missing an ear. Upon their filthy rags was a badge of service, the only mark of the mercenary. I spelled out the device. "It is the badge of Angoulême. They are the paid routiers of our host of last night . . . I thought he had the look of a traitor!"

From another direction came now the sounds of a galloping horse, and around the curve came Bernard the troubadour, his lute slung over his shoulder, his sword held high. He was alone.

"The others?" I asked. "Where are the guards behind and before?"

"I know not," he said simply. "But I came."

There was silence all about; even the horses were still, not pawing the ground. We three looked at one another; I think we all smiled at once, with the same thought.

"A lute player and two boys," I said, "but with stout hearts." I dismounted, and knelt; I felt the occasion demanded it. "What more," said I, "to take Jerusalem?"

We bowed our heads, not smiling now. For inside us all, whenever there was pause, was the thought of the Holy Sepulchre, in the hands of the infidels.

The forest was very still as we knelt beside the slain. We prayed.

CHAPTER 8

THE REAR GUARD caught up with us, finally, and the van, who had heard my rallying cry, turned back. They dragged the slain routiers onto the main road and left them there, with a sign reading "Beware, Traitor of Angoulême! Here is the justice of your Liege Duchess! Beware!" I was all for hunting down the rest of the outlaw band and punishing them all; it would have been Father's way, and in this I thought him right. But I was not yet lord of this domain, and Mother, being a woman and softer, decreed differently. "Two wrongs do not make a right. I will have Guilhelm up at the next law session, and he will make redress."

"He deserves to die!" I cried. "His mercenaries have preyed in our territory."

"Hush, Dickon!" she said. "We will deal with him later, lawfully. I am weary . . . let us push on now to Poitiers, so close as we are." I saw that indeed she looked pinched and exhausted, and held my peace.

Bernard said softly, "The Queen your mother had great fright for you, Richard . . . it might have been your end."

Mother looked at me sadly and said, "Yes, Dickon, it was folly to attack them so poorly armed as you were."

"They attacked us, Mother! One fellow had an axe raised to brain Alex here! Would you have me abandon my friend?"

"No." And she sighed. "You are a man already, and brave. A knight. I am proud of you." She came forward then, throwing herself into my arms and clutching me hard for a long moment; she was not often so demonstrative, though I knew she loved me dearly. She turned then to Alexander. "Let me kiss you too, dear lad. Another brave knight."

He shook his head, smiling. "I did nothing at all, Lady . . . but I spoiled the book when I threw it. The pages are all crumpled, and the binding broken." We all laughed then, breaking the moment.

"I will have it repaired," she said. "I promise."

And so we reformed ourselves, and rode on. Bernard

stayed behind with Mother and her ladies, and Alexander and I went ahead, among the guard. The day was still young, though fear and death had walked among us; it was a strange feeling, to see the peace of nature all about, unmarked. And I had killed two men, my brothers in Christ, foul as they were. I crossed myself, hoping He understood.

We rode along for perhaps a mile, not speaking, each in his own thoughts. Dust rose from the horsemen just ahead; the road climbed. At the hill's crest we paused for a moment, to rest the horses.

"Holy Jesu," murmured Alex, beside me, looking ahead. "How fair a sight!"

There was a little vale below, and then another hill. Upon it stood the city of Poitiers, gleaming white in the morning sun, my heritage. The site rose high on a grassy knoll, superb amidst its encircling rivers; bridges fanned out to little suburbs and great monasteries that lay beyond the streams that moated the city. Brimming with sunshine, the valleys ebbed far away below, hamlet and croft, mill and vineyard dissolved in a haze of soft misty blue. How fair a sight indeed!

I must have seen it before, when I was a child, for Mother had taken us there on visits, but I did not remember any such glory as this. Besides, Father, to do him credit, had recently enlarged and rebuilt the walls and restored many of the ancient buildings.

Poitiers was one of the oldest towns of southern Europe, built by the Romans long ago on an Etruscan site. Its arches and colonnades were Romanesque, as graceful as sculpture, its stone and marble rosy-toned and pitted gently with age. Father had extended the narrow old Merovingian area to include small parishes that had previously straggled over the outer slopes; ancient churches had been cleared of age-old decay and new ones had risen, magnificent as monuments, their spires like long straight fingers pointing to the sky.

In the center stood the tallest building of all, the beautiful tower that Count William the Troubadour, Eleanor's grandfather, had built for the pleasure of his wanton love, the Countess of Châtellerault. To this central tower recent additions had been made, to Eleanor's specifications, after the gorgeous palaces of Byzantium which she had seen in her youth, on Crusade. I remembered her, back in England, at the architect's elbow, prodding the man. "Open it up!" she had cried. "Sunshine! Light! Space! I want a look of endless space!" I spurred onward, Alexander trailing behind.

The drawbridge was down, the great gates open, spilling out a spate of foot soldiers, who lounged idly in the sun or squatted in little groups, playing at dice. I had not known we had such an abundance of guards here in this city, and thought they might have been better employed patrolling our roads. But then I saw, interspersed among our colors, the white and gold of Champagne, and realized that the Countess Marie had arrived with all her train.

Marie of Champagne was Mother's eldest daughter by Louis Capet, wed for many years now to the Count of Champagne. I had never met her, though she was my half-sister; I think Mother had not laid eyes on this daughter since she was a small child. I knew Mother longed for this reunion, and had planned and plotted for many months, till Henry of Champagne had finally given his consent to the visit.

And now she had arrived first, and Mother must come in to her all dusty from the road and unprepared! I resolved to lag behind and enter along with Eleanor; it was the least I could do. Besides, I was myself a little shy of this already illustrious lady, sister or no. She was the most famous patroness of art and music in all of Europe; her troubadour, Chretien de Troyes, had modernized all the old tales of Arthur and his knights, setting them to beautiful music that was so simple and tuneful that the lowest jongleur could make his living singing it.

We had been walking our mounts on the winding road that led to the bridge, waiting for Mother, with the rest of her followers, to catch up, when there came the long, full notes of a hunting horn, quite close, to our left. A party of hunters emerged from the forest's edge, like a flock of bright-colored birds, their voices light and chattering as birdsong, too, their plumed, silk-hung steeds stepping sideways, neat-hoofed, as though they were on show. At their head, like a spear point, rode a laughing lady all in green, a white falcon on her wrist.

She rode straight up to me, for I was nearest, and said, "The Queen . . . where is the Queen?" Her face was all dimples, enchanting me.

I stared, and stammered, "She . . . Mother is just behind—just back on the road."

"You must be . . ." She peered at me, coming close. "A brother. Which?"

"I am Richard," I said, still staring. Close to, I could see the little beads of moisture on her upper lip and the high flush of color that stained her cheeks; she had been riding hard, and was still a little breathless from it.

She laughed again, and put her hand to her chest. "Richard, of course," she said. "I had a picture, but I am shamefully nearsighted. Richard . . . my brother."

Too late, I snatched off my cap and bent over her hand, my own face reddening.

"Do not dismount," she said, and lifted my chin with her hand. "Let me look at you . . . Oh, you will be a handsome knight!"

I loved her from the first, this half-sister of mine. I loved her looks, much like Mother's, but of a fairer cast; her hair was a fine light brown, and her eyes were something between brown and green. I loved her manner, so free and open, and the sunny quality of her smile. And I loved her sensitivity, that had seen fit to greet her travel-stained mother in hunting disarray.

She held on to my hand, tight, her starry, nearsighted eyes searching my face. I felt a sharp sting in my other hand and looked down to see the white falcon a-tremble on her wrist, its feathers ruffled and its little red eyes furious; its beak had drawn blood. Without thinking, I snatched my hand up and sucked the wound.

"Oh, has he hurt you?" cried Marie. "He is a bad boy! Jealous!" Swiftly she cracked the bird across the beak; it chirped like a dove and hunched into its feathers, closing its angry eyes.

"It's nothing," I said. "Only a scratch."

"Still, I will punish him." She took from a little bag at her belt the tiny falcon's hood and slipped it over the bird's head. "There! Go to sleep! Bad boy! He is called Guillaume— William—after the Conqueror," she went on, trilling her lovely laugh.

I found my tongue then. "Perhaps after our ancestor too . . . William the Troubadour."

"Oh, no," she said, with a little piquant frown. "Falcons do not sing." And then, with a sly glance at my face: "And this bird-William is celibate too."

I blushed, hating myself for it; she would think she had a fool for a brother. I was still racking my brains for a clever answer when I saw her eyes go beyond me and stop, with a look of wonder.

"God, Richard, is that our mother?" she cried softly. "She looks exactly as I remember her, so long ago . . . I was six years old when last I saw her at the French court." A small sob checked her words. When she had mastered it, she turned to me, her great eyes unseeing. "Here, Richard, take Guillaume." And she thrust the hooded falcon at me. I held out my injured hand, gingerly, and felt the tiny claws grip my wrist. She turned her prancing horse then, and went to meet our mother on the path, all her gay train fanning out behind her. I sat my horse, quietly, and watched.

I saw Marie check her mount some paces from Eleanor and hold up her hand for her followers, who pulled up in a great milling mass behind her. Swift as swift, Marie dismounted; I saw a flash of striped stockings, and then she knelt before our mother, her head bowed, her green skirts ballooning about her in the dust. Behind her, all the lords and ladies followed suit, prostrating themselves before the Queen. A lute sounded from among the courtiers, the familiar notes of Bernard de Ventadour's famous ode, "Were the lands all mine/From the Elbe to the Rhine/I'd count them little case/ If the Queen of England/lay in my embrace."

It was a subtle compliment from one troubadour to another—for the lute must belong to Chretien de Troyes—and of course a tribute to Eleanor herself. I felt my eyes sting with tears, for Father did not encourage such gestures at his court, and I had never experienced such a moment. For Eleanor, it must have been a reliving of the adulation of her fair youth.

Bernard, at the first notes of the lute, had got down from his horse and knelt too; he had a feel for such things. Far back in Mother's train, all the minstrels and jongleurs had taken up the refrain on their various instruments; it was a stunning salute to their Queen of Love, for so such folk held Eleanor to be.

When the song was done, Eleanor held out her hand to Bernard, and with his help, slid down from her horse. Rushing to Marie, she raised her from the ground where she knelt. I was too distant to hear their words, and their faces blurred behind my tears, but I saw that they embraced like sisters. They were of a height, both passing tall, for women, and their two slim bodies merged, a lovely sight, the sky blue of

Eleanor's gown next to the green of Marie's, and behind them the darker colors of the cypressed hills. They did not mount again, but walked together, arms entwined, up the path to the drawbridge. As Eleanor passed me, I thought that she had never looked so beautiful, or so happy.

CHAPTER 9

THE GREAT HALL of the palace was flooded with light, though outside the sky was overcast. Huge arched windows lined three of its walls, reaching from floor to ceiling; at one end their mullioned panes were set in movable frames that opened onto the vast courtyard and the formal gardens beyond. The remaining walls, under fixed glazing, were lined with marble benches, cushioned in shining silk from Moorish Spain, a new weaving of blue and green, iridescent in the light. The same material was made into hangings, draped now above the windows; they could be let down against the heat of the sun, or to mask the night darkness when thousands of candles were lit in the magnificent gold chandeliers.

At the far wall were two thrones, delicately made and inlaid with ivory, upon a little dais. They were small, ladies' thrones, not built to bear a man's weight, and they were twins. The ladies who occupied them today might have been twins as well, at a little distance; they were Eleanor, Duchess of Aquitaine, Queen of England, and Marie, Countess of Champagne. The hall was filled with people, squeezed together on the benches, lounging on cushions on the floor or on the steps of the dais; many stood or strolled about, footmen going among them with trays of sweetmeats and honeyed wine. It was a session of the Court of Love.

These Courts were imitated everywhere now, even in the smallest castles, but they were an invention of Mother's, a pastime to lighten her days in the long winters of Britain and Normandy.

There, in the bleak Angevin castles, strewn with the straw bedding of Father's squires and knights, murky with the smoke of flares and fireplaces, and littered with flung weapons, armor, and the offal of hounds, the Courts of Love were no more than a game, a pretty mockery. But here, in the rich and decorous south with its refinements of Moor and Byzantine, they had become a way of life. Even the tavern wench had her suppliant gallant, and the shepherd piped love notes to the goose-girl. No knight entered the lists without his lady's colors at his helm, and pretty pages too young to lift a sword squabbled among themselves for a damsel's cast-off sleeve. The troubadours' songs addressed the lady as "Midons" or "Master," for women made the rules of Courtly Love, and men obeyed them. It was a topsy-turvy world, and we were all caught up in it. I had not been in Poitiers a week and I was already in love for the third time.

The first was named Lombarda, a dark beauty from a tiny duchy in Lombardy. She had a big bosom and laughed a lot; her black eyes turned my knees to water. I think she liked me too; she brushed against me in the hall, her flesh warm and perfume strong. I had already begun a poem to her, but Marie, my half-sister, shook her head. "She is not for you, Richard," she said. "She is a coquette, and her husband is jealous. He has already killed one knight over her; all Italians are hot-headed. No, you must look elsewhere." For Marie was my mentor in this, and promised to sponsor my cause, when I found the right lady.

The next one was Esme, from Touraine. I don't think she was truly beautiful, but she had great elegance, and a wonderful grace; I have never seen such a dancer, even among professionals. Her face was too thin and her features too sharp, but the whole look was pleasing, enlivened by wit and charm. But Marie was quick to strike her out. "She is far too old for you, Richard, almost thirty."

My third choice met with her approval. "Yes, Honorine may do," she said. "She is only seventeen, and her husband will be flattered. He took her for her beauty, with a small dowry, and has been criticized for it. Of course he does not love her—he has three mistresses already. But it would set approval on his choice—you are the heir, after all. Perhaps—if she accepts you—you might send him a little token, a ring or a brooch, so that he will look the other way."

"Is that how it is done, then?" I was amazed.

She shrugged and smiled. "I warn you, it will not be easy. Honorine has already refused two of our best knights. If she accepts you as a suitor, you will have to obey her in all things, no matter how difficult the trials she sets you. A true knight does not question his lady."

"Oh, of course," I said eagerly. "How shall I begin? Shall I write a song? A planh, or an alba?"

"Nothing so emotional at first," she said, frowning. "An ode . . . and bring it to me first. I will see if it is suitable."

My first two odes did not please Marie; the first she laughed at, saying it lacked subtlety, and the second, she insisted, did not scan! I was unused to criticism and anger rose in me, but I swallowed it. When I read the song over, I saw she was right.

The third song, like the third lady, passed. "It is banal— but not bad, for a beginner." And, so saying, she had tucked it in her sleeve. "I will give it to Honorine, and put in a word for you as well."

Two days had gone by, and I had heard nothing. I stood alone in the great hall, trying to pick out Honorine in the crowd. So many strangers. After a week, I still had not met all of Marie's train. It seemed she had brought most of Champagne with her! And there were others besides, all the younger nobility of Aquitaine jostling one another for a place in the court, to say nothing of clerks, musicians, jongleurs, and riding masters.

The clothes were impossibly gorgeous, fantasies in silks and velvets; any one of the costumes would have fed a family of villeins for a year! I was glad Mother had sent me to a Poitevin tailor the first day; I had outgrown everything lately, and besides, I had never had anything so fine. My tunic was tawny velvet, with yellow hose and the new pointed shoes, and the russet mantle matched my hair. I had thrown it back, to show the fox-fur lining, but still it was dreadfully hot on this April day, and the shoes pinched. But one must pay for this precious finery somehow, and I would learn to bear it; after all, everyone else was in like case, and no one seemed to mind.

I saw Bernard de Ventadour at Mother's feet, his usual place, his lute slung on his shoulder in a cloth-of-silver bag. He stood out, even at this distance, for he was all in black, even to the hose; Bernard was a wonderful showman, he had learned it from his jongleurs. But Chretien de Troyes was dressed like a clerk, in a long plain gown, his lute of some plain wood too, and unadorned. He was a little round man, running to fat, with balding head and a face as guileless and open as a child's. It was hard to believe he had written those glorious tales of Arthur and his court, so high and gallant. Another clerk, a true one, stood with Chretien beside the dais, holding a long scroll. He was Marie's chaplain, a man called André. Perhaps the scroll was his translation of Ovid's *Art of Love*. I knew Mother and Marie were both excited over this work; they said it set down all the rules of Courtly Love. I had not yet read the translation, only the original. I did not see how it could be used in mixed company, for it was very erotic; perhaps André had left those bits out.

Suddenly, not three feet from me, a little space opened, as it will sometimes in crowds, and I saw Honorine go by. She was in periwinkle blue, with a violet cloak, and her soft pale hair uncovered. It was braided in two thick plaits, all twined with pearls, and reached to her waist. She was in profile; I saw the long line of her throat and the rounded chin and brow, like a child's. She passed so close that I could see the small jewel in her earlobe, and the faint red mark where the flesh was pierced. She did not see me.

Honorine, at seventeen, was already a famous beauty. All the ladies were jealous of her. Her husband was twice her age, a noted libertine, and she was childless; she was said to have a cold heart. She came from Troyes.

Honorine was beautiful in the way of an image in a church, middling tall, delicately made, with narrow shoulders and long hands. Her face was oval, her mouth small, her eyes large. Her golden hair was very soft, and her skin was so white that the pearls at her throat looked yellow. I was proud to have chosen her, proud of her grace, of the way she sat at Marie's feet so charmingly, with her little feet curled under her skirts and her train flowing down the steps of the dais.

Music had been playing softly all the while, though I had not noticed it amid the laughter and the snatches of quick, light conversation. Now it grew louder and filled the hall, for all the musicians had taken their places in the gallery behind the dais. The noise died to hums and rustlings as everyone found seats; I settled myself on the floor, not far from the step where Honorine sat. When I looked up, our eyes met. She nodded gravely, and I bowed, wishing I dared moved closer. At least she had noticed me; had she read the poem?

A little hush fell; and notes cascaded from a lute; they might have fallen from Heaven, so sweet were they. The master troubadour, Bernard, was strumming a pastorale, new, for

I had never heard it before; he must have written it for the occasion. It was a charming song, fresh as a field of flowers, and his voice matched it, a pleasing tenor. He had a time range, Bernard; he could go deep for the planhs and albas, and mustered a cutting edge for his crisp tensons. But I saw that he was finished for today; the last notes had a final flourish, and he turned and bowed to Eleanor. She beckoned him close, gave him the kiss of courtesy, light, on both cheeks, and crowned him with a wreath of early roses. He looked silly, but he carried it off well, and there was great applause as he sank gracefully to his place below Eleanor. I noticed then that she carried a shepherdess's crook, beribboned and gilded, so the pastorale was meant for her, like all his songs. When his jongleurs came onto the dais, dressed in pretty rustic costumes and carrying crooks of their own, she took his hand and held it, drawing him close.

The jongleurs performed well, a girl and two young men; they had just the right touch, light and airy, singing pretty variations on Bernard's pastorale, miming the shepherdess and her lovelorn swains. Folk went wild over it, clapping their hands and shouting.

Chretien sang then, a new chapter in his latest work, the tale of "sad man" Tristan. There was not a dry eye in the hall, as the jongleurs say. Strange, Chretien had not much of a voice, and his person was unprepossessing. Indeed, he only plucked the lute softly and spoke the words in a kind of chant, but it was a thing of magic; one could not tell how he did it. Perhaps the magic was only in the song itself, a perfect thing; tender, moving, and infinitely beautiful, with all the sadness in the world in it. Afterward he got that rare tribute, a little moment of silence before the applause. Marie crowned him with laurel, which was fitting. He looked like a small statue of Silenus, with his round, smiling face, long gown, and the laurel a little askew on the polished bare knob of his head.

Then a hush fell, and Marie de France entered. She is the greatest of the glee-maidens, and my father's half-sister; even he respects her talent. She is the love-child of Geoffrey Plantagenet, got on a nun of Fontevrault; a sin, but that does not stop our family. And Geoffrey acknowledged her; she was raised in his house, along with Father, and given an education as good as a boy's. Geoffrey was dazzling fair, they say, handsome and debonair, and wore a sprig of the planta genesta, the common broom-flower, in his helm when he rode to battle. Which is how he got his name; now they call us all, his descendants, Plantagenets. My brother Henry wears the broom-flower already, since he was knighted.

Marie de France is beautiful, in her way—as a work of art is beautiful; she is painted as carefully as an illuminated psalter. Carmined lips, blue-shaded eyes, thin tracery of arched brows, on a face like ivory, and her hair so fair as to be almost white. This is her presence always, and dressed in white as well; it is very effective, for a performer. The other glee-maidens copy her, but disastrously; most of them end up looking like whores.

They call all these women glee-maidens, these performers, or jongleuresses, even when they are married, or old as crones. The young ones are often charming to look at, when one can see them; their menfolk guard them as carefully as nuns, for these are the girls who take the part of Our Lady in the pageants. When they are not performing, they are veiled, and they travel dressed as boys, to save their virtue. We boys are all curious as cats about these damsels, and scheme to meet one face to face—a lost cause, so far.

Marie de France, this sometime aunt of mine, is much more than a performer. She is a troubadour in her own right, though a woman; some call her a great poet. She is very arrogant; even Mother cannot get close to her, though I have heard her laugh with Father like a man. It is her pride to call herself Marie de France, as though no duchy were large enough to hold her genius. She will accept no money; one must present the rarest jewel as a reward, or she will scorn it.

She can play any instrument, even the great bardic harp, which leaves sore calluses on the fingers. Today she played on a little box, from the Saracen lands, called a zittur, or zither. Her song was long and complex, a story really, full of worldly wit. I cannot help thinking that if a man had sung it in this court, he would be driven out of the hall; it was ripe with innuendo, and the meanings were double-tongued and almost bawdy. Even I, used to Father's court and the rough talk of his soldiers, was shocked. But no one did more than smile or giggle, though a few of the younger ladies wore blushes, and Honorine hid her face behind a jeweled fan. It was the tale of a knight and two ladies; he was false to both of them, and in the end they had their revenge, for they became great friends and Sapphic lovers and set up housekeeping together. They banished the false knight, ruled their joint lands together, and lived happily till the end of their days. The epilogue had them in heaven, sitting on a cloud, their arms entwined, their golden wings spread behind them, wearing haloes and plucking at the same harp! I had heard most of Marie's songs, but never this one; now I saw why. Sister or not, if she had sung it in Father's court, he would have packed her off to a nunnery! But here in Poitiers, it was just the thing; even the pages would be humming it tomorrow.

Mother gave Marie de France a laurel wreath, but made all of gold. Marie thanked her prettily, but would not suffer it to be placed on her head, for fear of ruffling her elaborate coiffure, a thing of a myriad braids, snaking like Medusa's about her head. Mother was not offended, being a woman herself, but only laughed and waved Marie away. She was borne off, laughing, by two dainty gentlemen with coiffures to rival her own. They were all flashing gesture and high wild honeyed sound, the eyes of all upon them, until Mother raised her hand for silence. The session was to begin.

A little page, not more than six years old, came forward, dressed in a short Greek tunic of some airy stuff. His fat little legs were encased in cross-gartered sandals, and he carried a tiny bow; a quiver of little arrows was slung across his shoulder. He was got up to represent Eros, I think, or maybe Ganymede, and spoke some verse in Latin, saluting Love. He could not say his "s"s, lisping on them so that the court rocked with laughter, and he began to cry. As he ran off, his face all smeary and red, my sister Marie swooped down from her throne and caught him in her arms. She whispered a few words to him, wiped his face, and popped a sweetmeat into his mouth, sending him on his way with the loudest applause of all.

"Fair gentles," she said, addressing the hall, "our Eros is overcome with shyness, and cannot deliver Venus's message. Let the Court of Love begin!" She beckoned then, with both hands. "Come, sweet ladies, and sit in judgment."

At this there was a slow ripple of movement and color, and a surge forward like the tide; from all corners of the hall ladies detached themselves from their partners and mounted the dais. I lost count, but I swear fairly, there were upwards of sixty, their giggles silenced, their dimples vanished, all as noble and decorous in bearing as the two Queens of Love themselves. They ranged themselves behind and beside the thrones, wherever there was a space to squeeze into, and faced the court; their unwontedly solemn faces above their extravagant finery was almost laughable, though none of the knights made a sound above the tiny rustle of a cloak or the faint clang of a sword. There was now no lady left in the audience, save for a few half-grown girls, some glee-maidens, veiled to the eyes like harem beauties, and an old beldame or two nodding asleep.

A knight came forward then, knelt before the assembly of ladies, and placed his sword, hilt toward the dais, upon the floor, a token of peaceful submission.

"You may rise, Sir Knight," said Marie, in ringing tones. "Are you advocate or suppliant?"

"Advocate, Your Majesty." I was to learn that this was the answer of usage in the Courts of Love. A knight does not often seek judgment on his own; he must remain anonymous, to protect his lady's identity.

"What is your petition, Sir Advocate?" asked Marie.

"A point of conduct, if it please Your Majesty."

"You may present your case."

"Your Majesties, ladies . . ." he began, and took a scroll from his sleeve.

Marie raised a hand. "No written matter is admissible in this court," she said gravely. "Love speaks from the heart."

"Your Majesty, it was only that I feared to do love injustice with a stumbling tongue."

A little murmur of approval rippled along the dais. Marie inclined her head. "We will forgive your inadequacies," she said. "Speak on."

The knight's tongue did stumble and his voice rose and fell; I cannot recall his exact words, but this is the gist of his deposition. A certain knight, he said, had sworn to his lady, as one of the conditions of obtaining her love, that he would never boast of her merits in company. However, one day he heard some ill-wishers speak badly of her. He was so incensed at this that, forgetting his vow, he became eloquent in her defense. When she heard of this, she repudiated him, accusing him of swearing falsely. The question put to the court was: Does the lover, who admits he has broken his pledge to his lady, deserve to be driven from her presence?

There were cries of "No! No!" from the floor, and one loud "Shame on a false lady!" from the glee-maidens' corner. Marie raised her hand; the sounds died away, leaving only a buzz of conference from the dais. After a moment or two of deliberation, the verdict was given.

The lady in the case was at fault, declared the Countess Marie. She had given her lover too difficult a vow. Though the lover had been remiss in breaking it, he deserved leniency for the merit of his ardor and for his constancy. The jury recommended that the stern lady reinstate the plaintiff and release him from such an impossibly difficult vow. "Let this be a precedent," said Marie at the end. "Write it down, André!"

The next case caused quite a turmoil; the ladies on the dais buzzed like bees whose nest had been disturbed. It concerned a lady who, enjoining her lover to hold their love pure and spiritual—as all courtly love is supposed to be, ideally—then tempted the unfortunate fellow in the worst way. She admitted him to her chamber alone, and showed herself to him naked. When he could not resist, and laid hands upon her, she berated him for carnality and incontinence, averring that he had forfeited her love. The question before the court was: Should he be castigated for this lapse, given a term of penance, forbidden the lady's love forever, or forgiven? It seemed to be a hard conclusion to reach, for the court deliberated for a good half-hour. Suggestions from the floor were put down, and the ladies disappeared into an anteroom to make a private decision. When they came back and remounted the dais, I scanned the faces eagerly, for I hoped, like all the others in the court, to discover a clue to the lady's identity. They all wore red cheeks and shamed looks, so there was no way of telling.

Marie announced the decision: the knight had committed the gravest of all sins against courtly love. He had broken his vow, he had been weak, he had been bestial; a sterner court would be justified in banishing him from his lady's favor altogether. However, said Marie, the court recommended mercy, the knight being flesh and the flesh being weak. He should be given three hard trials and, if he passed them, and if the lady so wished, he might be admitted again to her favor, after a year. I thought it a chilling verdict; at my age, a year seemed forever. Although, of course, the knight had been very foolish; surely he must have known the lady was testing him!

Then came a petitioner, young, with fresh face and keen eyes. He advanced to the dais, bent the knee, and said, "Fair Majesties, I am my own advocate. The lady of my heart is far away and not known to this court, and my question is not personal, but abstract. I will acquaint the court with the circumstances. There is, in this aforementioned far place, a beautiful lady to whom I have given my heart. I would have given her my hand, my sword, and my service as well, but she refused my petition; she says that she is in love with her husband."

At this a great gasp went up, and all was consternation upon the dais. The case, it seemed, was unusual. After a moment Marie came forward. "Fair knight, what exactly is your question?"

"If it please Your Majesty," said the young knight, in firm tones, "the question I put to the court is: Can love truly survive marriage?"

The ladies on the dais looked thunderstruck; obviously they were at a loss for words.

Said Marie, "Fair knight, the code of love says that marriage is no obstacle to lovers." Her brow wrinkled. "Does that satisfy you?"

"No, no, Your Majesty . . . I know the code! From my point of view, I shall love the lady always. I knew she was wed, and in accordance with the rules of courtly love, might take a lover—in purity and chastity, of course. But the lady will not accept me. She says her husband is her courtly lover!"

Another gasp went up from the dais; all the ladies were shocked.

Marie said gently, "How long has your lady been wed, fair sir?"

"Three months, or thereabouts, I believe."

"Ah, well," said Marie, smiling. "Perhaps her husband is young . . . or kind."

"I know not," said the knight, a little impatient. "But, if she loves him . . . will that love last? Can true love survive marriage?"

"That is your question, Sir Knight?" He nodded. "Then, ladies," Marie said, beckoning them closer, "let us deliberate."

The ladies huddled together in animated debate. Then, finally, Marie said, with great solemnity, "The court feels somewhat divided on this matter. A few jurors feel that love can exist in the marriage bed . . . but the majority thinks otherwise, with regret. For myself, as judge, I must answer that love—in its ideal state, as among equals, and in purity and kindness—cannot exist between spouses."

At this there was a small uproar in the hall; the quiver of laughter, soft murmuring, and a voice, male, raised in an oath. Above it sounded the thin sweet notes of the zither, and Marie de France, singing a snatch of song. I recognized the words, her own, and famous. "Mortal love is but the licking of honey from thorns . . ." There was laughter again then, and applause, and a cry, "Well sung!"

Marie asked silence again, raising her white hand. "We will hear from Queen Eleanor . . . Your Majesty, your answer!"

Mother rose and stepped forward, her vivid dark face grave and sweet. "Fair knight," she said, "I cannot gainsay the Countess of Champagne . . . her judgment must stand." Then she sighed and smiled. "However, I hold it admirable that this wife—your lady, sir—can find love and marriage consonant." I thought that sadness colored her voice, and suddenly a series of pictures flashed on my mind's eye: Father raging and storming; Father dabbling in Rosamund's bosom; Father tickling the child Alys, my betrothed. Anger rose in me then, for, though I did not like little Alys, still she was mine.

Sunk in my own thoughts, I suddenly felt a silence, saw eyes turned to me, and, too late, heard my name called; I started up from my place, my clumsy practice sword clattering on the stone floor.

"Richard . . . Richard of Aquitaine . . . Sir Brother!" It was the Countess Marie, laughing softly at me before all the company.

I dropped to one knee, bending my head, but I had had one startled glimpse of her, standing tall upon the platform and holding a large, glittering sword.

"Come forward, Richard, and place your hands in mine. Repeat after me . . ." And Marie spoke the vassal's oath in fair Latin, ending with "I swear fealty to this court, to my lady, and to all fair ladies, and swear to be true knight and champion according to the codes of Courtly Love." She gave me the kiss of peace then, as it is done in all courts, and, stepping back, said, "Kneel, Richard."

I felt a light rap on my shoulder and heard, "Arise, Sir Knight." She was a little breathless from the weight of the great sword, but she held it out to me, clasped in both her hands, hilt forward. "Take it, Richard. It is a good sword

... it was our ancestor's. It was William the Troubadour's."

"And am I truly knight?" I whispered, for I was bewildered.

"In Aquitaine, you are ... and in my County of Champagne." Her smile flashed. "Elsewhere, perhaps it will not hold ... perhaps not in England." I laughed then too, to think of Father countenancing such a knighting.

"Thank you, fair sister," I said, and took the sword. It was Damascene work, the steel dark and shining, the hilt worked with rubies in the form of a cross, an old Crusader's sword. I tried the blade with my thumb. It was sharp, and a thin line of blood traced itself there in my flesh, my first sword wound. A thrill ran through my veins.

"Here is the belt and scabbard," said Marie, buckling them on. "And your spurs ... the Queen had them made."

The spurs were gold; I took them in my hand, and knelt before my mother. "I hope to be worthy of them, madame," I said.

"There is a horse too, Richard," said Marie, "and hauberk and helm as well." She drew me close and whispered, "Your lady looks with favor on your suit. Today at vespers, the garden walk near the little church. Be there." Then she spoke up loudly, saluting me before all. "Sir knight, be true!"

I got off the dais somehow, my head in a whirl; the rest of the session was a blur. I excused myself early and went to my chamber.

I dressed all over again, from the skin out, taking great care. My long gown was violet; it looked well with my hair, though one would not expect it, and it made my eyes look darker. I could not decide between the tawny velvet cloak and a black cape with ermine; in the end I wore neither. Hearing the bells begin for evensong, I buckled on my sword and hurried off.

Marie sat in the little garden, with three of her ladies; they were sorting out embroidery silks, frowning at the task and counting on their fingers. I saw no sign of Honorine.

"You may leave us," said Marie. They backed away, giggling. Marie patted the stone bench. "Sit here, Richard, beside me."

"The Lady ... Honorine," I stammered.

Marie frowned. "Know, Richard, that a lady does not keep the first assignation. It would be too bold." Then she smiled, relenting. "But she has sent you a letter." She reached into her sleeve and brought out a scrap of parchment. One side of it looked to be a market list, half scratched out. "Four oranges . . . a hen, not too old." I had a glimpse of Honorine's ordinary life; it was endearing. On the other side she had written, "Same time and place tomorrow."

Honorine was not there the next day, or the next, or the next; I was desperate, and complained to Marie.

"She is testing you," she replied, smiling brilliantly. "You did well to continue. Do not fail her now, Richard."

And so I went again to the appointed spot, the fourth time. I waited until the monks came out from the vespers service, walking two by two, and, downhearted, turned way. A hand plucked my sleeve. I looked down; at my elbow was an urchin face, all covered with freckles, a little lad dressed in the livery of Troyes. "The lady says come to the church, the last row but one." I started forward, but he hung on. "The lady said you would pay me."

I had nothing in my purse but louis d'or; I gave him one. He snatched the gold coin, his cheeky face splitting into a wide grin, and ran away.

The little church was dim inside, for the sun had almost set; two candles burned before the altar. There was no one there at all. I made my reverences to the Christ that hung there, an old, wooden image, badly carved, but with new paint upon it, so that the wounds seemed to run fresh blood. I went, in the empty church, to the row she had ordered, though I felt a fool, and that she had tricked me again. I bent my head, to cool my thoughts, and knelt, silently mouthing a little prayer to the Virgin.

A voice behind said softly, "Sir Knight . . ." My heart leapt; it was a woman. "Do not turn," said the voice. "Listen well. I liked your poem . . . I may look kindly upon your suit, if you be true. You have passed the first test, the test of patience. The second will be harder . . . do you still wish to endeavor for my hand?" The words were stilted and stiff, phrases out of the commoner romances, but they brought her close, somehow, and made her younger, like any dreaming damsel soaking up the minstrels' tales, though she was a wedded woman and a baroness; I remembered she was only four years older than I myself. The voice spoke on. "Fair friend, you do not answer."

I half-turned then; she drew her cloak across her face. "Look in front of you, Sir Knight!" she said reprovingly.

I felt the prick of anger; was this part of the game? "May I not see your face, Lady?"

"Do you doubt me, fair friend?" she asked sadly. "Love must rise above all doubt."

"Lady, forgive me."

"Will you, then, endure the second trial of true love?"

"With all my heart, Midons." She seemed pleased at the title; I heard her catch her breath.

"Take this letter, then . . . the instructions are in it." She slipped a parchment into my hand. "Go now to the end of the aisle and kneel, facing our Saviour."

I did as she said, hearing a faint rustle behind me. After a moment she said, "You may turn now, noble sir, and look upon the face of your Midons." I turned; she stood revealed in the light of the open church door, in the soft haze of twilight. Her cloak was thrown back, and she wore a gown of some simple light stuff, low at the neck. Her hair was uncovered, hanging unbound like a maiden's. I thought her more beautiful than ever. "Arise, fair friend," she said, and gave me her hand. Something broke in me, with the waiting, and the disappointment, and I clutched her hand and covered it with kisses. It was as soft and small as a child's, with a little wart too, like a child's, on the littlest finger. She snatched it away, her mouth opening in an "o." "What are you doing, friend . . . you go too far! I may permit you such a liberty when . . . *if* we become lovers. But now, you have only passed one ordeal!"

I fell again to my knees. "Forgive me, Lady. I was overcome by your beauty . . . but I swear my love is pure." I was talking like her now, but it seemed to be the correct thing, for she relented, and smiled a sad little smile.

"Fair friend, I will give you one more chance, for my heart is merciful. I must go now. Give me five minutes." And she was gone, her perfume lingering still, a faintness among the stronger incense of the church.

When I went outside, there was no sign of her, or of anyone. The light had changed, had become that strange and golden thing that happens sometimes just before darkness falls; the sky was a wonder of purple and red in the west, a splendor. I felt that God had made this show of pomp for me alone. I was so dazed with love that I held her letter, unread, clutched in my hand, all the way home.

CHAPTER 10

THE NEXT TRIAL set by Midons Honorine was not so easy; I whistled through my teeth as I read her round, childish scrawl. The spelling was atrocious, even for a girl, and it took me a while to decipher it, though it was short. She bade me enter the lists for the next tournament, and to challenge the Lord of Brécy, whom they called "the Lion Heart." I had seen him fight, of course, for who had not? He was the acknowledged champion of all the French lands, and had appeared at virtually every tournament for the last ten years; he had never been unhorsed.

This was to be my test for valor; most would have called it foolhardiness. My heart sank at the thought of suffering humiliation and defeat at my very first tournament. But for her favors I would do anything, even that. I resolved to make a fair showing, at least, for my lady's credit, and the pride of my house. The heart to fight him was not lacking either, for he was an ugly brute, only a cut above a routier, and hated by all.

Bertrand de Brécy was the younger brother of that lord who had knocked out the teeth of his wife, my mother's waiting-woman Louise. He had done it in drink, but his brother, cold sober, would as soon run you through as look at you; they said his own mother had cursed him. When the brother died, Bertrand had come into the inheritance, but there was pitifully little of it. The lands of Brécy had been mortgaged for years, and shamefully neglected too; the brother had been living on Louise's dowry. Bertrand sought to marry the widow, for he wanted to keep the monies in the family, but she was terrified of him and fled to sanctuary in the nearest cathedral. From there she sued for my father's protection, he being her overlord. He gave it gladly, taking charge of the dowry, and promising to find her a kinder husband. He never did; Father does not easily open his fist once it has closed on gold, and Louise has been in Mother's service ever since.

Bertrand did not find another heiress to wed with; his reputation had gone before him, and even the most desperate scarecrow would not have him. He was reduced to earning his living the only way a knight may, by the sword. Perhaps if he had not been so formidable a fighter, or so fortunate in his first tournaments, he would indeed have taken service with some lord, as a mercenary; the routier captains are made up of such as he. But at every joust he won some opponent's horse and equipment, selling them afterward for goodly sums. Many a knight has kept body and soul together this way, but after ten undefeated years, Bertrand was a rich man; by now he could afford to refuse a challenger who was not richly accoutered.

I could have no hope of this; my steed was princely, and the gold spurs alone were worth a duke's ransom! Bertrand would not refuse me; he feared nothing, and had nothing to lose. He had no kinder instincts either; the young, untried heir to all of Aquitaine would move nothing in him but greed.

At the thought of losing all, my first symbols of knighthood, my heart sank. Then, after a moment, a kind of fury rose, bursting, in my veins, Father's heritage; for the first time I understood how he could fall into a fit. After a moment I mastered the impulse, my stomach churning, and began to think, coldly. Need I lose, after all?

I began to remember Bertrand as I had seen him so often in the lists. I had been watching all the best knights for several years, since I had begun my training, watching like a hawk, adding up their best points, subtracting their weaknesses, planning imaginary strategies. I had made notes too, and kept them by me; now I rummaged through the coffer that held them. Yes, here it was ... Bertrand de Brécy. I scanned them carefully, smiling grimly to myself. Though they called him the Lion Heart, he was more bull than lion; short, stocky, built like a square cornerstone, ugly of visage, toad-faced. Thirty-eight years old, and most of them spent fighting. Well, that could be to my advantage; he could tire.

I resolved to wait until he had fought all other contenders; I had put myself down for the melee anyway, which comes at the end. Bertrand might be somewhat winded by that time. Already, when I had seen him last, I measured myself a head taller than he, and my arms were longer than most men's; I would have him on reach, if I could make it count.

I had been practicing with my horse every day since I got

him. He was as black as Galahad was white; I called him Bohemond, after the great warrior of the First Crusade. He had uncanny instincts, this horse, and could almost do my fighting for me, swerving to right or left to hit on target, and putting all his great weight behind my thrust. Still, I meant to spend all the daylight hours at jousting. My heart was lighter, but not by much.

I wrote to Honorine, promising to obey her and asking for her token, to wear on the day. It did not come till the morning of the tournament, a silk purse, heavy with something inside. I had expected a scarf or an embroidered sleeve, the usual thing, to wear in my helm, but when I drew it out, I saw it was a small round mirror of shining silver, marked with her initial, and hanging from a jeweled chain. I hung it round my neck, under my hauberk, after I had kissed it and murmured a prayer.

My young brother Geoffrey had begged to act as my squire. I could not refuse him, for he was almost as excited as I was; besides, he was certainly defter and quicker than poor awkward Will Longchamps. "You have a lady!" he cried, catching sight of the chained mirror as he armed me. "Who? What is her name? I will not tell!"

I shook my head, smiling, but as I raised my arms to pull on my jupon, the mirror turned, showing the initialed side. "The letter 'H'!" he cried. "It is Honorine! Oh, Dickon, she is the most beautiful lady at court! I am so proud of you!"

I put my finger to my lips. "It is by no means settled. She has let me wear her favor, that is all. I have only passed the first test."

He nodded wisely. "Patience, yes. The next is valor . . . Oh, Dickon, what is it?" His eyes widened. "Have you challenged someone?"

"Of course not," I muttered crossly, cursing his intuition or whatever it was. "Come, help me with this sword . . . the trumpets have sounded already."

"But you are only in the melee at the end. There is plenty of time."

"I want to see the beginning. Quick, now!"

The day was fine, cloudless and fair, but hot—so hot that even as the jousts began, the sun not yet high in the sky, I could feel the sweat trickle down beneath my padded jupon and my mail.

The tilting-field was about a mile's ride from the castle, a great plain of close-cropped grass; they had set the little goats to grazing there for a week, and it was as smooth as silk now. Brightly colored pavilions dotted the far end, where the knights from other parts slept and armed; there was not enough room in the castle to hold them. With their banners and nodding plumes and shining mail, and the ladies' section, rising in tiers of seats at one side, full of movement and delicate rainbow colors, it was a brave sight. Tournaments are always a fine show, but this was my first appearance in the lists, and my heart pounded away like a siege engine.

I was surprised to hear the herald call Bernard de Ventadour's name in the first set of six; I had forgotten he was a made knight. He did creditably too, breaking his opponent's lance, though neither was unhorsed, and going on to the next event, a display of sword fighting. Here, his natural agility stood him in good stead, and he was adjudged the winner. He received his prize from Mother, a purse of silver. As he bowed before her, I saw he wore her favor, a golden sleeve worked with lover's knots in silver thread; she had worn it last year at my birthday feast.

The tournament wore on, doubles and swordplay taking up most of the morning. It was a good showing; at any other time, I would have found it all most thrilling, but, waiting for my chosen enemy to appear, my hands grew clammy and my mouth dry. There was no bloodshed, though one knight, very young, got a blow on the helm that knocked him right out, and he had to be carried off the field. The contests were stopped while Mother sent to inquire after him. He was only stunned, and was coming round, so that was all right; it would continue. But the sun was high now, and the heat oppressive. I heard the twittering of the ladies in their stands as pages brought on refreshments, wine and cakes, and little birds roasted in pastry, served on skewers. My nerves were getting raw now, and the smell of the hot food sickened me, but I took a cup of wine, hurtling it down. "Not too much," said Geoffrey, sounding important. "It will cloud your head." I gave him a cross look, and took another, but I only sipped it, for he was right.

Some tumblers had come out onto the field now, while thralls rolled the churned-up parts smooth again. These acrobats were a wonder to see, making a pyramid of their bodies and hurling themselves through space like birds, but I could not enjoy it, for my mind was already with the next events.

74

"Some are girls," whispered Geoffrey. "How do they manage their skirts?"

Next came the wild animals, a striped tiger, a spotted great cat, and a rather mangy lion, all in cages, and not a growl out of them; they must have been drugged. Some little dogs put on a show, wondrous to watch at any other time, so clever were they, and dressed up like Christian folk. Then a bear danced, shuffling, and a huge ape, imitating the bear. At the last, a girl, in gauzy Moorish dress, put her head in the lion's mouth. It raised a great cheer, but I saw the lion yawn; it was clear he had no teeth.

Finally it was over, and the heralds called the next events, the single combats. There were three before Bertrand de Brécy came on; I did not notice them, for my eyes, and all eyes, were on this man as he rode before the stands to salute the ladies, his head uncovered. He was dark-visaged as a Moor, and hairy; his thick eyebrows met in the middle, and he had not shaved, his chin black with stubble. It was a face to frighten crows, so surly and baleful. I have seen such faces on mountebanks, cultivated to get a laugh, but no one laughed now; he had the dignity of pure vice.

He was marvelously arrogant too, for he had not deigned to polish his mail, and his hauberk was old, crusted with the sweat and dirt of ancient contests. But the lion badge on his breast was new, embroidered in gold, and twice as big as the custom; one could tell he was proud of his nickname.

I watched him closely; he unhorsed his first three opponents without much effort, and did not even dismount to claim his booty but sent his squire to sign for the knights' equipment; he was already above five hundred crowns richer. The fourth was a tall fellow who sat high in the saddle; Bertrand's lance caught him low on his shield, and only shook him mightily, his horse rearing and pawing the air. On the second try Bertrand got him in the groin and he fell heavily, lying motionless on the field. A great cry went up from all the ladies; he must have been a popular champion. He got to his feet, though, finally, and limped off, blood streaming in a long dark rivulet from his wound, and a surgeon running to meet him. It was the first blood of the day, and Mother raised her hand to halt the trials, till word was brought that he would live.

I had seen, though, what could confound my enemy. A shade lower, and his blow would have disqualified him; he was not used to fighting tall knights. If his opponent had aimed low and been quicker, he might have had the victory. It was what I had figured on in practice, setting the quintain close to the ground and grasping my lance at the level of my hip. I said another prayer to help my resolve.

The duels went on. Four were evenly matched and fought to a draw, and then it was Bertrand's turn again; he did not want for challengers. Twelve in all he fought that afternoon, and unseated them all, though the last two took a double try each. They were cheered as they left the field; crowds will always feel for the underdog, and Bertrand's defeat was long overdue.

Finally the listed trials were over and it was time for the melee. Geoffrey drew on my gauntlets and handed me my helmet, then brought up Bohemond and mounted me. All over the field were the sounds of armor clanking and horses neighing; everyone fought in the melee, even the younger knights and the old men past their prime.

I rode over to the starting line; I had picked the gold side, as soon as I heard that Bertrand had picked the purple. I got as near as I could to him, on the opposite side of the field; I did not want to risk losing him in the crowd. A melee is nearly as bewildering as a battle, with so many in the ranks.

The herald was reading out the rules, but I did not listen. I had heard it so often, and no one pays much attention anyway, after the fighting starts; it is all so confusing. Swords and lances are blunted, of course, and there is no hitting a man after he is down; those are the important things, and the rest gets forgotten.

The trumpet sounded, and we charged, clashing in a long line in the center of the field. I was lucky; the man I met had not set his shield straight, and he went down, though my blow was glancing. As we drew up for the next foray, I saw that many in our gold line were missing; we closed the gaps, reforming, I was three knights closer to Bertrand. By the time I faced him, having downed the opponents in between, our line was a good bit scanter than the other.

When the trumpet blew, I rushed in fast, lance held low; it struck Bertrand's shield square in the middle. But his lance met my shield, too, and the impact rocked us both. I thought I saw the gleam of his eyes between the slits of his helm, and fancied they looked angry. When his horse came down from his rearing, I had my gauntlet off and ready, and flung it, hard. The mailed glove rang against the steel of his helmet, and some heads near us turned. Bertrand swiveled his head around at me, a long look, and made a gesture, beckoning me off the field. I had no real hope that he would refuse the challenge, but still, now it was done, I felt my breath come short and fast.

We withdrew to the sidelines, giving our names to the nearest herald. I thought the man looked startled when he heard mine, as well he might, but he said nothing, and only wrote it down; he was well trained.

So I missed most of the melee, for Honorine's sake—and it was my very first. Watching the others, I was sure I would have done well. But I was none too sure of the outcome of my single combat, and dared not look in Mother's direction before my name was announced; even then, she might refuse to let me fight. I don't think she could have noticed me on the sidelines, where I stood by Bertrand; there were so many on the field, and so much movement. In the end, our side, the gold, was smartly defeated, and made a poor showing in the swordplay too, for there were not enough of us left. At least, I thought, my side would be sure too cheer me on, to make up our losses.

It is perfectly legal to challenge as I had done, informally, upon the field, though it is not often done. Still, a buzz of interest rose as soon as the contest was announced. I rode out and took my place, facing Bertrand at the other end of the tiltway. A gasp went up when my name was called, but by then there was not much Mother could do to stop it, or be shamed; it was what I had counted on.

He had chosen the western end, naturally enough; it was his right, as champion of the morning events, but now I would have the sun in my eyes, and it was strong enough to blind. My helmet had a visor and I pulled it down for shade and prayed again.

On the first note of the trumpet I shot forward, Bohemond responding beautifully to the light pressure of my knees. I met Bertrand closer to his side than mine, for he had not been so quick. I held my shield very low; at the last second I saw his horse's head go up, for the polished shield had caught the sun's reflection and flashed back into the creature's eye. He swerved a little to the right, and Bertrand's blow glanced off the edge of my shield. I barely felt the impact, and rode on, hearing a great cry of triumph from the crowd. I turned

77

about, and waited, this time the sun would be in his eyes, and he had not bothered to polish his shield.

We started at once this time and met dead center, hitting squarely, each upon his target; it felt as though I had run full tilt into a stone wall. Miraculously I held my ground, and held on to my spear as well, though all my insides were shaking like jelly. I turned and saw that Bertrand's lance was also still in his hand, so we must go the third and last trial. I knew it must not be a direct hit like that, for I could never have borne another. Amid the wild cheers my thoughts ran on; by the time I took my place at the eastern end again, I had planned my strategy.

The sun was now in my eyes again. But my shield was bright, and my mail new and glittering; my reflection must be almost as blinding to Bertrand as the sun to me. He was too old and skilled a warrior not to have seen his horse's movement to the right; this time he would compensate, but I was ready. And, for good measure, I pulled the little mirror, Honorine's favor, out of my jupon, so that its burnished disk caught the sun as well. I do not know, truly, what balanced the scales that day.

We galloped forward furiously. I saw he had risen in the saddle, and I rose too; he did not mean to take me in the groin, like the other man. I felt, rather than saw, that he moved a little to the left, inward, as his horse shied at the wink of light from my shield; I moved with him, and at the same time stretched to my full height, my feet standing in the stirrups. His head went up as the mirror's flash caught him, and he put his hand out; he missed. But my lance went in, full force, between his helm and gorget, into the soft part of his throat.

He must have been dead before he hit the ground. I jumped down to draw out my lance, and a fountain of blood poured over me; he never stirred. The noise from the stands was like thunder, or the baying of a million wolves, I forget which; I know it was loud. I was very calm. I drew my sword, hacked off the lion-heart badge at his breast, and held it high. It was all I claimed; his horse, poor creature, must have burst a blood vessel, for it lay beside him on the ground, its huge eyes staring, unseeing, at the sky. His arms were an insult to chivalry, the sword notched like a routier's, to mark his skills, and his lance black with old blood.

Slowly I pulled off my helm; sweat plastered my hair tight

and ran in streams off my face, and under my jupon I was as wet as if I had fought underwater. Geoffrey came running, his face white with shock, to take my arms from me. Slowly we walked toward the stands; I held the lion-heart badge high as I went. I saw Mother's face, white too, and trembling, and heard the crowd's cry, for the first time hearing the words they said.

"Richard Lionheart," they cried. "The new Lionheart!" And one voice, shrill above the others, "The old lion is dead! Long live the new King of Beasts! Richard . . . Richard Lionheart!"

CHAPTER 11

I WAS, FROM then, a hero of sorts, though there were some old soldiers who shook their heads and called it luck. All the younger knights flocked around me; I had a coterie of followers wherever I went, and had badges made up with my new-won emblem, the lion-heart. There must have been near a hundred who wore it, calling themselves my sworn men.

I felt no great pangs about the death of Bertrand; there is nearly always one fatality in a tournament, and this one was adjudged a fair accident. But Alexander spoke to me apart, his face stern and still. "And so you have killed your third man now." He had taken to wearing a heavy iron cross about his neck, over his scholar's gown; he fingered it as he spoke.

"The first two were villain routiers and would have killed us if they could . . . and Bertrand—it was fair combat!" I spoke hotly, for I resented his censure. "Besides, he will not be mourned."

"God mourns him," he said quietly.

I turned on my heel and left him, angry, but his words troubled me and I slept badly that night, spending the long hour before dawn upon my knees below the crucifix on my wall.

Marie gave a feast in my honor; she was delighted with her new-made knight. Bernard de Ventadour sang me a rousing lay, with the Lionheart name worked into the verses, a hearty compliment; it was tuneful too, and folk hummed it afterward. And Marie de France composed a pretty song, likening me to Saint George. But she made the dragon rather endearing and funny, so that it drew laughs and sighs, and I was somewhat put out, though I thanked her and gave a ruby ring that had grown too small for me. A jongleur troupe mimed the story of David and Jonathan; that had its sting for me too, for I could swear that my part—David—was taken by a girl, dressed up. Close to, when I gave her the complimentary purse, I saw lashes that looked to be an inch long and soft velvet cheeks, gently rounded.

It was a brave feast nonetheless, and many ladies sent shy glances my way, and some bolder looks too. But Honorine was not there.

"Did you not know?" cried Marie softly. "She is sick in her chamber . . . she collapsed the day of the tournament, after you came to victory."

"Oh, God. What ails her?" I cried.

"Fright for her lover, of course," said Marie knowingly. "It is the thing to do—Honorine is no fool." She looked at my shocked face and smiled. "She is well now, of course. But she *had* to stay away from the feast, to avoid the eyes of the court. It would not do to be talked about before she has formally accepted you."

"But will she accept me?"

"Rest assured," said Marie. "You will have a letter soon."

The letter did not come, but the same small urchin pulled at my sleeve again, just two days later, bidding me to a rendezvous at the same little church.

This time it was just after noon, and she was not alone, but had a maid attending her, a slight, silent girl, with big dark eyes, half-veiled. Honorine led me to a little glade, filled with soft shadows; bluebells covered the ground like a carpet, and grew right down to the edge of a little brook that made music as it tumbled over the stones. Honorine waved the girl away. "Fetch me in an hour," she said. The girl set down the basket she carried and withdrew.

"Will you break bread with me, fair friend, and taste my wine?" Honorine's cheeks were flushed and rosy and her eyes bright; little wisps of her golden hair had come out from under her white coif, stirred by the breeze. I thought surely there had never been a fairer sight.

"You do me honor, Midons," I said, bowing over her hand.

"We shall be informal today, fair friend," she said. "Let us sit together here, upon the ground. Bring me that basket."

"I have no cloak to spread beneath you." I had been remiss; I ought to have anticipated this! I felt the red flood up to my eyebrows.

She looked at me and smiled; it was a delightful smile, small, impish. "The ground is dry, and my dress is old," she said kindly. I saw that this was so, and felt, suddenly, overdressed in my tawny velvet; besides, it was very hot. Her dress, though it did not look old, was very simple, of some soft thin stuff, the color of cream; she had loosened it at the neck and I saw the white skin, disappearing into dusky shadows where the hollow between her breasts began.

Taking my hand, she settled herself gracefully upon the ground, among the bluebells, her little feet curled under her skirts, her slender back erect; I have seen cats sit so, straight and small, upon the hearth rug. "Open the basket," she commanded.

She spread a linen cloth upon the ground, and set out two silver cups, two plates, a round white loaf, and a roasted partridge wrapped in oiled parchment. I cut a cross upon the bread and sliced it, and poured wine from a leathern flask. The wine was the color of rubies, the partridge golden-crisp, and the bread still warm from the bake-oven; it was delicious. She licked her fingers like a child when she was finished, and laughed; I had not dreamed she could be so gay and free. "Often we go, my waiting-women and I, to the woods outside Troyes," she said, "and have our meal under the trees . . . never have I done it with a man before." Her eyes downcast, her face rosy, she might have been confessing a sin! I did not know how to answer, and wondered what came next. It was my move, I guessed, but I did not know the moves.

"I missed you at the feast," I began.

"Oh, I was indisposed," she said, with a sweet smile.

"Yes, I heard. I am sorry that I made you faint."

"Oh, it was not you! It was the blood . . . I faint if I prick my finger, I am of a delicate humor." She wagged her finger at me then, scolding as in play. "It was naughty of you to make him bleed so. My Baron had to take me home."

"Was he very angry?" I asked. "Your husband the Baron?"

"Oh, no. He was proud that I had chosen the best knight on the field. He gave me an emerald necklace."

I pounced upon her words. "Then you *have* chosen me!"

"To wear my favor, yes."

"To be your true knight."

"You have not yet passed the last test of all."

"What is that?"

"You will know it when it comes," she said cryptically. "And now, let us speak no more of it. Help me to pack this basket again. I must go soon."

"Oh, it has not been an hour, surely!" But I gave her my hand to rise.

She looked about her, a small frown marring the white of her smooth brow. "Where is she—that Melisande? I must not be late!" She sounded cross, and a little nervous; there was a fine dew of moisture on her face, and her tendrils of hair were dark with it. "Oh, I am so hot!" she cried softly, twisting her hands. "Come, I must bathe my face."

The brook was only a step away. She knelt beside it, dipped in her hands, and put them to her flushed cheeks. "Sweet friend," she said, "you will find a napkin in that same basket. Fetch it for me."

I brought the cloth; she turned her face to me, brimming and cool, looking like a mermaid, enchanted. "Let me," I begged, and held the cloth to her face, feeling, through it, the little delicate bones, the sweet pout of the small mouth; I dried it tenderly. She put her hands on mine, and took the cloth from me; then she raised her face, closing her eyes. I did not know if it was expected, nor did I care; I kissed her upon the lips, and felt her yield, her body swaying toward me, her mouth opening under mine.

It was a moment of bliss, but only a moment. She pushed me away gently. "The Baron waits for me," she said breathlessly, "and Melisande . . . I do not know if I may trust her, she may be a talebearer."

She looked about her again; there was no sign of anyone. She clutched my hand. "Listen, fair friend. The Baron goes to Troyes tomorrow to see to his estates. Come to me then, when it is dark . . . anyone will tell you where our quarters lie in the palace. But"—she pressed my fingers hard, so that her rings cut into my flesh—"be secret! Let no one guess our tryst! Go now, here is Melisande!"

Indeed there was a rustling in the bushes, and I saw a slender figure slip through into the glade where we had spread our midday feast. I raised Honorine's hand to my lips, then turned away, my heart like a caged bird clamoring in my chest.

Truly, I knew nothing of love, profane or chaste; I was terrified lest I make some misstep in the meeting of the next night. I knew no one to consult, for my companions were as ignorant as I; besides, I was sworn to secrecy. I kept to my room, and read *The Art of Love* from beginning to end, the Latin original, not the courtly modern version. I was no wiser; the Roman playboy Ovid seemed to look upon women as his natural prey, planning his strategy as one might mount a siege. Marie and her chaplain, André, had simply turned it all around! I decided to trust to luck, and the saints, though the only one I dared risk praying to was Mary Magdalene!

The next day came and, finally, the night. At first dark I presented myself at Honorine's door, having taken all the roundabout ways and unlit passages, like a spy. At my first tentative scratching, she opened the door to me; she must have been listening on the other side. "Shh," she whispered, drawing me inside. She held a great candle in her hand; by its light I saw she was fully dressed, her hair hidden in the white wife's coif, though she blazed with jewels at arms and bosom, and long diamond earbobs swung nearly to her shoulders. She wore no paint, and her features looked waxy and luminous; she was like some holy image incongruously hung with pagan offerings. "Do not speak," she said. "Come."

I followed her through the dark room and through two more doors. The only light was the candle she held; I saw dim shapes as we passed, amorphous in the faint aura at the edge of the wavering flame. A chair? A clothespress? Finally she turned to face me, holding the candle high. "There," she said, her voice expressionless. "Open the curtains." It was a great canopied bed, hung with some dark heavy stuff, winecolored or purple; I pulled it aside and smelled the odor of musk, overladen with the thin sweet fragrance of fresh violets. I supposed it was her perfume sprinkled on the sheets, for it smelled like her, but stronger. I turned to look at her face, but, like her voice, it told me nothing; her eyes were cool as rainwater. "Lie here," she said, "and wait. I will come to you."

I caught my breath for joy and reached out a hand to her. She moved away, her finger to her lips. "Shh," she said again.

"Do not speak." I could not understand. Was her husband, then, still there? I felt a little thrill of danger. "It will be dark when I come to you," she said. "Do not speak or try to see my face, or I will not stay." It put me in mind of the old tales of witchcraft and fairy women; my skin crawled, but pleasantly. Then suddenly she was gone, and the light with her; it was as dark as the inside of a cave. Not a chink of moonlight showed at a window's edge; they must be shuttered tight. Wondering, I obeyed her, and lay down, stretched out in my clothes. I had not buckled on my sword this time, but my table dagger hung at my belt. I took it off and laid it softly on the bed beside me.

It was a long wait. Perhaps she is waiting for me to disrobe, I thought. But no, she had said nothing; I had better follow her instructions to the letter.

I lay like a corpse, straight and stiff; my arms and legs were beginning to stiffen too. I felt ridiculous, and moved my ankle; it cracked, a loud noise in the dark chamber. I had begun to think she meant to leave me there, alone, all night—perhaps for a week, who knows? A test of endurance? We had already been through "patience," so it could not be that. My thoughts whirled on; I closed my eyes against the dark, and heard a ghost of a footfall, and a moment later felt the touch of a hand at my hip. Then I heard a smothered laugh and the little clucking sound someone makes when annoyed. Hands tore at my clothes, breaking the fastenings and scratching me with the prong of my brooch.

I put out my arms to touch her. She was naked and burning hot, her limbs writhing like snakes; the musk caught in my nostrils, under the drenched violet of her hair. I did not wonder any longer what to do; something informed me urgently, driving my hands to stray upon her body, my tongue to seek out hers, and my swollen flesh to bury itself in her. I was wild with a kind of furious rhythm; her legs got in the way and I wrapped them around my waist. She panted and moaned beneath me, thrusting upward. For her, it must be like riding a horse upside down, I thought. But the thought was the merest flicker and the red mist came down again; we moved faster and ever faster, intertwined. Suddenly her nails dug in, and she whispered hoarsely, "Wait . . . slowly . . ." I obeyed her, moving to her command, following her whispered words. When she whispered again, urgently, "Now!" it seemed to go on forever, the strange white bursting ecstasy.

At the end she was sobbing brokenly, like a child, but her hands were pulling, hard, at my hair and her legs were wrapped around my neck, strangling me. It hurt us both, I think, but we could not care. After a long moment while we lay together, slippery and soaked, I raised my hand and gently disentangled her fingers from my hair, bringing her hand to my mouth and kissing it. I felt the small soft bones beneath, and the little endearing wart upon her finger. She withdrew her hand, whispering, "God, Richard," and was gone, leaving me in a sticky pool of wetness upon the sheet.

How long I lay there I do not know. At last there seemed to be a small wind, cooling my nakedness and drying the sweat, and I saw a lightening of the shadows; a shutter had blown back somewhere. There was just enough light to find my clothes. I struggled into them, buckled on my dagger, and waited. It was a long time.

The moon had risen when she came, dressed and decorous, still hung with jewels; I had felt them upon her, sharp and scratching, but had not remembered until now. She stood with the candle high, her face a mask, as before; I rose to take her in my arms.

"No, do not touch me!" she said, her voice low and harsh. "Know, Richard, that you have been tested and been found wanting, for the last trial is . . . purity."

I stammered once, bewildered and angry, then found my voice. "But you gave yourself to me! You wanted me!"

"Not I, Richard." She shook her head. "Know, Richard, it was not I—but my maid, Melisande. You have ravished Melisande. She took my place." She turned away; her back was stern and straight. But when she spoke, her voice faltered. "I am sad that you did not know the difference." On the last word her breath caught; it might have been laughter or a sob. I could not see her face.

"Go now, Richard. Farewell. We shall never meet again." It had a final ring, so I said nothing, and went—out of her life, as she would have it.

But as I walked through the dark passages of the castle to my own chamber, something nagged at me, a memory, that I could not quite get hold of.

CHAPTER 12

"AND THE YOUNG knight lay with his lady in love, and she denied him nothing, far from it . . . she gave him all the sweetness of her fair body, and they two were happy beyond compare." A hush fell upon the great hall, and all the Court of Love hung upon my advocate's words. He was a persuasive youth, one of those who had joined themselves to me under my new lion-heart banner; I had chosen him for his strong voice and his frank and open countenance. For I meant to get redress, if possible, for the wrong Honorine had done me; I thought it a scurvy trick.

The young man told my story well. When he came to the part where she reappeared, fully clothed, and repudiated me, her sworn knight, there were gasps of shock from all directions. And when, in a moment, he related how she averred it was not herself at all, but her maidservant, there were loud cries of "Shame! . . . A sly trick!" We rested our case.

The ladies on the dais withdrew to deliberate. It did not take them long. Marie appeared, wearing a stern look upon her charming face. "Gentles all," she began, "a verdict has been reached—a sad one, for it must needs part the lovers. We have agreed that the young knight was tempted too far and too cruelly. By offering herself to him, the lady overstepped the bounds of reasonable trial. The young knight had sworn obedience to her, as his Midons; he could not go back upon his word, he must take her—though he knew it was the sin of carnality. It was not his place to reproach her with it, but to acquiesce in what he believed to be her earnest wish. It is not he who is proven false, but the lady. She is not worthy to be his Midons. As to the substitution of her maid in his arms, that is a trick this court cannot condone . . . in so doing, she has forced her knight to sin, unknowingly, with a stranger! She has forced two souls into jeopardy, and we condemn her for it, and hold her in contempt. From henceforth she is banished from this court. We will not countenance her among our ladies. That is the judgment of the court."

There was a long silence, and then a burst of applause and shouts of approval. It was the last case to come up, and the ladies left the dais then, Marie signaling for the musicians to begin playing. All the court began to move then, slowly, though no one danced. In little groups of twos and threes they left the hall, strolling outside onto the sunny terrace and the lawns beyond. There was not much talk and no laughter; it had been a shocking judgment. In a little island to one side, against a window, sat Honorine, her face very still and remote. Beside her sat her husband, wearing a mask of fury. I had not seen the Baron before, but I recognized him from his description, angry now to have been made the butt of innuendo and jest. For I had learned that in all these cases, everyone knew, really, who was meant, though they pretended not to. And in my case, I was the youngest, newest knight of all, and I had worn her favor in the now-famous tournament. How could they not put two and two together?

I tried not to watch as her baron rose and pulled Honorine roughly to her feet, dragging her behind him, going swiftly, so that she had to run to keep up. Under the eyes of all, he led her, stumbling, from the room. Poor Honorine. Now that I had my revenge, I did not find it oversweet. I hoped he would not use her ill, or beat her, in their banishment. She deserved it, of course, but still, I could not help but remember my love.

Nor could I forget my first night of carnal pleasure, which I owed to her; it was better than the love tales had pictured it. And in my inmost heart I knew—or thought I knew—that Honorine had lied. It was she herself who had lain within my arms that night; I knew her by the little wart on her finger.

I knew, I said to myself. I was sure, indeed. But just in case, and to make sure, I resolved to seek out Melisande, her maid. When I inquired, I was told that Honorine had sent her away, back to her parents' manor in the suburbs of the city.

It did not take long to find the little castle; it lay in a mean part of the countryside, almost a swamp. Melisande came of noble folk, but noble in a small way; the castle was not much more than a fortified wooden house, with some smaller buildings scattered near, huddling close, and a hill behind where some poorish vines straggled sparsely over the rocky soil.

I had not come alone, but with several of my new companion knights. The countryside was still unsafe, though I was making plans already to root out the insurgents and the lawless bands that plagued my inheritance. I bade the knights wait for me in a little wood out of sight of the castle, and rode alone toward the gate. At every step my horse sank in mud up to his ankles, and the smell was awful; he shook his head and whinnied, not liking it. I patted his shoulder, whispering, "Good Bohemond . . . be patient."

The gate was off its hinges, or nearly. When I pushed at it, it gave way, groaning, though we had to squeeze through a quite slim gap, for it caught again. We picked our way, through all manner of cast-off trash and offal, to what passed for the inner bailey; here the door stood open. It looked deserted, but was not, for there was a sound from somewhere in the rear, of an anvil being struck. I tied Bohemond to the post that stood outside, and I pounded with the hilt of my sword upon the open door.

It was a long wait, with nothing but the clanging noise of the beaten iron. I was just on the point of entering unbidden, when a fat slut in a greasy apron appeared, wheezing and puffing. She eyed me suspiciously and said, "They've all gone to the horse fair."

"I want to see the damsel Melisande," I said, smiling. "I understand she dwells here?"

The poor thing looked startled; she was not used to smiles. But she bobbed in a queer little bow and showed gap teeth, saying, "Oh, her'll be in the dairy house. It's cheese-making today." And she pointed to a small low building in the rear. I thanked her and gave her a small coin; she bit it, and bobbed again, grinning wider.

I smelled it before I got to the door, a fresh, milky, sourish odor, not unpleasant. Inside stood two young girls in big striped aprons, their sleeves rolled up to the elbows, their hair braided but uncovered. "Melisande?" I asked. "The damsel Melisande?"

The fair one turned at my voice, her mouth falling open. "Oh, God," she gasped. "It's Richard Lionheart!" Her arms were full of round white cheeses; one fell to the floor. "Oh, God," she cried again. "Father will beat me . . . it's all dirty now!"

The other one, the dark one, stooped and rescued the cheese. "Don't bawl, you silly goose. Wipe it off, he'll never know." So saying, she rubbed at it with a none-too-clean cloth and handed it back. "There! As good as new!" She turned to me then and said, "I am Melisande." She did not smile.

"I wanted to see you," I said, not knowing how to begin.

She stared at me, an insolent stare. "Well, you see me."

Her sulky look did not spoil her; she was very pretty, though her cheeks and lips were too thin and her eyes too big. She wore her hair in two tight plaits, the ends tied with twists of red yarn; her brown dress and black-striped apron made her look sallow. I had caught her in her ugliest clothes, her workaday things.

"I am sorry to have come upon you this way, without warning," I began.

"It does not matter," she said, shrugging. Then she called over her shoulder to the fair maiden, "Take the cheeses to the kitchen, Yvette. We will not need you." The fair girl backed away a few steps, and fled, giggling.

"Your maidservant?" I asked.

"My sister," she replied. "She only has one good dress, for church. She has never been to court. And now she never will, I suppose." Her dark eyes accused me.

"I am sorry," I said. "It was none of my doing . . . please believe me. I only obeyed the lady."

"I know . . . but still, Father beat me for it." She cast down her eyes.

I looked at her for a long moment. "May I see your hand, Melisande? The left one."

She held it out, with a wondering look. It was thin and long, with square-tipped fingers, like a boy's. The little finger was as smooth as the rest; there was no sign of a wart or blemish.

Still holding her hand, I said softly, "It was never you, was it? The lady lied."

She pulled her hand away, thrusting it behind her. "I have said nothing . . . nothing! She made me swear—" She stopped then; she had said too much.

"It was a sly trick the two of you played, Melisande," I said sadly. "What did she give you? A jewel? A purse of gold?"

"Nothing! She gave me nothing!" She tossed her head proudly. "Nor would I do it for pay . . . I come of noble blood!"

"Why, then?"

"She made me swear on the Virgin's milk—she had a drop in a vial . . . she made me swear not to tell."

"You have not told. I guessed," I said. "You will break no oath. Why did she do it?

She shook her head. "I know not . . . I guess she wanted to have her pleasure without the shame." She straightened her shoulders. "And so the shame is mine," she said bitterly. "And all the court thinks I am wanton . . . and my betrothal has been broken off . . . and I will never get another and will have to go to a nunnery. If they will take me!" She had begun to cry. I put my arm around her shoulders; she turned and sobbed against my chest. Brokenly she went on. "Father beats me every day; he has lost the dowry, the bridegroom will not give it back, calling me false. And Father has no other monies for another dowry—not for me, or even for my little sister."

I tipped up her chin. "Look at me, Melisande. Do you trust me?"

She nodded, and mastered her sobs, dashing away a tear with the back of her hand.

"Listen . . . I will explain it to your father."

She shook her head vehemently. "He will never believe you . . . he thinks all young people are liars."

"If . . ." I thought a moment, to put it nicely, and not offend. "If I gave him the amount of the dowry, in reparation . . . would that sweeten him, do you think?"

She nodded. "He loves money—though he seldom sees any."

"What is the amount?"

She told me, and I promised to bring the money the next day, when he would be home. I had none, but I resolved to find it somehow.

"Farewell, then, for now," I said, kissing her lightly on the cheek.

She smiled, for the first time. She had little teeth, with a space between the front two, like a child's milk teeth; it made her seem very young.

"How old are you, Melisande?" I asked.

"Fifteen on Michaelmas next," she answered.

"And did you want that bridegroom so much?" I asked, for she had wept so bitterly.

"Oh, no! He is old, with a long nose and bald head, a widower with grown sons. But he has a fair manor, and I would be mistress there, with servants, and keep the keys at my belt. It would be better than a convent—and better, maybe, than Father's rule."

I left her then, joining my companions and riding back to the town. I had thought to borrow the money from one of them, or several, but their ribald jests warned me off; I did not want to be the butt of them in earnest. In the end I had to get it from Mother, who borrowed it from Marie; Father always kept us all short.

Marie was struck by the plight of the girl, and offered to find a place for her at court. She offered in a half-shy, half-sly way, for she believed I meant to take Melisande for my mistress, having got a taste for her. I would never have betrayed Honorine so far as to tell the whole truth; the poor wretch was disgraced enough. Besides, in truth, the idea appealed to me.

I paid over the monies next day, and some to spare for the young Yvette's marriage portion; the father rubbed his hands in satisfaction, and smiled when I took his daughter away. He was not a bad man, and no greedier than the next; genteel poverty is the most miserable of conditions. I hoped the money would help him to some content and comfort in his latter years.

I had as good as bought the girl, but she did not see it so, and behaved abominably like a wife, after the first sweet days. She was a virgin and wept, and I wept too, for I was young and impressionable. For a while I almost thought I loved her. I wrote some of my best songs then, though they were rough and lacking in skill. They were unconventional, but the whole court hummed them; perhaps they were all a little tired of the stiff odes to a far-off Midons or a cold, pure lady. These were almost pagan, I see now—but they were fresh and sincere, and I trust that Jesus and His mother will forgive me in time.

Melisande was a strange and moody girl, the victim of her impoverished background. She could not read or write, and though I taught her her letters, she never got the habit. I could not talk to her, and spent more and more time with Alexander or the young knights who followed me. She hated this, and railed against me like a shrew when I was away from her half a day. She was intensely jealous, and if a court lady looked my way, she accused me of wild feats of love. It never occurred to me to take another mistress; I was not Father, and besides, Melisande was sweet and young, and very loving when she had me to herself.

We were together all that summer, or nearly, and most of the time I found her very dear. After a while though, I began to weary of her, and to wonder if my luck with women was running out before it had truly begun.

When Father recalled us to London, in August, I was not sorry to go.

CHAPTER 13

I HAVE BEEN called "the sword arm of God," but my heritage is surely far from pious, as all men must know. The Poitevin side was irresponsible and worldly, often heretic, and the Angevins were hag-ridden with bloodshed and sorcery, feared by all good folk. And then, to top it off, my mother divorced a saint, and my father murdered one.

Louis of France was not truly a saint, though many dubbed him so, for his monkish ways, and the irreverent mocked him for his unworldliness. He was merely a good man in a high place, a strange enough occurrence in this wicked world.

But Thomas, the Martyr of Canterbury, is another matter; his blood is precious and healing, and one drop of it in a flask of water can work miracles. Even as he lay dead before the altar at Canterbury, the sick and maimed dipped clothes into it where it ran, warm still, from his wounds, and were made well and whole again. He was beloved of his flock, and they, his people, canonized him before ever the Pope had a hand in it. And now Canterbury is a holy shrine, a place of pilgrimage, and the roads that lead to it are worn by the feet of the faithful. He is Saint Thomas à Becket now, who was once the King's archbishop; King Henry II of England, my father.

I was only fourteen at the time, but I knew, with the rest of the Christian world, that Father had killed him, as surely as if he had wielded the swords.

It happened in this way:

We were keeping Christmas court in Bures that year, the Year of Our Lord, 1170. The weather was miserable, as it often is, there in those northern parts; something between snow and rain fell continuously, with an icy bite, turning the grounds into a churned-up mess of black, half-frozen mud. The place was old-fashioned, with outside kitchens and butteries, and the wretched maidservants ran back and forth with blankets held over their heads and their bare legs spattered to the knee with filthy black ooze.

The castle was Norman, more like a heap of stones than a dwelling, and all of its stones dark with damp. Mother had hung several thick hangings on the walls of the great hall, but still they fluttered like rags in the fugitive drafts. The rushes on the floor were matted together and smelled as though they were rotted, though they were changed daily.

The only modern improvement was a huge new fireplace set in one wall; the old center hearth pit had been paved over and served as a performance place for the troubadours and jongleurs, who at holiday time played continually throughout the day. The fire blazed bright with a half-dozen great logs, and still our toes and fingers were numb with the cold and our noses red. It was worse than England; I wondered briefly if the Conqueror had brought his Norman weather with him to that island as well as his brutal ways!

We were all there, the whole brood of us, except for Henry, my older brother, who was keeping his own court in London. Father had had him crowned that year, though it was against the English custom to create a young king while the old still lived. Not that Father was so old, only thirty-seven, but he had been deathly ill in the summer, of a wasting fever, and perhaps feared for the succession. He was as robust as ever now, the danger long past, and it may be he regretted his hasty action; certainly he was cross as a bear on his best days now, and often purple with rage. That was nothing new, of course; we were used to it. Still, it was that same crowning that had caused the latest great quarrel with the Archbishop of Canterbury, Thomas Becket, and just when they two seemed to have made peace finally, after Becket's seven long years of exile!

Becket had been on his way back to England, to his See of Canterbury, and all forgiven, but Father did not wait for him; instead, he had had Henry crowned by the Archbishop of York, a breach of hallowed custom. The Pope had excommunicated the prelate of York and all those who had officiated in the coronation, laying most of the country under the Church's ban. Father had asked Becket to lift the ban, but he answered that it was not in his power, which was no more than the truth, for the Holy Father at Rome is supreme head of all Christendom. Still, it had driven Father nearly mindless with anger to be answered so; indeed, everything Becket did had for years now angered Father, though once they had been closer than brothers. This is by no means the whole story—it would take many days to tell it, sorting it out—but it boiled down to a clash between Church and State, no less.

Becket, in England, had all the commons with him, lining the roads wherever he went, prostrating themselves and weeping aloud, begging to touch the hem of his robe, praying for a blessing. When he reached Canterbury, folk crowded the church there, spilling out into the courtyard and clear down into the town, rejoicing at his return and giving thanks for their Archbishop's safety. We had been a week at Bures, and not a day went by that a new report did not come from across the Channel to drive Father wild. Becket was preaching against him, one report went; Becket was arming for a confrontation; Becket had threatened to depose him; Becket rode nowhere without a great army at his heels. All of them were garbled, contradictory, and no doubt false, but all wood for the fire that consumed my father, the King.

Father was no sullen brooder; he spoke his thoughts aloud for all to hear. He had been cursing Becket in extravagant language for a week now, every hour, every day. It was Christmas Day and the players from Nesle, the Blondel troupe, were performing, in mime, dance, and song, the story of the Nativity. They were very good, especially the glee-maiden who took the part of Our Lady Mary; very realistic she was in her birth agonies, making us all shudder for her, and beautiful later, holding the child, still weak, but happy in her new motherhood. The part is not usually done that way, but in a stylized manner, imitating the old pictures; this was very modern and fresh, and afterward Mother beckoned her close and handed her a fat jeweled purse, clinking with coins. I was near enough to see the beads of sweat upon her forehead and the flush beneath her paint.

I saw, too, that the girl was very young, as young as I myself; for some unknown reason it made me glad. I had been watching her on the sly all week as she sat, closely veiled, in the minstrels' gallery. She never looked my way, but I saw Alexander speak to her, their heads together, and smiling; they looked to have met before. It was the first time I had ever known Alexander to look at a girl, and I was instantly jealous—of both of them. Then I remembered that back in the spring he had mentioned a glee-maiden; he had spoken to her during a session of the Courts of Love.

I took him aside, grabbing him roughly as he served the wine and whispering, "Is that the Latin scholar—that glee-maiden?"

He looked startled; he had forgotten our conversation. "Yes . . . Blondelza speaks a good Latin—and writes it too. She is cleverer than most maidens, and loves learning. One can talk to her like a man."

"Blondelza," I mused. "Then she must be golden-haired under her head veil."

He laughed. "Not gold enough," he said. "She has to put gold stuff on it to live up to her name. A family name, it is, among these folk. Her father is the famous Blondel—Jean the Troubadour. He is a knight."

"I would like to meet her," I said. "Can you arrange it?"

His mouth tightened. "She is not for you to debauch."

I was angry. "What do you take me for? I am not a spoiler of maids!"

"There was Melisande," he said coolly.

"She was willing . . . and I have not seen her since August last. And that is beside the point! I only want to meet the girl!"

"I will see what I can do," he answered, shrugging. "Of course, I cannot promise . . ." He could be very irritating, Alexander, though I loved him well.

But I digress from my story, though truly I was more concerned, that Christmas Day, with this Blondelza and her fellow players than with Father, who was being his usual self. He could never sit still, even at meals, even at church—but would walk about the dining hall, gnawing at a bone, or pace the nave while the priest droned on in his Latin. This day had been no exception; he rose from his high seat, rustled parchments, played with his keys, and even talked to himself, throughout the performance.

This troupe was new to us, and had never played before Father. They went on valiantly, speaking a little louder to drown him out. Once, during the "visit of the Magi," Father's voice rose, querulous and bitter, above the words of the play. "Oh, that cur!" he cried. "That hound of heaven!"

The girl Blondelza had been speaking, the holy words of the Queen of Heaven. She fell silent, still wearing God's Mother's tender smile, and turned her head to stare coolly at Father, waiting. He felt the silence and, startled, stared back at her angrily, his eyes nearly popping; it was a breathless moment. Father's eyes dropped first; it was the Nativity play, after all. He muttered something, gruffly, and kicked a yelping little dog out of his way before giving the sign to proceed. It was not the little dog he had been cursing, though, but Thomas, and we all knew it.

Father took a seat, finally, and stayed in it till the close of the play, about ten minutes, but still a record, for him. The hum of voices around him went on, however, for he sat with some of his rougher knights, who aped him in everything, landless barons who hoped to curry favor. I had been puzzled to see these men at a Christmas court, for they were of little consequence in battle or policy, till I remembered that they were Father's hunting companions, and that Bures functioned mainly as a hunting lodge. Useless to speculate on what might have happened had the weather been better; perhaps all Father's ire would have been worked off on stags and boars!

During the music which followed, another messenger arrived, out of breath and mud-spattered, from across the Channel. Father raised his hand to silence the minstrels, so we all heard the news from England. It seemed that Becket had not only a train of armed knights, but an army of the commons, some thousand strong, armed with sickles and axes; they were marching to Canterbury to ask God's blessing on his war with the King. "And it is said, Sire," finished the quaking messenger, "that the Archbishop means to depose the Young King and seize the throne in London."

The poor fellow, drenched and weary from his long voyage across water and through more of it, almost cowered where he stood, and well he might! Father, his face purpling, gave a roar like a wounded bull's, throwing his head back and bellowing. He did not throw himself upon the floor, for there was no room between the tables and benches, but he took the edge of the long table nearest him and, with a great heave, overturned it. The huge wassail bowl, half full, went crashing to the floor, along with mugs and knives, platters and fruit.

There was a shocked silence; no one dared make a move to right the table or clean up. Father, beside himself with rage and having nothing in his hand to throw, reached up both fists and pulled handfuls of hair from his head while he howled like someone tortured.

"Oh, God! Oh, God!" he howled. "Will no one rid me of this evil churchman!" He began to rail at the whole company, cursing them. "I have nurtured you, given you my friendship . . . you are beholden, all, to me for many favors, countless benefits. Yet no man will avenge me on this wicked priest who seeks to disinherit my son and bring ruin on my realm!"

There was more of the same, of course; Father, once begun, does not run down easily. We must have listened to a good quarter-hour of shrieking and abuse before the doctors (Mother had summoned three) got a potion into him and led him off to his bed. It was one of his uglier seizures, but by no means the worst; we were used to them. I wondered, though, what the new troupe of Nesle thought; certainly no performer could follow that scene!

In the confusion, no one noticed that the low knights, his hunting companions, had left the hall. But it seems they had, and that they had taken horse for the Channel, and ship for Canterbury.

They burst upon Thomas Becket as he stood at the altar of his cathedral. They were fully armed; fearful cries rose from all the congregation at the sight of these iron figures with visors down, so that their eyes gleamed balefully through the slits. More than a dozen others had joined them, clanking in their mail, their spurs ringing on the church stones. The poor monks, without even a cross for weapon, had fled. Thomas stood alone in the half-dark of the sanctuary, and they cut him down there, striking many blows and almost severing head from body.

The murder shocked the whole of Christendom; some called it the worst thing that had befallen mankind since the Crucifixion. Before this, bishops, even Popes, had been done to death by pagan hands; never had a holy shepherd been slaughtered in full sight of his flock by men who called themselves Christian, and by order of a Christian king! Though my father, King Henry II of England, denied it, no man doubted his complicity. We, his family, had long lived with his hostility to the Archbishop, watched his struggle to destroy him. He had won at last, but paid for it with the calumny of the world.

If my boyhood did not end with my first battle, or my first act of love, it ended then—on the day that Becket died.

BOOK II

THE GIRL

Told by Blondelza, the Glee-Maiden

CHAPTER 1

I COME OF noble blood on both sides, but I am not proud of it. There is more honor, loyalty, and trust in our company of players than in all the castles of the Midi or the Vexin. My father's brothers, the knights of Nesle, cheated him of his inheritance, and my mother's people put her, an infant, out upon the barren rocks of Les Beaux de Provence to starve or be eaten by wolves. Neither tale is a pretty one.

Father, whom I call Papa Jean, was the third and youngest son of the Baron of Nesle. He was put early to the service of their overlord, the Viscount of Coucy. While he was away on Crusade with his master, the Baron, his father, died, and his brothers destroyed the will, taking Papa Jean's share and seizing the barony for themselves. Papa Jean got no spoils from the Crusade, only a knighthood on the field, a distaste for war, and a love for the beautiful songs of the Eastern lands. He was penniless, landless, and friendless too, for the old lord, his master of Coucy, had fallen in battle. He was talented, though, for he had the gift of music, and it did not fail him; he became a troubadour, in time one of the famous ones. He had been christened Jean, but most people do not know it; they call him Blondel, a name given to him long ago because of the color of his hair, a pale silver-gold. It is more silver than gold now, but the name has stuck, and I was named Blondelza, after him.

Mother's story is much more harrowing. Some forty years ago, on a dark, moonless night in Provence, our troupe of players was forced to take shelter at the foot of a desolate, rocky mountain, for the axle of their wagon had broken, and it was miles to the next inn. They huddled close to the fire, for the wind had a bitter winter chill to it. Above the crackling of the flames they heard a thin wailing, from somewhere high in the dark fastnesses of the mountain. Old Jacques le Gros, young then and thin as a weed, was sent up the mountain to seek out the sound, with a lantern for a light and a hound for company.

He came back bearing a woven basket he had found on the hillside, and cradled inside it, a tiny girl-child, wrapped in a white velvet cloak lined with ermine and worked with an unknown crest in gold. The babe had stopped wailing by then and stared solemnly from its velvet cocoon at the faces bent over its straw bed. The solemn eyes were large and bright, the little cheeks pink with the cold, and the small head covered with dark ringlets soft as down. She was pretty and they decided to keep her, even before they saw the long silk gown, the fine linen of the swaddling bands, and the three new gold bezants that fell from the folds of the velvet cloak.

They fed her with drops of goat's milk squeezed from a cloth, and in the morning light they looked up and saw where she had come from, the huge old castle at the top of the mountain, its turrets gleaming and rosy in the dawn, above high gray walls and iron-barred gates. They called her Castelloza, because she came from the castle. This was my mother, in her day the prettiest of all the girl mimes, pretty enough to catch the eye and the heart of the great troubadour-knight, Blondel.

We have passed that castle twice; it belongs to the signeury of Orange, but it is always close and shuttered, and the drawbridge up. The folk of the village below say the master is away on pilgrimage. He has been away a long time, so the sins he does penance for must be very great indeed. Or perhaps he has died on the way to whatever holy shrine he was bound for, this kinsman of mine—if indeed he is; assuredly I do not care. I am content to call Jacques le Gros my grandsire, and his wife Giselda my grandam.

Anyway, I have never seen any of Mama's people—or Papa Jean's either, come to that. His cheating brothers were both killed in some battle or other in Normandy, and the barony came to Papa Jean after all. It is not much of a barony; I saw it once, when I was very young. It was tiny, with only the gatehouse left standing; all the other buildings were razed to the ground, burnt by Norman routiers. But a little spring runs through it, very pretty, and there is good grazing ground, and a few beasts on it. I remember some peasants, too, who came out as we rode up and pulled their forelocks at Papa Jean; he knew them all by name, so I guess they were his people, the serfs who tilled the land, what was left of it.

Sometimes he speaks of going back there, building it all up

again and putting it in order, so that we could live there and I could marry some neighbor baron's son and be a noble lady. I know, though, that he will never do it; he loves this life too much. Thank God, for I do not want to marry a baron's son. I do not want to marry at all, not even a king. Though Giselda, who can read the cards, says that I will have a king for a lover. I suppose that could happen, if a gleemaiden became famous enough. But the only king I have ever seen so far was Henry of England, and all I wanted to do was slap his face!

I am too young to think of husbands and lovers anyway, just fifteen, though Papa Jean says many noble girls are already mothers twice over at my age. Another reason I am glad to be a player is that we keep young as long as we can, so that we can be slim and limber for dancing and tumbling, and can play the best parts. Of course, I am more than a player; I can play many instruments and sing all the troubadours' songs, besides making up some of my own.

I get my musical talent from Papa; Mother has a voice like a crow. She can still dance, though, if the steps aren't too vigorous, and she is a fair mime; she makes a stately goddess, because of her height and figure, and she can play some of the older saints. Poor Mother. One can see that she was beautiful once, but she is so worn and gaunt! It is from bearing all those children, none of whom lived. Most were stillborn, and some she miscarried; the last, a little boy, lived three months. I can just remember him. He would curl his tiny fingers around mine when I stood on tiptoe to look in the cradle, and he would stare so solemnly; he never laughed or cried. He is buried in the family graveyard at Nesle; that was why we journeyed there, so long ago. There is a stone at the head of his little grave, with his name and the dates carved on it; they called him Philippe.

I am their miracle, Papa says; I was the first-born, and was healthy and strong from the start. Indeed, I have never been sick, not even with a cold in the head when everyone else is coughing and sniffing in the winter months.

But that is another reason why I would not wish to wed—when I look at Mother. And she has a loving husband, not like most wives. Of course, she is better in these last years, since she has been converted to the Cathar faith. Her hands do not shake anymore, and the strained look is gone from her eyes. She does not try to have any more children now, for the

Cathar folk believe that all flesh is evil and do not want to bring any more children into the world to suffer in the vileness of their human bodies.

It is a strange faith, the Cathar one; they will not worship the Cross, for it is a symbol of suffering. And they believe that animals have souls as well as men, so they will eat no meat. I am not sure about the Cross, but I do not like meat either. I have worked with so many of our trained animals, and they are so intelligent and so sweet—why should God deny them souls?

I think the Cathars are good people, though there are many who hate and distrust them. Papa says folk will always hate what they do not understand; it is from ignorance. That is why he has given me an education as good as a boy's, Latin and philosophy. I used to fret when I was set to so many lessons, as well as the music and dancing and other crafts that players learn. But now I am glad, for I can read any book and I am not shy of entering learned conversations, even those of monks and scholars.

I met the great Cathar bishop, Nicetas, when he preached at Arles. He could not be anything but holy, no matter what the Church says; he looked like a being made of light—like an angel might look, or Jesus. That was when Mother became a convert, after she listened to his preaching. And now she is greatly changed, in just five years, with a calm face and easy movements, and a look of the spirit about her. And it has given her a purpose in life, too. Like all the other Cathar women, she has learned herb lore and nursing, and will go about the countryside, wherever we happen to be, tending the sick peasantry. She preaches sometimes too, for the Cathars have women preachers; afterward, she looks exalted, with that same look of light that Bishop Nicetas had.

Papa worries about her, though, for she will go anywhere, sometimes even into an armed camp, to tend the wounded. There are so many skirmishes and battles in this duchy, more even than in others, because of Aquitaine having had no ruler present to enforce authority. The Duchess, Eleanor, has been away so long, being Queen of France, and then of England; one or another of her vassal lords is always in rebellion, it seems, sending his hired routiers to besiege castles, burn fields, and destroy villages. But now there is to be a new duke crowned, red-haired Richard, who is young, just my age, but a proven knight already. They say he was vowed to subdue all these rebel barons and wipe out their strongholds, when he is made Duke. He has a great army of knights, all young and eager to follow him; they call themselves "The Knights of the Lionheart."

I saw the single combat when Richard got that name, when he killed the ugly knight and won the lion-heart badge. It was just like a romance, and all of us girls fell a little bit in love with him that day, he was so young and brave.

Richard is handsome too, as well as brave; I saw him quite close when he gave me the purse for the masque of David and Jonathan. His hair is not so very red, more of an auburn, and his face is tanned from the sun, with fine features. His eyes are a very light blue and so piercing that they seem to look right through you. I know, because he looked at me hard; I was the David, and I think he guessed I was a girl, though my long hair was hidden and nothing else showed. There was nothing much else to show then, I was so thin and flat in front. I am still thin, which is why I get all the boys' parts; we have no men of the right age or size. But lately I have had to bind my chest tightly to hold it in under a tunic, so perhaps there is hope. Before, when I played girls, I had to stuff my bodice with wool.

I am sure to meet Richard sometime soon—truly meet him, I mean, to talk to—because I am friends now with his best friend and foster brother, Alexander. We argue all the time, Alexander and I, but I like it, and I can see that he does too. He is the first boy my own age I have ever known, really, for Papa is very strict; he says glee-maidens should be above reproach, like Caesar's wife, for we play the holy saints and the Mother of God. He does not mind my friendship with Alexander, though, for everyone knows he is not a soldier or squire, to trifle with girls, and means to take Holy Orders as soon as he is qualified. Richard might be another matter, for there was that scandal with that woman Honorine, and the other girl afterward, Melisande, who said he fathered her child. I guess it is true, for the child, a little girl, has red hair and is called Richeut. Melisande is married now, to some old baron in the country, and never comes to court; they say Richard dowered her.

I would hate that, like being sold. But it would never happen to me, I am too clever. And I am a player and can wed where I choose, or not at all. Marie de France has never married; she is my ideal. Such wonderful songs! As good, or better, than any of the men's! And how she looks! So young! She must be at least as old as Mother, but there are no lines in her face and no gray in her hair. They say she is King Henry's half-sister, and that that is why she has risen so high in the profession. I think it would have happened anyway; she is a genius.

I wonder how she feels about being that man's bastard sister. Alexander says the whole family has suffered from the disgrace of Archbishop Becket's death; I supose it will always be hard for them to live it down.

It was almost two years ago that the Archbishop was murdered, but folk still make the sign of the evil eye when King Henry's name is mentioned, even in out-of-the-way places. The peasants think he has horns or two heads, or the look of Satan himself. Ignorance again, as Papa would say. I saw King Henry very close, when we performed the Nativity at Bures. He was just a man like any other, but spoiled, with a filthy temper; as I said, my fingers itched to slap him. Of course, no one ever does, he is the King.

He is not bad-looking, being Richard's father, and the man Queen Eleanor loved for so long. But he is short and square-built, with very bowed legs. And his face is the wrong red, against his red hair. His clothes look as though he had slept in them, and are not even very clean; no player would be seen in his coffin in such attire! Even so, I can see why he gets so many women, he looks so full of life—almost as though he would strike off sparks, like a flint. Richard is like that too, but in a subtler way.

Richard was at Bures Castle, too, for the Christmas season; it was a family occasion. He has three brothers and three sisters, imagine! I wish I might have had just one of each. They were all there at Bures, except the oldest, Henry, who is called the Young King, and was in London at his own court. They are a handsome brood, like steps in a ladder, all redheads, too, till the littlest one, John, who is dark like his mother. Joanna was my favorite; only a half-grown maid, but she laughed a lot and used her hands like a player, not shy at all. Also, she is most like Richard, something in the way they stand and walk. She had a beautiful green dress with pearls sewn all over the skirt and a border of fur dyed green to match. I wish I had one like it in orange-tawny.

It was terrible weather, rainy and cold, and everyone was cooped up together indoors. The Countess of Champagne had hired our whole troupe for the entire Twelve Days. She paid us well, but our quarters were poky and small, damp as a cellar; it is such an old castle. When we unpacked our boxes, the costumes smelled like wet dogs, and no place to air them. Mother sprinkled lavender on everything, but it was a vain hope; I was thankful we would not get near anyone but ourselves!

I was to take the part of the Holy Mother in the Nativity play, so I was not allowed to perform in any of the other entertainments, and had to sit in the gallery with the musicians and keep my hair covered. Even so, I know that Richard noticed me; he looked at me all the time, when he thought I could not see him. I hope he thought I was pretty; I was not allowed paint, but I kept biting my lips to make them red.

After the play, Queen Eleanor gave me a purse for myself and complimented me sweetly, speaking in the langue d'oc. I answered her in good French, and then in Latin, showing off. Papa was annoyed with me, but it made her notice me more. She looked very hard at me for a moment with those great beautiful dark eyes, then kissed me on both cheeks and asked my name. When I told her, her eyes widened; everyone knows Papa is a nobleman. "You are a credit to your blood," she said then, "and very talented, as well. Thank you, Blondelza la Douce." God, what a lady! I was too flustered to steal a look at Richard, standing close. And I did not see him again. It has been almost two years.

Now, though, at his ducal crowning, I am to sing one of his own songs; the Countess Marie gave us the air and the words. It is all about youth and hope and dreams, and I am the youngest, so it is fitting. I never thought to be nervous, for I have been performing all my life. But I am now.

CHAPTER 2

FOR MORE THAN a week before Richard's crowning, our entire company has been in a fearful bustle, rehearsing songs and dances, working out mimes, making costumes. For it is to be a double ceremony; Richard will be made Duke of Aquitaine, and he will also be wedded (symbolically, of course) to Saint Valerie. For the peasant folk of these parts, the Saint Valerie business is the more important; they are very devout, and she is their only saint. Valerie was a noble virgin who lived in the city of Limoges about a thousand years ago, maybe more, and she was martyred for her faith. Her death was not so exciting as some others, like Saint Catherine's on the fiery wheel. Valerie was only flogged and then beheaded. Still, it will be quite a spectacle, and requires a good deal of practice. The blood is easy, and the whip-cracking, but the beheading is always tricky, with the substitution of the dummy's head; there could always be a slip-up. But Gervase is confident. He is our magician, and has the whole thing worked out; the secret, of course, is in the timing. I am afraid Esmerelda will give it all away by her dreadful miming; she will be the Valerie, but Papa says it will be quite convincing, at a distance. It is a wonderful part, and she is too fat for it too, in my opinion. I would love to play it, but I would not even ask; she has to appear naked for the flogging. Sometimes noble birth is a curse, for a player. I should not feel that way, for if I were not noble, I would not have been given Richard's song to sing; one cannot have everything.

Richard's song has given me many sleepless nights, for at first I was at a loss as how to present it. It is, of course, written as a man would sing it; much of it is not suitable from a woman's lips. I thought at first of doing a razo; that is, a paraphrase of the song. Often we who are professionals can make a better thing of it, with embellishments of word and music. But this is a good song, and deserves a hearing on its own. It was Papa who finally came up with the solution. He said I must sing it in the guise of a boy, which is not difficult, for I have been playing boys for years now to great success. We all agreed, and I have rehearsed it so, but I have a surprise twist, which I shall put in on the day, if all goes well. I have rehearsed this alone, when no one was about to hear, and my costume, also, I have made myself; they have let me get on with it, for I am clever with a needle and thread, and God knows, every hand is needed elsewhere, with all we have to prepare.

Alexander comes every day to seek me out, but I have little time for him, I am so busy. Giselda says he is mooning after me, like a sick calf, and leers lewdly as she says it; she has played so many bawds it comes quite naturally to her. I know, of course, that it is not so; Alexander cares nothing for girls, and only likes to talk Latin with me and dispute philosophy. He wanders about, getting in the way. He has nothing to do in the castle, this is no time for a scholar; they are all busy there, too, for the coronation is a bigger show than any we poor players shall put on. Papa has set him to some scribe-work, for though all our company can read, few can write a legible hand, and there are many speeches and songs to be written out for memorizing.

I saw Esmerelda rolling her eyes at him and smiling, but he did not even notice. Poor girl. But she ought to know better; he has been like that always, since we met him first, two years ago, at the castle. He is not like other men, one must just accept it. Though he is handsome enough; Giselda says it is a wonder some fine lady has not seduced him before now. Perhaps they cannot see it in his old brown scholar's gown. Mother once offered to make him another, for it is patched and nearly threadbare. He was horrified, and said he had others at home but that this was his most comfortable one. We all laughed, and Giselda said what a shame he would not dress up for his Midons. He looked quite blank and said, "I have no Midons." At that, everyone laughed again, and I, to my fury, blushed. Later he asked me, with a worried look, if his gown offended me.

"I never notice how you look," I said, a trifle haughtily.

"Oh, good!" he said, smiling his white smile. "Then you are just like me!" And he threw back his head, as he often does, to get a lock of his hair out of his eyes.

I laughed. "You know," I said, "you look just like a warhorse when you toss your head like that."

"Yes," he said, smiling, not at all put out. "Richard calls me Saracen, after his father's stallion."

"So Richard has humor," I said, musing. "Perhaps, then, he will like the way I sing his song."

"Oh, he will. He likes you . . . at least, he likes your looks. He told me so."

"When?" I asked.

"At Bures. He saw you there, and asked your name. When I told him Blondelza, he said you must be a blonde. Your hair was covered in the play, you see."

"Oh," I said, for it seemed a paltry comment. "Did you tell him I dye it?" I asked quickly.

"Well, yes . . ." he said, and I cursed him silently.

The night before the crowning I did not sleep a wink, though my singing would come at the very end of it all, and the coronation itself would take two days. The day for the symbolic wedding ceremony dawned bright and fair, though there was a brisk wind that whipped the banners and made our tents creak; it was still cool when we set out for Limoges. You will get days like that now and then here in the south, even now, in June. I thought with a little malice of Esmerelda's white flesh coming out in goose pimples when they tied her up for the flogging. For after the ceremony proper we were to present the life of the saint; I had no real part in it, but we were all needed to swell the crowd scenes. I was glad, for I did not want to miss anything at all; I have never seen anyone crowned, and this was a person almost as young as I myself.

I was allowed to wear ordinary girls' clothes, for we would be in a great company, with the court poeple and armed escorts, and there could be no danger of ambush or routier raids. Usually when we travel anywhere, all the women of the company, even the old ones and the little girls, dress in men's attire, for protection. I had made a saffron gown for the occasion, cutting it from an old property robe. There was just enough good cloth to cut the pattern, for I am slender and do not need much, though I had to add a red band around the bottom to get the length. It looks good, even so, and the red matches the red gauze head veil I am wearing. It does not cover my hair and is just for show; for once I can go uncovered, since I am not playing anyone holy, just a town girl. I have put red paste on my lips and cheeks, too, and green color on my lids, with kohl drawn round my eyes. Papa is too busy to notice; he would say it is a waste, when I am only part of the crowd.

But I got a good look in the mirror, snatching it away from Esmerelda, who is always hogging it; I really look as fine as a princess, if one does not look too closely at my hasty stitches or at the pearls sewn on my veil, which are property too, and not real. My hair is not quite real either, I suppose, for the wave is from tight braiding overnight, and the color is from a jar and the sun. Still, I think no one would guess, and I must live up to my name. They say my hair was just the color of Papa's when I was born, a pale silvery gold, but it has darkened over the years, and now, if I did not work at it, would be light brown. No wonder, when you look at Mother, dark as a Moor! I have inherited her eyes too, but there is nothing I can do about that; only a miracle could turn them blue. Still, I know that I am handsome, for the contrast is arresting; I do not even really need the kohl, for my lashes and brows are so dark.

With my hair falling in waves to my waist, the color, almost, of my dress, I am pleased with myself today. If only I could have a horse! But there are not enough to go around, so Esmerelda and I must ride in Jacques le Gros's cart, with the caged animals. At least he has painted it freshly for the occasion and given us two chairs to sit on; they are more comfortable than mules would be. As we climbed up, Esmerelda gave me a filthy look and remarked that she was sorry for me, I would get all sunburned; she is only being spiteful because she must go completely veiled today. I pretended not to hear her over the dogs' yapping.

We make quite a procession ourselves, with our painted show wagon, our carts of costumes and props, and all our animals, though we are a small troupe, really. Papa keeps it small on purpose, for the sharing out of the monies; he is a good business man. He heads the company, of course, for he is our greatest draw. Mostly he only sings his own songs, but occasionally he will double in a small role too; he makes a good angel, with his stern but happy features, his pale hair, and his slender grace. He is still lithe as a boy, Papa; one would never guess he is well past forty years.

An then there is Mother . . . well, I will list us all. Blondel and Castelloza, my father and mother; Jacques le Gros and his wife, Giselda, who are older folk and play what we call "character," like innkeepers and bawds; Esmerelda, their daughter, who is sixteen and has black curly hair and a figure that all the peasants whistle at (I only call her fat because I am jealous); her two small brothers, Arnaut and little Jacques; Gervase the magician, and his wife, Yvette, another gleemaiden. Yvette is a real blonde, but she does not have much chin, so it spoils her looks. She is much admired, though, for her voice, as high and sweet as a singing bird's. Jacques le Gros's mother is still alive, though she has lost all her teeth and has grown tremendously fat, so that she must be carried everywhere in a special chair. She does nothing at all nowadays but eat and count her money. But she must have been beautiful once; she is still called Belle Aimée.

We are a small band, but it never seems so, for we can all double in dancing and tumbling, miming and song, and only Yvette is afraid of the animals. There is a brown bear, Ursula, that dances at the end of a chain. Only sometimes she will not, and sits right down; Jacques laughs and says she has "the temperament." Then we have a big lion, very old and tame; he looks fierce, but has no teeth or claws. A monkey too, from Africa, very clever, but messy; I know, for I used to have the job of cleaning out his cage. I still have the care of the little dogs; I am the only one they will behave for, Esmerelda is too rough, and so are the apprentices.

Limoges is not far, just over a few little hills, but we have to go behind the castle folk; we have already waited a half-hour outside the gates, and the trumpets have just now sounded. I suppose I *will* get sunburned, but I do not care. I do not want to be pale like a lady, anyway; I am an artiste!

Finally, they let the drawbridge down. What a creaking! You would think they would oil the hinges, for once. The horses' hooves sounded like thunder—so many men-at-arms, and all in mail, spears glinting, even the horses are wearing armor!

They went by us in a cloud of dust, as remote as silver statues, the horses high-stepping, beautiful to watch. Then came Richard, in gilded mail with a purple cloak, on his huge white horse. His head was bare and his russet hair hung to his shoulders, longer than I remembered it, with a strong wave. He sat very straight and tall, with a solemn face. Folk cheered wildly at the sight of him, but he did not nod or smile, only looked straight ahead, like a knight in a picture.

The royal litter followed, its purple curtains open; I swear Queen Eleanor looked straight at me and smiled! Then came the other royalty: Marie, Countess of Champagne, with her ladies, Richard's brothers and sisters, and many knights and ladies of the castle. The clergy was last, scribes, lawyers, clerks, in their drab gowns; Alexander was among them, and waved at me, though his fellow scribes frowned.

At a signal, we fell in behind them, our painted wagons lumbering and groaning like market carts. Papa, though, looked wonderful, as fine as any of the knights, on his roan charger. He wore his old Crusader's garb—the padded jupon, sky-blue, with a white cross upon the breast—red hose, and silver shoes with points. His hair, straight as silk, shone like moonbeams. His precious lute hung over his shoulder in a cloth-of-gold bag; together, bag and lute, they cost more than two wagons.

Mother looked lovely too, in a wimple like a great lady's, and a gown the color of old wine. She had the second-best horse, a dappled mare, Doucette, old as the hills, but she did not even stumble. We made a brave sight, we players all; I was proud of us that day.

Behind us, a band of men-at-arms made up the rear. It was a glorious morning, the grass all green and looking new-washed against the distant purple hills and the blue sky. We saw only one burnt-out field, unusual for these parts.

As we neared Limoges, the crowd thickened, swelled by the villagers. There was much cheering up front, where the great folk rode, but as we passed I heard a cry of "Witch!" and someone threw a clod of dirt at Mother. It missed her, but hit the mare, Doucette, on the chest, making her rear. Mother gasped and gave a little cry, and two men-at-arms rode up, pikes at the ready. But the man who had thrown it was down already, a knot of others beating at him with flails and kicking him; many of the villagers are Cathars too.

The soldiers watched for a moment, silently, then went in among the folk and broke it up. I saw one raise his pike, viciously, before the other motioned us on. Doucette was calm now, but Mother's cheeks were wet; she was miserable to be the cause of strife and pain. I should not have looked back, but I did. I saw one man lying on the ground, very still, and another all covered with blood, and beside him a woman, weeping.

But we had left the trouble behind, and were coming to the town gates, flung open and twined with ribbons and flowers.

Flowers were strewn in our path, too, all along the way to the Church of Saint Valerie.

Limoges is an old, walled town, and the church is even older, built on the ruins of a Roman temple. It is tiny, made of stones from the field, and has a crooked look; even the small bell tower leans to one side, as though it were tired. The bells had been ringing all along, but we could not hear them for the cheering.

I had hoped to see the ceremony, but the church was too small to hold us. All I saw was the Bishop kneeling and kissing Richard's ring, then Papa signaled us to steal away and prepare for the performance, in the center of the town.

The square was quite large for such a small town, with a ready-made platform to perform on, high up above the folk. It was the execution place, a grisly thought, but Papa whispered that it had not been used for years, not since King Henry's early oppressive days. It must have been so, for there was no gallows, and not even a flogging post; we had to put up our own property one to use in the last scene.

It all went off without a hitch, or almost. They had got to the end of the play—Esmerelda doing quite well, and the bloody welts from the flogging very real—when it began to rain, a slow, steady drizzle. Jacques le Gros, as the executioner, all in black and masked, had chopped off Valerie's head, a very convincing show, with the pig's-bladder blood working well. Esmerelda's body was covered with its burial cloth, and the dummy head lay, frightening and hideous, upon the platform. But when Jacques bent to grasp it by the hair and hold it up for all to see, the glue that held its wig came unstuck in the wet, and the hair began to slip, as though Valerie had had yet another trial, baldness, to plague her. Jacques recovered himself quickly and grabbed the head itself, raising it on high by the severed neck, his hands and arms all running with blood from the spurting bladder hidden inside. I think no one noticed except us players, and the scene was even more effective. Afterward, Papa said, laughing, "Keep it in!"—meaning play it the same way next time. We all laughed with relief, but of course there would be no next time—this was a play for this one occasion only.

It continued to drizzle all the way back to the castle; we were a sodden, sorry mess, we players, for our clothes are never of the best materials, and even the great folk looked a little subdued. Richard, though, was laughing as he rode by;

perhaps he was glad to have it over for this day. Everyone tended to straggle, returning, and his brother Geoffrey was riding beside him, eating an apple. I heard Richard say "English weather!" and Geoffrey sputtered with laughter, choking on the apple, Richard pounding him on the back and laughing louder. It was a homely little scene, making the great folk human, as it were, and I laughed too, watching.

Richard swiveled round on his mount and looked at me hard; it would happen then, with my hair plastered dark to my cheeks! But he stared for a moment, the laugh changing to a little smile, and then bowed low in the saddle, his hand on his heart, before he rode on. God, how my own heart beat!

CHAPTER 3

THE FIRST CHORD was too loud, and even startled me, but I pretended I was still tuning my lute, and bent over it, frowning. Then I struck two or three more chords, too loud still, deliberately, and sat as if listening, before I began the song; it is such little tricks that mark us as professionals.

From the first stanza I knew I had them; one can always tell. Of course, it was a good song. My boys' clothes fitted me well; I had taken much trouble with them, sky-blue tunic and hose, with a cloth-of-gold cape. My hair was out of sight under a scarlet cap, of the type called Phrygian that has been worn by players for centuries. I did not try to disguise my voice; it would be to no avail, for no girl has such deep tones, and, in any case, my identity was already known. After all, I, Blondelza, had been given Richard's song to sing!

"Oh, I am strong and fair and fit for battle . . ." I sang. "My mail glints, blinding, in the Eastern sun . . . My sword arm lifts, my heart is high . . . Oh, infidel, beware!" The song was true and simple, with high bright words and a lilting refrain that set the feet to tapping. It followed none of the accepted patterns, but was Richard's own, fresh and new. Although it sang of war, it was not martial; although its words spoke of the Cross and Crusading, it might have been any

115

quest, any adventure that called to youth. I was, I think, the first to sing it.

He sat upon his throne, in the great hall, wearing his new ducal crown, a slim circlet set with a single blazing ruby. He wore a sky-blue set of garments, with a cape of royal gold, the mate to my own, if one did not look too closely. Mine had the right effect—shocking—which I wanted; there is nothing to be gained by being timid. Everyone gasped when I took my seat before the new Duke, and the buzzing and whispering did not stop until I started my singing. I stole a quick glance at Richard and saw a twitch of smile upon a grave face, as quickly gone. It was a gamble, but in reality I had little to lose. For if he was not amused, then I did not want to know him anyway; I would not choose to people my world with dullards.

I sang the refrain four times in all; they would not let me stop. At the last, I beckoned all to join in, and set the hall to ringing. Amid the great applause, I rose, bowed low, and whipped off the cap from my head and the cape from my shoulders. I whirled, then, in a fast Moorish dance, the gold cape and my golden hair swinging free. When I came to a halt, finally, not quite breathless, I settled the long hair with a shake of my head, so that it flowed like a river down my back, and quickly wrapped the cape about my waist, making a skirt. Then I sank to the floor in a deep curtsy before Richard, and stayed there, holding the pose.

Richard rose from his throne, stepped down from the dais, and taking my hand, raised me to my feet. "Welcome to my court, Lady Blondelza," he said. I think if I had been a man he would have knighted me, there was such a look of surprise and delight upon his face.

"May I sing an encore, Sire?"

All the court had caught my words, though I spoke them softly. "Encore! Encore!" they cried. It was the sort of show they loved, easy but tinged with magic. I had practiced the metamorphosis over and over and I knew I had got it right and done it smoothly. I knew, also, from Richard's eyes, that I looked my best. I took my lute from his hands and let him seat me upon the bench again. This time he stood leaning easily against the arm of his throne, to hear my song.

I played a measure or two, without lifting my voice, just to make sure they knew it was Richard's tune, and then I sang it, my own words.

"Oh, I am young and fair and fit for love . . . My hair gleams golden in the setting sun . . . My eyes are beckoning, my heart cries out . . . Oh, ladies all, beware!" There were ten verses, all repeating Richard's meter and keeping close to the rhyme, and it went very well; I saw Marie de France, smiling and clapping, and Queen Eleanor too. The words were charming, seductive and innocent all at once, and with a sly wit underneath; it has been sung, my version, nearly as often as the original. It was the first song to bring me fame, and it not my own!

This first performance, though, I thought they would never let me go. I must have sung the verses, all ten of them, ten times over, before I pleaded hoarseness, and withdrew among my player company. Even then, I was called back; in the excitement, I had forgotten my rewards. I got no less than twelve garlands of flowers, a gold-mesh purse plump with coins, a length of shimmering tawny silk, finer than anything I had ever owned, and two pairs of flat leather slippers, one green, one yellow, with long pointed toes. I felt as though I had looted some Eastern bazaar!

Queen Eleanor beckoned me to her, crooking a long white finger; I knelt before her and bent my head. I felt a light touch upon my brow and knew she had placed a circlet upon it, and looked up, wondering. She laughed and held out a little silver mirror. "Look, child," she said. "See how you suit a princess's wear." I saw a slender wreath, laurel leaves fashioned in gold, and could not believe my eyes; I knew that Marie de France had the mate to it.

"Oh, Lady," I said, sincerely, "it is too good for me."

"No, child," she said. "It matches your talent—and your hair!"

By this time I was walking at least a foot above the floor for joy, and did not think there could be more. But Richard came forward to take me by the elbow and walk me toward my place beside Papa.

"Thank you, my lady troubadour," he said, promoting me and complimenting me all at once. "I too have a gift for you . . . but this coronation suit has no pockets, and I do not have it by me. May I bring it to your tent tonight?"

Oh-oh, I thought, and could not help but glance at Papa. Richard saw the look, and bowed toward him. "Sir Blondel, with your permission?"

Papa looked hard at him, the look he uses on apprentices

when they have not learned their lessons well. I hoped he would not make trouble, he is no courtier. But all he said was, "You will be welcome, of course, Sire. You are our Duke."

"I come not as a duke, sir, I hope—but as a friend," answered Richard. I was to learn he was very good at fancy speeches. He and Papa bowed to each other, unsmiling. As Richard straightened up, he turned to me, still grave, and winked; I hoped no one else had seen.

As he moved away, I heard Mother say, musingly, "He has a good face—like his mother." But Papa said nothing, and only busied himself ordering props and musical instruments to be gathered up, for our work was finished that day.

Back at our tent site, I took off my golden laurel chaplet and folded the beautiful shining silk about it, laying both gifts away in a trunk. It was as if I folded away my triumph with them, for none among our folk so much as mentioned my great success. It was a rule with players, to keep heads from swelling, and to keep, as well, the evil of envy from our midst. But, being young yet, I felt it a shame, and tears of self-pity rose hot behind my lids. To make it all worse, Papa stated that my fingering was off in two places, and set me to lute practice for the whole afternoon.

Perhaps it was just as well, for I did not have time to think about Richard's visit, or to wonder and fret when he did not come at twilight. It was near dark when I finished, for, like all artists, I had lost track of time. My fingers ached, and the tips were rough as sandpaper, grating on the soft stuff of my thin summer gown as I slipped it over my head. It was my second-best, a little short this year, as I had grown, but still pretty, a nice violet color with pale-pink hanging sleeves.

I bundled my hair into a net, having no time to tire it properly, as I thought. And I waved away all thought of food; who can eat when the gods have smiled and love itself, perhaps, beckons?

I paced the floor, trying out my new slippers; the green were good with my old violet gown, although they pinched a little at the small toe. Still, I would not be walking in them, only standing, or sitting maybe, so let the points show.

Mother had lit the cressets, standing them in the posts along the floor, where they would not flare to the ceiling, and setting one outside as well. It was full dark, and where was Richard? A cramp took me, suddenly, in the stomach; I went outside to the latrine, though I knew that it was only nerves. Of course that was when he came, as I sat moaning and holding my belly.

When I came back into the tent, weak in the knees and wan in the cheeks, I saw that he had come. Richard, our Duke, sat, wanner than I, upon Papa's seat near the fire. A white cloth, none too clean, wrapped him, like swaddling clothes, from neck to chest. He smiled and held up a pewter cup (our best) filled with dark red wine.

"I thank you, Sir Blondel," he said. "This is welcome, if anything ever was. I have a mighty crick in the neck."

As we watched, red seeped through the bandage, staining it; in the feeble light it showed black and almost greasy. I saw too that he was dressed in a simple jerkin such as cowherds wear, or stableboys; anger flew into my head that he should greet me so.

"My lord Richard," I said, straightening from my cramp, "you do me honor indeed."

"Hush, girl," said Papa, frowning. He, who was so fearful of Richard and my honor! "The Duke is wounded sore."

"Not so," said Richard, waving his hand weakly. "You should see the other fellow." And he smiled. "We were ambushed again," he said. "The second time. I ought to have known better than to ride unarmored. But I thought to attire myself simply for my Midons." And he bowed a little in my direction.

I was horrified. "Sire, it is never safe here, in these parts. How could you so endanger yourself . . . and your dukedom?"

He grinned then, whitely, as like Alexander as could be; they both had wonderful teeth. He shook his finger at me, as one does to a forward child. "Peace, madame," he said. "I cannot bear a scold."

Hot words rushed to my lips, but then I saw he was laughing at me, and, unaccountably, I blushed. "Your shoulder . . ." I said weakly.

"A scratch only," said Richard. "The sword was rusty and blunt as well. It could not cut butter." He grinned again. "And your Alexander was a hero, for once, forgetting his habit. He cut down two of them himself, with an axe he took from the first. I sent him on with the sole survivor—he who gave me this." And he felt, groping, for the wound at his shoulder; as he touched it, he winced. "A fine fellow. He almost did me in."

"Will you put him to death, then, Sire?" I asked. For I was shocked that our Duke—and the person who inhabited my dreams—should have been so attacked.

"Not I," said Richard, with a laugh. "He fought well. He was of Angoulême, my enemy's routier—but he deserves better than Guilhelm the Old for lord . . . I will double his pay."

"But can you trust him, Sire?" asked Papa. "These routier fellows—"

"For gold, yes . . . And it may be too . . . for something else. I cannot say. But there was a look in his eyes . . . Yes, I trust him. They call him Mercadier." It was a name I was to know one day as well as my own, and for long years, but I had no notion of it then. The name was unusual, so I remembered it.

Richard shuddered then, and the sweat sprang out upon his brow.

Mother, who had been standing in the shadows, came forward then. "Sire," she said softly, "let me have a look at that shoulder. I have some skill . . ."

He drooped then in the chair, and nodded. She gestured to me. "Quickly!" I ran to her herb chest and brought out the little bags, all of them that my arms could hold, frightened. "No, child," she said gently. "This one . . . and this." And she picked out those she needed. "There is a tree at the little spring . . . you know it?" I nodded. "A green moss grows under it. Fetch some of it . . . it will do for later, to bind the wound."

When I returned, Mother had cleansed the wound; it gaped rawly at the side of Richard's neck, the edges black. His face was almond-pale. Mother was white as a sheet, and looked frightened. I saw the iron poker that we used for the fire, its tip glowing red. "I had to cauterize it," she said. "It was festering already."

"Yes," said Richard, smiling. "This mother of yours . . . she is a cruel Midons." But he sat still while she laid the green moss upon the wound and bound a clean cloth upon it. "Who knows, Lady . . . you may have saved my life! For it grows easy now and does not throb."

"It will heal cleanly now," said Mother, smiling her rare smile. "But you ought to have a clean shirt before you go back to the castle. Queen Eleanor will guess . . . and *I* guess you do not wish her to." She laughed then, my grave and saintly mother. I had never heard her do it before.

"Yes, Lady, thank you kindly . . . it is true. My mother will be anxious. I must go . . . the wine has revived me—and the hot poker." He grinned again; I thought I had never seen anything so brave or so bright as that smile. If I had not loved him before, I loved him then—that boy Duke, so young suddenly, so sweet, looking at my mother, and not even glancing my way.

"I will ride with you, Sire," said Papa. "Here, lean on my shoulder."

"Oh, God's nails!" cried Richard. "I had forgotten! I must have taken madness from my festering wound." He fumbled in the purse that hung at his belt. "It was what I came for . . . to give the gift of triumph to Blondelza . . . the lady of the golden voice." His hand came out, closed tight upon something secret. "Here," said he. "Let me have a finger, any finger."

I held out my hand, with its chapped back and the fingertips roughened by the lute strings. He fitted a great heavy ring upon the third finger—the finger of love and troth—but it was too big. He slipped it on my thumb.

"Wear it till I come again," said Richard. "For I will come with a goldsmith to make it fit . . ." And he bent over my hand and kissed it, folding my fingers in upon the great gold ring.

I did not look down at it, or even open my fingers until he had gone, leaning on my father. When I did, I saw that the ring was yellow gold, set with a great ruby, carved with crest of Aquitaine, intaglio. It was the mate to the ruby that was set in his crown!

CHAPTER 4

RICHARD'S WOUND DID indeed heal cleanly, and quick—though he got another avenging it. It was a long shallow cut on the forearm, and he brought it to Mother to see to, as he said, "we have no such doctors in the castle."

"My lord, you are a flatterer," she said, shaking her head. "It is plain herb lore, mixed with a little prayer."

"And this cut, then?" He held out his arm.

"Needs only the prayer," she answered, smiling. "Though I will give you some ointment to take the stiffness out." And truly the wound seemed healthy, the edges closed already, and only a little pinkness and swelling around it. "I think it will not even leave a scar," she finished, rolling down his sleeve. "The other, at your neck, you will bear the mark of it all your life, I fear."

"Ah, well," he said, laughing. "There will be plenty more to keep it company, before I am done. Like bowlegs, scars are the signs of the knight."

"And of the routier too, Sir Duke," said Mother, not smiling now.

Richard colored, the blood flaring quickly in his thin cheeks; I saw he made an effort to control his temper, the legacy of his father, the King. But after a moment he laughed again, a short, rough sound.

"I see, madame, you make a brave warrior yourself, to speak so to your lord."

"There is only one Lord, Sir Duke," said Mother calmly.

"That is true, madame," said Richard, crossing himself. "And we are all in His hands, as the churchmen say. But the world has its rules and rulers too. Can you not concede that?"

Mother nodded gravely. "Rules and rulers of the sword, yes. And of war."

"I grant you, madame. But the sword can be for God . . . and the war a holy war."

"No war is holy." Mother shook her head, her face very stern.

"The Crusaders . . ." Richard began, his words trailing off.

"We Christians do not hold with Crusading," said Mother. "God has no enemy but the Devil—and the Devil cannot be vanquished by the sword."

"Christians?" said Richard, light breaking in his face. "You are of the Cathar faith?" For the Cathars believe they are the only pure Christians, and style themselves so. He was off then and running, as it were; I was to learn that Richard loved knowledge more than wine. Which is a silly saying of our times, and does not apply, for he was never much of a drinker. But let us say that he loved learning more than song; which is why his songs were somewhat studied; perfect, yes, in rhyme and meter, but something lacking in heart. I must say it, even though he was Richard and so dear to me, for I must be true to my art.

He questioned Mother closely then, on all the points of Cathar doctrine, and each time he visited he had some new argument to raise with her. She did not mind, for her faith made her bold, and they two took fire, each from the other. For weeks I was jealous of Mother, for he spent so much time with her; it was as if I did not exist. And when Mother was abroad on an errand of mercy or at her preaching, he then would corner Papa, begging for new lessons, on the rebec or the gittern; I might have taught him as much myself!

The long sweet days of summer went by, achingly, and never, never did I see Richard alone. The entire company came to know him as well, or better than I, for he spent much time in our camp, hanging about Gervase to pick up the tricks of his magic trade, or practicing juggling and tumbling with the apprentice boys; he even taught the monkey to handle a toy sword!

I was hurt and angry, bewildered too; he was no more of a swain than Alexander. I knew I was prettier than his Melisande, and cleverer, though not as elegant, than the woman Honorine. But Honorine was far away, surely; the Court of Love had banished her. Perhaps, now, there was someone else?

True to his word, Richard had brought a goldsmith to fit my gift ring with the great ruby seal. When the man brought it back, all neat and small for my troth finger, the gold was graven, inside, with the legend, in Latin, *Ricardus et Blon-*

delza, amor gravitas. I knew not what to make of it, unless Richard had ordered it before his ardor cooled. I sulked when he did not come, picked quarrels with him when he did, and at night, alone in my bed, I wept. I was a girl, young, foolish, and in love.

One afternoon in September, I sat upon the steps of our show wagon, on the side that faces the forest; I wanted to be alone, and quiet, for a song was teasing at my head and I wanted to get it into my fingers before I lost it. I tried over the notes softly, picking at the strings of the lute that lay in my lap. I had it, all but the last two measures, and it still would not come, though I fretted at it for more than an hour, cursing softly under my breath. Oh, let it go, I said to myself, it will come when the god wishes, and sighed heavily. The sweat was clammy under my arms, where my outgrown dress was tight; my concentration and the slanting rays of the sun had heated me, and now a breeze, cool, had sprung up, bending the dark green boughs of the great old trees that edged the woods and ruffling the hair at my brow. I rolled up the sleeves of my gown and opened my bodice top, shivering a little, pleasantly. The low westering sun made a band of light that struck across my face; I closed my eyes and turned my head aside, leaning back against the wagon, listening to the gentle whisper of the blowing branches and to the song in my head. When Richard spoke I jumped and turned a startled face.

"Oh," he said, "I did not mean to frighten you."

"No," I said, my hand to my heart, for it was still leaping. "No, I was silly . . . but you came so quietly."

"Like a thief . . . I know," he said, laughing. Then his face went all grave and his eyes strange and intent. "For there is much I would steal, Blondelza."

For once I knew not how to answer; my tongue felt stiff and numb in my mouth, and my heart was loud in the silence.

He leaned down and plucked a sprig of the bright-burning broom that grew between the wagon wheels. "Our emblem," he said, idly turning the yellow weed about in his fingers. "Since my grandsire first wore it in his helm." He pushed it into my hair above my ear, the touch of his fingers sending ripples down my spine. "It becomes you, Blondelza." He smiled, but his eyes held, still, that strange gaze. "You look like a sun goddess," he said.

I took it amiss; I knew my arms and neck were brown as a peasant's. "I do not have the time to loll about on cushions under shades," I said. "I am a professional, a joglarese. I must practice my art in the sun." And I raised my chin and sent him a dark look.

He laughed softly. "Oh, Blondelza, your skin is beautiful, like apricots with a blush." And he reached out to touch my cheek. "So soft." He rubbed his own chin, making a wry face. "Like nettle-cloth," he said, "for I did not shave this morning."

I thought he boasted, for surely he was young for so much shaving? I smiled.

He squatted on his haunches at my feet, laughing up at me. "There, I have made you smile! Am I forgiven?"

"For what?" I asked, and heard the coyness in my voice with shame.

"For . . . whatever," he answered, spreading his hands.

"You interrupted a song," I said. "A song in my head."

"Will you play it for me?" He picked up my lute, holding it out.

"I cannot get the end right," I said, frowning. "It will not come. Only a bar or two—but it will not come."

"Sometimes another ear . . ." he said. "Play it through to the stuck place," he urged. "If I find the right note, will you reward me with a kiss?"

I stared at him. "You are somewhat late in asking, sirrah!"

"I wanted to know you better."

I burst out with it then, all the resentments I had held for months. "You have not spoken a word with me—or almost none! None privately! Never have you taken me aside, or walked within the forest, or watched the stars with me . . . you will not even argue!"

"Have we differences, then?" he asked, smiling at me as if he were five and twenty and not barely upwards of fifteen. It fanned my anger; I was like poor Ursula when someone takes a stick to her—a baited bear.

"How would you know?" I shouted. "You do not trouble to find out what I think! And I am clever—and can read Latin and speak four languages, and talk philosophy with scholars! But no, you will talk with Mother by the hour—of nothing but religion, and Popes, and old doctrines worn thin by time . . ."

"Do not be jealous of your mother, sweet, for she and I

can never agree . . . and I think that someday you and I may."

"I am not jealous!" I cried, still incensed.

"I think you are—a little," he said quietly. "And I understand. Forgive me, Blondelza. Look, my own . . ." He took me by the arms, and rubbed his cheek against mine.

I felt he was gentling me, as he would a restive mare, and the thought made a bubble of laughter rise in my throat; I hid my face that he should not see me smile.

He went on speaking, soft words and sweet. "There is nothing I want more than to be alone with you, as we are now . . . but I could not show my hand so soon. You must see that. Duke or no, your father would spirit you away, or hide you from me. He is a proud man—not a man to see his daughter trifled with."

"You would not do that, surely?"

"What else would it be called? Be reasonable, my darling. The whole world knows me betrothed to Alys of France."

I raised my head. "What is she like, this Alys? Is she pretty?"

"She is thought to be . . . for a princess." He shrugged. "A thin blonde, delicate and pale, high-strung. And very young, when last I saw her." He let go of my arms, and turned away. "The truth is I cannot bear her."

"So young . . ." I murmured, a little shocked.

"She has whore's eyes," he said. "How old would she be now? Fourteen? And my father keeps her by him always." The dark blood rushed into his face; he looked frightening, old and cruel. "I will not take his leavings!" he said, in an ugly, choked voice.

"Richard," I whispered, plucking at his sleeve. "Surely you are mistaken."

"I hope so," he said curtly.

I watched him, again, ordering his features, willing the hot blood to subside. He accomplished it too, a strange and wonderful thing to watch, also a little frightening. At the end, his eyes cleared and brightened, his face smoothed out and wore a little smile. It was as if the storm had never entered him; only a small pulse beat, telltale, at the back of his jaw.

"Her sister," he said then, slowly, "her sister, Marguerite . . . *her* I could have loved. She was not beautiful like you, but sweet, so sweet. Small and dark, shy . . . she wanted to be a nun."

"And did she?"

His mouth was grim. "They married her to my older brother Henry. I hope she does not die of it."

"Richard!" I cried softly, shocked again.

"You do not know my family," he said shortly.

"They say he is fair, the Young King, and courtly."

"He is vicious." The words were hard and final.

"Richard," I said softly, with a pleading look; I could not bear this mood.

He smiled then, and said lightly, "Perhaps we all are. My father's blood is cursed." He laughed, showing those white teeth. "Have you not heard the saying, 'From the Devil they came . . . to the Devil they will go'?"

"Those old tales," I murmured. "They are said of all families. I do not know my own heritage—only the wickedness that happened just yesterday." And I told him all that I knew of my noble forebears; I had never spoken of it before, but it poured out now, like water when a dam is broken. When I finished the tale of my mother, with the words "and they called her Castelloza," I saw his face had a thoughtful look.

"I know that castle," he said slowly. Then he snapped his fingers. "And I know the tale . . . Raimbaut of Orange. When his sister bore a child, unwed, he killed her in a fit of fury. She never told the father's name . . . and no one knew what happened to the child, but it was a girl. Raimbaut has been on pilgrimage ever since. Or dead and in Hell. They say he murdered her with an axe." He crossed himself. I wept.

"Don't cry, Blondelza. I will get your castle back for you. There were no heirs of his body, and he was our vassal . . . I will get it."

"Do you think I want it?" I cried. "It's horrible . . . a place of carnage. I have seen it—dark and grim, high on a mountain. I cried for the poor girl, my grandmother, who loved and was betrayed . . . and kept silent. And paid for her love so dreadfully."

"I know," he said. " 'A woman's lot is not an enviable one.' My mother said that to me once, long ago, when I was a child." He was silent for a long moment, then he said, "I made a vow to myself then that I would never knowingly be the cause of a woman's sorrow." His smile was wry. "Already I have broken it several times over."

"How?" I asked.

"Well," he answered slowly, pulling on the knuckles of one hand so that they cracked, "you know of the damsel Melisande?"

I nodded.

"I grew tired of her and married her off. I know not if she is content . . . And the child—my child, a girl too—will grow up without a father. I have never even seen her, though they say she is pretty, and has my hair."

I was silent; there was nothing to say.

"And then," he went on. "I have killed. Each of those men, though he was a villain sure, had a mother—or a wife perhaps, or a woman who loved him."

I burst out then. "But they would have killed you! You cannot take that blame upon you."

"I must," he said simply. "Jesus would."

"Jesus," I said, "would not have killed at all."

"Yes, you are right . . . but He took the sins of all mankind on His head at the end." He crossed himself again; he was very pious. I was not used to so much Cross-signing; player folk are careless about such things, and my mother did not believe in the Cross at all. As for me, I had no god but my art, and no faith, except in myself.

I felt uneasy and a little frivolous, and, after a small silence, took up my lute.

"Ah, yes," he said, "you were going to sing me a song—or part of one."

I shook my head. "There are no words at all yet . . . only a little tune that teases at me." And I played it over softly, to the place where it would not come right, watching him.

Before I had finished, he began to tap his foot. "A good melody, a lilting air . . . play it again." He hummed along with me this time; he had a good ear.

"I think—could you perhaps go high on that last measure? Like this, perhaps?" And he took the lute and played, stumbling a bit on a note or two, but getting it right most of the way. At the end he made a climbing scale, finishing with a high birdlike sound.

"No, that is not it, not quite," I said. "But I see—" I took the lute back, almost snatching it, making him smile. "Thus!" I said, triumphant. "That is how it should go! When you started up the scale, my head cleared, and I heard the end." And I finished the song, playing it over twice. I knew then I had got it perfectly; one always does.

"Beautiful!" Richard said, clapping his hands happily. But then he stopped smiling, and his eyes seemed to darken and grow larger. "But now, I cannot take my forfeit."

"Your forfeit?" I stared at him.

"Had you forgotten? You promised a kiss if I helped."

"Oh, but you did help." Then I put my hands quickly over my mouth. Shame flooded me, that I seemed to ask for the kiss. My cheek was red as fire, I knew, but I turned it toward him, waiting for the touch of his lips. It did not come. He had not moved.

"I do not want the kiss of courtesy, my dear," he said softly, and took me in his arms. No one had ever kissed me on the lips before, except once when a patroness, a lady of Périgord, had clutched me to her, pressing a purse into my hand and thrusting her tongue into my mouth; it had felt nasty, and I had drunk a lot of spring water afterward to take the taste away. I stiffened, expecting the same, but Richard's kiss was nothing like it. It was soft and firm at once, and incredibly sweet; I knew then that the troubadours had not lied. It lasted a long time, though I could not say how long; it was a moment that did not seem to belong to this world at all. I trembled and melted and my lips parted of themselves, and I suppose he did the same thing as the nasty lady. But it was vastly different; I saw then how all the awkward and distasteful things that happened in love could take place easily, and a poor girl not know herself what she did, caught in this odd, transforming joy. It went through my head that drunkenness must feel so, before it wears off and leaves the drinker sick and spent.

I did not feel sick and spent now, though. When he loosed me, it was too soon, and I clung to him, feeling the hard muscles of his arms and legs, other places too, against me, and nearly swooning with it.

"Someone may come," he said, whispering into my hair, but still holding me.

It was I who should have said it, for it was my people who might come round the side of the wagon, and I was a maiden still. But I held him to me fiercely. "Not yet," I said, "not yet."

"Unless I put you from me, it will not stop at a kiss," he said, a little laugh sounding, low in his throat. "And this is not the place for it. Another time, love."

There was a practiced note in his voice, and I drew back,

affronted. "Another time I may not feel like it at all," I said sharply.

"Do not play the cruel Midons with me, Blondelza," he said. "Leave that to the court ladies. Be honest, as equal to equal."

His words struck me like a blow; I had thought myself as open as the sky. Of course it was not so; I lied every day of my life, though not always in words. Were women, then, born to duplicity? Certainly I had not learned it at my saintly mother's knee.

I spoke to him, slowly, coming out of thought. "I will try, Richard. I promise you. But it is true that I may not feel like it again. I have never felt so before."

"You will, I think. If you allow yourself to be kissed again."

"Yes," I said. "Kissing you is pleasant, Richard." I heard myself with some dismay; I sounded as earnest as a Cathar preacher.

He laughed. "You need not be so serious, girl!"

"I know . . . I shall have to aim for somewhere in between." And I laughed too.

"Well, at least," he said, "between us we have damped our ardor somewhat . . . and a good thing too, for here comes your father, and with a long face."

"We missed you, daughter," said Papa Jean. "I always worry lest some one of us should wander off alone . . . these routier bands . . ."

In my new awareness, I knew that he was not speaking all the truth, that he was uneasy to find me alone with Richard. Perhaps there is no truth, really—only half-truths and evasions. At least I saw at that moment that it was not the fault of my sex, but only of being human.

"I was working up a new song," I said quickly. "I could not get the ending, and Richard helped me."

Papa sent us a hard look, but let it go. "I hope it is a good song," he said lightly.

"I think so," said Richard. "And she is being kind to say I helped—for she listened courteously, and then finished it her own way."

"Like all song-makers," said Papa, with a laugh.

"Like all song-makers," said Richard.

Papa's face had cleared then, and he left us, with a word to mind the chill in the air.

"So that is how it is done!" I said, looking at Richard.

"It is always best to tell *most* of the truth if you have something to hide."

"I thought we must have nothing to hide."

"Between us two, yes. Let us make a pact."

"I will not swear," I said, holding back.

"No swearing. Only our word—and our hands upon it." I gave him my hand, and he took it, grasping it firmly. After a moment, he turned it, palm up, and planted a kiss in the middle. "To seal the bargain," he said, his eyes alight. We moved apart, but his eyes still held mine. He snapped his fingers, suddenly. "I came expressly to tell you something," he said, "and it had gone right out of my head!"

"Tell," I said, smiling.

"To ask a favor, really. It will be my birthday soon—on Lady Day." And here he crossed himself again, absently; it must be a habit with him! "You know I was born on the same day as Our Lord's mother? There will be a celebration, a double one, for the holy day, and for my part of it too. I had thought to ask you to come, on both counts. Do you think you could play something from Our Lady's life . . . is there a play we have not seen?"

"She appears in the Nativity, of course," I said, thinking, "and in the Passion play too—though I would not play the part then, she is too old. I wonder . . . when the Angel Gabriel speaks to her and tells her that she will bear the Christos . . . that could be a good scene . . . a small one, but good."

"Yes," he said eagerly. "That sounds like the thing."

"But there is not even a week to work it up!" I cried in dismay. "We will have to shape it as we go . . . and there are the costumes." I began to shake my head. "You have not given us enough notice."

"I am sorry," he said, humbly, for him. "Not being a professional myself . . . And, then, I thought that surely there must be a play already made."

"Not that I know of. And—" My hand flew to my mouth. "Papa! You must ask Papa! He is the head of the company . . . the decision must be his."

"I see," said Richard, smiling. "Even among players there is protocol."

"Of course," I said. "Come, we will ask him. Or you will. I shall pretend I have never heard it before." I smiled a little.

"It seems, now that we mean to be honest with each other, we are obliged to deceive all others."

"Do you think he will agree to do it?"

I nodded. "I'm sure of it. But"—and I turned a sad face to him—"I will not be able to dress up in my new tawny silk."

"For the other, you will. For my own celebration after the play. There will be dancing . . . all night perhaps! A secular entertainment." His lip twitched in a grave face. "And you see now that I had to stop the kissing . . . since you are to play the Holy Virgin."

I shot him a quick look, sidelong, before I ran ahead. "Even I, an innocent, know that a kiss will not take my maidenhead!"

I heard his steps behind me, and his laugh, low, in my ear.

CHAPTER 5

THE MARY PLAY went well. I was very good in the part, though I say it myself; but artists must know their worth, and their progress too. I had matured since I last played Mary, and there were many little nuances of feeling that I had missed before but that now came right. We had not many lines to learn, thank God. When one is a professional one can just improvise along the way; it works well, as long as the plot and action are clear. Our costumes were more or less pinned together, for we really were short of time. I was so anxious to have my beautiful silk to wear for the private party that I cobbled the Virgin's robe together in a shameful fashion. But I asked Our Lady's forgiveness; surely she would understand, for before she was the Holy Mother, she was a girl, and all girls love pretty clothes.

We did not perform the play in the castle, but in the nave of the Church of Saint Etienne, not far away. Though there were hundreds of candles burning, still, when I came out into the sunshine of the bright afternoon, the daylight dazzled me, and I stumbled on the steps of the church. A hand went out to steady me, taking my elbow. Then, shockingly, I felt it creep under my blue robe and grasp my breast, squeezing it hard. I pulled away, my cheeks flaming under the paint, for I feared that all the folk lining the steps had seen. But I saw that all heads were bowed, as befits them when holy things pass by, even when they are embodied in the person of a venal player. All heads but one, that is. I stared into the eyes, black and mocking, of a richly dressed young man. As I looked, he licked his lips, letting his tongue flicker at me; his lascivious intent was plain. I could hardly believe my eyes, and walked on down the steps, my whole being in a turmoil of shame and rage, nearly boiling over.

I could eat almost nothing at the feast, though usually after a performance I am starved as a wolf; I could only drink wine, my hands shaking on the cup. I drank three cups down before Papa put his hand on my wrist and shook his head. "You will be dizzy, child. Put the wine aside now and eat something—a little fruit, at least."

We players sat apart, at a table of our own, quite near the head of the big table; we never were given places at the regular feast board, for we are not vassals, either high or low, and do not fit anywhere. We are too low to sit above the salt, with the nobles, and too high to sit below it, with the clerks.

After a bit, the wine diffusing pleasantly, I nibbled at some nuts and ate an apple. My heart was slowing down now, and I looked about me. Far down the big table someone was waving his arms about, Alexander; he grinned and clasped his hands above his head in a gesture that meant "victory" or "bravo." I smiled and waved. We were still in our paint and costumes, though I had thrown off the Madonna-blue cloak and sat at table in the simple white gown that had served me for the part two years now. It was short in the bodice and the sleeves stopped at my elbows now, but I had brought my new silk to wear later, so I did not mind; besides, no one at the big table was near enough to notice. Even as I thought it, though, I felt eyes on me and, looking about, saw the black-eyed man staring. He showed his teeth at me; I turned away, haughty. At the head of the table, beside Queen Eleanor, Richard raised his great silver cup to me and drank; I bowed from the waist.

The feast went on and on. I was glad I did not have to do this every day, like the other folk; who can eat so much? Course after course was brought in, the cooks staggering under the weight of the heavy platters.

On one tray was a great stag, seated among parsleys and

herbs arranged like foliage; its horns were dressed with gold baubles and for eyes it had two green stones. It took four cooks to carry it; they bore it all the way round the table so that all could see and applaud. There was a roast peacock too, with all his beautiful tail feathers spread out, and surrounded by little partridges, in their feathers too, and swimming in a sea of gravy. There was a suckling pig, with an apple in its mouth—so pathetic, like a little dog, and great fish, carp and salmon, garnished with seaweed and lemons, and huge bright red lobsters, looking fierce and angry in death.

The pie of larks was a fiasco, for besides those cooked in it, just under the crust were live ones, meant to fly up when the crust was cut and soar, singing, into the air; of course the poor things were half smothered, their wings heavy with sauce, and they fell to the table like a plague of large locusts, where they fluttered feebly and then were still.

I could eat none of these things, they sickened me, though I did relish a new dish, smoked, from the east, called sausage; it was very tasty and neat to look at, served cold. One could pick it up and not get greasy or spotted from gravy. I heard afterward that it was meat too, all ground up—horrid thought—and encased in a skin made of intestines of some other animal. So I will think twice about eating it, too; it is a shame vegetables are so dull, by comparison.

At the end came the great pastries and ices, marvelous to see, and all food for the gods, in my opinion; I could live on them and be happy, if I did not know they would make me fat. I noticed that Queen Eleanor did not touch them, and most of the ladies who did were monstrously fat and had blackened teeth or none at all. Still, I sampled them all; I am young still, and besides, I do not often get a chance at such things.

Of course, wine was served in plenty, a different one to go with each dish. By the end, most of the men were too drunk to get to their feet, and some lay on the floor, snoring, to be swept out with the rushes. Hot Black Eyes was not among them, though he drank plentifully enough. He had stared at me the whole time, and it was only after the drink got to him a little and he began to nuzzle at his partner's neck that I was able to observe what manner of man he was to look at.

He was fairly young, I think, but with the most dissolute face I have ever seen. There were dark pouches under his eyes, and his mouth was loose and shiny-lipped, with an undershot chin; this, with the flat look of his head, gave him a kind of lizard-face that made me shudder. But for this, the rest of him might have been pleasing; he was slenderly built, with long bones, and his dress was handsome, rich and dark, finer than any of the other knights', though he sat just above the salt and could not have been important.

The lady beside him seemed to like him well enough, letting him put his hand down her dress, and laughing when he bent her almost double to kiss her. I thought their behavior unseemly, on Lady Day, but as I glanced round the company, I saw they were not alone. These nobles comported themselves in a way that would have been frowned on among honest burghers anywhere, and would have been out of place even around our tent fires, in the dark.

Music began to rise then, louder, from the minstrels' gallery; I realized it had been there all along, in the background, but the noise had been great. Some varlets threw open the doors to the big Hall of Windows, which had been cleared for dancing, and those who could still stand began to make their way toward the music, Richard going at their head. He stopped at our little table, where I sat tapping my feet to the tune, and bent down to speak to me, low.

"Come into the hall, Blondelza," he said. "I must lead off the dancing with Mother and then with my sister Marie . . . but then we will have a try at it."

"Oh, no," I said, shocked. "I cannot! I am wearing the Virgin's gown!"

He snapped his fingers. "God's feet!" he cried softly. "I had forgot!" And he signed himself again; I suppressed a smile, it was so automatic. Then he bent close again. "You did not bring your new silk?" At my eager nod, he said, "Well, change into it. I command it! For it is my day too!" He was laughing as he turned to Papa. "You permit, sir? I could not have my birthday dancing without Blondelza! And please, all of you, stay! We can use some professionals!"

He beckoned to Alexander, who came up to him smiling. Alex wore his old brown gown, stained black at the skirts with ink where he had wiped his pens. "Alex, old Saracen," said Richard, laughing louder. "Have you forgot it is your birthday too? You do none of us honor . . . even Our Lady might want to see you in a clean suit! Take Blondelza to my little dressing room so that she may change. And ask your mother to attend her, for my sake." He fisted Alexander's chin, playfully, but none too lightly. "And borrow a surcoat of mine, while you are at it." As Alexander opened his mouth to protest, Richard said, most lordly on a sudden, "It is a command!"

Alexander bowed and pulled at his forelock, mocking. "Yes, sir. Verily, my lord."

"Get along, you clown," said Richard, breaking into a laugh.

"Such a nuisance!" I heard Alexander say, as I followed him up some dark turret stairs. "Such a plague! Richard knows I do not dance!"

We came out, after a long, winding climb, upon a small round chamber, lit on all sides by high slit windows. There was little furniture, save for a three legged stool, a high standing cupboard, and a couple of large clothespresses. A woman, plainly dressed, was laying away garments in one of them; there was a strong smell of some dried herb, not sweet but with a sharp cleanness. I guessed that she was strewing it among the clothes, against moths or mildew. She turned, and I saw she was handsome and tall, very like Alexander, but with a sterner look. Her features softened when she saw him and she smiled a little smile, though she did not embrace him, and went on with her work.

"Mother, this is the damsel Blondelza, come to change into her fancy dress . . . will you help her? And, hang it all, Richard demands that I wear one of his gawds."

"I have been looking out one of them for you, Alex, for I guessed as much. You were ever careless . . . you must not shame your foster brother on his day. And it is your day too, remember." She held out to him a wine-red surcoat and a white shirt with very full sleeves. "Wait, I have the hose somewhere."

"Oh, Madame Mother, must I? Isn't the gown long enough?"

"Put them on," said Hodierna firmly. "I will not have your hairy shanks showing at the court. Get along now, lad, and let the damsel dress."

He went out grumbling, and she turned to me with a gentle smile. "Oh, a lovely color," she said, as I shook out the shimmering folds of the beautiful silk.

"Yes, my best color, I think," I said, suddenly shy. "It was a gift from the Countess."

"But you made the design." She nodded approvingly. "A severe style—but it suits the silk."

"It laces . . . so . . . over this peach-colored shift," I said, showing her. She helped me into the gown. "Tighter," I said. "Pull the laces tighter. See I will hold my breath." I let it out on a sigh, and felt the waist pinch satisfactorily, while she stood back to survey the effect. "It is a new cut, from Italy. One has to get used to it," I said doubtfully.

"It is daring," said Hodierna, "and not many could wear it. But it suits you, my dear. Here, look . . . there is a long polished shield behind this door." She flung open the cupboard, and I saw myself full length, as I never had before. I was much taller than I had realized, with a narrower waist, but I had estimated properly and allowed for a good length. It reached the floor and there was a small train in the back, just enough to gather up in one hand in the dance; I had practiced. My cheeks were too red, garish in the light of day; I snatched up the discarded Virgin's robe and rubbed at them. "It will never be used again," I said, feeling some apology was needed. "I have outgrown it—and, I fear, the part too."

"You are betrothed, then?" asked Hodierna, thinking, I guess, that I meant I would not long stay virgin.

I did mean that too, underneath, I realized, but my cheeks were redder than ever as I explained that I was indeed growing too old to be believable as the young Mary. "For I am almost sixteen," I finished.

"A very great age, indeed," she replied, her face very straight.

I bundled my hair into a net of our property pearls, but they looked shabby to me, beside the gorgeous silk, and I took it off, tying back the mass of hair with a ribbon of the peach stuff of the shift. "It is simpler so," I said.

"I agree," said Hodierna. "Your hair needs no adornment."

"Apollo Deus!" said Alexander from the doorway, swearing in Latin. "You look . . . splendid," he finished, rather lamely.

I thought he looked rather splendid himself, in a sober dark way. The wine-red gown made his hair black and shining as a crow's wing, and I saw for the first time that he had narrow, fine-boned legs and feet; I wondered idly if his father had been a nobleman, and then silently cursed myself for thinking as all the court did. I, who know that the lowest player, born in a ditch, can have the look of breeding out of nowhere!

"You took a brush to your hair," said Hodierna, smiling. "Good. Happy birthday, my son." She kissed him tenderly, holding his face between her two hands. I saw then that there was much love between them, for all their quiet ways.

As we turned to go, she let her hand softly touch my cheek, the merest hint of a caress. "Fortune smile upon you, my child," she said. "And bear my greetings to Dickon." It was the first time I had heard that nickname, but I felt it suited Richard well.

In the hall, the dancing was in full swing; the company had formed for some kind of volte, two lines, men and women, facing each other along the length of the room. Richard stood opposite a plump, dark-eyed Latin lady, who resembled Esmerelda somewhat, though she was older and as brightly dressed as a street-woman. This lady was very vivacious, tossing her black curls and dimpling her cheeks; I thought her very vulgar, but Richard did not seem to, for he held her very close in the first measures and swung her gaily off the floor, laughing, though it must have been an effort. I watched the two of them like a hawk; Richard was very graceful, but his lady danced like a country bumpkin, flinging herself about and bouncing at each step, so that her breasts shook like jellies. "Who is she?" I whispered to Alexander.

"Who?" he asked in turn, stupidly.

"The dark bouncer with Richard," I replied.

"Oh, that is Lombarda. She is very popular," he said. "She was widowed recently."

"She does not seem to mourn," I said, a little sharply.

He laughed. "No, she is enjoying her freedom. Her lord was very jealous, and killed two men on her account. The third got him first."

"Alexander!" I exclaimed. "I did not know you were so full of court gossip!"

"Oh, one cannot help hearing such things . . . and, for a while, too, Richard favored her."

"And now?" I asked, my chin lifting.

"Now," he said, turning to me with a grave face, "now, I guess, it is you."

I held his eyes with mine for a long moment. "Dukes mean nothing to me . . . I will give where I choose."

"I could almost believe you—" he began.

"You will see," I said, very haughty, my nose still in the air.

I felt then a warm breath on my neck, and a warm voice in my ear. "Come, girl, you must tread a fine measure," said the voice. "The next dance is mine."

I whirled about. It was the lizard, with the hot black eyes, smiling down at me, for he was a good height.

I blazed at him with my eyes and hissed under my breath, "Get you gone, sirrah! Get you out of my sight—or I will have the Duke's men on you!"

He did not move, but his smile broadened. "You think they will obey a joglarese?"

"I am a troubadour—and a guest in this hall," I said, keeping my voice down. "And I bid you be gone from my sight." At just this moment, the dance came to an end and the music stopped; my last words could be heard all over the hall, for my voice is trained to carry, even pitched low. There were a few titters, and a little shriek of laughter, quickly suppressed. Richard had heard too, and I saw him threading his way toward me.

"What's wrong?" he said, pleasantly enough, but with steel under. "You must have heard the lady. Betake yourself some other where." And he waved his hand in a lordly fashion, looking down his nose; tall as the man was, Richard was taller, the tallest man in the room.

Black Eyes stood his ground. "I only asked her for a dance," he said. "It is what she is here for, surely—a gleemaiden!"

"She is the Baroness of Nesle," said Richard coldly, "and her dances are promised already." He held out his arm, and I took it, like a very true lady. "Sir!" Richard snapped his fingers. "I have forgotten your name."

"Jocelyn of Fouquebrun," said the man.

"Fouquebrun. Ah, yes," said Richard. "A little place where two rivers meet, on the road to Lusignan . . . you hold fief of—Angoulême, is it not? Seisin is given by a white rose?" The man nodded. "You are a new-made lord, if I remember . . . my father took Fouquebrun in a raid three years ago."

"And gave it me," said the Lord Jocelyn. "I have his seal."

"His seal is obsolete now, since I am crowned," said Richard. "But let it go . . . it is my birthday, and I am in a generous mood." He did not look it; I saw the telltale signs, the dark blood flooding his cheeks and the quick pulse beating. Then his face relaxed into a faint smile, and he said, easily and lightly, "Find yourself a partner, Sir Jocelyn . . . the dance is beginning."

He swept me into it, a galliard; when I could get my breath, I saw that the man was gone.

"A fellow of no account," Richard said. "One of my father's nithings."

"I never heard that word," I said.

"Saxon . . . English . . . whatever it is called, the jargon. It means—" And he shrugged. "Just that, a shrug, no more."

His shrug was so overdone, like an eager mime's, that I laughed aloud, and soon forgot the whole incident.

CHAPTER 6

IT WAS THE kind of perfect day you get sometimes in October, before the rains. The air sparkled, with a little snap to it, and the sky was blue enough to drown in. The low hills were covered with vines, and stunted olive trees lined the road to Lusignan; they looked so gnarled and old they might have grown there since the Romans built it. It was a road straight as a die, and still smooth, though it crumbled at the edges where the soil had fallen away from the stones. Our horses' hooves rang loud upon it, the only sound except the running of the little streams in the hills. None of us spoke, for it would spoil the day, and then, too, we were lost, each, in our own thoughts.

Mother said over her own special prayers, I knew, for she had that look of light upon her face; Alexander read a book, he was the only person I ever knew who could ride while reading; Esmerelda, no doubt, dreamed of a noble bridegroom, and I thought, as always, of Richard.

We rode alone, except for the four men-at-arms that Richard had given us, two in front and two bringing up the rear. They were goodly fellows and young, though I could not understand a word they said; they had come from England in Queen Eleanor's train, and spoke the strange, harsh speech of that island, so unlike all the tongues I knew. Still, I felt I knew the men well, for they were the same four who had been with us now for a month, or nearly, even sleeping outside our tents at night. It lent us much freedom, for we need not travel everywhere in a body as before; today Papa was not with us, having stayed behind to work over some effects with Gervase and the others. Mother went to gather herbs at a place she knew in the forest; it was such a fine day we had all thought to ride along with her, not to miss it. Though I had another motive too, for I hoped to catch Richard, back from a hunting trip; Alexander had told me that his path crossed ours some way along.

I had a horse, a pretty mare, a gift from Richard, white with a brown mane and tail; I called her Blanchfleur. I so delighted in this little beast that she was already well spoiled, and would not be bridled without a lick of honey or salt. She had a special saddle and was used to skirts, but I was not; I had ridden so much in boys' gear that I still wore it, except for show. I went today with unbound hair, but in hose and shortgown, like a page, with my new silver dagger, another gift, at my belt. It looked like a toy, but was sharp; I thought it would do for cutting the tougher roots of the plants Mother searched out. Esmerelda was in skirts, but sat astride, so that they were bunched up, showing her ankles and her rounded legs. Only Mother sat sidewise, like a lady.

"This way," she said suddenly, coming out of her reverie. "The place is down this little path, to the right." Alexander called ahead to the Englishmen, who had gone some way along, directing them to the path we had taken; he had already learned some words of their tongue, from living among the Saxon thralls in the English castles.

A vine-covered hill led down into a new forest, sun-dappled; the scent of grapes gave way to berry smells, rich and ripe, and the darker smell of earth and leaf mold. The sound of water was louder here.

We came out onto a cleared place where a broad stream ran, but it was in spate, rushing down from a mountain somewhere high. It glittered in the sun and foamed white against the rocks; we could not find the ford-place, it must have been washed out. A boat rocked crazily at the water's edge, spinning at the end of its tether; there were oars lying in the bottom, but no ferryman. It was decided that we three women should ride in it. I said that I would row; that Alexander had best keep with the horses. I was not very good at it, I found; the rushing water kept turning us downstream, and my arms soon ached with the effort of keeping to the course. I had made little headway when we heard sounds of men and horses from across the river. "Oh, thank God," I sighed. "It must be Richard."

"No," said Mother, shading her eyes against the sun, "I think not."

My back was to the far shore as I pulled on the oars, and I turned about, craning to see. A body of horsemen had come right down to the water's edge, and armor gleamed, blinding me as the sun struck it. It was certainly no hunting party, I thought, and with the thought, I saw the first man heave the long spear in his hand, striking the nearest of our bodyguard; he fell into the foaming stream and did not come up. The others of our guard drew their own spears and advanced, but I could see no more, for the raging stream spun us about, while I sat helpless, with the unwieldy oars dragging painfully at my hands; Esmerelda shrieked continuously, a high thin cry like the wail of a sea bird. "Be still, or I will have you over the side!" I shouted, struggling to hold on to the oars and right the boat. It straightened, miraculously, and stayed afloat. I had lost one of the oars, but now I was facing the other way, and could see all. Two more of our men were in the water, and as I watched, one head went under; I saw the other man turn about and swim for the far shore, the water reddening around him, so I knew he must be sore wounded. Alexander, slower than the others, sat his horse in midstream, dumbstruck; my Blanchfleur swam, riderless, beside him, her reins hanging from his hand.

"Go back," I called. "Get help! Find Richard!"

"I cannot leave you," he cried.

"Go!" I shouted. "They cannot follow you—they cannot swim in armor! Go now, or you will be killed!" A spear fell short before him in the water; his horse reared half out, foundering and frightened witless. "Take Blanchfleur!" I cried. "She is quicker!" It seemed he could not hear me over the raging water and the tumult on the shore, but he must have, for he dropped down into the water, turning his own horse loose and swimming to my Blanchfleur. I saw them safe to the shore and galloping free on dry ground, before I turned about; I knew from then that we were lost, our last man fighting desperately in the shallows, four swords to his one,

142

and blood already pouring from his neck, staining his mail shirt like rust.

I paddled desperately, but the current swept us ever downward, on a slanting course toward the shore. It looked as if we might ground on a spit of land that jutted outward, about a quarter-mile down. The routiers, for such they must be, had seen it too, and a little knot of them were making for it, spurring their horses on, while their fellows rode into the water to bring our poor riderless mounts in. A good horse is worth more than a man, I had heard Papa say; how much more valuable, then, than a woman? And if they meant to rob us, we had nothing. Not even our wits, it seemed, for Mother, with closed eyes, was moving her lips in silent prayer, while Esmerelda whimpered and hiccoughed, her big cow's eyes almost starting from her head in terror.

"Shall we swim for it?" I said, keeping my voice steady.

"I—I cannot swim," whispered Esmerelda, her teeth chattering.

"Nor can I," I said sharply. "But then, I have never tried."

But when I made to stand up, the boat rocked so violently that the heart within me turned over. I saw that even a strong swimmer could not combat this raging, whirling angry spate of water. I straightened my shoulders and faced the shore, unconsciously gripping the oar that I still held. "Get down in the boat!" I ordered, my voice hoarse with fear. "Crouch down!" But I saw they did not mean to waste spears on us; already a pair of them idled their horses on the spit of land, waiting for the water to do their work for them. One man pushed his visor up. He was grinning; I saw there was a tooth missing at the front.

As we ran, tossing, into the shallow part, this gap-toothed one, still grinning, came wading his horse to meet us. He reached for me, passing Mother and Esmerelda. I swung the heavy oar with all my strength, aiming for his grin; his face smashed suddenly into a bloody pulp, and he fell backward off his horse. It made me deathly sick to see it, but I held on to the oar and swung it again.

This time a pike knocked it out of my hands and spinning into the water, and I felt myself grabbed roughly and lifted off my feet. Powerful arms swung me up and onto the horse's back, and the heavy saddle caught my leg, high on the inner thigh. I thought I would swoon with the pain—a metal buckle, it must have been—and I felt warm blood trickle down, wetting my hose. I saw nothing of my captor, for he had set me before him on his mount, his arm like a steel band crushing my chest and pinning my arms to my sides. In a daze I saw Mother and Esmerelda flung like sacks of meal across a horse's back, and another routier binding their feet with rope; then something dark came down over my head, and I saw nothing else. It must have been a woolen sack, it smelled like a wet sheep, and, faintly, too, of wood smoke and cured bacon. I thought they meant to smother me, and cried out; a hand was clapped, hard, over my mouth. I bit it, with all the force I could muster, right through the woolen cloth, and heard a muffled roar of pain. Then my ears nearly burst and a white streak of lightning flashed before my eyes, before everything went black. He must have hit me with something very hard; I remember thinking, on the instant, that I was dead.

I came to feeling I was still in the boat; it was rocking madly as before, only now it was night. And then I remembered, feeling the hard saddle punishing my crotch and the constricting arms that held me. My head hurt, and my breath came in shallow gasps, but I was still alive, and riding fast upon a galloping horse. After a bit I know the horse swerved, for I could feel it, and the sound of his hooves changed; wood clattered under us, a bridge or drawbridge, and the mount stopped short, whinnying and rearing into the air. The hood, or whatever it was was whipped off my head then, and I blinked, astonished, for it was still full daylight; I thought that many hours had passed.

"That's the one!" I heard. "I'll have that one ... the other two you can keep!"

The man who held me gave a snort of laughter, harsh. "This one's a wildcat, Baron! She made a blood mash out of Arnault the Black—killed him, maybe—and bit my finger to the bone."

"Never mind," said the voice, an oily voice that tugged at my memory. "I'll have her anyway. Bring her in."

I squinted against the slanting beams of the sun, and saw the speaker. It was the black-eyed man of Richard's birthday feast, Jocelyn of Fouquebrun. This must be his castle yard, dark and smelly, with pigs rooting in the flungout offal; Richard had said the fief was mean and small. The man himself, though, was clothed in velvet, ruby-hued, and his hair was sleek with Eastern oil. He saw my look, and smiled.

I did not smile back, of course; hot anger flooded up in me so that I was almost blinded with it, but I think I did not show it. I raised my head high and said, as haughtily as I could manage, "Good sir, are these your men? They have committed outrage, and I will have the law's extent on them! When Richard hears of this—"

He spoke then, angry too. "The new Duke is a puling boy . . . his father will soon have him by the ears! In any case"—and he smiled his sly smile again—"he will never hear of it."

I opened my mouth to retort, and shut it again. If Alexander got word to him at all, and if he came, surprise was best. It went through my head, sinkingly, that of course he would not know where we were. Unless, of course, Alexander might have recognized the badge upon the routiers' jupons; his mind was a storehouse of such trivial things. It might well be. I prayed a little prayer as my steel-armed captor lifted me down from the horse and pushed me, stumbling, after the Lord of Fouquebrun. My legs had gone to sleep and almost gave under me, and my arms were numb and stiff; besides, my head ached. I saw the rope in his hands and said wearily, "Let me walk free . . . I promise not to bite you again, and I have no weapon."

He gave me a snarl and a shove, but did not bind me, though he followed close behind with the rope ready. It flitted through my mind that I might push him down the stairs, as we began to mount them, but I was still dizzy and strengthless, and the stairs were steep and uneven, without a rail; I had to keep close to the wall and pick my way. At least, I thought, he is not throwing me into a dungeon!

We came out onto a small landing and a heavy door that led to a large chamber; my captor pushed me through after his lord. "Behave yourself now, wildcat, or I'll take it out of your hide later! Remember, Fouquebrun, I get first pickings," he said, turning to Sir Jocelyn.

"You can go now, Hébert," answered the lord, shutting the door on him and ramming the heavy bolt home.

"What did he mean—that varlet?" I asked, startled out of my cold manner.

He laughed, a nasty sound. "He is no varlet, but the captain of my mercenaries."

"A filthy routier—" I broke in.

He shrugged. "Filthy he may be, and a routier—but a valuable man to me nonetheless."

"What did he mean?" I insisted.

"We have certain . . . arrangements. When I have finished with a woman . . ." He shrugged again, and laughed at my face of horror and disgust. "They usually do not mind." He put his hand under my chin and lifted it, a soft touch, almost a caress. "But you need not think of that. If you are a good girl, I will keep you for myself." He drew me closer. "Be good to me, Blondelza."

His eyes had a strange, naked look, like the hungry pleading eyes of the poor in a famine year; though it made me sick and faint to look at them, in an odd way they gave me strength, for those eyes made him human. I thought perhaps I could strike a bargain with him, or play for time.

"Will you be good to me, Blondelza?" he whispered.

I lowered my lashes and tilted my head as if I were playing a coquette. "Perhaps . . ." I said, pouting a little. "But now I am so tired and thirsty."

"You shall have wine," he said eagerly, responding to my wiles. He loosed me and went to a small table where a carafe stood, pouring two cups. "It is good wine," he said. "Look. I will drink first." And he sipped from the cup. "Come, sit beside me here, upon the cushions."

I took the wine from his hands, and sat upon a little canvas-slung chair. "I will sit here, where I can look at you," I said, with a little pursing of the lips that might have been a smile.

"There is food too," he said, showing me a bowl of fruit and a platter with little cakes and sweetmeats.

I shook my head. "I am not hungry."

"You will see that this is a civilized manor," he said, "and no robbers' den . . . I have a lute, too, for you to play—and a gittern, if you prefer. And pretty robes from the East—a whole chestful. All girls like pretty clothes."

I said nothing, but turned the wine cup about in my hands; it was the mate to his, and of a good size, bound with silver. I thought of dashing the wine in his face and making for the door—or perhaps I might hit him with the carafe or the heavy bowl. But where would I dash to? His routiers held the castle; I might be worse off.

"What of the others?" I asked, suddenly. "The women who were with me?"

He smiled. "Routier meat. They will draw lots for them, I guess."

"Sweet Jesus," I cried softly. "One of them is my mother!"

"Your mother! The Cathar witch?"

"She is no witch, but a nobleman's lady!" I had forgotten my pretense of flirting with him. "If you mistreat her it will go hard with you!" I rose to my feet and held the wine cup high, ready to throw it.

"You are a wildcat for sure," he drawled, rising slowly. "I like that." He took the cup from me and held both my hands in his. I began to kick at him, but it only hurt my feet, in their thin leather slippers. I saw then, helplessly, that no matter how trained my muscles were, how lithe and strong for dancing, I was no match for a knight, even a fine-boned knight like this one. He was hard as steel, and his grip could not be broken; I remembered the knights' training, heavy swords, heavier lances, the weight of armor, and the warhorse between the knees. Still, I struggled on, panting and gasping, as he dragged me across the floor and flung me onto the cushions of the bedplace.

As he stood over me, loosening his shirt and grinning, I darted beneath his arms and ran to the door. I was very quick; I had the bolt half out, my fingernails torn with the effort, when he grabbed me from behind, chuckling. I could not reach my dagger; I turned and smashed my fist into his face. It left no mark, but the hunger in his eyes was mixed with fury now, and the good humor had left his voice. "That's how you want it, then . . . little slut!"

This time he handled me roughly, and fell on top of me in the bed, fumbling at his small clothes. The breath was knocked clear out of me; I could not even flutter feebly against him.

The fastenings of my tunic gave way as he tore at them; his tongue was thrust far into my mouth, and he kneaded at my breasts, while the whole length of him crushed me, his knee bruising my leg as he tried to push it to one side and get to my hidden woman's cleft. He cursed as he ripped at the drawstring of my linen hose. I heard the cloth tear; the stuff was weak with age and many washings. I lay naked except for the two flapping sides of my tunic. I scratched and bit wherever I could find a spot, but he only laughed and pushed my legs farther apart.

I got a glimpse, once, of his member, an angry red color, stiff and swollen, with purplish veins; in its nest of black hair it looked like some obscene root pulled out of the ground with grass clinging to it. He wants to put that in me, I thought, and struggled, stiffening myself against him. "Open up . . . open up!" he muttered hoarsely, stabbing at my flesh. It went in, agonizingly; I screamed. He brought it out, and in again, and each time I shrieked in pain; like a knife it was, cutting sharp into my insides. My fingers dug into his cheek, and I heard him laugh in his throat, while he thrust harder.

This is rape, I thought. I am being raped, and I am a virgin. A black lost sadness mourned in me, the tears ran down past my ears and onto the bed. I opened my eyes and saw his face above me. The expression on it was rapt, like someone listening to angels; his eyes were closed. Rage filled me that he could look so, while he tore my life apart. I fumbled for the little dagger that hung at my belt. It was caught beneath my body; when it came free, the sheath came with it. I could not get it loose one-handed, and the other was pinned to my side. His digging was faster now, and harder, but I did not feel it, only brought the knife slowly, stealthily upward. I caught the sheath between my teeth and drew the dagger out. His eyes were still closed and the look still transfigured his face; a large vein pulsed at the side of his thrown-back neck, the death vein, or so I had heard. With a prayer and a sob I plunged the dagger into it, so hard that it came out the other side.

His eyes flew open and he looked surprised; he stiffened, and slowly, slowly, fell onto his side, a jet of bright blood fountaining from his throat. I slipped from under him and looked down at his body. He never moved again, except for the jetting blood. The ugly root lay, collapsed and gray, looking shrunken, against his flaccid leg; there were streaks of blood on it, and, warm still, on my legs. I sobbed aloud, kneeling over the dead man, my long hair dabbling in his blood. "I killed you! I! I killed you! It was I!"

CHAPTER 7

I DON'T KNOW how long I lay there. I must have fainted. I was on my back beside the dead man; there was a noise like the end of the world, clashing steel, screams, thudding hooves and horses' frienzied cries, the shouts of men, wordless, and long, drawn out cursing, and the bumping and creaking of heavy wheels. One sound surfaced in my brain, close to me and loudest, a pounding at the door, and voices, muffled, I smelled smoke too, and sat up, awake and terrified. There was a roar of flames, sounding close, and, through the square of the high window, I saw the leaping red tongues of fire. It came to me where I was and all that had happened. They were trying to get to their master and I had killed him! In my mindless fear and shock I thought they had lit the fire to burn me up. I got to my feet, trembling; the caked blood on my legs pulled at the skin, and the wound I had got from the saddle smarted.

Jocelyn still lay where I had left him, my dagger transfixing his throat, but the blood had stopped and dried black, dyeing the bedclothes and cushions like a mourning pall. Whimpering low, I tried to lift him; he was already stiff as a board. I took hold of his feet and dragged; the body thumped on the floor, and the mouth jarred open, hideous. I flung a piece of bright cloth, part of the coverings, over it, for I could not bear to look, and dragged him slowly across the floor to where an arras hung, arranging its folds so that they hid him from sight.

The pounding at the door had not stopped. It was louder now; someone had taken a ram to it, and was running it home again and again, the door shuddering against its great bolt. They would have it down soon, I knew. My trembling was worse now, uncontrollable; I realized I must be cold, for I was naked as a plucked bird, except for the shreds of my upper garment. I remembered what he had said about the chestful of clothes. There were several chests in the room, serving as tabletops or seats. I swept a cushion off one and flung the lid up; it was full of old armor, rusty, and short swords. I took the best, a curved blade with an ivory hilt, and went to the next chest, nearly sobbing now; the door hinges were beginning to give, I could hear them creaking behind me. I pulled a green robe out of the chest and dragged it on, my fingers fumbling at the corded belt. I took up the short sword, it needed both my hands, and faced the splintering door.

The top hinge gave, but the bottom held, though the ram shook the door once more. A plank was left torn and hanging this time, and through the gape an arm reached in and felt for the bolt. I tightened my hold on the sword, hoping I had the strength to lift it for at least one blow.

The heavy door flew open and a figure burst in. I could see others behind, crowding the landing; there was a confusion of voices. I lifted the sword and swung at the first man; he raised his arm and caught the blade in his bare hand. "Blondelza!" I heard, and I knew the voice. Richard!

And then his arms were about me and I was weeping wildly; I felt, rather than saw, that it was truly he. "Richard!" I cried. "You must hide! This is a pack of wolves, a house of routiers! I heard them pounding at the door! Oh, hide! Here, come with me!" I tugged at him, desperate.

"No, No, my darling. Those were my men at the door ... we have taken the castle! You are safe now."

I knew, finally, that it was so. The chamber was crowded with men now, and I saw Alexander among them; there was a streak of blood on his face. For the first time I looked at Richard. His boots, his leather hunting clothes, his hands, his face, even his hair was spattered with blood; he looked as if he had walked through a lake of it.

"You too," I wailed. "I have hurt you too!"

"No, no," he said, puzzled.

"Your hand—you took my sword blade in your hand."

"Oh, that. Look, not even a scratch! The sword was blunt, poor darling."

"My dagger was not blunt," I said wearily. "It is sticking in a dead man now. There ... over there, behind the curtain." And I pointed.

Someone went to look, and came back dragging the corpse by one stiff arm, flinging it before Richard. "There he is! Black Jocelyn! Dead. God rot him!"

It was a voice so full of bitterness and despair that, even in my half-numb state, I had to turn and stare. He was young, one could see that, but his face was marked and ravaged, to match his voice. He was not tall, but strongly built, the muscles knotted in his wide shoulders and bare, bloody arms. He was dark, a Latin darkness, with a round head and hair like a black sheep's wool, clipped close. It was a face to look at more than once, cleft chin, broad low forehead, a short nose, a mouth full as a girl's but with two deep lines that ran down beside it, as sharp as scars. His eyes, when he raised them to meet mine, were startling, as blue as the lupine weed.

"You have forestalled me Lady, with this carcass." And he kicked the body, so that the head bumped, sickeningly. He gave a short, harsh laugh. "But you may yet be sure I will avenge you and yours." And so saying, he drew his sword, all bloodied, reached down and wiped it on a silken rug.

"You have found the men?" asked Richard, his mouth grim.

The man's shrug was eloquent. "I have found *some* men. Does it matter? They are all filth."

"Go than, friend," said Richard, "and have your vengeance."

"Richard," I whispered, looking after the man, "who is he?"

"The captain of my routiers," said Richard shortly.

I stared at him, aghast.

"One cannot do without them," he said. "Do you think I can take a castle with a hunting bow?"

I said no more, for I remembered something. "Richard," I asked slowly, "what was it he said . . . avenge me and mine . . . ?" He did not answer; I clutched at his arm. "Richard, my mother . . . and Esmerelda . . . ?"

"Esmerelda lives," he said, and turned away. I saw his shoulders shake and heard his hoarse, angry sobs. I waited, but I think I guessed what he would say. "Blondelza, your mother . . . the Lady Castelloza found peace at the end . . . she is with God." His face was all wet with tears, but I had none.

"I can guess," I said, in a small hard voice. "That man— that Jocelyn . . . he said the routiers would draw lots."

Richard shook his head. "They did not," he said. "They . . . shared her."

I could not speak at all; a hard lump grew in my chest and rose huge in my throat, choking me. I leaned over and retched, violently, over and over, while Richard held me close. Nothing came up; I had had no food, and you cannot vomit up evil.

After a while it stopped; I was weak and shaken. "Richard," I said, willing my voice to firmness, "I want to see her . . . take me to her. *Please*." For he had begun to shake his head. "Please . . . I must."

"As you will. Come."

He led me through the shattered door, his fellows making a path for us silently, then following close behind down the stairs. My snatched-up robe was too long, and trailed, nearly tripping me; I would have fallen but for Richard's steadying arm.

Through the slit windows beside the stairwell I saw that the flames were not so close as I had thought, but black smoke hung in the air of the courtyard; Richard's men must have fired the grain stores and the stables.

He led me into the castle hall, a dark and cheerless room with damp, sweating walls. It was of the old style, with a fire pit and an opening in the roof; you hardly see them anymore. The trestle tables, too, were old-fashioned, the kind that hang upon the wall and are taken down each time for dining. Two of them were down now, and laid across rough trestle supports. Long, low, covered bundles were set upon them. From one I saw black hair trailing, and a triangle of white face; as we came near, it moaned and sighed. Esmerelda.

"She is unconscious, but not hurt fatally," said Alexander, behind us. "There are no bones broken—she is only bruised and shocked." She was bruised indeed; her face and neck were all blue with it, and blood stained her legs, as it did mine. I bent and kissed the pale cheeks; she did not stir, but her flesh was warm.

I stood before my mother's body. The face was covered. I could not move to touch the sheet, but looked, mute, at Richard. He turned it back, gently. Her face was beautiful. And young, so young. All the lines of care were smoothed out, and the skin looked transparent, like the finest wax. The little hairs of her brows and lashes were feathery penstrokes against the perfect whiteness of her face; the lids and the curve of her lips had a faint bluish tinge. She looked like a maiden asleep upon her bed.

I gestured that he should uncover her body. His face set in hard lines, but he did it. I caught my breath. Her throat was cut from ear to ear, a gaping second mouth. The blood had dried on it now, as it had dried below. Above the torn flesh of her lower parts, a rough sign was carved, the Cross, upside down, symbol of Satan. I hoped that it had been done after they killed her.

"What will be done to them . . . the men who did this?" I asked.

"Castration," said Richard harshly. "And a slow death."

It was the routier captain, Mercadier, who did it, as though he were butchering pigs. It took place in the courtyard, on a rough platform raised above the ground. Old justice had been done there, in years past. A gibbet with a rotting rope hung over their heads, and the boards beneath were dark with the stains of vanished blood. There were seven men, I recognized my abductor among them by the marks of my teeth upon his hand, for I stood close enough that their blood spattered my green robe. Alexander stood closer still, holding aloft a small cross, but only Mercadier bowed his head and muttered a Latin prayer.

I watched them die, God help me, and heard their mortal cries. It was a long business, as promised, but I did not faint till it was over.

And I did not weep until later, much later, when we buried Mother in a clearing in the forest of Poitou.

CHAPTER 8

BLONDEL DID NOT live long after we laid his Castelloza in the ground. It was not six months before he followed her; he just seemed to wither away. His hair turned white, and his face gray, and he walked like an old man; one morning I found him dead in his bed. He was buried next to Mother, and Richard raised a small stone chapel over them, and two beautiful effigies, Blondel's wearing a laurel wreath and holding a gilded lute. It is still a shrine today, for troubadours and jongleur folk honor their own kind more than the saints.

Esmerelda, once so fair, never recovered from the shock of her ravishment. She lost flesh, and became as thin and fragile as a weed, her eyes enormous in her small, sharp-boned face.

She could not face a man's eyes, even her own father's, but cowered and shrank away, hiding in her tent. Kind words could not lure her forth; she would not take food, and spent all her time upon her knees in prayer. Finally Giselda, despairing of her daughter, took her to the nuns at Saint Valerie's. She is a lay sister there, and never sees a man, except her confessor; they say she is content.

As for me, once I had begun to weep, it seemed I could not stop. I wept for my mother, and the outrage of her death; I wept for my father, Blondel; I wept for myself, who had ached through a whole long summer to lose my maidenhead, and then had it snatched away in loveless cruelty. I was not afraid of men, like Esmerelda, for I had given as good as I got; my ravisher was dead, and by my hand. I kept the little dagger polished to a deadly brightness, and honed like a razor, and wore it always, even when I sang sweet love songs.

Richard was kind, too kind. I wept harder for that. I loved him still, but knew he could no longer desire me. I remembered his face, dark with fury, and his words, spoken of Alys, his betrothed. "I will not take his leavings," he had said. And he knew what the man Jocelyn had done. It was not my fault, but I was spoiled goods to any man. And so I wept, through half a year.

One beautiful May morning I walked to my father's grave site, to see the little chapel, still abuilding. Richard was there, talking with his masons. He stared at me, and came forward, smiling. I still wore mourning white, for Blondel, and though I was sad, I knew that I was fair. I looked at him, too, but neither of us spoke. It was the first time we had been alone together for many months, and we were both shy.

Inside the clearing the masons were at work; the walls were up, and they were busy with the roof tiles. A little boy, child of one of the workmen, no more than three, squealed in delight as he played some childish game of his own. We watched him as he ran, his little round head, covered with flaxen curls, shining in the sun. There was a great slab of stone, left over from the walls perhaps, set slanting against the building. The child ran up its tilted length as far as he could go, and then jumped down, laughing. He did this over and over again, farther each time, in the way that children will, daring themselves. On his last sally, the slab shifted with his weight, for he was near the top, and slipped. It settled some inches down, and did not fall, but the child was tumbled off, and hit his head, a glancing blow, as he fell.

I rushed forward and gathered him up in my arms, crooning to him. He wailed and wailed, louder when he saw who held him, for I was a stranger. "I think he is unhurt," I said, handing him to his father. Then I fumbled in the folds of my skirt, where I kept some sugar lumps for my horse in a pocket, and popped one in his mouth. His crying stopped so suddenly and with such a look of surprise that we all laughed. I left two more with the father before we turned away.

On the wilderness path through the forest, Richard spoke, after a bit. "Your face . . ." he said. "It was full of love . . . I never thought to find you fond of children."

"And why not?" I asked sharply. "Am I not human, then?" I knew my voice was bitter, but I could not change it after I spoke. "I am a woman like any other."

Richard put out his hand and touched my arm, almost a caress, a tender touch. "You are to me the most beautiful woman in the world, Blondelza."

I turned to stare, for there was a note in his voice I had not heard for many months; something in my throat ached. All my bitterness melted away; he must have seen it leave.

"I want you, Blondelza," he said simply, as humble as a varlet.

I could not speak, but felt the warm rush of tears and the small spill of their track down my cheeks.

"You were so . . . cold," he said. "I thought you hated us all . . . all men."

"Oh, no!" I cried, softly. "Not you . . . never you!"

He gathered me into his arms. Although I had not been there often, it was as though I came home. I sobbed a little, for my breath caught. "I thought you could not want a—such a one . . . a spoiled woman." I spoke very low, but he heard me.

"A hundred men could not spoil you, my own, my love," he murmured in my ear. He was very sweet in those days.

And they were sweet days, too, the days of our youth, blindingly sweet, days without number.

I say they were sweet, yet the first time I lay in his arms, naked, I was frightened. And I would not have a candle burning either, but must have the blanketing dark, remembering that other time and the horrid sight of Jocelyn's stiff member. It hurt, too, again, with Richard, though I pretended that all was well, and that my crying was of joy.

And, after a while, there was joy in it, and some little pleasure, so that I began to understand why men so prized this thing. But I would not have a candle, not for weeks—no, nor the curtains opened to the moon either. It must have been a whole month before I saw Richard naked, and that by accident.

We had taken a picnic lunch into the woods, quite near, a little clearing by a running stream, and, when we had eaten and drunk nearly a bottle of wine, we began to take turns with the lute, making a song. I had started the melody, an elusive thing, earlier that day, but now, the wine making me giddy, I put words to it, words too intimate for any ears but ours. He smiled slyly, took the lute from me, and sang some words of his own: I blushed and hid my face. He pulled me down upon the green grass beside him, laughing and fumbling at his clothes. "Help me with these thongs, darling," he whispered.

I did, and felt the whole huge life of him spring up, familiarly, under my hands. In the dark I had learned to flame to it, welcoming. But now I looked, in a kind of eager, breathless dread, as one will sneak a look at a scorpion or a snake. My God, I thought, if this had been coming at me in Jocelyn's bed! For Jocelyn had been a small-built man, but Richard was tall, the tallest man I knew, and long of limb— and everything conformed. The thing throbbed at me like a living creature, and I snatched my hand away. My own attraction broke the tension in my body, and I began to laugh and laugh, helplessly. It began to wilt, naturally, and I laughed the harder, while Richard drew away, puzzled and hurt. I knew I could never explain, though I began to try, stammering. "So big," I gasped. "So big . . . I was surprised."

I suppose, in spite of himself, he was flattered. His face softened, the lips curving. "Not now," he muttered.

"Yes, even now," I said, and the laughter came again, harder than ever, so that he too began to laugh, and clasped me in his arms. We rolled upon the grass, pressed tight together, in a kind of convulsion, like two happy idiots, until I felt him harden against me, and my own loins got hot and hollow with it.

"Shh," he whispered hoarsely. "Don't laugh . . . this is serious business."

And afterward he said, so earnestly, "It is only a part of me, after all, darling."

"I know," I whispered. "And I love it, too."

And truly the specter that had haunted me so long had vanished, never to return. I was wild and wanton, and silly too. I gave that part of him a name, which I will never say, though I put it in our secret song. I played with it like a toy, a tireless foolish game—calling it to attention like a soldier, and weeping when it fell in battle. All lovers play such games, I suppose, in their most private moments. But we were troubadours, both, and poets, and so we had a song as well, comprised of those moments—starting that day, and added to over the years. The words no one else ever heard, and the melody was intricate and difficult, so that it was always ours alone. Sometimes, at a tedious banquet, perhaps, or listening to tiresome state speeches—or even in a moment of taut creeping fear before a battle—Richard would catch my eye, curve his lips, and hum a snatch of the melody. And I would hum it back at him, under my breath, and our hearts would lighten, instantly. It was a thing we had together, among so many other things, a part of our love, and precious.

CHAPTER 9

RICHARD TOOK CASTLE after castle, in the years that followed, as though the capture of Fouquebrun had whetted his appetite. Some he took in his father's name, some for himself; some, also, he wrested from his father's vassals, those times when he was in rebellion against him. It is a complicated history, the settling of the lands of Aquitaine, and certainly no family was ever so torn by strife. At one time, the Young King, Henry, fought bitter battles with Richard and Geoffrey; the next thing, Geoffrey had joined forces with Henry. Now and then, one or all of the sons fought alongside their father to further their feudal claims in Normandy, Maine, Anjou, and

Aquitaine. Then, one or the other might be in rebellion against King Henry. It was like some grisly game, the rules a mystery except to the Angevins.

Queen Eleanor came into it too, quite early, inciting her sons to strive mightily against their father; they even had the aid of the French king. God knows she had reasons in plenty, aside from his long string of mistresses. He was gobbling up her inheritance, fomenting revolt among her vassals when it suited him, and high-handedly giving away her properties. Disenchanted with his elder sons, he had decided that John, still then a small child, was his favorite; in order to try to marry him off to the heiress of Maurienne, he carved out great portions of lands belonging to the others and signed them over to John, to sweeten the marriage bargain. None of the brothers would stand for this, much less their mother; their differences ripened into a full-scale war.

King Henry was intrepid, swift as a pouncing hawk, and richer than his young adversaries; he threw all his resources into the conflict, hiring the greatest force of mercenaries yet seen in Christendom. Castle after castle of the Midi fell to him, and town after town; he took Tours and Limoges, and, finally, stormed Poitiers itself. We all had to run, literally, for our lives—knights, clerks, ladies, troubadours, and jongleurs.

I was living in the Queen's household then, for Richard was fighting in the Vexin. I dressed her myself for her flight, hands trembling, in my own boys' gear—we were much of a size, for she had kept her youthful figure. She was unpainted, her hair bundled up under a close-fitting cap; her cheeks were flushed with the adventure, and she laughed as she viewed her mirrored self. "I like it," she said, touching the cap. "It hides the gray at the roots."

It was almost the last word I heard from her lips, except for a hasty goodbye; I made for the Vexin and Richard, and she turned her horse toward the boundary of Chartrain on the way to Paris. Our little band reached its destination, but hers did not. She was captured by the King's routiers, somewhere in the smoking wilderness they had made, and she was brought, bound and under heavy guard, to the King. He took her, with all her train, to England; she was his prisoner for nearly sixteen years.

This was, I think, the last straw for Richard; he had never had much love for his father, but now he was set, implacable, against him. One by one, his allies died; the Young King of a fever on campaign, Geoffrey of wounds suffered in a tournament, and King Louis of France of weakness and age. In the end, it was Richard against King Henry, alone; years upon weary years of strife; endless sieges, bloody battles; crimes against humanity, and sins against God—on both sides. Until at last, the King his father died, and Richard became the King of England.

I never wanted to be a wife, as I have said, though at one time I think Richard would have married me, when, at long last, I was pregnant with his son. But I lived the life of a wife, a chatelaine, much of the time. I was often alone, Richard away on campaign, with none but servants by me, and little to do except brood. I made songs, it is true, but I seldom had anywhere to sing them. In my high estate, mistress to the Duke, it was not seemly for me to continue my jongleuresse life. I missed it sorely. I missed the troupe, the crowds, the noise and applause; I missed the wandering and the fecklessness and even the tents. Sometimes I felt that this finely dressed lady, who had the run of all the great castles of the Midi, and sat sewing a seam and waiting for her warrior-man, was not me at all, but some other person; it was as though I were playing a part, often a rather tiresome one.

I cannot remember when I discovered that Richard had other women. I thought my heart was broken, but it mended. And I stayed by him, like any faithful wife—I, who had sworn never to humble myself in marriage! Though I threatened to, I did not leave him, even when I saw a two-year-old boy who must have been his, playing in one of the churned-up battlefields.

I did not leave him until later, much later, after our little Philippe was born. He was a lovely child, the image of Blondel, and named after my small brother who slept in the graveyard at Nesle. Richard adored him, as did I, and lavished great gifts upon him, fortresses and manors, and great tracts of land. The castellany of Orange he made over to him, and, when he was two years old, he betrothed him to the baby heiress of Cognac, a rich dukedom; he would be a powerful lord.

The King of France had left an heir, born late, a youth of fifteen years, Philip Augustus, now crowned, and Richard's overlord. The two became thick as thieves, allies against King Henry. They had, both of them, a question of honor to avenge, for the stories about Alys of France turned out to be true. She had borne a child to Henry, and he sued for divorce from Eleanor, hoping to marry the girl and start all over again. But the child died, and he changed his mind, announcing that he would marry her to young John instead. Now this was Richard's betrothed bride of many years, and Philip Augustus's sister; they were alike incensed.

I never liked Philip of France; he was ugly, to my mind, with the face of a pinchpenny clerk, and treacherous. Clever he was too, and cruel, and together he and Richard did deeds of horror, maiming and killing prisoners, lopping off hands and gouging out eyes. When I heard what was done to the women of LeChaillot, after the castle was taken, and they given to the routiers, I could no longer stay with Richard.

"They were my enemies," Richard said.

"Women are not warriors," I answered, and locked my chamber door against him. He did not batter it down, as he once would have done, for we were past that first flush of love. In the night I stole away to the south, to Jacques and Giselda and the rest, with only the clothes I stood up in, and our little Philippe, with his nurse.

I was not happy, for my heart was nearly broken, but I was, in a measure, content, for I felt I had come home. Our little troupe rallied round me, loving and kind, asking no questions; after a very little while it was as though I had never left the tents and the show wagons of my childhood.

Philippe had learned to finger his lute, a tiny one made just for him, and he could sing the simpler songs in a high clear treble, when Richard stole him away; he was four years old. His nurse disappeared with him, bribed, poor ignorant slut. In his little pallet, covered with his pillow, I found a chest of precious jewels, a fat bag of gold coins, and the deed to the castle of Le Chaillot; Richard was not without a sense of irony.

I did not destroy this purchase price, for so it was, truly, though that was my first impulse. Instead, I kept it all. It made me rich, in a small way, and in later years, when the land lay quiet, I took up my residence there, in my manor of Le Chaillot; it was known as "the House of the Glee-Maiden," for by that time I was the foremost of my calling.

I was famous for other things, too. But I never lay with a man who did not please me, and I never took their gold. I was my own mistress, and the whole world knew it. There were not all that many, either; such things are always exaggerated. We welcome them, we artists, for gossip makes good business.

I knew some few men, and had affection for them, but I never loved any man but Richard, and I never bore any child, either, but his.

My Philippe thrived, for I got news of him from time to time, but I did not see him again for many years, not till he was nearly grown. And Richard . . . But that is another story.

BOOK III

THE ROUTIER CAPTAIN

Told by Mercadier of Fouquebrun, Knight

CHAPTER 1

FOUQUEBRUN WAS NOT much of a barony, but it was the only one I knew, and my home. My father had held it all his life, since he came of age, some forty years, and his father and grandfather before him, back to the first Lord of Fouquebrun, who had received it from Charlemagne. In those days the great counts of Angoulême, our liege lords, were men of honor who protected their vassals in return for homage and loyalty, not like old Guilhelm and his sons, who would as soon kick you as look at you. I spent all the years of my boyhood in the stables and halls of Angoulême, since I was old enough to be sent there for squire service and knights' training, and there was not one day of those years that I did not long for the little hills and streams of Fouquebrun, and for the warmth and love of my father's old eyes.

I was the youngest of three sons, an afterthought, as it were, born when my parents were already gray. My mother died birthing me, so I never knew her, and my brothers were off in the Holy Land, waging God's war on the infidel; all my love was given to my doting old father. When I was five, word came that my brothers had fallen in the battle of Jerusalem, and Father made over the deeds of Fouquebrun to me, so that I should have it when he died.

Father was lame, with one leg shorter than the other, so that he lurched when he walked; a horse had fallen on him long ago, in his youth, and the bone had never set properly. He was never able to teach me anything at all of knightly skills, except a few sword passes and to aim an arrow so that it hit the mark nine times out of ten. I came raw to Guilhelm's court, the worst of all the squires that year. I was clumsy serving at table too, for without knowing it I imitated Father, walking with a cripple's gait and favoring one side. I was the butt of all the jokes that year of my sixth birthday, the other boys snickering at the sight of me. The old lord and his sons took it out of my hide too; often I slept on stable straw that stuck to my back, for the bloody welts upon it.

It was a hard school, but I weathered through it, and by the time I was twelve I was as strong as most men and looking down my nose at the new boys. I could walk straight, ride tall, bend a bow handily, and wield a lance and pike with either hand. I knew how to keep my ears and eyes open and my mouth shut, duck a blow, pick a fight. I said my prayers in Latin, strummed a lute, wrote my name, pinched the kitchen wenches' bottoms. In short, you could not tell me apart from any other boy in the castle. And, too, by that time I had learned that we were all more or less homesick, though none cared to show it.

It was the habit of the old lord, Guilhelm, to send us boys home at Christ's Mass and on the great saints' days, not for compassion, but to save our keep in the feasting seasons. So at least I saw Fouquebrun and Father from time to time, briefly. We were never given time enough off to help with the harvesting, or the accounts, or other estate matters. Never time enough to ease the burdens on my ailing father's shoulders. But there was time, just, to fall in love.

There was a girl on the manor there, the daughter of our reeve, a good man and true. It was able stock she came from, and they were not varlets either; he had saved up and bought his freedom years before. His name was Garsen, and she was Garsenda, after him; he had no heirs, only little girls, and she the eldest. I noticed her first at Eastertime, late that year and the land blooming already; she was fifteen, and I a year older. She was a dark girl, as dark as I myself, with straight, slender strong limbs and eyebrows dead black and tilted up like a spread bird's wing. Not beautiful, I guess, but something about her better than beauty—a kind of pride. An odd thing to say about a girl of the people, but it was there all the same, in the line of her jaw, and the firm way her wide flat lips pressed together. She walked like a queen too, in her short homespun frock and old wooden clogs.

It was in the little clearing we called the fairy glade that I took her, my hands trembling, for I did not really know what I was about. I had done it before, a few times, with the sluts that hung around the Angoulême garrison, but then the girls had helped; it was their business, after all, and they spread their legs willingly for a string of glass beads or a knot of ribbons. Garsenda lay staring up at me, her eyes wide and a tender smile softening her strong mouth. Like an effigy on a tomb she was, delicate and cool and straight, her hands and ankles crossed. I kissed her, and she opened like a flower.

In the end I managed none too badly, though the wonder of it shook me still. I gazed down at her afterward, her pride all gone in willing submission, her frank boy's eyes hidden behind her woman's lids. There was a bruised swelling on her lip; she looked exhausted. Tenderness filled me in a bursting flood as hot as passion, and I wept. She opened her eyes and cradled my head to her breast.

We were together there, in the fairy glade, five times in all, before I went back to Angoulême. We parted with lingering kisses and loving words, vowing to be true, like people in a song, but I saw her eyes were sad. I was to be knighted in the autumn, when I would receive my patrimony. I promised to wed her then and set her up beside me in my Fouquebrun manor. She shook her head, smiling. But I meant it.

The night before I left Angoulême to go home for my father's blessing and the knight's gear that was mine by right, we were very merry, all six of us boys who were to be dubbed and get our spurs the week following, in the great tourney. I set out in the morning, somewhat the worse for wine, but happy; the others had gone their opposite ways, on the same errands, an hour before. It was nearly a day's journey on horseback to Fouquebrun; three times I had to dismount and bathe my woolly head in a brook, before I felt like myself.

It was late afternoon when I came to the three-stream crossing that marked our fief's boundaries. I smelled it then, before ever I saw anything, the acrid odor of burning and under it, a ranker smell, rotten-sweet. I spurred my poor tired beast.

I came out onto the clearing and pulled at the reins, struck dumb and sick by what I saw. A thick black pall of smoke hung over all; a little wind lifted it in shreds, raggedly, showing the devastation that it hid. The drawbridge had been hacked to pieces, and blackened wood from it floated in the water, along with the dead. There was no sound but the soft lapping of water against the stones of the moat and, far overhead, the cry of a loon, like a mockery.

My horse was not battle-hardened, and the smell of blood maddened it. I had to wrap my cloak over its head before it would step into the moat, and, even then, it reared and tossed, neighing in protest and terror. The water was low; we forded it. A dog floated past, slit from throat to hindquarters, its insides gaping empty, washed clean. The water was sluggish with bodies; I had not known the manor numbered so many souls. I recognized one, a child with long black hair, Garsenda's littlest sister, naked and already bloated. My heart, which I thought had stopped, began to thud and pound within me, painfully.

The horse struggled up the other side onto dry land, the courtyard. The stones of the manor walls were black with fire, but there were no flames left, only heaps of ash, with here and there a stick of furniture or scrap of cloth to show what had fed them. More dead lay on the cobbles, mostly naked, the blood dried and brown; it must have happened yesterday.

A sharper wind gust blew, and the smoke cloud rose high into the air; a shaft of golden sunlight shot down through it, a long path across the yard toward the far side.

I recognized it from the long white hair, fine and thin, and the twisted leg in its built-up shoe. I rode forward slowly in deep silence, urging my mount on with my knee. At the foot of the makeshift scaffold lay his favorite white boarhound, its throat cut. The body hung long and thin, stretched out, like those Christ figures you see sometimes on country roads, where the carver's eye was off, or his hand unskilled. It swung, too, a little, in the breeze, the white hair ruffling. The face was not his, or anything human; mottled purple it was and the tongue sticking out. There were raw pits where the eyes had been, and his severed hands were hung round his neck, fastened onto the rope that had strangled him. I pulled the reins gently; the horse settled, quivering all over. I slid to the ground, drew my sword, and cut my father down.

It was a long time before I moved. I had fallen right down on the ground where I had laid his body, not sobbing or retching, nor howling in madness either; I was just numb, like a thing that has been hit too hard. Or not that either; I cannot remember. I know I lay like the dead all around me.

The next I knew, and it surprised me in that silence, I heard a voice calling, very weak, a man's voice. I got to my feet, finally, and followed where it seemed to call from, inside the castle.

In the hall, lying across the great table, too heavy to overturn except by giants, a figure moved feebly; I have seen half-crushed insects like that, moving so, not quite dead.

When I came close, almost frightened, I saw it was the reeve, Garsen. His eyes were open, and he knew me. He struggled to speak, his voice gurgling in his throat. "The English king ... King Henry's men ... coming back ..." It ended in a bloody froth and a great rush of water and blood, and he was gone.

It seemed he was the only thing left alive in that charnel place; the English king's men had been savage in their slaughtering, and even goats and cows lay lifeless, with gaping wounds. I saw now, looking for it, the royal badge of England on the breasts of one or two fallen soldiers; a few on the manor, it seemed, had put up some kind of fight.

There was still that unnatural silence, the wind blowing through it like a song. I went searching for Garsenda, knowing with a kind of fateful awe what I should find. She was not in any of the chambers, not in the dairy house or the kitchens, though I saw some women, flung like bundles of old clothes, in the dark passages. When I came out from the empty, shuttered bath house, half blinded by the light, I saw her, lying on the midden among the foul waste, staring up at the sky with still, sightless eyes. She was covered to the throat with a scarlet cloak; when I came near I saw the scarlet was soaked blood. I pulled it away. Her naked body had been slit like the dog's I had seen in the moat water, and the babe that had lived there thrust into her dead stiff arms; it was tiny, greenish-gray and curled, like a frog, not human yet—but I knew it must be mine, and would have been a man-child. Something burst in my head, and I swooned, like a woman.

When I awoke, a fiend had entered me. Before I buried my own, I sought out the fallen English—there were only a scattered few—drew my sword and went among them, stabbing at them over and over, and slashing their faces to pulp; I did not stop until my arm was too weary to obey me. I never thought to plunder their armor or their arms, though I was a pauper now.

When I had shoveled the last earth over my poor dead, the shadows had lengthened into twilight, and I straightened up, my back sore and aching, and raw blisters breaking on my hands. Wearily I set about finding fodder for my horse; there was a little grain, blackened and half ash, in one of the bins, and the water in the trough, miraculously, still ran sweet. I sluiced down my face and head, and drank a mouthful from my cupped hands, leaning against the stable wall. It was then

I heard it, faint and far away, but unmistakable, the sound of the hunting horn.

I went up to the top of the tower, fear lending my feet wings, and looked down at the road that wound out of the forest. I saw them then, with the banners of England, Normandy, and Maine blowing bravely above the long file of horsemen. They were not so far away, at that, but I stayed to take a quick count before I ran down the stone stairs, snatched up the bridle, and leapt up into the saddle.

The horn was louder now, and joined by the sound of trumpets, from the east road, where I had seen them. I rode the other way, plunging into the forest, already black; I rode all through the night, pushing myself and my horse, for Angoulême.

CHAPTER 2

AND THAT WAS how I became that most accursed of God's children, a despised routier. For, after I rode the poor beast to death under me on that wild ride back to Angoulême, and crawled, half dead myself, the rest of the way, to warn my lord of the English menace, Count Guilhelm, as I knelt before him, covered with the dust of those miles, cast me off.

"Fouquebrun!" he snarled, looking down at me with his hooded snake eyes. "What care I for Fouquebrun? A miserable fief not fit for pigs! Let the English king raze it to the ground! I care not," he raved, "so long as he stays there—and away from Angoulême!"

As I stared up at him, not believing my ears, his eldest son, Vulgrin, rose from his place at table and plucked at his father's sleeve, whispering something in his ear. The old count shook his head angrily, but Vulgrin snapped his fingers at me. "You, boy. What is your name?"

Stunned by the turn of events, I answered, though my neck reddened at his peremptory manner. "Mercadier, milord."

"Mercadier!" Vulgrin laughed harshly. "What a mouthful! What kind of name is that? Oh, never mind," he said as I reared back, offended. "How many did you say there were—the Englishmen?"

I swallowed; my mouth was dry. "By my best count, milord," I croaked, "upwards of two hundred."

He whistled. "God's wounds! So many? Well, your luck's out, Mer—Whatever your name. We have not the men to come against them and still keep the castle garrisoned." He looked at me, and something like pity moved in his face. They said his marriage had softened him; the Countess Blanche was a lady of great courtesy and kindness. "I had thought to get your fief back for you." He shrugged and started to move away, then snapped his fingers, but not at me this time. "You deserve a drink anyway." And he took the goblet that a squire came running with, and watched me intently as I drank. "Have you eaten?" I shook hy head. "Get something in the kitchen as you go." And then he turned away, dismissing me.

Later, in a corner of the long, low loft over the bath house that served as barracks for us squires, I told it all to my fellows.

"Does it mean he will not knight you?" asked one. "Could even Guilhelm be so crass?"

Another, quick to anger, cried, "Curses on him for a false lord!" Guilhelm was much hated, and feared too.

"Well, will he or not?" asked the first boy.

"I know not the law of it," I said miserably. "But I have no hauberk or helm . . . no horse even . . . now." We were all silent then, for a knight without equipment is no knight at all. "Still," I said stubbornly, "he owes me my spurs."

"That he does!" cried Robert, the angry one. "If he denies you, we will deny him! We will not accept knighthood from an untrue lord!"

"Oh, no," I said. "You must not. You must not give up your own rights! Swear to me you will not think of it!"

And in the end they swore. They were lads still, and could not so set themselves against family and custom. But Robert still muttered, "If he does that . . . if Guilhelm does that!"

But he did, his cold eyes gleaming with an inner jest. On the day of the great tourney, when all the contests had been fought to a finish, and the field strewn with broken swords and the bright rags of the ladies' favors, he beckoned us, the seven new knights-to-be. We had sat through it all, though the custom was that the ceremony should take place early, so that the new knights might fight in their first melee. Robert was not the only one who wore a sulky mouth that day, from resentment at the old lord; some families had ridden many miles, and beggared themselves too, for a sight of their young sons put through the paces, and he had cheated them. When we stood up to do homage and receive our dubbings, there were low mutterings from the stands and a scattered hissing. Old Guilhelm took no notice, and bade the first of us kneel.

The dubbings went without a hitch, and, in spite of all, the new knights' faces shone with pride; the vassal's oath is solemn and full of high words, and the heart swells to hear them.

I was the last; as I knelt before him, in my shabby old leather jerkin and hose, head bowed, there came a silence, and through it I heard a buzzing from the stands. Old Guilhelm cleared his throat and spat, close to my knees. Startled, I looked up, but his eyes were lowered and his hands held out to receive mine. I placed them between his, and repeated the oath; I did not stumble on the words. Then, head bowed still, I felt a hard blow upon my shoulder. "Arise, Sir Routier!" The words rang out. For a moment all was still, then from the stands rose cries of "Shame! For shame!"

Old Guilhelm stared them down; he had his own evil dignity. "There is no other title for you, boy," he said heavily. "You are landless and a pauper now . . . and you owe me for a round dozen years of training—to say nothing of the horse you rode to its death last week. I must get some good out of you . . . some of my own back. There is a place for you in the mercenaries' camp—and another horse too, for I bear no malice." His voice was oily now with false softness. "A sword and spurs too, I give you—out of the kindness of my heart." And he pressed them into my hands. I stared at them, stunned; the sword was old and rusty, the blade nicked from many battles, and the spurs were of twisted iron, broken and black. "When you have worked them off, you will have a wage."

I found my voice then. "Sire, my fief is gone through no fault of my own, and the oath of vassalage works both ways . . . you are sworn to protect me and mine. Fouquebrun—" I choked on the words. "Fouquebrun has been ours for three hundred years, held from your ancestors . . . and my father—God rest him—" And I crossed myself. "My father—he was faithful vassal to you all his years."

"Your father!" he roared. "That muling cripple! What good have I got from him!"

My blood rang in my ears and I ran at him, beating him with the flat of the ancient sword. He was old, and went down under the blows, down on his knees, his arms upraised to save his head. I beat him to the floor before a white light burst in my head and the world turned black. I did not even know what hit me.

I woke to another blackness, thick and heavy, with flames dancing in it. I thought at first I was at Fouquebrun, and the spoilers at their work again, and heaved myself up on my elbows; my head felt as though great stones were grinding at it under the skin of the skull. Then I heard the sounds of rough voices raised, cursing, and a harp twanged, out of tune; there was a smell of roasting meat and scorched fat and, somewhere close, the sharp sour smell of wine. A figure lurched past me, dark and crooked against the firelight, and a woman dodged its groping hand, twisting and giggling.

It came to me where I was: the routier camp. And now the other smell came, the pervasive smell I recognized, a mix of old sweat and midden, horse droppings and untanned leather, unspeakably foul and choking. We always used to hold our noses when we had to cross the common that separated camp from courtyard. I started up in disgust and terror; I *could* not be here! I got to one knee, laboring, before the huge pain in my head cast me down again. I lay there, groaning; I do not know how long, I must have slept.

I woke, shuddering and shivering; I felt I was encased in a block of ice. I heard a voice in a thick accented speech, the soldiers' jargon. "Ho, whore-son, rouse up! You've took my place by the fire long enough!" I stared upward and saw a face that seemed to be set into a giant egg; narrowing my eyes, I saw it to be a perfectly hairless man, the bald head round and gleaming in the firelight, the knobby forehead bald, too, and bulging where the brows should be. He was grinning evilly, and holding a bucket high. "Do you want another dousing, then?"

He was not unkind, in his rough way; he brought me a hunk of the meat I had smelled roasting. I did not ask its origin, but wolfed it down, black on the outside and almost raw within. "The broth's a hell-brew tonight," he said. "Fat Margot made it—and it's only fit for pigs." He ducked a bone someone threw; I guessed it was that Margot, for a string of curses followed in a woman's voice, and a cackle of coarse laughter. "The same to you," he said cheerfully. "The food's good here, most of the time. We get the leavings from the lords' table. But that's gone already . . . you been out a while, Sir Blackie!"

I was to learn that routiers seldom have names—only nicknames, often obscene. Sir Blackie was the mildest of mine. Routiers know everything that goes on in the castle; how, I never found out, but I suppose there are spies in every camp in the world. They thought it a rare joke, my knighting, and my knocking old Guilhelm down won me a certain standing among these scurvy fellows. After I ate, someone passed me the wine jug. It was not wine, but something thick and sweet that went down like fire; I choked and coughed, gasping, while a roar of laughter went up all around. "You'll get used to it, Sir Blackie," said Bald Rump, for that was what he went by, he that had befriended me. "Routier rot gut, they call the stuff, for none but us can drink it and live. Made from windfall apricots it is, pits, worms, and all."

I *could* not be there, but I was, and after a time I settled in. There was nothing else to do, short of begging my bread on the roads. Like the rotgut, you get used to the life—more or less. There was always plenty to eat, same as the castle folk had in the hall, with usually something extra roasting on our fires as well; a routier will poach anywhere, and no one dares to protest. And we were warm in winter too, firewood in plenty and tents, even, if we wanted them; except, of course, when we were on the march, or standing siege, and then all fared alike, anyway, the lords and knights lying down in their cloaks under the stars along with us.

And we got fair issue, horses and arms—serviceable stuff, though it was plain and unadorned. My first day, I got a decent sword and spurs that were in working order; those Guilhelm had given me at my knighting were just his idea of a joke. We did not have mail, but wore helmets and jerkins of boiled leather, hardened stiff, and almost as good for war. I never knew an arrow to go through the stuff, and it would take a strong arm indeed to make a hole with a sword. Some of us boiled the leather strips we wore wound round for hose, too; so in a way we were better protected than the knights. And then we got our wages, too. A sou a day was the going rate, and even stingy old Guilhelm had to pay it or do without an army; routiers can always get work somewhere else.

In the beginning I had some idea of saving my wages; I figured out that, in a year, I would have enough for knight's gear, and then, God willing, I might be lucky in a tournament and win some other knight's and sell it, and so on, making my fortune, maybe. But it was no use; they smelled it out no matter where you hid it, and a month's hoard would be gone in the morning. Robert offered to hold it for me, and that worked for a while; but alas, he was killed in one of our earlier skirmishes, and I never knew where he had kept it. By then I was almost past mourning anything but my lost coin, though I said a prayer for him, silently, in my head, where no one could mock.

I thought a lot, in the soft nights, alone in the dark; dark thoughts and white-hot ones too, splintering with dreams of vengeance. That same night sky stretched above my ruined Fouquebrun, with its blackened walls and pitiful graves. And it arched, too, somewhere above my enemies, the English king and his haughty brood of sons. In the routier camp they said that Richard, still a stripling, younger than I, would be heir to all these parts, Duke of Aquitaine and Count of Poitou. I concentrated my hate on this unknown boy; my dreams were full of his death throes, each killing worse than the other. It was the food and drink I lived on, more nourishing than routier fare.

Word came to us of Archbishop Becket's murder, and the English king's part in it. My fellows would as soon laugh as cry for a saint's death, but I had been gently bred and some shreds of honor still clung to me; I named the new saint in my silent, secret prayers.

Word came, too, of nearer interest, turning a knife in my heart. My Fouquebrun had been given to a Norman knight, name of Jocelyn, that King Henry owed a favor to. It was said that Jocelyn had sold his young sister to the King; the price: Fouquebrun. There was even a song about it, like that song of the Fair Rosamund. And now Jocelyn had taken up his residence there, in my old home, camping in its ruins, his own band of routiers trampling the earth where my dear dead lay.

I saw him once, from a distance, that Jocelyn. Three or four of us had been out foraging in the countryside—we had got a deer and two of his does, I remembered—and, from a little knoll, we saw him on the path below, riding at the head of his soldiers. He had his helm in his hand, at ease, and I saw him plain, a long lizard face with hungry eyes. I could have picked him off with my crossbow, but I had not time to wind it, and anyway, we were too few. I cursed myself for a dolt, and spat at his retreating back like the routier I had become. But now I had a face to hate, not just a name; he took his place beside the formless Angevin wraiths, and between them they filled my vengeful dreams.

CHAPTER 3

TWO YEARS PASSED, years like the long hopeless days of Hell. I killed and looted, burned fields and villages, guzzled and swilled like the rest. We burned the cornfields close to the town of Poitiers, on Count Guilhelm's orders. It was all his rebellion was good for; he did not run to deeds of bravery, like storming my Fouquebrun and gaining his vassal land back. Once, on a foray, some of our band ambushed Richard; he was not crowned yet, but he did them all in. I knew him a worthy enemy and gnashed my teeth that I had not had my chance at him.

He was crowned at Limoges. Some of us rode there, on the chance, I among them, but we could not get near enough to see him even, on the road there or coming back; he was guarded well, with all the force of Poitiers. It was not until he rode out in the shadowed twilight one evening that we caught him unawares, with only a paltry following.

We took them from behind, and we outnumbered them too, but the duke Richard fought like ten wildcats. With my own eyes I saw him slay three of us, without drawing his sword; his spear was bloodied to the hilt and he tossed it into the bushes before he wheeled his horse to face mine, raising his axe. He was laughing like a boy and shaking the hair out of his eyes; he wore no helmet and his long hair was tawny-red, like a lion's mane.

The sound of his laughter maddened me, and I rushed him hard. He took my lance point on his shield; it stopped me like the death stance of a wild boar. My horse reared high in the air and I fell backward over its rump, losing the lance. I took no hurt, for my hate protected me like a magic curtain; I scrambled to my feet. He had sprung down too, and stood waiting till I drew my sword.

His courtesy humbled me and my fingers would not work; I could not free the sword from its scabbard. I stood there, helpless and hating, fumbling at my belt. "Draw, man!" he cried.

I could swear his voice held joy. I got the sword out finally, and ran at him; he parried my thrust easily. But I put my foot out to trip him, and he stumbled, though he did not lose his footing. It was just enough; his guard was down. I raised the heavy sword to smash like a cleaver through his skull. Then, in the last instant, I saw his face, the features fine and straight, like an image's in a church, the teeth white in a brilliant bold smile. But there was more too—I saw his eyes and he saw mine, and something flashed between, something like knowledge, or fate, or love, perhaps. And my arm of its own will swayed to the right and weakened. My sword took him in the neck, above his mail, and I saw the bright blood well out. At the same instant I felt a searing pain in my left thigh, and my leg went out from under me.

I lay on my back, staring up at him; I had not known he was so very tall. His sword dripped blood, my own, and it ran down to meet that other blood that pulsed now in a jet from his neck wound. The pain made me light headed, and I whispered, "Brother . . ." He bent to catch my words, but shook his head. I opened my mouth again, still staring at him, but no words came out. In the hush that seemed to hold us there, halfway between light and dark, I heard a voice behind me, a pleasant voice and soft. "Shall I finish him, Dickon?"

Richard made a waving gesture with his sword, scattering beads of blood. "No," he said. "Let be. He fought well, and . . . there was something . . . I know not. I would have words with him, if he lives. Bring him to the castle keep." He turned to someone who came running up. "But gently. Make a litter. He is sore wounded. Tend him and bind the wound. I would have him healed."

I know not if they were his last words then, but I heard no more. The pain and the blackness overcame me, and I awoke to the light of morning, thin and cool, falling aslant between the bars of a donjon keep onto the pallet of straw where I lay.

"Well, Sir Blackie," I heard. "You are silent this morning, for a change." The Duke Richard sat beside me on a small three-legged stool. I knew him by his hair, lit to autumn fire by the light that fell upon it. His face was in shadow and dark; I could not read it.

"You!" I said. There was no pain in my head now, but my thoughts were in a whirl.

"Yes," he said, and now I saw his teeth flash white. "It is I, Richard of Poitou." He moved a little, and I saw a bandage at his throat, where the shirt fell open. "You had good nursing, my own foster mother, but not as good as my own . . . you have been raving in fever for three days now. It was 'Fouquebrun . . . Fouquebrun,' over and over it was 'Fouquebrun'—and a girl's name I could not catch. Garance?"

"Garsenda," I said. "But she is dead." I felt a slow tear run down from the corner of my eye, to trickle past my ear onto the straw. I tried to raise my hand to dash it away, but I was weak as a babe and could only turn my head aside. I muttered, low, "I wanted to kill you."

"Yes, I know," said the Duke Richard. "Why?"

I shook my head. I was too weak to answer, and besides, the hate was gone.

"You wear the badge of Angoulême," he said. "Did Count Guilhelm send you?"

"No . . . not to kill. No."

"Was it Sir Jocelyn? Are you in his pay?"

I shook my head then so violently that I heard my teeth rattle. "No! God save me, never! No!"

"So much talk of Fouquebrun . . ." he said wonderingly. And then, bending near, asked very gently, "Will you not tell me?"

"It was—I cannot—it was so . . . I hated you and yours . . . My Fouquebrun, you took it . . . it was mine. My fief, and my home . . . and so I have nothing now . . . and you took it."

He shook his head, and now I saw his face plain; it was very grave, and his eyes steady. "Not I," he said. "You are mistaken."

"King Henry," I said. "His men, so many . . . they burned and slew . . . all dead—all." My tongue would not work well, and the words halted. "All dead, the dogs even . . . and floating in the moat . . . And my father . . . his hands, they . . . And her . . . oh, her they were not content to— Oh, God!

Oh, Jesus!" I tried to rise, to look him in the eye, to make him understand. "And so, you see . . . I hated you."

"Listen to me, Sir Warrior," he said, still grave and gentle and his voice low. "It was not my work. I am not my father . . . I am not the King." A harsh note crept into his voice. "But I am Duke now in these parts, my mother's heritage . . . and if he has laid my lands waste he will pay for it!" I saw a small knot of muscle throbbing above his neck wound. "I swear it—he will pay! I will not take his sins upon me!"

"But he must take mine!" I burst out. "It is his fault that I am routier filth . . . and have done deeds of horror, routier deeds. When old Count Guilhelm knighted me with a broken sword and laughed, God rot him—" And then it all poured out, the ruin of my heritage, my landless state, Guilhelm's falseness and cowardice, my loved ones lost forever. I had not told anyone of Garsenda's fate, but now I told Richard; it was as though I spoke it to myself. When I was finished, the whole tale told, Richard sat silent, chin upon his hands, looking into space.

"A heavy tale," he said, finally. "And heavy sins . . . yours and mine."

"Not yours, Sire," I said. "It was your father that I named."

Richard smiled, a bare lifting of his lips. "It was a futile cry—that of mine against my father," he said, sighing. "For I know it well—all his sins are mine . . . and all those sinned against, my own oppressed."

He held out his hand; I kissed it. All at once I had fallen back into the old ways of knightly courtesy, my routier past vanished.

And so I became the duke Richard's man. When my wound healed, he offered me the post of captain of his own routier band. The salary was triple what I had had from Angoulême, with all new gear as well, a good horse, helm, and chain mail. Then he went about gaining a mercenary force, taking some from his own Aquitaine, some from his brother Geoffrey's Breton province, and even some from as far as England.

He paid better than anyone else, so he had no trouble getting good men; many of them were impoverished younger sons, or those fallen upon hard days, like me, and there were some as well who had fought in the Holy Land, old seasoned warriors. He did not mind if they lacked an eye, or a finger or two, so long as their sword hands were still intact. That way he got a clean camp, and one with discipline in it, for he meant to root out the trouble spots in his domain and force the rebel barons to own him as lord. I never knew a man of his who did not love him, even those who had long lived without a heart. Something moved there, within those hollow chests, when Richard rode before us, straight and tall and laughing, with always a word or a jest over his shoulder that a man could take to himself and remember.

For one thing, he never forgot a name, or a nickname, and could always put the right one to the right fellow. And he would turn his hand to anything, a broken saddle girth, or a lamed horse, or the felling of a tree that grew in our path. He was just, too, and open-handed with the folks that were lowly and dependent on him, though I have seen him haggle over a brass farthing with one of the great nobles.

CHAPTER 4

WHEN WE STORMED Fouquebrun, and took it, for the sake of that glee-maiden Sir Jocelyn had captured, Richard gave it back to me. "It is mine now," he said, "and you will hold from me ... it was never in my father's gift. Take it freely, with the vassal's oath." Seisin was always a white rose, and we found one, sprung up, as it were, overnight, from the earth we had piled over the rapists we had punished. It seemed right, somehow, that it should be so, a kind of hope ... but I could not voice it. Richard did, sometime later, make a song about it: "Oh, fragile flower, stronger than the mold of death and decay ... Sweet Mary's favor, rising pure from the flesh corrupt ..." I have forgot the rest; it was never very popular.

That was a good wench, Blondelza, and brave; though I ought not to call her that, seeing she was a noblewoman. But it was not to demean her that I thought of her so; she reminded me of Garsenda. I can't say why, because this one was beautiful; even with her lips all bitten, and white to the gills, with her hair in long squiggles, she was beautiful. But it was something in the way they walked, both of them, and the fearless gaze they had. I won't forget, ever, Richard's Blondelza, when we broke down that chamber door, her back to the wall and that old sword raised up in both hands. Or her face when I dragged out black Jocelyn, dead as a doornail, with her little knife skewering his throat, like a stuck pig. I saw her face, too, still as stone, but the eyes alive with hate, when I castrated the men who had ravished and slain her mother. I would not like to face that one in battle!

I got to know her later, and I never saw that look again. She was a generous and loyal lady, filled with a fire inside that made her shine; maybe it was what they call genius. I don't know much about music or poetry; I think it was just something in her nature. Richard had it too; they were a good match.

When she left him, he changed. Or at least I saw it then; I guess he had been changing all along. Not that he ever became very much like other men, ordinary men; he was always himself, and made of finer stuff. But when I first came to know him, I thought of him as one of those knights that sat around the Round Table with King Arthur, sort of misty and vague, in spite of his prowess at arms. And, although he could swear with the worst of us, I heard his words as poetry, almost; it's hard for me to express it, I never had much learning.

Maybe it was just that he grew up; he'd always had a way of making you forget how young he was, only sixteen when I first met him. Or maybe it was the endless fighting, brother against brother, father against sons. Anyway, all of a sudden I saw it; he had hardened, somehow. And I, who had been like an unfeeling stone to begin with—I had softened. Oh, I still did his dirty work; he was my overlord, and besides, I loved him well. But I took no joy in the maiming and the killing; I turned my mind off, as it were, like shutting your eyes.

In those years of fighting in the Midi, Richard won the name of best knight in the world—and it was no more than the truth. Not that he was always successful, no more than any other man—but if he didn't take a castle the first siege, then he'd get it later, a month later, perhaps, or a year; you see, he'd have ways of studying about it, and about the problems, and figuring out what the weak points were, and so on, just like mathematics. Sometimes he wouldn't sleep at all, puzzling over it, but you could see he liked it, just as much as the actual storming of the walls. That was what made him different; he could be cold, as well as hot. He had the name of Lionheart—and he deserved it, too—but his head was more important. And I don't know of any animal you could name that after.

We took so many castles I lost count, but, with the little unimportant ones, it must have been upward of a hundred, over the years. After a while they were all alike, and only one stuck in my memory, Taillebourg, which had been called impregnable.

Taillebourg was the important one in the eyes of the world; after he captured it, no one ever doubted Richard. It happened during the period when he had made it up with his father for a while; I think he hoped to get on the good side of King Henry, so that he'd release his mother, Queen Eleanor, from prison. But I guess King Henry didn't have a good side, at least where that lady was concerned, because it never happened.

It was May, 1179, and we had just taken the castles of Richemont, Genzac, Marcillac, Grouville, and Andeville; I can't recall a thing about any of them, it all took place within three weeks, like a hurricane running wild. So, on the tide of fortune, you might say, Richard moved on to Taillebourg.

I'll not forget the first sight of it, perched on an outcrop of light-colored rock, right under the sky, it seemed. From where we rode, winding below, it looked like a huge evil bird of prey, hunched and brooding. There was sheer rock face on three sides; on the fourth, where there was some kind of slope, though steep, you could see the fortifications sticking up against the sky, the wicked points cut jaggedly into the stone of the roof, and the long snouts of the Greek-fire engines, too many to count. And, from our distance, the spears of the soldiers were like pins in a giant pincushion; there wasn't a smooth place on the whole side of Taillebourg.

At the foot of the rock we could see a small town, nestled in behind its own walls, with green fields raying out from it, and vineyards climbing the foothills beyond. Richard sent a third of his party to burn and ravage these holdings, while he, with the main force, concentrated on that poor little town. It didn't take much time to reduce it to rubble; all the defenders were up there in the citadel feeling safe, with only a few unarmed villagers, old men and women mostly, and little children, left below. Richard gave orders not to hurt those people, but even so, some of them died. They went a little crazy, you see, smelling the smoke and seeing everything they owned smashed up, and ran every which way, under our horses' hooves, and into each other, even; there was nothing we could do except save the ones we could and rope them together for safety under a big tent. We pitched our camp there, right up against the castle walls, in the ruins of the town, and waited.

Now, there's nothing people hate more than seeing their property destroyed, and they had a good view from up there. If they hadn't been so greedy they would be there still, because it was true what they said about Taillebourg; it was the strongest castle in Europe, with walls three feet thick, at least. The walls slanted outward, too, so that you couldn't scale them. But Richard had that figured out; we camped so close that, no matter what they threw down, the walls' slope protected us. All night they hurled down fire and boiling oil, but it only went over our heads and made the town worse. Richard had given orders that our tent roofs should be watered, so a spark or a splash didn't have any effect either; we could hear it sizzle once in a while, that's all.

And all the time Richard was playing something over on his lute, and laughing to himself. Those of us who were near enough grinned as we listened; we knew it was some kind of dirty song. When he had it just right, he taught us the words, and spread it all over the camp. Toward morning we began to roar it out, some two thousand of us; there was no way they couldn't hear. And after a bit they made out the words, and we could hear them up there cursing us.

It wasn't all that dirty, even, just rude and insulting. But these little nobles are all alike, touchy as the Devil, and Richard knew it. I wish I could remember the song, but most of the words went out of my head, and I only recall the gist of it. Something about "The men of Taillebourg are born with tails. Lift them and . . ." And then it went on about what you could find and what you could put there, and so on. It was an English pun, but most soldiers seem to know a few English words, the dirty ones. In those days "tail" was just about the worst thing you could say, because of the Devil having one, I guess. It got overused later, in the Crusade, and now it doesn't mean much and even girls say it—but it was like tinder that night, and the whole garrison went up like flame.

Sure enough, the great gates opened and out came a troop of knights, all mad as bees and buzzing with it. Richard hissed quick orders, and a steady stream of us sneaked in through the gates, while the rest engaged those defenders in hand-to-hand combat. You can guess what happened. Once we were inside, that was the end. They made a few passes, half-heartedly, and then surrendered. It was like taking marchpane away from a child.

The best thing about it, to my mind, was that, once he heard about the fall of Taillebourg, Count Guilhelm came to Richard and surrendered Angoulême. Richard razed the whole place to the ground, filthy routier camp and all. So I got my revenge, at last. Old Guilhelm, almost beggared, and sick at the sight of his ruined stronghold, went on pilgrimage to Jerusalem, and at Messina he died. I almost missed having him to hate.

CHAPTER 5

I NEVER GOT to know Richard's brothers; they couldn't forget I had been a lowly routier, and always looked through me as though I wasn't there. From time to time, though, they were our allies, so I saw a good deal of them, and formed my own opinions.

The eldest, that was called the Young King Henry—well, he was a catamite, I guess, though it wasn't talked about much. Some of the common soldiers muttered or snickered when he appeared all tricked out, but I docked their pay, and they soon stopped it; after all, he was the heir, and somebody high above them. And he wasn't hurting anybody that I could see, except himself, and maybe his little wife, Marguerite. And maybe she didn't know; you have to be pretty wise to catch on to such things, because most of the high nobles dressed the same way, more or less. Even Richard could get himself up like a whore, in pink or mauve and with red paste on his lips; it was the fashion. Except I never saw a woman so tall or so broad; on him it looked all right, just fancy dress, like a jongleur.

But the Young King had a languid manner and a limp wrist, and he giggled like a girl when he was full of wine. Once he put his hand between my legs; it was one time he forgot I was a routier, I guess. I don't know what I would have done if Richard hadn't made a joke out of it, mincing around and screeching, "Stop that—he's mine you naughty boy!" Well, they all laughed, and the whole thing passed over; it was in the Young King's tent, and there wasn't anyone there except others just like him, or pretending to be. He was always giving parties; very generous he was, and wanting to be liked.

There was a lot of praise for him after he died, songs and such, and people went on as though he had been something wonderful. But I didn't think he was much, ever. He was handsome enough; it was a good-looking family. But he was low of stature, with bowlegs, and his face was spoiled by those white eyebrows and lashes; they gave him a rabbity look. I would have thought, with all the paint he wore, he would have darkened them, but he just put red on his lips and cheeks, which made his hair look wrong and carroty. They called him a great knight, but as far as I could see, he only fought in tournaments, for show; in battle, he sat his horse on the skirts of the action, and watched. Of course, he died young; it was hard to tell how he would have turned out.

Geoffrey died young too; a horse threw him and he broke his neck. He had a name for being sly and treacherous, but I don't know. It was true he always smiled and smiled, and seemed to be on everyone's side at once; what my old father used to call a "fence-sitter." And then it was whispered that he betrayed his mother, and guided her right into King Henry's hands. All I know is that he was the only one of her whole escort that escaped; he turned up later in Richard's camp, with some tale that he'd been sent out to scout ahead. Which wasn't likely, as he'd never be sent alone, a royal duke as he was. But then no one knows anything for sure. And I guess Richard believed him; he always loved both his younger brothers well, though he didn't get along with the Young King.

John—well, he was still a boy when I first saw him at Chinon. A small boy, really, for he was slightly built, with that thin, vulnerable-looking neck, hollowed at the nape, that you only find on children; he might have been about twelve.

He didn't resemble his brothers, who were all ruddy of color with light eyes, clear as the sea. John's hair and eyes were dark, and his skin had that look of cream, thick and shining. He had the face of a girl, full-lipped, large-eyed, in a pure oval; I realized suddenly it was his mother he looked like. Except that that startling beauty looked out of place on a boy. He was graceful, too, like a girl, with soft, boneless movement and long slender hands that were always moving as he talked. His only flaw, to look at, was his teeth; they were white and even, but too small, mouse teeth, I thought, and he showed his gums when he smiled.

John looked a likely candidate, with his girlishness, to step into his oldest brother's shoes when he was grown. Except that you knew he wouldn't. Even at twelve, he positively licked his lips at a pretty bosom, and he could not keep his hands off girls, even his own sisters. But for that, he was remarkably likable, witty and clever, able to make everyone laugh. He had been brought up till then in a convent; how he got so worldly all of a sudden I couldn't see; of course the nuns had spoiled him, everyone did. There wasn't a true or loyal bone in his body, and he made a joke out of everything, even the Sacrament. But no one seemed to mind; John was the kind that could twist you round his finger. Richard used to say, laughing, "Never mind. John has charm. God gave it to him, so He must love him, no matter what he does." I wondered if it wasn't the Devil instead.

I guess it seems odd that I, who was so low on the knightly scale and nobody, really, should have been as close as I was to Richard. But that's the way he was, if he took a fancy to you. That foster brother of his, Alexander—why, they were as close as two peas in a pod, even though it looked like they had nothing in common. And then there was that little gnome, Will Longchamps; they said that Queen Eleanor had *bought* him as a child, though I can hardly credit that, in this day and age. He was nothing to look at, one shoulder higher than the other, and almost hunchbacked, but he had a canny brain; he used to do all Queen Eleanor's accounts. But both he and Alexander had been with the Queen when she was captured, and Blondelza, who had been more than a wife, had run away, so Richard had to make do with someone like me. I think, except for a few jongleurs that he made music with, I was the only one he liked for company; certainly he never confided in his brothers. And you couldn't blame him, they were a self-serving brood.

It was a long time—years—before we learned whether Alexander and Will Longchamps were alive or dead; they weren't important enough to be included in our spies' reports. But finally, one day, Richard got a letter from Alexander. In Latin it was, to ensure that it wouldn't be read by the wrong people; Richard had to pore over it awhile—with all the fighting and so forth he had gotten rusty at his learning. But after a time he looked up with a smile and said, "He's safe, God be praised, and poor little Will too. They're both with the Augustinian monks at Gloucester Abbey—though he doesn't say how they came to be there, or if they're ordained or just lay clergy . . . Mother is safe at Salisbury, and well," he said, reading on. "But of course we knew that. He sends his love to Blondelza." He looked up, his mouth twisting bitterly. "So he doesn't know," he said heavily. "I had been fearing they were together."

I must have looked surprised; one cannot always govern one's face.

He nodded glumly. "Oh, yes . . . he knew her first. They were friends—long before I even spoke to her. I always suspected . . . more."

I was aghast. "But Alexander cared nothing for girls . . . and he wanted only to serve God."

"Have you ever known that to stop the clergy?" he asked, still bitter-mouthed. "Besides, Blondelza is not *girls*, she is . . . Blondelza."

It was not long after that that he ordered me to steal away his little son. He must have been brooding about it. I did it; it was as easy as snatching a pie that was cooling on the windowsill; the boy's nurse was goggle-eyed over soldiers, like most of her kind.

I did it, all right, but I counted it a sin—*his* sin this time— that I had to take on my shoulders. The child—his name was Philippe—was too little to take away from his mother, or so I thought. True, he cried all the first night, but after that he never even spoke his mother's name, he came to adore his father so. And that, I thought, was even worse.

Of course, Richard couldn't keep him with him long, on campaign as he was. It was dangerous for the boy—and then he came to be a nuisance, in a way, hanging about his father like a little dog. Richard loved him, but you could see how impatient he got; with all his greatness. Richard was no saint. The upshot of it was that Richard got rid of him, more or less. He had betrothed him to the heiress of Cognac when he was a baby, and when he laid siege to the castle there and won it, he made a bargain with the lord, Hélie. Richard would leave the castle and all its lands standing if Hélie would bring up his son like his own. So that's the way it was—the little boy growing up with his in-laws and his bride, and never even knowing his own mother.

Richard had women, a lot of women, during the years after Blondelza. None of them ever lasted more than a week, if that—even the noblest ladies. But it sometimes looked as though all he had to do was raise his eyebrows and they'd come running, married women or maidens, and the husbands or fathers behind them shoving them into his arms. It made me sick—but then I wasn't used to this courtly love game that all the high nobles played; I guess I was too simple. And it wasn't the way they pretended in all the songs—all spiritual and the knight never touching the lady because their love was too pure. Far from it. Richard was at home in every bed-chamber in the Midi, it seemed to me, at one time or another. But I think the whole thing bored him; he liked best of all the making of songs. Even so, the ones he used to make with Blondelza were better. He knew it too; I'd hear him playing them over and over, I knew just enough music to recognize them.

It must have been about the time of the Young King's death, or perhaps a bit after, that Richard first met the Navarrese princess Berengaria. Her brother Sancho was one of the first princes to come running to get behind Richard's banner; a hothead, crazy for fighting and tournaments, and just the age to fall under the Lionheart's spell, eighteen maybe. His sister was older, a good deal past the age when noble girls get married; I figured her to be twenty-one or so, because there was a sister in between and she the oldest. She didn't look it. She was small-built and dainty, and had one of those smooth, big-eyed faces shaped like a heart, a childish look. Pale cheeks, brown hair, a shy smile; butter wouldn't melt in her mouth.

Not the type to attract Richard, you'd think, but she did. Or maybe it was just that she was about the only eligible princess around, though Navarre was a little kingdom, hardly on the map. And now, you see, Richard was heir to England, and after Geoffrey's death, heir as well to all the Angevin possessions. And kings are supposed to get heirs themselves, legitimate ones, and if he wasn't going to marry the French princess Alys, he had to look around for another bride. That's how I figure it, but there was more to it than just that. For one thing, though Sancho had mentioned his sister (the other was in a convent) and he'd seen a picture of Berengaria, it wasn't until he'd actually seen her in person and talked to her that he began to think about marrying her.

We had been fighting there, near the border, and Navarre was the next kingdom over, as you might say; it was logical that after our victory Sancho should offer his father's hospitality. So there was a big festival in Pamplona, the royal seat, to celebrate, with a week of tournaments. Now Richard wasn't one for tournaments anymore, hadn't been since his early days; when you've had the real thing, this play-war seems very tame. But he accepted, an odd thing in itself. So, looking back on it, he must have wanted to see this princess for himself.

I didn't take part at all; I had a little wound, not much of a thing, but it festered, and made me feverish, so I was in my tent most of the time. But Richard won all the events he took part in, as he always did; it was only natural, with all his experience, and then he had the strongest arm and the longest reach. He was enough to turn any girl's head, just to watch, and little Berengaria was no exception, especially when he composed a verse in her honor as well.

Anyhow, riding back toward Poitou afterward—I was well enough to sit a horse by then—Richard said, "Well, Mercadier, what do you think of her?"

There was no use pretending I didn't know who he meant; the whole army had talked of nothing else for a week. "Pretty girl," I said. He didn't say anything, and seemed to be waiting for something more, so I said, "Very pretty girl."

"Is that all?" he asked, impatient. "Don't you think she looks like Queen Marguerite?"

I couldn't think who he meant for a minute, then I realized it was the Young King's little widow. Neither one of them was what you might call noticeable—so I had to think a bit, and try to remember the two faces. It was true, in a way;

they were both small and dark, with those wide-at-the-top cheeks. "Why, yes, Sire. You're right," I said.

He looked pleased, though I can't understand why he would care what I thought. "Yes," he said, in a musing sort of way. "Yes, she might do."

CHAPTER 6

BELLS. BELLS. EVERYWHERE the sound of bells, deep and low, like something ancient and wounded under the earth, mourning. From every great cathedral and every tiny parish church on the banks of the Loire they rang without ceasing, dark notes that tolled the fall of Jerusalem.

At every hamlet folk gathered, weeping, as roadside preachers proclaimed the tragedy and the danger to Christendom. Thundering voices exhorted service, commanding all pious men to go to the aid of the Kingdom of Outremer and the Holy Sepulchre. At the larger towns the artist monks held up huge pictures painted on cloth. In one, the Lord Jesus staggers, bearing his Cross, while a scowling black-visaged Arab strikes him; the blood on the Christ's face was wondrously red and lifelike. The monks cried to the crowds, "This is Our Lord, struck by Mahomet, the prophet of the Muslims, who has wounded him and killed him." So ignorant were the folk that they believed it; they had never heard of Calvary, except in the Latin Mass, which they could not understand. Many pulled out their hair by the handful and rent their poor garments, vowing vengeance on the infidel. But they were not encouraged, except to give of their few pence. The poor were not wanted this time—no pilgrims, no women, no children; this was to be a full-scale war fought by armed soldiers and commanded by belted knights. The mistakes of the Second Crusade were not to be repeated; this time the Christian world would see victory!

The shouting and the bells and the loud weeping followed us from city to town to village, seemingly borne by the river itself. At Tours, where we made camp for the night, the din was so great that it seemed the very walls of the city shook with it. Here the preachers were most bold, even venturing into our campsite and exhorting the routiers; the foulest words did not deter them. Jongleurs performed in the marketplace, their faces and hands dyed brown and turbans crowning their heads, miming the filthy deeds of the infidel and singing scurrilous songs. Here we saw the most popular picture of all, copies of which were being shown in Paris and London. Jerusalem was painted in all its glory, minarets and towers rising into a sulphurous yellow sky, the first scene. It was more than a hundred yards long, the cloth of the painting, held up by twenty acolytes from the cathedral. Then, further along, was the battle depicting the fall of the city, wondrously dreadful to see, with the Outremer knights and the Saracens clashing, and men and horses dying in their blood. Then there was the last scene, showing the Church of the Resurrection with the tomb of Our Lord. Above the tomb there was a horse, and mounted on it was a Saracen knight, who was trampling the tomb, over which his horse was urinating. At the sight of it, folk fell into the dust, groaning and crying, "Oh, the shame!"

The news of the disaster had come to us a week earlier, in Clairvaux, where the abbot himself, Bernard, whom men were already calling a saint, had taken to his bed with grief. It had happened in July, and now it was already October, so far away was the Holy Land, and the travel so hazardous. But the events were detailed, and could not have been in error. This is the gist of the sad story:

A powerful Muslim force was besieging the city of Tiberias, and Guy of Lusignan, the King of Jerusalem, left his camp in Galilee with all his Christian forces to march to the aid of Tiberias. He never reached it. Marching in the fiercest heat of summer and harassed continually by Muslim mounted archers, Guy's army was obliged to halt at Hattin, a region wholly desert, without even a watering place. The Christian soldiers spent a thirsty and sleepless night, their eyes smarting from smoke as the enemy built scrub fires around them. In the morning they joined battle, but it was hopeless; they were completely surrounded. They fought bravely, for they were inspired by the Holy Cross, which they carried with them, and led by the most famous fighting men in the West, the Knights Templar and the Knights Hospitaler. By the middle of the morning the entire army was annihilated, Guy of Lusignan and the Holy Cross were captured, and the Templars and Hospitalers executed. The Kingdom of Jerusalem lay helpless as the Muslim army marched through the gates.

Guy of Lusignan had been beaten by a greater man. The Muslim leader was Al-Malik al-Nasit Salah ed-Din Yusuf; we called him, for short, Saladin. It was a name I was later to know as well as my own, a name to hear every waking moment and every dreaming hour for a whole long, glorious, wretched year. For in Tours that autumn, in the Year of Our Lord 1187, Richard took the cross, and I with him.

A huge host of knights and foot soldiers stood before the new cathedral, half-finished, its raw stone blinding white in the midday sun, the scaffolding, empty of workmen, stretching like a thin web across its face. On a hastily improvised platform, high above us, stood the saintly abbot Bernard of Clairvaux, his face as thin and shining as a bleached bone, still marked with the fever and exhaustion of his sickbed. His voice, high and weak, cracking with strain, strengthened as he spoke on. The quiet of the crowd was hushed and breathless; you could almost hear its heart beat. The abbot's eyes were like lamps, brighter and more piercing than the sun's rays. He swayed perilously upon the wooden platform, as though the wind might blow him over; a soft gasp, fearful, went up from the host. The abbot held up his hand, his thin voice swelling with power.

"O mighty soldier, O man of war, at last you have a cause for which you can fight without endangering your soul . . . a cause in which to win is glorious, and for which to die is but to gain. Are you a shrewd business man, quick to see the profits of this world? If you are, I can offer you a bargain which you cannot afford to miss. Take the sign of the cross. At once you will have indulgence for all the sins which you confess with a contrite heart. The cross is cheap—and if you wear it with humility you will find that you have obtained the Kingdom of Heaven."

Richard walked forward to the foot of the platform and fell to his knees before the abbot Bernard. Through a mist of tears I followed him. Behind us was a great quiet rustle, a creaking of armor, a giant sighing. Then upon the still air rose a ragged cheer, "God wills it!" From every corner it came then, tentative, then louder, finally swelling into the great battle cry of the Third Crusade. "God wills it!"

CHAPTER 7

RICHARD WAS THE first among the great nobles of the West to take the cross, but it was not long before most of the others did too. Word of the fall of Jerusalem had spread through Europe; the monks and pilgrims carried it, and the jongleurs too. The churches were filled to bursting, and everybody wore hair shirts and relics of the saints; the merchants did a big business. Some folk gave all their money to the poor, and some joined monasteries. Poor knights pledged everything they owned, all their land, to buy hauberks and arms so that they could go on Crusade. The Army of God, as they called it, was forming up quick.

King Henry and King Philip of France joined too, taking the cross together, and the Pope declared a Truce of God. I don't know how sincere these kings were; I know Richard was. But nobody was really sincere about the truce. Because no sooner was it declared than it was broken, and England and France were at war again. Philip took the castle of Châteauroux, an Angevin stronghold, and then Henry marched into the French country and ravaged the royal city of Nantes and burned all the fields around it. They had a couple of peace meetings after these attacks, because the Pope ordered it, but they couldn't come to terms.

Then Philip sent a message to Richard, saying that King Henry had offered to marry Alys to John, and to disinherit Richard entirely. Maybe it was true, maybe not; I never did trust Philip. But Richard must have put some stock in it, because he went red in the face and shut himself up in his tent alone. The next morning he pushed us to get ready to march (we were in Limoges then), and we caught up with Philip just outside Châtillon. Philip must have given him some pretty bad details, because this time Richard turned white, not red, and just didn't speak. It seems nothing had been resolved between England and France, and there was another meeting scheduled in two weeks, at Bonmoulins, in Normandy. Now this place was within Richard's inherited lands, so he decided to go too, still white and icy calm.

This time I was up pretty close and saw and heard everything. I was shocked when I saw King Henry; he looked so old and gray, and he limped from an old leg injury that had turned into rheumatism with the fall weather. He seemed shrunken, a smaller man than I remembered, and his face looked really ill. You could see he was surprised to see Richard, but he only said, very mildly, "Where do you come from, Richard?"

"Beau Sire," said Richard, just as mild, "I happened to fall in with the King of France upon the road. It seemed too pointed, since I was so near, to avoid him. It is in the interests of peace to treat him with courtesy."

"Very well," said King Henry, "but be careful that it so turns out."

Well, I guess that Richard and Philip had agreed upon his approach, to test King Henry once and for all. Because Philip renewed his demands that Alys should be given in marriage to Richard, as promised long ago at the betrothal.

"For," said Philip, "I cannot countenance my sister's marriage with John, who, after all, is still nearly as landless as he was when he earned the nickname of John Lackland." That was supposed to be witty, but only Philip himself smiled. "She must marry Richard, the heir to England, Normandy, and Poitou, and all her husband's estates must be restored to him and the succession assured."

King Henry looked sicker than ever, and didn't speak for a long time. Finally he said, "So this is what you bespeak from me. Indeed, I see that you are interested in my son's preferment, but what you ask I am not prepared to yield." Well, you couldn't blame Richard; it certainly sounded like he not only didn't want Richard to marry Alys, but he didn't want him to be his heir either.

Richard just stood there for a moment, thunderstruck. Then his face got really desperate, and his arms raised up to Heaven. He came forward in front of all the nobles and the armies and all, and as he went he began unbuckling his sword. Right in the middle of the whole crowd he raised his voice and said, "Now I see it plain as day . . . what I always thought was incredible! I renounce you as father and as lord!" And he ungirt his sword and handed it to Philip, kneeling before him. "I hereby," he said, "do homage to you for all my continental domains." Philip received him as liege man, and they spoke the oaths of vassalage, which King Henry had renounced at Gisors.

So now Richard and Philip were allies against King Henry, and the Truce of God might never have been proclaimed. The two armies, Richard's and Philip's, rode south together, and at Amboise, the first night's stop, Richard stayed up all night, dictating letters. He sent out over two hundred, summoning his father's vassals to his banner.

Winter was drawing on, it was too cold to fight. Philip and Richard spent Christmas together in Paris, receiving those vassals who pledged to join with them against King Henry, and there were many. I could not help thinking that the poor old King, with all his faults, deserved pity, for so many deserted him. We heard that he lay ill, suffering from an old wound, in his native city, Le Mans. He sent messengers to ask for another peace conference in January, but January came and went, and he was still too ill to attend. It was not until after Easter that the peace talks were held. They were not successful either; in fact, everything was worse, for this time Richard asked point-blank if his father would accept him as his heir, and the old King just sat his horse, silent. There were four archbishops present, and they all threatened to lay interdicts on France and England if they didn't make peace, but it didn't help. King Henry just wouldn't speak, and neither side would give in.

King Henry withdrew to Le Mans, but Richard and Philip didn't just go home. Instead, they attacked—first five castles in the northeast, which they won without any great trouble, and then Le Mans itself. King Henry had to flee for his life, with us in pursuit.

Richard rode first, heading the pursuit. "He'll acknowledge me this time, the old fox!" I heard him say. But he wore no armor, and carried no weapons, and had forbidden any man to loose an arrow at his father, or to harm him in any way. We rode all day and finally, in late afternoon, we caught up with King Henry's rearguard. "No bloodshed," cried Richard. "It is William the Marshal who commands there!" That was his teacher, long ago, who had first taught him the knightly arts.

Well, we were pretty close to them, when all of a sudden this one knight turns about and rides back straight toward us—straight at Richard, really. He had his lance leveled, ready to strike, and he was only a yard or so away when Richard cried, "God's legs, Marshal! Do not kill me—I am unarmed!"

I got a glimpse of the knight's face through his open visor—high nose, thin lips, steely eyes—but not an enemy face either. Then he stopped his horse and dropped his lance lower. "No!" he shouted back at Richard. "No! Let the Devil kill you—for I will not!" And, so saying, he ran his lance through Richard's horse, so that it fell, and threw him. Richard lay on the ground as if stunned, and by the time we roused him the pursuit was lost.

Richard was not hurt badly, only a broken rib. The surgeon bound it tightly, asking, "How does it feel, Sire?"

Richard laughed. "What do you think? Like the tortures of Hell, you barber! Still, it served to keep me from the real tortures. If we had come to the fighting. I might have killed my father. So the Marshal deserves a reward."

Our armies overran Maine and Touraine that summer, for Henry had retired to his castle at Chinon and did not oppose us. All of these territories fell to us, and only the key city, Tours, remained.

We were at camp outside the city walls when a prisoner was brought to Richard's tent, where a few of us officers from both armies were getting our instruction for the morrow's strategy.

"My brother. Take me to my brother!" we heard, through the tent flap.

"Can it be. . . ?" cried Richard, rising. He flung open the canvas door, crying, "Loose him! Loose him! It is Prince John!"

It had been raining a little, a fine mist, and it hung, glittering in John's black hair and along the folds of his black mantle. He was laughing. Richard's arm around his thin shoulders. "God, brother, your bloodhounds nearly had me once or twice . . . don't they know the device of England? I kept sticking this ring into their faces, but it didn't keep them from shoving me."

"A shove is nothing, boy," said Richard. "If you had not had the ring, you would be dead now."

John looked startled, but then he laughed again, and shrugged, showering fine drops of water like a dog that shakes his coat. "Well, I'm in one piece, as you see. Only a little wet . . ." Richard snapped his fingers; a lackey brought a linen towel. ". . . and dry inside." And John winked, a wink that included us all. "Ah, Rhenish." And he held the goblet mockingly, high, as for a toast. "Drink with me, big brother," he said, in a soft, wheedling tone. "We'll drink to our father, the enemy."

Richard halted, goblet to his lips, and stared. "Then, you have left him?"

John shrugged again, smiling. "You see me here."

"God, John," said Richard softly, "you were his darling . . . he loved you well."

They stared at each other for a long moment. Then John spoke. "Perhaps . . . perhaps he thinks he loves me . . . but there is no love in him. He is an empty husk, our father. Don't be a fool, Richard. Don't be a hypocrite either."

"Ah, well," said Richard. "Me . . . I know he does not love me—never did, maybe. But—"

"Listen, Richard. Our father loved Henry, yes? What did that love do for Henry, then? Did he give him his inheritance? Did he trust him to rule? What will Father give me, do you think—if I am true? Another little castle? The hand of Alys, whom no one wants? Poor little bitch. He used her up . . . and how he wants to keep her lands. Well, I don't want to be used—like Henry, like Alys, like Mother. Look what he has done to Mother. Sixteen years!"

Richard was silent for a moment. "Yes. Mother," he said, and that was all. He had no longer tried to dissuade John from joining our rebel forces, but sat him down, gave him food and drink, and showed him the battle plans.

CHAPTER 8

Tours FELL TO US, as we had known it would; by now, we had most of the forces of Europe at our back. King Henry sent messengers to sue for peace. He was told to meet his conquerors the next day at Ballon, just outside the city. The messenger returned saying that the King was very ill, could not stand or sit, but that he would be there.

"He is faking," said John. "He is getting old, and won't admit it."

"He is only fifty-five," said Richard. "Perhaps he is really sick."

"Never believe it, brother," said John. "He was well when I left him. It is a ruse to get sympathy . . . I know him better than you do. Harden your soft heart, brother, or you will never have your will—or neither of us our rights."

Still, when King Henry appeared, bent almost double in the saddle, the whole great knighthood sent up a sigh. For he looked close to death, truly; his face was gray and contorted in agony. Even Philip, that cold fish, was moved. He called for a thick cloak and sent it, folded, to King Henry, that he might sit upon the ground and ease himself as they parleyed. I saw the old King raise his head and smile bitterly as he gave his answer. "I will sit my horse, as always at a parley," he said. "And now please tell me what you want of me, and why you have been destroying my lands."

Philip spoke. He was still a young man, only twenty-one, but he had the look of an old, cruel judge. "Know, Henry, that you are my vassal, and that you are here, not to treat of peace, but to hear sentence pronounced upon you." Richard put his hand on Philip's arm, but he shrugged it off and went on. "You must, first of all, renew your homage to me, and in all things defer to my judgment. You must pay the sum of twenty thousand marks to cover my expenses for this costly war which you forced upon me. You must cede to your son and heir, Richard, the territories of Poitou, Normandy, Maine, Anjou, and Touraine, and call upon your barons on both sides of the Channel to swear homage to Duke Richard for these possessions. We will hold all these castles we have taken as surety for your performance in these matters. As for my sister, Alys, you will at once commit her to five knights of Richard's choosing so that he may have his bride when he returns from Crusade." (I could not begin to follow this reasoning, for I was quite sure that Richard did not want Alys at all; perhaps it was strategy to appease Philip, I can't say.)

Anyhow, the two kings sat on their horses looking at each other, one sick, the other implacable, and it looked as if nothing would happen, and there would be more war. But all of a sudden—though the sky was perfectly clear—there was a loud clap of thunder. There was a deep silence in all that great body of men, and the Archbishop of Rheims, the mediator of the parley, fell upon his knees and bowed his head. It was the kind of thing that was always called an omen—but whose side was the thunder on? As I mused this way, there came a huge roll of thunder that echoed up and down the hills; this time, the entire assemblage fell to its knees. The horses neighed and reared, as though they felt it too.

I looked at the old King, and saw him swaying in his saddle. He fell forward, and would have fallen off, it seemed, had not the two knights near him swiftly caught him up. One of them I recognized as William the Marshal. I saw, too, that the King then raised his head and spoke, but his words were too weak to be heard, and the Marshal spoke for him. "The King of the English agrees to all the terms. He asks only that a list of those who deserted him be brought to him."

"Agreed," said Philip, with a wintry smile.

Richard advanced then, pulling up his mount beside his father. "Father," he said, just loud enough to be heard, "I ask the kiss of peace."

The King did not reply, but sat his horse stiffly, like an image on a wallhanging. Richard bent toward him, embracing him with both arms and kissing each cheek. The King did not move or turn his head, but I could see that he spoke, low, and I caught, too, the flash of his eyes. Richard whirled about, his horse rearing, and snapped down the visor of his helm, before he rode on at our head. And at Tours he turned off at the Chapel of the Holy Child and disappeared inside.

We waited for Richard inside his tent. "I shall need his signature on the list of deserters. Will he be long, do you think?" Philip asked, snapping his fingers at me; he never remembered my name.

I shook my head. "I cannot say," I answered. I remembered Richard's all-night prayer sessions, but kept silent.

"I can sign for him," said John, making a joke.

"That would be forgery," said Philip, looking at him with cold eyes.

John smiled. "Well, we are traitors," he said. "What is one crime more?"

"What is this talk of crime?" came Richard's voice from the doorway.

"Oh, nothing, brother," said John. "A feeble jest . . . and one that did not find favor with our liege lord."

"You must sign this, Richard," said Philip, ignoring John. "The messenger is waiting."

"Oh, yes, the list," said Richard bleakly, scanning it. "Well, it seems to be in order." He took up a pen and signed it.

"Let me see," said Philip. "Why"—he looked up—"John's name is not here."

"Oh, let it go," said Richard. "One rebel son is enough. Besides, there is not room, the document is filled."

"Here, at the top." Philip pointed with one long finger. "Let him sign here—the first name."

John took the parchment. "There's nothing I like more than being first." And he scrawled his signature in a bold hand, giving it to the waiting messenger.

Richard sighed heavily. He looked at John, putting out a hand to touch his arm. "I had thought to spare you." He buried his face in his hands for a moment, then shook his head as if to clear it, and said, slowly, "He cursed me, you know . . . Father. And refused me the kiss of peace." He looked once more at John. "I thought to spare you that curse, for you were his favorite, his most beloved son. I thought to spare you . . . and to spare him too."

But the thing was done, a sorry business. Three days later, Wiliam the Marshal came to tell of the old King's death. "He asked for the list of deserters. When he saw whose name headed the list, he turned his head to the wall and died."

King Henry II of England was buried in the abbey of Fontevrault, a hasty burial, and mean. His faithful followers had fled in the dozens, even his body-squires, and they had robbed his coffers of all that was goodly and needful. Some poor trappings were levied here and there, a sword, a cloak, a makeshift scepter. For a crown, a fillet of gold embroidery from some woman's gear was bound upon his brow.

The laying-out women and the embalmers had not done their work well either. The hands, crossed on the Crusader's sword, were tied clumsily with red string, already embedded in the flesh, and the lips were sewn carelessly, the stitches split at one side, so that the mouth wore a ghastly grin. And worse of all, when Richard entered the room where his father lay and stood looking down at him, the wad of wool waste that plugged one nostril fell out, and a thin trickle of embalmer's fluid ran out. I heard Richard gasp; he fell to his knees, and stayed there for the space of a paternoster. Then he rose, touching my arm, and turned on his heel and left.

When he had pushed through the little crowd outside the chapel and mounted his horse, he turned in his saddle and spoke, in a hoarse whisper, "Did you see, Mercadier . . . did you see? The blood from my father's nostril . . . they will say it is a sign, a bad omen."

"Sire," I said, "corpses do not bleed . . . I have seen many. It was the embalmer's fluid."

"Are you sure?" Richard's eyes were sick.

"I am sure," I said firmly, though the sight had shaken me too. We rode in silence for a bit. Then I said, in a steady voice, "The King is dead, Sire . . . Long live the King!"

BOOK IV

—

THE MOTHER

*Told by Eleanor, Duchess of Aquitaine
and Queen of England*

CHAPTER 1

How OFTEN HAVE I sat before this mirror! At least once a day for sixteen years! That adds up to—no, I cannot count it, figures are too much for me, they make me impatient. But a goodly sum, to be sure; in the thousands.

The mirror is only a polished shield, old when it was hung there. It has not changed, the scratches and dents that mar it are the same; I have grown used to them, and cannot imagine the flawless glasses that once graced my chambers. And Hodierna keeps it polished; even with her stiff joints she manages, and one can see in it passably well.

No, the mirror has not changed, but I have. I am sixty-eight. That, again, is a sum I do not wish to count to, but today I must. For today I am free. Henry is dead, and my glorious son Richard is King. Even De Glanville, my jailer, can no longer keep me mewed up here in grim Salisbury. He looks frightened of me today, he that was always a swaggering lordling. This morning I had white bread and honey with my thin porridge, and the sweet wine of France to replace this bitter ale of my captivity. I wondered why. It was not until Ebenezer bar Joseph came bowing through the door, wearing his secret face, that I heard. He has been my dear friend, the eyes and ears of my long imprisoned years; peddlers go everywhere. He heard of the death early, the day it happened, and sped across the Channel before they laid Henry out for burying. Even so, the news went before him. The tolling of the bells began at matins; I had thought it was for some local dignitary.

So Henry is gone, and the last lingering perfume of my youth with him. I had thought to feel a fierce joy on this day, but instead my throat is swollen with grief and tears prick behind my eyelids. I have sent Hodierna, that loyal soul, away from me, that she may not witness the shame of my womanly weakness. Oh, Henry! Henry, my lost sweet love!

I see in the mirror my sixty-eight-year-old face agleam with errant tears, and in their shining track a new wrinkle—

in the middle of my cheek, where surely, even now, it has no right to be! I smooth the wet away, and it almost disappears. I must get to work with brush and paint pot, for there will be other visitors—important ones—and soon. I thank sweet Jesus that Ebenezer has brought me some white lead for the orris-root paste; I have had none at all for the past month. I bought his entire pack this time, combs, perfumes, and all; now I can pay for it.

I see my fingers have not lost their old skill; at a little distance I can pass for fifty, and with my wimple . . . Oh, vanity! Shall I dye my hair? I think not. My son, Richard, the new King, is thirty-one, it would not be fitting. Besides, the gray streaks add dignity—I hope. I lose confidence, here, behind my walls.

A scratching at my door. "Enter," I call, squaring my shoulders. It is the fat worm, De Glanville, bending double now, like a courtier. What can he want? I have given him my orders, to release the others in his custody, wherever they may be—those others that were taken with me in my ill-timed flight, sixteen years ago. "Well," I say, haughty. "Speak up!"

"I have sent out couriers, Your Highness, to the other . . . places."

"Other prisons," I amended, in a flat voice. "Speak plain, man. Well, what is it? You cannot have heard from them yet."

"No, not yet, Your Highness. But—" And he held out a small coffer, plain and square, of some base metal. "Here are some letters. I saved them at my peril. The King had forbade you should have them, but now . . ." His voice trailed off. "They are all there. I saved them for you, Your Highness. A good thing, wasn't it? A good thing I saved them . . ."

"You disobeyed your King's orders," I said, holding out my hand for the box. "You are a bad servant." I loathed the man; he had made my captivity a sullen nightmare, and had enjoyed each wretched moment. "Go now." I waved my hand in dismissal. "I will send for you when I need you."

"Yes, Your Highness." He bowed himself out backward, stumbling at the door; I forbore to smile.

The letters. There were so many! I had been loved, after all. I had not been forgotten. I leafed through them. So many . . . yet few enough, for sixteen years. A letter from each of my Plantagenet daughters, two from Joanna. Four from my sweet Marie, written from Champagne, filled with court gossip, making me smile. A long poem from the other Marie, the troubadour Marie de France. "Poor prisoner," it went, a graceful planh. Odd, that. Was she not a prisoner too? I turned the missive over; there were none from the other prisoners, not one word. I supposed they had not been allowed pen and ink. There were none from my sons, except for Richard. And now I would never hear from young Henry or from Geoffrey, for they were both dead; it was years now since I knew. My tears were long shed for them, I would not weep again.

None from John either, but then he had visited me, twice— and he hated to write, being left-handed, and awkward with it. The rest were from Richard—a round dozen; or rather, from Blondelza, I recognized her hand. Richard was too busy to write, but he sent his love, and in one a scrawled message, covering a whole page. Dear Richard!

I picked up Blondelza's letter, the last in the pile; my eyes flew across the page. A son! A son to Richard! Oh, joy! But not an heir, of course. I shook my head, sad to think that true love could not be sanctioned by marriage. He wanted to marry her once, but of course no churchman would perform the rites, and no one in Christendom would recognize it. She is simply not eligible—not for him. Only a petty noble, if that, and a jongleuresse as well. Though she is a good girl, and beautiful. I smiled at myself, for of course she is Richard's age now, and only an old woman would call her a girl! I glanced at the date of the last letter. Nearly nine years ago. Then the boy—they had christened him Philippe—would be well grown now, a strapping big lad. I longed to see him, trembling with it.

I longed to see them all—Richard, John, Marie, my troubadour Bernard. I longed to look to the future instead of the past. I longed to begin life again, to leave these prison walls, to greet my people, to *go* somewhere. I longed and yearned and my heart raced. I found myself weeping again, and this time not for Henry. For myself, and for my freedom, and for joy.

CHAPTER 2

THE SMELL FROM the old keep was shocking; even with the whole length of the courtyard between us, we had to cover our noses to keep from choking. I recognized the smell; after so many years how could I not? On damp days it was borne, a ghost of itself, far upward to my high window in the tower; I had thought it was trapped rats, dead and rotting, in the stonework. But it was the living—if one could call them that.

That worm De Glanville had given us the keys and scuttled, pleading his duties. "Your most pressing duty, man, is to the Queen-Regent of England," began that fair knight, William the Marshal.

I stayed him with a hand on his arm, and nodded my dismissal to De Glanville. "Let it go, friend," I said. "We are better without him."

The stink rose, almost visible, from the ancient rusted iron grating set into the stones of the yard; the dungeon ran beneath it. It was reached by a small door in the side of the castle; the lock, long disused, grated and ground with the turning of the key. Steep stairs led to the cell below. In the light from our lantern, we saw that the steps were covered with black water, and slime ran, gleaming, down the thick walls. "Are you sure, Lady?" asked William doubtfully. "It may be unsafe."

"I want to see," I said firmly. "They are my fellow prisoners."

"Step carefully, then, and hold fast to my arm."

Though I had braced myself for horror, still the sight that met my eyes was beyond horror, a chamber in Hell. A tiny room, perhaps eight feet square, and dark, lit by the gray sky that filtered through the small grating. Figures, perhaps five, lay twisted together on the floor, around a central column of stone; chains were fastened into it at intervals, and these too were twisted and lost in the shadows below. Sir William raised the lantern, showing the floor, wet and shining with ordure, and the dingy gray-white of naked limbs. An arm went up, slowly, heavily shackled, to shield a face from the light; it was the only sign of movement.

"Can you speak, man?" said William. "What is your name?" There was the grating whisper of chain on chain, but no other sound.

I spoke then. "We will not harm you, friend. It is I, the Queen—your fellow prisoner—come to set you free. Speak!"

The arm came down then, and we saw the eyes, two black holes in a little space of gray set amid a wild bush of black; beard and hair must have had years of growing. The eyes shut once more against the light, and the shackled arm moved feebly; from the matted beard came sounds like croaking.

"He has forgotten how to talk," I whispered.

"No, Lady . . . I think not. His mouth is dry." Sir William bent to pick up a bowl of water. It was filthy, crusted with mold, and with small unspeakable creatures swimming in it; I shuddered.

"I have a flask of brandy," said Sir William. "But it might kill him," he finished shakily.

"Take this," I said, pulling a square of cloth from my sleeve. "Moisten his lips only."

The Marshal poured some brandy onto the cloth and held it to the man's lips. We saw him swallow convulsively; he croaked another croak or two, and then said clearly, "Raoul . . . Raoul of Winchester."

"The castle reeve," I gasped.

"His son . . . Raoul, his son," said the man.

"Of course," I whispered. "The father was a graybeard in my time."

"How long?" asked the Marshal. "How long have you been here?"

The man Raoul shook his head. "Long . . . long time."

"And the others?" asked the Marshal.

"Dead. All dead." He waved his hand toward the twisted mass. "For a week now . . . more."

I caught my breath. "He must be freed," I said. "Chained to dead men!"

"I'll see to it," said William. "Go now, up the stairs, Your Highness. Come."

"You will be free, Raoul," I called, as William gently moved me toward the door. "Your chains will be struck off. You will have freedom, in the name of King Richard!"

It was what I said, always, afterward. "In the name of King Richard. Your freedom, in the name of King Richard." More than a dozen prisons and keeps I visited, on the road to London. And in each one I freed the poor prisoners, that they should share my newfound liberty. That they should share it by the grace and bounty of their new King, Richard of England. Who would be the best king in the world, as he was the best knight in the world. And to the north and the west and in all parts, I sent my officers to open the prisons and unbind the chains of oppression, in the new King's name.

There were those who spake me nay, bishops mostly, saying that I had let loose all the felons of England to kill us or worse. But I would have it my way, for once. The prisoners I freed were those poor folk caught in the unfair poaching laws, endeavoring to survive in a world where plenteous game ran wild, but not for them—those who had strayed into the environs of king or noble and dared to take aim at a royal deer or a ducal rabbit. Or it might be one who had been condemned to a life behind bars for the snatching of a halfpenny loaf. I did not pardon murderers or highwaymen, or those who waited trial under due process of law; these must take their chances with justice, the Blind Goddess.

The next step was law reform, I knew; I had drawn up a writ already, and it only waited Richard's signature. Oh, I had been busy! I convened my assemblies, received the oaths of homage to my son, and transacted the business of court and chancellory, setting my own seal upon my sovereign acts. I appeared without hindrance in all the royal castles, not as agent or emissary, but as undisputed mistress. Richard's mandate had been clear on that.

Strangely enough, my long confinement within the walls of Salisbury had not impaired my faculties. My mind was keener than it had ever been, my spirits were high, and even my old body did not play me false. If I did not look often in my mirror, I could have believed that I was still in my prime. And the criticism that used to dog my footsteps, the foul gossip and the petty slanders, had vanished; I think that England had accepted me fully at last. Perhaps they felt I had been tempered in the fire, like fine steel!

My statesmanship was not subtle; I made an outright bid for popularity, for myself and for Richard, and addressed myself in particular to those who bore grievances under Henry's yoke. I knew that Richard, bred for the destiny of

Aquitaine, was not known, certainly not loved, in England. Since his childhood he had spent little time on this island; and had probably forgotten what little he had known of the language.

Fortune is a strange thing, and fickle. It might never have turned out this way, for there had been two heirs before him. Little William I could barely remember, only an infant when he died, so long ago; he had just learned to focus his eyes, I recall, and had lost that blind, blue, baby stare, when a fever took him. Or was it a pox? The memory has faded with the years. And Henry, the Young King—I mourned him, surely, and sometimes still do. But I always knew that Richard was the best of my sons. I knew from the start that here was something special—a happy blend of Angevin and Poitevin, the best of us both, and a child, still, of our love. Beautiful he was, always, and keen, even brilliant, with that quality, unexplained, that draws men to him and makes them follow without question wherever he will lead. Oh, he will be a great monarch. And he will make England the greatest power in Europe; the lands are there, and he has the strength to keep them safe. This island will be an empire, under him!

Or it will be, once he has got Jerusalem out of his system. There is that, of course; we all go through it—the Crusade, the Army of God, the Holy Sepulchre—it is the great broken dream of our lives. And he must have his fling at it, like the rest of us. Even I, a woman, was affected, when I was young and all afire. Hours on my knees I spent, and weeping, for the plight of the Holy Land. Hours in the saddle too, parched by the cruel Eastern sun and blinded by sandstorms, blisters on my lips and gripes in my bowels—but the flame still ardent in my heart. The churchmen called me frivolous and wanton, when I set out for Jerusalem in my golden Amazon trappings. But it was all as real and as earnest for me as for any man in God's Army. Even now, old and stiff as I am, my blood beats with a faster rhythm, my heart knocking at my chest, at the cry "God wills it!"

Oh, Richard, I can hardly wait! I have not laid eyes on you, the light of my life, for sixteen years! Finish your business in Europe and come quickly to your mother, and your people!

CHAPTER 3

I WAS IN my element, at last. I swear I grew younger and more vigorous every day! There was so much to do, and all of it important; my days were full. At night I lay down anywhere, royal couch or pallet of straw, closed my eyes and fell into a dreamless sleep, to wake refreshed. I traveled mightily, leaving in my wake all things in order for the coming of England's new King.

At Shaftesbury I found Marie de France, taken into captivity with me. She was now abbess of the convent there, and all her jongleuresses immured as nuns. She seemed content, and not much changed. Her habit was white, always her only color, and made of rich stuffs, fitted cunningly, and hung with gold crosses and relics. The walls of the nunnery ran with music day and night, bright birds sang too in jeweled cages, and little lapdogs ran about, wearing precious collars. Gold plate adorned the refectory table and luscious tidbits were heaped upon it; the merry little nuns had all grown sleek and plump, the worldliest of Christ's brides. It seemed a goodly place to come to, in the end. But not for me; I bade her a fond goodbye, and climbed into the saddle again.

At Gloucester Abbey I was joined by Alexander and Will Longchamps, both ordained now, tonsured and cowled. But to their abbot I pleaded that their country needed them, as indeed it did; they were too clever to waste their talents behind monkish walls. Alexander was loath to leave, he was novice-master there, and beloved of his pupils. "Dickon . . . King?" he said wonderingly, as though he had been living on a star.

"Yes," I said firmly. "And he will need you . . . you were always his dear friend."

"Oh, yes," he said, in a dazed sort of way. "If he needs me, of course. Oh, certainly." And he smiled his wonderful flashing smile that I remembered from the old days; it transformed him.

He was much changed, grown very thin, and with a stoop

to his shoulders, and a worried look. "You do not eat enough, Alex," I said. "We will have to fatten you up . . . your mother and I."

We fell to talking, and I learned that he had studied the stars in their courses, and could find his way by them on sea or land; that he had dug up old bones long dead and from them could discover the ancient customs; that he deciphered old writings, too and could read as many as a dozen languages, and write them as well; that he had read the Bible in Greek, its first rendering; and many other things.

"But you are very accomplished, then . . . and will be a great help to Richard. He goes on Crusade, you know."

"Yes, I know." His face was still, and shut upon itself. "But I have vowed to shed no blood, Christian or infidel."

"You will not be asked to, Alex. But he will need a chronicler . . . a true one, to record his deeds. You will not refuse him?"

"If he asks me, no. He is the only brother I have . . . and my sovereign prince."

"I am all afire to see this child of Richard's loins," I said.

"Blondelza's son," he said musingly; I fancied I heard a wistful note in his voice. "She was the fairest maid."

I glanced at him, curious. His face was still, and I could not read it, but his hands, where they clasped his breviary, showed white at the knuckles. Poor Alex. Was he a happy monk? As I watched, his clutching hand relaxed and moved upward to take the little cross that hung upon his chest; he raised it to his lips.

Will Longchamps, my little clever Will, fell in most eagerly with my needs, taking my muster rolls and my account books under his charge and reducing them to such order that I could well believe the sixteen years had been a day; I was so happy and relieved that I made him my Privy Purse and temporary Chancellor of the realm. With his help, I managed my affairs so competently that well before Richard's arrival from the Continent, the whole of England was ready for his coronation.

Richard landed at Southampton on the twentieth day of August, to the roaring of a crowd so thick and close that a fainting person could not fall down in it, but would be borne up by sheer weight of numbers. Some of them had been standing all night, waiting to greet their King; the press of people went right down to the water and into it, up to their waists. A path had to be cleared, and, even then, some of his men carried Richard on their shoulders to the shore, that he might not be crushed by his people's love.

That was my first glimpse of him, my kingly son, huge and laughing as he was borne slowly above the sea of water and of men. He was in mail, shining silver in the sun like the scales of a fish, but his head was bare, and his long hair hung down to his shoulders, a goodly mane, dark red in color and waving. His jupon was sky-blue and upon the breast of it showed the famous lion-heart badge, above his white Crusader's cross. In the wild din I heard shouts of "Lionheart!" and some scattered cries of "God wills it!"

They placed him on the landing stage; there was a little wooden tower upon it, and it shook beneath him as he climbed up to stand at the top, far above. I saw him raise both hands, long arms gleaming in their mail, to quiet the folk, still smiling down at them. When all was still, I heard him say, "My people . . . my people of England, here is your King!" They went wild then, throwing their caps in the air and shouting; I heard some women sob. He raised his arms again for silence. "Give thanks, good people. Give thanks to God, who kept me from the waves and winds and brought me home to you. Kneel with me, my loved ones, and thank Him . . . we are all in His hands."

He was a wonderful showman, always. Even as my heart swelled with love and the tears poured down my cheeks, I thought how canny he was, with what sure instinct he beguiled them. And that vast crowd, so noisy before, fell upon its knees in a silence so profound that the noise of the gentle waves lapping the ship in the harbor sounded loud in my ears. A moment of breathless glory, and over in a moment. He rose then and strode through them, the throng parting like a river before him, to where I stood waiting.

He, like Alexander, was much changed, close up—though differently. Of course, they had been more boys before, when last I saw them. I could not take my eyes off Richard, but must keep stealing glances at him, and each time with a pang of wonder: Was this mine . . . my son?

He was so huge, more giant than man—wide shoulders that blocked out the sun, legs like tree trunks, long and straight, not shaped by the saddle, powerful arms, big hands and feet. And a great head, like Jove, stern and smiling. His eyes were the same, blue as the sea and piercing, seeming to look right through you. But the skin that had been so smooth and beardless, sun-flushed, was weathered and seamed, dark as leather. Red patches showed on cheeks and forehead, and little white lines fanned out from the corners of his eyes, from squinting against the sun. He bore scars too, a long thin one near his ear and a small one that puckered his eyebrow; his nose, once so long and slender, looked beaky now, broken, I guess, in some skirmish. It made my heart melt to look at him.

"My son, my dearest son . . . it has been so long!"

"Mother . . . Lady, you have not changed at all." His eyes swept over me, a little smile lighting them. "Except your hair —what I can see of it under that veil." He bent close. "Dye it . . . little brother John has some new stuff from the East."

"John?" I asked; it seemed an odd thing for him to carry on campaign.

Richard laughed. "Little John has more white hairs than you . . . we are all growing older." He turned to look over his shoulder. "And there he is, taking his bows."

There was a rustle in the crowd, and high laughter; I could see nothing.

"Look, Mother." And he hoisted me high, ruffling my gown, and my dignity.

"Richard," I protested. "Put me down . . . my ankles!"

"You never used to mind showing an ankle," he said, "and it is still a goodly sight."

I blushed like a girl, and deeper when I saw the folk close by me smile and clap their hands.

"There, Mother, see? He climbs the tower."

I looked, shading my eyes from the sun. John swung up onto the topmost stair easily, waving and laughing, holding his arms high as Richard had done.

I heard Richard laugh. "That mountebank!" he murmured. "He loves to mock me!"

"But I cannot hear what he says."

"No. But be sure it is at my expense . . . he has a pretty wit."

And then I heard something, just the tail end. ". . . your Prince, your landless Prince, poor Lackland John!" There was a great burst of laughter. John, looking solemn, knelt, mock-pious, clasping his hands and gazing up at the sky. "Let

215

us pray, good people ... pray for poor John, that the heavens will open and rain down gold."

I heard no more, but turned a shocked face to Richard. "He must not be allowed to speak so," I said. "It is almost blasphemy."

Richard roared with laughter then. "Mother, darling Mother! Do you not know that our John cannot be stopped from doing what comes into his silly head? And it is not blasphemy ... even the clergy are smiling, I see!" And indeed, a little group of tonsured clerks were smiling behind their hands. "No, sweet my mother. John is incorrigible ... and the people love him. Listen!"

And as John climbed down, a great cheer, a merry sound, went up from all the great throng, and cries of "Go it, Princeling! Good fellow!"

Richard set me on my feet again, turning to face John, who came bowing and threading his way; a half-grown lad trailed behind him.

"Well, brother, what say you?" John twinkled at me as though I were one of his merry audience, and not his mother. " 'Tis a good ruse, hey? You cannot refuse me an allowance now."

Richard fisted his shoulder playfully. "You have an allowance, whoreson!"

"A pittance," John said. But then, in one of those lightning changes of mood I was to learn were a part of him, turned and sank to one knee before me. "Dearest Mother, beautiful as ever." And he kissed my hand.

I could not be angry with him; I raised him, put my arms about him, and kissed his cheek. "Dear John," I said, my eyes wet.

"Mother," I heard Richard say. I looked, and saw the little lad slip his hand shyly into my son's. "Mother, this is Philippe ... Philippe of Cognac. My son."

The boy bowed solemnly, going onto one knee. "My Lady Grandmother," he said. "I ask your blessing."

"Indeed you have it, Philippe," I said, charmed. I put out my hand to cup his chin and gaze down into his eyes. They stared back at me, unwinking, dark. Blondelza's eyes. They were all he had of her; he was the image of Richard at that age—ten, perhaps? Slim and fine-boned, with long knobby legs, like a handsome colt; only his hair was unlike, more gold than red, and straight as rain. He spoke the langue d'oc; I had not heard it for years.

"Will you visit me tonight at Windsor, Philippe?" I asked, raising him to his feet and kissing his cheek. "I have some toy soldiers—ancient things, but silver, and cunningly made. They were your grandfather's."

"Silver!" cried John. "I could melt them down."

I found myself laughing. "Are you so out of pocket, my son?"

"Always," he replied promptly.

"Well, you come too, then. I will give you a meal, at least."

"And I, Mother?" asked Richard, smiling. "Am I to be included?"

"Sir," I said, bowing, my hand on my heart, like a courtier, "I am yours to command . . . you are my King!" My words sounded very arch to my ears; I had not spoken in jest for sixteen years! "Yes, do come, Richard, of course," I said. "And bring—" I was suddenly conscious of the courtiers hovering near, and dropped my voice. "Bring whom you will," I finished, my eyes signaling to Richard.

CHAPTER 4

"BUT THEY ARE Saracen knights!" The boy looked up with such shock in his face, and such disappointment, too, that I nearly smiled.

"But you can *pretend*, Philippe. Play that they are our own knights, forming for battle in the Holy Land." I moved the pieces in a row, not knowing quite how to go about it.

"Let me, Mother." Richard took the ivory box of little figures from me, stood a row of them up quickly, then, with a sweep of his hand, mowed them down. "See, Philippe. They are the Saracen enemy, and you have felled them with one blow from your new secret weapon. Here, you try it." He began standing them again in a row.

"I can do it, Sir Father," cried Philippe, and knocked them down. "There, I got them all!" He clapped his hands joyfully, his dark eyes sparkling, and began to set the silver men up again. Before he had finished, a great yawn took him. "Sir Father . . ." Another yawn, bigger than the first. "What is the secret weapon?"

"Well, it is a secret," said Richard, smiling. "I cannot tell it in front of your grandmother. Come, lie down over here, in this soft corner, and I will whisper it to you."

The boy stood up obediently, swaying on his feet.

Richard gathered him up in his arms, laughing. "Come, little captain." And he laid him down on a low cushioned couch, then tiptoed back to where we sat. "He is dead tired, poor lad . . . it was a rough crossing, and none of us got any sleep."

"He did not say his prayers," said Alexander.

"I doubt if he knows any," said Richard. "It is a rough household, that of Cognac. Though rich enough."

"But you cannot let him grow up a very heathen!" cried Alexander.

"Why not?" said John slyly. "He will follow his uncle's example. Now, I never say my prayers—I make a point of it."

Both men ignored him; he must have been used to it, for he only smiled, and tipped up the last dregs of wine in his glass. I did not offer to fill it, I thought he had had enough.

Richard eyed Alexander gravely. "For the matter of the boy's heathen state," he said, "that will be up to you, old Saracen. Will you be his magister?"

"And your chronicler, too, for the Holy Land venture?"

"Why not?" said Richard. "You are well equipped for both. I *command* you," he finished, laughing.

"Well, in that case, Sire," said Alexander, pulling at his forelock and putting on a whining, servile voice. "I am at your service, Master."

I saw it was an old game between them; my heart swelled, it was such a homely scene. It might have been this same chamber, so many years ago. And then my throat ached; I remembered those that were gone forever. I took up the carafe and poured myself an inch of wine. John held out his glass, and I had not the heart to deny him anything. We raised our glasses in a silent toast.

"That is a goodly lad of yours, Dickon," I said. "Strong, and handsome too."

"He has her eyes," said Alexander softly. "How does she fare . . . Blondelza?"

There was a little pause, then Richard said lightly, "When last I heard, she was counted second to none . . . not even Marie de France has her fame. Her songs are sung wherever there are minstrels."

I set down my wine. "Where is she, Dickon?"

"She might be anywhere, for all I know," he said, as lightly as before, but with a strange look to his eyes. "She left me more than five years ago. Five? No, closer to seven . . . it makes no matter." And now he rose, tipped out the last of the wine into his cup, and drained it. His face was hard, and his mouth twisted. "She did not leave her address." And he smiled wryly.

"She left her child?" I could not credit it.

"No," he said. "She took him from me, too." And he stared at me with a kind of defiance. "But he is better off where he is. The heiress of Cognac . . . it is a good match."

"For a bastard," said John. "I should say so. What did you do, brother, bludgeon the heiress' father?"

Richard laughed shortly. "In a manner of speaking."

John laughed and raised his glass again. "Well, here's to the bastard of the Lionheart!" He drank. "He will be rich, that little boy." There was such regret and envy in his voice that we all, even Alexander, smiled.

"You will have your portion, John," said Richard. "I am not Father . . . What say you to speeding up that marriage with Gloucester? The girl is barely thirteen, but pretty, they say."

"And richer than Cognac!" John laughed. "Next week?"

"Wait till after the coronation . . . I will lend you monies till then." And now he was merry again, the shadow gone from his eyes. They fell to chaffering about money and women, horseflesh and armorers—men's talk, and a compliment that they had forgotten me and were so easy in my presence. After they had uncorked another bottle and were well into it, the conversation touched on Alys, the French princess, Richard's betrothed; I thought it oddly ribald, a little sly—not meet talk to bandy about a noblewoman.

"And they say she has grown fat," said John.

"Or maybe—" Richard's face wore a look I had never seen, foxy and cruel. "It could be she has another—" He stopped.

"Bun in the oven?" said John.

I banged my hand down upon the table, hard, to silence

them. "What talk is this?" I demanded. "What manner of speech, to so ill use a girl of blood?" I stared at Richard. "And your betrothed wife!"

Richard's smile vanished, and his mouth set in grim lines. "Never!" he cried, banging the table in his turn. I stared at him blankly.

For a moment no one spoke; I could hear Alexander running the beads of his rosary through his fingers.

"Can it be . . ." said John slowly. "Can it be, Mother, that you do not *know?*"

"I know nothing—except that you are both behaving like ill-bred varlets!" I said hotly.

They looked at each other, Richard very flushed, and even John a little uneasy, for once.

"Will you speak?" said Richard, looking at his brother.

"Mother," said John carefully, "she—Alys—bore a child to Father last year."

My jaw dropped; I was utterly stunned, unable to say anything at all. "What?" I stammered finally. "How do you know this?"

"It is the talk of Europe," said Richard bitterly. "Everyone knows."

"And songs, and jests in taverns," said John. "She is a byword, our Alys."

"Even in prison, Mother, I should think you would have heard something," said Richard. "Father sued to the Pope for divorce." He saw my face, and said hurriedly, "Sorry, Mother . . . It came to nothing, and the Pope refused—and the child died anyway. But I cannot believe you would have heard nothing at all."

"It is hardly the sort of thing my spies would have told me," I said coldly.

He nodded. "I think it was happening under our noses— when first we brought her to England. And none of us the wiser."

I was aghast. "But she was only a child!"

"Ten, yes. I remember well—she was my betrothed, after all."

"But that's monstrous," I whispered. "A daughter of the Capets, and his ward . . . and I wept for him!" I put my head down into my hands and wept again, silently. After a while I raised my head and said wearily, "You cannot marry her, then."

"No." Richard laughed, an ugly sound. "Even John would not."

I glanced at John; he showed no rancor. "Who, then?" I asked. "Who shall we wed her to?"

"No one," said Richard. "She shall not marry."

"A convent?"

"Not that either." There was a pause, then he said, "There is the question of her dowry—the Vexin lands."

"Oh, yes," I said, dully. "Of course. They must stay in our hands."

"Somehow, yes. They are strategic."

"So we cannot just send her back home."

Richard smiled. "Philip Augustus would like nothing better."

"He knows?"

"How could he not? I told you—the whole world knows." His smile twisted. "Saladin is probably regaling his troops with the news that his Lionheart enemy was cuckolded before he was even married!"

In a way, I had not yet taken it in. I groped for words. "She— Where has he kept her ... where is she now?"

"At Woodstock," said John. "In the little house built for Rosamund, in the convent yard."

"And Rosamund?" I asked. "Do they live together there? Surely, even he—" And I began to shake my head, nonplussed.

"No, Mother. Rosamund is dead. For years now ... the lung rot."

I crossed myself; it was almost as fearsome a disease as leprosy. "God rest her soul," I said.

"You are a good woman, Mother," said Richard, after a moment.

"No ... I hated her while she lived. But—" And I smiled a little smile, reaching out to take his hand. "But I have found all fires burn out at last, my son."

They were silent for a bit, then John said, uneasily, "You are not so old, Mother."

"Oh, yes, I am," I said, smiling still. "But not too old! There is still work for me. Now, what shall we do about Alys?"

"She must be kept safely somewhere," said Richard. "Woodstock is not fortified."

"Prison," I said bitterly.

"Harden your heart, Mother," said Richard.

"I cannot blame her, a child," I said.

"I can," said Richard. "She was not always a child. I think she gambled for power, and lost. She must take the consequences." He looked at me, a hot look. "When did she ever think of you?"

I bowed my head. "Where, then?"

"We will keep her at Rouen . . . let Philip think I mean to wed her. It will sweeten him, and we will keep the lands."

"Someday he will have to know," I said.

"We will cross the bridge when we come to it," said Richard, with a touch of impatience.

I went on. "And someday—and soon—you will have to wed. We must think of the succession."

He laughed. "Oh, Mother! That is another bridge to cross. Let us get me crowned first."

CHAPTER 5

"MOTHER," CRIED RICHARD, "I would sell England itself if I could find a buyer!"

He sat in a little chamber hardly larger than a closet, at a huge table which nearly filled it. Chests were open upon the floor, some half filled with coins. Upon the table other coins were stacked, in piles, according to their denomination. From time to time Richard referred to one of the ledgers in front of him, checking againt the list Will Longchamps held in his hand. Richard called this little room the "counting house," and it was here, on a morning the week after his coronation, that I found him, counting the money that had come in, by one stratagem or another, to swell the coffers of his campaign in the Holy Land.

Richard had not been minded to levy any tax at all upon the common people. "Why should they pay of the little they have, when there is immeasurable wealth in the hands of a few nobles?" So saying, he had proceeded to relieve these few of as much as he could. One way he accomplished this was by putting up for sale many of the state offices. "Behold," he said to me, his eyes alight with mischief, "how I have made, out of an old bishop, a new earl!" And he showed me the papers wherewith the Bishop of Durham had purchased the title of Earl of Northumberland. Many titles and offices had been bought and sold in this manner. "The trouble is," said Richard, "that there are not enough to go around!"

He showed me, for instance, that of thirty-one sheriffs, there were only seven left in office, the others having been replaced, after paying stiff fines.

"I am surprised there were so many as seven left," I commented dryly. "Seven honest sheriffs—unbelievable!" For the sheriffs of England were notorious bloodsuckers, having complete power in their shires.

"Oh, not honest," said Richard. "Just less dishonest. They paid, too, to keep their jobs. The other jobs I auctioned off to the highest bidder. Poor villains—little do they know the eagle eye I have set over them!" He pointed a finger at Will Longchamps; a grin split the little monkeyish face. "The Chancellor here has already taken share enough from those rogues to buy himself the bishopric of Ely."

I could not help smiling at Dickon's childish delight at his own clever ruses, but I said, "You are not overhonest yourself, it seems, my son."

His face fell. "But it is in a good cause! And besides, I have been scrupulous in all Father's wishes. Half-brother Geoffrey shall remain Archbishop of York, as he named him —and for free too. And John—I am giving John lands to the value of four thousand pounds a year, also as Father willed it. See." And he showed me a list of the counties, six of them, of which John would receive all revenues and profits.

I looked at it quickly. "But, Dickon, these are all adjacent. It is a formidable block of land, a good piece of the kingdom, in fact. Would it not have been more prudent to scatter them—give him lands separated by other territories?"

"John needs confidence," he said. "He has been babied too long. He must be given responsibility. I am making him my regent while I am in the Holy Land, too."

"He is so young," I said. "At least divide your power. Appoint Will co-regent."

Richard laughed. "Here, look! I have already done so. They can keep watch on each other." He caught my eye and winked. "And you, Mother, will keep an eye on both of them—unofficially. When you are here, that is . . . when I can spare you." He looked at me with a measuring eye. "It seems I need you for so many things . . . you must be in several places at once!"

"I had hoped to accompany you on Crusade."

"The Church has forbidden women to take the cross this time," he said, twinkling.

"Surely I am so old now that it does not count," I said, smiling.

"I doubt that you will ever be that old," he answered, smiling too. "But there is something else." He glanced at Longchamps and said, "Leave us, good Will. Stretch your legs for now. We can get back to this task later."

We watched as he gathered up his papers and left, bowing. Then Richard said, "You found a treasure when you found him, Mother. And I trust him, too. But this I speak of I want kept secret—for now." He rose and walked about, a little restlessly, I thought, and almost as though he were at a loss for words. "Take off your cloak, Mother . . . it is warm in here."

I smiled a little at this; he was so used to giving orders! But I threw it back off my shoulders, and loosened the head veil I wore.

"You never dyed your hair," he said, staring at me absently. "But let it go, it looks well; I am getting used to it." He paced again.

"You did not ask me here to talk about my hair."

"No." He flushed and turned away. "The fact is, Mother, I'm a bit nervous about this." He drew a deep breath. "Well, we decided I will not have Alys, isn't that so? Well, there is the succession to think about, before I leave. Well, hang it all, Mother, I don't want a wife at all, if I can't have—" He broke off, biting his lips. "A wife's a nuisance right now, with the Crusade and everything else, but I think I'd better settle it anyway. England needs an heir. If I— Oh, nothing will happen to me, of course, I've been in hundreds of battles. But the people will want it, so we'd better think of it, for the succession." He turned and looked straight at me, for the first time since he began this disjointed avowal. "Well, the upshot is, Mother, it's settled. I've found a wife."

I simply stared at him. "You have?"

"Yes. Her name is Berengaria—the King of Navarre's daughter, Sancho's daughter."

"Navarre! But that kingdom's hardly on the map! A tiny

place." I shook my head. "No. She won't do for you, Richard."

"It's settled, Mother," he said, in a lordly manner, most infuriating. He would make enemies with that look, if he did not take care.

"What kind of a dowry will a girl like that bring?" I said. "It must be a poor place, Navarre."

"That's where you're wrong," said Richard. "Sancho married well, and all the kings before him—and there is Moorish gold there too. The dowry is substantial—forty thousand marks, thirty ships, two thousand men, mounted, five hundred Arab horses, eight barrels of Greek fire—"

"All for war!" I cried.

"For the Crusade," he answered. "What else is there?" He smiled disarmingly. "With that dowry, I'd marry her if she had a squint in both eyes. But she doesn't!" he finished hurriedly. "She's . . . nice. A nice face. I like her."

"You've met the girl!"

"Of course, Mother. Would I buy a pig in a poke?"

"But when have you seen her?"

"Her brother—another Sancho—is a comrade . . . served under me in Aquitaine from the beginning, or nearly. There was a tournament there—in Navarre, in the city of Pamplona. I took part, to please him. And wore her favor—again to please him. But I met her afterward . . . and liked her well. She is a learned maiden, and virtuous . . . and fair too. And she is willing."

"But of course she is willing!" I cried. "What girl wouldn't be? You are the greatest catch in Christendom!" Though I had been nagging Richard about the succession, I was strangely disappointed; they say all women are jealous of their sons. I resolved to be different, and to love this Berengaria. "Berengaria," I said, "what do they call her for short?"

"I have no idea," he said, shaking his head and smiling. "It's a nice name."

"A very common name, there in the south," I said. "I had a washerwoman once by that name."

"Mother." He took my hand. "Mother, be good."

I smiled. "It's just that it's so sudden."

"Mother, I am thirty-two!"

"Well, you have been betrothed for years now." I looked sharply at him. "What does Sancho think about that? You are not yet free of it."

He waved his hand airily. "Well, I have settled all that,

Mother. Never fear." He was infuriating with his high-handed manner, telling me nothing. But I swallowed it, and heard him out, "And, now, finally, she has agreed."

"I should think so!" I said, properly indignant.

"Mother, you do not know these old-fashioned folk . . . she has never been outside Navarre. A life behind walls, it is . . . she might as well be a nun."

"Are you sure she is the wife for you?"

"One can never be sure of that, wouldn't you say? But there is no one else at all—literally. There is no princess of child-bearing age in all of Europe. I have checked and rechecked."

"I know," I said. "I have wondered who we could find. Well, if you think . . ."

"She will do, Mother. She is even intelligent. One can *talk* to her. Of course—" and he grinned at me, a wide, merry grin—"she has a wooden ear."

"She did not like your songs?"

"On the contrary, she loved them. But I knew she could not tell one from the other." His eyes looked blank. "Well, at least it will be a change."

I touched his arm. "Dear Richard, what happened . . . with Blondelza?"

"She left me." He gave a short, mirthless laugh. "Called me a monster . . . she barred her door." There was a little silence. "The next morning she was gone."

"What had you done?"

His eyes flashed at me briefly, a flicker of anger. "It was about some women . . . a castle we had taken. She thought they suffered too long a death."

"Women!" Shock made my voice hoarse. "I cannot blame her."

"Oh, yes," he said bitterly, "you women always stick together. Oh, Mother." He shook his head. "I will never understand you, Mother. A moment ago you were bristling that I had picked me a wife—" He held up his hand as I started to protest. "You were, Mother! Be fair! Yet for Blondelza—no wife—you are ready to take up arms!"

"I *know* Blondelza," I said, though I knew it did not make me sound more reasonable. "She must have had cause."

"Cause!" His words were hot. "She did not listen—would not see my side!" He stared at me resentfully, as though it were all my doing. "Mother, those women . . . she that was the castellan, they called her 'the she-wolf of Le Chaillot,' and her sister-in-law 'the red sow.' They caught a man of ours—a nobleman, not seventeen years—and flayed him alive upon the ramparts, in our sights. His cries—I can hear them still. And afterward they threw his head, with the bloody skin hanging in shreds from it . . . they threw it down to us."

We were both silent then, seeing that dreadful picture behind our eyes.

"And when the castle fell," he continued, "I gave them to my routiers for their sport, but even they would not rape them. They hung them in chains from the walls. The castle folk came out and stoned them and cursed. There was not one among them that had not had some husband or son tortured in the she-wolf's dungeons. Bones and rotting flesh were piled high there, underground, some from years before . . . we gave them Christian burial, poor wretched remains. But *they*—the wolf and the sow—we left to their perdition."

I made the sign of the Cross between us. "A terrible story . . ." I studied him; his face looked lost and miserable, suddenly young. I spoke, diffidently. "You were both wrong . . . Could you not seek her out where she had fled and speak fair words to her, so that she understood?"

"I could have . . . but I did not. I was angry, and counted her well lost." He did not look up; his hands, with a life of their own, kept twisting upon themselves, over and over. "I was a long time angry. I knew where she had gone—to her jongleur family, the company of players. I sent Mercadier to steal away the boy."

"Oh, Richard . . . to take her child! Perhaps she thinks him dead."

"No. I left a chest of monies and a deed to that castle . . . Le Chaillot. She knows he is with me."

"Le Chaillot . . . a little fief. A niggardly portion," I said.

"She has not complained," he said.

"No, she would not. Blondelza has no greed."

"Pride, though," he said, raising his head and looking at me. "That she has, in plenty. I have never once had word from her . . . not even to ask how the boy fares."

"No doubt she knows . . . jongleurs go everywhere," I said. And then, a little shyly, I asked, "Will you not seek her out?"

He shook his head. "Not now. She has another knight . . .

several, by now." His face sank down into his hands and he wept, a strained, harsh weeping. "Oh, Mother . . . she was so sweet."

I took him in my arms. It was the only time in his life I had ever known him to need comfort. My poor conqueror son. We clung together there in the little stone-walled chamber, weeping both, for the lost past.

CHAPTER 6

I CANNOT BELIEVE it is so many months that I have been free; my heart still leaps when I see, suddenly, the clear bright flight of a bird.

But now, at last, I am breathing another air than that of England; after sixteen years, France is inside me again—Normandy, Maine, Anjou—a crisper world, the fog drifting in shreds only, and disappearing as the sun climbs. Soon I will feel the little breezes of the south upon my cheeks and the backs of my hands, making me young. And, after that, the furnace breath of the East, shimmering white above golden sands, the sun white, too, in a bleached sky. I remember it imperfectly, my youth remembering.

The French air makes me drunk, or perhaps it is the great relief of having done with the crossing; I am not a good sailor. Twice the Narrow Sea, the channel between our island kingdom and the main coast, has nearly swallowed me up; this last trip they called an easy one, but it tossed our boat like a cork in a churned-up pond. The boat was small, one of the few spared from the Crusading fleet, which has left England sea-poor.

Richard had thought to do all quickly, and be in Vézelay with his fellow Crusader, Philip Augustus, by the end of Lent. But it is May already, and they are just now on their way to the rendezvous. He has been King of England for almost ten months. I might have told him it would take a while to mount a Crusade, even when you are thirty-two and called the Lionheart; even when men follow you at a flick of the eye, and gold pours into your lap as though the heavens rained it. But I never would say anything at all, for no one welcomes prudent advice, least of all a son.

He will go in a straight line, or as near as can be, to Tours, where the Crusaders will assemble; a goodly force of knights and mercenaries go with him, and the rest will follow by sea.

My journey, a slower one, has a twofold purpose: to see poor hapless Alys safely to the fortress where she must bide till her future is settled, and to fetch Richard's intended bride, Berengaria, to her wedding. So it will be a long trip, making a half-circle through Normandy and Rouen and from there to the little kingdom of Navarre, on the Spanish border. After that, I wait word from Richard; we will rendezvous somewhere on the way to the Holy Land.

We saw the fleet, nearly ready to sail, at Southampton, a wondrous sight, some hundred ships and more, their gilded decks shining in the sun, their sails marked boldly with the white cross of the English.

Everywhere that we lie over in this journey has memories for me; the castles of Normandy, dark, dank-walled, forbidding, yet holding for me the lambent sunshine of Henry's young manhood and my first wild passion; Bures, the scene of that fateful Christmas court which sent Thomas Becket to his martyrdom; Bayeux, more nearly a home, which has seen love and hate in equal measure, and where Henry, growing old, wrestled with death. I wept again at Bayeux, secretly, for death, which faces us all, and for Henry; I am too old now for hate.

I cannot even hate Alys, whom he tried to set above me. Though, truly, it would take a saint to love her; she is a foul slattern, empty-headed and totally devoid now of beauty. I cannot see any signs of a heart in her either; she does nothing but sulk and complain, stuffing herself with honey and sweets, and only changing her clothes when she is shamed into it. Sometimes I wonder, indeed, if she has all her wits about her.

She does not mourn him; often I suspect she has forgotten he is dead. "Hal gave me this," she will say, for that is her name for him. "Hal gave me this when I was fifteen," smoothing a length of cloth-of-gold which has gone rotten along the folds. "It is for my coronation." Or she will finger the pearls she keeps in a casket, smiling dreamily. When I suggest, impatiently, that we have them strung, so that she can wear them, she says, "Oh, no, they are for my crown, Hal says."

And she will laugh, an empty, high sound, like glass shattering; poor thing, she makes me shiver.

She is barely thirty, but her fair hair has faded and gone gray, and her white skin is pasty and unhealthy-looking, with eruptions around her mouth. Her waist is thick and she has a double chin, still I see that men look at her with avid eyes; she carries herself like a wanton and a flirt in their presence, tossing her head and making long eyes. Twice we have caught her half-naked with varlets, though, I hope before she had lain with them. I have had to double her guard of women, and still I am uneasy. If she were to become pregnant again, with no name to the father! Our relations with France are chancy enough as it is! I have counted the days till we reach Rouen, where I will leave her.

Yet, when the castle loomed in the distance, high, square-towered, impregnable, my heart misgave me. It is such a gloomy place, and lonely. We saw it first in the early morning, mists still swirling about its highest battlement, and the pointed lances of its guards showing through like sharp black needles. Alys rode beside me, slumping on her mount, for only ladies surrounded us, our men-at-arms in the guard and van. Suppressing a sigh, I glanced at her sidewise and said, "That is the castle of Rouen."

She laughed that high queer laugh and said, "It looks strong . . . how many soldiers?"

"Oh, it is well garrisoned," I answered. She seemed pleased, a little smile playing around her lips.

It was deep-moated, with a heavy bridge worked by stout chains. When it was down, our horses' hooves made deep, hollow sounds as we crossed over. The inner bailey was of dressed gray stone, five feet thick, with slit windows that gave little light. Inside, though, I had commanded cressets to be lit in all the wall brackets, and a fire glowed in the old-fashioned fire pit, for it is a chill place even in summer. There were Turkey carpets on the stone floor and fine, rich-colored wall hangings; it was a passable fair sight.

Alys stood in the middle of the great hall and looked about her, smiling. "And this is to be mine . . . my castle?" I nodded. "I like it," she said. "It is very big."

In a way, it was her castle, for it lay in the lands of the Vexin, her dowry land. I had given orders that she was to have the run of the whole bailey, the hall, and the apartments above, so that she would not feel like the prisoner she was.

She would have every comfort, luxuries even—not like my jail at Salisbury. It was in such wise that I quieted my conscience. But still she would live under lock and key, with waiting-women who were really guards, and no man's company at all, except for her confessor, an old, old priest, nearly blind.

The intrigues of royalty, the polices of kings; it was not the first time I had bent my will to acts distasteful and even cruel for their sake. In my softer moments I have thought, What profit these involved machinations? In a thousand years or so—only a drop in the bucket of eternity—will it matter at all who held the Vexin lands? Alys might go back to her brother, with her dowry—would it matter so much to England? But then I stiffened my mind; it might very well matter. It might matter just as much as an heir for the King of England mattered. My next task—to fetch the little bride out of Navarre.

I put Alys and her fate out of my mind for now, and set my face toward the southland, where Berengaria awaited me.

CHAPTER 7

PAMPLONA LOOKED LIKE a village in one of the cheap romans, those copies of the troubadours' tales that are all illustrations, done by some renegade monk or other for pennies and sold at fairs. It even had a faded look, like the poor colors that run in a week, and out of drawing. But it had the same childlike, unreal charm of those things too—at least from a distance.

We came upon it at sunset, one of those crude, southern sunsets, all red streaks and purple mists, with a raw bloody sun poised on the rim of the world. The little town nestled crookedly, its roofs rosy, at the foot of the hill that held the crookback palace of Sancho, King of Navarre. It was the oddest building, no rhyme or reason to it, sprawling there in the purple light against the garish sky. As we drew near, I saw that it must have been added to over centuries. Nothing matched, it was all angles, one of the twin towers leaning precariously over the village, an attitude which might have been protective or threatening. And yet, like the town beneath, it too had charm; it made you feel like smiling. I turned to Hodierna and saw that, indeed, her thin lips had begun to curve.

"A comical place?" I said.

"It looks as though a child drew it," she answered. It was so exactly right, her reply, so much more descriptive than my own fanciful thoughts; I marveled, as so often, at her wonderful simplicity. It was why, of course, I had loved her so much, for so many long years. Faithful, sensible, plain as an old shoe, my friend Hodierna. Associations, memories, joys, sorrows—they joined us like sisters. I felt a gush of warmth and reached out, my eyes wet, to take her hand. She patted my arm, a brisk, warm gesture, no nonsense about it. I dried my eyes and set my attention to the business at hand.

"They do not expect us," I said. "Everything looks asleep."

But no; as if my words had been heard, torches flared in the castle and the drawbridge came creaking down—a little bridge, over a little running strip of water that looked as though it could be leapt over. Sancho cannot have many enemies, I thought. I was to learn that the pretty moat was twelve feet deep, with a fast current, and the banks of it fitted with wicked spikes, and that the odd angles of the castle itself harbored sophisticated Eastern war engines, arquebuses and the long tubes that threw the deadly Greek fire.

We clattered over the drawbridge. The great gates of the castle stood open, and varlets in rose-colored livery stood ready to dismount us. A long, brightly patterned Eastern carpet was spread across the courtyard for our feet; Sancho had been an early Crusader.

The swift shadows of the southern night were already settling down behind us, but inside, all was bright as day. Wax candles stood on every surface, and the walls held elaborate sconces that burned with a steady yellow flame, the light from oil lamps, soft and welcoming. The hall was not large, but exquisitely furnished, with low tables, cushioned chairs with armrests, inlaid ivory chests, soft furry rugs. The walls had no hangings, but were painted, in the Moorish style, with flowers and leaves and trees. Stars and slender half-moons dotted the ceiling, and the floor was a cunningly worked mosaic depicting a hunting scene.

We were greeted by a sort of steward, richly dressed, who

immediately prostrated himself before us, kissing the hem of my skirt. He led us, Hodierna and I, with several of my women, to a bathing room, where scented water steamed in painted tubs and a dozen bath-women stood ready with towels and ointments. It was the most delicious feeling, after a day in the saddle, to lie in that warm fragrance, sipping honeyed wine and hearing, from behind carved ivory screens, the soft strains of some stringed instrument played by unseen hands. I had not lived such a moment since Antioch, so long ago, but it was not difficult to grow used to it, though I heard my women giggling and shrieking as the bath-women kneaded them with scented oil. Why had Richard called the kingdom provincial? I shook my head; I will never understand my sons.

Laid out for my convenience were the most modern cosmetics, such as I had not seen before; I was tempted to try them all, and grew confused. In the end, though, I settled for the paints I knew, and did a passable job on my face, considering the ravages of time. With my best robe, a violet-blue, and head veil to match, I would do; one needs such blandishments to meet a prospective young daughter-in-law.

Sancho was a small, rotund man with thinning hair, bright eyes, and an anxious manner; I saw, with a pang, that he was perhaps half my age. Then, with a mental shrug, I remembered that so many were. I smiled, and saw by his eyes that I was still, at moments, and in the softest lights, a woman, and admired. I gave him my hand; he kissed it, and I said, "Sir, we must treat of weddings."

"I hope so, Lady. Will you be seated?" He led me to a chair of state, set, for courtesy, a trifle higher than his own. I smiled again, and accepted the glass of wine a servitor brought. The wine was amber-colored, and the glass almost a match, cunningly wrought with bubbles trapped inside, so that the wine looked like sparkling water. I held it up to the light.

"A pretty goblet," I said. "Unusual."

"It was blown from the sands of the Dead Sea," he said. "And the wine is Cypriot."

"A good omen," I answered, lifting it to my lips.

"I hope so, Lady . . . Your health, Queen Eleanor." And he drank.

I tasted the wine. "Delicious," I judged. "All good things come from the East."

"Almost all," he said, his bright eyes holding mine. "But not quite."

It was the kind of compliment I had not heard for sixteen years. I felt a warm glow spread through me, languorous and golden, my youth creeping slyly back. Or perhaps it was only that the wine was strong.

"Lady, may I present my daughter, Berengaria?" The softness of his voice upon her name told me that he loved this damsel well; I hoped that she would not prove to be spoiled.

The maiden knelt before me, her head bowed in a deep curtsy. I saw an orange head veil, a purple mantle trimmed with yellow-dyed vair, and a glimpse of one scarlet slipper with a silver heel; truly the colors were obscene! I wondered who had dressed the poor girl. I bent down, cupped her chin, and raised her face, so that it looked into mine. She trembled under my touch, and I felt a stir of pity. I always forget, these days, that I had been a woman famed in song and ballad, and even, in this southern backwater, a little notorious.

I spoke softly. "Well met, daughter."

The face was small, triangular, shaped like a heart, and pale. Not ill-favored, but if she had been anything less than a princess, I would have called her plain. Except for the eyes, large, liquid, a soft brown, with an upward tilt at the corners; the eyes of a doe, her one beauty. I could not see the color of her hair; it was strained back into the ugly orange headdress, which was fashioned into two enormous curving horns that towered above her small head, a new style which I had heard of but never seen till now. I hoped it would not catch on; I could not imagine wearing it.

She used no paint, and the orange color gave her skin a sickly yellow cast. The rest of her costume was just as ugly, green surcoat over a scarlet shift, though all of the finest silks. But I saw that her laced waist was tiny and the little breasts, outlined by the clinging fabric, firm and high; as Richard had said, she would do.

Except for the ladies' dress, the evening was one of the most tasteful times I have ever spent. The food was delicious, like the wine, and beautifully served on glazed pottery-ware spun very thin. I tasted everything, thin cold soups, jellied little fish in a delicate sauce, meat subtly flavored with fruit, salads spiced with Eastern herbs, sharp on the tongue, and the wonderful sherbet from the Saracen lands, icy and fragrant; there was the Turkish beverage, kaffee, too, thick, strong, and sweet, served in tiny gold cups, and steaming hot. Much was as I remembered from Antioch, but much was new as well; I saw I must curb my appetite, or put on flesh, an easy trap for women of my age.

The little Berengaria ate next to nothing, I saw—but perhaps she was nervous. She spoke little, too, except when spoken to, her eyes downcast. But she was all smiles and courtesy as she led me, afterward, to the apartment that they called the "ladies' tower."

It was comfortable, even luxurious, but in odd disarray: books flung down upon the cushioned windowseat, a lute trailing ribbons, lying in a corner, a dish of sweetmeats spilled upon a silken divan. Berengaria brushed them onto the floor and threw a fringed shawl over the mess, indicating I should take a seat. She herself sank onto a cushion at my feet. "Ladies, be still, and settle somewhere!" she commanded, raising her soft voice for once. For the minute we entered the chamber they had begun to twitter like the bright birds they resembled. "Forgive us, Lady. We relax here . . . Pia!" she called to one of her ladies, a bold laughing wench with too much bosom, and spoke to her in a foreign tongue that was quick and clipped, strange to my ears. The girl nodded and went behind a curtain.

"The tongue you spoke—what is it?" I asked. "I cannot recognize the sound."

"Pia is a Basque, from the mountains," she said. "It is a strange language. I am the only one of us who can speak even a few words of it. Poor Pia, she must use sign language." She held out her hand as the girl returned leading a nun dressed in a black habit. "This is my sister, Blanche," said Berengaria, "home from her convent. She has taken a vow of silence, but she will allow herself a little music." The nun bowed gravely, and returned to the far end of the chamber, where she sat on a stool, folding her hands and looking as if she expected something to happen. And indeed it did.

Berengaria clapped her hands, and a hush fell among those noisy ladybirds. I heard the notes of a lute, teasingly familiar, and a voice, rich and golden, rose in a song I knew well. I knew the voice too, but I could not believe my ears. I heard it through, my heart pounding, my nails digging into the flesh of my hands so that I would not choke or sob. The sweet notes drew to a close, ". . . give all this grace, if the Queen of England lay in my embrace." Bernard's song, that one he had written for me so long ago. It was my turn to tremble now. I spoke to Berengaria, my words halting. "The—the singer...?"

"We must go to him," she said gently, raising me from my seat. I followed where she led, moving slowly, painfully. I felt, on a sudden, like an old woman.

Behind a velvet curtain Bernard sat, the lute in his hand, the lower part of his body covered with a silken rug. He was old, his hair white, his face all sunk to bone, and marked with lines of suffering, but I would have known him anywhere. "I cannot rise, Lady," he said, with a little smile. "My legs are useless, like twigs."

"Oh, my friend, my friend," I said, my voice shaking. "I thought you were dead!"

"As good as," he said, still smiling. "But now that you have come, I will go content."

I cradled his poor white head in my arms, not caring that Berengaria saw, and wept.

BOOK V

THE BRIDE

Told by Berengaria, Princess of Navarre, later wife to Richard

CHAPTER 1

WHEN I WAS twelve a Catalan witch-woman cursed me; the "cold curse," she called it. I have never forgotten the words.

It was my birthday, and I had been given my first full-grown palfrey to ride. A mare she was, and gentle enough, except she did not yet know my touch on the bridle. Snow-white, with a golden mane, pink nostrils, and large golden-brown eyes, she was Arab-blooded; I called her Fatima, the only Arab name I knew.

Spring had come learly that year, with much flooding from all the little mountain streams; the roads were mired and muddy as we rode back from morning Mass. I was happy, for, as well as the new mount, I had received a casket of gold coins and a pearl necklet, the match to the one worn in the portrait of Our Lady Mary that hung in the chapel. I pursed my lips to look more like the portrait as I rode, the necklet bobbing on my bony little chest.

Fatima stepped delicately, lifting her white legs high in the muddy way and a snuffling lightly in the golden, rain-washed air. I saw it before she did, a dark form crouched at the side of the road and rising up suddenly, but I was not quick enough; the horse shied, rearing high, so that I had to cling to the pommel, letting go the reins. Her hooves, coming down, struck the woman who stood there, knocking her to the ground and trampling her, before Father caught the bridle and pulled the mare aside.

I truly think the woman was not much hurt, for she got up slowly onto her feet and did not sway, but stood, staring at me with great black eyes like hard stones, her gaudy skirts all muddy and two dark hoof imprints on the front of her bodice where the horse's shoes had caught her. She was some sort of joglar-woman, her gown scarlet and trimmed with dirty, tarnished silver braid, and her lips and cheeks boldly painted. Lent had not yet started, and these folk had come in to the village for the fair-days that go before. They come every year to dance and tumble for pennies, carrying the round tambourines hung with bells that mark their trade; I had heard it jangle when she fell. Bells must have been sewn onto her skirt too, for, as she turned away, clutching the coin Father had flung her, her foot slipped, and a great tinkling sound went up in the air. I was startled, and nervous, and young, and the sound made me giggle, foolishly. She spun around, spitting the words at me.

"Curses on you, cold laughing maiden! I curse you! The cold curse it is I put on you!" And then she chanted the little verse that has sounded cruelly in my ears ever since. It was a Spanish dialect she spoke, but I understood it; we have varlets in the castle from all the Spanish provinces, and I know the tongue as well as my own.

"Cold hands and feet," she sang, the bright hoops swinging from her ears, "and a cold couch."

I stared at her as though I were turned to stone, and all seemed still as stone around me; even the mare did not toss her head or whinny.

"A cold bridegroom is yours, and a cold womb . . . and then, in the end, a cold grave."

Father was the first to move; he raised his hand, with the riding crop in it, and the woman scuttled away, melting into the crowd. I heard about me whispers and cries of "Witch! Black witch-woman!" and several folk made the sign of the evil eye against her going. Father laughed, putting his arm about me, and calling her words gibberish. "A foul Romany slut," he said, "and without the power to harm. 'Twas no witch, little one."

But I was not comforted. Those stony black eyes *had* the power; I saw it, and my heart turned to an icy lump under the new pearl necklet. That night, I remember, I took a chill, and fever with it, and was sick all through the Easter season. Our Moorish doctor said it was from going too early into thin spring finery. But I *knew*. And from that day I have suffered from chilblains in winter, and, even in the heat, my hands and feet are cold as the waters of a mountain spring, striking chill through my bedcovers so that often I cannot sleep.

I remember my mother only dimly, for she died when I was about four years of age, after my brother Sancho's birth. My sister Blanche was even younger and cannot recall her face. Mother was a beauty, I think, tall and queenly, with a vivid, laughing look. Neither of us girls takes after her, though Sancho does; he is uncommonly handsome. Father must have loved her very much; he has never taken another wife, or even a concubine. Perhaps, if she had lived, I could have talked to her, and eased my mind. But, brought up as I was, by peasant nurses, with only a sister more of a child than I, it was a thing I never spoke of, the cold curse that haunted my growing years.

Because of the great love he bore my mother, Father spoiled us all. He never betrothed us in childhood, as royal children are betrothed, to strangers of another princely house, but promised that we should have the choosing of our fates when we came of an age to care. He spoiled us in other ways too; little Sancho grew up wild as a mountain cat, and ran off when he was not turned fifteen to join the Lionheart, and Blanche was always strange and withdrawn, given to visions and long fasts. I was timid and compliant, by comparison, but even I was stubborn in my refusal to marry, finding excuses to reject suitor after suitor, and putting off the day of choice.

Girls usually get their monthly courses at the age of thirteen or thereabouts, but year after year went by and I remained a child. My breasts were no more than little buds, hardly showing beneath my bodice, and no hair grew in my secret places; my womb was dry. I wept, alone in the night, remembering the Romany curse, and fearing. Blanche had been already two years in her convent, and I was nearly twenty before I felt the first warm trickle of woman's blood between my legs.

There was a great festive tournament in Pamplona that year, to celebrate the end of the Lenten fast, and my brother Sancho came home for it, bringing his idol, Richard, Duke of Aquitaine, the Lionheart, that men called the best knight in the world. We all felt the honor greatly, Father decking the field of combat with silken flags and putting up new scaffolding hung with canopies. It was a brilliant sight, glowing with color and alive with sound. The morning sun was dazzling on the bright, wicked swords and lance tips, and polished the iron mail to shining scales, iridescent as the skin of dragons.

I was beside myself with anxious excitement, trying on gown after gown and hating them all. The Duke had asked to wear my favor in the lists, to honor the daughter of the house, though we had not yet met face to face. It threw me into a kind of frenzy, for I thought I had nothing fine enough. "Ah, sister," cried Sancho impatiently, "make haste!

He will never notice . . . he is a warrior! Anything will do—a sleeve, a head veil."

I stared at my brother in anguish, my hands full of fluttering silks, a clutter of them flung around me on the floor. "But what color shall I choose?" I cried, beside myself.

Sancho laughed. "Well, he is a redhead, you know . . . something green will do. And it is the color of love too," he added, laughing slyly.

I felt my face flame, and, in confusion and haste, snatched up a long scarf of some transparent stuff, blue-green. "Here, take this. And hurry! Don't keep him waiting!"

He turned to go, and I, gainsaying myself, caught at his sleeve. "Not yet, I beg you! What dress . . . what color dress shall I wear?"

He shook his head, exasperated. "Women! Why, wear the match to this, of course!" And he fluttered the scarf he held.

"Oh. Well, I usually wear it with a yellow satin."

He looked at me critically, as though he had never seen me before. "Not yellow, no—with your skin. It will make you sallow. Try blue or rose-color." And he dashed out the door, waving the scarf.

I had no rose-pink, except a velvet, too warm for the day, and so I settled for a gauzy blue, the color of the Virgin's robe, with a head veil of the same shade, shot with gold. It was too simple for the occasion, but the gold in the veil helped, and I carried an ermine capelet for show. When I looked in my mirror, I saw that there was a little color in my cheeks, for once; I pinched them to deepen it, and rubbed some red paste into my pale lips. My hands were shaking and, of course, as cold as ice.

Richard unhorsed all his opponents that day—there were fourteen, I counted them. But it was all done so easily, as though he and the horse beneath him took part in a fanciful dance. After each encounter, he made the horse prance and curvet, rear and walk backward, like a trained animal in a jongleur show. The stands buzzed and hummed with the wonder of the sight, and my blue-green favor floating free and clean through it all, untouched by dust or mire. My heart swelled to bursting with pride at the sight of it, and my hands, in my lap, twisted together at each contest, clammy with sweat, and warm, for once, so that they burned through the stuff of my gown.

After the melee, and he sitting horse, alone, the victor of

all, he doffed his helmet and, carrying it under his arm, rode toward the stands, straight toward where I sat. A violent tremor shook me so that I nearly lost my balance, as that godlike figure came closer, white teeth in a red-brown face, and the shining fall of auburn hair that waved to touch his iron shoulders. He reined in his mount and sat laughing up at me. Someone had put the victor's wreath into my hand, but I only held it, staring stupidly. There was a great hush all about.

"Princess fair," he said finally, squinting his eyes against the sun. "Will you not crown me with your white hand?" There was a little note of mockery in his voice, but gentle, so that I knew it was not meant unkindly, and he smiled still.

"Oh," I said, startled into action. I found the object in my lap, feeling it to be a slender circlet, leaves shaped of gems and set in gold. I thrust it forward suddenly, nearly poking his eye; he ducked his head smoothly to take the crowning, and then held out his hand for mine, his eyes holding a leaping light.

"You do me honor, sweet damsel," he said, and bent to put his lips to my hand; their touch was firm, cool, and dry.

I looked down at the thin white parting that divided the shining russet falls of his hair. It was then that I felt it, for the first time, that odd, disquieting rush within my belly and the quick hot flow between my legs. I caught my breath; my face was hot with shame, though of course no one saw, and my hand trembled in his.

"Fair hand," he said. "So small, like a little fluttering bird." I had forgotten he was a poet, and famous for that too.

I made to draw away my hand, but he held it fast. "Small bird," he said again. "So small, so warm."

So warm! So warm—*my* hand! A rush of heat went through me, borne on a rush of love. Richard had melted the ice within, and lifted the Romany's curse.

I knew that he was mine, the lover of my inmost heart. And that for good or ill, I was his, from that moment on—if he would have me.

CHAPTER 2

I KNEW THAT Richard had done no more than pay the usual court that is due a noblewoman in her father's house, where he was an honored guest. A few songs, a pretty phrase, a light compliment—and once a conversation, fully two minutes long. That was all . . . and yet I lived on it for months, until his letter came, the letter that changed my world.

It was not written to me, for that would be too bold, and I a damsel still. It was a letter to my father, the King, asking for my hand in marriage. And, though it was like a bolt from heaven to me, it infuriated Father. "That Plantagenet upstart!" he cried, tearing at his thin hair. "That churl!" His little pink jowls quivered with honest indignation. "So this is how he repays my hospitality! How can he dare? Descended from witches they are, or the Devil—the whole brood of them! I'll not have it! That he should dare!" And he threw the parchment with the ducal seal hanging from it on a scarlet ribbon—threw it onto the floor and trampled it.

"But, Father," I said, putting my hand on his arm, "I want him."

"You—you what?" he sputtered. "You are a little ignorant fool, a silly girl!"

"If I cannot have him," I said, very quietly, "I will have no one."

I had never been willful before, not in all my life; it set him back on his heels. I think he believed me bewitched, and perhaps I was, I knew all the arguments against the match; the doings of the Plantagenets, those showy, gorgeous creatures, have been common knowledge for years, even here, where all the news is late.

I knew of Richard's long-standing betrothal to Alys of France, and I even knew the gossip about her and the English king, his father; in a little court like ours, women have nothing else to do but whisper scandal. I did not mention this, however, but kept a prim mouth; it would not do for

Father to think me worldly. Strangely enough, he had heard nothing of the loose talk; the affairs of his kingdom are too much on his mind. But once, he scratched his head and said, querulously, "And there is something not quite right there, some mystery. *Why* has the marraige not taken place, after all these years?"

He could do nothing with me; I had made up my mind. Over and over he harangued me, stabbing at the letter with his quill to make the points.

"There is no peace there, in that family—no affection. All the sons have been at one another's throats for years, except when they have banded together against the father. And Queen Eleanor was in it too. She incited her sons to rebellion . . . even now she languishes in an English prison. He has kept her there for—how long? All the prime of her life! Do you want to share her fate?"

"Richard is not his father," I said calmly. "Richard is the best knight in the world, everyone says so."

"Knight! Knight! A whore-son brute! He has ravaged the Midi for more than a decade! Thee is not a castle he has not fired, or a field he has not burned! He is a murderer and a spoiler—and a rapist too! His routiers swarm everywhere, like locusts. He is not a man for my daughter!"

"He is the one I want," I said, still quietly. And then, "Richard loves God. He has taken the cross."

"He loves power and plunder!" This time he hit the parchment so hard that the quill made a hole in it. "What do you think this says? He wants such and such a dowry with you . . . so many men, so many horses, such numbers of arquebuses. Why, he is as much as asking you to buy him!"

"It is all for the Crusade . . . not for himself," I said.

"He is putting himself up for the highest bidder," Father said, growing weary.

"Then let us bid very high," I answered. "You can afford it, Father."

He was silent for a moment, all the lines of his face drooping. I knew I had exhausted all his arguments; we had been over it all for weeks now. I almost felt sorry for him, but, when I thought of life without Richard, my heart hardened. I waited.

He shook his head, sadly, saying, as he had said so often, "He may not even be King."

"I do not need a king," I said.

245

"There is talk that Henry means to disinherit him, in favor of John," he said, though he had not heard me.

"I do not care. Father, I *want* him!" For the first time, I bent my head into my hands and wept. From the corner of my eye, I saw his face crumple with concern, and knew that I had won.

"Well," he said. "I will send to him . . . I will open the way for negotiations. Now, don't cry!" He patted my shoulder awkwardly, for I had fallen at his feet, sobbing. "Now, now . . . I will write. But I must get to the bottom of this Alys business, there is something odd there."

A reply came back from Richard, promptly—very promptly, considering that the letter had to go halfway across Europe to catch up with him.

He accepted our offer, on condition that Father double the amount of men and horses. Father read it aloud. "'. . . I will let the gold stand as it is . . .'" "Oh, good of him!" interjected Father, his face red "'. . . though I have much need of gold, always, for this Crusade. Still, the maiden pleases me. I shall hope to come to a fair agreement soon and get on with this marriage, before I leave for the Holy Land. As to the old arrangement with the French court, know you that I shall never marry Alys Capet. The betrothal will be set aside by law and by Church canon, as soon as the truth is made public. I have held off thus long in deference to her brother of France, Philip Augustus, my fellow Crusader. But now I shall put it at risk—now that I am like to be committed elsewhere. It is an open secret, at any rate, and the shame long worn thin. Alys, my betrothed, is my father's mistress, and has borne a child to him. You need not tell the Princess Berengaria this, but simply say I give my solemn word, under God, that I am free to wed, if she and you be willing.'"

And he signed it, a great scrawl that covered the page, "Richard, by the grace of God, Duke of Aquitaine, and heir to England."

I lowered my eyes, pretending shame at the revelation; how I was learning to dissemble already! But Father was truly shocked; to him, the laws of land and Church are sacred, he is very old-fashioned. "God, how can this be! What a monster this England is! Murderer of saints and defiler of virgins!" He tore at his hair again; at this rate he would nave none left.

"It is only one saint, Father—and perhaps only one virgin," I said mildly. "And we do not know the whole story ... perhaps she was wanton."

He rolled his eyes to heaven, deploring my words. "Holy saints, the Plantagenet has corrupted you already!" But there was a light note in his voice, and I could tell he was coming round to accept the whole thing, and even to see its advantages for me, and for the kingdom of Navarre.

I could not believe that I had done it, that I had got my way, finally. I dared not smile in triumph—it would offend Father, and I had been unmaidenly enough already. I was never alone, so throughout the day I must strive to keep the curve from my lips, turning it into a hiss of deprecation at some fancied flaw in my needlework—easy enough, it was always hen tracks!—or laughing outright at the antics of my little dog. Even so, my Spanish duenna, Caterina, glanced sharply at me more than once, and finally asked me outright what I was mooning over. "I am dreaming of my wedding," I said, with a high trill of laughter. She stared at me as though I had gone mad; perhaps I had, I had always been such a mouse all my days. For of course, no one knew anything yet; it must all be kept quiet until it was truly settled.

That night, in the great bed, beside my woman Gratiana, I lay staring at the pale gray square of the window, waiting for her to sleep. I never liked the nights when it was Gratiana's turn, she was always restless. But finally I heard her snore, soft and snuffling. I pressed my hands to my hot cheeks and whispered, "Richard ... oh, Richard." I smiled, now, in the dark, running my hands down my body, under the light coverlet. My breasts, which had been growing, hurt. I touched one, softly, feeling the tip harden under my hand. "Richard ..."

CHAPTER 3

AND NOW BEGAN the waiting that was to become a part of my life.

Even after the betrothal agreement was signed, month after dreary month went by, and still no word from Richard. We heard rumors that there was war in the duchies around Paris; that he had fallen out with Philip Augustus; that they had made a new alliance, against his father, Henry of England; that the English king was old before his time and sorely ill. And, finally, came the report that, in weariness and defeat, the King had died at Chinon. Richard would be King, and I would be Queen of England!

Soon the whole of Pamplona buzzed with it, for within the week Richard's token came, a slender gold circlet, set, between the royal arms of England, with a large ruby. "This is the crown of the English queens, worn by my grandmother, Mathilda," wrote Richard. "I would have Berengaria wear it at our wedding, which will be soon, God willing. Now that I am King of this realm, I must get me a wife."

"He means an heir, the whore-son!" cried Father, with a look both tipsy and lewd; he had broached a keg of the best amontillado, rich and sweet, for the occasion, and we were all a little drunk. My brother, Sancho, had brought the letter and the heirloom crown, riding all day and night from Fontevrault, where King Henry lay in state, in his last repose.

"A toast," cried Sancho, raising his glass. "A toast to the unborn! To the heir of England and Navarre!" He drained the glass and, swaying slightly where he stood, fixed me with his glassy, drunkard's eye. "It's important, you know, sister. Richard's got plenty of the other kind—from the wrong side of the blanket . . . but none that can rule after him." He pointed a not-quite-steady finger at me. "That's why he'll have to do it before he leaves. If he should die in the Holy Land . . ."

"Oh, don't say that!" I cried. "He *cannot* die!"

"No, nor will he, sister! I have seen him walk through a rain of arrows as thick as a sheep's hairs and come through without a scratch. But just in case . . ." He mumbled a little now. "Bear it in mind, sister, and do your duty!" He poured another glass and, quaffing it, said slurringly, "An heir for England . . . a little, little heir."

"That's enough, lad . . . you've had enough," said Father, pushing him gently toward the door. "Go now and sleep it off."

"And you too, now, My Lady Princess," said the duenna Caterina, with a sniff of her high Spanish nose. "You come to bed." She sniffed again and raised her dark eyes to heaven. "Such talk—before a damsel!"

I rose and drew myself up, standing on my toes to look taller, and holding my head high. "I am nearly twenty-one," I said, "and betrothed now . . . soon I will be a wedded woman and a queen. And I will go to bed in my own time." I nodded firmly as she stood staring like a codfish. "You may leave us now, Doña Caterina." And I waved my hand in dismissal. My heart was beating like a caged bird's, almost making me sick, but I kept my eyes forward and did not watch her go.

"Why, pigeon . . . little pigeon," said Father, his eyes chiding. "You have offended her, the good soul! Go after her now, like a nice child, and make it up!"

"No, Father," I said, standing my ground, though I trembled. "I am *not* a child. And she is not good . . . she is a cross-hatched scold! Forever at my elbow or peering over my shoulder, and covering her ears if any of us laugh or sing! Richard loves light hearts and music—he said so! Oh, Father! Send her away!"

"But, pigeon . . . you must have women about you."

"I have plenty of women—young ones, like me! Send her away! Send all the old women away, I do not need them! Oh, why do I have to have a duenna? We are not even Spanish!"

At this Father had to smile; it was so like the child I had sworn I was not. He took me in his arms and tipped up my chin. "My poor little pigeon, you will be a wife soon enough—and a queen . . . it is none so easy." At this, a chill went through me; I did not know why I shivered. "Don't fret, little one," said Father. "It shall be as you say . . . for this time left to us, at least." His words were sad; I had not thought of leaving him, and what it would mean. He had been my whole world, up till now.

"Oh, Father, we will see each other often, when I am with Richard . . . he will not come between us."

"Oceans will lie between us, little one," he said, his eyes bright with tears. "But it is your destiny . . . a high one."

I was to remember his words, and bitterly, in the years that followed.

But, for now, I had my way. Doña Caterina was packed off to wherever she had come from, and the old waiting-women with her, pensioned, or sent to nunneries. And I was free to order my own life, within my woman's domain, to laugh and sing with the flighty Navarese girls who made up my train, to sew feverishly at my bride's gear, pricking my fingers, and to wait for Richard's summons.

It was a whole year, or nearly, before it came, sending us all into a wild flurry of activity. Richard was on his way to the Holy Land, and his mother, Queen Eleanor, freed from her long imprisonment, was journeying to Navarre as his envoy, to fetch me to him, somewhere on the Crusaders' Road. Father was to send my dowry, men, horses, and arms, over the mountain trails and along the sea wall to Marseilles.

With Richard's letter came his captain of mercenaries, the famous Mercadier, bearing the birde-gifts: gorgeous lengths of bright silks and glowing velvets, thick, rich furs, caskets of gems, and boxes filled with silver and gold plate. I had not expected anything, I was so happy to get him! And with Mercadier, whose dark brooding face I remembered dimly from Richard's first visit, came a courtly old gentleman with white hair and burning eyes, borne in a litter, with a gilded lute in a cloth-of-silver bag, borne on a cushion all to itself.

"This is the great troubadour, Bernard de Ventadour," said the letter. "I beg you to do him honor. He has been cruelly used, tortured and half starved, kept in dungeons, and his legs smashed to jelly so that he can never set foot to the ground again, but he still has a voice and a store of glorious songs that must not be lost to posterity. Give him a refuge and a home; the world will thank you. Remember, for me, that he was, for long years, my mother's faithful friend. She knows, as yet, nothing of his unhappy state, though it was for her sake that he suffered. I would have you break it to her gently, and, by cherishing this great man, give her peace."

Father said that it was King Henry that had misused the troubadour, out of pure malice, and jealousy of the Queen he had scorned. Bernard had been among the Queen's party when Henry's soldiers captured them sixteen years ago; I supposed he was lucky to be alive, considering the late King's insane rages. But Bernard never spoke a word against him, or indeed, ever mentioned his past trials at all. He took up quarters in a little apartment we readied for him, in the ladies' tower, and became our very own troubadour, playing for us in the evenings all the splendid music of his glorious past. We gave him our Ethiopian eunuch, Bilbo, to serve him, and I think his life will be easy from now. God knows, he cannot have long to live, for his death is in his face already; I can hardly look at him without weeping.

It was a wonderful thing to see the meeting between the old Queen and her longtime swain. Her proud face softened with love and pity, and her whole being seemed to melt. It almost made me like her—but not quite.

It is strange; Richard's mother, and beloved of him, and yet I took against her from the first! I know she is a remarkable woman; I have heared tales of her all my life, like everyone else, and some not of the most savory, either. They say she has had hundreds of lovers, and that she slept with her own uncle, Raymond of Antioch, and that that is why the King of France, her first husband, divorced her. Also that she rode to Crusade half naked, in men's clothing, to the scandal of all who saw her. It is whispered, too, that she poisoned King Henry's mistress, the Fair Rosamund, but that cannot be true, unless she could pass through stone walls. That lady died while Queen Eleanor was in prison, so it is just an ugly tale, told by the Queen's enemies. Perhaps they are all false, the old stories; a beautiful woman in a high place will always be talked about, I must be fair.

And certainly, I can see that she must have been beautiful once. But she is very old now, thin and ravaged, with a wrinkled face and brown grave spots on her long white hands. Yet she still paints and prinks like a woman in her prime, full red lips drawn on with a brush and black lines outlining her eyes, and her ancient bony frame hung with gorgeous silks and jewels. When she made long eyes at Father at their first meeting, it was a gruesome sight, like a death's-head grinning. He did not think so, obviously, for he held her hand too long, his eyes glistening, and preened himself for all the world like a partridge strutting before its mate; I could have smacked him, poor silly Father!

No one shares my opinion, I must admit. My ladies fawn over her, oohing and ahing over her clothes and hair, and falling all over themselves to serve her. Even the varlets are dumbstruck when she passes, and she had our cross old cook, who bars his kitchen to all, eating out of her hand from the first. He even took her on a tour of his domain, bowing and scraping—and all because of a casual compliment about a sauce. And now he creates special dishes, just for her! "Dear man, you will make me fat!" she says, batting her lashes like a girl. "Oh, never, Lady," says he, all smiles. "Nothing could spoil your figure." And it is the same with everyone; Queen Eleanor can do no wrong.

I must admit she has good teeth, for a woman of her age; none missing, and only a little yellowed. Better than my own; I have a crooked eye tooth. And she is still tall, for a woman; even in my new heeled slippers from Genoa, I must look up to meet her eyes.

That first evening, when I was presented to her, falling upon my knees before her, as was only her due, she tipped my head up and looked me full in the face. Though her expression did not change, I knew, somewhere within me, that she did not like what she saw. It was a quick judgment and, I thought, unfair. For of course I was dreadfully nervous, shaking with it. Her measuring look, a long one, summed me up, and found me wanting. It was the first time I had felt disapproval; after all, I am a princess, and gently nurtured.

I know I am not beautiful; many of my ladies surpass me in face and figure, for, even now, filling out a little, I still have the body of a child, and my eyes are too large for my face. But I am cleverer than any of them, cleverer than my sister Blanche too. I can read and write Latin, and speak several languages, and I know something of numbers and the stars. And, I am sure, from the way he looked at me, and the words of his songs, that Richard, at least, found me passably fair. Perhaps Queen Eleanor would not like anyone he chose; it is clear that he is her favorite son, and that she dotes on him.

Looking inside myself, perhaps, too, I am jealous of her, his mother. For it is equally clear that Richard adores her above all other women.

Even so, I cannot help feeling that she is unkind. She says things—sharp judgments or careless comments—that are meant to wound. And I cannot fight back, for she is old and venerable, and Ricahrd's mother besides.

When, shyly, I asked Bernard to play a song that Richard had made for me—one that I had written down—she listened, nodding sagely, and afterward said, "Yes, I know it well . . . it is an early song, written to some lady of the court at Poitiers. Even the words are the same."

It took the wind out of my sails, as Father would say. But when I replied, with a valor that surprised me, that the words described me very well, my face, my hair, even my low stature, she smiled and said yes, but that it also described the little Marguerite of France, his brother's bride, ". . . and I should have known, he always fancied her, poor boy." She stared at me for a moment. "Yes, it is true. You are very like. Except—" And she broke off. Then, after a bit, "But that is all to the good, my dear. We must play up the resemblance."

It was then that she began to make me over, as it were. I am sure that she enjoyed it, but it made me feel a fool, stupid and tasteless. "Marguerite had great delicacy . . . your clothes are all wrong, my dear. So rich, such strong colors . . . meant for someone far more imposing. Forgive me, my dear, but you look like a little dressed-up doll. These fashionable gawds are not for you. You must aim for simplicity, an ingenuous look . . . no furs, no jewels, a few flowers braided into the hair . . . soft colors, white, blue, gray. And no headdresses . . . your hair is very beautiful." At this, I must say, I gasped. For my hair is my despair, so curly that it never will stay in plaits, and hurts to comb. And then it is no color at all, just a plain brown. But Queen Eleanor says not, that it is a perfect glossy chestnut. "One cannot get that shade with dye," she mused, narrowing her eyes. And so she bids me wear it loosely, falling as it will about my shoulders and face, or bundled carelessly into a net of pearls; it is forever getting into my eyes and mouth. "And wash it often," she says, "having your maids rub it with silk to bring out the shine." She clucked over my fingernails too, and painted them with some bitter brew so that I will not bite them. Still I do, without knowing it; I have got used to the bad taste. Some things will not change, no matter.

But mostly the change is great. Or no, it is not change exactly, but an intensification of what is *me* . . . my qualities. I seem softer, smaller, younger, and more pliant, almost fragile—all the things I tried to hide. And I can see that it is right that I should look so; for the first time eyes follow me where I pass, on my way to church. She even instructed me how to behave at such times! "Acknowledge them, my dear, they are your subjects! A gentle wave of the hand—so . . . and a smile. Remember, you are to be a king's wife."

"Your skin worries me, dear," she said, while I swallowed the offense. "It is just a tiny bit sallow. No. No rouge! You must play the natural nymph!" And she smiled brilliantly. "Perhaps a touch of the sun?"

"Oh, madame," I replied, alarmed, "I will look like a peasant!"

"Nonsense, Berengaria! A little sun will not hurt you." Her face changed, suddenly, a quick, annoyed look. "By the way, what do they call you for a 'little' name—a pet name? I cannot keep on saying that mouthful. What? Berrie? Berenza?"

"Sometimes," I said, blushing, because it sounded so silly, "sometimes the girls call me Ria."

"Ria," she repeated, trying it out. "Excellent! I like that! Well, little Ria, we must rig up something—a tent, a shelter—on the highest roof, where you can sunbathe."

I was absolutely aghast, and stared at her with my jaw dropped.

"Close your mouth, Ria dear, you look like a fish," she said, laughing. "You must not be such a little provincial, you know. Richard warned me that you were."

At this, I felt tears rise to my eyes, but held them back; I was too proud to cry, little provincial that I may be to these worldly Plantagenets.

She went on, not noticing. "When I was in the East, in the Outremer court, sunbathing was all the rage. No doubt it still is. I envy you, for I can no longer take the sun. It makes me look like a prune, so I avoid it. But what a lovely feeling it is! And what a glow it imparts! You will see."

There was no gainsaying her, of course; there never was. So, every afternoon, while the fine weather held, I lay for an hour, my arms and bosom bared and my face upturned to the sun's rays, upon the flat roof of our ladies' tower. She was right, of course, as usual; my color, after only a week, became a lovely rose-gold, looking as if it were painted. Some of my women begged to be allowed to "get a suntan," as Queen Eleanor called it. I had started a fashion! *I!*

And so, I see that my humiliations served a good purpose; I am certainly closer to beauty than I ever imagined I could be. And if Richard found me acceptable before, he is bound to like me better now. So, I thanked Queen Eleanor, gravely, for all she had done.

She waved her hand airily. "Oh, I love to do such things . . . I should have been an artist, I think, instead of a queen!" And she laughed, as she often does, a great, unwomanly ha-ha-ha! with her mouth wide open and all her fine teeth showing; it is infectious, and all my women began giggling and tittering, and even I smiled wide, forgetting my crooked tooth. At such times she is uncommonly good company, and one can almost forget she is so old, a grandmother several times over—a thing which she never hesitates to brag about. "My girls are good breeders, I'll say that," she says. And then, suddenly remembering, she will point her finger at me and ask when my period is, noting it down in a little book she carries at her belt. I am afraid to ask what it means, or whether the time of the month has significance, or how; I do not wish to seem ignorant. And also, I have lied to her. For I do not know, truly, when my periods come; they are so irregular. I am afraid that means I am not normal or something, so I lied, and gave a date, near the end of the month. I hope she does not try to check up on it.

She must have read at least a part of my thoughts, for she kindly explained that it is well to know the exact times, so that one can judge at the fertile times in between. I nodded, as though it set my mind at rest. But of course it did not. If I am so irregular, can it not be possible that fertility, too, is infrequent, or— But I will not think about that.

And so I did not, by day. But at night I lay awake long, troubled with icy hands and feet, though it is still full summer. And when I slept, I dreamed of the Romany's curse, and woke, weeping.

CHAPTER 4

I WELL REMEMBER the day I first saw Joanna Plantagenet. If her hair, a russet mantle, had not reached almost to her hips, I would have mistaken her for her brother Richard. Even so, the likeness was breathtaking. She was on horseback, and even the way that she handled her mount—boldly, imperiously, and with a touch of the mountebank—was the same. All eyes were on her, and she knew it, and her own eyes flashed fire and she laughed, her head thrown back to show her long white throat.

We were in Messina, finally, after a whole winter's weary journeying, and my own head a jumble of the sights and sounds of strange places. We had set out from Navarre in

November, accompanied by Father and many nobles of our court. Indeed, we were such a large party that quite often folk in outlying districts thought we were a contingent of the Crusading army; Richard's soldiers, sent to escort us, wore the white cross of England, and each of us had, somewhere upon his equipage, on horse, litter, or baggage mule, the blazon of the same intent. We began to accustom ourselves to the sight of rows of kneeling worshippers lining our way, reaching out to touch the hems of our robes or to kiss the prints where our horses' hooves had sunk into the dust.

I had never seen so many poor people, for Navarre is a fruitful country, if small, and Father has always been a generous overlord. These could break your heart; men crusted with the grime of years, their limbs and their very faces gnarled as the roots of old trees, looking as though they grew out of the earth they stood upon, twisted, dull-eyed, colored like the soil. The women, too, things of the earth, but paler, thinner, their eyes sunk deep in bony sockets, tears tracing white runnels down their wasted cheeks. The little children, most heartbreaking of all, hid, naked, behind their mothers' skirts, only their huge, solemn eyes and shock heads showing as they watched our passing. Even so, those poor souls thrust out at us rough baskets of coarse bread, country cheeses, or windfall apples, and sometimes a hand pressed upon us a brace of skinny fowl; once a young girl, incredibly dirty, with matted hair crawling with lice, but whose shy eyes were the color of violets, touched my skirt, and I looked down to see, in her hand, the offering of a single egg.

I made to protest, but Queen Eleanor, beside me, hissed, "Take it, child! Would you spurn a sacrifice?" I took it, smiling my thanks; the rest of the day I rode, with the egg warm in my hand, wet with my tears of pity and guilt.

Such sights made our journey wretched, and the towns were worse, for there refuse and excrement fouled the lanes and byways, and dwarflike children fought desperately over scraps of offal, while old corpses rotted in the gutters, black with flies.

So we were glad when we came to the foothills of the Alps, and gladder still when we began to climb the steep, winding roads that crossed them and breathed in the clean, pure air. Higher up, the same air was like a knife, cutting sharp into our lungs, and the way grew very hard and weary. Sometimes we had to go single file, and slowly, the rock face rising beside us on one side, and on the other, a steep fall of rock going down far below, miles perhaps. I looked down once, seeing rolling valleys and hamlets like children's toys nestled among them, and a tiny moving speck that was a farm wagon, its horse and driver smaller than ants. But I grew dizzy and swayed in the saddle, and Queen Eleanor caught my arm, saying sharply, "Have a care, child. Keep your eyes on the road!"

Ahead of us the long ribbon of our train wound, disappearing into the mists above, while, behind, it stretched again, longer still. We rode like this, creeping like snails, a whole day and night and part of another day. When we came down onto level ground, we were so stiff we had to be helped from the saddle, and our legs gave way beneath us when we tried to stand on them. We lay then, resting in a mean inn, for two days; I slept the whole time. And so, after another week, and the saddle sores hardened to callus upon us, we came to Marseilles.

Here Father was to part from us, returning to Navarre, though many others wished to continue on and celebrate the wedding. Of course he was the only one I cared about, and I shed bitter tears. But I am a king's daughter, and I know a little kingdom like ours cannot be left long without a protector.

And so, the parting; but I could not grieve too much, for I was getting closer and closer to Richard and marriage.

At Naples, five galleys awaited us, sent by Richard to bring us to Messina. On the sea journey, I lost all the aches and pains of travel, and put on a little flesh, so that there was some curve to me, at last. And, too, the sun was out in these parts, like full summer at home; in a few days I got back my pretty sun-color. "You have grown much lovelier, my dear," said Queen Eleanor. "Richard will be pleasantly surprised." I was used to her double-tongue by then, and thanked her, without rancor.

At Messina was a huge crowd, every inch of land covered with humanity; even from a mile out we could see them, and all under Richard's banner, and wearing, each, the white cross of England. My heart swelled. Surely, with so many on our side, the infidel would turn and flee at the sight!

I searched along the dockside, shading my eyes, for Richard. It was then that I saw Joanna, prancing her mount in a little space all to herself; folk had drawn back as if in a pattern, though probably they feared the flying hooves. Beside her, mounted too, was a monk, all brown—habit, cowl, hair, and horse; from where I stood, even his skin looked a fine smooth pale brown. He leaned toward Joanna, pointing straight at me. Beside me I heard, "Alexander . . . it is Alexander! Oh, God be praised!" I could hear the tears in Queen Eleanor's voice, and when I turned, surprised, she made a little embarrassed gesture, smiling, and dabbed at her eyes. "Hodierna . . . someone fetch Hodierna!" But the woman was already beside her, taking her arm; together, they turned to wave to the pair on shore. The tonsured clerk must be Hodierna's son, and Richard's foster brother, who was traveling as chronicler of the Crusade.

No one could miss Joanna, so like Richard, and so magnificent to look at, in her own right. Though Queen Eleanor spoke, low and faltering, "Is it. . . ? Can it be Joanna . . . my little Jo?" Of course, this daughter, too, she could not have seen for many years; probably she had been only a child when she was sent to Sicily to wed King William, a man older than her own father. Fleetingly I felt pity for that girl I had never known, and again that surge of joy at my own incredible good fortune. But old William was dead now, and Joanna, from the look of her, would have no trouble finding another husband, young, rich, and royal, too. I thought her quite the handsomest creature I had ever seen, except for Richard.

They were letting down the boarding planks now, the chains squeaking, and we began to surge forward. But I saw that Joanna had jumped down from her horse and, gathering her skirts up over one arm, was running up the swaying walkway. She pushed her way excitedly through the sea of shoulders and flung herself, panting and flushed, into her mother's arms.

"Oh, Mother, isn't it wonderful! Richard has got all my dowry back from that awful Tancred . . . and more besides! And Tancred was keeping me prisoner too, the devil! But now I am free! Oh, if only the Pope would let women go on Crusade . . . I long to set foot in the Holy Land! I can fight for God as well as any man!" She caught her breath, laughing. "But Mother, let me look at you . . . You look just the same! Oh, but you've gone gray! Well, no matter. I have marvelous dyes . . . we can try them. Have you seen Alexander? Look at him, the little monk! I would never have believed it—such a waste! How many girls must be weeping."

She threw the monk, behind her, a teasing look; a thin red came up in his brown cheeks, though he did not look offended. "Come, kiss your lady mother, little monk! Hodierna, you too are unchanged . . . just as I remember you!"

She talked so very much, this Joanna, but all so naturally, as though it spilled out of her, like her ready smiles and the bright beam of her sea-blue eyes. She was so big, and so colorful, and so glowing, there seemed to be no room for anyone else; even Queen Eleanor paled and grew small beside her. She was like some healthy, half-wild animal—though it seems odd to describe a young woman so. I had never seen any lady like her, and could not take away my eyes.

She must have felt me staring, for she turned suddenly, and with a kind of swoop, bent toward me, crying, "You must be Richard's Berengaria! But how adorable you are!" She kissed me quickly; it was like a hot wind rushing by. Then she stood back, surveying me. Taking my chin in her hand, she tilted it upward, for of course I was much shorter. "Look at that enchanting little face! I don't wonder Richard chose you! Mother, don't you adore her?" Joanna did not stop for an answer, but kissed me again, holding me close. "We shall be sisters, true sisters, you and I, shall we not? I cannot remember either of mine, it is so long now since we parted, and besides"—she laughed merrily—"we always used to quarrel."

"I, too," I said. "I, too, with mine. And now she is a nun."

I did not think this funny until I had said it and saw Joanna's eyes dancing, then the two of us burst out laughing. I held out my hands; she took them. "Oh, we are good friends already!" she cried. "What a happy morning!"

Queen Eleanor, speaking quickly, so as to get a word in edgewise, said, "Richard has not come to greet us?"

"Oh, Mother," cried Joanna, "I forgot. He sends his apologies . . . and us as emissaries. He is busy salvaging some barrels of meat . . . the ship that brought them collapsed her hold, or something—and everything fell into the sea. He said it is a matter of life and death for an army in an alien land."

A little frown came between the Queen's brows. "Could he not have left it to his squires? It is not every day that his mother and his bride arrive from far places, and after so long a journey."

"I know," said Joanna, her bright face all concern. "It is too bad of him, but you know Richard! He must always do everything himself! Forgive him, Mother . . . and Berengaria . . . he is so pressed—and yet so wonderful with it. Nothing escapes him. Oh, you cannot know what a giant of a creature he is. He promises he will attend us this evening. And wait till you see our quarters! It is the brand-new palace that Tancred built for himself . . . Richard just took it! Said we must have the best! And so old ugly Tancred must live in a tent, for Richard had already requisitioned all the other palaces and court buildings for himself and his knights. Serves Tancred right, of course . . . he is only a usurper, with no more than a bastard's claim." She shrugged. "Well, he is welcome to it. It is a throne I do not want. The people are always at sword's point—so many nationalities, the Griffons, the Lombards, the Muslims . . . now Richard has come, they must behave, or die. He has had to execute fifty a day, sometimes more—a nuisance."

It seemed a quaint way to put it, but Joanna was a Plantagenet—and they were a law unto themselves, as I was to find out.

CHAPTER 5

IF I HAD thought Joanna filled a room—and I certainly did, this one at least, where now we sat by lamplight, all we women together—then I had not counted on Richard, bigger, bolder, brighter, more alive; a man, and now a king. Noisier, too, he was; we heard him from the time he entered the courtyard, and all the way up the broad marble stairs. He was singing at the top of his lungs—or perhaps not, perhaps for him it was merely whispering; one could believe anything of him, he was already a legend.

Suddenly a hush, then the great double doors flung open, hard, so that they clanged against the marble walls, and there he stood, a giant, laughing, his red hair plastered dark to his huge head, his teeth and the whites of his eyes flashing in his burnt-red face, long legs planted wide, long arms outstretched, and dark pools of water dripping from him onto the polished floor. In one hand he held a forked stick, bleached driftwood, smooth from the sea. "Enter Neptune, dripping," he said in a hearld's voice, and struck a pose. Then he shook himself like a wet dog, so that the drops flew, flung the stick aside, and bowed low. "Ladies, I am yours!"

The room was full of them; Joanna's, the Queen's, mine. They twittered like caged birds, fluttering, gasping, and giggling; I think any one of them would have gladly walked back into the sea with him. But he was mine, or would be.

Though I trembled, I cast down my eyes, pursed my lips prettily, and waited while he greeted his mother and sister. When I raised my eyes to meet his, I saw a startled leap within them, and knew that I had pleased him.

"Lady, you have been patient." He bent over my hand; his lips were dry and warm, but water from his wet hair splashed my rose-pink gown. "A saint's patience in a nymph's body. I am the most fortunate of men." It was a pretty speech, the words of a troubadour, but his eyes told me he meant it; they were ice-blue, as I remembered them, but their look was hot, and seared me. When he turned away, after a long moment, sweat ran down my body under my clothes, and my face flamed. My prim and pretty mouth had vanished, for I felt it hanging open. I shut it quickly and wiped my damp hand on my gown; it was ruined anyway.

He did not address me again, but spoke to the room at large, telling of the day's adventure. Through my bemusement, I heard him, dimly. "A thousand barrels—and we saved all but ninety! For this day's wetting, there will be three days—more!—of life!"

"What was in the barrels?" cried Joanna, laughing.

"Salt pork, sister . . . the army's roast pheasant!"

"Would not the seawater damage it?"

"It is all salt, sister. When they have dried out, the rations will be as good as new . . . better!" He laughed hugely, as though a day of scrambling in the shallows was a great joke. "And, speaking of rations, I am starving!" He snatched up a handful of the little sweet cakes that were set upon a table, cramming them into his mouth, and washing them down with a great draft of wine, tipping up the carafe.

"Dickon!" cried Queen Eleanor. "You will spoil your appetite!"

"Never!" he insisted. "I could eat a horse . . . and have"—he laughed again—"in sieges!" Gasps went up from all the ladies. "But I am comforted to find that you can still sound like a mother, madame," he said, bowing to Queen Eleanor. "I had thought us both past it."

"Well, then, Dickon," she said, with a little mock of dignity, "I shall not suggest that you change to dry clothes—but order up whatever horses there may be in the kitchen!"

"That's my girl! And more wine! We must all have wine!" He caught her up so that her feet in their scarlet slippers swung clear of the floor, and whirled her round and round. When he sat her down, the front of her surcoat all dark from damp and her head veil knocked askew, I saw that she was as pink-cheeked as I myself. She looked like a girl suddenly, and I knew then what the troubadour songs had sung of so long ago.

It was a wonderful evening, spent almost entirely watching Richard eat and listening to him talk. It was well past all our bedtimes when he took his leave, but I think no eyelids drooped; we would have watched and listened the whole night through if we had the chance. Though, truly, I doubt if I could recall a word of what he said, I was in a kind of hectic dream.

He did not address me till he rose to leave. "Lady, I must kiss your apricot cheeks." And so he did, most heartily, the kiss of courtesy, but something more too, and his blue eyes spoke again. "Lady, I have nothing to do tomorrow, and there are any number of chaplains here . . . shall we marry tomorrow?"

It was my turn to gasp. I caught at my throat, for it seemed that my heart had jumped up into it. But I heard the Queen say, "Richard! It is Lent!"

He clapped his hand to his forehead. "Sweet Jesus! I had forgotten!" He turned on his mother, looking quite angry suddenly. "Madame, you might have timed this thing better!"

"Dickon, the fault is not ours! We have worn ourselves to the bone, rushing to meet up with you—and at your leisure! And you dare—"

"Of course, Mother. It is not your fault, or mine either . . . it is fate."

"Well, Richard," said Joanna brightly, "Lent does not last forever. You can wait."

"I cannot," he said, shaking his head. "All is ready. We *must* set out without delay." His frown cleared, and he snapped his fingers. "But there is no reason I cannot be married anywhere—on the way to the Holy Land. The chaplains will still be with us, those black crows. Yes, that's it! Why not! So do not bother to unpack, ladies. Be ready to embark when I give the word. Tomorrow, perhaps . . ." His voice trailed off; he looked as though he might drop, swaying where he stood. "And now, forgive me . . . I must be off to my bed. I rise at dawn, for those barrels must be stored away properly, before they are lost or stolen." And he was gone.

It was as though life had gone out of the chamber; we stared at one another in the silence.

"Well," said Joanna, "he does not ask if his bride is willing to be married somewhere, anywhere—just 'somewhere on the road to the Holy Land'!"

"Oh," I said, quite clearly and steadily, "I am willing."

I would have followed him anywhere.

CHAPTER 6

IT WAS THE tenth day of April, in the year 1191, that we set sail from Messina, on our way to the Holy Land. There were over two hundred ships, all laden with men, horses, siege guns, and provisions, and riding low in the water; at the head went the flagship, the largest, carrying the King, my Richard. It was a brave sight, strung out like a giant necklace, the crimson sails marked with the white cross of England, billowing in the sea wind.

Our ship was far back in the line, being small, and carrying little except our people, and Joanna's and my belongings. Queen Eleanor had taken her leave, preparing to return to Normandy; Richard had received word that affairs there were in a pretty mess, his vassals protesting vehemently against a new tax levied by Prince John and the Chancellor, Will Longchamps. "I can trust no other than you, Mother," he had said. "You will know what to do with my foolish regents. I give you full power."

If she was disappointed at being sent back, she did not show it. Indeed, her eyes sparkled like a girl's and her step was light and firm; I think that statecraft went to her head like wine. But oh, that weary journey, over hill and dale, the saddle sores, the flea-ridden inns, the ill-cooked food and watery ale! I offered her my Saint Christopher medal that I had worn through all the months of journeying. "No, child, you keep it, you will need it more than I," she said.

She was right too, as it happened, for three days out, upon the open sea, a great storm blew up and raged for four days before it blew itself out, as the sailors say. The master of our ship, Sir John Dawe, a small, square man with a rolling gait that somehow planted him foursquare on the slippery deck in the wild gale, came to us where we huddled behind our lashed-down canvas on the foredeck and asked if he had our permission to head for the southern shore of Cyprus. "Good God, man," cried Joanna, pale for once, "what do we know of seamanship? Do whatever you may to save us!" I nodded to show my agreement; I could not have opened my mouth, from sheer terror.

"Well," Sir John said, "it was the King's orders. Meet up at Crete, he said. But *her*"—he jerked his thumb downward to the boards under his feet—"her doesn't want to turn about." He was chuckling, but then, looking at our wide eyes, something like concern showed in his broad North Country face. "Don't 'ee be anxious, ladies . . . her'll weather it. Her's a good ship. Wind'll blow itself out."

How many times we were to hear those words, before we sighted the port of Limassol! Each time a sailor stumbled into our canvas, knocking it down; each time the cook came with his covered pannikin of rations; each visit from the ship's doctor, doling out the bitter brew that was to allay our queasy stomachs! But it did not in fact "blow itself out" until we had rounded the sandy Cypriot shore into the comparative safety of the harbor of Limassol.

What a dreadful, nightmarish three days and nights! Like some watery, tossing Hell it was, the ship scudding forward like a wild frightened bird, then caught up and whirled, tossed into the air, pitched down nose first, and whirled again, only to miraculously right itself and skim onward. The captain bade us ladies lash ourselves to whatever solid parts there were, mysterious iron spikes in the deck, the iron rail, the mast. Even so, one of Joanna's ladies was swept, her bonds broken, clear across the desk, through the open gate where cargo was taken on, and into the sea. I will never forget her face, white as milk, and her shrill cry, suddenly cut off. One of her little slippers was torn off by the force of the gale, and floated all that day, ribbons trailing from it like seaweed, in a puddle of bilge water not two feet from where I stood, lashed to the mast; it was pink silk, sewn with pearls, I remember. During the night, though the wind howled fiercely and the boat tossed like a demon, I must have slept, my hand hanging onto my breast, exhausted; in the morning, the pink slipper, that last lone relic, was gone.

On the fourth day, we limped into the harbor of Limassol, our decks awash, the doors blown off our hatches, and the mainmast cracked at the tip, so that the sail, with its great white cross, dipped low, touching the sea, nearly calm now. We were green-faced, battered, and soaking wet, yet we were fortunate beyond belief. For we saw, in the sudden brightness of a cloudless sky, the whole great coast scattered with wreckage and flung dead bodies.

I thought, in my ignorance, that it must be that most of the fleet had smashed there, driven onto the rocky shore. But the master said no, it was only a matter of two ships, three at the most. "For I count two crosses. See, ladies." And he pointed shoreward. I could make out nothing in the wild confusion of broken wood and the bright rags and tatters that were the drowned sailors' wear. " 'Tis true, ladies. Two only, praised be God. Sailors have trained eyes, far-seeing, begging your pardon . . . take my word for it. I can even make out the name of one—the *Saint Bridget*, she was."

The harbor was filled with shipping: small fishing boats, cargo ships carrying the Cypriot flag, and some strangely built, graceful ships, long and slender, manned with hundreds of rowers, and the sails painted with the crescent moon of Islam. "Infidels!" I gasped. "Can we not flee?"

"Them're trading vessels, little lady. Old Isaac, he trades with the Saracens. He and Saladin made a pact of friendship—drank each other's blood, they say. That's a fact." And the master shook his head and made the sign against the evil eye.

"Then he is our enemy!" I cried.

"It may be," said Joanna. "We must go warily, at any rate."

"I'll get the lay of the land, ladies," said Sir John. And he, with some of his sailors, strongly armed, put into shore in a little boat, leaving the ship anchored far out in the bay.

I was woefully ignorant of the history and politics of these parts, and much shamed before Joanna, who knew it all. But she, with the easy good humor of the Plantagenets, was happy to tell me everything, and did not think it strange that I had to ask. "Women never pay attention to such things," she said. "But my husband, old darling that he was, always consulted me."

It seems that the island of Cyprus had long been a part of the Byzantine Empire, but five years ago Isaac Ducas Comnenus, a member of the imperial family, had arrived in Cyprus, claiming, on the basis of forged documents, to be the island's new governor, just sent out from Constantinople. His deception was successful, and the island's fortresses were placed in his hands. Then Isaac came out into the open and pretended no longer. He announced himself Emperor of Cyprus and governed as an independent ruler. In order to maintain himself against the government of Constantinople, he made an alliance with Saladin. "Therefore," she finished, "it is not likely he will be well disposed toward Crusaders."

"But he is a Christian!" I cried, aghast.

"Well," she said, shrugging, "we are not all saints!"

It was not long before we saw the little boat with Sir John and his men at the oars; they made for shipside, rowing very fast. As they climbed aboard, I could see that the master was disturbed; his face was very red, and his little eyes looked angry. "The survivors!" he cried, almost sputtering on the words. "They've imprisoned all the survivors! Isaac is not in residence . . . they wait word from him, and will not release them into my custody."

"Sir John," said Joanna firmly, "I think it best that you keep on board for now. Who knows, they may think it expedient to seize you as well!"

He shook his head, fingering the cross he wore at his throat. " 'Tis to be hoped the fair weather holds, ladies. I dare not venture farther into the bay."

Meanwhile, we gave thanks we were still in one piece, and no longer buffeted by the wild winds. We spent the rest of the day tending to our persons, repairing the damage, so to speak. With a wash, and dry clothes, and the ship no longer rearing and plunging like an unbroken stallion, we were ready to face the first decent meal we had eaten in days; even the salt pork (probably the very barrels Richard had saved from the sea) tasted delicious. When we saw, toward sunset, seven more of our ships sailing toward us, battered but still seaworthy, we raised a ragged cheer, Joanna leading it with a hearty will.

The next day Isaac returned, evidently, from wherever he had been, for he sent envoys to invite Joanna and me to come ashore as his guests. I would have been glad to set foot on dry land, but Joanna drew herself up, looking lordly as Richard himself, and said, "Thank your master—what does he call himself, 'Emperor'?—but tell him that we are content here, upon our own decks, where we feel at home."

When the envoys had left, I turned to Joanna, mystified, and almost in tears at the prospect of spending yet another night upon the swaying, dipping decks. "Why?" I cried softly. "Why did you answer so?"

Joanna looked at me, a wise, knowing look. "Have you not heard the fable of the spider and the fly?"

"Oh," I said, feeling stupid. "You think he means treachery."

"I am sure of it," she said.

For three days Isaac pressed us to accept his hospitality, each envoy visit bringing another rich gift, wine in great handsome amphoras, and luscious fresh fruits in huge woven hampers, and each gift Joanna politely but firmly refusing. One basket was filled with oranges, bigger than any I had ever seen; my mouth watered. "So many," I said sadly. "Oranges are so rare at home."

"You will have your fill of them soon enough," she said, "but let us eat them in freedom."

And so we put off the "Emperor's" sly proffers, while we watched men on the Cypriot shore erecting barriers to fortify it. They were putting up doors, benches, planks, chests, blocks of stone; even the abandoned hulks of old ships were pressed into service. It grew into a veritable wall—oddly shaped, to be sure, but formidable enough to defend twenty Limassols, or so I thought. Also, on the far side of the bay, the slender Saracen ships were lined up, their broadsides facing us.

Joanna's forehead puckered. "Sir John," she said, "those ships . . . do you see anything on their decks—engines or catapults? You have far sight—what can you see?"

He squinted. "Hard to say, milady. They got them canvas curtains." He shook his head. "No, I can't rightly say."

"Do you think they mean to attack us?" she asked. I gave a little cry.

267

"Don't 'ee be anxious, Lady." Sir John fixed an earnest look on me. "It won't be today, anyway, light's nearly gone. And soon as it gets more shadowy-like, us'll sneak a bit further out. Then we'll see them coming. Never fear, little lady."

His words did little to set my mind at rest. I am not like Joanna, who visibly brightened at the prospect of a possible sea battle; I am a coward. I could not get to sleep that night. There was no moon, and the darkness was like a thick, stifling blanket; I stared into it, seeing nothing. Joanna snored softly, moaning once or twice in her sleep. The water lapped against the sides of the boat; twice I thought I heard the splash of a flying fish, and once a distant shout, but that was all. When the sky lightened to a dim gray before the dawn, I fell into an uneasy doze.

I woke hearing the shout again, closer this time; I sat up quickly. A pale dawn streaked the sky; the pale sun, rising, threw a pinkish path across the water. Across the path, on the very rim of the world, the sails of a galley moved, swiftly, then another, and another; behind stretched a great fleet, soundless, like a flock of birds. I watched, my heart pounding, as they moved closer. Suddenly I saw clearly, where a stray beam of sun glinted on it, the unmistakable outline of a white cross against a dark blue sail. Richard! It was Richard's fleet, come to search for us! Quickly I shook Joanna awake, almost stammering in my excitement.

She stood up, looking where I pointed. After a moment she said, "Yes . . . yes, you're right! What sharp eyes!" She yawned, and sighed. "Just in time, too. I was beginning to be afraid we'd be fired on." I stared at her. Afraid! She didn't know what the word meant!

I said, a little indignantly, "You never showed it . . . you snored all night!"

She smiled—smugly, I thought. "Yes. I have nerves of steel. My old William always said so."

We watched as the great fleet of ships came on, skimming swiftly across the ocean toward us. Sir John by now had seen it too, and was standing beside us, grinning broadly. "I knew he'd find us, little lady. Now eat up your breakfast . . . there may not be time later."

"You think Richard will fight?" Joanna's face lit up like a torch.

"May have to," he answered, quaffing his morning ale.

The flagship, Richard's, loomed large now, and coming

closer every moment; we dashed to the starboard side, trying to pick him out. I saw the figurehead, new, and bright with fresh paint, a maiden dressed in blue, with long snakes of curling hair, and beneath it a new, fresh-painted name. I cried out, joyful. *Berengaria*, it read; when last we saw it, the ship had been called the *Sea Serpent*. Joanna turned, face vivid with excitement, to hug me hard. "You are his fancy, sweeting," she whispered in my ear.

Then we saw Richard himself upon the foredeck, dressed in the short canvas drawers of the sailor, his head bound up in a bright checkered kerchief and gold hoops swinging in his ears, catching the light, his smile white and wide. He cupped his hands to his mouth and shouted, trumpetlike, "So we have found you . . . runaways!"

The *Berengaria* came on swiftly, so close that it looked as if it would ram our sides. When the ship lay alongside, Richard climbed the high rail, balancing above the blue water. "Closer, man, closer!" he called to his captain.

But there still yawned a great gap of blue when he leaped, clearing our ship's rail and landing on all fours. He picked himself up quickly, grinning like a small boy. "Not bad for a landlubber!" he cried. Then, looking at me, his face fell into soft lines, and he said softly, "Ladies, I feared for you." He took me in his arms, tenderly, stroking my hair. "You are safe . . . my little bride is safe."

He stayed thus for a moment only. Then, his eye encompassing all those who gathered behind us, gawping, he said, rubbing his hands together, "Now we must deal with this upstart emperor."

CHAPTER 7

I HID MY eyes, so I did not see when Richard's foot touched the ground of Cyprus, in the forefront of his men. When last I looked, from our ship, drawn close now for battle, he had leapt from the little boat, impatient, before it yet came into shore, and splashing through the waist-deep shallows, stormed the beach alone. He carried, held above his head, a huge battle-axe in one hand, in the other his long sword, bright silver in the sun. He had no helm, and only a shirt of light mail thrown over his sailor garb; his red hair looked like a gout of blood above the blue of the sea. Upon the shore was a line of warriors, waiting to repulse him, waving long spears. I covered my face and murmured, "Mary, Queen of Heaven, protect him."

Joanna, beside me, squeezed my arm so hard that I cried out. "Oh, sister, look!" she shouted, in accents of joy. "He is a very god of war! Oh, look! They are afraid to look at him ... are running away!"

I took away my hands and saw that red head in the midst of what looked like a horde of the enemy, and a writhing, flailing mass of arms and legs. I saw one go down, and then another, and another, all falling beneath Richard's whirling axe and slashing sword. By the time the first of his men reached his side, Richard had slain seven, by count, though it is hard to believe.

Afterward, I could not believe, either, what I had seen. Perhaps it was his great height, so much more than the defenders', perhaps he had taken them by surprise, or, more likely, his ardor, greater than a mere man's, intimidated them. But the whole defense was crumbling after his first lone assault, and when the others of his force joined him, it was quickly over. Not one of our Crusaders fell. When half the Cypriot defense lay dead upon the sand, out from the town came a frightened legation, bearing the white flag of peace; Limassol had surrendered! That was the only battle I ever saw, and that from a distance. But I never again feared for Richard. I saw he led, indeed, a charmed life; God loved him.

When he handed me down from the boat onto the shore, his face was streaked with dirt and blood; I caught my breath. He raised his hand to his face, seeing it come away all red. "It is not mine, I assure you," he said, smiling. "I am hardly winded. A poor showing, these Limassol dandies."

I began to laugh. It was nerves, I guess, and the relief. And then with his smeary face and bright eyes, he looked like an urchin caught at the honey pot. And there were arrows all over him, too, sticking out, the heads caught in the chain of his mail. I pointed at them. "You look like a porcupine," I said, not knowing now whether to laugh or cry.

"Oh," he muttered, pulling one out. "Where did all these come from?"

Alexander spoke up then; he was carrying a little book and a stick of charcoal, marking in it. "They shot arrows at you as you left the boat . . . didn't you know?" He looked at Richard curiously, as if he were some other breed of man than himself; of course, Alexander was a monk.

When Richard answered him, I saw that he paid close attention to this Alexander, and was carefully sincere with him, not jesting as he often did with others. "Why, yes," Richard said slowly. "I think I did. Part of me knew. Another part did not. When I go into a fight, there is a kind of a wall goes up, but like glass to see through—a wall between me and the enemy. And afterward, it is gone. As though I had drunk a heavy brew."

"And you have no fear?" asked the monk.

"Fear . . ." said Richard, wrinkling his brow, as though he had to think what the word meant. "No, no fear, not then. Before, yes. If I think about it." He smiled, a dazzling show of teeth in his filthy face. "I try not to think."

All this time, Alexander was nodding, and listening, and marking with the charcoal in the little book.

"Why, man," cried Richard. "You do not have to chronicle that!"

"I must," said the monk gravely. "For it explains you."

This exchange took place at the very edge of the water, while the little waves lapped gently at my feet, and Joanna, still standing precariously in the small skiff, sighed impatiently. But Richard was always like this with Alexander, his foster brother; he would stop anything for him.

"This wall, you say . . ." asked Alexander, still marking, "like a protection?"

"Yes," I said quickly, not like myself, intruding on them. "Yes . . . a protection from God."

The monk crossed himself. "Let us hope," he said.

"Indeed!" said Richard, laughing. But he smiled down upon me tenderly and stroked my hair with his dirty, battle-bloodied hand.

He brought us ladies then, under escort, to Isaac's palace, our quarters. "You have no host, ladies," said Richard. "For Isaac has fled into the hills. In the meantime, Limassol is yours."

Isaac had refused to release the men who had been shipwrecked on his shore, calling them hostages for Richard's good behavior. But Richard stormed Limassol, Isaac fled into the hills and the townspeople surrendered. That night, while we ladies slept in Isaac's palace, Richard and his army found Isaac's camp, about five miles outside the city, and came against it with sword and Greek fire. The hastily garrisoned camp surrendered too, and Isaac barely escaped, fleeing farther up the high mountain. He had not time even to dress, and left behind his crown, his treasure-laden mules, his horses, and his imperial standard.

These two crushing defeats within twenty-four hours were too much for Isaac; he decided to sue for peace. Hostages and envoys were sent, but Richard said it must wait, for he was going to be married! It was the first I had heard of it, but I was not about to demur, though my wedding gown had been ruined in the great storm. "It does not matter," said Joanna. "Take him while you can! It is not often that Richard will stand still long enough to attend Mass—much less a wedding ceremony!" This was not strictly true; Richard was very good about Church, better than I, certainly. But like all the Plantagenets, Joanna exaggerated as easily as she breathed.

So, on the first day of May, we were married in the Chapel of Saint George. Bishop John of Evreux performed the ceremony, and afterward crowned me Queen of England. And Alexander wrote that in a Cypriot town an English queen was crowned by a Norman bishop, for all who follow Richard range thus through the whole of Christendom. It was a pretty thought.

I was terrified, you can imagine—not least of the wedding night. For I was woefully ignorant, and did not know what was expected of me. Even so, I was grateful I did not have Queen Eleanor to instruct me! The day before, Pia, my Basque waiting-woman, brought me, secretly, a fertility charm, a hideous thing, the root of a tree or bush, I think, but shaped like a woman—or rather, a fantasy of a woman, all breasts and stomach, and no face at all. It was very ancient, rubbed smooth by the hands of suppliants, but I could hardly bring myself to touch it, though for courtesy I thanked her, hiding it in my hanging sleeve. At my timid questions, she became all smiles and eyes, making explicit gestures even I could understand. I turned fiery red, even though we were alone, and was more terrified than ever. I even wondered if I might die of it, being so small and weak. Of course no one ever did, at least I had never heard of such a thing.

The night before the wedding, exhausted from our hurried preparations and my great ever-present fear, I steeled myself to speak to Joanna; after all, she was a widow!

Our ladies were all asleep in the anterooms; we sat together on the great bed we shared, sipping honeyed wine, our bedtime drink. I spoke haltingly, my voice hoarse with emotion; she stared at me over the rim of her wine cup. Then she interrupted, very businesslike. "Well, you have seen animals, of course?"

"Oh, no!" I cried softly. "I cannot . . . on all fours!"

"Well, he will not expect you to do that, I suppose," she said musingly. "Not at first." There was a considered pause, then she made those same gestures Pia had made, looking to see if I understood. "On your back, you see, your legs spread—like so."

"Oh," I whispered. "Does it hurt?"

"Only a little—and it is quickly over." She stopped short then. "Of course, my William was old . . ." She giggled. "Not much bigger than a lapdog." I stared at her, aghast.

"I mean his—what do you call it, his . . . thing. About as big as that." And she measured a short length with her fingers. "Richard, of course . . ." And she giggled again at my frightened face. "Don't worry—it cannot be so bad . . . after all, you love him, do you not? It makes a difference, to a woman."

I faltered, seeking words. "The love songs—songs of the troubadours, all the tales of love . . . It sounds so . . . beautiful."

"Oh, it is not so much," she said, tossing her head. "And men have all the best of it. Think of them, all hard and scarred with sword wounds, and with hairy legs and chests, and smelling of old wine. And when they are old—like William—wrinkled, with potbellies and skinny shanks. Whereas we are soft and curving—smooth as silk, and white as pearls. Think of it . . . we have these pretty breasts." And she reached out her hand to stroke mine softly. "I don't blame them for writing that way—the troubadours are all men, after all."

"No," I said stubbornly. "Some are women . . . and their songs tell of firm lips and broad shoulders, of narrow hips and strong arms to hold you. Marie de France makes it sound lovely . . . and Blondelza—" I broke off, for her face had changed; it looked sly and wary.

Joanna smiled. "Well, then," she said, and spread her hands in a shrug. "Richard must be different."

"Perhaps," I said hopefully, "perhaps *he* is like the songs."

"Well," she said, looking wise, "it would seem so."

My expression did not change; I waited, expectant, while she peered close, looking into my eyes.

"Is it possible you do not know?"

"Know what?" I asked, smiling now.

"That Blondelza was Richard's mistress . . . for years, maybe ten. She bore a son to him." She was still looking hard at me. "You knew he had a son?"

I said, out of a sudden deadening misery, "Sancho, my brother, said he had several bastards."

"But that one is the only one he acknowledges—Philippe, Count of Cognac. Blondelza's son." She saw my misery then, and put out her hand to draw me close. "But it is all over—for years now. He has not seen her for years. And it is plain to see he is very taken with you, little Ria. I am so happy for him."

Tears snaked down my cheeks, not warm, but cold, like rain.

"Oh, you mustn't weep, Ria. Richard has forgotten her long ago. He never mentions her name . . . it was a youthful passion. And you . . . you will be his queen, and give him heirs for England." She hugged me close. "And anyway, you are so very different, you and she . . . as different as night and day."

I raised a wretched face to search hers. "Did you know her, then?"

"Not to say *know* . . . I saw her once, when I was just a child still. She was young too—only a glee-maiden then, a nothing. Though they say she had noble blood. Her father was a knight, the Baron of Nesle."

"She is a great artist," I said sadly. "Was she very beautiful?"

She thought a moment, pursing her lips. "I'm not sure . . . people thought so. *I* thought so then. She was so alive . . . one *had* to look at her." She smiled suddenly. "She was like Mother—you know? But with golden hair. Strange, I never thought of that before. But yes, she was like mother. Like a queen, or a duchess at least, in her bearing, though she was so young and a nothing, really. I guess it was all that playacting, and being in front of crowds—like a queen."

She held me very close, stroking my hair and whispering into my ear. "You are so much prettier, little Ria . . . so soft and sweet. I love to touch you." She pressed me gently, so that I fell back upon the cushions of the bed. She leaned over me, her vivid face laughing and a little wild in the light of the candle. Then, swiftly, she put out her hand, palm down, and snuffed the flame; I had seen Sancho do that sometimes, but never a woman.

I felt her kisses in the dark, on my cheeks and neck, and her hands upon my body, so that it tingled and glowed. "Little Ria . . . sweetheart," she murmured. "Richard will love you—as I do." I felt her teeth then, hard against my mouth, and opened my lips; her tongue, swollen and warm, probed. I gave myself up to her mouth and hands, and afterward I slept. In the morning she was gone from my side, and at the wedding later I did not meet her eyes.

CHAPTER 8

MY GOWN, CLOTH-OF-GOLD, had been ruined, soaked with seawater in the great storm. But the veil was still good as new, for it had been kept in another chest. It was a shimmering, gossamer thing; when Pia threw it over my pale pink dress, it covered me from head to toe like a dawn mist. With it I wore the pink pearl chaplet and heeled slippers of rose-colored silk. It was not the fashion to wear one hue, but the Queen had taught me a style of my own, and, after a misgiving or two, I saw that I did indeed look rather sweet, and the slippers added three inches to my height. We were a sanguine pair, Richard and I; he was clad all in scarlet, with gold lions embroidered upon the chest of his surcoat, and wearing the new pointed shoes. It would seem the wrong choice, for his tawny coloring, but it was not. "Two wrong reds make a right," he said; there was so much that he knew.

The Bishop of Evreux had a stern face; it looked angry. I trembled all through the ceremony, like a scared rabbit. I was ashamed, but I could not help it; I despaired of ever behaving like a queen, though the weight of the crown upon my head was heavy. But I made the Latin responses in a firm voice, if small, and afterward, to my surprise, the angry Bishop smiled at me, showing big yellow teeth.

Richard kissed me heartily, on both cheeks, the kiss of courtesy, and then very hard upon the lips, sweeping me off my feet and holding me for a long moment. I do not know what happened to my beautiful veil, after he whisked it off; I never saw it again. I suppose it got trampled in the dust. There were great rude calls of "Go to it, Lionheart!" and "Dickon, prick-on!" from his knights; I was as pink as my gown as we walked to the litter that would take us on a circuit of his army.

This was even worse, I am sure, except that many of the bawdy words were Saxon, and I could not understand them. His men, even common foot soldiers, crowded close, halting the litter to push red faces in between the curtains and wish us well. They seemed to have no discipline at all, but Richard took no notice, and seemed to bask in all the rowdiness, shouting back obscenities and making rude gestures, laughing, giving as good as he got. So strange it was, he seemed to know the name of every soldier, even the lowest! There were one-eyed old warriors, gnarled as tree roots, and veteran Crusaders from the last Eastern campaign, burnt permanently black by the desert sun, their eye-whites startling in their dark faces, and not a few missing an arm or a leg, or showing the purple chain-scars of an old captivity.

But most were young, squires and petty knights, joined up for the adventure and for love of Richard. One face I will never forget, it wore such a look of worship: a young, young boy, not much more than half grown, who stood at a little distance alone. He must have been a squire to some great noble, for he wore a sort of livery. Richard called to him, "Ho, Yves! Wish me good fortune, man!" The boy stood transfixed and speechless, as though he looked upon the angel Gabriel. For him, I guess, it was so. He had a round guileless face, still rosy at the cheeks, and great light-blue eyes. The love that showed in them was boundless, a sky, an ocean, full of love. And all for Richard. I felt my own eyes water at the sight.

The banquet lasted for hours, going on and on till the candles were lit, and, one by one, men dropped to the floor to sleep off their drunkenness. Music played continually, for Richard never liked to be without it; he had brought, in his train, upwards of sixty minstrels of one kind or another, and they all wished to do him honor on this day. I never heard, I swear, nor ever will again, so many songs sung to my person; if I believed the words, my head would have swelled far too large for the crown! There were Eastern musicians too. Saracens! I do not know where they had come from; a strange kind of sound they made on their pretty golden instruments, whining and monotonous. I am not very musical, and it grated on my ears and made my head ache. My head hurt anyway, the crowd had grown so heavy and pressed so hard upon my brow.

"Poor little pigeon," Richard said, smiling at me. Did I look like one, I wondered. Father, too, often called me pigeon, in affection. "Poor little one, let us take it off." And, so saying, he lifted the heavy crown off my head and set it on the trencher before me. Bishop John frowned, for this was against all custom, but Richard paid no heed to him; he was always very unconventional.

I was too excited to eat at all, though I emptied my wine cup many times, not counting. I began to grow bewildered, and found it difficult to remember who I was talking to. Richard was up and down all day, now and then coming to rest beside me in his proper bridegroom's place at the high table, but mostly ranging widely round the dining hall, jesting and joining in the singing; several times he took up the lute himself, and played and sang, to great and thunderous applause. I think they were his own songs, but I could not always recognize tunes, and especially now, with my senses all fogged with wine.

I remember that Guy of Lusignan sat beside me part of the time; this was the man who had been King of Jerusalem until a week ago, when Conrad of Montferrat had seized his throne. Conrad had the backing of Philip Augustus of France, so Guy had come straight to Richard, seeking redress for his wrongs.

Guy was very courtly and pleasant; he was also the handsomest man I have ever seen, even more beautiful than Richard. His hair was the purest gold, and fell straight to his shoulders, shining like moonbeams, and his eyes were violet, with lashes a girl would envy. His shoulders were broad and his hips narrow, his new-style short coat fitting like a second skin, so that one did not know where to look. He paid me compliment after compliment, but I saw that his violet eyes roved as he spoke. He was always watching to see who noticed him, or looking for a woman's attention; I think it was what he lived for, truly, admiration and dalliance. I could not think he would make a very good king, but perhaps Conrad was worse; at any rate Richard was pledged to him, so I went out of my way to be courteous. They say, also, that he had brought a great army, which was all to the good, for Richard's cause.

Richard's chair beside me stood empty much of the day, and from time to time another would sit in it, to court me and make pleasantries. I was not used to this, but the Plantagenets do everything differently, and certainly it made for a pleasant ease. After a while I did not notice; the wine had made me as casual in manner as all the rest of them.

Once, even Alexander, the monk-scribe, sank into his chair, pushing away trencher and meat, cups and bowls, to make room for the parchment and ink he carried. I asked him what he was writing. "Why, I chronicle everything," he said. "It is my job." He stared at me, abstracted, and then wrote, looking up in a measuring sort of way as he scrawled upon the page. I leaned over to look at his writing, but I could not make head or tail of it, and thought perhaps the wine had affected my eyesight. I rubbed my eyes and blinked, but the characters on the page still looked like hen scratches.

Alexander smiled. "It is a kind of code—my own . . . a way of writing briefly. I will copy it all out later in fair Latin."

"I wanted to read it," I said, pouting, the wine making me bold. "I wanted to see what you had written about me."

"How did you know it was about you?" He seemed astonished.

"I knew," I said, looking sidelong at him like a flirt. "Will you not read it out to me? Or is it something bad?"

"Oh, no, Lady," he protested. "It is nothing but praise."

"Read it, then," I commanded.

He peered close at the hen scratches, frowning; I think he was shortsighted. "Let me see . . . 'Richard wore scarlet.' No, that's not it." He flipped the pages forward. "Ah, here it is. 'His bride, the princess Berengaria of Navarre, is neither tall nor short, blond nor dark, but somewhere in between. A maiden to the liking of all who see her, prudent and wise, with a kind heart. Our glorious King may rejoice in his choice; a maiden both virtuous and fair.' " He closed the little book.

"Is that all?" I asked, obscurely disappointed.

"Well," he said, sounding offended, "I have not polished it ... and I am no poet either." He smiled. "It will sound better in the Latin," he said.

He had a lovely smile, so I forgave him his scanty praise. And, it was true, he was never much of a courtier. At least, I thought, *he* meant it.

While we talked, they had cleared the floor for dancing; I saw that Joanna was already whirling in the arms of Guy of Lusignan. Richard took my hand, laughing, to pull me into the dance.

I had been seated all the afternoon, and now it was full dark. When I stood up, my legs would not support me, and gave way, but Richard, laughing harder, bore me up. I stumbled twice, treading on my long bridal train, and finally caught my pointed heel in it, tearing the silk.

"You are tipsy, little pigeon," Richard whispered in my ear. "Let us go to bed." And, so saying, he swept me up in his arms, pushing his way through the dancers to the foot of the marble stairs.

Ribald voices rang in my ear, coming from all sides. But I did not mind, for once; I felt a drowsy, happy smile curving my lips and, over his shoulder, waved gaily at the blur of faces that swam at me. I was dizzy, and saw two of everything, making a throng.

I had never thought to go drunk to my bridal bed—but perhaps it was just as well. I remember nothing much at all, and need not have worried about anything. I can just recall squealing when I saw him naked, and his hand palming the candle flame out, as Joanna's had. And, also, I know that I found myself in all sorts of indecent postures, but I did not care, and laughed aloud. The pain was much larger than Joanna had said, an unbelievable pain, like being torn apart. And it hurt each time all over again; I think, three times. But, afterward, I slept.

I awoke to a taste like rabbit fur in my mouth, a pounding head, and a leaden, all-over ache. But through all these, my pulse raced; I had got through it, the thing I dreaded, and without mishap. And I had pleased Richard, my lord. The bed beneath my haunches was sticky still, proving it.

A thin silver light came through the shuttered windows,

cutting narrow bands across our bodies; it was dawn, or nearly. Beside me, Richard breathed noisily, a comfortable sound, like bees humming in a bush. I cast a look toward him, a smile beginning on my lips. They were swollen, though, and hurt when I stretched them, so I stared at him gravely as he slept.

I knew he was thirty-two. A great age, certainly; soon he would be past his prime, as such years are counted. But he looked young, so young. His red hair was dark, like garnets, in the pale light, and was rumpled and rough, like a child's, where it met the soft yield of the pillow. All the stern lines of his face were softened with sleep, his mouth half-open upon a gentle curve; the lids of his eyes were blue, as some sleeping children's are, seeming to take color from the eyes closed under them. He stirred and sighed, his breath going silent; I drew back, quiet, so as not to wake him. But he must have heard my movement, or felt it.

His lips drew back, showing the gleam of teeth, and his eyelids fluttered, but he did not wake. He sighed again, and a look of great happiness came over his face, transfiguring it; my heart swelled as though it would burst my chest. He flung out his arms, turning, still asleep, and laid it, heavy, across my body. "Blondelza," he murmured, upon a sigh. And then again, "Blondelza." His arm tightened around me. "My own."

Silent, I lay like a stone, and growing cold as stone, as he settled back into sleep, the tender smile still hovering upon him.

Slowly, slowly, I felt my hands and feet grow cold, though the air was warm. The sheet beneath me grew cold and clammy, and my bridegroom's arm was heavy as lead, oppressing me. Something within my chest was heavy, too, and icy hard.

The words of the Romany's curse came back to me then, and never left me. ". . . cold hands and feet, and a cold couch . . . a cold bridegroom, and a cold womb."

BOOK VI

THE SCRIBE

*Told by Alexander the Monk,
Chronicler of the Third Crusade*

CHAPTER 1

"A MAIDEN BOTH virtuous and fair." Thus it was that I wrote of Berengaria, Richard's bride, and by her look of shy dismay, I knew that it did not please her.

"I am no poet," I answered her, and that is true. And yet there is more to it than that. Am I to write down that during the wedding ceremony she trembled like a leaf in the wind, and that her eyes shone large and still and listening, like the eyes of a deer when it meets the hunter's knife? Or again, should I put down that had I been a man like other men, and not one vowed to celibacy twice over, I should have gathered her close into my arms to comfort her?

I think not, for I am only a scribe, my task to set down the story of King Richard and the iron men he led into a holy war. So I shall make my notations as events happen, and later put them into the formal Latin of the chronicles. And my thoughts and my feelings I shall express only when I am alone, inside my head, as now.

King Richard. I ought to know him, surely, as does no other man, for we share the same stars. We two were born on the same day, Our Lady's Day, September 8, of the same year, 1157, in the royal mansion at Oxford, and something less than an hour apart. We were attended by the same midwives and doctors, christened by the same bishop, and suckled at the same breasts—my mother's. We were friends too, always, and very close—closer, I swear, than proper brothers; closer, certainly, than Richard was to any of his. As for me, I never had any—or sisters either. And I never knew my father; Mother let me think that he had died, but she put no name to him. For years, till I was about twelve, I said a prayer for his soul every day, silently and in secret. And then she told me, deeming me now a man.

Mother was a knight's daughter; he held the little fief of Trois Rivières, in Maine, and was a vassal of the Angevins. Mother, called Hodierna, was betrothed to an old knight, Garnier of Ausseton, who died before she reached a marriageable age. Then she was promised to a second cousin, but the Church would not sanction the union, it was too close. So it was that she reached an age where most girls are wives and mothers, and still unwed. Her father had a squire, young and orphaned, who had loved her long, but it was thought his birth was too low, so there could be nothing but friendship between them, and this young squire was sent away, removing temptation, as it were. The night of his going, he begged Hodierna to meet him, alone, upon the road, so that the pair might make their last farewells. She was fond of the lad, having known him all her life, so she consented, and stole out after the household was asleep.

While they embraced tearfully, exchanging innocent vows of undying love, four horsemen came upon them, slew the young squire, who drew sword to protect her, and raped the daughter of the house, leaving her battered and bleeding among the bushes. Mother lived, but in due course found herself pregnant. The father, a harsh man, blamed her, as often happens with these poor wronged girls, and cast her from him. My mother, though, was a maiden of some mettle, and made her way to the big castle, where the King and Queen were in residence. Queen Eleanor, still young then, and with child herself, took pity on the ill-used creature, and made room for her in her own household, hiring her as waiting-woman, and as nurse, when the two children should be born. And that is how it came about that a high-born damsel served as wet nurse to a prince. My mother and Richard's were dear friends from the first, despite the difference in their stations, but Mother did not confide in Queen Eleanor, even so. She let it be thought that the dead young squire was my father; the ugly rape shamed her.

I know now that my mother, Hodierna, was a woman in a thousand, for she did not visit her disgust and hatred on me, or warp my nature with thoughts of revenge. She could not have done that anyway, for she never saw the faces of her ravishers; all she knew was that they were mounted, and that they wore mail emblazoned with the King's badge, and swore in the Norman tongue. She could not know, even, which one fathered me. "It was a knight, at any rate," she said, "so you can be sure, for what it is worth, that your blood is good." Her mouth twisted wryly as she spoke; her own "good blood" had availed her little in this world.

At first, after I knew the story, I used to scan faces, furtively, when the King rode in with his knights, hoping, in a twisted sort of way, to come upon a fugitive likeness, but I never did. I resembled Mother, except for my coloring, and there are many dark Normans.

But it was then, so early in my life, that I secretly vowed to live a celibate all my days; I did not want to risk the sins of the flesh, or be the downfall of some innocent maid. It was hard, at first, for I was just beginning to notice girls, so pretty and so soft, so unlike myself. But I was able to hold to it, with the help of prayers and a hair shirt worn under my smallclothes. In time I came to think of myself as neuter, a mind without a body; I am sure that others held me so.

I have said that Richard and I shared the same stars, and so had many like traits—though, for sure, he would not see it so. But I was not born a monk, nor he a warrior and tumbler of wenches; these things we wrest from life, according to our opportunities. The girls who have taken his eye have hidden behind my eyelids too, and many of the blows he has dealt have twitched along my unused sword arm. His little bride is such a one as I myself might have chosen, had my destiny been different, and Blondelza, God knows, stirred my senses too. But then she could stir any man's, and has, so it is said; I fear she is a great sinner, and I pray for her every night, remembering that Our Lord loved well the Magdalene.

But my foster brother and I share much: a love of learning and of new things; a zest for adventure—in my case, adventure of the spirit; and, above all, a love of God. How fortunate I am in this great journey! To go to Outremer, the Land Beyond the Sea, and explore the wonders along the way, and in such company!

CHAPTER 2

To GET ON with my chronicle...

It was certain, after his first encounter with Isaac Comnenus, that Richard had no choice but to press for a full-scale conquest of the island of Cyprus.

Isaac had come to Richard's camp, smiling all over his

swarthy face, swearing that he had surrendered, and would abide by the peace terms that his envoys had offered after the fall of Limassol.

Isaac was a man in his middle years, running to fat, with a black beard that hid his expression, and narrow, yellow-green eyes set on a slant. He was as richly dressed as an Eastern emir, and the gold upon him sparkled blindingly in the sun; he was so heavily encrusted with it that I swear his garments could stand alone! He wore upon his balding head the ancient crown of Byzantium, a wonder to behold; its value in gold would keep our vast army in food for a month.

Richard greeted him pleasantly, embracing him and planting the kiss of courtesy upon both bearded cheeks. Isaac's Latin was poor, strangely accented and interspersed with Greek words, and Richard, out of politeness, switched to the speech of the Griffons, a corrupt mix of Greek and Turkish; he had picked it up in Messina, where the population was made up of these mongrel Griffons. It was obvious that Isaac found it easier going; he smiled and bowed at the end of each sentence. It looked as though he made no objections at all to Richard's terms, which were very stiff, and put Cyprus under the overlordship of England, almost vassal status.

When the talks came to a close, both men still very cordial, Richard sat Isaac down to a luncheon, a feast really, and—a pretty irony—served off the gold plate that had been captured from Isaac himself when he fled before our army!

After lunch, Richard proclaimed that it was time for a siesta, a Spanish word for a nap in the middle of the day. He stood up, making a great show of stretching and yawning, excused himself, and went into his tent, leaving Isaac and his envoys in the palatial guest tent, unattended.

Sometime during the siesta, while his hosts slept, Isaac, with his adherents, slipped away. We were awakened by trumpets, shouts, and a wild din, and a disheveled knight burst in, gray-faced, to announce Isaac's defection. Richard, however, did not even rise from his couch, but smiled and nodded, calling for wine.

After a few giant yawns, he sat up, took the wine cup that was offered him, and raised it in a toast. "To the conquest of Cyprus!" he cried, quaffing it. My face must have been as much a study in consternation as the knight's, for Richard laughed loudly and then, pulling a long face, said, "I have no choice . . . Isaac has asked for it! Now let him look to his kingdom!" And, so saying, he took up his lute and played one of his earliest songs, a tune as well known over the world as his red hair, one that armies marched to, a war song, brisk and bold. And all afternoon he hummed it, as he made his preparations for a full-scale conquest; I could hear he was well content.

First off, he dispatched his newfound vassal, Guy of Lusignan, with a goodly portion of his army, upon the pursuit of Isaac. Then, dividing the remainder in half, and boarding the galleys, he circumvented the island, putting half the forces under the command of Robert of Thornham, and heading the other himself. So, divided into two fleets, they sailed in opposite directions, with orders to capture all enemy ships and all the coastal towns that lay in their paths.

To the surprise of all us Crusaders, there was not a shot fired in defense; ships and cities laid down their arms and surrendered, welcoming King Richard as their new ruler, come to save them at last from the long oppressions of a usurping tyrant.

Richard received them all graciously, refusing tribute. All he asked, with a glint of his ice-blue eyes, was that they shave their beards. "That way," he said, laughing, "I can distinguish you from the Saracens!"

Only Isaac himself held out, perched high in the mountains of Cyprus, in the great fortress of Kantara. Days went by; Richard prepared for a siege, moving up his siege towers and erecting his scaling ladders below the rock where the fortress was built. "We will smoke him out, never fear!" he cried. Richard, after his time in the Midi, thought nothing of a long siege.

But the thing had hardly begun before it was all over; it happened in this way:

At nightfall there rose a small commotion in our camp, shouts and a clash of steel, and then, quite clear, a loud "Ho! Ho there, King Richard!"

"Mercadier!" cried Richard, jumping up from his couch and yanking the canvas tent flap so that it tore. "Ho, Mercadier!"

And there came that Mercadier, his dark face alight with laughter, and a swagger sitting on his shoulders, though it was plain to see he was drawn with exhaustion and ready to drop in his tracks. "Ho, King! I bring you a prize!"

In his right hand he held two swords, and his left grasped

firmly the wrists of a small, slim maiden, tied together; she held back at every step, digging in her heels, so that he had to drag her. Her face was oddly like his own, dark, smoothly dark, with black, close-curling hair and eyes of a startling deep blue; and now she had, also, his habitual expression, a fierce, innocent scowl.

"A long-lost sister, man?" said Richard. "She has your eyebrows."

Mercadier drew in his breath, an exultant sound. "Isaac's daughter," he said. "His only child."

Richard whistled. "God, man, what a find!" He stooped forward a little to peer at the girl. "Are you sure? She's very dirty."

"Well, we have come by a long and dusty road. It's his daughter, all right. Name of Zenobia."

At this the little maid twisted like an eel in his hands, so that he had to drop his two swords and get a fresh grip on her. She was a flailing mass out of which came bare legs, kicking. I was reminded of a housecat when it suddenly turns, hissing, and strikes with its scratching hind claws.

Mercadier grinned as he dodged the kicks. "Ow! She's a handful, King, I'll tell you. Has been all along. I hope they haven't poisoned those claws."

She had managed to bring her bound hands close enough to score his cheek twice, and it was bleeding. Richard, laughing, got behind the girl, thrusting his long arm between her arms and body from the rear, thus effectively putting her out of action; it forced her back to arch and she could not even get a purchase for kicking, but she turned her head suddenly and spat at him, very catlike. She was short, so it missed his face, but showed gleaming upon the breast of his red shirt.

"Little witch!" he said, laughing, "that will come out of your father's hide."

At this, she hissed out a stream of invective in what sounded like the Griffon tongue, but I did not recognize a word of it.

"Where did you learn that?" said Richard. "Did Isaac bring you up among his whores?"

The little body gave a great shudder, trying to twist out of his hold, and the gray robe, fastened at the shoulder with a huge pronged pin set with a red stone, fell away. I wanted to cover my eyes, for she was dressed in nothing more than two gauzy bands about her hips and chest.

"Sweet Jesu, what is she wearing?" cried Richard.

"It is a disguise," said Mercadier, unnecessarily. "I threw the robe on for decency. It is mine, though I stole the ruby brooch." And he bent to pick the garment up from the floor.

"Keep the bauble," said Richard carelessly. "It will pay you for your scratches."

We saw then that the little maid had grown still and drooped where she stood. Her eyes were closed, and tear tracks showed on her flushed cheeks; I guessed she was worn out. Slowly, carefully, Richard slid his arm from where it held her.

"Will you be good now, little one?" he asked, smiling.

She nodded, and mumbled something; he bent closer, listening, and then snapped his fingers. "Toss me that velvet bedgown, Saracen, there's a good fellow."

Evidently she had asked for something to cover her near nakedness. He took the gown and wrapped her in it, pinioning her arms again, but tenderly this time; there was almost a caress in it. He held her close, smiling, and tipped up her chin. The blue eyes stared defiantly, but the scowl had smoothed out; she was uncommonly pretty, if somewhat dark for Western tastes.

Richard held her so for a long moment, staring in his turn. Then he sighed and said, half-turning to Mercadier, "Too young, you think?"

"Twelve years they said, Sire."

"Too young, then," he said. "But I regret it, little one. You will make a good armful one day."

At this she opened her mouth, ready to curse at him again, but he covered it with the palm of his hand.

"Gently, little princess. I only spoke in jest. I would not harm you, were you ever such an enemy."

The tears began in earnest then; her face was suddenly wet with them, and the slight shoulders shook in long shuddering sobs. Richard held her close, stroking her hair; his face was as gentle as I had ever seen it.

"Poor little Zenobia. Poor little girl . . . so tired. Are you hungry?"

She nodded, sobbing aloud.

"Saracen, fetch that covered tray beside my couch. If the flies have not been at it, it is still fresh, and I have not touched it."

I held the tray while Richard fed her, bringing small morsels to her lips with his own fingers, and watching her swallow like some old doting nurse. "A little wine now," he said softly. "Not too much at first . . . Good! There now, that is enough for the moment. Now you must rest, little princess." And so saying, he lifted the child—for she was not much more—in his arms and laid her down upon his own couch. Almost before he had straightened up to his full height, she was asleep, breathing in soft, regular childish breaths, almost like sighs. He smiled. "She will be out till morning, if I am any judge. You must have led her a pretty journey, my friend," he said, turning to Mercadier.

"From Kyrenia, on the coast," he said. "She was hiding in Isaac's harem there."

"God's nails!" cried Richard softly. "Poor little maid." He looked up suddenly. "What happened to the rest of the girls?"

"I left them there," said Mercadier, "under guard." At Richard's wry look, he went on. "They will be safe. They are too fat, even for routiers."

CHAPTER 3

"ON THE FIFTH of June, in Whitsun week, Richard's fleet, with his entire army, the two queens Berengaria and Joanna, the Damsel of Cyprus, Zenobia, and all the minstrels, clerks, cooks, and laundresses, set out for Palestine. The conquest of Cyprus had taken, in all, fifteen days. So easily was the mastery of that island won for the service of God."

So wrote I for the chronicles. I did not put down the description of the Damsel's shameful undress, or that she had been found in the abode of her father's pampered whores. Nor did I write of Isaac's pitiable state, his unkempt beard, his torn hair, his knees raw and bleeding where he had knelt begging for his daughter's life. He was a villain, sure, a usurper and a foul oppressor. But by his great fatherly love, he had redeemed himself in my eyes, poor weak soul that I am.

He gave all of Cyprus for his little Zenobia, gave up all his great wealth, his castles, his wives and concubines, and gave over his person into bondage. All he asked, after her life, is that he might see his darling once again.

Richard, moved, stood up from his improvised throne of judgment, put out his hands, and raised Isaac up from his knees, giving him the kiss of courtesy and seating him in honor by his side. Then he called for Zenobia to be brought before them for her father's farewell embrace.

Tears flowed down Isaac's swarthy face, streaking it where the dirt had struck and matting his curly thicket of beard. He stood up, swaying, and gathered his child into his arms, sobbing aloud, while she added her tears to his.

I was not the only one moved by this view of the fallen tyrant; as one, the assembled host gasped and sobbed, even the most hardened routier among them, at the sight of the lovely child, decently garbed now in a blue dress cut down from one of Queen Berengaria's, her unruly curls tamed under a silver-shot head veil. Demurely, her sapphire eyes cast down, long lashes shadowing her cheek, the little maid, in fair Latin, implored Richard to grant her father one privilege.

"Gladly," he said, his face tender, as always, when he looked upon this Damsel.

"Spare my poor father the indignity of irons, O King!" She spoke in a throbbing voice that carried through all the lines of soldiers; this little maid, like Richard himself, was a fairish mountebank, knowing well how to gain sympathy. A soft groan went up from the watchers, and one of the women, laundress or camp whore, cried out, "Oh, woe!"

Richard frowned. A long moment went by while the host waited, holding its breath. Then his face cleared; he nodded. "Granted," he said. "His chains shall be of silver."

And Isaac was sent, under the charge of Guy of Lusignan, straight across the sea to the nearest point on the Syrian coast, the fortress of Markab in Tripoli. He had been a tyrant in every sense of the word, unmanned though he was now, and the whole island of Cyprus rejoiced, the people giving to Richard, their new ruler, half of all they possessed; he swore to use it only for the great conquest of the Holy Land and the recovery of the Holy Sepulchre. Little Zenobia was given to the two queens for a handmaiden; she dwelt with them in their royal cabin, the largest chamber on the largest boat. After the acquisition of the Cypriot navy, the total of our ships numbered one hundred and sixty-three, the largest fleet, it is said, that was ever assembled on any waterway.

We sailed down the coast past Tortosa and Tripoli, glittering cities, white in the Eastern sun. We reached the port of Beyrout as the sun sank into the sea, dyeing the sky purple and pink in a brief display of God's glory, before the swift descent of the dark, a phenomenon peculiar to these parts. So strange to our Northern eyes, the bright white day, the sky barely tinged with blue, with shimmering waves of heat rising above the diamond waves of the sea . . . then that soft wash of color, lasting no more than a moment or two, and then, in a flash, a pall of heavy black, pierced by the silver jewels of the night sky, the stars.

When one looked up, it seemed that the sky grew ever closer, enveloping us in its spangled cloak, a strange, unearthly sensation. At first I felt as though it would strangle me, I swear I could feel the heavy folds of black in my lungs, and tore at the neck of my robe to ease my swelling throat. But it was only an illusion; after a while I grew used to it, and welcomed the closeness of the heavens.

But this night, to get back to my tale—this nightfall at Beyrout, Richard took a notion to visit his bride, embarking in a small boat from his flagship, in the lead, to the great galley in the rear that held the two queens. It was still warm from the heat of the day, and he wore only his sailor garb, the short canvas drawers and thin open shirt, with sandals on his feet; how I envied him, in my heavy woolen monks' wear! Over his shoulder he had slung his lute, in a fair cloth-of-silver bag. "Come too, Saracen. And bring your lute as well . . . the ladies may fancy a night of music."

"Oh, Dickon," I protested, the old nickname slipping out in the warm dark and the closeness. "I—It has been so long . . . there is a broken string."

"Easily mended," he said airily. "We can have a tenson or a duet, like old times."

"Very old," I grumbled. "I have forgotten the fingering." But I fetched it anyway, the battered old thing from the days of my boyhood, and all the way over in the boat I puzzled the fingering, getting it in my head again. Despite myself, I felt a pleasurable thrill; perhaps is was a sin; the Church does not look kindly on the troubadour art.

But, strangely, as we neared the galley's side, there came a floating music on the air, soft and sweet—a fugitive tune that died away, unfinished, as we climbed the ladder to the deck. "Joanna has been practicing," Richard said, laughing softly.

"The touch is surer than her usual one . . . and poor Berengaria is cursed with ten thumbs."

The lute player proved to be neither of them, but the little Damsel of Cyprus. When the waiting-woman opened the door to us, we saw her, seated cross-legged on a low divan, her dark head bent to a pretty gilded lute, small and with a foreign shape. The sounds that came from it, though, were lute notes, no mistake, thin and silvery.

Richard kissed his bride and his sister quickly and, without pausing, strode to stand above the little Zenobia. "So, small one, you are a troubadour!"

"I hope to be," she said demurely. "Someday." All the while she played, softly; it was deceptively simple music, but I saw, looking close, the flying fingers and the strained swollen muscle in her small forearm, mark of the musician.

"You have had a good teacher," he said.

"The best." She lowered her eyes, frowning a little as she came to a difficult passage; when she got through it she smiled and tossed her head, her fingers loose and easy now as the song drew to a close. I did not know the song—I have been far from such frivolities in my last years—but I heard Richard humming, a look of pleasure on his face.

When she finished, he clapped loudly and shouted, "Well done! Gaucelm Faudit is not easy."

As he unslung the lute bag from his shoulders and began to undo the drawstrings, she started up another tune, one that even I knew well. "Oh, I am fit and fair and ripe for love," part of the raza that Blondelza had sung at Richard's ducal crowning, in Aquitaine, all those years ago. I stole a look at Richard, seeing his face still and carven, looking as if he were holding his breath. Slowly he took up his own lute, felt for the strings, and began to play, softly, the alto part, swelling stronger and stronger as the girl's playing came to a close. He raised his voice then and sang, too, the old words, his words, that he had written and that Blondelza had countered in her raza. His voice was deeper than it had been, but still true, and it rang out, resonant, in the small chamber. When he finished, ". . . O Infidel, beware!" I saw that his light eyes glittered in the candles' light. He smiled a little, and reached up and dashed away a tear, not shamed, but looking happy and content. There was a little pause between them, their eyes meeting; then he said, almost on a sigh, "Blondelza."

She nodded. "My teacher."

After a moment he said, "You know . . . Yes, I can see it, you do . . . you know Blondelza and I . . ." His voice died away.

She nodded, grave-faced. "She wore the ring . . . the crest of Aquitaine. Besides, King, the whole world knows."

"Do they?" said Richard, looking surprised.

She smiled. "How not? The King of England is always news. And if he is also the best knight in the world, and a famous troubadour as well—" She shrugged, spreading her hands. "And Blondelza could not get the ring off, either. Even with soaping, it will not go past her first finger joint."

"She has put on flesh, then?" Dismay was in his face.

Zenobia laughed. "Not she . . . slim and sleek as ivory she is still. But she has the lute picker's hands, muscled and strong." And the little maid looked down at her own, still tiny and delicate. "I wish . . . Well, one must sacrifice something for art."

I stole a glance at the two queens, after this exchange. They were gawping like hooked fish, listening to every word. I thought Joanna's eyes would pop, but little Berengaria had gone white; if all the world knew, then I suppose she did as well, poor lady.

The two lutists were still talking intently; I caught Richard's words. "And so, how long since you have seen her?"

"Oh, just last year," said Zenobia airily. "She comes to me every year, at about this time. That is how your captain caught me . . . I was at Kyrenia, our palace on the coast, waiting for her. Father built a little guesthouse there, a private place, just for Blondelza."

Richard's face froze. "A private place . . . among his whores? Then—"

She shook her head. "No, King. Father would have had it so, of course, for her fame would have brought him honor. But she would not. She will be no man's mistress, she told me once. She will not be bought. She loves where she will."

Richard was grim, his voice harsh. "And that is . . . where?"

Zenobia smiled; it had a mocking look, old for her years. "I am not her confidante." She shrugged again. "Many names have been whispered—it could be all of them . . . or none."

"I see," said Richard. He spoke quietly, but a little pulse

beat strongly in his jaw; I could see it even from across the room.

And so they played and sang all the evening, a pleasurable thing to hear. Not just Blondelza's songs, or Richard's, but many of the great troubadour lays—Piere Vidal, Marcabru, Faudit. At the end Richard struck up the peautiful planh of Bertrand de Born, that which he had written for the Young King's death. It was so very moving, so tender; I felt my own eyes water, though I had not really liked young Henry. And when I turned about, I saw that Joanna, his sister, had completely broken down, and was sobbing in Berengaria's arms. I remembered wryly that that same Henry had teased her unmercifully in her childhood, long ago. But such is the power of sweet music.

It served, as well, that lovely planh, to break the spell that held the two singers, and to bring us all together. Berengaria, still pale, but wearing a smile, rang for wine and little cakes, and for a while we were all merry together, and Richard kissed her heartily upon our departure. "Dear little love," I heard him say softly, "I would be with you this night . . . but, short of banishing all your ladies to the slippery decks, I cannot." He smiled, and kissed her again; color flared in her cheeks, making me content.

Joanna, a little flown with wine, and having known me from boyhood, threw her arms around me in a boisterous hug and kissed me full on the lips. "There!" she cried. "That's for old times!" Berengaria, bright-eyed now, gave me her little hand; I bent and kissed it, afterward stumbling and turning red as fire at the laughter about me. I do not know what came over me, and clutched at my beads as at a lifeline.

Somehow I heard Richard's last words to the Damsel of Cyprus; I hoped that Berengaria had not. "But she had not arrived?" His voice was very low. "When had you thought to see her?"

"She was due any moment . . . depending upon the sea winds." She gave that little worldly shrug again, and laughed, low. Then she raised her voice. "Good-bye then, King, for now."

"Good-bye, little one," he answered, fisting her cheek; it was a way he had with pages and boy children; I never saw him touch a little maid so. She liked it though, it was plain to see, tossing her little dark head and looking at him sidelong. Women always took to Richard, even small girls and old

295

crones; it was a spell he cast. And also how he got a name for tumbling one and all; I know for a fact he did not.

When we reached our own ship, Richard strode forward purposefully toward where the men-at-arms lay, under their canvas lean-tos upon the starboard deck, I stumbling along behind him, feeling foolish. I tried not to go among them this way, if I could help it; I knew it constrained them. But I could not avoid it this time, for he had not given me leave to go to my pallet. He took up a flaring cresset, holding it high; a few heads poked out, blinking and tousled. "Mercadier . . . where is he? Which is his place?" Others took up the word, calling the captain's name. Mercadier rose from his place; he had been squatting with some others, around a small fire, playing at knucklebones.

"Ho! King Richard!" Mercadier grinned whitely. This man seemed never to tire; he might, at this moment, have just risen from a long night's rest. "You are abroad late, it seems."

"I have been making music," said Richard. "Time is no matter. But I need your good services, as usual. Friend, I ask you . . . turn about, and go back upon the sea path we have traced. Go to Kyrenia. I have heard that someone may be there, someone . . ."

"The glee-maiden?" said Mercadier, too low for any ears but ours.

"She was expected. Perhaps . . . Who knows? She may be there now. She may still be there—if you hurry. Bring her to me."

They moved away, Mercadier gathering up his winnings, with a rough, goodnatured oath and that swagger he wore always, that seemed to mark him from his fellows. He turned to the King. "Shall I have men at my bidding? There may be difficulties."

Richard frowned; I could see it in the light still, as it faded behind us. "Just take her, man! I do not care how! But unharmed, of course. Bring her to me here, at Beyrout. I will lie over, waiting."

"Yes, Sire," said Mercadier evenly. "I shall do it . . . as I once brought your son to you."

"Mercadier, friend," said Richard softly. "There can be no morals between us . . . our sins are one, remember?"

"Not that sin, King," said Mercadier. "You must pay for

the theft of your son, alone. This—well, if I can do it, she is only a woman, after all."

I forgot my lowly status, forgot my place, and spoke then. "Dickon," I said, "you must not do this thing! You are free no longer. You have a wife."

Richard turned on me, swift as a lion. His face was in darkness, but his voice had a sharp edge to it. "I care not for a thousand wives!" he said. "I care not!"

I was silent, though a knife thrust through me, for Berengaria's pain.

"Am I to have nothing that I love?" Richard said. "Nothing?"

"You have more than most men," I said, taking my courage in my hands.

He must have read something in my face, even in the uncertain light of the stars; he stopped then and laid his hand upon my arm. "Forgive me, Saracen. None knows another's heart." For a long moment I felt, rather than saw, his eyes searching mine. He turned away, but then, in a moment, turned back. "But you are not my conscience, either."

It was true. And, in any case, I was a monk, and should be proof against the winds of fancy. I went below, to my bedplace, and could not sleep; I prayed, and watched the dawn upon the waters.

CHAPTER 4

RICHARD, DRESSED IN red surcoat and hose, with the white Crusader's cross upon his breast and the thin gold fillet of royalty set upon his brow, paced the deck of his flagship, *Berengaria*, looking now toward the shores of the infidel city, Beyrout, now behind him, past the great line of his halted ships, to the far horizon. The fleet stood at anchor, rocking gently.

Since break of day, there had been hails from the nearer ships of the fleet, questioning the delay. No answer had gone forth, only "The King's pleasure." So, we waited, hour after weary hour, while the sun climbed high in the sky and the oven heat beat down, until one expected to see the very water boil beneath it. The fast ship bearing Mercadier and his mission had set sail before first light, headed back toward the little port of Kyrenia. With favorable winds, it could return before nightfall, perhaps with its precious booty, perhaps not.

Richard could not settle. He had eaten nothing, and drunk only a cup of watered wine; there was a tremor in his hand, and from time to time he took a cloth from his scarlet sleeve and wiped his sweaty face. The men crouched over dice or knucklebones, swearing softly; the sailors went about their business, swabbing the decks and polishing the rail; a lookout clung to the mast, high up.

The day wore on, the sun climbed, Richard paced. Suddenly there came a low cry from the lookout on his perch. "Ahoy! A sail!"

Instantly Richard ran to look up, shading his eyes. "What is it, man?"

A pause, while we strained our eyes. "Sorry, Sire, 'tis nothing. Someone has hung out laundry on the queens' galley."

Richard clicked his tongue against his teeth, exasperated. "Silly fool women."

"Surely it is early still," I said. "He cannot have got there and back. Richard, will you not rest? Come into the shade, take some refreshment."

He threw me a filthy look, his footsteps creaking on the boards, forward, back, forward, back. I gave up, and sought shelter from the sun under the forward tent, where I took up my chronicle, adding and correcting.

Later, much later, the afternoon sun slanting along my scrolls, there came another cry, louder this time, and a sudden bustle and scurrying of feet. Richard pulled aside the folds of my tent, smiling; his eyes looked alarmingly wild. "Come, Saracen, I want you! She has come!"

I stumbled from under the shelter, blinking in the golden light. There, far in our rear, was another ship, tiny in the distance; I could just make out the square of tawny silk that hung from the mast, Mercadier's signal. "She is aboard," cried Richard. "They are flying her colors! Oh, hurry!"

I followed him, climbing down the ladder and stepping into the little unsteady boat manned by two wooden-faced sailors. "Row for your lives, men!" cried Richard. They bent to the oars, still wooden-faced; it was all the same to them, a king's whimsey, worth no more than obedience. But Richard, bursting with excitement, took his lute, which he wore slung over his shoulder, and played a lively air, one new to me, a rowing song. Soon, one after the other, the sailors joined in, pulling with a will, and singing the words, a meaningless chant, roaring loud above the sea.

The distance had seemed great, but we were there in minutes, or so it felt to me. I was nervous, for I had not seen the lady Blondelza for so many long years, a frightening length of time.

Mercadier stood at the low rail of the little ship, leaning forward to give us a hand up. Since the ship rode low in the water, it was only a few steps.

"Where is she?" demanded Richard, first up the ladder.

"There," said Mercadier, gesturing over his shoulder; a striped tent, gay in yellow and red, covered the whole port deck. As we looked, soft sounds came from within it, the faintest lute notes, blending into the lapping of the waves.

For a long moment Richard stood, as though struck by a god; then, with a long sigh, he turned to me, saying quietly, "Go before me, friend. I cannot make my legs behave." He laughed shakily. I moved forward to the tent, Richard laggard at my heels. A hand flung back the tent door as we approached, and we heard a voice. "Enter, fair friends."

The tent was full of people, or so it seemed, gay with bright colors, and humming, somehow, with unsung songs; the lute was silent, but the reedy notes of a pipe played on, thin and high as birdsong. I did not see those other folk, though, for my eyes went to Blondelza, where she sat, still as a statue, against the painted canvas wall. She was beautiful still—more beautiful, indeed, than she had been in her youth; a woman now, thinner, but with a deeper bosom. Her hair, which had been thick and golden-bright, was smooth and palely gleaming, half hidden by an azure veil. The same azure veiled her body, the flesh of her arms and neck showing rosy through its folds. A lute lay in her lap, her hands still and crossed upon it. There were pearls in her earlobes and at her throat. Her face was dazzling fair, thinner, too, than I remembered it, and her eyes deep and dark as shadowed waters. Unsmiling, she held out her hand; I dropped to one knee, like a courtier, and kissed it.

She gave a little, low laugh, husky. "Alex, you have put on courtesy with your cowl." She did not speak then, for a long moment; I heard the quick breath come and go in her, like a sob, and then she whispered, "So long ago, dear friend . . . so long ago."

Tears came to my eyes, stinging. Confused, I stepped back and turned. "Here . . . here stands the King," I said, and moved away, leaving those two face to face.

They were silent and did not move. I held my breath, it seemed, forever.

Then, "Oh, Richard," she said. In one movement he was upon his knees, his arms around her, his head buried in her lap. Her face went soft, seeming to crumple; she bent over him, stroking his hair. "Oh, my dear, my dear," she said, over and over. When she raised her head, her eyes were dark and swimming. Her cheeks were wet, but she smiled. "Leave us," she said, and waved her hand.

Richard spent the rest of the day and the night on the little ship with Blondelza, giving orders that we return to the flagship and send the rowboat for him the next day at first light.

She had, traveling with her, many jongleur folk; it was these that had crowded her tent as she awaited us. Among them I recognized several that I had known well in the old days; we fell upon one another's necks with joy, remembering our youth. The two young lads, apprentices then, were now strapping great fellows, each with the lithe body, hard as rock, of the acrobat. Their mother, Giselda, that good dame, had died two years earlier of a pox, but Jacques le Gros, her husband, was still head of the troupe. He mocked at himself, saying he was close to the century mark now, and indeed he looked it, in a way. For he had lost weight, belying his nickname, and he looked sad and shrunken, though his black eyes were as bold and bright as ever. I counted up the years, in my head; he was younger than Queen Eleanor, so lovely still!

Gervase, too, I greeted with gladness; the magician had another wife now, his first having run away with a lion tamer; I remembered her, a whey-faced rabbity girl, and thought him well rid of her. His new wife was pretty, and they had three half-grown sons, learning the magician's trade. There were others too, musicians and tumblers, but all new faces to me. These lively artists followed Blondelza about, performing with her, as they had in her father's day; they still called themselves the Blondel Company.

I had such joy in these good, merry people, exchanging

tales and hearing of their adventures, that I quite forgot to pray for Richard's soul, trapped now in the sin of adultery. I fear I am not much of a priest, God forgive me.

CHAPTER 5

ACRE . . . THE FAMED city of the ancients, a great citadel, reaching out, southward, to the sea. Eastward, far away upon the tree-covered hills, Saladin's camp was spread, tent after tent, blinding white in the sun, like a great flock of birds. To north and west the Christian banners waved, standards of the kings and nobles, bright with many colors, red and white, blue and gold, purple and green, with another city of tents beneath—a city swarming with life, like a nest of ants, gray and brown, sparkled here and there with the silver of mail. High above rose the golden tents of the kings, facing the ramparts of the infidel garrison.

A huge crowd lined the shore; the shouting tore at our eardrums, tore at our hearts. Acre . . . the outer plains of Hell.

The first thing, after the noise, that smote our senses was the smell. Far off the shore it drifted toward us, faint at first, like a hot breath, then stronger, sweetish, sickening. It was everywhere, like an invisible cloud, a fog that closed round us as we set foot on the shore. Too soon we grew used to it. It was the smell of death.

I was ashore with the first, my charcoal slippery in my sweaty hand, my little book hanging, closed, at my belt. There was too much, too many sights, too much suffering. Soldiers, starved and sick, stared at us out of hollow eyes, reached out worn hands to touch the air that held us. Gaunt women rolled upon the ground at our feet, their skull-faces frightening; they held up children, human weeds with great swollen bellies and limbs like sticks, their eyes hopeless, staring, the eyelids clustered with black flies. Beggars held out their hands, rotting stumps of flesh. Whores, ragged, filthy, smiling skeletons, offered themselves for a crust. Hell. Acre.

I turned seaward, seeing what that poor suffering horde

saw. Our ships stood in the harbor, filling it and on beyond, hiding the horizon, darkening the sky; upon each sail a white cross blazed, hundreds of crosses. On every deck stood the glittering masses of mailed knights, shining like the angels of God. From the first, the flagship, poured a silver river of men onto the shore.

And from those hundreds of throats came a great triumphant roar, answered by those on shore, swelling to a crescendo as Richard left his ship, huge in his mail, his red head bared, a scarlet cloak flung over his wide shoulders. He stepped down into a broad barge hung with bright pennants, taking his place between two of his nobles, the Duke of Bedford and the Earl of Leicester. The barge came swiftly on, its oars cutting through the dark, foaming waters. Standing high, under a crimson canopy, Richard raised his long arm in a salute. The canopy shed its rosy glow upon him; he was as if bathed in blood. The roar rose to a high, piercing shriek.

King Philip Augustus of France stood under another canopy upon the wharf, waiting to welcome his fellow Crusader; his face was dark, unsmiling.

Richard landed, and the storm of sound rocked the sky. The Deliverer was come! The white cross on his breast blazed, holding the sunlight; the crown on his head became a halo. Slowly he turned, raising that long, scarlet arm again, and smiled, a smile like the smile of heaven, friendly, simple, wide.

He embraced Philip of France like a brother, stooping to him, so tall was he. The two moved forward together, slowly, against the hands stretched out to touch, to worship, to give thanks. They came to a long canopy; under it flew the Christian flags, all the nations', held by young knights, beardless as girls, fair skins peeling from the fierce sun. Two of them brought forward a white charger and handed Richard the silvered reins. As he mounted, delirium broke again, as though his every move were a cause for wonder, for adoration. He rode forward very slowly, the horse's feet dainty, its huge head proud; the young knights in the first row cast their cloak upon the ground under its feet. Richard raised his arm again, smiled again, his eyes—large, bright, sea-blue—moving along the ranks.

I saw one face as it met that smile and those eyes; a boy's face, thin, wasted with fever, his own eyes glittering beneath the dirty white cloth that wrapped his head. Beneath the cloth

302

were clustered curls red as Richard's own hair, a rare color. Richard's smile widened at the sight; he nodded. The boy smiled back, tremulous, bursting with joy. Love, overwhelming love I saw there, pure, untarnished, simple; he would never love like that again—with his whole heart, and asking no return—never again, if he lived. And I saw that look of love mirrored in a dozen faces; the flower of Europe's chivalry gave its heart that day. I was to see it many times, over and over, in the days and months that followed; through blood, through tears, even shining from the ugly face of sudden death. Never was man so beloved as Richard of England; never so fiercely adored.

After the King came troop after troop, spilling off the ships in turn, men in their thousands, each greeted with roars of welcome. Onward they came, the knights and foot soldiers of Guy the King of Jerusalem, the Duke of Bedford's men, the Earl of Leicester's, their helmets starred with plumes of white or scarlet, their tunics long, rich, gleaming with gems. Little by little the crowd thinned out, following the newcomers in thin trickles, begging for notice, hope, a crust of glory.

Some barges capsized that day, so heavy were the great engines, so wild the penned-up steeds. Thin wrecks of starveling Crusaders waded into the water to lend a hand, grinning their comradeship, splashing each other with the already tepid water. It was still morning; not till the shadows lengthened did the ships empty of their human cargo, so many were they. The queens came near the end, stepping gracefully from their barges onto the trampled shore, big, handsome Joanna and the shy-faced, small Berengaria. They passed through the lines of siege-weary soldiers like a breath of new air, their clothes rich and bright, their spangled veils floating behind them like a soft mist, their perfume cutting through the fetid stench like a mass of flowers, making their presence real.

The poor sick wretches stood staring after them, still as posts; some of them had not seen such women for years, not since their mothers and sisters bade them goodbye in the courtyards of their own manors. More than one face gleamed wet with tears after they had passed. Lackeys came running with carved gilt litters, hung with velvet; they mounted into them, their ladies with them, and were gone from sight, mounting the long slope farthest from the main camp, where they were to be quartered.

After them came Blondelza and her troupe of jongleurs.

She dressed as they did, in the gay garb of the minstrel, striped yellow and red, her hair bundled into a red silk net, little heel-less yellow slippers on her feet; she carried her lute, slung into a silken bag. Some of the company turned somersaults as they went, and one fellow played the pipes. The faces round me lit with shy laughter; they clapped their hands in time. Blondelza smiled and waved. "Give us a song, Lady! . . . Don't go! Give us a song, a short one!" She called out, "Later . . . tonight! The king's criers will announce it . . . you'll have a concert!" And they passed on in their turn, piling into a big wagon, which then trundled up the hill. "Blondelza . . . it is the glee-maiden Blondelza!" went the whispered cries.

They were the last. All the boats had emptied; it was almost evening. I gathered my habit up out of the dust and hurried up the path myself; I must find my quarters before dark. Or find, at least, a corner out of the way, where I could sit and jot these happenings down while they were fresh.

Acre. City of Hell. City of welcome. Our camp, the first camp of the Holy Land. I reached down to the earth and took up a handful, kissing it, kissing its holy dust.

CHAPTER 6

GREAT FIRES OF driftwood from the beaches and brush from the wooded hills flamed like pyres against the black of the night sky. The whole vast army of Christendom gathered round them, eating the roasted meats off the spits, drinking the Cypriot wine, Richard's bounty. Torches and cressets flared, too, lighting up the festivities as far as the eye could see, right up to the walls of the besieged garrison. Arrows and bolts fell harmlessly along the outskirts, shot from the enemy walls. The men laughed, raising greasy fingers in a gesture of contempt, their eyes bright with drunkenness and hope. The enemy's fire was not returned. Joy was in the Christian hearts this night, and the fighting due to resume next day, alas; too soon for these weary scarecrows.

They had been fighting, besieger and besieged, for more

than a year, ever since Guy of Lusignan had made daring camp here, right under the walls almost, and, by a miracle, held on. Now they were at a stalemate, the garrison still standing, Saladin's troops in the hills beyond, the Christians battering at the walls and the infidels battering too at *their* backs, harrying them.

But, for once, all was forgotten; for once, each man had his fill. The great King of the English had come; victory glimmered like a marsh fire within the celebratory flames. Richard's minstrels and jongleurs played and sang; the men, their hoarse voices sharpened by the wine, sang along with them.

Slowly, the fires burned down, and only picked bones strewed the ashes. The huge bronze wine vats, tipped over on their sides, lay empty; the army slept.

I had drunk nothing, not wanting to take some weary wretch's share. I had slept little, and, when the dawn paled the sky, I rose quietly from my pallet in the scribes' tent and crept forth into the half-light. The smell was stronger now, choking. Borne on the wind, it gusted toward the nostrils; it was almost impossible to breathe.

I held the hood of my habit up to my face, wrapping a corner of it over my nose and mouth, and climbed the rampart of hard-trodden earth that rose between our camp and the Saracens'. A vast plain lay before me, a living mass of corruption, a charnel house. Bodies in every state of putrefaction, swollen, black, covered with flies, picked at by crows. Bleached bones gleamed white among them, and grinning skulls; here and there a head fluttering with a rag of hair, or a limb, yellow and blood-streaked. On, on it stretched, right up to the city walls, thousands of bodies, flung like garbage upon a midden heap. Flies buzzed in great clouds above, and covered the whole mass, so that it seemed to heave, sickeningly. I saw a jackal streak past, a hand with flesh still upon it held in its jaws, and, from the hills beyond, another barked, like a signal. And, high above, a harsh chorus, loud, so that I raised my head; I saw a great flock of vultures wheeling against the sky, wide-winged, sailing. They dropped to the stinking ground and dove into the rot and bones; ugly as sin they were, with raw necks stretched out, and open beaks. I felt my scant supper rise, sour, into my throat, and turned away, pressing my face into the muffling cloth.

There was someone watching me, standing a pace below,

looking up. Another cleric, but in a habit I did not recognize, with a curious cut. I saw his tonsure, though, and the wood cross with the ivory Jesus, hanging on a thong about his neck. He saw me and smiled; a good face, burnt almost black, with dozens of tiny wrinkles fanning out from the eyes, and the eyes themselves, light in the brown face, sparkling like rainwater.

"Brother Alberic," he said, answering my look. "Greetings, brother in God." And he made the sign of the Cross in the air between us. "You came with the King of the English."

"I am only a scribe," I said. "Brother Alexander is my name . . . from Gloucester, in England."

"It is good you have come," he said simply. "And your King. There is great need." And he gestured, silent, to the great plain of the dead.

"Infidels?" I asked.

He shook his head. "Not one but bore the cross upon his jupon."

"Christians!" I shuddered, signing myself.

"Christians all." He lowered his voice, moving closer. "The first layer—those that are picked clean—is a contingent of knights, French and Burgundian. They tried to force the Turkish camp. Desperate, I guess, and wild with fever. Lacking leaders, they were mowed down like wheat by the Saracens. The French king, and his barons, and the Burgundian count, and, God save us, my own master of Austria . . . they stood and watched, and did not raise a hand to stop the slaughter. No orders were given, no succor . . . they just let them die." Neither of us spoke; I could not take it in, the horror.

"That was only a month back," he said. "But the vultures, and the heat . . . they might have died a century ago. And since then, when any man dies—and there are hundreds every day—they are just tipped in on top, and left to the jackals and the filthy birds. No burials . . . just the army's offal."

Shocked, I felt for the beads that hung at my waist, mumbling a silent prayer. For a moment we two stood there, heads bowed, praying together for the poor unshriven souls, while the birds of death cried, black, against the sky.

Then Brother Alberic raised his head; his eye, with a glint in it, held mine. "I think," he said, sniffing, "the wind has changed." And so it had; the smell was bearable now, not so rank, and a little breeze from the north ruffled his hair. I saw it was not white, as I had thought at first, but a pale tow-color, thick and straight under the tonsure. He was still young, though famine-thin, his face like a blade.

Slowly we walked down together from the yellow hill of earth, talking of this and that, companionable. He said he came there each morning at sunrise, to pray. "For sometimes it is cool, for a little while . . . and, then, I cannot sleep." He smiled. "Hunger is no good opiate."

"Last night," I said, "surely every man had his fill."

"Oh, yes," said he, laughing. "Thanks be to your good King . . . but then I could not keep it on my stomach, poor wretch that I am."

He was very easy and open with me, telling me of his life now and in the past. He spoke a flawless Latin he had learned in Rome, during his novitiate. It was a pleasure to listen to him.

Brother Alberic came from a place in the German lands, called Swabia, and was the youngest son of seven. "Pure Swabians all, they are . . . living for hunting and horses, women and wine—and I the only changeling in the nest." His face fell into grave lines as he talked. "I miss them, you know . . . though I never thought to feel so. I saw them often, back in the homeland. Our monastery is in the town, below Father's manor, and the order is lenient." He looked at me, a very straight look, and lowered his voice. "But I think I shall see them soon now . . . for Duke Leopold has come to the end of his monies. He cannot hold out much longer. His men have not been paid for six months. Austria is a poor dukedom, and Leopold must beg every penny from the Duchess, his mother. She keeps him on a short rein, always has, poor lad."

"He is a young man, then, your duke," I asked, "like the French king?"

"Not so young as Philip Augustus, no—but seems so. He is one of those unfortunates born to power and wealth and having neither—and not one to snatch it for himself, either." He shook his head. "No. I think we will be going home soon— those of us who can make it there. Much sickness is in our camp; every day a few more die, without having drawn sword or spear."

"Not from hunger only . . . you don't mean from hunger?"

"No, not that. We have rations . . . rotten as they are, and scant. But there is sunstroke." He glanced at my uncovered head. "You must get a turban," he said. "It is the first rule in this land. A cloth, any kind, to wrap your head from the sun." He went on, frowning at his own words. "Then there are the fevers, and the chills when the sun goes down. And the fainting and the nausea . . . the hair falling out, and the fingernails . . . and the skin just erupting and never healing, the sores getting bigger and bigger and suppurating. But the worst of all is the loose bowels. The worst. We lost many from that alone, before we ever got to Acre. Men could not march—just kept falling out to relieve themselves, over and over, and finally, so weak, they just fell and could not get up."

"Have you had one of them—one of these diseases?" I asked, thinking he exaggerated.

"All of them," he said, with a harsh laugh. "Every man has had all of them. At one time or another. If you're lucky, you live. You don't recover. You simply live with it, the fevers, the chills, the nausea, the running bowels . . . Saladin's Curse, the men call it. It's as good a name as any. There's no cure."

"What do the doctors say?" I asked.

He laughed. "*I* am a doctor . . . ours is an order of healers." He shrugged. "We do what we can," he said simply.

We parted then, for morning sounds were coming from the camps, as the men arose and made ready for the coming day; he had his duties, and I mine. We promised to meet again. He was the first friend I had made in the Holy Land; I counted it a good sign.

The sun had just risen, showing white and pale in a whitish sky; already it was hot. I hurried to find a cloth, to make a turban for my head.

In the lull at midday—the morning had been spent in raising the great siege engines from our ships, the men dodging Saracen arrows as they worked—there was a great meeting called of all the kings and dukes, the leaders. Richard bade me be there, to record what was decided.

I saw them all, then: King Philip Augustus, with his young face set in the hard lines of an elder statesman; thin-lipped, with a grudging smile, and pale eyes that bulged slightly, giving him an angry look. Hugh, Duke of Burgundy, dark, sallow, and fleshy, a man who loved hard living and hard fighting, a brute in satin. The young Henry, Count of Champagne, fair-faced and long-legged, though wan from a recent bout of "Saladin's Curse." Henry, a mere boy, was nephew to both Philip and Richard, being the son of the Countess Marie, who was daughter to Queen Eleanor and the late King Louis, Philip's father. He asked, first off, and making no bones about it, for a loan from King Philip. "For I cannot stay otherwise—no ships have come from Champagne, no money, no gold. My men must have their pay, they are already pawning their horses and their armor."

"I have barely enough for my own expenses," said King Philip, his face very stern. "But I will advance you a hundred marks, if you agree to pawn Champagne. I will have the papers drawn up."

"I cannot do that," cried young Henry. "I cannot put my country at hazard! No one knows what this war will bring." He was weak from his illness, and sounded near to tears. "And, anyway, a hundred marks is not nearly enough."

"Be calm, sister's son," said Richard, smiling. "I have plenty. How much do you need, in pounds?"

Count Henry turned, amazed, almost stammering in his eagerness. "Sire. Uncle . . . I think— Well, it's a lot, I know, but— Well, I'm afraid I'm three thousand in arrears of wages."

"You shall have four thousand," said Richard, clapping him heartily on the back so that he nearly choked. "And I will undertake to feed your soldiers for a week and redeem their horses too."

"Oh, Sire, you are generous! Oh, Sire, I cannot thank you enough! You will have it back as soon as—"

"No hurry," said Richard gaily, waving his hand. "I cannot let the war be lost for lack of Crusaders. You have all spent a weary time here, before me—preparing the way. It is only right I should carry some burdens now." He looked around the table where they sat. "Good fellows all, speak up! Is there any other who must give up for want of money? We must keep the army a solid force here, or suffer defeat. Speak up!" There was a movement at the foot of the table; Richard turned. "Ah, Austria! Speak, brother!"

Leopold, Duke of Austria, was a neat, small man with flaxen curls and a pouting mouth like a girl's. But it was his eyes you saw first. They were a hot blue, intense, wild, and he carried himself tall, with his chest thrust out, like a strutting pigeon. Almost laughable—but Richard only smiled affably, and waited.

Leopold turned those mad blue eyes upon him, seeming to accuse. "My men are hungry, thin as weeds, and in rags. Many of them are sick. They have not been paid for a half-year, and are not pawning their horses, but eating them. I cannot stay another week, or we will not even make it home to Austria."

"How much?" asked Richard mildly. "How much will put you on your feet and keep you here in the Holy Land for another half-year?"

"Oh, sweet Jesus. I cannot say offhand. I must have my accountant figure it out. It is a great deal, though, I fear."

Richard raised his hand. "You shall have it. It will not make a dent in my fortune at the moment, however big a sum. Know you, brother Crusader, I have just this morning sold half of Cyprus to the Knights Templar!" He laughed loud and long. "All the world knows their wealth! So don't be shy, good Leopold . . . take it while you can get it!" And he threw his great red head back and laughed again, till all the council laughed with him.

"I can give you no surety," warned Leopold. "It all belongs to Mother, till—" And he broke off.

"Never say it, friend!" cried Richard. "You will inherit soon enough! No, I want no surety . . . only that you will fight for Holy Sepulchre and that your men will fight too!" And he rose, holding his wine cup high. "Let's drink to that! Holy Sepulchre! Fight for Holy Sepulchre!"

They drank, all their weary faces fired anew with him at that moment, a good moment. I know they did not love him, those dukes and that king, his peers—but at that moment, there in the tent, upon the holy ground of God, it did not matter.

CHAPTER 7

"KING RICHARD!" THEY shouted. "King Richard the Lionheart! We follow the Lionheart!"

Small hordes dogged Richard's footsteps wherever he went in the camp, and clusters of soldiers hung about the trodden earth outside his tent. Many wore the colors of France, Burgundy, and Austria, and shoved and pushed at one another to come close to the King. "Our deliverer!" they cried. "The conqueror!"

"Poor devils," said Richard, speaking low and smiling, "they want the gold."

For no sooner had we made camp than Richard had sent criers throughout, offering four gold bezants a month to any who would take service with him. This was one whole gold bezant above the wages offered by Philip Augustus—offered, but, it was said, seldom paid. Thus it was no wonder that all flocked to Richard's banner. Still, it was not all for the gold. A decisive leader was long awaited, they were hungry for him. Many fell upon their knees, begging him to set to at once and win back the face of God, so long turned away.

"They need you, Sire," said young Henry of Champagne, with a shy smile. "Our men are dying like flies."

"I am no doctor, nephew," said Richard, shaking his head. "Nor a worker of miracles either."

"No. No, I know. But—for the *spirit*, you see—they need you. The others, Philip Augustus and Burgundy and Austria . . . they do nothing. King Philip—" he burst out, his face reddening. "King Philip has set up his war engines, but he will not use them—they are quite new, he says! They hate Burgundy—he has flogged men to death for a surly look or a slow step! Oh, Sire, they need *you*! They are dying, and they are afraid! If the heat and the fevers do not pick them off, or the spoiled food, the polluted water, the mosquitoes—then it will be the great stones hurled from the walls, the burning oil, or the Greek fire."

Richard's eyes narrowed in thought. "There is no wall that

311

cannot be scaled," he said. "It needs planning. Come." And he strode off toward the ramparts, where his own men were setting up the war engines that had been taken off the galleys.

About twenty men were needed to man each siege tower. These towers were, like Philip's, handsome structures, very modern; a strange, spindly sight against the sky, like an animal from some other world. And, like such animals, they could not walk this earth. For, when it came time to push them forward against the wall, the ground, muddy, grooved, rutted by the wheels of so many others, stopped them. They would move forward a few paces, with the sweating soldiers pushing from behind, and then totter, like drunken men, totter and lean, their wheels caught in the mud, or stuck in a rut. They looked handsome, it was true, but they were top-heavy—made for show, on a new road.

After two had been dug out, and two lost to Saracen fire, Richard called a halt. "I see," he said, rubbing his unshaven chin. "I see now what the trouble is." And straightaway he threw off his mail and his heavy boots and, taking shovel in hand, began to dig out the ground beneath the wheels. "Tell all the men to do likewise," he said. "We must make a level roadbed."

But he labored alone, except for Mercadier, who shoveled beside him. The knights stood about with long faces, unwilling to dirty their hands with serf labor—though a king was their example! I threw off my robe and took a shovel, and Brother Alberic, who had been looking on, followed my example. In a few hours the four of us had a smooth roadbed, leading right up to the walls.

There was a ragged sort of cheer then, and a rush to man the towers, but Richard held up his hand. "Wait!" he cried. "It won't do much good if we're burned to a crisp inside them." Which, of course, had been happening all along. "Go over to the pen where the animals are kept," he said to Mercadier. "Take about thirty of our sickest goats and slaughter them, and bring me their hides."

"They've been dying of heat and hunger anyway," said Mercadier, smiling grimly. "There won't have to be much slaughtering."

As he started off, Richard called, "Give the carcasses to the men—they can have a goat-meat roast!" And he made a wry face; goat is very tough. Still, we soon smelled the roasting flesh. We were lucky to get anything.

I saw several Frenchmen grinning behind their hands, and heard some sniggering. Poor fellows, they were probably dead already before they could see what Richard's strange command meant. But it was to save many lives.

The fresh goat hides were stretched across the wooden structures, forming a roof and walls about them. The road now being smooth, the towers were pushed up to the garrison walls, the men inside protected by the stretched hides. When the Greek fire or the boiling oil was poured down, it simply fizzled out, for the raw green hides would not catch fire. Thus were we able to do much damage, with no loss of life. And the others imitated us, the French and Burgundians, so that in twenty-four hours there was hardly a goat left in the whole Christian camp!

In a week, Richard had designed another top for the towers, tapering and light, easy to handle. With the green hides as protection, these towers were practically invulnerable.

Around the fires at night men sang the "Goat Song" and another, "Richard Our Lord," and even the knights of France and Burgundy bragged of their new leader. It was felt that soon the walls would crumble, the defenses melt into air. "Yon garrison cannot stand against Red Richard!" cried one, and "God and the Lionheart!" cried another. And poor sunken eyes followed him where he walked among them, devouring him; lips dry and cracked with fever smiled tremulously. It was felt that a hero led us, a being like no other, inviolate, charmed; even the Saracen arrow would not, could not, pierce that ruddy skin, nor could a bolt find that canny brain. "We are saved," they said. "Richard will bring down the walls! We have only to follow. None can withstand him."

But one morning I heard a sort of hoarse cough from Richard's tent, and heard my name called in a croaking voice. I started up, and saw him, hanging on to the tent pole, swaying, his shirt plastered wet to his body and his eyes wild, his orderly hopping about trying to put a rose water poultice to his head and clucking like an old woman.

"Get him away, Alex," cried the hoarse voice, and a hand, burning, clutched me so that I swayed with his weight. The teeth were chattering in his head, though he was so hot that the air about him was hot too; he gave out heat like a bonfire. "Get the fool away, and fetch a surgeon."

The surgeon-doctor was a man called Iselin, a Moor but a baptized Christian. He called me to him, for I had some knowledge of leech craft. "I have bled him," said Iselin, "and he is resting now. But I am sorely needed upon the battlefield. You must be his nurse."

It was not a task to enjoy. Richard was the worst patient in the world. A dozen times a day he struggled up from the cot, hollow-eyed, burning with fever, and scarcely able to stand upright, to pull aside the tent flaps and look out, as though he were expecting an angel to come and take him from the grip of this malady. Watching the fighting, he would call out in that hoarse croak, giving orders that could not be heard and cursing when they were not obeyed. Often he fell, but he would not be helped, and would crawl back to the couch upon his hands and knees, weak as a baby.

"There is nothing for it," a voice behind me said. It was the third afternoon of his illness, and I was bone-weary. "We must tie him down," said the voice. I turned; it was Blondelza, enveloped in a great apron, once white, but now so streaked with blood and filth that it might have been any color at all. Her bright hair was covered in a thick twist of cloth, for she had been ministering to the wounded under the burning sun. Brother Alberic had told me of this, but I had not had time to give her a hand; she looked weary unto death.

"You must rest, friend," I said, "or we will soon be nursing you."

She shook her head, smiling wanly. "I am never sick," she said. "Help me with him—now, while he is still asleep."

I rummaged in some boxes and found a length of ship's rope. "Will this do?" I held it out.

She took it, laughing shortly. "He will hate it—but I will take the blame." Her hands, covered with still-wet blood, left ugly marks upon the new white rope. Together, we bound him to his couch, passing the rope beneath it and across his chest and legs; he only stirred and sighed.

We stood looking down at him. He looked as if he had just been fished out of the sea; he was covered with slimy sweat, his red hair dank with it, and his face a frightening, unhealthy green. She touched his forehead. "I think the fever has broken . . . pray God! Perhaps he is on the mend." She took a towel and wiped his face tenderly. "He feels cool," she said, turning to me a face alight with sudden hope. "But—oh, sweet Jesus—what is this? His hair . . ." She held a tuft of it in her hand. "It just came out as I touched it." She bent over him. "And look—here, and here . . . bare spots upon his scalp! Oh, God. What can it be?"

Iselin, when we had fetched him, called it "Arnoldia," and shook his head. "So many have it," he said, "the French king too. We know not what its cause may be. Sometimes the fingernails, too, loosen and fall out, and the skin peels off in patches. But I see it has not come to that yet."

"He has no fever," said Blondelza.

"Yes," said Iselin. "The hair loss is an after-effect—or so we believe. He may be on the road to recovery. Let him sleep."

Blondelza, with a hard glance at the doctor, bent to kiss Richard's cheek, a light touch that he did not stir under, then, turning, said, "I'll go back now with you, good Doctor . . . those poor men. And Richard has Alex."

Iselin's dark face softened. "You are worn out. You can do more good here, when he awakens. The King of England is worth a hundred men."

"Ah, God—don't say that!" she protested. "Every mother's son deserves all we can do for him. They are all one, in God's sight."

He smiled, patting her cheek. "And *you* say that! King Richard is the lodestar of this holy war . . . without him there would be no hope. We must pray for his recovery." He gave a little unhappy laugh. "But now there is no time for prayer. I must go to them . . . poor wretches. It is hard—we can do so little." As Blondelza moved to accompany him, he turned a stern eye on her. "Blondelza, I *order* you to stay here. Let the good brother go in your place. He is fresher, and stronger too. I need strong arms—there are two amputations, and we are short of poppy juice."

I held the men down, thrusting knives between their teeth for them to bite on in their agony. One was no more than a boy, and called piteously for his mother; he died under the knife. Iselin, covered with blood like a butcher, raised a face that streamed tears. "I can never get used to these sights," he said, "though I have seen them in the hundreds."

I too found it all too harrowing; the faces smashed to pulp, the ruined flesh of arms and legs, the guts—and this the worst—spilling out between the hands of the poor bewildered victim. The blood, bright red and flowing, and the old blood dried black or brown; the pus, sticky, yellow; the slow viscous trickle of gray-white corruption; the vomiting and the diarrhea; the hopeless eyes, already like the dead. And the noise, the groans and rattles, shrieks and howls, all against a background of rumbling, creaking wheels, whistling arrows, and crackling flames. The smells I had grown used to, except for the acrid odor of burning flesh when the Greek fire found its mark.

We worked all day, and all the night through, the light of torches flickering uncertainly above us, so that the surgeon's knife often blundered. I prayed.

CHAPTER 8

FOR THREE DAYS and nights I had no sleep, but labored beside the doctors, after which the good Iselin banished me to the scribes' tent, where I fell into the deep sleep of the exhausted. I woke refreshed, but with a nagging feeling of guilt. It was too long a time to leave Richard—or, at least, too long a time to leave him on Blondelza's hands. I threw some water, tepid as always, on my face, swallowed down some sour thin wine to moisten my dry tongue and throat, and hurried to the royal tent.

It was empty, the cookfire burned down to ash, the invalid's cot empty, and all the sheets and coverings upon it pulled straight. The cups and dishes had been washed, and were set in a row upon a low table, with the fever cloths, fresh-washed too, folded neatly and stacked beside them. A large bowl of fruit was set in the middle of another table, oranges, pomegranates, grapes; my mouth, still dry, began to water at the sight.

There was a rustle, and the tent flap was pulled aside: Blondelza, her arms piled high with clean laundry, came in. She shook her head when she saw me, raising her dark eyes to the roof in an eloquent look, and shrugging. "I could do nothing with him. He is feeling better—or so he says." She laid down the bundles of stuffs and took me by the hand, leading me outside. "There," she said, "see for yourself!" And she pointed to the walls of the town. "But be careful!"

There were now many siege towers pulled up under the

walls, their graded platforms filled with sharpshooters, hides covering them in a slant, deflecting the bolts and arrows of the defenders. One or two arrows, aimed very high, fell beyond and into our camp, but they were spent and nearly harmless; I went forward cautiously. In the thickest part of the bombardment was a new structure, the raw wood not yet marked with fire or blood. As I came near, I saw that, incredibly, Richard sat under it, upon a kind of improvised couch, his legs stretched out before him, his back supported by a great mound of rugs and cushions. The lower part of him was wrapped in a coverlet of red silk, but he had thrown over all a light mail shirt; already several arrows were sticking in the rings of the mail, harmlessly, but his neck and head were bare. He held a crossbow, firing it over and over, handing it to a nearby knight to be wound anew each time, and shouting hoarse orders to the men on the towers beside him. The damp goat hides crackled at the snap of Saracen arrows, but they fell without doing any hurt.

Though he lay immobile upon his siege couch, or whatever he called it, he still seemed to be everywhere at once, calling his instructions up and down the whole battle line. As I came nearer, I saw that his face was white as new cheese under the hot flaming of his hair; I saw too, giving thanks, no new bald patches; perhaps the disease had abated. Indeed, it seemed so, judging by the vigor of his constant cries of command.

As he handed the crossbow over to be wound again, he caught sight of me. "Ah, Saracen!" he shouted. Then he laughed, very loud. "I should stop calling you that now—here in this place! Could cause confusion! Well, Alex, see how I am fighting today. A new fashion! I have sent criers to my brother of France, describing it, with the offer of this structure, or another like it . . . they say he is felled by the same fever. But I am better now . . . I am well! A week more and we will have the walls down!" He turned from me then, to cup his hands and bellow, "No! No, not there! Pound them here, in the weakest spot. Up, lads! Up!"

He did not turn round again, but seemed ensconced for a whole day's fighting; I wondered if I ought to report it to Iselin, but dismissed the thought. What could he do? Nobody could pry Richard away, once his mind was made up, and besides, he was needed everywhere at once. Richard's towers were now functioning beautifully, but where the engines and structures of the other king and the nobles were employed, carnage was still rampant. I saw a tall, spindly tower, filled with soldiers, blaze up suddenly, engulfed by Greek fire; behind the curtain of flame men screamed, horribly. In minutes its black, skeletal arms showed against the sky, stripped bare. Others rushed, frantic, to push the towers near it away before they caught. I could not watch any longer; I crossed my breast, and walked back toward Richard's tent. Far to the south, some of Saladin's troops were harrying a contingent of our army; this was the third time they had tried these tactics, and twice they had been successfully repelled, led by young Henry. I prayed our lines would hold again now, for the third time.

Brother Alberic sat in the royal tent, cross-legged on the floor, making his breakfast from a plate of oranges and grapes. Blondelza was gone. He looked up, smiling. "The glee-maiden told me to help myself . . . said they would spoil before the day was out. They were a gift from Saladin." At my look of surprise, his smile broadened. "I swear it, Brother," he said. "Huge baskets brought in by runners under a white flag. I did not see it myself, but I believe the lady. Besides, here is the note." He held out a thick square of paper, covered with black letters, printed close together. "Keep trying—you will see it is Latin . . . of a sort."

I studied the heavy black marks, finally making out the end of the message. ". . . for my illustrious enemy, Malek-Rich, in his illness. May the God of Islam grant him a swift recovery." And there was a signature, very long. It must have been Saladin's full name, though it was scrawled wildly, in the way of all monarchs.

"The glee-maiden said that Richard had it divided, and portions sent to the King of France and the other leaders." Alberic shook his head. "Still, it will not sweeten them. They are eaten up with jealousy—except for the young count, the nephew. I fear Saladin is a gentler enemy."

There was no answer to this; I only hoped that Richard realized it, and would not depend upon these, his allies, or trust them. "Where is Blondelza?" I asked.

"Gone to take my place with the nursing. She is a good woman, the glee-maiden. I only wish she were a good Catholic." And he shook his head sadly.

"Well," I said, "her sort—jongleurs and such—were always careless in such matters." I sketched a cross in the air; it had

318

become an automatic gesture with me. "They are almost pagan, God save them. But they have good hearts."

"If that were all . . ." Brother Alberic raised frightened eyes. "But Blondelza . . . Blondelza holds with the Cathars."

I was startled, for I had not known this. "Are you sure?" I asked.

He nodded firmly. "Oh, yes, she told me. With tears in her eyes she cursed the Cross that has led so many to dreadful death. Cursed the Cross!" It was his turn to sign himself. "It is blasphemy, of course—but I could not gainsay her . . . sometimes I think myself it is a waste." He looked at me worriedly. "You will not tell?"

"No," I said a little sternly. "It is between you and God. He will be your judge, not I."

"Yes . . . He is the judge of all. And yet—" He was silent for a bit, then spoke. "Yet He has not struck down Blondelza or the others. Or even—not even the infidel." His eyes were troubled. "Do you think God sees?"

"He must," I said. "He sees all." But I too was troubled, and miserable with it. This carnage, this sickness and death, this corruption, this evil: Why? It was a thought that plagued me always.

There was a lull in the battle sounds; they seemed to die down and become a murmur, soft and low. And above them we heard the ringing cry, "God wills it!" From the south, where the infidels harried us, it came—and in a moment, clear upon the air, the answer, from the wall ahead, again, "God wills it!" From a thousand throats it came, shaming us, two men of God.

"You hear?" I whispered softly.

"Yes," said Brother Alberic. We bowed our heads and prayed.

CHAPTER 9

"AFTER A HARD siege of nearly two years, the city of Acre fell, and Frankish banners waved above its walls. The courage of its Muslim defenders was tremendous, and can only bring praise from us, the conquerors. As King Richard said, 'If only these brave infidels had been of the true faith it would have been impossible, anywhere in the world, to surpass them.' Nonetheless, on July twelfth, Acre surrendered to the Army of God. Christ and His soldiers had triumphed. The victory was ours!"

So I wrote amid the clamor and celebration of that great day. But in my nostrils was still the stink of death and corruption, behind my eyelids were printed forever the ghastly sights of blood and carnage, and in my heart lay great sorrow for the fallen of both sides, Christian and infidel. I am no soldier, nor ever was, though the great bishops of our host, clad in warlike mail, fell upon their knees that day and gave thanks to God for the vanquishing of the enemy and the taking of the great stronghold. In all that great host of Christian souls, only Brother Alberic, a monk as lowly as I myself, Blondelza, a heretic troubadour, and I—only we three did not rejoice, but offered, behind the walls of Richard's tent, silent prayers for the souls of the dead thousands. But I believe, inside of me, that Christ Jesus, too, mourned with us.

The next morning in a great assembly at the Templars' quarters, the two kings, of France and England, with the sanction of the entire host, made an agreement with the two emirs of Saladin who came to treat for peace. Acre was to be turned ever immediately to the Christian army, and its entire garrison was to be kept as hostages for the fulfillment of three conditions, pledged in Saladin's name: the restoration of the Holy Cross, the release of sixteen hundred Christian prisoners, and the payment of two hundred thousand bezants to the kings. The emirs returned to the city; a herald proclaimed throughout the camp that all molestation, injury, or insult to the Turks was to cease at once. The gates were opened, and the defenders of Acre, unarmed, were brought out and placed under guard in our charge. The kings sent representatives to take formal possession of Acre by planting their banners on its walls and towers.

The next day an equal division of the city was made with all its contents, including the hostage-prisoners. But immediately quarrels arose as to which king should have which half. I looked up from my writing as angry, querulous voices rang throughout the great assembly; suddenly they were like schoolboys at a game of ball gone sour. And there was, of course, no mediating force, for those here assembled were the great kings and nobles of Christendom. It was enough to make a poor scribe smile, and I bent my head to hide the twitch of my lips.

The turmoil went on about me; I heard the sounds of swords pulled from their scabbards, and the furious iron whisperings of mail as it swished about like ladies' trains, or like serpents' tails. I hoped it would not come to blows on this, a day of peace at last.

Suddenly, loud above the others, rang out a voice I knew well, rich and robust, edged with laughter. "Come, lads," Richard cried. "Enough! Let us cast lots . . . it is the only answer!"

I looked up to see Philip, red-faced and tight-mouthed, staring, and Burgundy, darkly passionate, arrested in the act of raising his sword. Little Leopold stood flushed but calm; he did not stand to gain much anyway, his forces being so small.

"Come, my good brothers, my fellow Crusaders," said Richard, more quietly. "King Philip and I will hazard it, for all our adherents. What shall it be? Drawing straws, or casting dice? Or shall it be coins?" And he flipped a gold coin, a bezant with the sides notched in the Roman fashion, tossing it high into the air. He watched as it spun, shining, and fell to earth, then placed his large mailed boot upon it. "Well, friend Philip, it is yours, the first call! Heads or tails—which shall it be?" He looked about the great company, challenging with bold eyes. "Is it a fair toss, Crusaders? Speak now!"

A cry rose. "Aye! Oh, aye, Lord King!"

"Well, good Philip, say then—heads or tails! And fair acceptance of the result. This scroll"—and he held up one list of spoils that had been drawn up—"this to the call of heads . . . and the other one to the poor tail end!"

By now he had some of the wrangling nobles laughing, and from his own men and those of Champagne came a ragged cheer and a whistle or two.

Philip, after a long moment, nodded. "Well, then," said he, "I will call heads!"

Richard lifted his boot, bent down, looked at the coin closely, and held it up, smiling. "Heads it is," he said cheerfully and, handing the list he held to Philip, made a flourish and a bow. "And this one"—he held up the other list—"is for me and mine. So let it be. And will you swear to abide by this decision?"

He spoke to all the company, and with one voice they called out, "Aye!" Philip, thus pinned down, had no option but to agree.

"So!" cried Richard, scanning the list he held. "I have drawn the royal palace—which is but right, as I have by me my queen and my sister. And you, fair temporary bachelor, good Phil—you have drawn the Templars' great house, which"—and he laughed loud and long—"surely has no accommodations for women at all!"

At which the whole hall roared. For the Templars have their vices, known to all.

So it fell out that the city was thus occupied, most of the host finding quarters there. Many petty knights were taken in by noble families of the city, with whom they shared their army rations, eating from the gold and silver plates of the starveling conquered. Many unsuitable love alliances were made too, chaste maidens of good family lying down beneath rough warriors, sighing out their cherished maidenheads in the arms of low ruffians. There was no way to prevent this, or to protect the innocent; winner takes all in war, even in a holy one.

The men of our army, the victors—drawn, dirty, half dead from fever and wounds, and long deprived of the society of any women but poor camp whores as worn out as themselves—ran wild in the beautiful streets of Acre, grabbing at the first female form they saw, tearing at clothes and hair, raping, coupling in the gutters like dogs. More than one sinner dropped dead from his efforts—God forgive them!

The days in the city passed, day after day of turmoil and riot. The great victory, coming after so many long months, had gone to the men's heads like wine. They roamed the alleyways and lanes, filled the taverns, slouching narrow-eyed like jackals, searching for some overwhelming joy, some great reward, to offset the pains and sickness they had endured for so long without ease.

They lay with anything that had breasts and bellies, and drank themselves insensible. They fornicated and drank prodigiously, despite the protests of their prelates and the orders of their captains. They fought over women, almost tearing them apart, slashing at their comrades savagely with knives or smashing them with pikes. They drank all night, emerging into the day with glazed eyes and hollow cheeks to vomit up their guts, then drink again all the next night, and the next. Many died of it; no one knew how many.

The knights drank and fornicated in the mansions and the gardens, the soldiers in the streets and marketplaces. No decent woman dared leave her house; some starved within, from fear.

Every day ships arrived, coming from every port in the Eastern world, crowded with beautiful, richly dressed prostitutes and their bawds and pimps. There were gorgeous Venetians with pearls woven into their loose hair, Persian girls, their eyes made long with black kohl, their bodies gleaming through gauzy trousers caught at the ankle with jeweled clasps; Syrians with oiled black hair, hung with gems, glittering with gold, accompanied by slaves as beautiful as themselves. And there were the poorer sort too—simple little slave wenches, naked, unadorned, offered by their masters for a couple of sous. No man went hungry for love. It engulfed them, crammed itself down their throats, bloated them with surfeit. The whole port seethed with female flesh, reeking of perfume and hair oil, flowing with scarves and veils, bare arms writhing like snakes in a vast open cage. By order of the kings they came, the girls, the women, the paid whores—taking the burden of shame and disgrace from the townswomen, giving them breath, giving them life once more.

Never had such waste been seen. Good wine wasted, running in the gutters; women wasted like the wine, flung aside, spoiled, the pretty ones, the young ones, the old and diseased. Men and women, sodden with drink, exhausted with pleasure, lay like so many dead upon the battlefield; lay snoring, stretched across the streets, blocking the thoroughfares.

Horses could not pass through the streets of the city, nor the supply wagons; detachments of men had to be employed to drag the sated, drugged bodies out of the way. Even on foot it was difficult, and dangerous too. For it was no certainty that the soldiers lying there were truly unconscious; suddenly an arm might come up at you, holding a dagger or a dirk. Many an innocent was maimed in this manner, even killed; the drunken are mindless. I was thankful, indeed, to be quartered in the same place where my work was.

From the Church of Saint Anne, bells rang night and day: bells of jubilation, of victory; bells that tolled the passing of souls. After a while one could not tell the sounds apart, they became a clamor, tuneless, meaningless, almost unnoticed.

Every day there were a hundred funerals, perhaps more; in the Holy Land the dead could not wait. The great cemetery in the eastern sector of the city became crowded; graves upon graves, the raw earth drowning the brown grass, the bright flowering shrubs. Over some, banners waved, sadly, the colors of some petty castellany, faded in a day. Some had stone crosses, some were merely marked with two sticks tied together in a cross shape, some went unmarked, except for the mourners stretched flat upon them, soaking the dry earth with their tears; most had lost someone in the siege, a father, a son, a brother, a comrade. Few of the great nobles had suffered death, though many had been wounded, and almost all had been grieviously ill with that same "Saladin's Curse."

But one of Philip Augustus's vassals, a high baron of the French lands named Thibault, had been killed in a street brawl on the first day of our occupation of the city. A Mass was said for him by Hubert Walter, Richard's bishop, and Richard himself attended, out of courtesy.

The two kings, of France and England, walked together in solemn procession down the short way leading to the church; for once all signs of riot and disorder had been cleaned up and the streets were clear. Neither king had a large retinue, only a few of their leading vassals and prelates, and some pages and scribes. By chance I found myself placed a pace or two behind the kings, and so heard and saw all that passed.

The colors of England, Normandy, and France fluttered from every building, in tribute to the deliverers of the city. (It must be remembered that Acre had been Christian up until the time the Saracens had taken it, a few years earlier.) Richard and Philip were the undisputed leaders of the Crusade, had been since the beginning. They had the largest stakes in the enterprise, had furnished the most men and monies, led the richest vassals. Suddenly, against the sky, among the blue and white, red and gold, of the two kings, rang a harsh note of color: an orange banner, huge, striped diagonally with purple, and fringed in silver. Whipped by a stray gust of hot wind, flattened out to its proud full length atop one of the highest towers, upon it, plain, was worked the device of the Austrian dukes; Leopold's flag. I bent my head, pretending not to notice, and plodded on. But I nearly ran full tilt into the King of France; he had stopped short, looking upward, his face tight with fury.

"That whore-son . . . that whelp! That Austrian upstart!"

he cried, in his thin voice. Richard, who had walked on, turned. "Look!" shrieked Philip, like a housewife whose wash has been muddied. "Look! There, atop that round tower . . . Leopold's banner!"

Richard looked where Philip pointed; he shrugged and smiled. "Well," he said, "the poor little bastard . . . he fought too."

"With a ragtag hundred or so and our monies," said Philip, angry.

"With *my* monies, dear brother in Christ," said Richard, an edge in his smile. "Remember it was I who furnished him the wherewithal to fight on beside us."

Philip waved his hand impatiently, royally. "All the more reason you should not allow it to be there! He has no right to boast of triumph—it was our men and machines that vanquished the enemy. It was France and England, no others, who took Acre. We are the victors!"

"Well," said Richard, still mildly, "our vassal flags fly . . . call him my vassal." And he, in his turn, waved that royal dismissing wave.

"On the highest tower!" Philip was still red-faced. "Besides, it is not so. Austria is an independent duchy."

"Under Flanders, was it not?" asked Richard. "And when Philip of Flanders died, it was left to little Leopold to represent all that was left of the German contingent."

"They all left, all the others. The German states have no stake in this victory. It must not fly there! I forbid it!" And Philip, incredibly, stamped his foot.

Richard smiled. "Hold on, friend . . . we are mourners, remember. It is unseemly to argue points of protocol in the street. I agree, of course. Leopold's banner has no business there. But, for now, let us proceed."

"I will not go another step!" Philip was shrill; the prelates ahead of us had begun to look over their shoulders, curious, and a crowd had collected. I saw Hubert Walter's worried face under his mitered hat, and the round eyes of the tonsured abbots.

"Oh, for Christ His Mother's sake!" cried Richard, his face beginning to color and his jaw tightening. "Here. Hold these!" And taking off his crown and red cloak, he thrust them into Philip's hands. "I will take care of it!"

He ran lightly to the base of the tower, studied it for a moment, and then, finding a foothold, began to climb. It was one of those uneven roundish structures, built of some local stone, with edges protruding here and there; it was easy. Richard quickly, like a schoolboy, picked his way upward, his face flushed now and laughing, his red hair tossing free. Faces looked up in wonder, following his progress; a soldier somewhere behind me gave a long low whistle, which brought a laugh from his fellows. Having reached the smooth part at the top, Richard flung out his long arms and, encircling the tower with his long legs, shinnied up to the top. He stretched out his hand and grasped the flag, pulling it free. So doing, holding on with one hand, he held the Austrian banner aloft, as though he were leading a charge. Richard always looked as though he were doing some heroic action; he had an instinct for it. The crowd below roared with pride and delight, and there were cries of "Lionheart! Richard Lionheart!" "England! Normandy! "On to Jerusalem!"

He smiled, turning his face to show himself to all, and sketching a perilous bow; then he started down, slipping, sliding, almost falling, but still with that smile on his face, and the flag still clutched firmly in his hand. About ten feet up, he let go, and fell, landing on his hands and knees, but rising swiftly, as cries of wonder went up all around. Any agile boy could do it as well, but it was Richard, King of the English, Richard, the lion-hearted one, Richard, their darling, and they loved it. As from one throat came the roar of acclaim and delight, loud enough to drown out the great bells.

He faced them, raising the banner, and then held up his other hand, palm out, for silence. A hush fell, and he made the sign of the Cross in the air, bowing his head. The little crowd fell to its knees; I heard a woman sob. A moment to remember; as I have said, he had a talent for them.

When it was over, he walked lightly, easily, to Philip's side. "So, friend France," he said in a low voice, "are you satisfied now? And what shall I do with the thing—now that I have climbed for it?"

"What you will," said Philip, shrugging. "Certainly *I* have no use for it." And he began to walk on, continuing in the procession.

Richard turned, spied a fellow dressed in motley at the edge of the crowd, a mountebank, a jongleur fellow of some sort. "Here, catch!" cried Richard, laughing, and threw it, walking on.

And that might have been the end of the matter. The fellow caught the flag, made some sort of foolishness with it, miming a strutted-up prince, or the like—I did not watch longer. But, as I turned away, I saw a face, dark with anger, staring at Richard's broad red-clad back. I did not recognize the face, but I knew well the livery he wore, the livery of Austria; Leopold's man. A chill went over me; I shrugged it away, hoping vaguely that I was not coming down with a fever, and walked on, following my King.

CHAPTER 10

"AMONG THE PROUD banners of England and France showed another, orange striped with purple, the flag of Austria, atop the tallest tower. It was misplaced, for Austria had small stake in the victory, a fact all men knew. Urged on by Philip Augustus, King of France, King Richard of the English climbed the tower and took the offending banner down."

Behind me, as I labored over the record, a voice sounded. "No, no, my Alex. No, dear friend! It does not look well in the Latin. Take it out!" And a long forefinger stabbed at my script. "Here. Leave Philip's name out of it . . . I will take the responsibility. You make it seem as though I moved as puppet to his strings!"

I looked up at Richard's face, questioning. He frowned a little, though I could see he was not angered, only irritated. "Well, if you say . . ." I agreed, and drew a black line through the words.

"Leopold will never forgive the insult," said Blondelza, her head bent over some sewing she held in her lap. "He is like his mother, much as he would deny it. These Hohenstauffens, they never forget, and never forgive." She bit through the thread, and held up the mended hose. "There. It is the best I can do . . . they are threadbare. The other knee will go by the end of the day."

We were in Richard's quarters in the royal palace of Acre; a scene as domestic as any cottage hearthside. She sat crosslegged, clad in her jongleur tunic and hose, upon a pile of low cushions, Eastern style, though Richard had brought in

Frankish-height chairs and tables for our comfort. He wore only a loose shirt, and was bare-shanked, his long legs showing oddly white against the baked-in reddish-brown of his face and hands. He held out his hand for the hose and began to struggle into them; mended tears showed now in three places. We were all ragged beneath our clothes of state, the siege had gone on so long.

I scribbled away, and Blondelza took up her lute, trying out a little tune, softly. All was quiet for a bit.

"Where are my slippers, the whore-sons—they always disappear!" Richard slammed a coffer lid.

Blondelza, not looking up, said mildly, "Under the bed. See, a tip of the toe is showing, just behind you."

Richard cursed under his breath as he bent to fish them out. "The beggarly things ... the soles are splitting!"

"You have others. There." Blondelza nodded to a chest under a window.

"I am used to these," he said curtly. And then, in a different, lighter voice: "You knew him, then?"

"Who?"

"Leopold."

"Oh," said Blondelza, running her fingers through a scale of notes. "Yes, a little. I was his mother's favorite troubadour for a while." She smiled. "She liked to sponsor the cause of women—and so would have none but a woman to make songs for her. I was at home in all the castles of Austria ... such as they are. Some of them are quite barbaric."

"But Leopold ..." Richard insisted. "You said you knew him. You never told me."

"I never thought of it," she answered. "It was a long time ago. He was very young then, just a boy, really. And sweet—in those days. Sweet, and very shy. I felt sorry for him."

I looked up then, seeing Richard's jaw tighten and his eyes narrow. I wished I were in some other place. These two often behaved as though I were invisible, and I was forced to witness intimacies I had no mind to. I began to gather up my papers, quietly.

"And so—" Richard's voice was choked with feeling, held in rein. "And so, you let him into your bed."

"Not quite." Blondelza raised her eyes. "His mother had a hawk's eye—and never wished him pleasure." She spoke demurely, but I heard something else beneath.

"But you would have, otherwise." Richard spoke softly, with a kind of menace.

She shrugged lightly. "Probably. I told you I felt sorry for him." She looked up at him, her eyes cool. "And remember, there were to be no chains like this between us—no recriminations, no accusations. I swore it, and so did you, when first I came back to you." Her head went up. "I am my own mistress, and not your minion—king though you may be, and the darling of the world. I love where I please."

He sighed heavily. "It is a hard lesson, Blondelza. Hard for a man, king or not."

"Women have had to learn it, from time untold. Someday it will be otherwise. Not yet . . . but someday the two genders will be equal, in this thing at least. What is it, after all, but a pleasure of the flesh—and of the heart, too, sometimes—shared?"

"Yes," he said softly. "I understand. Truly. And we are artists, both, is it not so?" He reached down to pick up her lute. "Sweet Jesus," he said, shaking his head. "It has been so long . . . I cannot make my fingers find the strings." He began to play, softly. "Our private song . . . remember?"

She smiled. "We must make new words for it now. We have both lived so much longer . . . and learned so much." Her smile deepened, she looked like a sleepy cat.

"Oh, Blondelza," he cried, throwing down the lute so that it jangled all out of key. "You are the only woman for me— or ever was! Come kiss me, jongleur wench."

And so before my monkish eyes they sank into the cushions, clasped in each other's arms. Not knowing where to look, I took up my papers and my pot of ink and tiptoed toward the door.

Before I reached it I heard him say, "Blondelza mine . . . is it true, what they say—that you have had a hundred lovers?"

And she answered, quick as quick, "Is it true, my lord king, that you, for some lady named Margery, thrust your arm down a lion's throat and tore out its heart—and thus gained your nickname?"

Richard threw back his head and laughed loud and long. "And ate the heart too, with relish—if I remember the story right. Ah, Blondelza." His voice came very low now, muffled. "So, it is something less than a hundred, then?"

"And something more . . . counting you, my darling. Something more—and more than more."

I was glad to get out of there, for such words, such scenes, stirred my blood. I drew my girdle tighter, so that I felt the bite of the hair shirt I wore, and, reluctantly, turned my way toward the apartments of the two queens.

Berengaria had summoned me that morning, a note sent by a little half-grown page. Summoned me, in her gentle way. ". . . when you can find time from your duties," the words had gone. I had dawdled at it all the morning, but now I squared my shoulders, like the soldier I had never been, and climbed the stairs of the women's wing.

The two queens had been given the grandest quarters in this very grand palace—painted walls, inlaid marble and gold floors, thin silk hangings, gorgeously embroidered, couches of tortoiseshell and ivory, carved tables set with precious jewels. And they two went attired in the loveliest Eastern gowns, layer upon layer of thin floating stuffs, as fine as cobwebs and gleaming in the light from the great wall of windows that faced the sea. But Joanna's handsome face was peevish, and Berengaria was pale and sad, with dark circles beneath her great soft eyes.

"Where is my brother?" Joanna demanded. "We have not seen him since they brought us here—nearly two weeks ago!"

"Has he recovered?" asked Berengaria, in her timid fawn's way. "We heard he was very ill." She clasped her little hands together. "Oh, tell me true, Brother Alexander. Is he truly well?" She hung her head, but I caught the sheen of tears. "For I fear they are keeping it from me . . . and surely, if he were himself again . . . he would visit us here . . . now that we are settled in and . . . and the war is over."

"Well, of course the war is not over, little ninny," cried Joanna, impatiently. "Acre is only the beginning. But—" And she tossed her head, the red braids flying, and the set of her jaw and the blue steel of her eyes so like Richard's that I all but smiled and called her Dickon. "But what is happening? No one seems to know anything. Has Saladin delivered the prisoners yet? Has the Cross come? Has Richard met with him?"

I held my hand up, laughing a little. "I am only a poor scribe, my lady. I know as little as you."

"Oh, Alex! You are privy to all of Richard's doings . . . always have been! Why has he not come near us here at

330

least? Has something gone wrong? Has Saladin backed down? Tell! Tell!"

"I really know nothing, I swear it. Nor does Richard, nor anybody. Saladin is delaying . . . that is all. Whether he means some treachery or only wants to gain time, I cannot say. Nor can anyone. At least there is one thing that has happened. All is in readiness for the exchange of prisoners. Conrad of Montferrat has finally brought them from Tyre, some three thousand Muslim hostages. He was hedging, but Richard hounded him to it—and they are here. Or rather there—back in the camp."

"I didn't know about them," said Joanna. "You mean there is to be an exchange?"

"Yes, part of the bargain for peace. Now Saladin must send the Christian captives to seal the bargain. Richard waits for this . . . but impatiently, of course. For every day, another hundred of our men die, from disease or . . . other things. And rations are consumed, money slips through fingers, and spirits fall lower and lower. The last I heard, Saladin had sent to ask for a little more time. The date set now is the eleventh of August, the end of the Muslim year, or the beginning, I forget which."

Joanna narrowed her eyes, again like Richard. "I suspect some treachery . . . Saladin is only an infidel dog, after all!"

I said, mildly, "Richard thinks well of him. Says he wishes he had friends so courteous and true."

"Richard has a naïve streak . . . always has had. Look what he lets our little brother John—that fiend—get away with! The news from England is always bad."

"Queen Eleanor is there, and Longchamps. Richard trusts them."

"Mother is getting old, and Will Longchamps is a commoner—out for the main chance."

"Well," I said, "I know nothing."

"Oh, nobody asked you!" she cried impatiently. Although, of course, she had. Joanna was a true Plantagenet, all arrogance, temper, and spirit. But I suspected her heart was large; she loved little Berengaria. I saw her now, her eyes anxious, staring at the sad-faced Queen. As Berengaria took her seat again and picked up some embroidery work, Joanna beckoned to me.

"Come aside. Here, by the window," she whispered. "We have a fine view of the harbor here, is it not so?" she began, in a loud voice. Then, dropping to low tones, she said, "It is that glee-maiden, isn't it? Blondelza is with him! Tell me!"

I evaded her eyes. "I don't . . . Well, maybe . . . I have not noticed."

Joanna flashed me a look of scorn. "I am no baby, Alex! Besides, it is all over the palace. I see the varlets' eyes leering at poor Ria, and they snicker when she passes. How can Richard be so cruel!"

I was miserable under her accusing stare, and felt guilty, a bad priest that condoned adultery. But, for my life, and risking God's wrath, I could not see it so inside my heart. I kept remembering those two together, now, and the long years before, and a perverse thought struck at me—that the adultery was the other way around! And yet I pitied his little Queen, so small and childlike still, not quickened with all those Cyprian love nights. I wondered if she knew of the boy, Philippe, growing up, there in the Cognac duchy, so like his father.

Joanna hissed at me, "You must *make* him visit us, Alex! He is insulting his lawful wife. And besides, I want to see him!"

"Shh," I whispered. "She will hear."

Joanna nodded and, as we moved back to where Berengaria sat, said loudly, "So, you think Richard will be well enough to take dinner with us this evening?"

"Oh, is it truly so?" asked the little Queen, her hand going to her breast as if to quiet something that leaped there. "Oh, what shall we serve him? Oh, I must make ready." And she made as if to rise.

"Richard never notices what he eats," said Joanna. "And the cooks will attend to it—if he comes."

"The King is always harried—by messengers, and suppliants," I temporized. "In the city, morale could not be worse. If we are forced to wait here much longer . . ." I spread my hands in resignation. "Well, there simply will not *be* an army. Oh, the King has much on his mind . . . and is still weak from the wasting sickness. But perhaps he . . . I will tell him of your invitation."

"Oh." Berengaria was flustered, and looked agonized with shyness and a sort of shame. "Oh," she said, wringing her hands, "you mustn't bother him with our silliness. Just sometime . . . when he has the time . . . anytime at all . . ."

"Tell him to *make* the time!" cried Joanna, imperious. "I

am sick of being shunted off into a corner! We saw nothing of the battles, and now we see nothing of the victory. It is a disgrace!"

"Be glad on both counts," I said wryly. "For neither is pleasant."

Joanna stared. "How strange you are, Alex! Certainly victory is a wonderful thing!"

"A city that has been under siege for nearly two years, and is now occupied by the military, is no sight for ladies' eyes. Take your comfort here, and be glad of it!" For once I spoke sternly; Joanna was a provoking creature.

"Oh, the poor people!" cried Berengaria softly. "How they must have suffered! And our own soldiers too . . . sick and wounded . . . and so many dead! The bells toll day and night." There were tears in her sweet eyes, the lovely little lady. "No, Brother Alex. Just send him our warm regards, and tell him he is always welcome here." Something of dignity had come to her, her head was high. Then she flushed a little and said, touching my arm, "Look, Brother Alex. But don't speak of it to him, it is for his birthday. Look what I am making. Do you think he will like them?"

In her hands was a pair of great gauntlets, red leather, cunningly stitched. They were covered with thickly embroidered designs, flowers and crosses entwined, and two leopards facing; one was very cross-eyed.

"It is beautiful," I said. "Beautiful work."

"They will have pearls sewn all over them too, and the beasts will each have a great ruby in his collar. Will he like them, do you think?"

"He has nothing so fine as these," I said. "I am sure he will prize them highly . . . a wonderful gift."

"Oh, you are kind . . . I hope so."

"It is so fine," I said. "Better than a court embroiderer."

"Oh, I do thank you. You know, it's odd—once I thought I could never even sew a seam!" She laughed merrily. "No, truly, I was all thumbs! You should have seen it! My duenna despaired of me . . . but now, well . . ." And her little head went high again. "Now I have so much time on my hands."

"You speak true, sister," said Joanna grimly. "Thank God we have Zenobia to play her songs for us, or we would all go mad!"

Isaac's daughter, I had forgotten her—but of course, she had been given into the two queens' care.

333

"Poor little Zenobia," said Berengaria. "I think we demand too much of her, sister."

"Don't talk foolishness, Ria!" snapped Joanna. "She is a lazy Greek, lying abed half the morning. I'll warrant you she is still there, and it is nearly noon!"

"She is only a child."

"She is our waiting-woman, our slave even! You spoil her, Ria . . . you spoil all our women!" Joanna was working herself up into a temper, but I saw a stubborn look come over Berengaria's face, dainty as it was, and knew she could be a match for her. She stitched away, as Joanna's voice rose high about us, and, deaf to the sound, stretched out her little hand to me.

"Go now, good Brother Alex. And thank you for coming. Tell Richard . . . well, tell him I await his pleasure." Her voice was soft, but easily heard amid Joanna's rantings. There was a pause; Joanna stamped her foot and flounced away as if to fling herself out the window. "It is so dull, dull, dull, in this place!" I glanced at the tall figure, its arms thrown out in a Plantagenet pose, turning away quickly before she caught my eye.

"Go now," Berengaria whispered, smiling small. "She will tire soon, and then there will be tears."

I tiptoed out. A household without men—spare me! And a strange, unlikely pair. But I could see, in spite of all, that there was much love between them.

CHAPTER 11

"IF THE KING of France leaves undone the work for which he came here," declared King Richard, "he will bring everlasting shame and contempt upon himself and upon France." For Philip Augustus had sent four of his barons, who, with tears in their eyes and shame in their voices, explained that their master of France had made up his mind to go home, for he was indeed so sick that if he stayed on in this land, he would surely die.

"Sick!" roared Richard, astonished and aghast. "He is no

more sick than I am! Nor was he ever in such a bad state as I, or most of the knights and men. Why, every day he goes hunting in the hills—and every night makes merry in the Templars' Palace!"

At this Philip's envoys broke down, sobbing and declaring their intention to stay despite the orders of their lord. "We follow you, great King. We will not leave till Jerusalem is ours!" And they insisted that he take their oath of vassalage then and there, calling as witness Henry, the young Count of Champagne, and bidding me, as scribe, to take note of it. After the vassal ceremony, they took their leave, their scarred and lined faces smeared with tears of shame.

"Sire Uncle," said the young Count Henry, "King Philip has one aim—to get back to France and secure the heritage of the Count of Flanders. Since the count Philip died, early in the siege, it has gnawed at his mind; I have even heard him voice it!"

Richard sank onto a stool and sat, face between his hands, frowning darkly. "And not only that. I'm sure he hopes to make profit of my absence in my duchies too."

"I would not put it past him," said Count Henry, smiling a little. "He is not my favorite uncle." And he looked upon his other uncle, Richard, with the same adoration that I had seen on the faces of so many young knights.

Richard jumped up and threw his arm about the boy's shoulders. "You are a good lad and true, sister's son . . . you have your mother's loving heart. Marie . . ." Richard's face softened as he spoke her name. "How I worshipped her when I was a boy! And she is as dear to me still. She is my favorite woman, after my own mother, Eleanor, and . . . one other."

The young count blushed; he was still young enough for it. I suppose, like all the rest of the host, he had heard the tales of the glee-maiden, though Blondelza discreetly kept out of sight when Richard had dealings with his peers.

Richard laughed and flicked the boy's red cheek with his long forefinger. "You need not blush . . . I will not make you privy to my secrets." He laughed again and gave the young count a little playful push. "Go now, sister's son . . . while I sit me down and think how to foil this enemy of France."

The next day Philip signed over all that he had gained in Acre to Conrad of Montferrat (taking a good price for it, of course). It seemed his mind was made up; he was determined to go home. Richard, fearing for the fate of the Crusade, offered Philip a half-share of everything he had gathered together for the war effort—gold, silver, provisions, arms, horses, ships—if he would stay on and fight.

But Philip shook his head. "This cursed land will be the death of me," he said, pulling a sad face. "France will lose her King."

Richard pleaded and threatened; all was in vain. At last the only thing he could do was to insist that Philip take a solemn oath not to invade the Angevin lands or work any mischief there while their lord the King of England was still on God's work, nor within forty days after his return. The oath was sworn; Hugh of Burgundy stood surety, and Conrad of Montferrat, who had arrived from Tyre to receive Philip's gains from his own hands.

I was interested to see Conrad with my own eyes, this man who had been so talked about, so hated and feared, and by some so loved, as well. I saw a man in his middle years, a commanding figure straight and tall, with power in his glance and voice, deep-set eyes in a dark hawk's face, and an overbearing manner. He spoke the speech of courtesy, but there was something savage under it; the beast of prey beneath the silken coat, or so I fancied. He had abducted his bride, the heiress of Jerusalem, on her wedding night; snatched from her young bridegroom's arms, or as good as. At least that is how the story went, and I could well believe it, looking at his face. It was a deed not done for love or lust, but for gain; he wished to mount the throne upon the heiress's body. The native knights, the "Colts," who admired him greatly, hailed this as proof of his quick wits and canny mind, but in our ranks he had forfeited our good esteem by this unchivalrous behavior.

"I do not trust the man," said Richard to me privately. "But then I do not trust Burgundy either. And certainly not Philip, oath or not."

Conrad made his way back to Tyre, and Philip made preparations to go home. Richard called Mercadier to him. "When he sails, friend, follow him, with as many routiers as you need. I would keep you here, but there is greater need there, to protect my domains. I count on you to keep an eye on things for me. Watch him well, and send word of any treachery."

The French king's share of the Muslim prisoners was separated from Richard's and placed, together with the French troops which were remaining in Syria, under the command of the Duke of Burgundy. And, on July 31, in a galley lent by Richard, King Philip of France sailed to Tyre; on August 3, he set sail for Europe. King Richard was now the undisputed leader of the whole Crusade.

At once, his first act upon assuming command, he loaded up his ships with his military engines and with provisions for man and beast. Then he issued orders that all the Crusaders should make ready to follow him, with their arms and horses, to Ascalon. He also summoned all the common archers and, addressing them as if they were knights and not landless men, announced that by their fighting in the siege they deserved a reward. "To tell the truth," he said, grinning broadly, "every man of you ought to be knighted!" This, of course, raised a great cheer, even from those worn-out scarecrows. "But I cannot do that, for then my knights would ambush me—and it would be an end to all!" Cheers and huzzahs, and a great sound of clapping. "But know you, my men of England, Wales, and Normandy . . . you are the great oaks of my realm, its hills and dales, its wheat and its wool. You, and no others, are the gold and the treasure of this our empire! Long may it rule! Long may you live to see its banners wave over Jerusalem! On to Jerusalem! Holy Cross! Holy Cross! With me, lads! God wills it!"

And from a thousand throats it came again, that thundering cry, "God wills it! God wills it!"

"So, lads," Richard went on, "gird up your loins, bind up your wounds, and, with good crossbows at the ready, wait for the signal to march on Ascalon."

Again the roar of many throats, "On! On! We follow the Lionheart!"

He waited, smiling, looking down from where he stood upon an upturned barrel, holding up his hand, waiting for silence.

When the cheering died down finally, he said, in a conversational tone that somehow managed to penetrate to the farthest reaches, "By the way, lads. From this day I have raised your wages. Every man of you shall have one gold bezant a month till this holy soil is shed from your heels and you tread good Angevin earth again. God bless you and attend you, till the day we assemble for the march!"

Well, you may imagine the uproar then! Most of those

poor archer fellows had never seen a bezant, much less held one in their hands or felt it in their pouches. But I saw Hugh of Burgundy's black eyes meet the hot blue eyes of the Austrian duke, and the sour smiles that twisted their lips.

That afternoon in council some of the nobles protested this—which they called high-handed, this raising of the archers' wages. But Richard countered, smiling, "They are *my* archers, after all." And when Burgundy grumbled that his own archers would desert because their wages did not match, he said, still smiling, "Well, I will match their wages, whatever is needed. Gentlemen, I have hazarded my realm for this holy war . . . I cannot let the cause be lost for a paltry few thousand bezants. What are they, anyway, but coins—manmade? We will find greater gold stored up in Heaven, when all is counted—and travel lighter for the lack of it in our pockets, too!"

They could do naught but abide by his words, but privately I thought the faces in that room looked sourer than ever. I have learned, even though I have been cloistered from the world so long, that no man really looks with favor upon the one who gives him favor, unasked. A riddle, a paradox—but there it is. Richard made enemies by those same qualities that marked him apart—his generous heart, forgiving nature, largeness of spirit. All these were mistaken for arrogance and high-handedness, if, indeed, they were not suspected as covering a subtle guile. So will the small pull down the great. God protect him in his ways, my foster brother, my King.

Of course, in spite of all these preparations and the high words, it was impossible to leave Acre till the treaty with Saladin was put into effect. The delays stretched on, Saladin sending emissaries every day with some new excuse. He could not gather the money together so quickly; the Christian prisoners needed Western dress before it was seemly to deliver them; the Holy Cross was here, there, and everywhere. It was maddening. Richard sent envoys to Damascus to bring Western-style surcoats and inspect the prisoners; they were received politely and allowed to choose four from among the prisoners to bring back as an earnest of Saladin's good faith.

What a sight! Burnt black as Saracens they were, bent, and old before their time, only their fair or brown hair and light eyes attesting to their European origins; their native speech came haltingly or not at all to their lips, and they cringed at a sudden move. One, bigger-boned and stronger than the others, had a back so criss-crossed with scars that it resembled nothing so much as burnt steak that has been softened by pounding with the flat of a knife. He had no tongue either, his captors had cut it out long ago; he could talk only by a kind of sign language, his eyes staring white and angry when it was not at once understood. His companions, though, had learned the signs, and could translate, but in the Moorish speech. So pandemonium reigned, until Richard sent for the good doctor, Iselin, a converted Christian, who could interpret for us. Then all talked at once, happy to tell their various tales of horror and degradation.

They had all been slaves, of one sort or another, some from childhood, for these infidels make slaves of their captives; the economy of all the Eastern cities is founded on it. Our big scarred tongueless man had been a rower in a galley, and found a way to attack his masters, during a moment when the decks were washed down and the slaves unshackled from their benches; he killed a half-dozen, if his signs could be believed, before they mutilated him and strung him up for flogging to the death. He had been hurled overboard to the fishes, but the water revived him and he managed to swim to shore, where he lived in alleys and ratholes, half starved, until he was captured once again.

And all the other stories were as dreadful, full of the terror of nightmare, yet these poor souls still survived! One, a boy who swore he was seventeen but looked closer to forty, had been castrated and used as a male whore; he still bore traces of the beauty that had earned his fate, though his eyes were like the eyes of a dead man, dull and staring. Richard ordered that all four be taken to the infirmary and their poor bodies mended as best could be. "God grant," he muttered, "that no man of mine be taken alive."

A list of the Saracen prisoners held in our camp was brought to Saladin, and four sent along, to equal Saladin's act. These were four of the bravest defenders of the Acre garrison, still hale and hearty, if as thin as the rest of us. "For I would scorn to send my enemy such examples as those we have seen, poor victims of savage cruelty." And he outfitted each of the Muslim prisoners in the best uniforms that could be found. "So that Saladin will understand Western chivalry," he said, "and perhaps, someday, emulate it."

On August 2, Richard sent envoys again, to ascertain if the holy Cross was truly in Saladin's hands or not. They returned, saying yes, they had seen it, from a distance, wrapped in cloth-of-gold and lying in a jeweled coffer.

"And you did not demand a closer look?" asked Richard, his voice hard.

"Sire," replied one, quaking in his mail, "we dared not. They held those curved swords—those scimitars—at our heads throughout the meeting."

I saw the dark red flare in Richard's cheeks, but he said nothing, except, "Fair friends, you have done well. Feel no shame . . . the scimitar has a wicked blade."

A few days later, emirs came again to Richard's quarters in the palace, this time bearing rich gifts upon a train of camels. "They are for your ladies," said the spokesman, who spoke a tolerable Latin. "For your sister and your wives."

Richard, thinking the emir's Latin was off, shook his head, laughing. "I have only one wife," he said, holding up one finger and nodding vigorously.

The emir bowed, head almost touching the floor, as they always did. "A thousand pardons," he said. "We understood—"

At this, another, who had been sitting silent, astride a richly caparisoned black stallion, threw back the white burnoose which had nearly hidden his face and made a gesture of command. The first emir prostrated himself, crawling backward. He of the white burnoose slid down from his mount, disdaining the hands stretched up to aid him. He bowed toward Richard, inclining his head and putting his hand to his heart. "Illustrious Malek-Rich," he began, his teeth and the whites of his eyes very startling in his darkly handsome face. "In the name of the prophet Mahomet, and the one God, Allah, forever blest, I greet you . . . I, Prince Al-Adil Saif ed-Din."

"Saladin's brother!" cried Richard, stepping forward and embracing him with a huge smile. "The great victor of Hattin! God, man, you do me honor! Well, come inside. Come, do! You must take some refreshment with me, we must talk! Come." And, in his easy way, his arm still about the Muslim prince's shoulders, he led him into the palace.

This prince was one of the few men I have seen who could match Richard in height, and in length of leg and arm; together, they were spectacular, the red-gold Plantagenet and the flashing-eyed dark Saracen in his white robes and silver turban.

"I shall call you Safadin," said Richard, chatting easily, as they took seats in the great hall, Richard, for courtesy, sitting on the footstool that was drawn up near the throne. "Your true name is a mouthful for our Frankish tongues."

I had followed them, for I knew I would be expected to record this visit, and Richard, catching sight of me, said, "Oh, settle somewhere, Saracen, do." He turned to Safadin. "My secretary, and foster brother."

Safadin bowed. "You called him . . . ?"

Richard laughed. "A nickname—from our childhood. He looked much like a horse of that name." He held up a protesting hand. "There was no offense, I assure you. We Franks worship our horses. But his name is Alexander."

"After the Greek conqueror," said the prince, looking hard at me.

"No, Sire Prince," I said. "I am no soldier even, but a monk."

The dark face was puzzled. "A religious," said Richard. "A uh, dervish."

"Ah, a holy man! But you are so young!" Safadin exclaimed.

I shook my head, smiling; somehow I liked the man. "I am . . . more of a scholar," I said, speaking slowly in the Moorish tongue; I had been working at it for weeks now.

He looked delighted, the wide white smile spreading in his lean dark face. "You speak our language! So few Franks can."

"King Richard speaks it as well, or better," I said. Which was true, though I had never known him to study; it had to do, I think, with his musician's ear, which picked up differences in cadence so quickly.

From then they switched to the Turkish tongue, and I hope I got it all right for the record. First off, Richard explained that in the West men take only one wife at a time, and that Berengaria was his Queen.

Safadin wagged his finger at him, with a sly look. "The other one, the fair one, the famous singer . . . she is nothing to you?"

"A fellow troubadour, and a friend," said Richard.

"Ah, come now, Malek-Rich," said Safadin. "There is a child."

Richard reddened. "My doings are such a byword, then, even in your heathen cities?" And he laughed a little. "Yes, there is a child . . . and the lady is much more to me than friend. But . . ." I could see it was difficult for him to explain. "In Europe we marry . . . especially high nobles . . . for dynastic reasons. Blondelza was not my equal in birth . . . she was not eligible in the eyes of the Church. And so . . ." And he spread his hands in a curiously Eastern gesture, with a shrug.

"So, by the other one, your Queen, you have fine sons too? Heirs?"

"No," said Richard. "Not yet. But the marriage is still new."

"Well, don't wait too long," said the Moslem. "If she does not quicken, put her away. A barren wife is no good. Put her away, and take another. I have put away five already."

"Five? Divorced?"

"No," said Safadin, drawing his hand across his throat in a cutting gesture. "There is no divorce in Muslim law."

I was shocked, but Richard did not bat an eye—one reason he was such a good diplomat. He merely nodded and said musingly, "Well, divorce is not so common with us, either . . . the Church does not approve. But there are ways of getting around the problem." And he shrugged again, and smiled a little. "My mother, Eleanor, was divorced—from the King of France."

"Ah, Ali-Anor. There was a woman! I saw her once, in Beyrout, when I was a small boy. I never forgot her." And he chuckled, a rich sound. "My father wanted to marry her—he only had six wives then—and I was jealous. But of course, it came to nothing."

Richard smiled. "Yes, Mother is a woman in a thousand."

"She is still alive? But she must be—" And the prince began to count on his fingers.

"Yes, she is nearly seventy now. Still strong and beautiful. And keeping my kingdom for me."

"Ah, a great woman—a legend," sighed Safadin. "We have some such too, in the old tales. But, alas, there are none left."

"They are rare with us too," said Richard.

"Your blond lady, though . . . she must be . . ." He paused delicately. ". . . no longer young."

"Blondelza is just my age," said Richard.

Safadin nodded. "Old for a woman."

Richard laughed, and walked to the door leading to an inner chamber, calling, "Blondelza, can you come out, please?"

I had not heard the lute, but it jangled now; she must have been playing very softly. In a moment she appeared in the doorway, a little diffident. "Richard," I heard her say softly, "I am in my working clothes."

"He will not know the difference," said Richard, laughing. "Come."

She walked into the room and, seeing the richly dressed Eastern stranger, made a jongleur's bow, graceful and quick. She wore her player's clothes, tunic and hose, none too clean. But her face was like a ripe apricot from the sun, and her hair, spread out loosely upon her shoulders, was a mantle of spun gold. I saw that, in Safadin's eyes, she had a wondrous, alien beauty.

He stared at her for a long moment, holding on to her hand, which she had extended. "What will you take for this one, Malek-Rich? Ten thousand dinars, a hundred thousand?"

"Not all Saladin's kingdom," said Richard. "She is not for sale."

"I know," said Safadin softly. "I jested. You have good taste, friend enemy." He bent and kissed Blondelza's hand. "A Frankish custom, no?"

Blondelza spoke a few words, in the Moorish tongue, offering him wine.

Safadin shook his head. "It is forbidden in our faith," he said. "Until Paradise, when there will be many such as you to sit beside me on soft cushions, and share it with me . . . or so the Prophet promises."

"Some sherbet, then," said Blondelza, and left the room, calling softly to a servant.

Safadin shook his head. "Ah, you poor Franks," he said. "If you were a Muslim, you could marry her."

And so the extraordinary conversation went, between those two great foes. But, in spite of the amenities and courtesies and all the great gifts lavished by Safadin upon Richard and his women—a string of camels and a pure-bred Arab horse for Richard, gorgeous silks and jewels for the two queens, and a dulcimer wrought of ivory and gold for the "other wife"—it all boiled down, really, to more delays. Saladin, that wise monarch, had sent his personable younger brother to ask for time and concessions.

Twice more the Muslim Prince came, laden each time with more and finer offerings, to spin out the days till the treaty should be kept. First it was August 8, then the twelfth, then, finally, quite stern, Richard gave the last deadline, August 20. "And after that, if it is not met, tell the great Saladin that all is still war between us, no more excuses, and the infidel prisoners in my hands shall be mine to do with as I will, and as the council of Frankish knights decides."

Safadin smiled, his charming, flashing smile, and said, spreading his hands in resignation, "Then shall all those true souls of Allah be your slaves . . . so be it."

"Know you," said Richard, his face grim, "we in the Western world do not keep slaves, nor no man owns another, enemy or friend. And these accursed infidel prisoners are eating me out of camp and castle."

And it was true, of course. The knights and foot soldiers were grumbling at having to share rations with these strange folk who did not speak our tongue and did nothing to earn their keep. And the great nobles whispered behind their hands that Richard was betraying them, treating with Saladin's brother; at any moment, they said, he would forsake the whole Crusade for his friendship with the cursed sons of Allah. Rumors began to circulate in the camp that Richard was a traitor, that he was converting to Islam, that he found the enemy more pleasant than his allies.

"God's nails!" cried Richard, tearing at his red hair. "They shall have me writhing on the floor like my father! These whore-son highnoses drive me wild! Give me Saladin any day . . . at least I know he is my enemy!" He saw me eyeing him warily and laughed harshly. "Never mind, Alex. It is only a little rage—I will not foam at the mouth. But, God forgive me, it is hard to suffer fools!"

He sat, controlled, but very bleak of countenance, for nearly an hour, not moving, staring into space, while I fussed quietly with my papers, trying to look invisible, in a corner.

"Finally he rose, stretching himself, and held out his hand. "Will you help me, brother?" His face was very weary. "Will you pray with me this night? Perhaps God will give me counsel."

CHAPTER 12

THE TERM OF treaty with Saladin had been set for the twentieth of August; the deadline, noon.

The day dawned, like any other there, in that land, pale pearly pink, quickly bleaching to white under the fierce sun. Like any other day, I said, but this day is seared now forever upon my heart.

At dawn the council of nobles sat, voting upon terms. Richard was to meet Saladin upon the plain outside the walls, and there hand over the Saracen prisoners and receive, in return, our own.

We were solemn as we rode out to the great plain where our tents were pitched, below the mountain of Keisan, where the infidel waited, out of sight.

It was a long morning. No sign came from Saladin, no word. The hours wore on. Face looked into face, oddly fearful; eyes met fleetingly and turned away; men rubbed sweating hands against their jupons. Horses neighed, restive. The sun climbed.

Noon passed without a move from the infidel; no message, no signal. The deadline had come and gone.

From my place behind Richard I sighed heavily, a sound broken, tearing, like a sob. He turned to me; his face was like a rock, and bleak as rock. "Go back, Alex," he said. "Get back behind the walls. We do not need a scribe." I did not protest, for his face told me something his words did not.

I saw, from my place upon the walls, safely inside, the Muslim prisoners led out, bound with cords, the whole of the Christian host assembled beside them. So far away they were, looking like ants, but still we saw, we watchers on the walls.

It was now three hours past noon. There was no stir from the Saracen camp, in the hills above. Slowly Richard raised one long arm. There was a heartbeat, the space of a heartbeat only, and then, at Richard's signal, the Christian host fell upon the prisoners with swords and spears, slaughtering every one.

It was over in a short while; so many men, all dead in a matter of minutes, and all in silence, or so it seemed, far away upon the plain.

We watchers did not cry out at the sight, though some of us hid our eyes. When I, for I was among them, looked up, the Christian host stood knee-deep in a lake of blood. Richard, in his shining mail, sat his horse, fetlock-deep where the blood had flowed like a river, reaching the farthest corner of the plain. He did not move. I saw his hand fall to his side; he bowed his helmeted head.

Then came a howling as of fiends from Hell, as the infidel knights swept down from their eyrie in the hills. Shrieking and crying vengeance, they joined battle with our host. They fought so fiercely that they were not beaten off till nightfall.

And, through the night, even from such a distance, we could hear the wailing voices of a multitude of mourners, repeating over and over the Islamic prayers for the dead.

In full dark, with flaring torches lighting the way and cressets burning in all the streets and upon the walls of Acre, the Crusaders returned, spent and weary, bearing many wounded comrades, and some few dead. Richard, at their head, all but fell off his horse at the entrance to the castle, still clad in full mail, spattered with dark blood, his sword dripping from all its length. He slowly climbed the marble stairs, each mailed boot leaving its bloody imprint, his head still hidden in the round metal casque of his helmet.

Below, staring up at him, were Hugh of Burgundy, Leopold of Austria, and some of their Burgundian and Austrian nobles; they wore the faces of awed children. "Is it done?" asked Burgundy in a hoarse voice.

Richard's voice came, hollow, sepulchral, from behind the mask of his helm. "It is done—as was voted in the council this morning. The deed is done, we have beaten off the avengers, there are no more prisoners to hinder our progress. Be ready to march for Ascalon tomorrow, at first light." And he shut the chamber door upon their astonished faces.

I stood within, waiting, with his squire and Blondelza. None of us dared speak. Richard, huge and heavy, leaned against the great door; he looked like a great iron man, a statue, set there by its artisan while the pedestal was made ready for it. For a long moment we waited. Then, slowly, the iron arm bent, raised itself upward, loosened the helm, and the other iron arm rose too, meeting it, pulling off the great closed helmet. Behind it Richard's face looked shrunken, and white as a bleached bone, the hair dark and matted like seaweed, plastered to his skull. We could see that it ran, gleaming, with sweat. One iron arm made a ghost of a gesture, and he said, through lips that did not seem to move, "Get me out of this mail."

The squire's fingers shook like aspen leaves, as he fumbled with the latches of the mail. I hurried to help him, peeling off the stiffened dragon-scale pieces one by one. Inside them, Richard's leather tunic was dark and heavy with the sweat of his body, and his shirt dripped like a washcloth. "Help me to a seat," he said, in a wooden voice. "My legs will not work."

Blondelza knelt beside me, each of us tugging desperately at a boot. The frightened young squire came running to help, getting in the way.

A wraith of a smile flitted across Richard's face. "Easy," he said. "Take it easy. We have all night."

Finally the armor was off. Richard's whole body trembled, and ran with sweat; his flesh felt cold and clammy. Blondelza snatched up a quilted silk coverlet from the bed and hung it over his shoulders. He shrugged it off. "You must bear with my nakedness for a while." His voice had still that dead, hollow sound. He waved his hand wearily at the squire. "Leave us. You have done well . . . but leave us now."

The squire left, stumbling on the threshold. Richard raised his head, slowly as he did everything this night, and looked at us. Never have I seen such eyes, not on a human. I remembered a dog that had been crushed by the wheel of a wagon; its throat was destroyed and it could not even whimper, but the look in its eyes was like those blue ones that now stared up at me.

A long, long moment. Then, "Unarmed men," he said. "Two thousand six hundred unarmed men."

"You could do no other," I whispered hoarsely.

And it was true, though I never thought that I would need to give comfort to the great Lionheart. There was nothing else to be done; the prisoners could not be taken on the march, so many, without weaponry, dragged at the heels of an army. Neither could they be left in the Acre garrison, for a huge guard must be left to keep them, and it could not be spared. The prisoners were able-bodied soldiers in their prime; even unarmed, they could overpower their captors. They could, of course, have been chained, and left upon the plain to starve and die. Was that mercy? Only easier. It was clear that Saladin had gambled with these lives, thinking to encumber our army for so long that the war would be well lost. But *he* had lost. I ventured to say it.

"Saladin has lost the gamble," I said.

Richard stared still. Then, harshly, he said, "And I have won . . . A heavy victory." And he put his weary head into his hands and sobbed, great racking, tearing sounds that we listened to, sick at soul.

For a long while the sounds went on, dying at last to choking breaths. He raised a haggard, old face, the lines cut sharply in it; I had never noticed them before. "Every man of them cried out Allah's name, and some went to their deaths, smiling, with a look of joy. Allah . . . and God. Do you think," he whispered, "they are the same?"

"I know not," I said miserably. For I knew a good priest of Jesus would deny it, or warn of blasphemy. Yet I could not, nor say a word of comfort either.

Richard spoke again, haltingly. "And my men . . . upon their faces was the same joy—a fierce joy. They cannot both be right."

"It is an evil world," said Blondelza, very low. They were the first words she had spoken. Her face shone wet in the candlelight, her eyes dark and swimming.

"And my whore-son fellow Crusaders, they who voted so strong for death . . . the filthy buggers stayed within the walls while the deed was done. Damn them to Hell, the whoresons!" He was coming back to life, though his curses were feeble still; I let out my breath on a ragged sigh.

"At least"—and a bitter smile twisted his lips—"I have sent Mercadier to harry Philip in France. For once he will not have *another* of my sins upon his conscience."

Blondelza made a little move, and moaned softly.

"And you, Blondelza," he said, looking at her with his burned-out eyes. "Will you leave me now? Will you leave me once again?"

"I will never leave you, my dear." And she reached out her long hands and took his head between them, bearing it close, cradling it to her bosom, like a child's.

CHAPTER 13

Two MAIN ROADS led southward from Acre to Ascalon: the inland one, built by the Romans and still in good condition after centuries, and the coastal road, decaying and fallen away in places, but safer, for it faced the sea, thus leaving only one side of the ranks of marching Crusaders vulnerable to attack. This was the road that Richard chose, for he wished to gain control of all the coastal towns, thus keeping clear the lines of communication to Cyprus and to Europe by sea, and also blocking the enemy's route to Egypt, the source of much of the trade of the Muslim world. The entrance to Egypt, by both land and sea, was commanded by the great fortress of Ascalon. The directive, issued during that night after the massacre, was to regain, one by one, all the cities of the seaboard along the way, and, ultimately, to capture Ascalon itself.

No one slept. Richard rested on his couch for something under an hour. Then he rose, took a hot bath, ate some soup and bread, drank a cup of watered wine, and, fully dressed, went forth to rouse his captains and men and alert his peers. None, seeing him then, would have recognized the anguished creature of just a few hours earlier. His step was firm, his back straight, his eyes bright; only the set of his jaw, and the pulse that beat there, betrayed him, and then only, perhaps, to me.

I was issued a suit of mail, and a hauberk to wear over it. I did not know how to put it on, and had to be helped by Blondelza, both of us giggling foolishly from nerves. "I wish I could go too," she said.

"I wish I could stay," I muttered crossly. Which set us off again, laughing helplessly.

"Oh, why are we such fools?" she said, suddenly sobered. "Sweet Jesus, keep him safe . . . keep you both safe!"

"We are all in His hands," I said, bowing my head and sketching a cross in the air. It was not easy, my arm felt like

349

lead. I had never worn mail before; it must have weighed, in all, about fifty pounds.

"He has given me a sword too," I said testily. "I don't know how to use it . . . I doubt if I can lift it!"

"It is only to defend yourself," she said mildly. "You will be riding with the squires and the baggage, well in the rear. No one expects you to do knights' work."

I glanced at her sharply, unaccountably miffed, but her face was bland; I suppose I was tired. "By all the saints, stay here, in this wing of the palace," I said. "It would not do for you to run up against that other household."

"Do you take me for a fool?" she said. "I will not leave these chambers, not even to wave farewell." Her face dropped into sad lines; she sighed. "It is a strange life, mine," she said. "Empty . . . without him."

"You have your music . . . and you have companions too, your troupe. Think of the two queens, in the other wing. All they have is each other."

She nodded. "Yes. You are quite right. I was falling into the sin of self-pity." She smiled a little smile, half mocking. "You see, I know how you think, Sir Monk!"

"I only meant to cheer you," I said.

"There is little cheer in war. One can only put a good face on it. I wonder—" she said suddenly. "I wonder how she feels . . . that other one. Berengaria."

"Much the same, I expect," I said.

"You know, I've never even seen her . . . not a glimpse! What is she like?"

"Oh, very small and very shy, with curly brown hair and deer's eyes."

"Not like me at all, then."

"Oh, no. She is not beautiful. Not accomplished. Only sweet . . . and young."

"I wonder why he married her."

"She was a princess," I said simply.

"Yes," she said. "She can give him heirs." She was silent for a moment, then she asked, touching my arm, a tentative movement, "My son, my little Philippe . . . I never asked you, but you were his tutor. Is he . . . What is he like now?"

"Not so little anymore. He will be tall like his father. A good, clever boy, learns quickly—but loves his jousting practice more than books."

"He was much like my father, Blondel . . . when he was small."

"Yes," I said. "Fair-haired, but like Richard too. No one can doubt whose son he is."

"Is he musical?"

"How not?" I said, laughing. "Richard has hired Piere Vidal for his teacher."

"Oh, that is good . . . I like that."

Richard burst in; for the first time I wondered how he moved so fast and so lightly in his cursed mail. He looked from one to the other of us, curious. "What are you two whispering about? There is no time for dawdling. Have you all your papers and gear?" he demanded, looking at me.

"Yes . . . somewhere. They are somewhere about."

"Well, get them together. It is getting close to daybreak."

"Richard," said Blondelza softly. Their eyes met, and their hands. "Take care."

"I promise," he said, their eyes still locked. With a sigh, he gathered her into his iron arms. "Keep well, my love." And he kissed her firmly upon the lips. Then, abruptly, he turned on his heel and stalked out the door, waving to me to follow. I murmured a good-bye and hurried after him, noisy in my awkward new suit of mail.

Downstairs, Richard turned and looked at me, laughing. "You will get used to it—sooner than you think." He laughed again, more harshly. "Some of my knights have got too fat for theirs. Christ, the whore-sons! Knights and soldiers too. Still lolling on their whores' couches! Half of them are unfit for marching, much less combat, and the other half are hiding! The life is too good . . . we cannot pry them loose, the rotted wine-heads! I have given orders that no women shall accompany the army—only the old dames that wash the clothes. Even they are probably not safe from ravishment . . . the men are like goats! I am going now into the stews to rout out some of them. Go, Alex. Tell that company over there to follow us. I'll need help."

"Richard." I plucked at his sleeve. "Richard, will you not bid farewell to the ladies . . . the two queens? They must be anxious, hearing all the bustle."

"Oh, Jesus' feet! I forgot! Yes, yes, of course! Tell the company—they are some of the Duke of Bedford's men—tell them I order them to proceed to the 'Flesh of the Lizard.'

They'll know the place. Tell them to knock the men over the heads if need be, but bring them!"

I ran to do his bidding, while he gave orders to another detachment. I heard the name "Silver Bellies" and a roar of laughter. Strange names for taverns, I thought, then realized they must be whorehouses, and blushed violently, glad it was too dark for my face to be seen.

"Some will have to be left, and rounded up later . . . it takes time to smoke them out." Richard was walking very fast through the long, winding corridors, and it was all I could do to keep up; I was weary already, and it was not yet day! "But we must get going now, there have been enough delays. Besides, Saladin will not expect it, after yesterday . . ." His voice tailed off. After a moment he said, his voice very crisp, "We may steal a few days' march on him—put the river of Acre between us, at least."

The door to the queens' quarters was ajar; Richard pushed it open wide and walked in, each mailed footfall sounding heavily on the marble floor. "So, ladies, where have you got to? Are you hiding or still abed?"

The curtains that veiled the great windows moved; a head appeared, then two. Joanna, flushed with excitement, cried, "Richard! We could not tell . . . we thought you had gone! We have been watching since daybreak."

"So much bustling about, and so many men in the courtyard . . ." said Berengaria. "I wondered if Saladin had attacked."

"Well, I didn't!" exclaimed Joanna. "We would have seen Muslim banners or heard the catapults. But what has happened, Richard? Will you attack them again?"

"We march today for Ascalon," said Richard.

"Without us?" cried Joanna. "You cannot leave us here! It is so boring—shut up here forever!"

"And Saladin—maybe . . ." Berengaria's face was white with fear.

"I am leaving a goodly force to man the walls, with two constables to command the city, Bertram de Verdon and Stephen de Longchamps. You know those knights . . . if you need anything, call on them. You have no cause for alarm. Saladin has seen us already, and you may be sure he is making ready to harry us on the march."

"Oh, dear Jesus," cried Berengaria softly. "Keep well out of danger. You are so conspicuous in your red hauberk . . .

can you not disguise another knight so that they may make a mistake?" She kept on wringing and wringing her hands, her face working with fright and grief.

"Richard would disdain such tactics!" cried Joanna. "It is the coward's way!"

Richard smiled at his little Queen, ignoring Joanna. "I think it's a very good idea . . . if I can find another as overgrown as myself, so as to fit my armor. He could act as a decoy, and draw off the enemy. A good idea! I'll think about it." His face was kind as he looked down at her. "But be of good cheer, little pigeon. I told you, I have a charmed life!" And he flicked her under the chin, playfully. "Hold your head high, my Queen . . . be brave. Now give us a kiss . . . until we meet again."

Joanna had been peering shortsightedly at a map. "But it may be weeks! Ascalon is at the very tip of the coast!" She flung herself into a chair, wailing. "We may be immured here for months! Like being in prison!" Suddenly she jumped up, her eyes brightening. "Why can't we come with you? We could keep out of range . . . in the middle of the host. Or we could wear mail shirts! Mother did!"

"That was in another time—and a different war. And besides, everyone agrees it lost the Crusade for Louis of France."

"Nonsense! It was the fortune of war! You can't blame the whole failure of Louis's war on Mother and her Amazons! But that's just like a man. I thought better of you, Richard."

Richard's face was darkening with anger. "Be quiet, Joanna! I command here! And I have said there will be no women."

"Not even the glee-maiden?" Joanna's voice had risen, shrill. I shot a quick look at Berengaria; her face looked as though it had crumpled.

"No. No one," said Richard. "What is this catechism? I came here to make my farewells, as was seemly. I am late already." He was very curt, his face hard.

Berengaria stepped forward; it was at such moments that she showed the stuff she was made of. She looked small but regal; her face was still pale, but composed and serene. "Farewell, my husband, and may God and His mother watch over you. We shall be quite safe here, you need not worry on our account."

The hard lines left his face; he smiled down at her, then

took her in his arms and kissed her. "I shall send for you soon—when we have taken a proper city. I am sure it will be long before Ascalon." He flashed a sudden smile. "But keep the reins tight on this sister of mine . . . she is too big for her skirts!" And, so saying, he turned quickly and left the chamber. I murmured a quick blessing and a word of farewell, and hurried after him.

The host assembled on the coastal road outside the city numbered, so far as it could be counted, about three hundred thousand archers, foot soldiers, and knights, with their squires, baggage-bearers, cooks, and servants. It seemed, to my untrained eye, to be a plenteous array, even without the laggards still lurking in the stews and taverns of Acre. Of course, it was true that many of them were still weak from wounds not quite healed or from the fevers and ills that had affected so many.

Richard rode out before them as they lined up for his inspection. He was riding a famous steed, captured from Isaac at Cyprus, a black gelding with a white blaze down its face; it was very spirited, and took all his great strength to hold it still while he spoke to the troops.

At the first loud huzzah the creature's head went up, its ears flattening; it reared high, pawing the air, for all the world like one of the pictured lions rampant upon Richard's standard. Richard, after a brief tussle, got it still, four hooves on the ground, then bent and whispered to the horse. It seemed to listen, gentling, then nodded its head three times. The crowd roared a laugh and a cheer.

"See," said Richard, in his parade voice, "I have told him our mission—to take all the coastal towns, to take Ascalon, and to capture, finally, Jerusalem. A threefold task—and he has agreed. Did you see him nod?" There were louder cries and cheers, and scattered bursts of applause. Richard held up his hand. "Listen well, lads. We march close to the seashore—there"—and he pointed—"to the right. Thus will our entire right side be protected by the sea, and by my fleet, where it shares our progress. The other side, the left, is vulnerable, so we will take turns—like watches on a ship. Shall we say six hours at a time—alternating danger and safety? Are you willing?" He waited for the loud favorable response, then went on.

"Now know you this. Our knighthood is our striking force, our ultimate weapon. The Saracens cannot withstand their heavy charge. But that force must be husbanded. The time to strike must be the right time, when it will do the most damage. Our knights and their horses must be protected until this crucial moment. That is where you, lads—my foot soldiers, my archers—come in. It is your task to make a defensive screen for our horsemen—a screen which the Saracens cannot penetrate. So the knights will march near the coastline with their left side protected by foot soldiers, both spears and bows. *Half* our men—do you understand? Then—at the next watch, as it were—after six hours the other half, which has been taking it easy with the baggage train between the knights and the sea, will exchange places with the first half. So each man will have a double chance. It will ease the burden. What do you say?" He had put it very simply, and all understood; it was probably the first time in history that a commander did not consider his common foot soldiers expendable. The cheers were wild, mixed with cries of joy.

Richard held up his hand again, smiling grimly. "Make no mistake, lads . . . it is no picnic you are going on. You are still at hazard. But remember, I am with you every step of the way. I ride the left side, you will hear my commands and reap my curses. I ride with you! So, take care! I will be watching!"

This drew a great laugh, as tight nerves eased.

"And now, look to your leaders. Take your formations. And remember this . . . I never saw a finer sight than you! God go with us! God wills it!"

And the huge thundering cry came again, heating the blood and ringing in the ears. "God wills it! God wills it!"

CHAPTER 14

When to pursue them one essays,
Their steeds, unrivaled, like a swallow,
Seem to take flight, and none can follow.
The Turks are so skilled to elude
Their foemen when they are pursued,

That they are like a venomous
And irksome gadfly unto us.

So wrote Ambroise, the poet in our ranks. He put it very well, though Richard said the verses did not scan. It was true—they harried us at every step. Our men were hard put not to return their sallies, they so angered them. "Ignore all provocation!" cried Richard, riding up and down the ranks. "Keep to your close formation! Never break ranks!"

Saladin, unable to goad our men into disorder, began to concentrate his attacks on the rearguard; our foot soldiers had to turn and walk backward, fending them off. The first batch that held the dangerous flank were Richard's soldiers, and it worked very well, for they followed his orders. But on the second day, it happened that it was the turn of the Burgundians and Austrians. Somehow, after a few hours on the march, they began to lag behind, leaving an open place in the ranks. Immediately the Saracens swept in, like a cloud of fierce dark birds, and began attacking the unarmed wagon train, where I rode. Oh, then I was thankful for my heavy mail! The Turkish arrows flew thick and fast among us, whistling through the air; many found their mark, for the squires and baggagemen were lightly armored, if at all.

"Sound your trumpet!" I cried to the trumpeter, a lad barely big enough to sit the pack mule that he rode. He raised it to his lips; the first blast was shaky, but the second swelled loud and ringing, and King Richard heard. Turning back swiftly from the van, he swept upon the enemy, his steed's hooves thundering above the lighter Arabians'. There were two or three knights behind him, a Templar, I think, and the Earl of Leicester, but all I saw was Richard, blazing bright in his mail, red head bared, and his long sword, raised high, catching the sun like silver. I never knew how he did it—though I saw him this way many times—but they seemed to scatter before him, as though he *willed* it. Perhaps he did. I know he left six dead, tumbled from their trembling mounts, before the other knights came up to join him.

His sword dripped blood and his mail was spattered with it, but I saw his teeth flash white; he was laughing! It had all happened too quickly for me; I had, however, drawn my sword, and, forgetting its weight, held it straight out before me, where a Turkish knight ran into it, his whole lower half immediately streaming with red blood. I was still staring, shocked, when Richard pulled out the sword and handed it to me with a laugh and a flourish. "Good work, Alex. It is baptized now . . . wipe it off!"

Dazed, I looked about me, seeing the dead upon the ground, my own Turk among them, and the Turkish horses dancing, riderless, above them.

"Get the horses!" cried Richard. "Don't let them get away!" He jumped off his own horse then, and picked up the trumpeter boy, who had fallen among the slain Turks, a slender arrow piercing his forearm. "His trumpet saved the day," said Richard. "Pray God our good Iselin can save his life."

I saw then that the Turks had been beaten off, leaving more than a dozen dead; among our ranks, miraculously, there were no serious casualties, only a few small wounds. Richard's left hand had a gash across the back. "Only a scratch," he said, when I pointed to it. He stared at me curiously. "Can't you feel it?" he said. "The arrow through your ear?"

I thought he jested, but when I put my hand I felt it, thin as a wood splinter and slippery. My hand came away wet, and I stared at it, seeing my own blood. Only then I felt it, a stinging pain that worsened when I moved my head.

"Get you over to Iselin," said Richard, and, turning, cupped his hands and shouted, "On! Keep to your formations! All is well!" He spurred his horse ahead.

When we made camp that night, Saladin's campfires glowing in a long line across the distant hills to our left, Richard called a council of war.

"There must never be a repetition of today's fault," he said. "I have ordered over and over—keep close formation, never separate, keep close! It is the only way we can push ahead and give these cursed gadflies the slip! Burgundy, you must keep keen watch on your men."

Hugh of Burgundy, insulted, hotly denied his men were to blame. "It was the Austrians," he said. "They are lazy curs . . . they fall behind."

Leopold leapt to his feet. "My men are not lazy, but sick! They have watery bowels, and some fell out to relieve themselves; the others slowed to cover them."

Richard held up his hand, laughing. "So have we all, friend! But, after this, let he who must drop out, but the others must march on. My men—and I, also, with them—do not drop out. We wear no smallclothes and, when we must, let it drop on the ground as we march, like our steeds. There is much to be learned from nature." Gasps of horror were heard, and cries of protest. "Come, comrades," cried Richard. "What are we, a gaggle of women? We will never win Jerusalem in skirts and blushing smirks. We all have this complaint. We all suffer. We must not let it be our death!"

At length, a compromise was reached. It was agreed that the Templars and the Hospitalers would bring up the rear at all times, for they had the most experience of this desert warfare, and, also, of that same Saladin's Curse. It was agreed that if any man dropped from fever or exhaustion, two of his fellows must make a sort of chair with their arms and carry him, if he still lived; if he fainted, he must be dumped in a wagon; if he died, he must be abandoned to the vultures, and prayers said for his soul when camp was made at night. "It is a hard campaign, friends . . . but it is God's campaign! Every soul will fly straight to Heaven!" Richard held up both arms as the cheers went up. "Hear me, lads! Let who will fly to Heaven . . . I call upon you to hold firm, stay close, and march with me to Jerusalem the Golden!"

Day after day the great army marched on, past Haifa, over the ridge of Mount Carmel, and on past Caesarea. And at each town, each fortress, it was seen that Saladin's advance had gone before, razing buildings and walls to ruins and scorching all the crops. The poor farmers and their families lay dead in ditches, speared by their own army's zealots, or heaped in blackened, stinking heaps within their burned-out fields. Those few poor infidel souls left alive might have been better with their dead companions, for they held out raw stumps that still oozed blood, where once their hands had been, or crawled on mangled legs. Many were eyeless and missing tongues or ears; my own ear throbbed under its bandage at the sight. We had no spare rations to give them, though many, moved, thrust a crust of bread or a handful of meal into the small hands of the starving children who wandered alone or in bands like wild dogs across the countryside.

And day after day the heat pressed down, white, intense, heavy, out of a sky of pure cloudless blue. Some of us died of that too, even with the improvised turbans we wore over our helmets; there were always one or two each day who turned red, then purple, then gray, and, finally, dropped like a stone, and dead as a stone. There could be no stopping for them; I knelt beside each one—I or Brother Alberic—and murmured a hurried prayer, anointing them with the precious drinking water from our hoarded skins. And, after the terrible heat, the sudden drop that came at fall of night, when the sweat that bathed us under our mail turned icy cold and we shivered in it as in a bath of snow, wishing each time, vainly, for a blanket. We carried a few, kept for the wounded and the feverish, or for the horses, more precious than the men. Each morning there were a few who did not rise, their poor punished bodies unable to bear the sudden extremes of temperature. I, a monk, have cursed this land many times, God forgive me—this Holy Land. No wonder the God of the Jews was such a stern God. He must be, to be born of such a climate, to rule in such a sky!

And day after day others were lost too, to Saracen arrows; in closed ranks, even a stray one will find a mark. Richard himself had three new wounds, the "scratch," as he called it, upon his hand, a long graze down one thigh, and a spear thrust in the side. "Our Lord bore a deeper one, remember?" he said, grinning, as it was being dressed at the end of the day.

I stared at Richard, stripped; there was not an inch, I swear, upon him that was not scar tissue. A strange effect, like a statue wrought of some rough, pitted stone. Still, he was beautiful as a god, a pagan god; I flushed at the thought, there, in the dark. The sin of Sodom is always with us, in an army; I prayed not to be guilty of it, even in my secret heart. There are some of us, within the cloisters, who hold that celibacy is only the forbidding of traffic with women. But if they be true believers, underneath, they know their souls are in peril. Flesh is flesh, and the love of it forbidden to us, the brothers in Christ.

All through the month of August we wore on, day after weary day; our army, in close formation, doggedly marched forward, not to be deterred by death or Saladin.

The Sultan must have realized this, for by early September our scouts reported that he meant to risk a huge force of his troops in pitched battle with us. The place he chose, the plain to the north of Arsuf. The spy who brought us the news was missing a hand, for he had been caught behind the enemy lines, but he was cheerful; a Welshman, by the lilt of his voice.

"Look you," he said, a thin smile playing on his lips, "the black devils thought they got my sword hand; they could not know, the poor heathens, that the best Welshmen are left-handed!"

Richard, as reward, gave him ten gold bezants and a good sharp sword with a silver hilt and the red dragon emblem of Wales worked into it in rubies. "What is your name, lad?"

"Cadwallader ab Owen y Cymry," he replied, rolling the strange syllables on his tongue.

"Sounds like a king's title," said Richard.

"Only a prince," he said. "We are all princes in Wales."

"Well!" cried Richard, clapping him on the shoulder. "You are a prince of a fellow, that's for sure! Go now to the surgeon's tent and let him take care of that hand."

"Oh, look you now, Sir King, that hand will never cause me trouble more." And the Welshman threw back his head and laughed, loud and long. He had a big, lean frame, near as tall as Richard, a thin, beaky face with ice-blue eyes, and a head covered with red-gold curls, matted now from his leather helmet.

Richard stared at him. "I had thought all the Welsh were a small, dark people."

"Ah, those are the hill princes, King Rhys," he answered. "We of the valley are 'goch'—red, like yourself . . . true Britons."

"I am flattered," said Richard. "But I fear I am Norman—and, who knows, old Merovingian perhaps."

"All lost tribes of the Cymry," said the Welshman, his eyes dancing. "Lost on the long migration from Troy . . . back in the mists of time when it all began." They moved away together, heads close, as Richard led him to Iselin's quarters. I strained my ears, but could follow no more, for I could not leave my post; I was lookout that evening. But it was the kind of conversation I loved most, and sorely missed in the grim business of war.

But such musings were not all the Welshman had to offer. He brought back a rumor, heard in the Saracen camp, that Saladin meant to set the forest of Arsuf ablaze while we marched through it. So this time we all carried extra water, and a blanket or a rag end of one, whatever cloth could be found to muffle the flames.

It was a poor thing, for a forest, not like the forests of Europe. Here the trees were more like bushes, thin and straggling, many not as high as our heads. But they were all dry, bone-day; they would go up like tinder if a spark fell. We went warily, looking from side to side, every man of us, though Richard had given orders to march on the double. Every step was a terror, like walking in a nightmare; once someone cried softly that there was a smell of smoke, and others, hysterical as women, took up the cry.

"Softly," hissed Richard, riding tirelessly up and down the ranks. "Go softly, and go quickly, as I bade you. There is no smell, except dryness and dust. This is a dead forest, overcome by sunstroke." Even he could not raise a laugh, but I, who had been fancying that I smelled burning, took a deep breath, and knew him right.

It seemed a lifetime till we got through it, though I think it was not so very large. But we were a great host, and it seemed to swallow us up.

Later, much later, we heard noises from the van, gasps and muffled cries. As we came out, line after line of us in turn, onto the plain, we saw what the commotion was about. The plain itself was vast, and the army that filled its farthest end was vast as well. From this distance the infidels looked thick as flies in a cluster; the gaudy colors they wore in battle merged into one huge black mass, but above them flew the bright colors with the half-moon of Mahomet, hundreds of them, it seemed, making a tent under the sky. They were all massed together solidly, like a crowd in a city square, not drawn up in battle formation. Suddenly we saw, as our eyes began to gain strength in the bright sun, that there was someone exhorting them, someone on a tall black charger; from time to time the figure waved a flag, and there would come a distant roar. After a bit, as we watched, a great rippling wave seemed to pass over the Saracen host; they were kneeling to pray.

"They are facing east," said Richard, "praying to Mecca. They will not fight today. Let us make camp."

And then we saw that it was indeed sundown; the western sky was a bloody red, and purple rimmed the horizon. We would not fight, as Richard said; the Turks will not do battle after the evening prayer. Still, our camp was a restless one that night; we made no fires, but gnawed on cold bones and crusts, and drank spare mouthfuls of wine to wash it down, saving our water for the morning, when we would need it more.

Richard gave careful orders. "At the first hint of gray in the sky, we are up and forming our ranks for battle. They mean to attack us. We are outnumbered, but we will stand firm and take them as they come."

I did not sleep at all; I think there were many who did not. We lay on the fringe of the forest, or within it, and all night I smelled the false smell of burning; when a sentry's boot snapped a fallen twig, it sounded like the first crackling of flames. A camp of soldiers is never quiet; horses whinny and snort, mail creaks, a spear scrapes against a stone. And then there is the breathing of the thousand upon thousands, like the wind in the trees, with here and there a loud snore or a muffled cry.

In the chill, clammy gray, like ghosts the sentries came among us, shaking us awake. My mouth was dry as dust, with a taste of iron in it; I took a long swig from my waterskin, blessing it. Does fear have the taste of iron? I never found out. Quickly we took our places, forming our ranks closer this time than ever, so solid and tight a formation that one could not have thrown an apple between one soldier and his fellow. The steeds of the knights rubbed their hides together, roan and white, black and dappled, so close were they packed.

Richard rode up and down as always, seeming to be everywhere at once. "Wait for them. Do not charge till I give the signal," he exhorted the knights. "It will be six clear trumpet blasts, two in the van, two in the middle, and two in the rear. Upon your souls, do not charge before! Let the foot soldiers get the Turks in close, let them wear them out, wait till they tire and their horses tire . . . that will be the moment. Watch for it and charge on signal! Hold, knights . . . and, lads, take them on the run—butcher them, slaughter them, hold them for the charge! Now . . . they come! God be with you! God wills it!"

He cried the war cry softly, and softly it came back, like a sound in a dream, "God wills it! God wills it!"

The ground beneath our feet began to beat like thunder, as the thousands of hooves pounded toward us from the distant rim of the plain. We could not see them yet, only a dark cloud rimmed with yellow from the light of the rising sun, and another cloud above them, a cloud of dust, yellow too.

The din was amazing; thunder of hooves, clash of cymbals, blaring of trumpets, wild, savage drumbeats, and, above it all, a high, thin cry as from one throat torn open; their war cry, no doubt, the invocation to Allah or his Prophet. Closer and closer they came, the ground shaking under our feet from it, the air filled with war-mad music. I gripped my sword in two slippery, sweaty hands, and planted my feet hard; there was nothing I wanted more than to turn and run away. But I could not if I dared; we were too close-packed. My horse rubbed skins with a pack mule; it turned and fastened aggrieved eyes upon me. On the other side my spurs grated against the wood of a wagon. I remembered Richard saying "When it starts, Alex, get down from your horse and stand between him and a wagon—it is the safest place." I had forgotten it, and now, in some obscure way, it offended me; I gripped the sword harder.

No one who has been right there in the thick of battle can describe it; it takes an observer on a hill above, or a general, or God. But when it explodes around you, all you see is the face that bares its teeth before you and the arm that lifts the sword or axe, and all you hear is a curse or a cry of pain and surprise. And something works inside you, raising your arm, striking, and striking again. Something; it is fear, or love, or hate, or all three.

I was in the middle, with the baggage train, squires, and pages, but I was mounted, like a knight, and held a sword. It should have taken a good while before the Turks got to us there, and I suppose only a handful trickled through our lines of foot soldiers, but I saw a great curved axe poised over the wagon with its wounded, and I raised my sword and chopped downward. The axe tipped sideways, harmlessly, attached to a lean brown hand; as in a dream I watched it fall to the ground, while a jet of bright blood painted the side of the wagon from the stump of the wrist. There was the taste of iron in my mouth again, and a sour taste behind it, but I raised the sword and struck again, for the man still stood. This time he went down, but immediately I saw, under my horse's chest, another brown face, turbaned, with the curved scimitar slashing upward like a sickle. My horse, smelling blood, reared, and brought his heavily shod feet down, smashing the brown face. I took the scimitar from his outstretched hand as he fell. Now I had a weapon in each hand. A fighting monk! But I did not think of that then; I was delirious, as with fever.

And then I heard the trumpets; the first two, distant in the din, then the middle, sounding next to my ear, and, almost at the same time, the last, the rear. And then came the charge, a clash so loud it seemed to burst the eardrums, reverberating till the very air seemed made of sound. I felt myself sway in the saddle, and, amid the wild tumult, soft but clear, I heard a voice. Iselin. "Here. Climb in here, Brother Alex, over the side. Your horse has been hit, he is falling."

I let the steady arm guide me, and stumbled, stiff, into the wagon; someone let out a groan as my foot hit something soft. "Your pardon," I mumbled, groping my way. It was near midday, I suppose, but strangely, I felt as though it were full dark. Iselin told me later that patients in shock often feel so. I was not wounded, except for my nearly healed ear, so the shock in my case was to my spirit, knowing that I had killed, and killed again.

We were in the eye of the storm, as it seemed, there, in that wagon, unmoving, the action swirling, dizzyingly, around us.

The first charge had smashed the Turkish line to pieces; the enemy lay dead upon the ground, heaped in piles, uncountable. Here and there a Frankish knight stood over his dead horse, but the bulk of our horsemen, unhurt, had reassembled for another charge. I saw one knight pull desperately at the painted reins of his fallen horse, trying to bring it to its feet, while it struggled feebly, its whole throat torn out; the knight had pushed his helmet back and was crying like a boy. A companion came and led him away; I do not know where, for without a horse he was helpless and could not fight again.

There were five charges in all, and in all Richard led, slashing to right and left, carving a wide path for himself, cutting down the enemy as a reaper mows corn with his sickle. It seemed as if he was everywhere, his head rising right above the others, his red hair swinging free, his white teeth flashing—a portrait of a war god.

I watched as he cleared an open space around him. Suddenly he looked like the victor in a tournament, his sword raised high, his horse rearing. He pulled hard on the reins, subduing the blood-maddened animal. He was alone among the fallen; the field was empty.

The Turks had fought fiercely, but that day they left upon the field more than two thousand dead. We, with God's help, had lost only thirty foot soldiers, ten archers, and one knight.

But Richard looked across the bloody battleground, his

eyes bleak. He dismounted slowly and, laying down his sword, knelt upon the ground. "Forgive me, God, for these I led to death." He spoke very softly, but I heard the words.

CHAPTER 15

*There was great wealth of pasture ground,
And there did grapes and figs abound,
Almonds, and pomegranates, too ...*
                              Ambroise's Chronicle

Joppa, blinding white jewel against the dark blue sea, city of gardens, city of trees. We took it three days after the Battle of Arsuf, took it bloodlessly, quietly, in the hush of a white-hot noon.

The Muslim host had retreated, leaving their thousands of dead, leaving a desert, a bloodstained ground where grass had grown only the day before, a desert churned and rutted with wheels and the passage and strife of men and horses. Wearily we plodded and limped our way through it, recognizing their passage, a bright scarf caught on a thorn bush, a shoe thrown from a horse, a dirty rag of bandage trampled into the ground; the pitiful refuse of war. Towns were abandoned, fields burned, bridges broken, the very roads hacked into rubble. The fleeing remnant had not done this; Saladin had made sure the Franks' hands would close on nothing—this had been long planned. We knew his forces were many; any stand of trees, any cave, might shelter them; we went warily, sending scouts ahead. But we saw nothing, heard nothing; it might have been an empty world.

Bone-tired, bruised, bleeding, our mouths parched, we saw it. Joppa! Stumbling round a bend in the road, the first men halting in wonder, we came upon it, its walls glowing like opals in a nest of dark cool green.

The Saracens had left it hurriedly, destroying what they could, wantonly, haphazardly. The great walls were breached in several places, the huge gates sagged drunkenly on broken hinges, most of the graceful buildings were rubble. But the olive orchards, the orange and lemon groves, the vineyards were lush and fragrant with the scent of the heavy golden fruit, the great clustered blue and amber grapes; streams ran sparkling and noisy through them. The men fell upon their knees, thrusting in hands and faces, lapping up the precious water like cattle, crying aloud in joy and wonder.

The city had so many gardens that the whole army found room to camp within them, their tents shaded by leafy trees; cool, cool and good it was to rest there from the marching and the sun, the battles and the din of battle.

Two months we had there, in the cool gardens of Joppa, resting, our wounds healing, eating the wondrous fruits of the East, drinking the juice of pomegranates and figs, while masons of the English camp set to work to rebuild the city's walls and churches. Native Christians there were there, too, black as any Moors, who crept out of hiding to rejoice and weep at their liberation. Many had been born there and could speak no tongue but the Turkish, but they were Christians all, baptized souls, wearing gold crosses round their necks and at the belts of their outlandish heathen costumes. Weeping, speechless, talking with their hands like Jews or jongleurs, they clustered round the masons, carrying stones to put into the rebuilt walls of their destroyed churches, kissing the feet of the rough English laborers, blessing them with tears and broken Latin. "Colts," our men called them—I never found out why. There was little love lost between Frank and Colt, they were too different. "Might as well be Turks or Jews," said the soldiers, eyeing them with distrust.

But among these strange, heathenish Eastern Christians there were some whose fathers had settled there during the last Crusade, who spoke a little French, or German, or Saxon, and could still say their prayers in Latin. These begged for news of the homes they had never seen, bringing old gaunt men, wrinkled and burnt black by years of the Outremer sun, speaking haltingly of some little place in Arles or Normandy that no one had ever heard of. "You must know it . . . on the road to Lisieux. Mallon it is called, the priest was named Father Jacques . . ." insisting, growing angry, at last coming to blows, till one of our own priests had to be called in to quiet them.

And there were a few, the educated among them, richly dressed, bearded, hung with jewels, turbaned like Turks, who would not speak, except to knights, and then only contemptuously. They had nothing good to say of the Crusade or the Crusaders; King Philip was a soft French coward, Hugh of Burgundy a predator, King Guy of Jerusalem a worthless puppet in the ruthless hands of the overweening King of the English. Only Conrad of Montferrat had they any respect for. "There is a leader," they would say, fingering their gold earbobs. "There is a man, fearless as a hawk, strong as a lion, clever as a fox. He is worth all the rest of them put together."

Ugly were the disputes between the Frankish knights and these patronizing knights of Outremer; there were daily clashes and duels. Finally, Richard put a sullen end to it by the threat of fines, whereupon the Coltish knights disappeared behind their courtyard walls, so stingy were they.

The foot soldiers and the archers were still not fit for much more than sitting in the shade, and an hour or two of practice with bow or lance; most of them had been wounded more than once on the long, hot march. But the knights had suffered little more than the loss of a horse or a sword. Richard went among them, trying to enlist help with the rebuilding of the city, for it was going slowly, and he could not move on, leaving it unfortified.

"Jerusalem awaits us!" he would say. "The next city is Jerusalem! Let us turn to and get the job finished. I will buy you other horses and new mail, new swords . . . only take up a shovel or a pick. Look, I am doing it!" And it was true; he had recovered from his fevers now, and was tireless, digging and hacking at mortar in the high heat of the sun, cheerfully wringing the sweat from his shirt and headcloth. The youthful knights of Champagne and his own seasoned veterans turned to with a will and toiled beside him, but the Burgundian knights gave scanty aid, and that only after they had received their new destriers and burnished blades. The Austrian knights, under their haughty Duke, would not touch hand to spade; they said Leopold had forbade them, under pain of punishment.

"Can it be?" cried Richard, stalking into Leopold's tent without ceremony. "Is it true you refuse to help? It is your Crusade too!"

"My men are noblemen, not varlets—and I am of the royal line of Austria. We cannot labor like serfs!" cried Leopold, his blue eyes starting from his head like angry round marbles. "My father was no upstart prince."

"And mine was?" said Richard quickly, with a grim smile,

looking down from his great height. "He was of the line of the Conqueror."

"William the Bastard," said Leopold, standing on tiptoe and glaring; he had a terrier's courage, I'll give him that. "And on the other side—the Angevins are descended from witches and warlocks! The Devil's spawn!"

"God's wounds!" cried Richard in a great voice. "You try a saint's patience! And I am no saint—nor no devil either, but a plain man wanting to get a job done." I could see his fists clenching and unclenching, but still at his side. Very calmly he said, after taking a deep breath, "Will you not remember that the Apostles were plain fishermen, and that Christ His Holy Self practiced the carpenter's trade?"

"Oh, very pious-mouthed you are, indeed, King Richard," replied Leopold with a high scorn, "but the whole world remembers that your father murdered a saint!"

"It was his sin, not mine," said Richard levelly. "And he has surely paid for it, by now—God rest him." He put out his hands and took Leopold by the shoulders, gently. "Look, friend Crusader, what is the good of bringing up old sins, and lineage, and time past long before we saw light of day? Be reasonable . . . all I want is a little goodwill and help, man to man. We might be at it all day—the calling of names, the blackening of father's fame and mother's honor."

"Not mine!" cried Leopold. "*My* mother was no troubadour's whore."

At this I saw, from my place behind him, Richard's sun-reddened nape flare to crimson under his headcloth; his hands, already on Leopold's shoulders, gripped hard and shook him, pulling him clear off the floor. I could see no image but a terrier being shaken by a mastiff; Leopold's eyes rolled in his head and his teeth clattered like castanets. I made to step forward, but Richard flung the Duke at last into a corner. He glared for a moment, as if to make sure there was nothing else he wanted to do to him, then turned on his heel and stalked out, saying, "God save you, for I will not."

The little Duke lay motionless, his eyes closed, his limbs awry. I crept close and bent down. "My lord, are you hurt?"

The blue eyes opened, and the look in them seared me to the soul; I have never seen such pure hatred. I stepped back, startled. "Get you gone," he hissed. "Base-born catamite!"

I had never been called any vile name before, much less that one; I felt my own hands close into fists, before I remembered my calling and made the sign of the Cross between us. As I turned, I saw he had got to his feet. It would take more than a shake and a push, even from Richard, to undo him; he was a hardened knight, after all, if small of stature.

The next morning, as we labored to raise the walls of the Basilica of Saint Stephen, word was brought to us that the Austrians were going home; it was Hugh of Burgundy and two of his men who told us. "Thus it is that I am late," said Hugh. "I did not mean to shirk these duties, but he held me in my tent, for I tried to persuade him otherwise."

"And did not succeed," stated Richard. "I thought as much. Well, it seems I must apologize." And he started to lay aside the trowel and wipe his hands, all gray with mortar.

"It will do no good," said Burgundy, with a twisted smile. "This time he will go. This time— Well, he will 'brook no more insults,' were his words."

"He!" barked Richard. "It is the other way around! *I* called no names!"

"Only threw him across the room, as if to dash his brains out," said Burgundy. For the first time I saw a hint of humor in his face; both men burst out laughing, holding their sides.

"Oh, Hugh, you should have seen him . . . eyes rolling like a scared rabbit, and flopping like a rabbit too!" Tears of laughter stood in Richard's eyes.

"You may laugh on the other side of your face one day, my friend," said Burgundy, sobering. "For the tale will grow in the telling . . . and he has King Philip's ear."

"Ah, yes, I know—God rot the little bugger!" said Richard gloomily.

"What in Hades made you do it?" demanded Hugh.

"Well, among other things, he called my mother a— He called her a filthy name. I could not let that pass."

"I suppose not," said Hugh. "Though Queen Eleanor has been called many things, by better men than he, and it has not put her beautiful nose out of joint."

"Still, I could not let it pass," said Richard heavily.

"You could have kept your hands off the man . . . he is a good deal smaller than you, after all."

Richard gave him a long hard look. "Yes . . . Well, I must go to him. I must try what I may to atone."

"I tell you it will do no good," said Burgundy, shaking his

dark head. "His mind was made up anyway; this is only the excuse."

"But why? We are so close to full victory."

"Oh, Richard, face the facts! His men are dwindled to nothing—and that nothing a sorry, sick lot. He has no money, no provisions, no arms—and none forthcoming."

"I will offer—" began Richard eagerly.

Burgundy held up his hand. "Not again. He will take no more help from you, or at least no more than will help him on the journey. He *must* go. He must get the remnant of his army home—while they can still be called an army." He sighed. "I, too. My men are grumbling . . . they say we are wasting time."

"This great city must be made strong," said Richard firmly, "or we will never hold it. We must have bases behind us, so that provisions can get through, so that we have free passage. Gird up your loins, my friend!" He broke into a smile. "So much sooner it will be finished then . . . and Jerusalem awaits!"

And indeed Richard believed this, for he wrote to his mother, Queen Eleanor, on October 1: "With God's grace we hope to recover the city of Jerusalem and the Holy Sepulchre within twenty days after Christmas and then return to our own dominions."

CHAPTER 16

"THE MUSLIMS AND the Franks are bleeding to death, the country is utterly ruined. The time has come to stop this," said Richard, in a tone of mild reason. He was meeting for the first time since the occupation of Joppa with Safadin, the Sultan's brother, in a tent which flew, for courtesy, the standards of both armies. "Look," he went on, "the points at issue are Jerusalem, the Cross, and the land. Jerusalem for us is a holy city which we could not give up if there were only one man of our host left alive. The land from here to beyond the Jordan must be consigned to us. The Cross, which to you is simply a piece of wood, is all-important to us and our faith. If you will return it, we shall be able to make peace, and both sides rest from this devastation and death."

Safadin's dark eyes flashed as he replied, "Jerusalem is as much ours as yours. Indeed, it is even more sacred to us than to you, for it is the place from which our prophet, Mahomet, made his ascent into Heaven, and the place where all Muslims will gather on the Day of Judgment . . . never imagine that we will renounce it. Even if my brother, the Sultan, wished to do so, for the sake of peace, his people would not allow it; they would topple him from his throne, and drive you out with your entire army cut to ribbons. No, it can never be." And he leaned forward to pound the low table in emphasis, making the tiny cups and dishes rattle. "The land too—it was ours long before it was yours. Your people took it in unlawful conquest; Allah gave it to us!" He shook his head. "No, you have no right to it at all." And then he smiled, a sly, Eastern smile. "As for the Cross . . . well, think, King! It is the greatest card in our hand!"

Our spies had brought word that Saladin had razed the great port of Ascalon to the ground, upon hearing that Richard had taken Joppa. Saladin had divided his army, leaving a small contingent to guard the port of Ascalon, and moving the greater part to Ramlah, to lie in wait for the Frankish forces on their way to Jerusalem. Therefore, the entire campaign had to be reconsidered. Richard had intended to take Ascalon and then push on to Jerusalem, thus holding all the great ports and cutting off Saracen supplies. But the devastation of Ascalon would mean more delay; it was a dilemma. Thus, the King decided to open negotiations, and this was only one of many meetings with Safadin.

At another meeting, a bit later, in the rebuilt palace where Richard had taken up his quarters in the city, I was startled to hear the King call Safadin to the window and point down to the courtyard, saying, "There goes my sister, Joanna—there, upon that tall white mare. What do you think of her? Is she not fair?"

Safadin looked down. From my place at my writing table I could see what he saw. The two queens, who had been fetched from Acre, now that there were quarters for them, were taking the air with their ladies, seeing the sights. Joanna, as usual, had chosen a spirited mount; it kept rearing, pawing the air, and trying to throw her. She was laughing and flushed, above her green gown; her veil had slipped and her red hair loosened, falling in wild locks about her vivid face. We could hear her, too, cursing like a soldier, as she held the unruly horse; I wondered what this Eastern lord thought of our free Western ways, then remembered that the oaths were in Saxon, which he could not understand.

"She is the King in skirts," said Safadin, bowing. "A great resemblance, surely?"

"Well, red-haired, yes," said Richard. "But, otherwise, she is thought to be beautiful."

"Beautiful, yes . . . but a trifle large?"

Richard laughed. "More woman, then!" He turned to study Safadin's face. "Joanna is a widow."

Safadin said nothing, but a little smile played about his lips. "The small one, in violet, with the face of a flower . . . she is much like the women of my race—but thinner, of course."

Richard spoke sharply. "That is my Queen."

"Ah, the barren one."

"Not barren," said Richard. "We have been married for a short time only." And he laughed, clapping the emir on the shoulder. "Give the lady a chance, my friend!"

Safadin bowed, smiling in courtesy, and murmured, "Of course."

"But Joanna," said Richard, his face keen with interest. "Does she please you?"

"What I see, yes," said the emir. "How not? She is beautiful, as you say."

"I have a proposition," said Richard, his eyes on Safadin's face. "Give up the Cross, and all the land . . . I will give you my sister to wife, and as dowry she shall have all the coastal cities from Acre to Ascalon. You will live in Jerusalem, and rule over it, and all our Christian pilgrims shall thus have free access to worship there. Thus are all our problems solved!"

Safadin smiled blandly. "I am honored . . . but I must take up the matter with my brother."

"And I," said Richard, laughing, "with my sister!"

Saladin, who took it as a fine joke, agreed, but Joanna did not. She flew into a towering rage, swearing she would never marry an infidel.

"He is very handsome," Richard said.

"I know." Joanna clapped her hand to her mouth.

"Ah, you have seen him, sister?" asked Richard, smiling.

Joanna was sullen. "I—we looked out of the window when he rode in."

"And then managed to be seen in turn beneath this window."

Joanna tried to put on a haughty face, but could not keep it up, and burst out laughing. "Well, Richard, none of us have ever seen an emir before! They wear splendid clothes."

"But their women go veiled," said Richard. "Safadin indeed thought you beautiful—but, I fear, in need of taming."

"Well, don't worry, brother, he will never get the chance! How dared you propose such a thing!" Joanna's head went up and she flounced across the room.

"Calm down, sister. It was a diplomatic ruse. Naturally I have no idea of such a marriage. But it has come to my ears that there may be a rift between Saladin and his brother . . . I was testing, probing, that is all. If he had jumped at the bait . . . But he said he must clear it with his brother. So perhaps it is only a rumor, after all."

Joanna looked pensive. "Did you say he thought me beautiful?"

"Oh, yes . . . he was enchanted!"

"Perhaps . . ." Joanna was shy, for once. "Perhaps you might ask him if he would become a Christian."

"I will," said Richard gravely, too gravely. "A good idea."

But he exploded into laughter when we left her presence. "Oh, poor Joanna, she has been a widow for too long." After a bit, his laughter fading, he said, with a shrug, "Well, I could try it. We have nothing to lose by asking . . . and perhaps . . ."

But Safadin, with a flash of dark eyes, refused. "I live by my faith," he said, with a fine dignity.

"I respect that," said Richard equably. "And I, of course, by mine. But, by my faith, I like you, friend Safadin!"

"And I you," said the Muslim, smiling.

"Friend enemy," said Richard, solemn, holding out his hand.

Safadin took it. "May Allah grant us an honorable peace," he said, and made to take his leave. At the door he turned back. "A word of warning, friend enemy. Beware of Conrad—Conrad, the Knight of Montferrat."

"Ah, yes," answered Richard, nodding. "He holds aloof,

Conrad—and will give us no aid in this struggle. I sometimes wonder whose side he is on."

Safadin's face was hard, his eyes steady; he shook his head. "Not that alone. Friend, I tell you this in confidence . . . he is not to be trusted. Twice he has met with my brother, Saladin, behind your Christian backs. He has offered to break with you, to betray the Christian cause."

Richard's face grew red; his hand went to his sword, instinctively. "The whore-son!" he cried.

Safadin held up his hand. "Slowly, friend, slowly. My brother will not honor such an ally. A traitor once is always a traitor. If he will betray his own, how much easier to betray us, his avowed enemies? My brother knows this. Besides"—and here Safadin smiled—"Conrad asks too much. He wants the towns of Beyrout and Sidon in return. It is a high price to pay for one defector."

But when Richard reported these findings in council, the nobles were enraged, accusing Richard of collusion with the enemy. "We know of all your secret meetings with Safadin," they cried.

"Not secret," said Richard. "We have met openly; it is diplomacy. It is how you come to understand the enemy . . . to know his tactics. We are civilized men, though we worship different Gods."

But the muttering and distrust went on, though they must have known Richard was no traitor. "I will show them," he said grimly.

And the next day he rode out on a foray and came back with near a dozen Saracen heads hanging from his sword belt, grisly things. "They stink," he said, his face stiff with disgust. "But the council shall have them!" And every day he brought in more grim trophies, sometimes as many as twenty heads at a time. Then the council called him a savage.

"It seems I cannot win!" cried Richard, washing his bloody hands in his tent, and calling for wine. "These allies of mine will be my undoing."

He spoke lightly, but I could not help agreeing. They were all jealous of him, and resentful of the love the army felt for him. And for once I spoke out. "Go carefully, Richard," I said. "They want to discredit you."

He smiled and shrugged. "Good Alex," he said, with a hint of impatience, "good old Saracen . . . how can they? I have done nothing to be ashamed of—and will not."

"I only mean to warn you . . . think before you act."

But of course he did not—or not in the way I meant. A few days before we resumed our march, there came a strange messenger to his tent, a thin, wiry, dark fellow, turbaned in black, and naked except for a black loincloth into which was thrust a great curved knife with a silver hilt. Already a chill had been felt in the air, but the dark body gleamed with sweat, where he stood between two sentries. "A spy, Sire," said one. "He will not give his name."

"Shall we finish him off, Sire?" asked the other. "He looks an ugly customer."

The fellow's eyes rolled wildly in his head, and he struggled in their grasp, hoarse, guttural sounds coming from him.

"Wait," said Richard. "Speak, man!"

The sounds grew louder, but there were no words, just that choking noise, and the chin all slobbery with spittle.

"Loose him!" commanded Richard. "Now, man, speak!"

The fellow pointed, frantic, to his mouth, opening it, still making those dreadful sounds.

"I think that he has no tongue," said Richard. And he pointed to his own mouth in turn, opening it and showing his tongue.

The fellow nodded vigorously, his eyes alive, and began to fumble at his loincloth; the sentries drew their swords.

"Leave him alone!" said Richard. "I think he wants to show me something."

The thin hand came out with a roll of thick parchment, or so I thought; on closer inspection it proved to be some kind of uncured skin. Hairs clung still to one side of it; on the other was a strange writing, heavy and blackish-brown, smudged and dirty.

"It looks like dried blood," said Richard. "Wait, here is a signature. Alex, can you make it out?"

I peered close; it looked as if it had been drawn with a thick brush, and was very hard to read, but I said, finally, "I think . . . Rashid . . . ad-Din . . . Sinad," I said.

"The Old Man of the Mountain!" cried Richard softly. Everyone in the Eastern lands had heard of him, but no one had ever seen him. The fabled religious leader of a fanatic Muslim sect, the Old Man was Saladin's bitter enemy, and more feared than the Devil throughout the Islamic world.

I bent again to the piece of hide. "Look, Richard, it is

375

Latin!" The words were oddly formed and barely discernible where the ink—or whatever it was—had run, but after a moment I made out a little of the message. "He wants to meet with you, Richard . . . says it will be to your advantage. This man—" I nodded to the tongueless messenger. "He says this man will lead you to him and—" I looked up in wonder. "Dress warmly, it says."

Richard laughed; his eyes were as eager as a boy's. "Come then." And he snatched up a fur cloak.

"Richard, don't go! This is a madman! Everyone says so! Even the Saracens will not own him! He is a renegade, a wild, butchering hermit who lives up in the hills and sends out murderers to do his bidding! Oh, don't go!"

"What can happen?" cried Richard gaily. "I will take a dozen of my biggest Englishmen, fully armed . . . they will be match for any scurvy monks or holy men." Something in my face must have caught him, for he laughed again and said, "Oh, come now, Alex, you never used to be such an old woman! And I'll need you . . . bring your notebook." He turned to the messenger. "Can you lead me, then?"

The man nodded. Richard looked hard at him, then said, "See that he has food . . . he looks half dead. Wine, soup maybe, whatever he can manage. You, sirrah, go to my English knights and ask for volunteers. I'll need at least ten, ready in an hour. And now, arm me." He issued orders fast, right and left, without stopping, all the while rummaging in a coffer. "This, I think . . . and these pearls . . . and this dagger with the ruby set in." He had spread them out on the floor, sorting them. "Gifts . . . not too many, but the richest. There, that will do. Wrap them up."

We left camp openly, on horseback, and armed, the tongueless fellow in the lead, taking the road toward the east. A few heads poked out of tents, and then were withdrawn. All knew of Richard's constant forays; this seemed only another such adventure.

After we had ridden for about an hour, with three turnings, and the road now not much wider than a footpath, we came to a thick growth of forest, tangled bushes and creepers hanging down from them, and no path at all. From out the wilderness of foliage stepped about a half-dozen men, naked like the first messenger. Silently they took our bridles, motioning us down from our mounts and making signs that we should follow on foot. I suppose they were all, like the first, dumb. "It's all right, lads," said Richard. "I'll go first."

There was no path, but some kind of track was there, through the woods, known to these men, for they pushed aside the hanging branches, turning this way and that, and led us on. We began to climb; the trees grew sparse; and in a few moments we saw bare rock beneath our feet. It was hard going, our feet slipping and sliding on the loose stones. I don't know when it was I realized how silent it was; nothing sounded in that fastness except our panting and the rasp of our feet upon the rock. I looked up, but I could not see the top of the mountain, just a long stretch, bare and gray, covered with jutting rocks, and steep; high above, in the sky, some birds sailed on wide wings.

We toiled on, upward, stumbling, grazing our hands against the rocks as we felt for holds. I don't think I could have gone much farther; my breath was rattling in my chest, and my legs ached. But then, suddenly, we came to the end of the climb and out onto a level plain, as flat and open as a city square. And, fanning inward toward the far side, were shining walkways of marble, leading to a sort of temple or mosque, set among dark swaying palms, a miracle of the builder's art, here at the top of nowhere.

Terraced gardens blazed with color below the building, which seemed to hang in the air, so high were we, so close to the clouds. It had a strange beauty, as so many of these Eastern palaces have, long and low, columned in golden marble, with those onion-shaped domes topping it. Our naked, silent escorts beckoned us on; the knights' mailed boots rang against the shallow stairs, and the wind made soft music through the palms.

We were led into a great hall, open on all sides; it felt like the top of the world. A dais stood at one end, upon which a figure sat cross-legged, muffled in rich robes. We passed between rows of naked backs, prostrate, with their heads touching the floor; then our guides motioned us to stop. It seemed, suddenly, that the wind stopped too; there was a great, thick silence. I stared at the figure on the dais and a chill ran through me. I got the impression of eyes—just eyes, black as coal, stabbing. He snapped his fingers; a curtain rustled, and another figure appeared beside him, but I did not look, held by those eyes.

"Hail, O Rashid," I heard Richard say, in Latin. The eyes

shifted to him, and I looked at the face, dark, bearded, still, under those blazing eyes. I could not tell whether he was old or young, for he was covered in rich robes, and turbaned and bejeweled as well. His beard was a silvered black, like another jewel. He made no denial, so I guessed he must be the Old Man of the Mountain. The eyes did not leave Richard's face as Richard greeted him with courtesy, and asked why he had been brought there.

The Old Man spoke then, in a voice oddly thin, with a wheeze in it, and in a dialect of Arabic I had never heard. The hidden figure beside him interpreted in flawless Latin, a voice low, pleasant, sweetly modulated, unmistakably a woman's.

She wore a shapeless black garment like a shroud, which covered her completely, leaving only an oblong slit for the eyes; I caught a glimpse of them, long, gleaming like jet, rimmed with kohl. It was the dress of the Bedouin women of the desert; now and then one saw them, in pairs, in the markets of the native quarter, or behind the curtains of a litter, passing in swift silence on the road.

She replied, saying that the Master wished to pay his respects to the greatest knight of the Christian world, and to offer his services.

"What services?" asked Richard sharply.

"What do you need?" the interpreter countered, a beat behind the Arabic.

"Jerusalem," answered Richard quickly, with a smile in his voice.

"It is not mine to give," said the Old Man, "as you must know. There are obstacles."

"Many," said Richard.

"But there I can help you. I have the means to remove obstacles . . . if they are human."

"How?" said Richard bluntly.

"Observe." And the Old Man clapped his hands, once, twice.

We heard a stir somewhere behind us, and two of the naked mutes appeared below the Old Man's feet. He held up his hand; they fell to the floor, foreheads touching it, in obeisance.

"Observe, O King, our situation upon this mountain," the Old Man went on. "On three sides it slopes downward. But on the fourth, behind me, there is a chasm, the bottom lost in fathomless deeps." The shrouded figure moved forward, beckoning. "Please look."

Beside Richard, I stared downward where the ground fell away sheer; the building rose from it as part of the rock. Below, there was nothing, just black depths, though I thought I saw the gleam of water, far below.

"Observe," said the Old Man when the interpreter had led us back to our places. He clapped again; the prostrate men rose, staring straight ahead, like sleepwalkers. Suddenly he barked a command, Arabic. Upon the instant the two mutes ran past him and jumped off the cliff into the chasm; there was a strangled, wordless cry, and then silence.

"My servants, as you see, do my bidding."

"But they are dead," said Richard.

The Old Man's eyes flashed. He clapped again. Two more ran to their deaths. And yet again, and again, all in silence.

"Are you convinced?" he asked.

"Well," said Richard gravely. "I might say no . . . and let you strip yourself of servants."

"Never. They are as flies. But"—and the voice of the woman sharpened as she repeated the words—"I may please to give another command—and they will tumble you over, O King!"

"You jest," said Richard easily. "It was not for this you brought me here, for who would carry the tale of your might?"

"True . . . I would make a bargain with you. So swift as they go to their deaths, so swift can they bring death at my bidding. For twenty thousand marks . . . the death of your enemy, O King!"

Richard laughed. "I have so many . . . Saladin?"

"I would take no money for that one. But he is too well guarded. Name another."

Richard paused, then said, "It is not the Christian way, Old Man."

The despot gave a short "Ha!" of derision, and the translator went on; following his words as before. "Bribery was not invented in the East, and the bishops of Rome are not innocents."

"Say then, Old Man, that it is not *my* way." Richard broke into a grin. "Besides, the price is too high."

"Ah . . . too high for the King of the French, with his tightened purse strings and his greed for English land? Or for the arrogant one who would be King in Jerusalem—for Conrad of Montferrat?"

Richard shook his head, smiling. "Not yet, Old Man. I do not fear them—yet. But thank you for your courtesy, and for the wonders you have shown me." And he bowed, low. Too low, there was mockery in it. But the Old Man seemed not to see it, though the black eyes still stared. He inclined his head. The interview was over.

"You may go now," said the interpreter.

Richard turned away, then, as with a sudden thought, turned back. "Old Man," he said, "may I compliment you on your interpreter? She has perfect Latin. Your daughter?"

There was a little short silence. Then the Old Man, incredibly, threw back his head and laughed, the evil eyes crinkling to slits.

The interpreter spoke, softly. "The master is a holy one ... a celibate."

"But you?"

"I serve him." The shrouded woman turned, disappearing again behind the curtain.

The Old Man's high laughter rang in our ears as we went down the mountain.

That night, beside a flickering fire, Richard spoke of our adventure, making much of the strangeness of those naked mutes who did the Old Man's bidding. "Did you see their eyes?" he asked. "Pinpoints they were, the pupils, and glazed over ... they must have been drugged."

One of the Colt knights spoke, nodding, his Eastern beard wagging up and down as he said the words, as if in emphasis. "Yes. Here in Outremer they are called Assassins ... eaters of hashish."

But Burgundy's eyes narrowed. "Why you?" he asked. "Why did he show you these things? And what did you answer when he offered to kill at your bidding?"

Richard looked at him in surprise. "I said it was not the Christian way ... not our way. What else?"

But Burgundy made no answer, and his face was dark and secret where the flames played upon it.

CHAPTER 17

THE WALLS OF Joppa were rebuilt; the army resumed its march. The heat had gone, and a chill wind blew. The sea had changed color; no longer blue, but a sick greenish-gray. It was the day before All Hallows' Eve; the men crossed themselves repeatedly as they went forward, huddled against the wind.

The next week, for the first time, we were no longer in sight of the sea; the great man-made hills—the "tells"—rose before us, grim and frightening in the twilight days of a bleak November. We fancied ranks of Saracens lurking behind each one; often they did. Many skirmishes were fought, our foot soldiers slipping in the thin mud, for a light mist of rain fell now almost continuously.

Castle after castle we rebuilt on the way, fort after fort; Saladin had destroyed them all. Our journey was slow, hampered by the constant halts. The rain, now turned to sleet, soaked us, soaked our provisions. Our clothes stank of mud and frozen sweat, our food was a sodden mass, unrecognizable.

Richard sent out foraging parties, but they were lucky if they brought back a basket of bread or a dozen eggs, and luckier still if they avoided Saladin's patrols. More often than not, they were caught and cornered, Richard then sallying forth to the rescue, always first, raising his battle-axe high. How often I saw it from the ranks, the huge figure in its red and gold, mail black and glistening in the wet, riding into a cloud of striving warriors, the great axe coming down again and again, the long sword whirling through the air, cutting a space around him, the infidels falling back before him, confused and scattering, turning suddenly and spurring away. Then Richard riding back, laughing, exultant, at the head of his knights, those Turks' heads bobbing bloodily at his saddle. And the young knights looked at him with love that was close to worship, the archers and foot soldiers, too, gazing at him as if he were an angel of God, marveling that he rode with them, set to building fires with them, roasting meat alongside them, always with a song or a jest. Who would not love him? Who would not follow such a leader?

But low in the gathering dusk, I heard Norman voices too, thin with malice, shrill with spite. "The hypocrite! The devil! Putting on a show for routier filth!" And I saw through the silver sheeting rain the colors of Burgundy limp upon the horses, and heard the Duke's answer, low, "Let it go . . . he has the commons' ear." And again those other voices, "Saladin's ear too . . . and the Old Man's." "Hush," said the Duke. "Let it go for now."

At Ramlah we were forced to make camp for three weeks while the winter rains beat down, unceasingly. Many were short of clothing and shook with the ague; many fell ill. It was hard to say which was worse, the terrible heat we had endured in the summer, or these pitiless icy rains of winter. It was an accursed land, holy or not.

We pressed on to the next town, Toron of the Knights, left in rubble by Saladin's fleeing army. By day we toiled in the driving rain to build up the walls; and at night white frost covered our tents and the provision lean-tos, and the cold wind turned it to ice.

At last word came that Saladin had disbanded his army for the winter, leaving only small garrisons to man his holdings outside Jerusalem. Richard decided to move on to Beit Nuba, only twelve miles from the holy city; here we spent Christmas, rejoicing that God had brought us so near.

It was Christmas—a day of joy, a day for repenting, for forgiving. Yet it was dark outside, even at noontime, the hills hemmed us in, the wild wind blew out torches and candles. But candles and torches were lit again, their flames reflected in the tears of all; from King Richard down to the lowest baggage carrier, there was no man whose eyes were dry, no man who did not rejoice in Christ Jesus on His birthday. "He suffered for us . . . He that is so much greater than us all!" they cried. "Great is His mercy!" And they fell upon their knees in the improvised chapel and wept again. "Gladly will we die for Thee, O Merciful Lord Our God." Not a man among them who regretted joining the holy Crusade, not a one who regretted his fallen comrades, his lost family, his broken health; it was worth it, to free the Lord's land from bondage.

But there were others who did not see it so, those who

knew the country, who knew the weights that filled the scales: those Templars, those Hospitalers, those holy knights who had spent their lives here in this land. "Jerusalem the Golden," they said sadly. "It is but a dream, a mirage. Better men than these," they said to Richard, "have gone down to darkness in the fight to save it. Look clearly, King. If you lay siege to that city, you will most certainly be caught between the garrison and a relieving army. You are far from the sea ... how escape from that trap?"

"I think it is ripe now for the taking," said Richard. "Saladin's troops are dispersed, only a half remain there in the city, if that. They will not be expecting us ... it is winter for them as well as for us, remember? Armies go home in the cold months ... they will be grumbling, those that are left. Morale is low. I think we could take it—if we strike now!"

An old Hospitaler, his face seamed with a score of scars, shook his head. "Friend, you take the city, yes? What then? The pilgrimage is over ... the great adventure finished ... all vows fulfilled. No one has promised God to stay here and settle. No one will remain to defend it. Will you? Your nobles? The French have already gone home, and the Austrians. It will be only a matter of time before it is retaken. We are too few, those of us who are native here. The coastal cities, yes—we can hold them if they are fortified. We can win much ... but not Jerusalem. Not to have and to hold. Face the reality, for this is it."

"We will have to take a vote in the council," said Richard heavily.

The vote was taken, and the decision went against him; he was forced to give the order to retreat. It was a bitter blow. For the first time in Richard's life, he stood before his soldiers and was not cheered; many fell upon their knees and sobbed aloud, and there were jeers and catcalls from the Burgundians. Richard stood before them, straight and tall; he held up his hand. "Trust me," he said. "When have I played you false? Trust me! We have won much ... we will yet win all. Trust me! Trust God!" And he knelt before them, his head bowed, his red hair hanging before his face.

For a long moment there was silence. Then came a hoarse, ragged cry, "Richard! God and Richard!" The host took it up, more sob than war cry. "God and Richard! God and Richard!" And then, from the ranks of the loyal English,

"We follow the Lionheart!" It swelled into a roar that reverberated in the icy air, even seeming to stir the limp banners at the side of the kneeling King.

But afterward, in his tent, Richard said bitterly, "And now I, the conqueror of Cyprus and of Acre, the victor of Arsuf, am the general who turned back at the gates of Jerusalem."

CHAPTER 18

EASTER AT ASCALON, the great port city won from the infidel, now rising from its ashes. For more than two months our armies had toiled here, in the rain and the snow, buffeted by the icy winds from the sea. Toiled to raise the walls again, to rebuild the marble temples and mosques, to lay the paving stones of the streets. Was it for this they had come to the Holy Land, warriors all? But Richard had commanded it, and they obeyed, these few English and Normans. The French and Burgundians had fled to Acre, to Joppa, to Tyre; it was a much diminished army that had followed Richard here on January 22, and it had been nothing but hard labor, sickness, and cold ever since. No help came from Conrad of Montferrat, nor ever had, and now Hugh of Burgundy had joined forces with him.

Acre was in chaos. Those two, Conrad and Hugh, had tried to seize the city; a few loyal Pisans had beaten them off for three days, till Richard arrived, whereupon the traitors fled by sea, beating a hasty retreat to Tyre.

Easter at Ascalon, and Richard returning after a brief visit to Acre with more men, fresh from their long rest, now sorely needed to swell the dwindled ranks. He brought, too, many minstrels and jongleurs to celebrate the Eastertide; among them was Blondelza, with all her troupe, gay in their motley. Richard looked happy, the lines of care all smoothed away. I could not grudge him this, though I felt pity for the little Berengaria, left idling at Joanna's side in Joppa.

There was great merriment at Eastertime, for it was long since that the men had been treated to such entertainment. Minstrels played all day long, acrobats and jugglers livened every corner, the jongleurs sang new songs of the Crusade. There was one about Saladin, a scurrilous thing but full of wit, that caught on; we heard it all that spring on the soldiers' lips. Blondelza sang; a love song it was, with many stanzas, and very sad, all about the girl left at home and a flower, cherished for years because her Crusader had given it to her the day he left, and now all faded and dry. Many wept, great tears dropping down into their wine, for there was hardly a man among them that had not left a loved one behind, a wife or sweetheart.

"A pretty song, my sweet," said Richard softly in her ear. "But very melancholy."

"But a nice melancholy," she answered. "Better than that they should fear they've been forgotten. Now they can picture her waiting still, faithful still."

"I wonder how many of them are?" said Richard, smiling.

"More than you think, milord. Women are made that way."

"Some women," he said, his eyes searching her face.

"I," she said, softly, "have waited these long cold months, waited with doors barred against rioting . . ." She was still for a moment, twisting her hands together in a gesture unlike hers. "Waited, too, and saw you ride in . . . and ride out again to Joppa, with the queens. Without a word, without a glance upward at the window where I sat."

Richard, miserable as a callow boy, and flushing to his brows, bent his head and mumbled, "Forgive . . . it was a vow—a vow to God, made when I took her to wife. I must . . ." His voice was so low it was less than a whisper on the air; yet I heard, and so did she. "I must make an heir for England."

Her back straightened; her voice was cool and clear. "And did you?"

He stared at her for a bit, as cool as she. Then he grinned suddenly, a schoolboy's grin, full of mischief. "It was not for want of trying."

A light leaped in her stern eyes; her face collapsed suddenly and she fell against him weakly, laughing and crying at once. "Oh, Richard, I ought to beat you to a pulp!" she sobbed, and pummeled his chest with her fists.

"I wish that you could," he said, clasping her to him. "For I deserve it." He held her for a long while, stroking her hair, kissing her long fingers. Then a thin smile curved his lips. "And yet . . . it was not so hard a task."

She sat up, drawing away, not smiling. "I know. Such tasks are seldom difficult."

"Not difficult, no," he said softly. "Not difficult—but different. Different from us. From the way we are together."

"I know," she said. "It has always been so with me, as well. Never the same with others. Pleasant, but not the same."

The flush was back in his cheeks, but darker now, and I saw that small dangerous pulse at his jaw. His knuckles whitened on her arm, where he held her. "I could beat *you*, you know."

"To a true pulp, I know," she answered. "You are the Lionheart." And she smiled. "But I am not afraid."

And they two laughed again, like tavern roisterers, like comrades in arms, clutching each other and rolling about on the couch. I could not fathom these lovers, and kept my head low for shame. The noises from the couch were changing now; even I, a monk, could recognize the intimacy that colored the lowered voices, that slowed the wanton limbs. I shuffled my papers together, gathering them up; I was on the point of making a run for the door, when a loud knock sounded. With my heart leaping a welcome, I opened it a crack. An orderly stood there, a young squire barely out of his teens, looking important, and a little frightened. "A letter for King Richard," he said, holding it out.

"I'll take it," said Richard, smoothing the folds of his robe as he rose. "Tell the boy to wait."

The scroll was wrapped in several layers of heavy cloth and tied with twine. Richard cursed softly as he picked at the knot, snapping it finally with his teeth. More wrapping, fine linen this time, and then the letter; I saw a red seal, and a ribbon dangling from it, blue and gold. Richard scanned it quickly, frowning as he read. "Sweet Jesus," he cried softly. "You, boy." He snapped his fingers at the squire, who stood miserably, shifting from one foot to the other, a nameless fear showing in his young face. "Where did you get this?"

"Sire," he said shakily, wetting his lips. "A messenger, just now—just come into the camp."

"Fetch him," said Richard. Then, catching sight of the boy's state, he flashed his dazzling smile. "And stop shaking . . . we do not murder the bringers of evil tidings. Just ask him to attend me here. Go now." The squire fled, tremulous with the excitement of being spoken to and smiled upon by a creature so far above him, by the magnificent King; we heard him stumble on the stairs.

"God's eyes!" cried Richard, studying the script again. "John—and Philip! God rot them both! John is up to his tricks in England again, and Philip, that whore-son villain, has broken his oath—he is threatening the borders of Normandy!" He began pacing the floor and tearing at his hair. "I must go home! I must go as soon possible! God! How many weeks has this"—and he tapped the letter he held—"been on the road here? Six? Eight? The situation may have worsened by now. God, what shall I do? I cannot leave this land without a leader—without some semblance of accord. They will never listen to Guy—they never have. And Conrad will not cooperate with him . . . they have always been enemies. We stand to lose all, divided in this way. Outremer must have a king!" He sank down upon a stool, his head in his hands. "I have always backed Guy—he is my vassal, his rights are my affair, but—"

At this point the little squire appeared, followed by the messenger from Europe. This was a knight who had been wounded at Acre and sent home, a certain Sir Anthony. Richard sprang up and embraced him, "God, man, are you not endangering your health by this kind of thing? There must have been another to take this letter."

Sir Anthony waved his hand wearily. "I am tired, that is all—my arm healed long ago. And Queen Eleanor trusts me."

"So it is from her, the letter! I thought I recognized the phrasing, but it is not in her hand, and not signed."

"She thought it better so." The knight's face, already gray from exhaustion, went paler still. "Sire, it is most grave. Prince John is trying whatever means he may to make himself King . . . taking power from the loyal nobles, discrediting your chancellor, gathering troops. He is busy making a pact with Philip of France, who is pounding at Normandy's borders already. They say John will marry Alys, in return for French recognition as King."

"That old story! Poor little fool . . . what a life she has had!" He eyed Sir Anthony shrewdly. "And Philip will get back the Vexin lands, is that the way of it? Of course . . . he cared nothing for his sister's honor. I think, in any case, he never laid eyes on her . . . Oh, what a mess!" He peered more closely at the knight. "You look as though you are holding something back. Come, what is it? Can there be worse news?"

"Sire, Geoffrey Plantagenet is in it too . . . I know not how. But he has been the go-between, at least."

Richard's face lengthened; the eyes were sad. "Geoffrey . . . He was good to me, when I was young . . . I thought he loved me well. And I did Father's will—I made him Archbishop of York, the highest office."

"He craves more worldly things, Sire."

A little smile flitted over Richard's face. "Yes. Mother did not trust him . . . she reminded me that William the Conqueror was himself a bastard."

It was indeed grave news. Wasting no time, Richard called a meeting of the council of Nobles, telling them of the dangers to his realm.

"If I should be obliged to depart from this land," he said, "I will leave three hundred knights and two thousand men at arms to serve here at my expense." He then turned to his barons and asked them to decide whether they would go or stay. "For I will put no constraint upon any man." The barons then asked to speak together without him, and he left the council room.

When the council called him in, after deliberating, they said that each and every one of them would leave the land unless he appointed a leader to rule in his stead. "The King of Jerusalem, you mean," said Richard. "Unfortunately, there are two claims to the throne, and I cannot decide that alone . . . you must vote on it."

Without leaving the room, they all spoke up loudly for Conrad. Richard was taken aback by their vehemence, for many of these same lords had been bitterly opposed to Conrad's abduction of his young queen, and of all his autocratic ways, and had fought against him, too, at Acre. "You want this man to rule here?" he asked. "Can you be sure? He has sown dissension among you, and conspired with Saladin."

"Sire," said the Earl of Leicester, "I detest Conrad—but he is a soldier. Guy—" And he shrugged eloquently. "Guy is a good enough monarch, if you are here to enforce him—but he is no leader of men. And the local baronage will follow no one but Conrad. Also, he has the confidence, it seems, of the French and the Burgundians." A wry smile twisted his thin lips. "And he has married the heiress of the ruling house, and has got a child on her—no matter how it was done, it was done. He has the only claim now."

So a delegation, headed by young Henry, Count of Champagne, was sent to bring the news to Conrad at Tyre. But three days later Henry sailed back into harbor, with a black flag at the mast of his galley. He came ashore in a small boat, and leapt out to walk the last few yards through the water, standing before Richard dripping and hung with seaweed. "Sire," he cried, falling upon his knees, "Conrad is dead! Murdered!"

The news was like a thunderbolt out of the blue. Conrad was indeed dead, killed by stab wounds in the street as he walked to his home unattended. He was stabbed repeatedly, the body left in a pool of blood. Those who did the deed were captured, naked brown men, tongueless, followers of the Old Man of the Mountain, Rashid ad-Din Sinan. There was nothing to be got from them by torture, since they could not speak, so they were put to death with the murder unsolved.

Most folk believed that Saladin had bribed the Old Man, some saying that Richard was a target too. "Oh, Sire, walk carefully!" cried his loyal knights, fearful of the same treachery.

But there were whispers, too, that Richard was implicated, for did he not pay a visit to that same Old Man? It became new food for his enemies' bad thoughts, and there were many fights over it, and many heated arguments within the Christian camp.

The "Colt" knights of Outremer insisted the Old Man had done it on his own, for, they said, he had always hated Conrad, as an oppressor of his people.

One thing was certain, the mystery was never solved, then or later.

Conrad's death made chaos in the land. The Duke of Burgundy tried to seize Acre, but the widow, Isabella, shut herself up in the fortress and refused to hand over the keys, except to Richard or to the new King of Jersusalem. But who might that be? Would Guy now make a bid for the throne? What about her husband, Humphrey of Toron, from whom she had been abducted by Conrad? Did their marriage now stand? (There were some rumors that hinted that he planned the assassination.) All was confusion.

Richard took matters in his own hands, as he usually did. He knew well by now that no one would accept Guy as king;

his next candidate was Henry, Count of Champagne. "You must marry the lady yourself," said Richard. "And speed is essential."

"But is it legal?"

Richard smiled grimly. "We'll worry about that later." And so, to the amazement of the whole host and the land of Outremer, on May 5, after a week of widowhood, Isabella married Henry. At twenty-one, she had been three times a bride.

The marriage was celebrated with gorgeous splendor in the cathedral of Tyre. Henry, a fine, fair youth, looked neither happy nor sad. He accepted the crown that had been thrust upon him without joy or fear; it was all too quick, poor lad. He stood by the side of his new bride, his face flushed and solemn. Isabella was beautiful, pale and almost staggering under the weight of her jewels and her embroidered robes; pearls covered her arms and neck, her breasts, her head, her veil. She was four months pregnant, but no one mentioned it. Jerusalem must have a king, and the king must have a queen; did it matter if there was no love lost between them, strangers that they were?

After the wedding, with all speed, Richard rode out with his forces to Darum, ordering an attack on that coastal town, and summoning the new ruler, Henry, and the Duke of Burgundy, now docile again without Conrad, to his aid. He wanted to take as many of the coastal towns as he could, before he had to leave for his own domains.

After five days of fierce fighting, Richard took the town; the new King and the Duke of Burgundy did not arrive until a day after. However, Richard, elated that he now had cooperation again among the Christian leaders, handed the town over to Henry. "It is yours," he said. "A wedding present. Rule it well! I wonder . . ." he said, in his newfound optimism, "I wonder if this time we might try once more for Jerusalem—now that we are in accord, and there is no ice and rain, but only fine weather."

But lo, another messenger came, one John of Alençon, this time from Aquitaine; now Philip had sent routiers into the borders of Richard's own duchy! Also, the news had worsened in Normandy; John and Philip were thick as thieves, and, like thieves, were plundering Maine, Anjou, and all of England's holdings on the Continent. So far, Mercadier had held Poitiers, but he was sadly outnumbered, and begged for more money to hire other fighters.

"What to do . . . what to do!" cried Richard. "Jerusalem is at hand again—but the Angevin empire is at stake."

The council, now that everything looked easier and winter had passed, reversed itself and insisted that, whatever Richard did, they would go on to storm Jerusalem. Somehow the word got out to the pilgrims of lower rank, who had never understood why he had not attacked the holy city before; there was great rejoicing and dancing in the streets until well after midnight.

But Richard sat alone in his tent, pondering the problem, for he knew well the risks involved. Still, the next morning he gave orders to push on.

Five days later we reached Beit Nuba, without having seen any Turks on the way; it looked like a good sign. "We will wait here for Henry," he said. For he had sent the young King to Acre for reinforcements.

Days went by while we waited; the men, once so fervent, became listless and impatient; they felt nothing could stop them, if only Richard would lead them up to the gates of Jerusalem.

"We must wait," said Richard, weary of explaining. "Saladin has mustered all his forces at Jerusalem. We cannot do less . . . we cannot go against him with so few."

At last Henry came, with a huge force of men. We rejoiced and gave thanks. But, alas, how cruelly were we deceived! For, as we marched, so many thousands strong, so many thousand parched throats, we found that well after well, watering place after watering place, had been poisoned. Horses and mules, led to drink, dropped in their tracks, mouths frothing, legs convulsing, struggling, and stiffening, finally, in death.

The wells showed yellow and brackish, bubbling as with some devilish brew. Richard gave orders that no one should go near them. But, after long hours of unbearable dust and dryness on the march, two men, driven mad by thirst, broke out of line and threw themselves down at the water of Wadi el Dassi, plunging in their faces and gulping it up like cattle. Upon the instant, before our eyes, they turned black, went into violent convulsions, and died.

Richard gave the order to retreat, back to Beit Nuba.

From Wadi el Dassi he sent scouts ahead to see if Saladin had poisoned every well.

The news was bad; there was no unpoisoned water from Beit Nuba to Jerusalem. Not one well; not one sweet spring; not a trickle. There was no way to carry enough water to survive in a waterless region in midsummer.

Richard wept. "God has shown us the face of death," he said. "I will not lead my army into a trap."

He called the council and announced this decision, citing the poisoned wells, but as usually happened, he had thought of another tactic. "Let us march to Egypt," he said, "and attack at the Nile Delta. Our great fleet is already assembled; we can transport all our arms and supplies, with no fear of privation. I myself will send seven hundred knights and two thousand men-at-arms, paid out of my own pocket. What say you?" I think this idea had been in his mind for months. Egypt was the Saracens' great supply source; if it were cut off, Jerusalem would fall like a ripe plum into our laps.

The great majority of the council now were Templars, Hospitalers, and the native knights of Outremer; they voted immediately for this plan, understanding the strategy. But Hugh of Burgundy refused to join in, and the French contingent voted with him. "Jerusalem or nothing!" he cried, and they took up the cry.

Richard, angry and bewildered at this evidence of bad faith, shed tears of frustration, but they would not be moved. "Well, I will go, if you insist, to Jerusalem—but I cannot lead the host. I know it is useless and that many lives will be lost . . . I will not take this upon me."

They could not insist, of course. The Crusaders were hopelessly split, and neither venture was feasible without the entire army.

In misery, Richard gave the order to turn back to the coast. "I have risked all to stay here, giving my word before God," he said. "Now Jerusalem is beyond us, and Egypt too. And perhaps, for all I know, I have lost the Angevin empire as well."

On the march back to the city of Darum, we went another way, to avoid the poisoned watering places; it led us through the foothills, winding north. A longer way, and roundabout, but most beautiful, now, in the green glory of the summer; every turn opened a vista more magnificent than the last. So full of wonders was this hilly path that all my sadness fell away, and my heart lifted at the glorious works of the Lord.

It was Richard's habit to ride back and forth along the marching men, tightening the line, giving a word of cheer, or starting up a marching song. Though his spirits were low, he did not change this habit, but wore a vital, laughing face, and sat straight in the saddle before his men. He had just passed me, riding, when we rounded a wooded bend in the road. There was a rise here, and our tired mounts snorted and hung back, for the march had been long and it was now nearing sunset. Above the rise, the slim poplars stood like sentinels against a rosy-golden sky. I heard the knight in front of me catch his breath, almost in a sob; it was the Earl of Leicester, as I remember. Then my steed climbed up beside him, and I saw what he saw.

Here, upon the crest, the hill fell away before us, and a great valley lay, green and golden, as far as the eye could see. At its farthest part, almost lost in the gold mist of sunset, rose a distant city, golden too, its spires and turrets glowing, burning, against the setting sun. So beautiful a sight I have never seen, before or since; a city of Heaven, it was. Beside me, Leicester whispered, "Jerusalem . . ."

We stayed there, filling our eyes, filling our hearts, for a long moment. Then the Earl turned in the saddle, calling out, "Sire! Oh, Sire, look!"

Richard heard, and we felt his horse's hooves pounding the earth as he rode up behind us, his eyes questioning.

"Sire, look! Before you—there, over the hill . . . Look, it is Jerusalem!"

Richard's eyes saw, I know, for I could not mistake the stricken leap in them. But he lifted his great shield before his face and cried out in pain. "Fair Lord," he wept, "I pray you . . . do not ask me to look upon your holy city—since I cannot deliver it from your enemies."

CHAPTER 19

WAR WAS OVER, or nearly. Men rejoiced, though the peace had not yet been signed. All were weary, sick of battles. Still, there was one more battle yet to come, a battle beside which all other battles paled, a war won single-handed, or so it seemed. Those men in the Holy Land who saw it, who wielded sword or spear, who fell wounded in the fray—never will they forget it, never forget Richard of England that day. Scribes have written of it, and minstrels sing of it still. Bohadin, Saladin's poet, and Ambroise, our own, told the tale, more eloquent than I; yet I shall try.

Joppa was besieged, and swarming with Turks who sought to breach the walls; Turkish banners streamed along all the sea strand, and Turkish arrows flew thick as black flies, darkening the air. For few were the defenders within, and help had not yet come. Henry had not arrived by land with his host, nor Richard by sea. The helpless folk inside the walls wailed and prayed, for none believed the city could hold.

Joppa was thought to be safe, as safe as Acre; I had been sent there to join the two queens, along with most of the noncombatants, among them all the musicians and jongleurs, while Richard negotiated for peace. If it had not been for the perfidy of those Turks who attacked the city, Berengaria would never have laid eyes on the glee-maiden, but, in the circumstances, we were all crowded into the fortified tower, waiting to be rescued, or to die.

Blondelza, fierce as a warrior, distributed knives from the kitchen among all those gentle ladies. "Aim for the throat," she said, "or the soft part of the belly, beneath the mail shirt."

Berengaria gave a weak cry, like the cry of a bird. "Oh, I couldn't."

"Nonsense!" cried Joanna, taking the longest knife. "It is better than rape!" She looked at Blondelza, a measuring look, and said, "Thank God someone thought of the kitchen . . . we have no weapons here!"

"I think it will not come to that," said Blondelza, for the little Queen looked as though she might drop any moment. "The King will surely come . . . he is long overdue. The winds have been against him, but now they have changed. See." And she pointed to the window, where the curtains blew inward from the sea.

The din outside was hideous; shrieks and moans, clanging of arms, war cries, and a kind of awful, steady beat of some kind of drum, hollow and hoarse, as from the depths of Hell. "That will be the Mamelukes," said Blondelza. "It is their music."

One of the things we always forgot was that the Muslims were made up of as many races as we Franks ourselves—many languages, many sorts of men, in all colors and hues, from purplish-black to a strange milky fair, the Circassians. The Mamelukes were tall, proud, black-skinned warriors, the bodyguards of the emirs. They disdained horses, and strode into battle, clad in feathers and armed with light spears; many of them carried the drums, small as cooking pots, which they beat curiously with their knuckles and elbows, while their eyes rolled white in ecstasy. I had an unreasoning fear of them, as some folk have of snakes; under my breath I muttered a prayer that I would fall into any hands but theirs, if God willed that I should meet my death here, in His Holy Land.

I heard, beneath the clamor all about us, a small, soft cry. Berengaria. "Is it . . . ? Oh, yes! There! I see a sail!"

"Let me look," cried Joanna, crowding into the window. "Yes, it is the English banner! Richard!" And the poor fool began to shout toward the far-off galley, her hands cupped to her mouth. "Here, Richard! We are here—in the castle!"

"He will never hear," said Blondelza. "We must signal. Your skirt! Give me your skirt!" For she herself wore only her spare jongleur tunic and hose.

"Here, have mine!" said Berengaria, stepping out of it quickly.

"You are a good girl," said Blondelza. "Surely he can see this." And she began to wave it up and down outside the window.

Joanna, not to be outdone, pulled off her own red gown and waved it frantically, while Blondelza snatched up the silver cloth from the table. There they stood, three curiously meager creatures without their wide, spreading skirts, crowded into the window opening; the queens looked strangely indecent in their short shifts and huge-sleeved bliauts, their bare knees knobbly beneath. I pushed away the thought and leaned out the window alongside them.

The Turks below had seen us. Arrows shot upward, but fell short, harmlessly; the tower was very high. The din rose; they were trying to frighten us. Looking down, I saw that all the windows in the tower were filled with others like us, desperate prisoners, waving improvised banners toward the great royal galley. It had come in swiftly, but stopped now, about three hundred yards offshore; the swarms of people on its deck looked like ants, even the flags were tiny. I thought that the red figure clinging halfway up the mast might be Richard, but there was no telling at this distance.

"They don't see us!" wailed Joanna. "Richard will just let us die here!"

"It must look as though the whole place has been taken over by Turks," said Blondelza. "There must be a way up to the roof."

"There," said Joanna, pointing. "See—the trapdoor! And there's a ladder somewhere."

"Behind the arras," said Berengaria. "Remember? You stubbed your toe on it yesterday."

Blondelza was already staggering under the weight of the ladder. I ran to help her. In no time we were on the roof, jumping up and down, waving desperately.

Berengaria's dark head, uncovered in her disarray, showed above the trapdoor. "Could we light a fire perhaps? The smoke . . ."

"A good idea, if we had flint and tinder . . . though they might think the tower had been fired by the enemy." Blondelza stared at the sea. "It's no use," she said calmly. "They simply cannot see us." And she kicked off the pointed slippers she wore, and shrugged out of the tunic, standing in her thin shirt near the edge of the parapet. "Well, lend me your prayers, friends."

I caught her arm. "No! No, you cannot swim!"

She fought me off. "Let me go, Alex. It is shallow down there . . . and I have made higher jumps."

"No!" And I summoned strength from somewhere, I pulled her forcibly away from the edge, in my zeal throwing her to the ground. "Forgive me," I heard myself say, "but this is man's work." And, so saying, I hiked up my cassock, twisting it through my rope belt, and kicked off my sandals. Holding my cross aloft, I ran, starting far back to give myself momentum, and leapt as far as I could, out and over the astonished Turks below us, my gray gown belling out like a tent and bearing me up.

I landed in the shallows, not feeling the great stone that crushed my foot, but treading swiftly out till I reached waist depth, and then swimming. The moment I hit the water, an arrow hissed next to my ear and splashed down, throwing up spume; the Turks were quick. I could not think of that, and blundered on, the hiss and thwang around and behind me, until, swimming, I felt the breath in me sear at my chest, like a raw, raking hand. I could go no farther; I lifted my head, treading water, taking great gulps of air. A glistening dark hull rose before me, I had nearly gone headfirst into it; a shoregoing skiff. I could hear Richard's voice, calling my name in wonder, but dimly, for water filled my ears. "My hand. Take my hand, Alex."

I reached up and felt the strong warm grasp and the pull that lifted me over the side. I was dazed, and wondered what I was doing there; I shook my head, cupping my hand to my ear as we used to do as boys in the River Thames. Suddenly a voice boomed at me, loud, hearty. "God, man, what are you doing?"

"The queens," I said, "and Blondelza . . . in the tower . . ." I gasped, my breath all squeezed out of me; it had been a labored, frantic scramble, that swim, what with the whizzing arrows and my monk's gown up around my ears and threatening to smother me in its folds.

"Alive? They are alive?" The King grabbed my shoulder, shaking me; it hurt so much I nearly cried out.

"The whole garrison is alive," I gasped. "Most of the town . . . immured in the churches and towers. The Turks have not gained entry—yet! Oh, go quickly, Richard! Save them!"

The boat had drifted or been rowed in closer to shore. I cannot remember much of who was in it, other than the King and myself. Richard, in a short, sleeveless mail coat, with bare head and legs and sandals on his feet, jumped in, the water just up to his chest, holding aloft a battle-axe in one hand and a sword in the other and crying, "To me, Christians! Follow me! God wills it!"

I know the boat rocked dizzingly three times as some knights jumped in after him, but I do not remember who. I got a glimpse of Richard striding onto the shore, both arms flailing about him like the arms of a windmill, and the gaudily dressed Saracens falling before him, going down under his blows, and turning—yes, turning to flee. By the time the other three knights had joined him, there was a clear space on the shore, empty, strewn with the fallen enemy.

I felt arms dragging at my armpits and lifting me; before I swooned away, I saw—dimly, yet I am sure I saw it— Richard's legs, running up the beach. I thought to myself, How stupid you are, Alex, he had boots, after all, long red boots, not sandals. Long red boots, to match his surcoat and his hair . . . It was my last thought for a long while; my foot had been thoroughly smashed, and though Iselin worked assiduously, he could not save it. No doctor can put together bone and pulp and mangled tissue; I was lucky, they said, to have the rest of my leg, from the ankle up. And I am lucky, too, that a clever bootmaker has made me a boot, with a lead foot inside it, cunningly contrived. I can almost, but not quite, disguise the limp, though when I am very tired, the foot is a heavy burden to drag about.

But I am ahead of my story, already back in the English countryside, in my home monastery. And the story must be finished.

This is how Ambroise told it:

Then did the King waste no time, but saying, Follow me, though it be our time to die! jumped straightaway into the boiling sea, his legs unarmed, and in his boating sandals— and swim and wade he did, and came apace to the dry ground, the first to land, as was ever his custom. And all the other knights leaped in after him, and went against the Turks with whom the shore was filled and attacked them. And the King slew many in his own person, with axe and with spear. And, when the lance splintered in the armor of a slain Turk, then did the King draw sword and swing it about, laying low a round dozen with the length of his arm. Oh, then did the hated foe flee before him, crying Malek-Rich is come upon us! They durst not face the great King and his knights, who smote them like folk gone mad, but ran away down the strand, howling of Malek-Rich.

And so did they clean the shore of Turks, and strowed their bodies high as a wall upon the shore. Then builded they a great bulwark and up it the King ran light foot and laughing, and calling to the besieged folk within. The bravest King in all the world entered first of all and gat him into the city where he laid about him with a merry will, till the streets ran ruby red with Infidel blood. And the folk within did arm themselves, taking heart, and issued forth to battle. And from the galleys, laggard, came the knights who followed, and between these and the knight of Champagne, who also arrived, did they clean the city of Joppa of its foe. And in less than one hour was this accomplished, to the great glory of God. But the great King tarried not inside the walls, but with only three knights did he pursue them and they fled before his fearful aspect. Nor ever, even at Roncesvalles, did any man, young or old, Saracen or Christian, acquit himself in such fashion as he. And over the bodies of his foe he sped, and routed them for two leagues, even drave them from the camp they held, whereupon he took that camp, and raised the banners of Christendom over it.

And when the news was brought to the great Saladin in his stronghold, he cried, Who pursueth you? Hath the whole host of the Christians come among you that hath drave you out? And they answered, Sire, it was the Lionheart. And that brave Sultan bowed his head in shame. But asked he then one more time. How many horse and horsemen hath the great King? And they answered, Sire, not one. For he hath been unhorsed and fought to the last on foot, though now he bides within our tents."

And the Sultan, thinking on it, bade them saddle the finest horse in the kingdom of Jerusalem and take it to the English King. For surely, said he, so great a King must not go without a mount to match him. Thus did all, even the enemy, bepraise the magnificent King our own, calling him the best knight of all that lived.

And thus, by Richard's prowess, did the war end, and the peace begin.

All the world knew Richard's valor; he is called the best knight in the world, and I think perhaps it is true. He was larger than other men, and stronger too, and without physical fear; he was always first in any fray, and the wild glory in his face terrified his foes so that they ran from him. They say that, even now, Turkish mothers frighten their children thus: "If you are not good, England will get you . . . Malek-Rich will get you!" And, shaking their fingers at a bad boy, they will say sternly, "Watch out, evil one, England is coming!"

And all those at Joppa, and at Acre, and at Arsuf, where his glory blazed so brightly, remember him still—how could they forget the god, the giant, the shining knight, the great red king! He is legend, already, like Arthur.

But I say—and I have said it always—that the greatness of Richard was within . . . in the heart that wept for his fallen comrades, and for the brave foe . . . in the head that planned the battles during all the long hours of night while the army slept.

The battle that Ambroise writes of, when the Franks held the routed enemy's camp, outside Acre, the battle where the infidel so outnumbered us that men wonder how the victory happened . . . I was there. I saw it, saw how it happened. It was no miracle, except the miracle of great generalship. Richard bade the foot soldiers dig trenches and stand firm, no matter how close the foe came, till the signal was given. Every second man had a crossbow, and—because they are devilish things to wind again, and a man could die ten times over in the time it takes—the man next to him was charged with winding it while the fellow fired the next one. And so it went, in continuous fire, a solid block of men who did not budge, but fired into the enemies' faces, blasting them over and over, till whole lines fell, and, finally, the rest broke and fled. And we lost none. Only horses. No one had thought of it before, in all the history of the crossbow, though it seems simple enough. But then genius is always simple, is it not? So I believe. And therein lay Richard's glory.

No, Richard did not win Jerusalem, and and it broke his heart. But he won much more—more than had ever been wrested from the infidel in all the years of Outremer.

On September 2, a truce was made with Saladin, a truce which was to last three years. The entire coast would remain in Christian hands, and Jerusalem, untouched by war or siege, would remain a holy city for both sides, free and open to any pilgrims, Christian or Muslim. From now on, it would be the Great Christian Pilgrimage, to see the Holy Sepulchre, to visit the places where Jesus lived and died.

All over Christendom, churches and cathedrals were thrown open, lit by thousands of candles, filled with the sweet music of choirs, fragrant with incense, to celebrate the great victory, so hard won, so precious. Many were the men, rich and poor, who would not be coming back, who lay in unmarked graves, moldering in the dry soil of the accursed Holy Land. Many were those sold into slavery, wretched, done to death, remembered only in the prayers of their loved ones. Many were those others, too—lost to God—who remained there, seduced by the Eastern riches, by the cushioned life of Islam. God forgive them!

Did I love Richard too well? But I cannot help it, we were so much more than blood brothers, our very stars were the same. I have tried to tell the tale truthfully, without bias. But that is not easy. For Richard stood head and shoulders above other men, even to me, who knew him so well.

And if I loved him too well, I am not alone. Every foot soldier, every petty knight, every half-grown squire, would have laid down his life for the Lionheart. Never was man so beloved, never so revered.

I was sent home, maimed as I was, by sea, while the Atlantic was still safe, before the winds of autumn. Richard did not leave until all the peace was concluded, late in the fall. And even then, he had to ask leave of the churchmen, to absolve him from his vow. For he had promised to stay till Easter. If he had stayed . . . But one cannot ever think of what might have happened, it is fruitless. One sees it all afterward.

Three weeks before Easter, Saladin, the great Sultan, our enemy, died. And Richard, by that time . . . Well, you will see.

BOOK VII

THE MAN

Told by Richard, King of England, called the Lionheart

CHAPTER 1

JERUSALEM WAS LOST. But the Holy Sepulchre was ours, free for Christian pilgrims and worshippers. We had gained Cyprus too, the gateway to the East, and all the coastal towns were ours; most of the Holy Land was now in Christian hands. We had gained more on this Crusade than had ever been won before. So, though I grieved that we had not taken all, I took heart. Now I had to get back to my domains in France and my English kingdom, for the peril to them was grave.

I could not set out till October; the truce with Saladin was still not truly settled, and then, also, I had to be absolved of my vow to stay till Easter. These things would take time.

I had to dispose of my women, too, sending my queen and Joanna with Zenobia to Brindisi, where they would surely be safe, until these ugly troubles were cleared up in my realm. They protested, of course, Joanna passionately. But I could not take them with me; it was bad enough to put Blondelza to such hazards as might await us on the road back. One can never order *her* anywhere, of course; she is her own mistress, as always. And then, I had promised her she could see her son again; I had wronged her deeply all those years ago, and truly repented of it. I had sent word ahead to Mercadier, in Aquitaine, that he should bring Philippe to meet us on our journey.

We made good time, homeward bound from Acre. On average the journey to Venice takes ninety days, and in winter even longer. But our ship, the *Franche-Nef*, was huge and seaworthy; in less than sixty days we were nearing Venice. But at every port the news was disquieting. Raymond of Toulouse had rebelled and was ravaging the Midi; any hope of returning overland through Provence had to be set aside. France too was closed to us; Philip had routiers guarding the ports. "Head for Marseilles," I told the captain. "Anchor offshore and wait. I have scouts all along the coast, perhaps they will have news."

We sat at anchor a day and a night before we saw anyone slip through the ships that guarded the port. But then it was better than news that came toward us in the little boat. I stood at the rail, Blondelza beside me, shielding my eyes from the sun, squinting to make out the figures that rode there, two at the oars and two passengers. Blondelza caught at my arm, her nails digging into it. "Can it be . . . ?"

"I think it is Mercadier. Yes!" I cried joyfully.

"And the other . . . ?" I felt her tremble beside me. "Oh, God. Is it my little one, my Philippe?"

As the boat drew near and the sailors let down the rope ladder, I saw that, truly, it must be the boy, though he had grown a full head or more, as they do at that age. He was first up the ladder, Mercadier steadying him from below, and, his face all alight, he threw himself into my arms.

"Oh, Father! Sire, it is I, your Philippe!" When I could extricate myself, and held him at arm's length, laughing, he cried, "Oh, Father, you are as black as a Moor!"

"So are we all," I said. "It is a fierce sun in Outremer, and has baked us for over a year." Then I gave him a little shake, smiling. "Where are your manners, sirrah? Here, beside me . . . here is your lady mother." He stood gaping, until I pushed him, annoyed. "Upon your knee, little churl. Have they taught you nothing there in Cognac?"

He dropped to one knee, but still stared gawpishly at her face. With a lovely, shy grace, Blondelza held out her hand. "Philippe, my dear one."

He had the sense then to take the hand and kiss it, but it was awkwardly done; I saw he needed some training. Though he had stared long enough at first, now he dropped his eyes, still holding her hand, and I saw the bright blood stain his fair skin. I held my tongue, remembering how fiercely I myself had blushed at that age.

"You don't remember me." Blondelza spoke softly; it was not a question.

The boy raised his eyes then; there was confusion in them, and a kind of defiance. "I . . ." He shook his head. "I thought . . . they said—you were beautiful."

Her face did not change, nor her voice. "So I was, I believe," she said evenly. "Once."

"And are still," I said, and took a step forward. He stood his ground, but in his eyes there was a kind of flinch, as though he feared a blow. And she too held out her hand as if to stop me. "I do not hit boys," I said curtly. "Even when they answer like villeins."

"Richard." Blondelza took my arm. "Richard, you do not see me with fresh eyes." She laughed then, a high, silver sound, that held neither rancor nor wildness. "Look again, my lord." And her sweet wide smile flashed in the sunburned leanness of her face. I turned then and saw that old cloak of my own, threadbare and with the squirrel fur of its trim flattened and wet, whitened by the salt spray, that she had pulled about her shoulders against the cold. Beneath it hung her motley player's gown, and beneath that the long points of her narrow slippers, hung with bells, that gave out a whispering tinkle in the wind. She had cut her hair straight off at the shoulders, as the pages wear it, to free it of the smell and the fierce lice, too, of the Holy Land; it lay limp and flattened, like the squirrel fur, with all the spring and life gone out of it, and I saw, too, that there were many silver hairs mingled in among the yellow-fair. Her face was thin and drawn, for we had all gone on short rations for more than a year, and her unpainted lips were chapped. Pity and love stirred in me, and my voice went harsh as I spoke to the boy.

"It is for Christ Jesus Our Lord that she suffered the burning sun and sand of His Holy Land, the bite of hunger, the fevers—"

Blondelza put her hand upon my arm, a firm but gentle touch. "Richard, he is only a boy, and spoke thoughtlessly." And again she laughed that sweet merry laugh, and said, "I swear I have not looked in a mirror in weeks, but tonight I will brave it. And I will hunt out women's gear, and paint, and wash my hair . . . and if you do not remember, my Philippe, at least I will not shame you."

"Oh, madame, I did not mean—"

"I know, little one."

Later, closeted alone with Mercadier to hear the reports he brought, I saw those curious blue eyes of his darken as he looked at me; he sighed heavily. "She looks exactly the same, your lady," he said. "Such a one does not change with clothes or paint, or even time." He did not take those blue eyes off me, but said, blunt as an old saw, "There is something wrong with the boy, Sire. They have done something to him there, in that castellany you sent him to. He is another boy now— all ups and downs, and sudden frights, and quick angers."

"It is a noble house, Cognac," I said. "Powerful too. He will be a great lord."

"Noble!" And he gave a cluck of his tongue, impatient. "I saw his back. All scarred it is, old scars—"

"They *beat* him?"

He nodded. "It was the old lord did it, the boy said. Old Hélie, that is half mad, with one foot in the grave. For spilling the wine, the boy said." And he gave a mirthless laugh. "Puts me in mind of my own early days and old Guilhelm, God rot him! They are mad dogs, those old lords . . . and the closer they get to the grave, the worse."

The anger in me was like a pain. "I can take him away from there, have the match annulled. They are still only children."

"No. He's fond of the little maid. Ally, he calls her. Wanted to bring her along."

"Alamanda," I said, remembering. "She was a winsome child."

"Lame, now," Mercadier said. "She is lame in one leg. The old lord again. Pushed her down the stairs or something. But, pretty still." He shook his head. "No, the boy would never hear of abandoning her . . . he is her knight."

"Then he's not a bad lad, after all."

"No, but there's been some damage . . . I'd keep him by me if I were you, Sire—till the old lord dies, can't be long now."

I was sick inside; it was another sin to atone for. I had never probed into the House of Cognac, just dumped the boy there in my zeal to get to the Holy Land.

Mercadier read my thoughts, I suppose, for he said, "There is no way you could have found out, Sire. These things happen. The boy's young still; he'll mend."

And that night, when Philippe saw his mother all bedecked and bedizened, with red lips and cheeks, the eyes made long with kohl, and her cut-off braids woven in with her short locks and studded with pearls, he fell to his knees, his face all shining, and said, "Oh, yes, I remember now . . . *Maman*, I remember! Except that your hair was loose, spread out on your shoulders, and you wore a blue gown."

"Not always, surely." And she smiled.

"No. At night, when you sang to me, and played the lute. It was some kind of loose, shiny gown, blue . . . with gold at the sleeves."

"My bedgown!" She turned to me. "Richard, do you remember it? It was a gift for my lying-in . . . lined with ermine it was. The moths got into it later, and I had to let it go. It was the most beautiful bedgown—fit for a queen."

And so she should have been, I thought, but said only, "Not good enough for you, the fairest . . . and the mother of my son."

The boy took up her lute then and was bending his head to it, bending delicately, and in that moment I saw her father, Blondel, in him, as he looked, listening inward to the tuning. A fleeting thing, and gone when he raised his head. "Listen, *Maman*. I hear it still, the song you sang to me before I slept . . . something about angels." And he played, softly, exquisitely, a song I had never heard, a lullaby, secret between those two. Blondelza hummed along with the lute, and then, very softly, came the words, "Close, oh close your shining eyes . . . Angels, angels tread the skies . . . Hear the music of the night . . . Angels, angels bathed in light." It was not much longer than that, a line or two, but lovely, and very sad, as such lovely things so often are.

There was quiet for a long moment, and she taking him in her arms, soft smiles upon both faces, looking alike. And then she took the lute, and played and sang, and I too, in my turn, and the boy, who played well, with the sure touch of one who has music inside, making me proud. We sang late into the night, like old times, Mercadier even lending his frog's croak to swell the merriment.

And afterward, in our cramped little seacot, Blondelza and I lay together in love, and were content. But music still wrapped us round with its wonder and glory; she picked up her lute. "Remember?" she asked softly, playing a measure. It was the song, the old song, private, known only to us, that we had made together years ago, in the first days of our love.

I took the lute from her and played too, the notes coming as from some enchanted place; I had not thought of it in years. "Have you ever played it with another?" I whispered.

She shook her head gravely. "It is too difficult," she said, with a wicked little smile.

I caught her in my arms, laughing. "Oh, you are a bad girl, a witch . . . and I love you for it!" For she was everything at once, my Blondelza—and she had wit too, a rare thing in a woman. But when I held her close, I felt the wet of tears upon her cheek, and felt them, too, behind my own eyes. Was it a premonition?

Before dawn, Mercadier tapped upon the door. "I must be off now," he said, "while I can slip through unseen."

"Friend," I said, "come inside a moment." Shutting the door behind him, I said, "I trust you to hold off Philip where you can. Have you forces enough?"

"Sancho of Navarre, your brother-in-law, is pledged to you. He will help."

"Thank God," I said. "For I must get home, to England, or to my Norman lands, or the Angevin empire is lost. The whole of Europe swarms with my enemies, it seems. I can get safe-conduct nowhere." But then I snapped my fingers. "Germany!" I said. "My brother-in-law's territories. Henry of Saxony . . . his lands will be open to me. It is just a matter of a few hazardous miles to get through."

"Austria," he said, his face somber.

"Leopold will be watching like a hawk," I said, smiling. "But I will slip through." I took up the map I had been studying. "Here, just this narrow corridor . . . and there—" I pointed. "There is Saxony, Henry and Mathilda's realm . . . not far to go. We will slip through, disguised. There are so few of us."

"The best way," said Mercadier. "You will get through . . . you are Richard," he said simply.

I laughed. "I am not colored like a fox for nothing." I clasped his hand. "Go now, friend. God be with you."

He left then, promising success against my French enemy. But he refused to take Philippe. "I got through with him once, but twice I will not hazard. He is your only son."

"Yes, he will be safer with me," I said, and then, with a smile, "and I am getting used to him."

And then, wakeful, watching for the dawn, the thought went through my head that I was happy, here and now . . . truly happy. We were a family, we three . . . though not the family that I had ever known, God knows!

The sun rose over the eastern rim of the sea, a perfect ball, like a child's toy. Blondelza's hand touched my shoulder lightly, and she sighed. "I could not sleep. Mercadier is gone?"

"Yes," I said. "He is needed back there, in the Midi."

We were silent for a moment, watching the pearly pink grow in the sky and the dark waters lighten to purple in the path of the rising sun. It was cool, the air fresh and sweet as wine.

She sighed again. "It is so beautiful, here upon the water . . . so beautiful."

I turned, catching her close, as a sudden thought struck me. "Why not?" I said. "Why not go back by sea? My galleys came to the Holy Land by way of the sea . . . so shall I return to England."

But the captain would not hear of it. "There are the Straits of Gibraltar," he cried, his eyes bulging from his head in fear. "Both sides are held by Muslim powers!"

"I have conquered Muslims before this," I said, reasonably.

"No! No, Sire!" he cried, his jowls shaking. "I cannot risk my ship!" He looked as if he might collapse any moment, turning red and purple, looking like my father long ago. Which thought saved me from doing the same thing myself; instead, I grew calmer, listening with a smile as he raved on. "And even"—his voice went up to a shriek—"even if we got through the Straits, winter is upon us! No ship ventures upon the Atlantic Sea in winter! No warship, no trader—none! Only the rash English—"

"But I *am* English," I said quietly.

"No! No, Sire! I cannot! Even if you kill me—I cannot do the impossible!"

"Good God, man," I answered. "I am no killer!" The idea struck a chill in me. Was this how the world perceived me?

I spoke again. "Stop your shaking, man. I cannot force you. It is you who are the master here, upon the sea. Put us into a port, and I will find another ship."

And he fell upon his knees, sobbing and kissing the hem of my cloak. "Oh, thank you, Sire! Thank you!"

This groveling upset me, and a worm of disgust wriggled within me. But I did not show it, and said only, "Get up, man. You are the master of a great ship. Behave so, and bring us to a port, losing no time. For I must get back to my domains."

CHAPTER 2

WE PUT IN at Corfu, where we disembarked; it seemed the mere idea of sailing upon a winter sea had unmanned the poor shipmaster, for there he stayed, and would not budge.

We hired a goodly boat there at Corfu, a made-over war galley, not very large compared to the great ship we had been sailing in, but still she seemed seaworthy enough. I had been informed that her captain and crew were pirates, and indeed they looked villainous enough for it, but they were happy to get the two hundred marks I offered in return for our passage.

We were a small party, a handful of knights, headed by Baldwin of Béthune and William L'Étang, four Templars, and a clerk, Philip of Poitiers, to take the place of Alexander, who had been wounded and sent home early. Not that any could replace him—but someone must keep accounts and records. Or so I thought. No doubt they still lie on the floor of the sea, and may be there, for all I know, till eternity.

For no sooner had we embarked, those I have mentioned, the crew of pirates, and Blondelza's little company of jongleurs, than we hit contrary winds and were becalmed. A day and a night we lay, just offshore and almost in sight of it. The morning after, dawn came with a bite and a blow, and no brightening of the sky, and for full five hours the wild winds punished us. Even "the best knight in the world" cannot fight tempest with sword, or shield his people from the thunder and lightning. Somewhere I had heard, or read perhaps, to lash oneself to mast or rail, and so I did that, and thus we lived out the storm, those who deigned to take my advice. But eight of the crew, the captain, two of the Templars, and Master Philip were lost before the galley dashed itself to pieces on the rocks of a lonely island. While we tossed in dreadful peril, I swore a solemn oath, in my heart, that I would build a church upon whatever spot we came to land, if God so permitted us to come to land at all.

When I saw we would break up upon the reefs, I cut us all

loose from our bonds and bade my people to hold hands and stand firm as the sea engulfed us, so that we would not be separated. A huge wave washed over us with a roar like the sound of the earth splitting in two, but, miraculously, from the sea floor where we were hurled, we rose up, still close upon each other, though the waters had forced our hands apart. We stood, our legs atremble, knee-deep in shallow water, with no more harm done than that our feet were scratched and cut upon the sharp rocks and shells that strewed the beach beneath the shallows. Before us rose, through the lashing rain, a large, low building of rose-brown stone and, at one end of it, the unmistakable slender finger of a steeple pointing through the swirling mists at the angry sky. I gave a shaky laugh and said, "God has been here before me." Of course, no one understood these words; I suppose they passed for the deranged prattle of a storm-addled brain. And as the wind died down, I heard the sound of bells, and a host of brown-clad monks came out to greet and succor us.

It was a monastery of the Benedictine order, and not a church, and the island was called Lacroma, part of the territory of a mainland republic, very tiny, named Ragusa. We were welcomed with joy and awe by both the monks and the inhabitants of the little republic, somehow they recognized us as returning Crusaders, which, to these simple folk, seemed no less than a visitation of angels.

Our welcome by the Ragusans and the monks was so sincere that I took heart. I had thought my enemies to be everywhere.

"Ah, but they are," said Blondelza, with a black look. "Everywhere important, and in every land that stands in our path. These Ragusans are decent folk that love God and fear him—they are not like Philip Augustus Capet of France, the king of avarice!" She rolled the syllables of the French king's name upon her tongue with scorn; like all minstrel folk, she held herself above mere noblemen, princes too. For these folk, there are two classes only, the talented and the untalented; it is quite simple.

I leased a galley from the Ragusans, then, complete with crew and captain, we set forth once more upon a calm sea. Which did not remain calm long; three days and nights we sailed, and upon the fourth were driven mercifully to shore before another great wind, which tore the sails to rags but spared the ship and all it carried.

"'Tis soon mended," said the captain, squinting his eyes against the lashing rain, which seemed to be turning to ice as we huddled under it. "But I cannot risk my ship further, Sire," he went on, shaking his head lugubriously, as mariners do whenever the sea rises or the gales blow. "She'll not give up afore a fortnight, by my reckoning." The weather too was feminine, like the ships; I took him to mean the wind, this time.

"Where are we, Master Mariner?" I asked, avoiding his name, for it was all "c"s and "z"s and unpronounceable, except to a Ragusan.

"Well," he said slowly, keeping us in suspense, as authorities will, "somewhere between Aquileia and Venice, as I take it."

That was not much help. I saw, at any rate, that we were stranded in a remote corner of the Italian borderland; every local magnate would be bound to claim kinship or dependency either to the House of Montferrat, the Duke of Austria, or the Emperor—perhaps all three, and all my implacable foes. I saw that the danger was immediate.

There was an inn of sorts that stood sentinel upon an old Roman road that followed the coastline; the man who kept it, a surly varlet, demanded an ungodly sum for shelter and a greasy fish stew, but vouchsafed the name of the most powerful noble, Mainard of Gorizia, pointing out the Count's castle upon the hill. I dispatched Sir Lucien, one of the knights of our party, to seek an audience with this nobleman and ask him for safe-conduct. To sweeten him, I sent a present, a ruby ring of some value, bidding Sir Lucien to describe us as pilgrims returning from the Holy Land, naming myself as leader of our band, a merchant named "Hugh."

Lucien's heart sank, as he told us later, when he saw that this Count Mainard flew the colors of Montferrat, but he felt he had no choice but to go on, as he had been spied by the Count's lookouts. When he gained access to Mainard, the Count, having heard the tale, took the ring and, turning it about in his fingers, said slowly, "His name is not Hugh; it is Richard, the King of the English. I have sworn to seize all pilgrims and to accept no gift of bribe from any of them. But for the worthiness of this gift, and of him who has so honored me, I return it and give you leave to depart."

This alerted me to danger. I bought some horses, and we set off in the middle of the night, not sleeping on our filthy pallets at all, but galloping fast through the night, disguised as best we could, in our haste, in the gowns of Templars and pilgrims.

I was right to flee that place, for Mainard pursued us with a large force of men, and in a pitched battle at a crossroads, captured three of our party, two of the pirates and a squire. It was a fierce fight, and we left more than a dozen lying dead, my own sword bloodied with a good half of them, before we escaped that coil.

Riding hard, we came, after three days and nights, to a place called Carinthia, where we rested in a pilgrims' hostel, run by some good monks who asked no questions and shared with us their own spare pallets and plain fare.

I was for pushing on, but only the knights could have kept up. Jongleurs are hardy folk, but not trained to the saddle, and Philippe was not much more than a child; they needed rest.

At the close of our second day at the hostel, there came riding up to the gate a man alone, a merchant, judging by the glimpse I had through the window. We were at supper, the porridge cooling in the wooden dishes. Blondelza gazed at me with a white, fearful face. I sprang to the great fireplace, where a spit hung, and began to turn it, pulling my hood forward and trying to hunch over and look like an old, bent monk.

"Turn the spit *away* from you, not toward!" cried Blondelza, a hint of hysteria sounding in her voice. I saw I had spattered myself already by my awkwardness; cookery is one of the few things I have never turned my hand to. The fat hissed and crackled in the fire. I never knew what cooked there, a joint of mutton, I think; it had a fainty musty smell.

Boots rang, hollow, on the flagstones; we heard the man's voice raised in a question, and the monk's reply.

Blondelza snatched up her lute and began a tune, and the other jongleurs followed suit. Two of the apprentices began to sing, but it was in the langue d'oc, a giveaway. I turned and hissed, "No! No singing!"

The intruder entered; quickly I turned back to my spit, bending over like an ancient. The bench creaked as the man sat down. When the song was over, he applauded, saying something in German, and then, surprising us, in French, Norman French. "The Count is waiting for a troupe of minnesingers, Twelfth Night jongleurs. Perhaps you are the ones? He has paid in advance."

"Ah, no, we are not expected." Gervase's voice was rich with regret. "But if perchance they do not arrive . . ."

"Well," said the stranger, "show me your company . . . I will relay it to the Count."

"What count is that?" inquired Blondelza, politely, playing for time. "This district is new to us."

"Frederic of Pettau," he answered. "You are in the County of Pettau. But introduce me, please, I beg of you. A small troupe, is it?"

"Not large," said Gervase cautiously.

"But we are all very versatile," said Blondelza, who should have kept her pretty mouth shut, since there was no question of pride of calling here. I suppose it was second nature with her by now, to advertise herself and her troupe. But the man had taken another look at her, obviously, for he rose and went forward, his boots stirring the rushes, freshly strewn that morning; a scent of marjoram and thyme filled the room from the herbs scattered among them.

"And what do you do, pretty youth?" I heard him say, with a note in his voice, half amused, half wooing. I felt him to be close to her and, flushing with anger, turned to look. I saw she had bowed, a low obeisance, nearly touching the floor with her forehead, hiding her face. But the stranger had either sensed or seen my movement, for he swung about. Our eyes caught, and for a long moment we stared across the room.

I saw a man of middle height and middle years, but with a youthful set to his shoulders and hair of a goodly light brown, cut short below the ears in the Norman fashion; he was as freckled as a thrush's egg. Something tugged at my memory, something from long ago. I could not place his face, and yet . . .

Suddenly he moved, his look changing, and fell on his knees before me. "Oh, Sire! Oh, please, flee for your life, I beg you!"

I was greatly shocked, but pretended not to understand him; playing the part, I tugged at my forelock, mumbling and ducking my head.

"Oh, Sire, never mind that . . . I know you well! Please. You are in danger here, milord! The Count has sent me expressly to look in all the lodging places to find the King of the English! You are not safe, Sire!"

By now I knew there was no use going on with the pretense. We were all frozen in our places, staring. Blondelza, intrepid, darted to the table and snatched up the bread knife. I shook my head. "No, no, my dear. The man knows me . . . he is warning me. Let us listen." I turned back to the stranger. "Who are you, sirrah? I have seen you somewhere before, I think."

"I am Roger of Argenton, Sire. I have seen you many times, Sire. You are my sovereign lord. I was squire to the young lord of Argenton, young Sir Thierry. I saw you many times, at Rouen, at Le Mans, at Bures. You were only a boy then, but I would know you anywhere."

"Well, Roger, get up, man. I cannot keep on talking to the top of your head . . . That's better. Now, tell me, Roger of Argenton, what quarrel has this count—what is his name?—with me?"

"Frederic, Sire," he answered. "He is Mainard's brother."

"Ah, I see," I said wryly. "We had thought ourselves shut of him. So, kinsmen of Conrad, eh?"

"And on the other side, of Duke Leopold also. Oh, Sire, they mean to do you a mischief. You are not safe in these parts, you must flee!" I suppose I must have looked my utter exhaustion, for he said, with a worried frown, "I wish, Sire, there were some other way . . . that we could hide you. But there is nowhere safe, truly. Look how quickly I found you. I shall report to the Count that he is mistaken, that you are not in the region. I will try to convince him that you are not even in the country, and have gone home by sea, that the rumors are false. But, oh, my lord, I fear it is only a matter of time! Someone is sure to recognize you . . . yours is the most famous face in Christendom."

"And the most hated, so it would seem."

"Oh, no, my lord. The people love you, even here. But the great lords are jealous. They cannot bear to know one is so above them . . . they will do their utmost to pull you down. So was our sweet Lord Jesus served."

"Oh, no, my good man, you must not blaspheme." I gave a little shaky laugh. "I am no saint or prophet . . . and my sins are many." I let my hand fall upon his shoulder. "But you are a good and faithful vassal—I had thought to find such loyalty outmoded in these sad times." I sighed. "Well, we must get to practical matters. I shall take your advice, Roger of Argenton."

"Yes, Sire, go now. Don't wait."

"Horses. Where will I get fresh horses? Our poor beasts are spent."

"I will find them. Have you monies?"

"Yes, that is no problem."

"Then make ready. I shall return within the hour. "Let me see, how many horses . . ." He began to count, looking at our company.

"There is my son as well, asleep in an upper chamber."

"Can he ride at a gallop?"

"Oh, yes. He is nearly grown, and trained to the saddle long ago."

"So, I'll waste no time then." He knelt again for a moment, kissing my hand.

I had been long without these shows of royal obligation, and felt strangely uncomfortable. "Go, man. Arise and go," I said gruffly, pulling my hand away. "I know you are faithful."

He was back, true to his promise, well within the hour, and we were ready to depart, though Philippe was still rubbing his sleep-swollen eyes. Roger brought good horses, bridled too, and a roll of maps, which he spread upon the table. "Look, Sire. You must turn here, at this crossroads, to avoid Vienna, where you may be recognized. This is the way . . . if you ride hard, four days should take you to the Guelf country, where you will be safe." This was the domain of my brother-in-law, Henry of Saxony, bound to me not only by virtue of his kinship, but by his own rebellion against the German crown, and his enmity to both Leopold and the Emperor.

We rode hard, but we must have read the map wrong, or missed the turning. After four days, we drew up, nearly starved, and falling from the saddle in our weariness, before a small, mean inn; the host said it was just outside Vienna. But there was no help for it, we could go no farther.

Here we were, in hostile country in the full fury of winter. We had all taken fierce punishment in our wild ride, but I, the "best knight in the world," had fallen ill, with a return of the old sickness of the Holy Land, sweating, shaking, coughing. I was as weak as a puling babe, and cursed myself.

Blondelza's Cathar potions did little except relieve my cough for an hour or two; we dared not risk the services of a doctor, here in enemy territory. I could not sit a horse, so here we must bide, trusting in God, until this sickness left me.

CHAPTER 3

THE WEATHER WORSENED; a heavy snow blanketed the land, and the roads were impassable. The inn was drafty, and only the common room heated by a great old-fashioned fire pit. We could not sleep in our beds, but gathered round on pallets, close to the fire, the innkeeper and his servants crowding in as well to keep warm; it was worse than an army camp. The inn folk complained bitterly that we were eating up their stores, though much of them had been bought by us in the first days. I had no appetite, but I felt for the others, for all were now on short rations. The jongleurs laughed and pulled in their belts. "Good for the figure," quipped Gervase, smacking his pretty wife's bottom. In truth, she was pretty no longer, her Outremer sunburn yellow now as cheese, and her elbows sharp as needles. I saw, with a little shock, that we were none of us very appealing, not even clean; melted snow does not go far when it must be used for everything.

Four days the snow lay thick as far as the eye could see; another time it would have looked like an enchanted fairy country, but now we saw no beauty in it, only a vast prison, frozen and still. On the fifth morning I woke early, seized, as usual, by a fit of coughing. Blondelza, who lay by my side, was up quickly to throw a handful of herbs into the pot that hung over the fire pit; sometimes the scented steam eased the constriction in my chest.

The fire had died to a soft glowing ash, yet the room seemed warm. In the quiet we heard a steady drip outside the shuttered windows. Leaving me huddled in my blanket, still breathing in the steam from the pot she had placed by me on the floor, Blondelza tiptoed to the window and drew back the heavy shutter, sending a cold gray shaft of light across the floor. "It is a thaw!" she cried softly. "The icicles are all melted, and there are bare patches on the ground already! Oh, thank God!"

As the winter sun rose, the melting snow ran off the roof in a steady stream, and puddles lay in the roadway before the inn; the air was sharp and thin, but the icy feel of it had gone, and by noon it was almost warm. Faces visibly brightened; you would have thought we were safe at home in England. There were arguments as to who should go into the town for food from the market; voices rose, almost angrily.

"Let me, Mother."

"No, definitely not, Philippe! We cannot risk it . . . you are too like your father. Gervase, dear friend, not you either. You have made the trip so often—someone may suspect our presence here."

"I'll go," said Baldwin, the knight of Béthune, in a tone that brooked no opposition. "I am known nowhere in Europe. I will surely pass safely as a holy pilgrim. If the landlord will lend me a serf who can speak this barbarous tongue."

Baldwin made a passable Templar; these men are always sun-darkened, and it is natural for them to go armed; they are God's warriors. I looked up from my pallet, approving. "Good, good, Sir Baldwin, is that short cape warm enough?"

"Surely," he said, smiling. "Only—" And he looked down. "Drat these hands." They were covered with chilblains; after a mile of holding the reins, they would be bloody and raw.

"Have you no gloves, man?" I asked.

He shook his head. "Lost somewhere."

"Take mine," I said lightly. "Philippe, will you fetch them?" They were goodly gauntlets, of rich dyed leather, ruby red, and lined with ermine; Berengaria had made them for my birthday, and they were almost new. I was very fond of the cross-eyed beast that adorned the back, a touching testament to her long hours of labor.

Philippe handed me the gloves. "Here you are, good Baldwin," I said. "Some of the pearl embroidery is missing, but they are still fine, if you do not look too close."

"Now," he said, as he drew them on, "now I feel like a king."

"Not *this* king, I hope," I said, laughing and coughing.

As he rode away, the inn servant mounted behind him, Blondelza called out from the doorway, "Try to get some dried figs. And some comfits—sugarplums, if you can. It is almost Our Lord's brithday."

"I doubt he'll find anything like that," I said. "Vienna is off the beaten path. Where would they get sugarplums?"

Sugarplums, indeed. It was not sugarplums—or even a bag of grain—that Baldwin got, but a shallow gash on his temple, and the strong bonds of a prisoner.

Not two hours later the inn servant galloped in, all in a sweat, his teeth chattering with fear, babbling a tale to make our blood run cold. He spoke a kind of routier-Norman, brokenly, but, after he calmed somewhat, I could just follow it.

It was the cursed fancy gloves, my brithday gift, that had done it; upon the underside of the cuffs, traced in seed pearls, were my initials and a minuscule copy of the royal arms.

While bargaining at a market stall, Baldwin had removed the gloves and thrust them through his belt, and some sharp-eyed toady of the Austrian Duke had spotted the insignia upon them and challenged him with my presence. The good knight drew his sword and fought valiantly, but he was greatly outnumbered, and soon overpowered; it was just our luck that Leopold was in progress in the area, staying in some vassal's castle in the town. They trussed up Baldwin, but the servant, in the confusion, was able to slip away.

"Were you followed?" I asked, shaking him, for he was nearly incoherent in his fright.

"I think not, milord," he answered, pulling at his forelock.

The innkeeper, a little sparrow of a man, gray-faced now, hopped from foot to foot, his hands clasped, beseeching. "Your honors, I beg you, go! They will find you . . . there is no other place, this is the only inn! They will clap me in irons! I cannot stand the torture! I am only a poor man, untrained to arms. Oh, go, please. I beg you! They will tear at my flesh, beat me! Oh, go!"

"Yes, Richard," cried Blondelza. "The road is still clear, maybe there is yet time to get away. Gervase, see to the horses! I'll grab up what I can, or we'll leave it all behind. Come!"

I held up my hand, making my face stern. "No. I cannot. I cannot leave the knight of Béthune to suffer in my stead . . . it is not his quarrel. Besides, I could not ride at a gallop. I am sick . . . it would kill me. No. Make ready and go. Leave me here, and get away while there is time. It is Richard that Leopold wants . . . I am the prize, such as I am in these days." She made some movement of protest and I cut her words short. "They will not harm me—the King of England is no good to them dead." I shook my head. "Don't argue with me, darling. I cannot flee . . . I have no strength."

She put her arms around me. "Then we will stay with you. There are swords here, we can defend ourselves for a while, at least."

"I want you to go. I command it! You are all my subjects . . . you must obey!" While I spoke, I felt a kind of strength seeping through me, a thin and fugitive heat that fired my blood and cleared my head; it would not last, I knew, but at least I would go down in some kind of dignity, upon my feet and with sword in hand. I turned to the landlord. "Hide yourselves, you and your people . . . I would not have you suffer for your kindness. Get you below, to the cellars, and do not venture out." As I spoke, I moved with some of my old decisiveness, pulling off my night robe, buckling on my sword belt. "Don't stand and stare, Blondelza. Make ready and go! Gervase, the horses!"

The magician moved first, opening the inn door that led to the stables. With the freshening wind that came gusting in, there came also the sound of many horses, making the roadway tremble with a hollow thunder, and then we heard voices, as of a rabble aroused, and swelling with each flying instant. "It is too late," I said, calm now. "Arm yourselves, and bar the door and the windows."

Hastily the company snatched up whatever swords and daggers lay at hand; Blondelza had only the little sharp dagger that had served her so well those many years ago, but she held it in her left hand and with her right pulled down the great spit that hung, idle now, in the fireplace. Gervase's wife, her pretty face pinched and grim, held the poker into the heart of the glowing coals, watching the tip grow red. Women are shockingly bloodthirsty, when they are pushed to it; a man would never think of such a weapon.

"Philippe," I said, "take my small battle-axe. See, there it is, among my mail. Is it too heavy for you?"

He shook his head, hefting it, his small face solemn, the eyes too big.

"It will not come to it—we will not fight. But the feel of these weapons will help you." I laughed shakily. "So, my warriors, raise the battle cry! God wills it!"

"God wills it!" came from those trained singers' throats,

the sound surprisingly strong, and Philippe cried, his voice breaking, "God and the Lionheart!"

"Good lad!" I said, a hard lump rising in my throat. "Now here they come. Stand fast!"

The noise outside was deafening now, pounding hooves and clashing mail, and, rising above all, the voices, strange and guttural, shouting in the heavy German tongue. They began to pound against the door, but the strong bolt held. Then someone thrust in a heavy pike, splintering the wood. I felt something flood through me; my weakness had gone. I strode to the door, flinging it open and making a blind slash with my sword, almost a half-circle. I saw a round, half-helmeted head, wisps of yellow hair upon the cheeks and a yellow beard, the eyes surprised, topple sideways, almost cut through, and next to it, a severed arm fall to the ground, as that man fell too. Behind were a host of others, swords raised, still as a picture, shock upon their faces. I stepped forward into the gap and swung the sword again, drops of blood falling from it like rain; two more went down, and I saw the ranks fall back. A fierce joy rose like a flush, up into my head, intoxicating me like wine; thus had the Saracens given way before my face. I shouted, in a voice like the voice of their German thunder god, "Back! Back, you German dogs! For I shall take twenty with me when I go! The King of the English will not bow to the peasant's yoke! Back! Back, I say!" I swung the sword again, on empty air this time; it hissed as it cut, swift and fearsome, and I saw that they were stopped. They could not understand my words, but the sword spoke for me, and something, too, in my face—something, I know not, an accident of expression—but better men than these have run from it. They fell back, leaving a space between us, empty except for the fallen, who looked sad and diminished, as they always do, like dirty laundry stained with blood. Blood stained the snow too; in the clear winter sunlight, it was the delicate rose-pink of a lady's gown.

It was partly fear that held them—but I knew, too, that their orders must have been to take me alive. I was in no danger from them. But I also knew that I could not attempt to cut my way through them, not with all those souls inside dependent upon me; some of them would surely die. And my son and his mother stood in gravest peril. No, there was nothing for it but to surrender, with what dignity I could muster, and what safety I could bargain for them. I raised my voice again.

"Leopold," I said, knowing they would recognize the name of their Duke at least. "I will surrender to none but Leopold. Fetch him!" I raised the dripping sword I held, and mimed handing it over, hilt first. "Leopold!" I shouted again.

In the front rank of men I saw a kind of rude light dawn; heads nodded. "Leopold, *ja*!" After a moment of consultation, a small group of horsemen turned and clattered away, back toward the town.

I nodded vigorously, and raised my sword. "We will wait," I said, and raised a hand as though for silence, turning about to face the entire circle of barbarous villains. "Wait!" I said again, and, turning, went inside the inn, shutting the door. I waited a moment to see what they would do, then opened it. They stood as I had left them. "Be at ease!" I shouted. "Sit!" And I made a gesture as one might make to a dog. Like good dogs, they sat; I almost smiled. But I nodded gravely, nodded my approval, said "We wait" again, and went back inside the inn.

"I think they understand. Now, Blondelza, make ready. I will make a bargain with Leopold when he arrives. I will surrender my sword to him, in return for his prisoner, Baldwin, and for your safety, all of you. You are to go freely—or I will fall upon my sword." She made to speak, her face alive with horror. "No, listen. He will not let me fall upon my sword . . . he cannot raise ransom on a dead king. It will work, he will make the bargain. He has no choice. But I want you ready to gallop fast, in case of treachery. I will insist on waiting here, with him and all his men . . . I will insist upon an hour's grace. Get as far away as you can. Baldwin will go with you. Get word to my mother in England, my Chancellor. Tell them that I am taken prisoner and where."

Again there came the sound of pounding hooves; Leopold must have ridden fast on the heels of his men, and those who had gone to fetch him met up with him on the way. He had a goodly force with him, all in knightly garb, and armed with lance and sword; Baldwin rode among them, between two of the largest and fiercest warriors. His arms were bound to his sides, his head bared, and blood trickled thinly from a slash upon his temple; I remember offering up a prayer that it had missed his eye.

"Leopold!" I called from the open doorway. "Stop where

you are! Hear me out! I will surrender my sword and my person to you—but in one hour." And I outlined the bargain I had thought out in my head.

He sat his horse quietly, listening with a brooding look. When I had finished, he nodded. "It shall be done," he said. "I give my word."

"Your word is not enough," I replied coldly. "Do you think I expect fair dealing from a slanderer and a predator? Stay as you are, your men with you, for one hour—or by Heaven, I shall cheat you and fall upon my sword!"

I set the sword, for emphasis, into the hard ground before the door; its blade pointed upward toward my heart, stained with blood but glinting wicked-sharp along the edge. Without turning my head, I beckoned my son to my side. "Philippe, my dear son, kiss your father."

Leopold, by no means all varlet, called out, "A truce, King Richard. We shall not take up the gage of battle. You have full leave to make your farewells. Do you think a knight of Austria is less knight than one of yours?"

"Send Baldwin to me, then. Loosen his bonds, and give him back his sword!" I waited while it was done, then, turning to Philippe, I said, "Kneel, fair son." I held out my hand. Baldwin, divining my purpose, put his sword into it. "Philippe of Cognac, son of Richard of England, whom men call Lionheart, I charge you with these duties: Do valiant battle; respect your enemies; succor the poor; honor ladies; love God." I tapped him lightly upon the shoulder with the flat of Baldwin's sword. "Arise, Sir Knight!"

He rose, nearly stumbling in his pride and confusion, tears starting in his eyes. "Oh, Father! Oh, thank you, Father! Am I true knight now, Father?"

"True knight, my son." I smiled down at him. "It is early days, but no matter . . . behave as a knight, and the rest will follow." I embraced him and kissed him on both cheeks. "I give you the kiss of peace. Go now. I put your mother into your care . . . watch over her. Farewell, dear son. Remember your father."

Blondelza then came into my arms, weeping, making my cheeks wet with her tears. "Farewell, my dearest love," I whispered. "Ride swiftly. Go to my mother, tell her my captor's name."

"Where will he hide you?" She spoke, low, into my ear.

"I know not." I laughed softly. "Somewhere strong and remote, we can be sure."

"I will find you, I swear it."

"No, no, my darling. You must ride hard and far. Get word to my kingdom! Promise me!"

"I promise." She kissed me. "Farewell. God and His Angels keep you."

I listened, standing still as stone, while the little party gathered themselves together and took horse. I listened till the sound of their galloping died away. And still I stood, poised over my sword, staring at Leopold and his men. We were like a painted picture, or figures in a tapestry. Now and then a horse whinnied restively, or a man cleared his throat; once I heard a muttered curse and saw Leopold frown and turn, quelling the culprit. My legs shook, and the cold sweat broke upon my forehead, chilling me, but still I waited, till I felt the hour was up and more. Stiff and sore, I bent, painfully, and took up the sword. "Dismount, Duke," I said; it was a command.

He got down from his horse and stood before me, holding out his hand, making a sign that none of his men should stir. His head came somewhere below my chin; he tilted back his own chin and looked me in the eye, proud. I'll say this for him, he was a fearless little bantam.

"Richard, King of the English, render me your sword, as promised," he said, in a voice fit for the parade ground.

"Leopold, Duke of Austria, take this symbol of my surrender." And I handed it to him, hilt forward. "I charge you, by your knight's honor, use me well." My knees buckled then and I toppled forward. "A doctor. I need a doctor."

A blackness came before my eyes, then cleared to gray mist. I felt hands lifting me, and the hard saddle under me; hands closed my hands upon the reins, and tied rough bonds upon them and upon my ankles, binding me to my mount. I heard a word of command, German or Austrian, and the animal beneath me swayed and swerved; the whole world spun about me, and I slumped, closing my eyes, smell of leather and horse strong in my nose. There was movement, sickening, and a noise like thunder rumbling in far hills, and then I knew no more.

CHAPTER 4

BRIGHT SUNLIGHT FELL in four narrow stripes athwart the dark stone floor; I could just see it from where I lay, stretched out upon a flat cot or couch. Raising my eyes, I saw, far above my head, a rough-plastered ceiling, hung with cobwebs. From somewhere near there came a faint resinous smell, and a spot of warmth; a brazier fed with pine knots. I turned my head and saw it, small and glowing, quite near. A hand touched my shoulder, gentle, and I smelled another smell, soup; I even felt its steam.

Into my vision swam a face, slowly taking shape; a face I knew. I had lost all sense of time and place, and fancied myself back in my tent at Acre, for the face was the face of the good monk Alberic, who had nursed me there.

I opened my mouth to speak, but no words came, only a kind of husky growl that hurt my throat. I swallowed, and tried again. "You," I said. "Is it you?"

The monk smiled, wrinkles seaming his cheeks like well-worn leather; the eyes were kind, familiar. "It is I, Brother Alberic, Sire. Your wits are back again; I had feared them flown forever."

I shook my head slowly; I did not understand.

He spoke again, bringing the bowl of steaming soup near. "Try to sip a little, it will ease your throat and bring strength. You have been gravely ill."

Obediently, like a good child, I opened my mouth and let him feed me. I had no idea what broth it was; it tasted better than anything I had ever known, like Heaven or the fruits of Heaven, like love. I felt the warm, weak tears trickle down onto my lips. "Salt," I whispered. "It needed salt." And laughed, a ghostly whisper.

He smiled again, and brought the spoon up again, and so it went; I ate it all up, every drop, and let my head sink back again, still weak but happy.

Slowly, as from some time long ago, some other country far distant, I began to see images, darkly, becoming sharper as my memory groped deeper. I remembered our flight, our hiding, my surrender. I saw dead men upon a snowy ground, other men, armed and live, the face of my son, blurry with tears, Blondelza's eyes, like shining pools, and my own sword, red with dark blood. I looked at the monk. "I am a prisoner," I said. "The prisoner of Leopold."

It was not a question, but he nodded. I asked him then, "Where? Where does he keep me?"

"You are in the fortress of Durrenstein, on a high hill above the Danube."

"How long? How long have I been here?"

He began to count on his fingers, then, smiling, gave up. "My guess is a month—maybe more. I came here three weeks ago. You were unconscious then, and Leopold feared for your life."

I gave a twisted smile. "My money, you mean."

"It is the same thing," he said gravely. "At any rate, you are better now, and likely to recover. Not many do."

"What is it I had? What ailed me?"

He shook his head. "We do not know its name. Some call it the tertian fever, some the little plague. The old wives name it the lung rot. There is no cure but rest."

"I strained God to the limit of His mercy, then. For I had no rest at all for weeks on end, riding day and night, spending my strength." I looked up at him, trusting what I saw. "I knew, you see, that I was hunted . . . by many. Though I cannot, I swear, know why . . . it is against the laws of chivalry."

"Against the law of God, too, and His Holy Church—as they have found out." He dropped his voice. "The Holy Father has put all the German lands under interdict. The poor souls . . ." His voice trailed off; he made the sign of the Cross upon his breast. "There can be no Mass, no Communion . . . not even the Last Rites."

I shuddered, and crossed myself as well. "That I should have brought this upon Christian souls!"

"Not you, Sire. The Duke. And the Emperor."

"The Emperor? He is in it too?"

"So the rumors have it . . . I am not sure. There are rumors of France too, and—" He broke off, and his eyes were sad and somehow ashamed.

"My brother John. Do they name him too?" It was almost not a nod at all, but I read his face. I laughed harshly. "Well,

I may take heart then. For whatever John puts a hand to will not prosper. He has no luck, poor child."

"Hardly a child any longer—well into his twenties now, surely." The monk's lips had a wry twist.

"He will always be a child," I said, smiling. But as I began to take in what he had told me, I frowned, wondering. "You know of no one who has come asking for me? No one has tried to make contact or treaty?"

"Well," he said, "the Pope must know. Someone has written him. And the rumors . . . Well, there is no smoke without fire, they say. But no, no one has come here. Nor are they likely to. This place . . . it is the back of beyond, nearly inaccessible. The Danube side falls sheer to the river, all dense forest, and the village is tiny, clustered at the foot of the castle. The village folk are all servants here, there is no trade."

"You," I said, a little shy. "Can you not get word outside, word of my imprisonment here?"

"If I could . . ." He spread his hands eloquently. "My order owes no fealty to Leopold, or to Henry the Emperor either."

"Well, then. A letter to my mother, or my Chancellor . . . a message by word of mouth even."

He shook his head sadly. "I am as much a prisoner here as you, Sire. I have the run of the castle, and of the courtyard. The village—Well, no one ever leaves it. Men are born and die there, and see no other folk but the occasional peddler or tinker." Seeing my disappointment, he added, "But I will try. If it is in my power."

He left me then, that good monk, saying I must not tire myself with too much talk, but rest that I might recover the quicker. He would see me again at suppertime, and bring my food and medicines.

The next day I could sit up, and the day after left my bed and paced about the chamber, though it made me dizzy. I tried to take its measure, as best I could; ten paces the long way, and six the narrow—though my legs are beyond the normal length and so not a perfect measure. There was one small window, very high near the ceiling, crossed with iron bars. There was the low cot and a stool, and a bucket in the corner to serve my bodily needs; it stank foully, though only I had the use of it, and the good monk emptied it every day. It told me something about kings, if I had not known it before; a lesson in humility. I saw no one at all except Brother Alberic. He came twice a day, often breathless, for he carried my food, and the bucket too, and it was a climb of one hundred and fifty steps; I was held up in the topmost part of the tower.

My recovery was quick now; before the week was up I was walking the floor, backward and forward, over and about, and ravenous all the time. I had soup twice a day, and beer, and coarse brown bread, and always asked for more; he said it was a good sign.

One day he brought a basin of water and set it over the brazier to heat; I realized then how dirty I must be, and foul, for the wash felt so good.

"You are thinner," he said, "and paler too. But take heart—I think you are still a man one would think twice to tangle with." He eyed me closely, and felt the muscles of my limbs, testing them. "They have not atrophied, that is good. But you are all gone to bone and slack flesh. You must exercise—a little each day, and more as you grow stronger. It is a thing we learn in our order, when we fast. Stretch and bend. Flex your tendons. Running in place is good too. But easily at first—don't overdo it." He was showing me what he meant, bending from the waist, twisting his torso, running lightly. It was the kind of thing that jongleurs do, but gentler. I had watched Blondelza at such antics day after day, amused. Now I saw the benefits.

In two days I felt improved, more fit, and my breath came easier. But one cannot do this every moment, and time hung heavily upon me. I pushed the cot under the little window, then stood upon it and jumped, hoping to catch hold of an iron bar and pull myself up, so that I might see something of the countryside where I was kept. But it was too high; tall as I was, I could not come near it. At least, not yet. My fingertips just grazed the sill; perhaps at full strength I could make it. I exercised harder and longer each day. It began to seem an end in itself—to reach that window, to look through the bars.

Alberic was wonderfully kind; he stayed most of the day with me in my little cell, talking, teaching me German words, though he laughed at my accent. "You are quick, though, Sire. I have never had a brighter pupil."

I cherished those words. It was as though I had never been praised for anything before; I found myself repeating them at night when I lay awake. Imprisonment plays strange tricks upon us. I could see how men have gone mad in these circumstances.

"A book," I said. "How I long for a book! Could you—do you think . . . ?"

"I doubt if there is such a thing in this place." But then he said shyly, "I have a *Life of Augustine* . . . you may have that." He reached over and removed the volume from his cloth bag.

I grasped at it greedily, though I must have read it a hundred times and more. "A lute, or a mandolin even . . . could you get such a thing? I am something of a musician; it would pass the time well."

"Perhaps," he said, a trifle doubtfully. "One of the guards, maybe . . . I will try."

"And pen and ink, and something to write on . . . I could use that too."

He shook his head. "That we could never manage. It is forbidden. They would not risk you getting messages out, you see. If I asked, they would send me away—or worse."

"I see. Of course. Well, what you can find . . . And many thanks for old Augustine here." I tapped the book, already well worn; I had been thumbing through it for hour after hour. I had never cared for the saint, a bumptious old pontificator, I thought. But he was all I had; I knew his musings by heart already. I would sit by the hour, arguing with the man, thus and so, as if he were there before me, instead of moldering for centuries in his grave.

We were having a particularly fierce discussion, the saint and I, when next the good Alberic climbed the stairs to my cell. I was shouting doctrine at my unseen debater, and my face was as red, I think, as Father's used to get, in a temper. The door opened, tentatively, and a surprised look came upon the face that Alberic showed around it. I laughed, a little shame-faced, and said, "See to what I am reduced! Arguing with Saint Augustine! I hope it is not the onslaught of madness."

"No," he said, smiling broadly, relieved. "It is a good sign. I bow to your resourcefulness, Sire."

"I wish you would call me Richard," I said impulsively. "I command it!"

"Oh, I doubt if I could do that! I come of very small folk."

"But small folk are fine people!" I said. "You must try. I will not be content if we are not good friends."

"Well . . . perhaps," he said, flushing. "But look, Sire . . . Richard. Look, I have found a lute! A poor thing, but with all its strings."

"Oh, wondrous fellow!" I cried. "You are a worker of miracles!" I fairly snatched it out of his hands, my fingers trembling with excitement. It was foully out of tune, but even so, the very notes, flat as they were, sounded sublime to my ears. And with a little work . . . I bent my head to the task, forgetting Alberic.

After a moment, I heard him say, "Can you use this? The fellow I got it from gave it to me, said it might come in handy."

It was a lump of resin, just what I needed; another miracle. I raised a glowing face, and took the sticky mass from him. I never noticed when he stole away; it was darkening into twilight by the time I had the lute tuned up and true. The sound it made was thin, but not all that bad. Not the best lute in the world, but not the worst either. I was happy.

I practiced hard all next day, playing to my audience of one. At least prison has given me this, I thought; it had been years since I had had time to play my favorite songs or try my hand at some of my own.

Alberic looked up timidly. "Can you play a sacred song?" he asked.

I shook my head, smiling. "They do not sound well on the lute." I swung, though, into another tune, "Marching to Jerusalem." "Do you recognize this one?" I asked.

"Oh, yes," he sighed. "I shall never forget it. Strange, I did not know this while I was there, but it seemed the only time I was really alive . . . there in the Holy Land."

"I know," I said. "It is so for me also." My fingers wandered over the strings with a will of their own; it was coming back easily to me now, the old art. I swung into a sprightly sirventes—onle of Gaucelm Faudit's I think—and then into a slower song, a song about love and lovers, honey-sweet, the notes drifting like flower petals upon the wind. I let the lute rest quiet then, my thoughts stirring deep within me.

After a moment I raised my eyes to Alberic's face. He looked away, and said, "That song . . . I know it too. It is *hers*."

"So many are," I said lightly, putting aside the lute and

standing up to stretch my cramped muscles. "I have played too long. I must give my fingers a rest."

But my thoughts I could not put to rest, nor even my dreams. That night, when I finally slept, after hours of restless tossing, I awoke to a fugitive memory of the days of my youth—our youth—and the soft hauntings of the little song we played together when we were alone. I tried it on the lute, picking out the melody with the fingers of one hand, but it made me weep, and I set it aside, and out of mind.

But after I had paced the floor and run and stretched, after I had had my daily argument with the good Saint Augustine, after I had run through my repertory of songs, and lain down upon my cot to rest, I jumped up, startled. For it seemed as though I heard the notes of that private song again; I was sure I had not been asleep.

I shook my head to clear it, and rubbed my eyes, blinking against the strong shaft of light that poured down from the lone window. Yes, there it was again! I was not dreaming! I listened, rapt, not daring to breathe. Yes, the song was drifting upward from the outside, far below, sounding strongly now, as the wind gusted through the open window. I reached for my lute and began to play, the return of the melody; the sounds below had ceased. When I stopped, wondering if somehow the song had been copied, unknown to us, I heard it again—the razo this time that she alone could play, that only an accomplished performer could even hope to get through; I could not play it myself, it was too complicated.

I listened, my throat full, my heart seeming to stop. It was Blondelza, down there somewhere; it could be no one else. My thoughts ran wild in my head, fraught with fear and hope.

Frantically, I pushed the cot under the window and jumped; this time, in my extremity, I reached the sill and held it fast, pulling myself upward, straining, till my eyes were level with it and I could see the tops of black-green firs, a snow-covered mountain, and blue sky. But that was all, I could see nothing of what went on below. But as I strained my hands and arms, inching upward, I heard a great burst of music and singing, old songs that I had heard a hundred times, the standard repertory of the jongleurs. There were others down there too. I could see the show in my head, listening: the roll of drums that heralded the magician's act; the quick plucking of strings and tapping of feet in the jig; the staccato noise of the juggler's wooden balls. There were voices, too, raised in song, but indistinct through my prison walls, I did not recognize them. There was great laughter then, and clapping, as of a crowd. When it had died away, I heard the private lutesong again, thin and pure, and dropped to my feet to take up the lute and answer, hitting the strings hard, standing just beneath the window to make sure it was heard. When I stopped, the lute below spoke again, but very softly now, and dying away each moment, until, at last, I could hear it no more.

Trembling, I sank upon the cot; my knees shook so hard they would not hold me up. Sweat sprang out on my forehead and ran down inside my woolen garment. I clenched my hands together, caught in a tension tighter than a stretched wire. Suddenly I heard footsteps upon the stairs below; I jumped up, holding to the wall so that I would not fall, and stared at the door. When it opened I thought that I would faint, and when I saw Alberic's face, I let out my breath on something close to a sob; so foolish of me, for who else could come through that door?

We stared for a moment, eye to eye; then he said, clearly but very low, "It was she down there in the courtyard. The glee-maiden. The Cathar."

I nodded, not trusting my voice.

"I spoke to her for a moment only, and in Latin—it was safe."

I nodded again, searching his face with my eyes.

"She got word to England of your capture. The Queen your mother has gone to Rome, to the Pope. Now she will know where you are as well."

"Blondelza . . ." I wet my lips and went on. "How did she find this place?"

"Her troupe has been traveling in Germany, playing in every castle yard. Last night they came up the Danube by barge."

"Then I did not dream the song," I said wonderingly. "She—how is she? Will she be safe? And my son? He is with her?"

"They are both well, and they will be safe. Here in these parts they have never seen a jongleur before . . . they will not be recognized." He smiled. "And now they will set out for Rome too, to take the news. Leopold will be forced to action now."

"Yes," I said. "Yes . . . it is good. She is my truest friend. I thank God for her."

"I told her," he said shyly, "that you were well . . . and that you sent your love."

"Good man," I said.

My heart raced. And, though the day was darkening to evening now, for me it was light, and lightness. For now there was hope, and I knew that the door must open, sometime.

CHAPTER 5

THE DOOR TO freedom did not open to me until one year, six weeks, and three days of captivity had passed. There were times when I had all but given up hope. I cannot think of anything worse than imprisonment; that my poor mother endured it for more than sixteen years is a miracle, and a testament to her great heart and spirit.

For more than a year kings and princes haggled over my body—the body, moreover, of a Crusader and supposedly, therefore, under full protection of the Church. But I see now that, to the political mind, the most valuable piece on the chessboard of Europe had come onto the market; the bidding was fierce!

The first deal to be made was between Leopold and the Emperor, Henry VI of Germany. Neither trusted the other one inch, though the Duke of Austria was sworn vassal to the Emperor, and this should in knightly honor bind both parties firmly. To begin with, my only friend, dear Brother Alberic, who I do not doubt had saved my life—and certainly, by his unfailing kindness and sympathy, my sanity—was dismissed immediately as soon as it was reported that I was well again. Leopold then had me brought in chains to Regensburg, for the inspection of the Emperor. It was as though he said to his overlord, "Look what I've got . . . look at my prize. What will you offer?" As for me, poor prisoner, I thought of nothing on that journey except the cruelty and humiliation of the chains. And I had condemned—so blithely!—that poor prisoner of my own, Isaac Comnenus, to the same fearful bondage! I had ever made a jest of it; hearing his plea not to be put in irons, I had ordered for him chains of silver!

I resolved, each time I looked down at my own hands and feet and heard the hollow clanking, that I would atone for this callous behavior as soon as I was out of bondage myself, accepting whatever penance the Holy Church imposed upon me, even a public scourging, like my father's.

The meeting at Regensburg was brief, for Leopold did not trust me with his overlord, the Emperor; we were, after all, the two rulers who dominated Europe, never mind Philip of France's pretensions. Leopold shipped me back to Austria as soon as the first amenities were over, and did his own private bargaining with Henry, a matter of six weeks' work. Out of the total of 100,000 marks, the price put on my head, Leopold, who had possession, was to have 75,000 marks, 50,000 of this being part of the dowry for Eleanor of Brittany, my niece, who was to marry Leopold's son. In addition, I was to release immediately the prisoners Isaac Comnenus and his daughter. Leopold was related to the Comneni, so he got good marks for loyalty, but alas, poor Isaac died almost as soon as he was released. He had immediately tried to seize the throne of Constantinople and, defeated, died in seclusion. Some said he deserved his death; but I resolved that this would not stop me from atoning for my cruelty to him.

Another condition was that I should come with fifty of my own galleys and help the Emperor invade Sicily. Also, the Pope had excommunicated Leopold; I was supposed to arrange for that to be lifted!

Meanwhile, the Emperor had notified Philip of my capture, I suppose to see what offer would be made! Philip begged him not to release me without consulting him. Henry the Emperor then wrote my brother, who assured him of total cooperation; I wept when I heard this, for I truly loved John. I heard all this from two Cistercian abbots who visited me at Wurzburg; it was the first news I had heard from outside since my capture. Leopold allowed these men to accompany me to Speyer, where he was taking me to be tried at the imperial court. It was an unheard-of thing, and inside I was wild with righteous anger, but God had put into my head the proper course. I resolved never to show that anger, never, by sign or word, to reproach my enemies or to feel sorry for myself, but to keep at all times an even, cheerful countenance. I was always mindful of my father's fatal choler and the dreadful havoc it had caused; I did not want to remind others of the sins he had committed through giving rein to his emotions. It was not easy, but it counted in the end.

At Speyer, I was accused, before a court of ecclesiastics and lay judges, on three serious charges. I refused counsel, and stood my own defense. I was accused of betraying the Holy Land, by making peace with Saladin; of plotting the death of Conrad of Montferrat; and of breaking agreements with the Emperor. I cannot repeat now all of what I said to clear myself, for I spoke at great length on all three charges, long enough, indeed, that I was hoarse at the finish.

"Is not peace holier than war?" I asked in a reasonable tone. "Is it better that men should die horribly, and their wives and babes as well, or that leader should treat with leader, honorably, to save the destruction of two great peoples? Because I negotiated with Saladin, Jerusalem, that golden city of our dreams, has not come under siege, has not been laid waste. Blood does not run in its holy streets, and pilgrims of every sort may visit without peril, while the sacred places are forever intact. Also, this peace has given us the whole coast of Outremer; never shall Christian be forced to fight for what is his by right. Ships come and go, our people live without want, the Holy Sepulchre is preserved forever!" There was more, too. Suffice it to say that when I finished, as Blondelza used to say, there was not a dry eye in the house!

As to the charge of murdering Conrad, that was nonsense, and I said so. Fortunately, Hubert Walter, that great and faithful bishop, had arrived in the nick of time from Sicily, a long and arduous journey, undertaken for my sake, in his hand a document from the Old Man of the Mountain absolving me of all blame in that assassination. It was a forgery, written by a Muslim scribe, but no matter; another instance of peace serving well. Hubert Walter was a tireless diplomat, and a great favorite among the Saracen enemy. Never had ruling prince so loyal a bishop; he testified well, and when this was over I would make him Archbishop of Canterbury.

I had made no agreements at all with the Emperor, I told the court, for before my imprisonment I had never laid eyes on him. I said that I supposed he meant my support of my brother-in-law, Henry of Saxony, who was in revolt against the Emperor's unfair seizure of his lands. But what is a knight worth if he will not defend his kin? Not a fig, I said. Not a withered orange. Oh, fine words came tripping from my mouth, and my eyes clear as a summer sky, and I meant it all. And the great lords and bishops knew it, and wept and applauded like children at a fair. Even William the Breton, Philip's court poet, was moved to tears, and wrote afterward, "The great king spoke so eloquently and regally, in so lionhearted a manner, that it was as though he had forgotten where he was, and did not feel his chains, but imagined himself seated upon the throne of his ancestors at Lincoln or at Caen." I can just see Philip gnashing his teeth as he read it!

The Emperor was very canny; he sensed the mood of the onlookers, dropped his accusations, and heaped great praises upon me, offering the kiss of peace, and striking off my chains then and there. "I will promise to bring peace between you and Philip," he said, with a pious air. As though he had done nothing wrong himself and had nothing to do with my circumstances! He was a wily crook, no question.

But kiss or no kiss, I still had to pay. One hundred thousand marks, fifty galleys, and two hundred knights' service for a year. I made the promise, expecting a speedy release. But instead I was sent, though not in chains this time, to the castle of Trifels in the western mountains, under close guard. It was obvious that he feared I had done my cause so much good at the court at Speyer that I might raise troops and money from my sympathizers there.

Again, God gave me the grace to behave well. I was never alone, but constantly watched by the roughest guards the imperial army could dredge up. Germans are giants, everyone knows; a few of them were taller than I was, and most were heavier. Rude peasant creatures they were, nearly sub-human; it took close to five minutes for even the simplest thought to get through to them. But once they got it, it was lodged there; I can see they would make wonderful servants, loyal to the death. At first I amused myself by playing jokes on them—the sort of jokes that children play when they are very young—but they were so simple and so easily gulled that it soon lost its savor; besides, I saw that it was cruel, whether they knew it or not. So, slowly, patiently, I began to win them over; if I must have these poor dolts always with me, they might as well be friends. I sang to them, drank with them, practiced my German on them. In turn they brought me food, the sausage-and-cabbage soup of the region and the delicious, cream-topped pastries. They brought me women too, though it was strictly forbidden, I am sure; yellow-haired girls with eyes as round and blue as cornflowers. They were pretty if they were young enough; they ran to fat early. Later, much later, there was a legend there, among the country people, that every other child of the right age was mine. Like all the legends that kings inspire, it was without foundation. There were only two girls I favored; and if either of them bore a child, it was not in my time; they were still slender as dryads when I was taken away from there.

Under pressures from Mother, Cancellor Longchamps, and the Pope, Emperor Henry brought me back to court at Hagenau, and now he, the monarch, became my jailer. He was more difficult to win over than the untutored soldiers of Trifels, but eventually I managed, with two weapons; I taught him the lute fingering and some simple melodies (which was not easy, as he had no ear), and I let him win at chess.

In the end, I had to play politician, or I would be there still.

The Emperor had agreed to meet Philip, bringing me along, ostensibly to make peace between France and England. But I knew that somehow, given Philip's wiles, I would end up in a French prison from which there would be neither ransom nor escape. Actually, Philip was offering the Emperor aid against the rebels of the empire, in return for my custody; it was as plain as could be, once you knew Philip. I had to prevent this. So, month after month, I worked on the Emperor, flattering him shamelessly, inching him toward my purposes, which was for him to make peace with those same rebels. It worked. The meeting with Philip never took place. Instead, with me as mediator—no chains this time—the Emperor came to terms with my brother-in-law, Henry of Saxony, and with the other rebels of Thuringia and Meissen. At the same time, my ransom was renegotiated and finally settled. I would be freed when the Emperor had received 10,000 marks and the promise of an additional 50,000, for which hostages had to be given for seven months after my release.

Philip made one more try; pooling his resources with my brother John, he offered to pay 150,000 marks, or a thousand marks for every month I was held. The Emperor was sorely tempted, and kept putting off the date of my release, but in the end his vassal princes and the princes of the Church forced him to hold to his bargain. So, on February 4, more than a year after I was captured, I was set free.

Philip sent a hurried message to my brother John. "Look to yourself ... the devil is loose!"

CHAPTER 6

THE WORLD. THE world outside Germany. So beautiful it was, even in February, and the winds piercing and raw, laden with the moisture of the misty lands of the north. I threw back my hood and drank it in, the pungent salt air of the Narrow Sea, blowing from England.

Beside me at the ship's rail a little cough, with a laugh in it. Mother. I put my arm around her, sheltering her with my great cloak. Mother, old now, suddenly old and seeming to have shrunk, her skin pale, thin, almost transparent where it stretched over the bones of her cheek and temple. Her hair, still thick, abundant, matched the silvery gray of the furs she wore. Her long hand, when she took it out of the muff she held against the cold, seemed to have extra bones in it, knobs and protrusions, and the curving nails were like claws. Something twisted in me; pity, regret, love, shame? Her face looked up at me, questioning my silence, the large eyes faded to violet, luminous.

"I always thought your eyes were black, Mother," I said. "Not this pansy color."

"No. They were always like this, but darker. You never noticed." She sighed, then smiled.

"We had not spoken, not really, since our meeting at the port of Swyn, in Flanders, where we had come on board this vessel an hour ago. My throat was still thick and swollen with emotion, and the traces of tears shone upon her cheeks.

"Philippe is with Berengaria," she said. "They have journeyed from Ostend, overland. They had safe-conduct from the Pope. I expect they will be here by tomorrow or next day at the least ..." Her voice tailed off; she did not look at me.

"With Berengaria?" I said, my voice sounding harsh, even in my own ears. "And Blondelza ... ?"

440

She did not answer; her head was bent.

My hand clenched involuntarily, the fingers digging hard into the soft flesh of her arm. "Mother! Mother, for God's sweet sake, tell me!" I felt my heart, a choking pain in my chest. "Is she dead, then? Mother, where is she?"

"Oh, no! No, dearest." Her eyes looked up at me again, her turn for pity. "No, she is well. She gave me a letter . . ." I heard a rustle within the great fur cape; she was fumbling at the satin of the lining, a pocket. And then she brought it out, a small, tightly rolled parchment, the edges sealed with wax and a blue ribbon dangling from it; at any other time I would have called it a pretty thing.

I tore it open, savagely. The writing blurred before my eyes.

"Mother," I said, rolling the thing up again, "will you give me leave? I cannot keep the parchment flat in this wind."

"Of course. Go, darling. Go below to your cabin. And the letter is not for my eyes, at any rate." At least, I thought, she had the grace not to look at me. She lifted her chin, smiling. "Look, here is young Baldwin, to keep me company! We do not need you. Go!" She gave me a tender little push. I had a glimpse of the boy's face, awed by hers, before he dropped to his knee in obeisance.

I waved my hand. "Be at ease, lad. Have you your lute? Play for the Queen, then." I waved my hand again, vaguely. His young eyes looked startled; everyone knows not to expose the strings to such damp. I left, nearly stumbling on the steep stairs that led below.

"My dearest dear," went the letter,

> I pray God you will not hate me—or not for long—but will understand, when you have read this. I must break my promise never to leave you. For know you, my darling, that my very soul stands in peril. Forgive me.
>
> For my faith—my mother's faith—I mean to renounce the world. I shall not find it difficult, except for the loss of you. You know I believe—have long believed—with the Cathar folk that this world is evil, and that it was created not by God, but by Satan, and that the better world awaits us, when we have been purified, stripped of our vanities, our pride, and our fleshly love. I know I can never persuade you of this, and so I have never tried.
>
> I have lived for my music, and for you, though I know

both to be deceptions and false lures of the Dark One, holding me back from my salvation.

You know already my feelings about the Cross, the symbol of suffering humanity, and about the war, not holy to me. And you have been kind, and tolerant, and have not denounced me as a heretic. I think you will not now—once your anger has passed. And it will pass, believe me, my friend.

Our Philippe, though he has heard my arguments, holds with you and would follow in your footsteps; I have not tried to persuade him otherwise, but made my last loving farewell, as I do now with you. I beg you to cherish him and hold him dear, for the sake of our love. (For even now I cannot name that love false; the flesh is still so dear and wounding, and I am not yet one of the Pure Ones.)

There is a Cathar convent near Montsegnur; by the time you read this I will have begun my novitiate there. If all goes well with me, in a year I will be given the grace to go among the poor and tend the wounded, and in another year I may perhaps be deemed worthy to preach the faith. I live for that day.

Do not come after me, or send, I pray you, for I am lost to you from this time. I pray you, forgive me, and forget.

Farewell, my dearest love,
Your Friend in God, Blondelza

I crumpled the parchment in fierce, trembling fingers—for it was too thick and strong to tear—and threw it into a corner. The cabin's ceiling was very low, like all ship's cabins. A dark beam showed close to my forehead, and in an intensity of passion and rage I dashed my head against it, over and over. Perhaps I hoped to knock myself into insensibility, I do not know; I welcomed the pain. I heard a roaring in my ears, and knew it, finally, for my own voice. I took my throat in both hands, squeezing hard, to still it—for, even in my agony, I was mindful of my poor father's witless bellowing. In the end, I sank down upon the low bunk, my fist jammed into my mouth, and a flood of tears streaming from my eyes.

I wept and whimpered like a child, how long I do not know. I saw the rough-balled parchment in the corner and snatched it up, kissing it, smoothing it out, wetting it with my tears. When that was over, and I was still, like a fire that has been put out, I shivered, suddenly cold. I pulled my heavy cloak around me close, and lay down, the parchment held to my chest, my eyes straining upward at the ceiling, at nothing.

CHAPTER 7

WE LANDED AT Sandwich, in England, on March 13, contrary winds having held us on the far side of the Narrow Sea for more than a fortnight, another sort of captivity.

The shore was lined, nay, filled, as far as the eye could see, with welcoming folk, some even standing in the freezing waters. Never have I seen such a multitude, not at my crowning, not even in the Holy Land with armies arrayed against me. A roar came from them like the roar of another sea, and beyond that, the bells of all the seacoast towns, merging. It was a sound not of the earth; a sound like an army of angels, stern and beautiful, swelling the heart.

As I rode in to shore, standing in the little boat under the whipping flags of the Plantagenets, hands reached out to touch me, to touch my cloak, to touch the air that held me. I saw faces, young, old, glowing as if lit from within, gleaming with the jeweled tears of joy. It was a fine, crisp morning, the sun so bright it hurt.

I stepped upon the shore; moved by something beyond thought, I knelt and kissed the English soil, the grit of its sand rough and dear upon my lips. Behind me Bishop Walter knelt too, with all the clergy; I had stolen their scene, as Blondelza would have said. I was still in the habit of thinking of her.

I rose, and raised my arms. "Home . . . I am home," I said. And, under the wild thunder of noise, I could hear sobs and the sounds of weeping.

There are those who would say I spoke for show, but it was not true. This England was not the home of my heart, for that belonged to Aquitaine, to youth, to Blondelza; and it was not the home of my soul either, which was God's and the Holy Land's. No, it was closer still, dark and deep, like the womb, like the cord that bound me to my mother, like the very air I breathed. I turned, took my mother's hand, and brought her forward to stand with me upon this soil of home. "Queen Eleanor," I said. "Your dear friend, you know her well."

Hands took her from me, Hubert Walter's, I think, and bore her forward, while I reached out my own again for Berengaria. How small she looked, and young, the little heart face framed in white fur, the eyes solemn and scared. "This is my Queen," I said. "Love her, and do her honor."

Behind us my son stood with the other boys, young Baldwin who was the son of my friend, the knight of Béthune, and two others. They had been marked for hostages to the Emperor, but, for once, I had bested him at chess, letting myself go, and won the freedom of these little ones. One of them was not yet turned ten, and all three were boys still; it would have gone hard for them, life in a hostile land, among unknown enemies. I can still remember the Emperor Henry's face, shocked; he had believed me an inept player. But I held him to his promise, and these, at least, were safe on the soil of their fathers.

God grant we might redeem the other hostages! My ransom had beggared my kingdom; I would have to fight now in my Angevin lands to win back some of the fortune spent on me. But not yet, not just yet; my English kingdom must be set in order once again, and John's mischievous hand checked. Then, too, I must wear the crown again, going in progress with my Queen and all my train, a tradition from the old Saxon rulers of long ago. And first of all, there must be another task done, for my soul. I ordered the route set for Canterbury, and the shrine of the saint, Thomas Becket.

It was a leisurely progress, for crowds of folk lined the ways and spilled out into the road, and there were the castles of my loyal vassals too, where feasts and entertainments had been laid on; they had been waiting for weeks, even months, for my return.

In Dover square, outside the church, John waited for me, kneeling in the rutted roadway, clad in sackcloth, with ashes on his head. "What a mountebank!" I exclaimed, and held out my hand.

He kissed it, washing it with his easy tears. "Forgive me, brother," he asked, bowing his head till it was nearly in a puddle.

"Get up! Get up, John, do!" I said impatiently. "Of course

I forgive you . . . you are only a child. You have been led astray by villains, like better men before you. Come, walk along with me. And brush that ash out of your hair, people are watching."

I have been criticized for this, but what else could I do? He was my brother, and the only one I had left. Besides, I loved him. Everyone loved John; let no one tell you otherwise. If not, he would have met an assassin's knife before he was out of the nursery.

Ae we walked along, he began to chatter, pleasantly, with wit, as only he could do; I laughed, for the first time in many months. He shrugged out of his sackcloth as he walked, dropping it where he went, like a courtesan dropping her garments as she entices you to bed. Under it, he was dressed in rich blue velvet trimmed in vair. I laughed again.

"You have not met my Queen yet, Dickon. Oh, you must see her! What a sweet little witch!"

"Later, John, later. Here. Come into the church with me. We must offer up prayers for our reunion."

"Oh, not me, Dickon. You go. I'll wait for you. I hate churches!"

"I command it," I said sternly.

"Oh, all right," he said, as petulant as a girl. Then, his dark eyes flashing, he said, "I won't promise to behave, though."

"You *will* behave," I said, keeping a straight face. "People are watching. If you want to be King after me—"

"Oh, Dickon, shall I? Shall I really?" He turned and threw himself into my arms, his face transformed into a happy angel's.

"Yes," I answered gravely. "You are my heir."

"Oh, Dickon, I am so happy!" He drew away, looking at me with a kind of exasperation. "You might have told a fellow!" Then, in another lightning change, he said, "What happens if—" He tossed his head toward my followers. "You have your Queen with you . . . she may quicken. And then I am out of luck."

I shook my head. "It will not happen," I said. "She is barren. And now she is already past it, past bearing. Her monthly courses have dried up—she told me last night."

"Really?" he asked, like a gossip. "She doesn't look it. Looks like a child . . . almost as young as my Isabella she looks."

"I know, but there is something . . . something wrong, I guess." I sighed. We were silent for a moment, a rare thing with him.

Then he said, slyly, "Well, you could put her aside. A divorce . . . another girl, another Queen." His lips turned down, sad. "I could still be done out of it."

"John," I said firmly, "I promise you. I always keep my promises."

"You will not divorce her?"

"No. Never. She is a good child. It is not her fault. And she loves me . . . that is a rare enough thing in this world." For once he did not interrupt my thought. But then, John had a sixth sense; he knew how to be the way you wanted him to be—when it suited him. As it did then, of course. I knew him well, you see. Yet I loved him well, also. And he made me laugh. That is almost as rare as love.

I clapped him on the shoulder, almost knocking him down. I had forgotten how sedentary he was; he hated exercise. He winced and straightened his velvet. "Besides," I said, watching his face, "no one wants a child for a king! So I would have *you* grow up, for that matter."

He threw back his head and laughed, a joyous sound. I smiled, happy. It was something—to make John laugh at a witticism not his own.

"Come now, John," I said. "You cannot put it off any longer. The church is waiting."

"Oh, I shall enjoy it for once," he said. "I shall burn a candle to a saint. Lots of candles. To all the saints!"

CHAPTER 8

CANTERBURY. THE SPIRE of the cathedral rose out of the mists; it was the first thing you saw. The road to the shrine had been widened recently, to take the feet of the thousands of pilgrims; six men on horseback might ride abreast now, where once it had been little more than a lane.

I reined in my mount, motioning to Hubert Walter to go before me; it would be his domain, after all. He nodded gravely and, with several of his clerks, passed me; they bowed as they went by, as if apologizing.

John had caught up with me, and chatted companionably. "Your Queen," he said, "she gets along well with my Isabella, is it not so? They have been exchanging compliments like any pair of girls before a court masque."

"Yes," I said, "Berengaria has beautiful manners. She was brought up in the Spanish way." She would never in this world show her recoil to the other, that common little creature with whore's eyes, who cannot even sign her own name. But what in the world can they find to talk about, I wondered.

John was running on, his mouth unceasing, giggling now. In anyone else I would despise it as girlish, but with John, even the giggling and the silliness were infectious; I found myself smiling, though God knows I contemplated nothing joyous!

"And the churl dropped dead of fright," he cried. "Pure fright!"

"Ah, yes," I answered. "They brought me the report this morning." The messengers had come at first light, while I breakfasted on my host's good capon and French wine, with news of those strongholds not yet subdued by my troops. The commander of the fort at Mont-Saint-Michel, it seems, upon hearing of my release and my return to this country, had given up the ghost rather than face his punishment; the garrison had been in revolt for more than a year. Tickhill too had surrendered; they had brought me the keys to the place. Only one rebel nest still held out.

"What of Nottingham?" I asked, cutting short John's spiteful gaiety.

His face fell. "They will not believe me, Richard. They will not believe you are alive. What can I do?"

"You command there, do you not?"

"Oh, Dickon, you know what Nottingham is like! Always a den of thieves and outlaws."

"The outlaws, I understand, were on *my* side."

"Well . . . depends how you look at it," he hedged. "They use the forest of Sherwood as though it were common property—the King's forest!"

"It *is* common property now," I said. "I repealed Father's poaching laws when I came to the throne. Sherwood is no longer King's Hunting."

John changed sides; it took only the twinkling of an eye. "To tell the truth, Dickon, it is that awful sheriff there. A notorious money-grubber. And now he has his hands on the tariffs, he will not let go."

I sighed; it was common knowledge that all the crooked dealing was with John's consent, and at his instigation. "Oh, John, you weary me. I had thought you might have straightened this out yourself. It is your mischief, and I know it."

"Well," he whined, "you will have to show your face, Dickon. They will not listen to me." I looked at him sharply. "It is true, Dickon. I can't do it by myself. It has got out of hand up there."

"Well, I'll think about it after the business at hand." Suddenly I meant it; he *did* weary me. "Leave me now, John. I have other things on my mind."

"Willingly, Sire," he said, with a mocking grin. "Old sourface!"

It was good to be alone again; my thoughts were deep, and the sound of the horses' hooves upon the new paving was soothing and gentle. The new folk that lined the way here were silent, showing respect for the saint and for my mission. I bowed gravely in the saddle, acknowledging them.

We rode through the town, crowded as on a market day; I suppose it was always like this, since Becket had been canonized. There were stalls where relics were sold, vials of the saint's blood, bits of dried brain, slivers of bone; so long ago, the murder, there cannot have been anything left of him now, but folk, when they are believers, will believe anything. The vendors did a lively business.

Outside the cathedral was a huge pile of crutches and canes, said to have been discarded by those who had been cured at the holy shrine. A long line of the uncured stretched clear to the door: blind men led by children; children, too, lame or halt, some on litters; there were even a few lepers, standing apart, the sound of their little bells mournful and hopeless, their figures shrouded from sight. The Bishop, going before me, blessed them all with the sign of the Cross, his face alive with pity; a good man.

At the church door I dismounted and knelt for his blessing. Inside, the cathedral was dim, the vaulted ceiling arching into darkness. Before the altar a great candle burned on an iron stand; this was the spot where Thomas fell at the hands of my father's minions, a sacred place. In the flickering light I seemed to see Thomas, tall and straight and deep-eyed, as I remembered him from long ago, when I was a child. I fell to my knees, weeping. "Thank thee, Thomas, for my salvation ... I give thanks for my release. I pray thee, intercede for me with God in the forgiveness of my sins, which are many."

I lay there, stretched upon the stones, my arms spread out in the shape of Christ upon the cross, welcoming the cold hardness of the stones, feeling the bruising upon my face and chest, the healing tears that poured from my eyes.

I do not know how long it was I lay there; a long, long while. When I rose, my arms and legs were so stiff I could barely move them. I whispered to Bishop Walter, who was kneeling in prayer. "I wish to confess. Here, in this sacred place."

"Certainly, my son," he said.

"Not to you, my friend," I said, smiling a little. "You would impose too light a penance. It must be a stranger."

He nodded, as if he understood. "Brother Archibald ... he is made of stern stuff. He was a novice here when the saint was struck down."

"I will have him," I said. "He sounds the man for me. I have not made confession since before I left for the Holy Land."

"God save you, my son. Come."

The confessional was dark and dusty, the hangings smelling of camphor, against the moth, a homely smell. I felt beneath me for the little stool and sat down. "Father—" I spoke tentatively and low. "Father, I have sinned."

"Speak up, my son. My ears are not what they used to be." He had a high-pitched voice, disconcerting. I pictured the unseen face, thin and querulous, a little peevish. It stopped me. After a moment, I cleared my throat and began again. Began, shyly, with the small sins—shunning the Mass, forgetting my prayers, eating meat on Friday. After a while I grew used to it, used to the replies, dry and automatic, the small penances, the paternosters, the donations of candles to the poor.

Then, taking a breath, I said, "Father, I have sinned. I have killed more than two thousand unarmed men."

There was a silence, then the voice said, "Where was this, my son?"

"Outside Acre ... after the siege. The prisoners, the whole garrison."

"But they were infidels, my son. It is no sin."

"They were brave men—and they were defenseless," I said. "I count it a sin."

"It was war . . . a holy war. And they were doomed anyway . . . they were not Christian souls. It was no sin, my son." The voice had a final sound.

I sighed. "I have killed Christian souls too, Father. Or been the cause of their death. Helpless Christian souls, women and children . . ."

"Two lashes," said the voice.

"I have kept a prisoner in chains—a cruel punishment. And laughed at him."

"Two lashes."

The list was long; two lashes added each time, a goodly penance.

The list came near to the end. "I was the instrument of my father's death. I hounded him to death, pursued him when he was ill. I was a rebel son, and did him no honor."

"A grave sin, my son. Do you repent?"

"Yes."

"Five lashes."

"Father, I have consorted with a heretic."

"Man or woman?"

It made me smile in the dark, sincere though I was. "A woman, Father."

"More than once?"

"For many years."

"Do you repent?"

"No, Father. I love her as my soul, and cannot forget her."

I thought I heard a gasp, but perhaps I imagined it; these priests have heard so much, surely he was inured to it by now. But there was a long silence. Then the voice, softer now: "You must try to put this woman out of your mind. You must not see her again."

"*She* will not. She has renounced me, and gone into a nunnery."

"A Cathar?"

"Yes, Father."

"Poor, misguided soul. I will pray for her. But she is wiser than you."

"Yes, Father, I know. What penance?"

The priest sighed heavily. "Ten lashes, my son. But I cannot absolve you. You must renounce her in your mind."

"I will try, Father. Perhaps the scourging—"

"Yes." A dry sound. "But you will pay a substitute for that, surely?"

"Why, no, Father. I mean to endure it."

"Are you not Richard, King of England?" His voice was amazed.

In the end, I had to command him to it. At first he wanted to carry out the scourging privately, but I insisted upon a public penance as my father had endured; insisted it be here— in the cathedral where the holy martyr died. The date was set for Good Friday, two days hence. My mouth twisted wryly in the dark. An imitation of Christ, a kind of blasphemy. But it was the custom, and who better to imitate?

I was led into a small cell, at my own request, to pray and meditate, until the day.

I heard the rain before dawn, as I woke on the hard straw pallet. My tiny room, once used by a holy anchorite, was built onto the side of the cathedral proper. A heavy door separated it from the church, and in it was a small square window, where the recluse had received the sacrament and his daily bread and water. Its roof must have been made of tin, for the rain clattered with a thin sharp noise upon it, sounding as if the heavens had opened. I remembered that, as a child, I had thought it always rained on Good Friday, in mourning for Our Lord; I suppose it had happened once or twice.

Unlike the anchorite before me, I had received no bread and water through the little door; I had been given nothing for these two days, and seen no face. When you finally get them down to it, they will punish you properly; the Church knows how, you can be sure. I was already a little weak; my head felt light, as though it would float away.

There was an almost imperceptible lightening at dawn; it would be a dark day. The rain was beating down harder than ever when they came for me, just after the dawn, two friars in brown cloaks with hoods, carrying the short bundles of split willows that were the scourges of penance. They were thick as a man's arm, many twigs tied fast together, and the stinging ends left free. These, I saw, were peeled new wood, raw, almost white.

I peered curiously at the friars, wondering if one of them had been my confessor. But I could tell nothing from their faces; they were as blank as parchment that has not felt a pen. "Come," the taller one said. "We are ready."

I had been given a black robe to wear, open at the front; my feet were bare. They placed a black hood upon my head, and led me forth, hands guiding me at my elbow. It was not far, just down a few steps. There was a soft murmuring sound all around me; was the church then filled?

"Here," said a voice. "A step up, Sire." I was turned about, the hood was whisked off, and, blinking in the light of many candles, I saw the multitude that watched, blank gray faces in the yellow light.

One of the monks, in a quick gesture, ripped off the black robe, pulling it down from my shoulders till it was held by the rough cord at my waist; I was naked before the congregation and my nakedness was vulnerable; I felt it, felt aware of my body, with its whiteness and its scars, my rib cage thin still from the deprivation of my war years and my imprisonment. It was with an almost painful effort that I stood straight and tall; I felt like cringing, a felon before God.

My eyes were accustomed now to the candlelight, and I had a glimpse of faces I knew: Mother, white and strained, a shocked look upon her; Berengaria, her eyes cast down as if I embarrassed her; Philippe, looking ready to throw up his breakfast. Then I was turned around and saw no more, only the wall behind, with the great tortured Christ hanging upon it.

I heard a kind of low whistling sound, and the first lash hit, like a dozen wasps' stings. I can stand this, I thought, surprised. The second, from the other side, was heavier, a stronger arm. I heard a gasp, quite loud, from many throats, and the sobbing of a woman somewhere in the rear.

Two more blows, and I fell to my knees. Hands placed a small table before me, oaken and heavy, something to hold. I needed it. It got worse with each blow; worse, and becoming agony. I do not think I cried out, or even moaned, but I cannot be sure; the whole cathedral was filled with the moaning and sobbing of the onlookers, and the woman who had sobbed first was shrieking now, a dreadful sound.

At last it was over. I slumped against the table, a taste of blood in my mouth; I had bitten my tongue. After a long moment, they lifted me, turning me around to face the people. From somewhere Bishop Walter came forward, his face grieving, a white robe in his arms. I winced as he threw it

452

over my nakedness, as the soft cloth touched my raw back. Winced, and smiled, and, painfully, knelt for blessing. "God be with you this day, my son, and make His countenance to shine upon you."

I was led forth then, out of the cathedral, into the sight of the people who stood waiting in the rain. Lackeys rushed forward to hold a canopy over me. Above the rain noise rose a swelling sound, cheering from a thousand throats. The throng stretched into the distance, I could not see its end. Soldiers cleared a path for me, and I moved forward, the canopy above me still. Every step was agony; the robe stuck to my back and shoulders. Someone brought me a goblet of wine; it stung my bitten tongue, but the warm gush of it going down gave me strength. I moved on, bowing as the people strained to come near me, their faces streaming with the wet. I had found my inner strength now, and shrugged off the hands that sought to bear me up.

As I passed the line of suppliants, the maimed and the halt, the blind, I saw a face that I remembered, young and thin, with red hair, the eyes huge and incandescent, above hunched shoulders borne up on crutches. I stopped, searching the face. "I know you . . . I know your face. Acre! Yours was almost the first face I saw when I stepped off the boat onto the shore there. We smiled. Do you remember?"

The face was split by a wide smile, as before. "Oh, Sire," the boy sighed, hardly breathing. "How could I not? You *saw* me! Just once . . . but I have never forgotten."

"Nor I," I said. "It was a welcome—a welcome as from an angel. But I had not known you were English."

"Half," he said, still smiling. "I was with the men of Champagne, my father's fief is of those parts. I am only half English."

"Like me," I said. "You do not fare well, it seems." And I nodded toward the crutches.

"I caught a crossbow bolt in my spine, Sire. I was not running away, but bending to pick up an arrow. Someone from the walls . . . It healed well, but now I cannot make my legs work. Mother brought me here, to the shrine."

"I pray the saint's good prayers will help you," I said.

He shook his head. "No, it will never be. I felt a twinge, I thought, when you took the last blows . . . but I think I imagined it. Oh, Sire!" he burst out. "Oh, Sire, your poor back! Why did you do it?"

453

I smiled thinly. "A man's sins are his own."

"Oh. Oh, yes, I did not mean—" The boy cast down his eyes.

"Come close. I will tell you something," I said, beckoning. "Do you remember the massacre? The massacre of the prisoners there?"

He nodded, and brought one hand up to cross himself.

"They did not count it a sin, the men of the Church, because the slain were infidels. But I did." I searched his face. "Do you understand?"

"Oh, yes, Sire. It was—it was Hell that day. But, Sire, it was the others did it too—the other kings and nobles. The council voted, I heard . . . we all knew. It was not you alone . . . it was their sin too."

"But that is for *their* consciences, you see. As for me . . . Well, that is part of why I did this—only a part."

"Oh, Sire, I cannot kneel . . . But, Sire—" And his face shone like a light through the silver slashing of the rain. "You did it for all of us . . . all of us at Acre."

"No," I said, shaking my head. "Only for myself. If you thought it sin, you too must pray for forgiveness."

"I have, every day," he said. "And God has only taken away my legs. He has kept me alive till this day."

"Yes, we have met again," I answered; I could not deny his adoration. "But I do not know your name."

"It is Gaucelm, Sire. Gaucelm of Port-sur-Lanne."

"You are knight?"

"I was," he said. "But now my brother wears my hauberk."

I smiled at him; there were no words. But in a moment I said, "Fare you well, Gaucelm. And my prayers go with you."

"Farewell, King Richard."

I moved on, my step almost light. This boy, this knight, maimed as he was . . . Well, we are not all brutes, we knights. There is some good in us, after all.

As I went forward, nodding to left and right, I saw the faces clearly, for the dark was lifting. The rain was only a mist now, and would stop soon.

EPILOGUE

—

ANNO DOMINE 1204

Told by Queen Eleanor, at Fontevrault Abbey

"ELEANOR, BY THE Wrath of God, Queen of England." So I had signed myself in a letter to the Pope, when the news of Richard's capture was brought to me. And later, to another Pope, I confided, "I have lost the light of my life . . . the staff of my age," when Richard died. My pen was eloquent in those days. I cannot hope to equal it now. For now I am very old, and perhaps, at last, tranquil. I am eighty-three.

All of my wild, bright children, all my high-hearted brood, are gone, except for John. John who is King of England, and keeper of all the vast lands of Angevin and Poitevin; one by one he is letting them all run through his fingers, poor feckless John. And I can do no more, I am tired. It seems, in these latter years, I have been an old crazy woman, scurrying across Europe, up hill, down dale, over waters, stirring this pot, snatching this one off the stove, brewing up simples, with Death behind me, breathless at my foolish heels. Now I have turned and looked him in the face, an old friend, and have come here, to Fontevrault, to wait for him to catch up to me. It is a sweet and noble place to rest, all marble and dusty sunlight. Rest and remembrance, all that is left. Rest and remembrance.

My daughters, long gone from me, have died, and are buried beside their husbands, the youngest, another Eleanor, far away in Spain. I saw her grave not long ago; it was my last far journey, an emissary, a matchmaker. Well, I brought back a bride, my granddaughter, for Philip Augustus's son; perhaps it will help us to peace. But I lost Mercadier on that journey; he was killed defending me from footpads in the streets of Bordeaux. I counted him almost a son, so devoted a captain, so fair a friend.

Life and death have mixed me up, confused me, in these old days; I forget, sometimes, who is left alive. Forgetting little Zenobia, my hand maiden now, I called for Hodierna yesterday, quite annoyed, and knitting my brows, wanting her to lend a hand with some needlework; she has been dead two full years! They sat this is typical of ancient crones, but I had been determined it would not be so with me. And my stormy Joanna, the last to go, seems just over a mountain or two, in her bridal palace of the Count of Toulouse; I think of her still as a child, my great baby. But alas, she died in childbirth, and the little one too; it was a late marriage, her second, to the new Count there, and perhaps she was old already for bearing.

The others too, Marie, Mathilda, Alix . . . I forget their deaths. My boys have been gone so long, I remember them only as they were as children. Except for Richard—the light of my life, the staff of my age. His loss is always with me, an agony in my breast, like a canker eating. A loss to us all, who knew him, a loss to the world.

He was the idol of Christendom. For more than a month after his death bells tolled in all the churches of Europe, and the streets were hung with mourning black in every town. Folk lay weeping, covered in ashes and clothed in sackcloth; hordes of them, pitiful, gathered at all the crossroads. Poor knights, rough foot soldiers, young squires who had served under him long ago in the Holy Land cried aloud to all who would hear, "How can I live? Seeing that he is gone, the best knight in the world is gone." And some, sore wounded, and hanging on by a thread, gave up, in sorrow, turned their faces to the wall and died. Hubert Walter, his prelate, said, "Even the angels wept."

His only son, the love-child Philippe, shapes well, a good fighter, trained, as his father was, by William the Marshal. He is handsome too, and very like Richard, tall and strong; sometimes a look, a turn of the head, a movement, catches my breath, it is so nearly his father. But he is Richard-with-water, as it were; the rich wine, the heady brew diluted. Still, he might have made a king, if he were not a bastard; a better king than John, or than Arthur of Brittany, Geoffrey's son, the Pretender—my grandson too, but tainted with his mother Constance's leprosy and filled with the poison of her bitterness.

Men whisper that John has done away with Arthur. This I cannot believe. Not with his own hands, surely; John has not the stomach for such things. But Arthur has disappeared, no longer a threat, no longer "the hope of Brittany." He had joined with Philip the insatiable, Philip Augustus, our enemy of France, to do the Angevin empire what harm he could. It is better that he is gone, God forgive me. He was only seventeen.

And my own, my darling, the world's darling, was only forty-two; Richard, the *"preux chevalier,"* the best knight of all. His like will never come again.

Ever since his release from Germany, Richard had been plunged into warlike pursuits; he had no rest. England itself was easily settled; the rebel fortresses capitulated at the very sight of him, and the country cheered as he toured it, wearing his crown once more, with his little queen by his side. But those rich possessions on the Continent were continually threatened by sedition, stirred up by the French enemy. Richard, short months after his home-coming, took ship for Normandy. He never saw his island kingdom again.

There were many battles fought upon Angevin soil, the accounts of which I will leave to the chroniclers. My thoughts are scattered, my heart weighed down, and there is, after all, only one battle that matters, the little siege of Chalus, in the Limousin.

By the advent of Lent in 1199, just five years after Richard had emerged from his imprisonment, he had very nearly won back all the castles and holdings that were his by right, and which Philip Augustus had seized during the German captivity. And he had built to his own specifications the finest, strongest fortress ever seen, upon a place known as the Rock of Andelys.

Two-thirds of the way from Paris to the sea, the River Seine describes a deep loop beneath the chalky cliffs of a huge promontory; upon this height one can see the whole region for miles in every direction. It was there that Richard built Château Gaillard, almost with his own hands. Since his earliest days Richard had studied the massive strongholds of Aquitaine and Anjou, of Maine and Touraine; in the Holy Land he had found wondrous examples of new architecture, at Margreb, at Acre, at Ramlah and Ascalon. His wild enthusiasm pushed the work forward; it was finished in a year. He altered the face of nature, rerouting tributaries of the Seine, marooning the site by waterways, and building upon the very topmost eminence, islanding his fortress high in the air.

I watched him excitedly laying this masterpiece out with stones and woodwork, even acting as stonemason. I marveled at the genius that informed him, as I had marveled at his songs; if we had not lived in a world where war was the ultimate monarch, my beloved son might have been the greatest of architects, or the finest musician. I swear this is not motherly pride; one has only to hear his music, or gaze upon this wonder, Château Gaillard, his "saucy castle." As it is, I must be content to know him the greatest warrior of his day; ashes in my mouth, for no woman loves war. If women ruled the world, it would be abolished. Perhaps, in some far-off day, it will.

But I digress; I cannot bear to tell what I must tell.

There had been an uneasy truce between England and France for some time. When I say uneasy, I mean that it was continually being broken by one or the other vassals of the two kings; there were always skirmishes, small battles, forays into hostile territories. One such battle was the siege of Chalus. Philip's allies, the Count of Angoulême and the Viscount of Limoges, had not been included in the truce, for some reason I cannot fathom now. These nobles were at the same time the hereditary vassals of Richard, holding their lands from Angevin lords since the time of Charlemagne. They were in rebellion again, so, in March 1199, Richard brought up his troops to lay siege to the Viscount's castle at Chalus-Chabrol. It was a little place and poorly defended. The Viscount Aymar was not known for his generosity to his poor dependents, and there were no more than forty of them behind the walls. But they were brave, and fought loyally for their ungrateful overlord. From their battlements they rolled down stones on their besiegers and from the vents in the barbicans exhausted their supply of arrows. On the evening of the third day there was left upon the ramparts only one lone defender, a crossbowman using a huge frying pan as a shield.

"Sire, you must come see this fellow!" cried Mercadier, sticking his head through the flap in Richard's tent and grinning broadly. "He is a wonder. The garrison has no arrows left, so he is catching ours in that fry-pan, fitting them to his crossbow, and firing them back at us!"

"Brave fellow!" cried Richard. "We must cheer him on!" He snatched up helmet and shield and dashed out, wearing no armor at all.

The lone figure was still visible in the twilight, though the shadows were gathering. As Richard watched, the man deftly caught a half-spent arrow sent up from the besiegers; it hit the iron fry-pan with a sharp pinging noise and fell harmlessly to the stone roof where he stood. He stooped to retrieve it, fitted it into his bow, and fired down into the ranks of Richard's soldiers. With a great roar of delighted laughter, Richard laid down his shield and clapped his hands, shouting, "Bravo! Well done!"

But the fellow had been better than brave; he had been clever. Another crossbow, already wound, lay at hand upon the walls; he took it up, fitted another spent arrow to it, and coolly fired at the King.

Richard saw the bolt coming, and heard the singing of its flight. He snatched up his shield, but just a fraction too late; the barb, a heavy one, for it was one of his own and well made, went into the flesh of his shoulder and lodged deep in his spine. His men, working beneath the protective hides of their siege engines, saw nothing; Mercadier had ducked his head under one of them to give an order, and was unaware. Richard made no sound; he did not wish to alarm his own soldiers or to give heart to the desperate garrison. Calmly he returned to his tent as though nothing had happened.

Once inside, he tried to pull out the bolt but succeeded only in breaking off the wooden shaft, leaving the iron barb, the length of a man's hand, still deeply imbedded. He cursed aloud, rousing young Philippe, who was acting as his squire on this comparatively safe siege. The boy, exhausted, for he was unused to the warrior's life, had dozed where he sat, at work oiling some leather straps. "What, Father? Did you call?" he cried rubbing his eyes.

"It is nothing . . . the sting of a gnat only," said Richard. "But I have snapped the shaft and the damned thing is still in there." He wriggled, trying to smile, and groaned. "It *does* sting. Hell and damnation!" Richard sank onto his cot. "Philippe, fetch Mercadier. He is at the siege engines. But go quietly, no one must know. And go carefully, take my shield and helm." The boy, frightened, stumbled out into the twilight.

It was the evening of March 26; on the first day of April a summons from Mercadier reached me in my Lenten retreat here at Fontevrault. The wonderful Abbess Mathilda set out northward to Maine to fetch Berengaria from Richard's castle there and to inform John, who was fighting in the area. I left at once for Chalus, a distance of one hundred miles, traveling night and day.

Richard was beyond any help except God's. The army surgeon had dug out the barb, working by the light of a lantern, but the flesh was torn and mangled, and the wound soon turned gangrenous, getting worse each day.

Except for Mercadier, Philippe, and the surgeon, no one had been admitted to the tent until the garrison of Chalus fell, but then the news could no longer be kept from the army. By the time I arrived, all the tents were hung with black, and the soldiers, hardened routiers that they were, gathered morning and evening in the chaplain's tent to mourn and pray.

When I arrived, with my little escort, the first thing I saw was the black banners. "God," I cried, swaying in the saddle at this sight. "Is it too late? Am I come too late?"

Mercadier reached up his arms; I almost fell into them. "Tell me! Oh, tell me, friend! Is Richard—"

"He lives still," said Mercadier. "Steady now, Lady. He is very weak, and he may not know you, for sometimes the fever mounts. Be steady now." And he led me toward Richard's tent. "The smell," he murmured as he pulled aside the tent flaps. "Be brave, dear lady."

He had warned me, but still the smell was shocking, like a blow. They had burned fragrant herbs against it, but nothing would avail. It was the odor of corruption, of death; I caught my breath in a gasp. At first I could see nothing through the thick clouds of smoke from the herbs; then, in the half-dark, I saw him, stretched out, long, so long, upon the raised pallet, my dear, my dying son. I ran forward, my feet unsteady after so many hours in the saddle, and flung myself upon my knees at his side. "Oh, Dickon," I said, very low.

I had never seen him so pale. I had never seen anyone so pale; it was as if all the blood had been bled out of him. Above his drained white face, the hair blazed like a torch. His eyes were closed. "Dickon," I said again, and touched his hand.

He opened his eyes; they were wildly blue in that marble face, and brilliant with fever—but they saw me clear. "Mother," he said. "What an irony. Such a little siege . . ." He tried to smile; it looked painful.

"Lie still," I said. "Don't speak. You must save your strength."

He *did* smile then, showing a gleam of teeth. "Mother, never mind . . . No lies, Mother. I am done for." I opened my mouth to protest. "Mother, I have seen too many men die

... Let be. Just sit here with me and hold my hand." He sighed, and closed his eyes again. "I want to sleep."

The smell grew worse, grew stifling, so that I thought I would die from it, there, with my son. But then I grew used to it. Day wore into night; the fever mounted. Richard began to cry, like a baby, and call for me, though I sat close and held his hand. "Mother, where are you? I want you. Mother, come. I need you."

The night wore on; he tossed upon his couch, weeping and calling piteously. Toward dawn he grew quiet again; when I touched him his flesh was wet with sweat, and beneath him the coverlets were soaked.

"Has the fever broken?" I whispered, hoping, lying to myself.

"No, Lady," said the surgeon. "It is this way every night. Another man would be dead long ago."

Sometimes, during the day, he was rational, and would talk of John and the kingship, giving me instructions, naming his bequests. Thus and thus for this one or that, these monies here, these troops disposed there.

"And Alexander must have a large bequest . . . he has a great project in hand." His eyes wandered. "Oh, and he must be made abbot. Make a note of that," he said to the scribe who sat writing out these items.

"He *is* abbot already, Richard," I said gently, but I do not think he heard.

He went on, counting off on his fingers, naming this one and that. "And there is Will Longchamps. John will try to get rid of him . . . but he has been a good and faithful servant. Put him down for, let's see, a hundred marks a year."

It was no use telling him that Will had no need of his bounty, that he had lined his own coffers long ago. Richard never understood greed.

But I spoke up then, fearing his mood would pass. "You must make provision for Berengaria, my dear."

"Oh, God. Yes. Is she in her nunnery yet?"

He had forbade her to go when she requested it, miserable that she had not given him an heir; had forborne to divorce her and take another. But he had forgotten all that.

"Not yet," I whispered. "But, in any case, she will need an annual sum. She must not have to depend upon her brother."

"No. Of course not. Would five hundred marks be enough, do you think?"

Five hundred marks was a fortune, unheard of; she would have a hard time squeezing it out of John every year. But he was beyond reasoning this. I nodded my head. "That will be ample." And, after a moment, I said, "She has been summoned, Dickon."

He nodded, somber.

"And John, as well. They are both in Maine. I hope they will—" I broke off at a loss.

"Hope they will be in time?" he asked, almost jauntily. "Poor Mother. Never mind, Mother . . . I have accepted it. If only—Well, John will have to behave soberly, for once. Surely, when he is King . . ."

He worried much about his kingdom, fretting that he would not see England again, fearing that Philip Augustus would trick John as he had so often. His poor feverish head tossed to and fro upon the pillow.

"Rest, darling," I said. "Oh, rest."

The surgeon gave him a strong brew that made him sleep, and Mercadier persuaded me to lie down in his tent, out of the smell and the sight of death. "I will call you, Lady, as soon as he wakes." I was grateful, for I had been awake the whole long journey, and could still feel the jolting of the horse's gait in my bones.

I slept, and did not wake till full dark, when I heard Mercadier call my name.

"Lady, come. He is out of his head. No one can calm him."

Richard had dragged himself out of bed, streaming sweat, his bandage soaked with blood and the gray viscous matter from his disturbed wound. He stood, wild of eye, in the center of the tent, holding on to the tent pole, babbling.

"Where is she, my own, my dearest? Where? She has forsaken me . . . I would not forsake *her*. Oh, girl, my girl . . . come back. Once more, come back!" And he fell to weeping, great anguished, tearing sobs that racked his poor wasted frame. "I cannot die . . . cannot die without her! Without a sight of her . . . it is too much to ask! Oh, Blondelza, come back to me!" Over and over he called her name. Strength seemed to come to him from somewhere, and his voice was as loud as if he were at the head of his troops, though his whole body shook with the fever chill. I tried to pry him loose from the pole, but he held on to it as though he were drowning, and threw me off from him, so that I fell to the ground; he did not notice. "Blondelza. Oh, my Blondelza! My bad girl . . . come to me!"

I think the whole camp was roused, or perhaps they had not been sleeping at all; Richard was much beloved of his men. Voices sounded outside, and running feet, a half-muttered curse. There was a scratch at the tent flap, and we heard someone speak. "Sire . . . Sire."

Mercadier drew back the flap. I saw a head, tousled, young, anxious-eyed. "Captain, begging your pardon . . . is it the glee-maiden?"

"Yes," said Mercadier, tersely. "He calls for her."

"I know where she is, Captain. A few of us was there last night, praying for him . . . and she along with us."

Mercadier grabbed the poor boy's shirt in an iron grasp, frightening him. "Where? Is she near, then?"

"Yes, Captain. Over in the next town. Just a little place, but quite a crowd it was, to hear her preach. She's the best of them."

"Will she be there still?" Mercadier's voice was hoarse with emotion, rough with grief.

"Oh, yes, Captain. All week, they said."

"Fetch her. Take a battalion. Force her if need be."

"Oh, she'll come, Captain. They'll go anywhere they're needed . . . Them Christians are fine folk, not like the whorish proud Romans. And she'd come to *him* anyway. It was him she was praying for, spoke him by name, she did—saint though she is."

"Get her! Make it quick! He may not last long."

"Yes, Captain!" The voice sounded awed, very frightened. "Straightaway, sir!"

They had got Richard back onto the couch—it took four men—and then only with the promise of her coming. The surgeon had cleansed the wound and changed the filthy bandage, and bled him again. He lay still, very still, but I saw his chest rise and fall, slowly, and once he groaned and muttered.

We had not long to wait. The clatter of hooves sounded outside, quite near, and a jangle of spurs, then low voices. A hand drew back the tent flap, and a lantern glimmered in the darkness beyond. "Thank you, friend. Go with God."

I think I would not have known her. A white woolen robe covered her body and hooded her head. One hand held it close; the other held a small lantern. Noiselessly she approached the couch, looking down at the long length of him who lay there; I could not see her face, shadowed by the folds of the hood. He did not stir. Silently she bent closer, lifting the lantern to study his face. Her own swam out of the darkness, like a ghost. I do not know which of us, she or I, caught breath on a sigh.

All prettiness had fled from her face, as if frightened of the stern saint who lived there. Her skin was stretched white over bare bones, her nose was high and arching, her mouth was pale, and her eyes were like great caverns where light flickered deeply, fitfully. And yet, in a way, she was beautiful still, as though an artist had found the spirit and drawn it there, upon her spare flesh.

She stood looking down at him, in the light of the lantern. There was not a sound within the tent, and I could no longer see the sheet that covered him lift with his breath; I thought he had passed beyond us already, and felt it in my heart. Then his eyes opened, opened wide, and he smiled. I have never seen such a smile; all grace, all good, all happiness was in it. He held out his arms and she came into them, kneeling.

"You came to me." His words were frail and insubstantial as the motes that dance in a sunbeam.

She nodded. "Yes."

"You are not too good to love me still?" A faint, old mockery lit the smile.

I saw her cheek curve sweetly, rounding. "Not too good ... not yet."

He nodded then, very grave. "I can sleep now." He caught at her hand. "Sing to me, sweetheart ... once more. Sing me to sleep."

She laughed, low, and made a little gesture. "I have not sung for many years ... and I have no lute."

"Take mine." His hands held hers, gripping them hard. "A lullabye."

Hands pressed the lute into hers, Mercadier's hands. She took it, still kneeling by Richard's side, and struck the first note.

Then there was no sound in the tent, only the song.

Close, oh close your shining eyes ...
Angels, angels ... tread the skies.
Hear the music of the night ...
Angels, angels ... bathed in light.

Soft the passage of their wings...
Angels, angels... pluck the strings.
Close your eyes, my dearest one...
Angels, angels... veil the sun.

When it was finished, a great sigh went up from the tent, and beyond, and the sounds of soft sobbing, Philippe. We crept close, all of us who loved him, Philippe, Mercadier, and I. And from the night came the rough routiers crowding in, silently, their heads bowed. We stared at Richard, lying there, our beloved. He did not breathe, though his eyes were open still. A long moment. Then Blondelza's hand went out, softly, softly, and brushed over the eyelids, closing them. It was over.

NOTES AND ACKNOWLEDGMENTS

THE CHRONICLERS SAY that Richard forgave the man who killed him; I could find no place for this incident in my narrative. The story goes, with slight variations, that, the man having been brought before him, a mere boy, Richard asked, "Why did you shoot at me? I was applauding your bravery." The boy replied, "Sire, you killed my father and both my brothers." At this Richard said, without rancor, "Well, then, you were right, and I absolve you of all blame." This seems to have occurred before the wound turned gangrenous; after Richard died, the man was nonetheless put to death, some say by order of Mercadier, others by order of Joanna.

Joanna, like Berengeria and John, did not reach Richard before he died. Joanna, pregnant with the child of her new husband, Raymond of Toulouse, miscarried on the journey, and later died from complications. Berengaria entered a small nunnery, where she lived out her days, never remarrying. (She did, in fact, have trouble getting her annuity from John; it was often as much as three years late.)

Blondelza, if she had been real and not invented, would assuredly have died in the infamous Albigensian Crusade of the early thirteenth century, for not one Cathar (sometimes called Albigensian or Bougar) survived. Whole cities were put to the sword, but most of the people of this sect died at the stake; these were the first days of the Inquisition and the first great holocaust of Europe. Zoé Oldenburg has written of them with anger and compassion in two novels, *Cities of the Flesh* and *Destiny of Fire*.

This novel could not have been written without consulting a great many books pertaining to twelfth-century life; it would be impossible to list them all here, but I would like to mention those few which proved indispensable to me.

Of the dozen or so biographies of Richard, I found most useful the intensive, detailed, and meticulous work of Kate Norgate, *Richard the Lionheart* (Russell and Russell, 1924), though her footnotes are almost entirely in Latin and therefore somewhat taxing; and John Gillingham's *Richard the Lionheart* (Times Books, 1978), which is clear, concise, and unbiased.

Of the biographies of Eleanor, I like best the charming and scholarly *Eleanor of Aquitaine and the Four Kings*, by Amy Kelly (Harvard University Press, 1950). Another I found useful is *Eleanor of Aquitaine*, by Regine Pernoud (Coward-McCann, 1968).

There are many sources on the troubadours—the Ezra Pound translations are spirited and fine—but I feel the definitive book is *The Troubadours*, by Robert Briffault (Indiana University Press, 1965). I would also recommend *The Women Troubadours*, by Meg Bogin, a study long overdue (Paddington Press, 1976). I like best for twelfth-century warfare, including tournaments, sieges, and the use of mercenaries, *Crusading Warfare*, by R. C. Smail (Cambridge University Press, 1956).

The Crusades, by Zoé Oldenburg (Pantheon, 1966), gives a clear insight into the whole picture of these great phenomena.

The contemporary sources are, among others, Roger of Hoveden, Ralph of Diceto, Ralph of Coggeshall, Richard of Devizes, Gerald of Wales, Geoffrey de Vigeois, and Ambroise (or Amboise), all available in translation.

I wish to thank Carleton Kelsey of the Amagansett Free Library, Amagansett, New York, for his help in finding out-of-print works and for his great patience and understanding.

ABOUT THE AUTHOR

A former Broadway actress who played with the Lunts and Helen Hayes, Martha Rofheart has written several novels, including *The Savage Brood, Glendower Country, The Alexandrian,* and *Fortune Made His Sword*. She was born in Louisville, Kentucky, and lives in New York City.